USA [illegible] orth Texas with [illegible] nd, three beautiful children, a spunky golden retriever/standard poodle mix and too many books in her to-read pile. In her downtime, she plays video games and spends much of her time on or around a basketball court. She loves interacting with readers and is grateful for their support. You can reach her at barbhan.com

Carla Cassidy is an award-winning, *New York Times* bestselling author who has written over 170 books, including 150 for Mills & Boon. She has won the Centennial Award from Romance Writers of America. Most recently she won the 2019 Write Touch Readers Award for her title *Desperate Strangers*. Carla believes the only thing better than curling up with a good book is sitting down at the computer with a good story to write.

Also by Barb Han

Undercover Couple
Newlywed Assignment
Texas Kidnapping
Texas Target
Texas Law
Texas Baby Conspiracy
Texas Stalker
Texas Abduction
Cornered at Christmas
Ransom at Christmas

Also by Carla Cassidy

Desperate Strangers
Desperate Intentions
Desperate Measures
Stalked in the Night
Stalker in the Shadows
Scene of the Crime: Bridgewater, Texas
Scene of the Crime: Bachelor Moon
Scene of the Crime: Widow Creek
Scene of the Crime: Mystic Lake
Scene of the Crime: Black Creek

Discover more at millsandboon.co.uk

EYEWITNESS MAN AND WIFE

BARB HAN

CLOSING IN ON THE COWBOY

CARLA CASSIDY

MILLS & BOON

First Published in Great Britain 2022
by Mills & Boon, an imprint of HarperCollins*Publishers* Ltd
1 London Bridge Street, London, SE1 9GF

www.harpercollins.co.uk

HarperCollins*Publishers*
1st Floor, Watermarque Building,
Ringsend Road, Dublin 4, Ireland

ISBN: 978-0-263-30346-9

0622

MIX
Paper from
responsible sources
FSC™ C007454

This book is produced from independently certified FSC™ paper to ensure responsible forest management.

For more information visit: www.harpercollins.co.uk/green

Printed and Bound in Spain using 100% Renewable electricity at CPI Black Print, Barcelona

EYEWITNESS MAN AND WIFE

BARB HAN

All my love to Brandon, Jacob and Tori,
the three great loves of my life.

To Babe, my hero, for being my best friend,
greatest love and my place to call home.

I love you all with everything that I am.

Chapter One

Agent Quinton Casey stood on the porch of the two-bedroom bungalow with his fist raised and ready to knock. This visit was supposed to be him showing up with a suitcase in hand, ready to personally measure Ree Sheppard's bed to see if it was big enough to fit him and her together. The invitation to try a sleepover unrelated to their jobs as undercover ATF agents—they'd been partners on the last two cases—wasn't something Quint had intended on wasting. Halfway down the Texas highway in between Fairfield and Madisonville, things had changed when he got a call from Agent Grappell, the desk agent who had been assigned to their previous cases. Now, Quint had to deliver the news that the person they'd arrested a couple of days ago had been killed in jail, along with any hope they would be able to get a name from him or a trail to follow like they'd hoped.

Quint lowered his elbow and put his hand on his hip instead. The direct link to a crime ring responsible for killing his best friend and fellow agent was gone forever.

Raising his fist once again to knock, the door swung open. Emmaline Ree Sheppard stood there with a confused look on her face. His lips still sizzled from the heat in their last kiss, but he couldn't let himself think about that right now.

"Are you going to stand here all day or decide to knock?" Ree asked. She crossed her arms over her chest, shifted her weight to one side, and chewed on the inside of her cheek as she studied him. She glanced at his hands, no doubt noticing the lack of suitcase. "What is it? What's wrong, Quint? Because if this is about you letting me down easy or telling me there will be no sleepovers, you didn't need to drive all the way out here to do th—"

"Constantin is dead." Ever since hearing the news, Quint had felt lost.

"What? How did this happen? He was in solitary confinement," she said, bringing her hand up to cover her mouth, all color drained from her face. She'd been there alongside him in Houston for the undercover sting that had ended with Constantin in handcuffs and the promise he would talk for a more lenient sentence. She clearly realized the trail to finding and locking up Tessa's killer had dried up once again. All the work done on the last two undercover cases that had led to this bust had gone up in smoke.

"Prisoners get an hour a day outside in the yard. It's supposed to be alone, but the guards said there was a paperwork error and he ended up with the regular population," Quint informed her, clenching his back teeth in a failed attempt to bite back some of his anger. He knew full well a guard had to have been paid off for a prisoner to be strangled to death in the yard. This also brought him back to the men who'd been arrested the night Tessa was shot. A-12 was the group he and Tessa had spent weeks cracking. They'd gotten in, but since drugs were involved the DEA showed up on bust day. Politics had been involved, since there were political ties to the case, and the governor needed a win against crime. Everything about the case got complicated. They busted five guys, but Quint always felt it was the tip of the iceberg. One of his informants gave him the name Dumitru as the head of the A-12 crime ring before the bust went down. Once the dust settled and he checked back, no one arrested went by that name. All five of the others, however, died in prison within two weeks of each other—two suspected suicides, and two had been outright killed. The last guy was put in solitary confinement for his own protection, but he was poisoned.

And now Constantin was dead.

"This is bad, Quint." Ree opened the door a little more before turning around and walking away. He'd noticed that she'd glanced at his empty hand twice and decided this wasn't the time to tell her that he'd left his suitcase in the car. The whole point of bringing it in the first place was to see what might happen if they were together for personal reasons.

He closed the door behind him before walking to the small dining table next to the kitchen, where she was putting on a pot of coffee. He'd left his case folder in the vehicle, too. It was never far despite the fact this was supposed to be a social visit.

"A guard 'found' him about an hour and a half ago facedown in the grassy area behind the basketball post, strangled to death," Quint explained, smacking his flat palm on the small table. "What the hell am I supposed to do now?" Every person who could have helped him get to the person responsible for Tessa's death had ended up dead.

"We'll find another trail," Ree said, pouring fresh coffee in a pair of mugs. She handed one over, then took a sip from her own. "Give it some time."

Quint issued a sharp sigh.

"I do realize patience isn't your finest asset," she said

with a smile that caused a little bit of the ice encasing his heart to chip away. This visit was supposed to have gone a whole lot differently than this and should have ended up with the two of them tangled in the sheets. He wanted nothing more than to get lost with Ree, if only for a couple of hours. But it would be a temporary break. The demons would return and he would be right back to this same spot of anger and frustration. “I always thought it was your eyes.”

“Keep saying stuff like that and I’ll be forced to lean across this table and kiss you,” he said. The round table was small for a person of his considerable size. At six feet three inches he’d never be accused of being short. Closing the distance between them wouldn’t take much in the way of effort.

“What’s stopping you?” she asked. It was a distraction, but it was also working.

“Your wish is my command.” He leaned over and pressed his lips to hers, releasing a little of the pent-up frustration burning him from the inside out. There was something about Ree that helped him remain calm, no matter how irritated he got with a case. She had a soothing presence underneath that fiery red hair of hers that reminded him of all things fall, his favorite time of year. Those auburn locks fell well past her shoulders and brought out the emerald green in her eyes—eyes that were shielded by the thickest, blackest lashes he’d ever seen. Those eyes had a piercing quality that made him relieved he wasn’t sitting on the opposite side of an interrogation table from her. She would see right through lies and into the depths of a person’s soul.

After pulling back from the kiss, he rested his forehead against hers. Memories of the line they’d crossed on their last case flooded him. Having sex was supposed to tamp down some of the ache he felt whenever she was in the same room. Instead, it only made him want to be with her even more. *Great job there, Quint.*

"I did bring it," he said, referring to the suitcase.

"I know," she said without missing a beat.

"Then why did you give me 'the look' at the door?" he asked, leaning back in his seat and grabbing his coffee mug. He needed a caffeine boost to clear his thoughts.

"Because you didn't have it in your hand, which meant you had second thoughts." She picked up her coffee mug and stared inside.

"About us taking our relationship to the next level? Never," he confided. "The timing? There's where the doubts come in."

"Working together is a problem if we're going to date," she agreed, her lips compressing into a frown.

"Right now, I need you as my partner," he said. "I can't risk you asking to be reassigned because our chemistry fizzles."

"Is that what you think is going to happen?" Ree stood up and crossed into the kitchen like she needed to put space between them. She didn't stop until she was at the farthest point from him, and she rolled the coffee mug in between her palms, fuming. It seemed to be taking great effort for her not to speak her mind.

Quint's cell buzzed, interrupting the moment, and he couldn't decide if it was a good thing or not.

"Hold that thought?" he asked as he fished the phone out of his front pocket.

Ree gave a slight nod. Not a great sign but at least she was still willing to talk to him. The fizzle comment had sounded so much better inside his head. It never should have slipped through his filter and come out in a way that put whatever was happening between them in a bad light. But he also couldn't give her what she deserved until he put the bastard who'd been responsible for Tessa's death behind bars. An annoying voice in the back of his head picked that moment to ask if locking up Dumitru would be enough. It wouldn't bring back Tessa or her unborn baby.

"It's Agent Grappell," he said, checking the screen before answering.

"I have good news," Grappell said. Working weekends came with the territory of an undercover agent, but Grappell always went above and beyond the call of a desk agent. "Well, not exactly good but better."

"Okay. Mind if I put you on speaker?" Quint asked. "Ree's in the room."

"She is?" Grappell didn't hide his surprise. Considering it was the weekend and their last case was closed, there wasn't an official reason for the two of them to be together. Quint's personal life wasn't up for discussion. For all Grappell knew, Quint could have shown up to tell Ree the news about Constantin in person.

"Yes," Quint confirmed.

"Of course. Put her on the line."

Quint tapped the screen and motioned for Ree to come closer. She stood her ground in the kitchen and shot him the look that said she was in no mood. He realized in that moment just how big his mistake with her had been.

REE COULD LISTEN just fine from where she stood in the kitchen, tapping her toe. The word *fizzle* would forever be on the list of words she never wanted to hear again in any context. Right now, it needed to go on the back burner so she could focus on what Agent Grappell had to say.

"We have a name of the prisoner who is being held responsible for Constantin's death," Grappell said after perfunctory greetings. "Of course, the warden said he is conducting a full investigation. However, Bjorn was able to pressure him into providing details since they pertain to our ongoing investigation."

A few thoughts ran through Ree's mind. Was this person aware of whom he'd killed? Another thought—did he really care? Was he a patsy? Was he given a pack of cigarettes and extra privileges to take out the new prisoner?

"And?" Quint asked. The rim of his coffee cup suddenly became very interesting. She didn't need to look him in the eyes to realize he would have those same questions.

"You've been granted permission to interview him," Grappell said.

Quint lifted his gaze toward her, but Ree turned to look out the kitchen window.

"You'd have a voice box, of course," Grappell continued. A voice box would distort their voices so they wouldn't be identifiable later to the person being interviewed or anyone else around. "And you'd be able to see him, but he'd be looking at a two-way mirror."

The usual protocol would be in place.

"Why would this guy tell us anything?" Ree asked.

"If he's convicted, he would be facing the chair. Says he'll be killed long before then and it'll be made to look like a suicide. All the guy says he wants is to live long enough for his daughter to graduate high school in four years. She's a freshman," Grappell informed them.

"Strange request from an inmate who just committed murder," Ree said.

"The guy says he had no choice," Grappell said.

"Isn't that what they all say?" Ree quipped.

"He wants a transfer to a prison closer to his wife and

daughter, too," Grappell continued. "Said if he gives up names, he'll have a target on his back if he isn't moved."

"What's he in for?" Quint asked.

"Weapons charges," Grappell said. "The arresting officer in this case was almost one-hundred-percent certain this guy was covering for someone else when he was busted."

"He was willing to take a fall for someone in A-12?" Quint asked. Ree already knew the crime ring was notorious for running guns and had been difficult to pin down because they trusted few people, kept their operation slim and efficient, and the few people on the lower rungs of the ladder had to be willing to take a fall when necessary. It was part of their code. The business was lucrative for those who were able to make the commitment.

"He was in A-12," Grappell stated.

"Why would he turn on them now?" Quint asked.

"First of all, he already gave a statement denying involvement with the death of the new inmate. He said a guard did and that he can prove it. He was a witness to the crime," Grappell continued.

"Is he threatening with a lawyer?" Quint asked.

"No, not yet anyway," Grappell stated.

"I'm confused. Why would he go against a major crime ring with the power to kill someone on the inside who is supposed to be in solitary confinement?" Ree asked. "It doesn't make sense."

"He says his wife and kid are in danger and need to go into Witness Protection immediately," Grappell stated. "Someone will come for them the minute word leaks that he's talking or being moved. He begged for protection for his family. Said we could lock him up for the rest of his life and throw away the key, but please keep his family safe. He finished by saying once he was gone they would come for his family."

"What did Bjorn say?" Quint asked. Lynn Bjorn was their boss. She would have to approve any moves they made.

"I called you first," Grappell admitted. "I'm in the process of writing up the request now but I know how important this case is to you. This guy is willing to talk and, if what he's saying is true, we can't waste time."

"Where does his family live?" Ree asked.

Grappell rattled off an address in North Dallas. Ree opened a kitchen drawer in search of a pen and paper before realizing she could just plug the address into her encrypted phone.

"Do you trust him?" Quint asked Grappell point-blank.

"Can we afford not to?" Ree asked, jumping in before Grappell could answer.

"Ree makes a good point," Grappell said. "How do I write this up?"

"This inmate is promising names with A-12, correct?" Quint asked.

"That's what he said," Grappell confirmed. "He seemed very nervous someone might already be on the way to get his wife and daughter."

Quint looked to Ree. "What do you think?"

She was already grabbing her purse and running shoes. "I think we have no choice but to get to them first."

"Call Bjorn and let her know what's going down," Quint stated as he followed Ree. "She won't want to read about this in a report. Especially if two innocent people end up dead—three, if they get to the inmate."

"Got it," Grappell confirmed. "I'll send over the inmate's name and information. He said his family might take some convincing, so you'll want to tell them some personal details about him. They'll ask about his birthday and his favorite book. You're supposed to give them his daughter's birthday and his favorite movie. The trick is that he doesn't like to read because he's dyslexic. That's how they'll know you were sent by him."

"You drive." Ree ushered Quint out the front door before locking it behind them. From the looks of it, they were headed to Dallas, and back in the thick of the case.

Chapter Two

Quint raced to his vehicle and slid into the driver's seat as Ree hopped into the passenger side. Cell phone in her palm, the target address filled her screen after a couple of taps. The urgency of the situation demanded they table any relationship conversation, which was probably for the best. No one had ever been able to hurt her the way Quint Casey could. She needed to remember that before she ended up with her heart ripped out of her chest.

At forty-two years old, the man had aged to perfection. He was tall and, basically, a solid wall of muscle. Don't even get her started on those sapphire-blue eyes of his, the storm brewing behind them making him even sexier. His muscled torso formed an improbable *V* at the waist and even with day-old stubble on his chin, the man would be considered hot by most standards. He had the kind of body most athletic recruiters would kill for if he was college age. He had the whole look—chiseled jawline, strong, hawklike nose and piercing eyes. Being intelligent put him in a whole new stratosphere.

Intense would be a good word to describe his personality, but he seemed like the type to intensely love someone if he ever truly let them inside. His upbringing had hardened him. He'd been born in a trailer park and raised by a single mother whom he unabashedly referred to as a saint. She'd worked two jobs after his father walked out not long after Quint was born, and she was the reason he got his act together when he'd gone astray in high school.

Now, he blamed himself for his former partner's death and the fact would probably haunt him for the rest of his life. Tessa Kind had been pregnant. She'd convinced him not to tell Bjorn right away, saying she needed time to adjust to the news. The child's father took off after she'd told him. Tessa had asked Quint to be the baby's godfather. The bust that took her life had been complicated by DEA involvement. Someone went left when they should have gone right. Tessa had been killed by mistake. One person had escaped the bust that night, Dumitru. Ree had read the file in detail after the Houston case.

A person like Quint wouldn't take letting down someone he loved lightly, and he'd loved Tessa more than if he'd had a blood-related little sister.

It was most likely the real reason he'd left the suitcase in his truck. He would never allow himself to be happy. He wouldn't see it as fair to Tessa. Since Ree couldn't compete with a ghost, she probably needed to protect her own heart. Quint Casey could wreck her.

The ride to Dallas was quiet as Quint concentrated on the road, gripping the steering wheel like he was about to make damn sure it didn't go anywhere. *Brooding* would be a good word to describe the agent sitting next to her. He had his game face on, and a family was at stake.

"GPS says we're almost there," Ree said, breaking the silence.

Quint glanced at the clock. "Do you want to do the honors?"

"I'll shoot the text," Ree said, firing off the okay to Grappell to send in the federal agents, who'd been parked outside the prison gates in a white minivan for the last twenty minutes. "Axel Ivan will be in protective custody in the next five minutes."

Quint nodded but he didn't speak. He didn't have to for her to know what was running through his thoughts. Ivan might already be dead. He could be hanging in his prison cell by now. He'd taken a huge personal risk in speaking to Agent Grappell on the phone. One that could cost his life. And since the death rate for prisoners related to this case was high, Quint would be tense with worry until he knew Ivan was safely in custody.

Getting to the family before anyone else just took on a new priority now that they'd given the okay to extract Ivan. The North Dallas address was near, so Quint exited the Dallas North Tollway onto Frankford Road. He headed east toward Preston Road. Ivan's wife and daughter lived in a gated community to the right, past the grocery store and strip mall that was on the left.

Beyond the entrance was a large lake. The waterfall was visible from the turn-in. Quint stopped at the guard shack and flashed his badge. The rent-a-cop was short and hefty. He didn't look like he could outrun a turtle. The weapon strapped to his side was most likely a commercial-grade stun gun. Not exactly stellar security but he would probably have 911 on speed dial, anyway.

"Go on through, sir." The security guard pressed a button—the gate almost immediately opened and he waved them in. Grappell would have already made arrangements for them to get past the first line of defense.

"Ivan's wife lives in a town house along the road that circles the community," she informed him. The houses in this area probably started at close to a million dollars. The place where his wife and kid lived would probably be about half to three quarters of the starter-home price in this neighborhood. Ree sighed. Unfortunately, crime paid.

It also came with a price and Ivan's family were targets now that the text came from Grappell, confirming the extraction.

"He's alive," Ree said to Quint. He grunted an acknowledgement. She didn't take offense. He was focused, concentrating all his energy on the task at hand, and probably fighting off the instinct to ask her to wait in the truck. He'd never treated her like anything but an equal.

Ree scanned the street. No one in this neighborhood parked out front. The road was quiet and clear. Too quiet? Too clear? Adrenaline kicked her body into high gear. Her senses sharpened as she went on full alert. A front-gate guard could be bought.

From the side-view mirror, Ree caught sight of a vehicle barreling toward them. Based on the map she'd studied on the way over, there were woods at the very back of the property. If leaving the way they came, which happened to be the lone entrance, was out of the question, they could get to the back wall, climb it and run into the woods. On the other side was a nice neighborhood that wasn't gated, and possible freedom.

If they'd had time, they could have planted an agent there. But the fewer people who knew about this extraction, the better.

"Do you see that?" she asked Quint but he was already studying the rearview mirror. He reached underneath the driver's seat and pulled out a Glock at the same time Ree gripped hers. Cell phone in one hand, she tried to snap a picture of the license plate of the black Acura gunning for them. The suspension had been tweaked, turning the vehicle into one of those lowriders with oversize tires.

"I'll swerve as he gets close, blocking the road. You

bolt out the passenger side and get to Ivan's family," Quint said. Neither had to point out all this would be for nothing if they couldn't save Ivan's wife and daughter. He would clam up faster than a metal trap that had been stepped on by a bear.

"Let's do this," Ree said.

Quint stomped the brake, causing the truck to slant sideways before coming to a screeching halt. The second it slowed down, Ree wasted no time in making a run for it. The town house was half a block away and the Ivans lived in unit number three.

Thankfully, Ree had on tennis shoes and joggers. The August heat threatened to melt the bottom of her shoes before she reached the target. Summers in Texas weren't for the faint of heart. Gunfire caused her to duck and then run in a zigzag pattern to make herself a more difficult target. Cell phone in hand, she managed to fire off a text to Grappell. He would be on standby, waiting to hear from her. The only word she needed to send was help.

QUINT HAD POSITIONED the truck at an angle, blocking the small one-lane residential street as the souped-up Acura with blacked-out windows skidded to a stop fifteen feet away. Rubber tires scorched the pavement. The sun glared against the windshield, making it impossible to see who was driving or how many were inside the vehicle. He had no idea if the gunshot had come from the driver or a passenger. Either way, Quint lowered himself in the seat, making as small a target as humanly possible.

There was no way he could identify himself as an ATF agent if he wanted to stay under the radar. He glanced over to the passenger side of his truck and saw Ree disappear around the block.

The driver of the Acura revved the engine. A threat?

Quint couldn't get a look at the driver or a decent shot. He was responsible for every bullet fired and wouldn't risk a civilian getting hurt.

A front door swung open, and a woman stood at the threshold with a cell phone to her ear, looking more angry than scared and no doubt calling the cops. She must have thought the gunshot was a car backfiring. It would make sense with the Acura.

The Acura driver reversed the vehicle and then gunned it. The woman stepped onto her perfectly decorated porch and behind her impeccably designed landscaping. The houses, lawns and people were flawless in this million-dollar neighborhood.

Quint had to stop the driver before he got to Ree and the Ivans first. She had a decent head start but was on foot and would have to convince Axel's wife to trust her. Not exactly an easy accomplishment given Axel's criminal history. His wife would be trained to be suspicious of strangers, especially those trying to rush her from her home with her daughter to keep them safe. She would be reluctant to accept help from anyone without first receiving word from Axel.

Rather than chase the Acura, Quint backed up, then turned around to the direction he'd been going before jackknifing his vehicle. He would idle his truck in front of the town house and wait for the Acura to make a move. Either way, Quint could block access long enough to hopefully give Ree time to work her magic and get away.

The Acura came up behind Quint. The driver must have figured out Quint's plan. This way, he was at a slight disadvantage because he'd have to do everything in reverse. The driver was smart—Quint would give him that.

After putting the gearshift in reverse, he backed up before the Acura could get close enough to get a good shot off. The sound of a police siren split the air, but it was clear to Quint the squad car wouldn't arrive in time.

Quint grabbed a ball cap from the seat and threw it onto his head to shield as much of his face as possible from the Acura driver. He bolted out of the driver's seat, arms out in front of him with his Glock leading the way. Keeping low would allow him to use the truck to block any bullets as he came around the front of the vehicle. No matter what else happened, he couldn't allow the Acura driver to get to the town house before him.

A quick glance to his left as he rounded the front of the truck said Ree had either worked her way inside the town house, or gone around the back. Using the back door would be tricky considering the Ivans would most likely have some form of protection. An aggressive-sounding dog barked nearby. Close enough to belong to Mrs. Ivan? Other random dog barks had already been filling the air. Then, there was the siren. Close enough to let Quint know help was on the way. Far enough that people could be dead by the time it reached them.

He needed to stack the deck in his favor. For the moment, at least, the driver seemed hesitant to make a run for the town house on foot. Quint needed to make sure he stayed where he was.

The crack of a bullet echoed, and it pinged off the side of the truck. Quint ducked.

New game plan. He dropped down on all fours and took aim. His marksman training came in handy, as he fired a shot and hit the front left tire of the Acura. His second shot was dead on, as well, nailing the front right tire.

That should slow down the bastard when he tried to drive off.

The door of the Acura opened and closed. Suddenly, Quint was staring at a pair of black running shoes. The driver was either abandoning the vehicle or about to charge the town house. Either way, Quint couldn't let the guy off the hook and he sure as hell couldn't let him out of his sight.

At this point, Quint had no idea where Ree was or if she'd gotten the wife and kid to agree to run.

Not knowing was the worst feeling. His mind momentarily went back to when he'd paced up and down a hallway on the sterile white tile of Parkland Hospital's trauma unit, where Tessa had been airlifted to. Minutes had ticked by. Then, an hour was gone.

The news had been delivered by the ER doc and Bjorn. Quint snapped out of it before he hit the point of no return on that road again. The one that always led to a vicious cycle that kept him beating himself up.

The man from the Acura was making a run for it. Quint shook out of his funk and popped to his feet, bolting after the guy. The runner was much shorter than Quint and lighter. He was quick, with less bulk to carry, and the guy ran fast enough to make the college track team. Too bad he'd wasted his talents on being a criminal instead. An adrenaline push probably wasn't helping matters.

Since Speed Runner had abandoned his vehicle, Quint figured it was probably registered to a phantom person if it had a registration at all.

Speed Runner jumped a fence and Quint cursed. His lungs already burned as much as his thighs, but the jogging-suit-in-August-wearing bastard didn't get to win.

As Quint scaled the fence, Speed Runner turned and fired a wild shot. The bullet pinged the bricks on the corner of the home ten feet away because he hadn't taken the time to aim. In the next second, he was already scaling the ten-foot-high wooden privacy fence this area was famous for. No one wanted strangers to have the ability to see what went on in their backyard. No fences in the front, not even wire ones. North Texas backyards were sacred. Quint wished Speed Runner would have taken them on that tour instead. His chest wouldn't be burning nearly as badly right now. He was also fairly certain he'd be picking splinters out of his fingers long after this chase ended.

Five blocks over, Speed Runner started slowing. The first sign he was running out of steam at this blistering pace sent a wave of relief over Quint. He was a couple of steps behind the younger, faster runner but Quint had something this kid didn't—stamina.

The sirens were closing in on the neighborhood. Could Quint get this guy and keep his own identity a secret? Security would have been alerted to allow them passage, but he wouldn't necessarily be told why. Quint would have to allow himself to be arrested, which would leave Ree on her own. She was fully capable of doing her job without him there to hold her hand.

And yet the thought of leaving his partner vulnerable ate at him from the inside out. Let this guy go and he could be a problem for Ree. He was still armed and dangerous. She was out here somewhere.

Speed Runner continued slowing down, and Quint maintained his pace. At this rate, he would catch up to Speed Runner in a matter of seconds. His lungs gasped for air but he knew exactly how far he could push his body, and he had a little more gas in the tank.

He was almost within reach, but Speed Runner whirled around and jabbed a knife into Quint's side. Quint was close enough to knock the weapon out of Speed Runner's hand as it went off. The bullet shot through a fence. Quint winced, praying there'd be no scream to indicate an innocent civilian had been hit.

Quint dove at Speed Runner's knees a second after he turned to run. He connected and heard an immediate snap. A broken bone would slow down this bastard. Stopping a second ago to shoot had cost the jerk his freedom. Speed Runner bounced to his good foot. From the corner of Quint's eye, he saw security running toward them. Speed Runner tried to shake him off, but his grip on Speed Runner's ankle was unbreakable. Quint rolled onto his back, grabbed Speed Runner's other ankle and squeezed. Speed Runner cried out in pain as Quint jerked the man's feet out from under him.

Speed Runner landed with a thud and a grunt as all air seemed to whoosh from his lungs. Before he could make another move, Quint rolled on top of him, flipped the guy facedown before he knew what hit him and then practically crushed him with powerful thighs as he secured him in place.

"Freeze," Security said.

"Detain this jerk until the police arrive while I check on my friend. His gun is over there," Quint motioned toward the metal glinting through blades of green grass a few feet away. "Do it now. I have to go."

Security complied, handcuffing Speed Runner before securing the weapon and calling it in. With no sign of Ree, Quint could only hope Speed Runner had acted alone.

Chapter Three

"Keep your head down and stay as quiet as you can for me. Okay?" Ree crouched in front of Axel's wife, Laurie, and his daughter, Ariana, as the two huddled together in between the brick home and Japanese boxwoods. The common shrubs had been elevated into a row of perfectly symmetrical round balls.

The sound of shots being fired nearby had caused her to duck into the shrubs. Could she circle back to the truck near the family home? Could she risk calling Quint? He could be hiding somewhere and even the slight buzz of his cell could give him away.

She couldn't risk it no matter how badly she wanted to reach out to him, to know he was safe. Their recent romantic relationship had nothing to do with how much her heart was hammering her ribs at the thought something had happened to him. He'd used himself as a distraction so she could get to Ivan's family.

Police sirens had abruptly stopped. Cops were on the scene. Since they were still undercover, no one could know about their ATF affiliation, so it was best for her to hide for now. Otherwise, she would be arrested along with Quint if he wasn't already in cuffs. They would have to go to jail, leaving Laurie and Ariana vulnerable to the next attack. And there would be another. News was already out about Axel turning witness based on the fact Speed Runner came after Axel's family. It was the only logical conclusion after Speed Runner showed up.

Laurie nudged Ree at the sight of two officers walking across the street, checking bushes. The hopeful look in her eyes said she had no idea. The so-called cops wore black uniforms, not navy blue. And they had on white sneakers, a dead giveaway that they didn't work for the DPD. Officers there wore black shoes. Their belts were all wrong, too. All they wore were badges and shoulder holsters. These men were imposters. Ree needed them to keep moving, as they continued to poke sticks into shrubs far away from the ones she and the Ivans were in.

How long could they stay hidden?

Ree gave a slight headshake to Laurie. Her brown eyes grew wide as she pulled her daughter a little closer. The teenager was a mini version of her mother, with a slightly longer nose, no doubt inherited from her father.

The Ivan women were beautiful, though. They could model for the Italian version of *Vogue*—both had brown eyes, long, slicked-back ponytails, and were tall with some curves along with olive-colored skin. They were the picture of perfection, all high cheekbones, small nose and soft lips. Their silky black hair framed their perfectly symmetrical faces. Laurie was dressed in a silky cream-colored pantsuit that hugged her figure to perfection while Ariana had on a jumper that fell to midthigh. Laurie's clothing could be described as sexy without crossing the line of being vulgar.

Axel was a beast of a man from the pictures Grappell had just texted to her, large frame, large head, and large nose. He seemed to hold those old-fashioned, gender-biased rules that meant a man was the sole provider and protector of his family. Ree couldn't relate to any of it, but to each his own. Some women wanted to be protected. Some women wanted to be handled like breakable china dolls. Some women wanted a credit card without a limit and all the free time in the world to look and be some wacked-out version of perfection.

Ree preferred the messy chaos of her own closet. She threw outfits together that sometimes worked and sometimes undeniably did not. Perfection was unattainable and, quite frankly, boring.

But that was just her opinion. She had to admit perfection looked pretty great on the Ivan women.

The fake cops moved from house to house, and it was only a matter of time before they would head this way. The street was quiet. If anyone was home, they seemed afraid to step on their front lawns. Rightfully so, since a police chopper was overhead. There'd been the screech of rubber burning, gunshots fired and police sirens in the last fifteen minutes. She didn't blame everyone for locking their doors and staying inside. In fact, she preferred it. There would be less chance of a civilian being in the wrong place at the wrong time and ending up with a bullet in their chest.

Come on, Quint. Why hadn't her partner called?

Ree held on to her phone, using the camera feature to zoom in and snap a few pictures. They would most likely be too grainy to get anything usable, but it never hurt to try. Her stomach clenched as she thought about any of those bullets ending up in her partner.

She checked her cell. There was no word from Quint or Grappell.

Laurie nudged Ree again. She looked up in time to see the "officers" cross the street, coming onto their side five houses down. It wouldn't be long before they were right on top of the trio.

Ree nodded and tried her level best to give a reassuring look to Laurie. Ariana's eyes were still squeezed shut, as she looked like she was blocking out the world. One look at the kid said she'd been overprotected to the nth degree, but this also demonstrated how much Axel Ivan loved his family. Ree couldn't stand her family's overprotective side, but she appreciated the amount of love and care he'd put in. The pair of them seemed to love him just as much. Laurie's first question once Ree had established her identity was whether or not her husband was all right. The concern that had etched lines in the near-perfect woman's forehead had been real. To her, Axel was like any other businessman who worked and took care of his family. It seemed easy for her to forget that he was on the wrong side of the law.

The second thing that had come out of Laurie's mouth was that her husband was a good man and couldn't possibly have killed someone in prison. Her argument was that he'd gone to mass every week before prison. Strange argument for a criminal's wife to make on behalf of her husband. Apparently, moving weapons that killed others into the hands of very bad people who used said weapons to murder and maim didn't register as bad in Laurie's book. As long as her husband wasn't the one pulling the trigger, she seemed fine with his line of work.

This didn't seem like the time to educate his wife on the fact that Ivan would have had to kill for his boss if asked to, and probably already had. Ree decided to let the woman live in her fantasy world. It wasn't Ree's job to educate a criminal's wife. It was, however, her job to keep the woman and her daughter alive.

The fake cops were three houses down and time was running out. Ree had no qualms about outrunning the men in "uniform" herself. Laurie and Ariana didn't seem like the fast running types. She needed a diversion or a break. Since luck hadn't exactly been in her favor of late, she figured a distraction was her best shot.

Glancing around, she searched for something she could throw. She'd played enough softball in her youth to realize she could chuck a rock across the street. If she could get Dumb and Dumber over there to look in the opposite direction, maybe she could get Laurie and Ariana to run around the house to the backyard.

Then what?

"How well do you know your neighbors?" Ree asked.

"We keep to ourselves since Axel went to prison. We used to throw amazing parties..." She paused in dramatic fashion, like her life was somehow harder than most because she could no longer fire up the barbecue and have the neighborhood over for dinner now that her husband had been busted.

Sorry. Ree left her sympathy for criminals who deserved to go to jail at home.

Two houses. Ree could always point her gun at the men and hope like hell they listened to her when she made them handcuff each other. Oh, right. There were no handcuffs on their belts, either. Another dead giveaway.

She texted her exact location to Grappell and begged for a squad car to circle the street. Then held her breath and prayed he would get the message in time.

OUT OF BREATH, Quint pushed his legs to keep going despite the burn in his lungs. Ree had to be around here somewhere. She couldn't have gone too far without the truck. Could he text her without putting her at risk? She hadn't reached out to him. The annoying voice in the back of his mind picked that moment to remind him that she would if she was able to.

The thought wasn't exactly reassuring.

Quint figured Ree had two options—the trees in the back of the neighborhood, or get to Frankford Road, a busy six-lane street that led back to the tollway to the west and Preston, another busy street, to the east.

The path she chose would have depended largely on the situation. There was no way to reason it out. She would follow the path of least resistance. Trees or road? At this point, it was a coin toss.

Of course, he could go back to his truck that, by now, would most likely be guarded by cops along with the Acura with the shot-out tires. A neighbor might be able to identify Quint in his ball cap. He took it off, and tucked it inside his back pocket. The guard shack might have a security uniform he could "borrow" for the time being.

Quint circled back toward the gate. A street over, he stopped in his tracks as he saw two cops smacking shrubs with a stick.

"Hey," one of the cops shouted, but something wasn't quite right about the guy. Even from halfway down the block, Quint could sense something was off. The uniform? The way the guy walked as he moved toward Quint? The cop didn't have the usual swagger. There was also another indicator. The belt was a little too light, and missing a few key tools.

Quint took off running, circling back to the way he came. He figured he could run a couple of blocks over, get these guys on the wrong track and then head back to the guard shack from a different angle.

As he turned the corner, he caught sight of something in the shrubs near one of the fake cops, a bright floral print of some kind. Could it be Ree and the Ivans?

Since only one of the "cops" was following him and the other was moving toward the shrubs in question,

Quint needed a new plan. He spun around, pulled out his Glock and aimed at a mailbox on the opposite side of the street. He fired a round, figuring it would get their attention.

The move worked as planned, so he booked it out of there. With both supposed officers on his tail, he needed to hop the wall blocking the neighborhood off from Frankford Road so he could get the lay of the land. His cell buzzed inside his pocket and relief washed over him.

Continuing in a dead run, he fished the phone out of his pocket and checked the screen. It was her. He answered and tried to speak through labored breaths.

"Thank you," she whispered, and he could hear the rustle of shrubbery.

"I'll bring these guys out to the front of the neighborhood. Can you get to the trees?" he asked.

"No can do," she said. "Cops are already there."

"Then I'll get these guys over the wall and to the strip mall across the street. I'll lose them in the grocery parking lot," he offered.

"I'm already requesting a car to meet us at the gate," she stated, sounding winded.

"If I'm not there in ten minutes, leave without me," he instructed.

"Got it," she said before ending the call. Neither could afford to take their attention off the goal. Hers was to get the Ivans to the guard shack safely. His was to lose the jerks following him and join up with Ree. Easy peasy.

Quint knew he was in trouble when he started whipping out corny lines. He'd been ignoring the red dot on his shirt that was flowering like lilies on a sunny morning after a spring rain. There was no way he was seriously hurt. The bullets had flown near him, some getting a little too close for comfort, but he would have registered a hit.

Exhaustion was setting in because he'd been running, then in a fight, and now back to running without much in his stomach in the way of food. Or caffeine. He never got a chance to finish his cup of coffee at Ree's, he thought as he leaped over a bush. He misjudged the height, caught his toe on a vine and went down face-first.

Branches stabbed his arms, torso and neck as he tried to tuck and roll out of the shrubbery. Whoever planted that thing deserved to be shot. But he couldn't allow himself to wallow in self-pity because the fake cops had rounded the corner and their smirks told him everything he needed to know about what they planned to do to him if they caught up.

Pain be damned, Quint untangled his shirt from the grip of the shrub and pushed up to his feet. There wasn't anything to grab hold of as he got hit with a bout of light-headedness.

He tried to take a step forward, but did a face-plant instead, eating grass and dirt. This was not good. This wasn't part of the plan. This wasn't supposed to be happening to Quint Casey, one of the ATF's finest agents.

The sounds of heavy footsteps and panting breaths drew closer as Quint tried to force open his eyes. Darkness tugged at the back of his mind, but he refused to give in. *Shake it off, Casey.*

Why couldn't he?

Chapter Four

Quint had distracted the fake cops. Ree stayed put as the text from Grappell said Dallas PD was coming. An SUV rounded the corner as she stepped out from the bushes. She waved her arms in the air, uncertain where Quint had gone. This scenario had gone south and Grappell had been forced to divulge information about her and the Ivans. As of now, Grappell was working on a safe house.

The officer stopped the vehicle. Over the loudspeaker, he asked for the three of them to come out of the bushes with their hands up. Ree's were already held up high.

"Do as the officer says," Ree urged Laurie and Ariana. The teen clung to her mother as though her life depended on it. They complied as the officer exited his vehicle.

"I understand the three of you are in need of a ride," he stated as they walked toward him.

"That's correct, sir," Ree said. "However, there are four of us."

"I was told three." The officer shook his head.

"I'd like to verify the information once we're en route," Ree stated. Bjorn must want Quint arrested if she didn't make provisions for him yet. He might be able to get information while in jail.

"I'm Officer Reinhart. I need to pat you down." The tall

officer with a runner's build wore Ray-Ban sunglasses. "My SO said I need to put on a show for the neighbors."

Ree gave a slight nod.

"Hands on the vehicle," Officer Reinhart demanded.

She gave a slight nod to the Ivans before walking to the front of the vehicle and placing her palms on the hood. Laurie and Ariana followed suit, daughter sticking close to her mother.

The officer gave a quick pat-down, nothing to cause concern of abuse of power. Ree climbed in the back of the vehicle along with the others. She slipped her cell phone out of her pocket, careful to hide the fact she was texting to any watchful eyes. She bent forward, resting her elbows on her knees as the officer took his seat. A tow truck passed by on the road behind them. It was the same direction Quint had taken off to.

She texted Grappell that the three of them were safe inside the back of the SUV. And then she asked about Quint.

When Grappell commented on her and the Ivans but not on Quint, her heart sank. It meant there was no word from him. This seemed like a good time to remind herself he was a professional who was the best at his job. He'd most likely been in stickier situations than this and would come out the other side just fine.

Pinching her nose, Ree leaned back in the seat as the officer finished typing on the laptop that was affixed to his vehicle. He drove off as she kept an eye out for her partner.

"Where are we going?" Laurie asked in barely a whisper.

"To a safe place," Ree commented. She couldn't tell Laurie what she didn't know—an exact location. She could only pray Quint had been picked up and was on his way to the safe house, the same as them.

The officer pulled onto the North Dallas Tollway, NDT, and headed south. Ree read the signs as they passed. First Campbell. Next, Arapaho, followed by Beltline. Then Spring Valley to Alpha. Reinhart took the Alpha Road exit then made his way to Midway Road and headed north again toward the Addison Airport, where he navigated his way into the parking lot of Million Air Dallas.

"This is the end of the line for me," Reinhart said, nodding toward a waiting Suburban with blacked-out windows.

"Thank you," Ree said, then added, "but you'll have to open the door for us if you're ready for us to exit the vehicle."

The officer exited the driver's seat and then opened the door. "If you ladies need further assistance, I'm sure your boss will let mine know."

"My name is Henry and I'll be driving you today. Agent Grappell said to make you comfortable," the driver said through a rolled-down partition. All she could see was a traditional blue chauffeur's hat along with mirror-lensed glasses. "There's cold water in the cooler, sealed bottles."

"Thank you. We're good," Ree said before the partition came up and they were effectively sealed off from the outside world. The Ivans made themselves at home immediately, relaxing in the leather seats. Laurie pulled two bottles of sparkling water from the small cooler, handing one over to her daughter as she exhaled.

These two looked like they belonged riding around in a vehicle like this with a driver at the ready and refreshments at arm's reach. Ree couldn't decide if she was sad for them. Everything in their world seemed manicured and catered A strange ache filled Ree. She'd come to resent Sunday suppers at her mother's ranch due to her mother's disapproval of Ree's career, but they'd been good once. Thinking back, it was a tradition her father had started since long before she could remember before he died when she was eleven years old.

Ree pulled out her cell and palmed it, praying for a message from Grappell about Quint. She started to request an update but realized she would probably be the first person he contacted the second he received word.

Rather than try to sit back in her seat, which she realized was impossible under the circumstances, she leaned forward and checked her inbox. Scrolling through names that barely registered, her thoughts kept drifting back to Quint. If he was safe, he would have made contact by now. The fact he hadn't checked in with Grappell after luring away the fake cops distressed her.

Was he still in the neighborhood? She'd watched for him on Frankford Road, past the apartments to the right and the shopping center with the Albertsons grocery store and her Tex-Mex favorite at the end of the mall. There'd been no sign of him on the brick wall encasing the neighborhood to the left. She'd kept an eye there as well.

The fake cops had to have caught up with him. It was the only explanation that made sense. He couldn't outrun them and now he was…

Ree stopped herself right there. It was possible Quint had escaped and his cell phone had gotten lost in the process. Again, she reminded herself how fully capable he was of taking care of himself. She also decided to point out her concern wasn't more than caring for her partner. They'd been through some rough times on the cases they'd worked together so far and they'd bonded.

Caring about what happened to each other was part of what made them good partners.

The partition rolled down.

"This is where I'm supposed to drop you off," the driver said. A text came through as he added, "You should be receiving a message any second with an address."

She thanked the driver and ushered Laurie and Ariana out of the vehicle. Neither looked too thrilled to be exiting the safety of the Suburban.

An address came through via a text from Grappell. Ree brought up her map feature as the Suburban pulled away—2436 Briarwood Lane. They'd been dropped off at the Farmer's Branch Moose Lodge across the street from the neighborhood. They would walk Towerwood Drive across Webb Chapel Road, which would lead them into the neighborhood of the safe house on Briarwood Lane.

"How much farther do we have to go?" Laurie asked, holding tight to her daughter, who looked ready to burst into tears. They were sweaty and breathing hard.

"Almost there," Ree reassured her, thinking gratitude might be a better tact to take instead of whining. Then again, she would never understand anyone who chose the kind of life they lived over the straight and narrow. Ree's life might not be champagne and Italian leather shoes, but she had a lot of pride in knowing she'd worked for everything she owned. Her car. Her home. Her furnishings.

The safe house looked like any other home on the block, a one-story tan-and-brown brick. The wooden door had a peephole. Ree stood in front of it so she could clearly be seen. She texted Grappell the second they were standing on the small concrete block porch. The grass in this area was a patchy yellow-green. There were more weeds than lawn. The trim on the house was in severe need of a paint job, but it fit in with the neighbors. This safe house had a pair of ATF agents acting as spouses while on another case.

The door swung open, and an agent ushered them inside.

"I live here with my 'wife' and have a lot of cousins come visit," the agent said by way of explanation of their cover. He was a solid six feet tall with curly brown hair that looked to be in need of a cut. He had on a Gap T-shirt and cotton shorts with flip-flops to round out the look. Ree guessed him to be close in age to her, in his mid-thirties.

"Is there a place where my daughter and I can wash up?" Laurie asked.

"Yeah, sure," he said, then pointed to a small hallway right off the living room.

Laurie thanked him and scurried off as Ree shot him a look.

"They can't go anywhere. Bars on the windows," he reassured her. "My name is Lucas Hoover."

"Like the vacuum?" Ree asked.

"Like the president," Lucas stated with a hint of pride and a smirk.

"I'm Ree, but you probably already know that," she said after a firm handshake. He wouldn't know much else except who she was and that she was bringing friends. She checked her cell in case there was a message from Grappell.

"No word on your partner yet?" Lucas asked.

She shook her head.

"What can I set you up with?" he asked. "A quick tour?"

"Sounds good," she stated, thinking the living room was a relic from the nineties. Gold wallpaper with a print design. The seating was decent—a sofa and a couple of leather club chairs and benches positioned in a circle for talking. The room immediately opened up to a dining area with sliding glass doors behind the table. To the left was a standard kitchen with all-white appliances and hunter green wallpaper. The table seated six and had laptops set up at two of the spots. She imagined those were for him and his "wife."

He walked her down the same hallway Laurie and Ariana had disappeared to a few minutes ago. The sink water was running as they passed the bathroom. There were two bedrooms on the left and at the end of the hall to the right was the master. It had its own bathroom, which Ree assured Lucas she didn't need to see.

"Are you hungry?" he asked as they made their way back into the kitchen area.

"Not me," she said, checking her cell for messages again. "I'll ask A and B," she said, referring to the women they were assigned to protect.

"There's food in the fridge. Drinks, too. Make yourselves at home. My wife's name is Chelsea Ridder. She 'works' a regular job and our cover is that I work from home. We both work in tech. She's a graphic designer and I'm a programmer."

"Sounds good," Ree said. She was listening despite the fact she checked her phone two more times. And then it buzzed in her hand. Her heart pounded inside her rib cage as her pulse skyrocketed.

Quint has been shot at, stabbed, and arrested.

Ree glanced up at Lucas. "My partner has been stabbed."

"Where is he?" Lucas immediately reached inside his pocket for what she assumed was keys.

"Jail," she said as a half-dozen scenarios raced through her mind, none of them good.

THE LAST THING Quint remembered was hearing sirens, then heavy footsteps. As he'd blacked out, the perps bolted in the opposite direction. He woke in a jail cell. No phone. No gun. No wallet. Since he didn't keep his badge inside his black fold-over wallet, anyway, he had no way to ID himself as law enforcement. Plus, he was still undercover.

His shirt was soaked in blood. His? He'd been bandaged up.

Quint tried to sit up. Pain shot through him as the memories came back of being chased, the fight and being stabbed by Speed Runner. At least Speed Runner was locked behind bars somewhere inside this place.

As Quint tried to move, he felt the effects of being in a knife fight. Still, his thoughts flew to Ree. He'd drawn the fake cops away from her. Did she get away? Was she safe? His chest squeezed at the thought anything could have happened to her. The Ivans were the least of his worries. The lead drying up wouldn't matter if he lost Ree. Catching Dumitru would have no meaning if there wasn't something to look forward to when the case was closed.

A uniformed officer came into the room with a set of keys in hand. His tan shirt and matching pants with brown stripes down the sides of his legs signaled he was a jailer. He had salt-and-pepper hair, wrinkles that said he was closing in on retirement age and a thick enough accent Quint that figured the guy said *y'all* a fair amount.

"You're out, Matthews," the officer said. His name tag read Rex Davis. Given his height and lankiness, he probably grew up with a nickname like T-Rex.

"How is that?" Quint asked, playing the part. He'd

been arrested dozens of times for the sake of a case in the past. It was nothing new. The charges against him included disorderly conduct and disturbing the peace. An investigation was pending that might add charges.

"You made bail. Sally Struthers posted for you. Said she was your mother," Rex continued.

Sally Struthers? Quint shook his head. Grappell should definitely get a gold star for that one. He always referenced stars from old TV shows his dad used to watch. Once Quint got his cell phone back, he'd text his response—*All in the Family.*

Speaking of which, he asked, "Any chance you have my cell inside there?" He motioned toward the paper bag in T-Rex's hand.

"Just a black wallet," the officer said.

No keys? Then Quint remembered he'd left them in the vehicle near the Ivan house. "Is my mother outside waiting?"

The officer walked Quint to the front, closing and locking doors behind them. A few minutes later, they stood in the lobby, where Quint was handed the paper bag. "Said she'd be in the blue Honda."

Quint's heart stirred at the thought of seeing Ree again.

Chapter Five

"Thank you, sir," Quint said, figuring he needed to leave on a positive note. His thoughts raced and he wouldn't get information until he got inside the Honda.

Outside, a blue Civic waited. An agent sat in the driver's seat, motioning for him to hurry. He did, covering his disappointment it wasn't Ree in the driver's seat. In fact, he couldn't get away from the jail fast enough.

The sun was setting, which at this time of year, meant it was after 8:00 p.m. He'd been out cold for hours. He hopped into the passenger seat. His body screamed in pain with the slightest movement. Fresh blood soaked a bandage as he checked underneath his shirt.

He didn't exchange names with the other agent. There was no need.

"I have a partner," Quint said once the door was closed and he was able to strap in his seat belt. "We got separated."

"All I know is that she's fine and at the safe house, where I'm dropping you off," the agent said. "Sally" was really a man in a wig. Once they pulled out of the parking lot and stopped at the first red light, he took off the wig and tossed it in the back seat. The wig meant he'd been pulled from an undercover assignment to help out.

"Thanks for picking me up," Quint stated. Granted,

it was the guy's job but Quint always appreciated a fellow agent's time. Being undercover was difficult enough without being tagged to pick up someone from jail and risk blowing their cover.

"Not a problem," the agent said.

Quint didn't spend a whole lot of time memorizing the details of the guy's face. He stopped at the bright red lipstick and overdone rouge. The rest of the drive was spent in silence. Quint leaned his seat about as far back as it could go.

Before long, the agent stopped the Honda in front of a one-story brick house in a suburban neighborhood.

"Sorry if I bled on your seat," Quint said.

"Don't worry about it," the agent said. "It'll only help with my credibility."

Quint cracked a smile that felt like it broke his ribs in half.

"Mind if I ask a personal question, though?" the agent asked.

"Go ahead." Answering was the least Quint could do.

"Are you, by any chance, *the* Quint Casey?" the agent asked.

"Guilty as charged" was all Quint said as he opened the door. Getting in and out of the sedan was painful.

"Interesting," the agent stated. "It's been a pleasure working with someone like you even for a quick pickup."

"I appreciate the compliment," Quint said and meant it.

"You're a legend in the agency," the agent said.

All Quint could do was smile at that one.

"Believe about half of what you hear about me," Quint joked.

The agent laughed. "Will do, sir."

Quint closed the door and headed to the house. As he

stepped onto the concrete block porch, the door swung open and Ree came bolting toward him. He was so damn happy to see her that he forgot to warn her not to touch him too hard. When she barreled into his chest and wrapped her arms around him, he let out a grunt.

Ree pulled back and apologized.

"Don't be sorry," he said. "You're the best thing that's happened to me today."

She looked him up one side and down the other. "This blood is fresh. You're turning ghost-white. Let's get you inside."

Ree moved beside him and wrapped an arm around him for support. He leaned on her, needing the extra help to get inside.

Quint stumbled. He was dizzy and saw stars as he was led to a bedroom, where he was helped onto the bed. "I should clean up first before I bleed all over the place."

Those were the last words he remembered saying.

The next time Quint opened his eyes, there was a worried-looking doctor hovering over him. Then, later, he awoke to a dim light on the nightstand and Ree asleep in a chair next to the bed between him and the door.

By the first light of morning, Quint felt awake enough to sit up. The second he moved, Ree bolted up.

"How do you feel?" she asked. The concern in her voice told him it had been a rough night.

"Better," he said. "I have one helluva headache, though. Any chance there's coffee brewing?"

"I heard one of the agents named Lucas up half an hour ago. I can check." She pushed up to standing and started toward the door.

Quint figured he could make it across the hall to the bathroom on his own. Standing made him feel woozy. The room started to spin, so he took a step toward the dresser and held on for the ride. He'd had worse benders than this, he tried to convince himself. Except he wasn't much of a drinker. A beer here and there was as far as it had gone. He'd grown up around too much alcoholism in the trailer park to ever fall down that hole.

His stomach gurgled and growled. He probably should have asked for a power bar before trying to put any caffeine in his stomach. At this point, he'd take either.

Making it across the hall took some effort. He was certain "Sally" from the Honda wouldn't be too impressed with his skills at this moment. Quint made himself laugh, and that just hurt.

He washed his face and located a toothbrush still in its wrapper. Safe houses kept various supplies on hand for when they were needed. There would be clothing in various sizes. After brushing his teeth, he felt half-human again. The walk back to the bedroom went a bit easier. He shrugged out of his shirt, and the simple act was more painful than he ever imagined.

It slid out of his hand and onto the floor. Quint looked down at the crumpled shirt. Too bad. There was no way he would be able to pick it up. A clean one waited in the dresser. He located his size and tossed it onto the bed for later.

Ree appeared at the doorway, carrying a tray. She stopped the second her eyes dropped to his bare chest. Suddenly, her cheeks flushed. She cleared her throat. She'd seen him completely naked before, so her reaction caught him off guard. Was it the circumstances or did she regret going there with him on their last assignment?

The suitcase. Could this tie back to the fact he'd shown up at her doorstep without it in his hand? Did she want to dial back the relationship?

"I brought food," she said. "And coffee."

Without making eye contact, she moved to the bed and set down the tray.

"Do you need help sitting down again?" she asked, her gaze steady on the bandages on his chest.

"I got it." At least, he hoped he had it. "Mind if I take your chair instead?"

"No. Go right ahead." She scooted the tray closer as he grabbed both arms of the chair, steadily lowering himself down. "What hurts?"

"Everything," he said, wincing as he reached for the fork. The scrambled eggs and bacon looked and smelled amazing.

"Lucas made this for you. Chelsea, the one who drove you here, had to leave so she said she'd check in later," Ree stated.

He didn't like how easily Lucas's name rolled off her tongue.

"Have you been getting to know each other?" he asked, realizing how jealous that sounded.

"Us three, you mean?" she quipped, cocking an eyebrow. "Not to mention Laurie and Ariana Ivan."

Point taken.

"GRAPPELL SENT A message an hour ago stating we can watch the interview with Axel Ivan since we were rerouted to save his family earlier," Ree said, steering the conversation to work. There was no way she was letting him get away with the jealous routine now. He'd been clear on where he stood with her when he'd left the suitcase in the car. Fizzle.

"Good. Did he say when we should leave?" Quint asked, wincing as he leaned forward to grab the tray and position it in his lap.

"You're hurt," she reminded him. "There's no reason

to start making plans to ditch out of here in your condition. Plus, you haven't met Laurie and Ariana yet."

"Where are they?" he asked.

"In the bedroom. I'm giving them a minute to adjust and process everything that has happened and changed in their lives," she stated.

"Good idea. As for me, I've felt worse, looked worse," he said before taking a bite of egg and chewing. He followed it with a sip of coffee and some of the tension lines in his face eased.

"Not on my watch, you haven't," she stated. "You'd be a liability if we left here and something happened."

Quint looked poised to argue, then took another bite instead.

"Your health has to come first and the doctor said you need to take it easy," she stated.

"Can't," he said without missing a beat.

"Or won't?" she asked.

"Does it matter?" He sounded annoyed.

"It does to me," she countered. His anger was him covering the fact he was weak right now. It was also his frustration coming out. Despite those things being true, she couldn't let him run around half-cocked and in terrible physical condition. In fact, she needed to tell him what she'd been thinking since finding out he'd been stabbed. "You know, you could stay here until WITSEC arrives. Hand off Laurie and Ariana, then heal. You have to give your body the time it needs, or you could end up in real trouble, Quint."

"Did you have a replacement in mind?" He picked up the toast and ripped off a piece before tossing it in his mouth.

"I mean, the obvious choice is here on property," she

continued, and she could almost see his temperature rising by the redness in his cheeks.

"Tell Lucas that he can—"

"It's not Lucas I was suggesting," she said, cutting him off. "It was Chelsea. Why would your mind automatically snap to him?"

"Guess I was wrong." Quint didn't say another word while he finished every last bite of food and then drained his coffee mug. "We both know this is my case, Ree."

"Plans can change," she stated. Having grown up with four brothers, she knew a thing or two about being stubborn. Quint was digging in his heels due to his personal involvement in the case. "And we both know this is how cases go sideways."

"If you don't think I'm competent, that's fine," he said. "But this is my case and I can easily request to be the one to work with Chelsea instead of you."

"What do you think Bjorn's response is going to be?" she asked. There'd been a whole lot of desperation in his voice.

Quint picked up the tray from his lap and bent forward to set it on the bed.

"For what it's worth, I was worried sick about you," she finally said on a sharp sigh. "I have no doubts about your abilities as an agent, Quint. But you have to admit, sometimes it's better for someone to stay back and call in plays from the desk. Or, in your case, bed."

"We can work my injuries into the cover story," he said. "We used the fake boot before and it worked."

"Because it was a fake injury," she reminded him. "This is very real. You were stabbed and I had no idea where you were or what kind of condition you were in."

Quint managed to join her at the foot of the bed. He

pulled her against his chest, where she heard the staccato rhythm of his heartbeat.

"I don't know what I would have done if anything had happened to you," she admitted, leaning into him.

He brushed a kiss on her lips before resting his forehead against hers.

"I'm right here," he reassured her. "I'm a little damaged but I'm okay."

He was alive and there was a difference.

A hot tear rolled down her cheek. It was all she could afford since she didn't want to give away the fact that she and Quint had crossed a line in their professional relationship. The sound of footsteps coming toward them from down the hallway caused her to sit upright and start checking his bandages.

She cleared her throat as she heard Lucas at the door. "The doctor said these have to be redressed every night. You have to wrap yourself in Saran Wrap to take a shower so they'll stay dry."

Lucas stepped inside the room and introduced himself. He and Quint shook hands and then he thanked him for the meal.

"There's more coffee if you're ready for another cup," Lucas said. His gaze bounced from Quint to Ree and back. He was on to them. Based on his expression, he'd picked up on the attraction simmering between them.

"I'll be right there," Quint said and his voice was husky, basically a dead giveaway.

This wasn't good. News like this could get around and damage both of their reputations. Ree bit back a curse. They weren't used to working so closely with other agents, people who would pick up on their underlying chemistry.

"Right," Lucas said. "Good to see you sitting up again."

Ree stood. "I'll refill your coffee."

"Okay, thanks," Quint said in what must be one of the most awkward conversations Ree had ever been engaged in with coworkers.

She grabbed his mug and made a beeline for the kitchen. She'd go pretty much anywhere to get out of that room at this point, so she could regroup and figure out how to spin what Lucas had just seen happening between her and Quint.

Chapter Six

"I'd like to get up and walk," Quint said. "How about we join Ree in the kitchen?"

"Sounds good to me," Lucas agreed.

Quint managed the trip to the next room without letting his face give away the sheer amount of pain he was in. He immediately locked gazes with Ree as he headed to the table and sat down.

"Your phone has gone MIA. Service was shut off and data was erased remotely," Lucas informed as Quint motioned for the agent to take a seat. Lucas obliged. "It's great to have an opportunity to work with someone of your caliber."

Quint never knew what to say to a comment like Lucas's, so he went with "Thanks."

"I've heard about some of your busts," Lucas continued. He smiled like he was about to start recounting them and then his expression became solemn. "Tessa Kind was an amazing agent."

"Yes, she was," Quint confirmed.

"I was sorry to hear," Lucas continued.

The subject was still sore with Quint even though he appreciated how many lives Tessa had touched. Others seemed genuinely sorry about the loss. It warmed Quint's heart to think her memory was still alive in the agency.

"I appreciate the sentiment," Quint said. In a surprise move, even to himself, he added, "I miss her."

"How could you not?" Lucas stated. "She was intelligent and knew her stuff. Her sense of humor was legendary. She kept me on the straight and narrow early on in my career. She was a damn fine agent."

"Did you know Tessa personally?" Quint asked, caught off guard at all the compliments.

"I worked with her on my first undercover case," Lucas admitted.

Quint rocked his head. Tessa had the patience to work with newbies, whereas he'd rather stick tacks in his eyelids. Patience in a case was one thing. Patience in working with new people wasn't something Quint had ever been able to tolerate despite Bjorn's pleas for him to make an exception every once in a while. It just wasn't in his DNA.

"She kicked my butt more than once," Lucas said, his gaze unfocused, like he was looking inside himself for details of the memory. "We were working a tobacco case. Truckloads were being moved across the border and sold illegally out of the back of a store with no license. The owner had a record and couldn't qualify for a liquor license. We took the guy down but I probably made every stupid mistake in the book."

Quint closed his eyes, thinking all the quips Tessa would have had about a case like that one.

"Tessa not only walked me through how to bust the guy, but she tripped him when I lost my grip and he started to get away. She made eyes at me because I was standing there dumbfounded at how this guy could have slipped right out of my hands. She gave me a look that said I better get my act together and bust this guy," Lucas continued. "Training kicked in and I've never hesitated on a bust since. The thing is, she never teased me about it or told anyone."

Quint knew how that would have gone over with a few agents—not so well. They would have given Lucas a nickname based on something they witnessed during the bust that would have stuck with the young man the rest of his career. Law enforcement was like a fraternity and the hazing could get intense with some officers.

"She would never do that if she believed in you," Quint said. "If she didn't, she would have taken it to Bjorn in private after telling you she thought you might want to consider another profession."

"So I've heard," Lucas said. "She gave me the confidence to keep going when I faltered, and I've never forgotten it." Lucas looked down at the carpet. "I would have liked to say something at her funeral but there was a line of agents in front of me."

There was a time in the not-so-distant past that hearing Tessa's name used to make Quint sad. Now, it didn't. It only served to remind him what a good person she was and oddly made him feel closer to her memory.

"Tessa had this crazy laugh once you got her going," Quint said.

"Like an elephant, right?" Lucas chuckled.

"Exactly, and then she'd snort when she really got going," Quint stated as Ree joined them with two mugs in her hand. He took one from her as she took a seat.

"She once spewed tea on the windshield of my service vehicle," Lucas said.

"And then probably blamed you for it since you were the one who made her laugh," Quint said.

"As a matter of fact, she did." Lucas laughed. "She threatened to make me clean it up if I ever made her laugh that hard again."

There was something special about having Ree in the room while Quint and Lucas relived the memories of Tessa. Ree had a calming presence that took away some of the ache in his chest.

"I usually got socked in the arm," Quint revealed. "And she could pack a punch."

"For a tiny person, she had the strength of a bear," Lucas added.

The two shared a few more stories, then Ree's cell buzzed. She checked the screen. "A message from Agent Grappell."

Quint took a sip of coffee, pretending not to be hanging on by a thread to learn there's been a breakthrough in the case.

"He says a marshal will be by in an hour to pick up Laurie and Ariana. Once they're safe, Axel will be ready to talk," she stated as she read the text.

"We'll be ready." Lucas pushed up to standing. "I better get some food in them. I'll go ask what they're hungry for. No telling how long they'll be on the road when they're relocated."

Quint nodded, appreciating a few minutes alone with Ree.

The minute Lucas was out of earshot, Ree said, "That can't happen again. He almost caught us in a very intimate moment."

"I know," he said.

"It's unprofessional and word will get around, ruining both of our reputations," she continued, as if he hadn't just agreed.

"You don't have to talk me in to anything," he said. "I'm on your side on this."

"Good." She pressed her lips together like she was biting back what she really wanted to say. "Because I can't have a mark on my file or every single male agent I work with from here on out wondering if he has a chance with me if we work a case together because Lucas walked into that bedroom at the wrong moment."

"Agreed," he said. The thought of Ree being hit on by another agent sent anger boiling in his veins. The suitcase incident was the equivalent of one step forward, two steps back, in their relationship.

"You can't afford female agents to wonder if they should make a move or wait for you to, either," she said emphatically. "It'll hurt both of us for promotions if Bjorn got word."

"Maybe we shouldn't spend a whole lot of time worrying about it," Quint said, figuring he had to stop her momentum before she talked them into a harassment case.

"You are a decent-looking guy," she continued. "Women are going to want to date you. Look at you." She threw her hands up in the air.

"If it matters at all, I don't want to date other women. I'd like to date you but I realize how complicated I am, so that's not as easy as it probably should be," he finally said. "Let's move on and not worry about looking back right now."

Those words were meant to be reassuring. Instead, Ree reacted like she'd been punched in the gut.

RATHER THAN LET the comment get to her, Ree lifted her chin and took a measured sip of coffee. A couple of slow, deep breaths later and she could think more clearly. "Tell me how you really feel."

He started to open his mouth but she stopped him with a raised hand.

"I mean physically," she said with a cautionary tone. They'd reached a standstill instead of moving forward with their personal relationship. It happened. It was called hitting a wall. Neither had the equipment to tunnel through. "Be real with me, Quint."

"The stabbing hurts. I still bleed a little when I move but I imagine that will scab up after another night of sleep. I'm banged up pretty good but I've pushed through in worse shape, so I know I'll be able to handle whatever comes my way," he stated. "I'll have to be quicker with a gun and back off from a fist fight. I'd say by tomorrow, I'll be in decent enough shape to sit in on the Axel Ivan interview."

Ree listened, taking in the information. Bottom line, she could request to have Quint removed from the case, but she couldn't do that to him yet. He needed a chance to prove himself capable and she needed to help him see this thing through. She'd made a promise she had no intention of going back on now. Besides, with two undercover operations under her belt and a need to find justice for a fellow agent, Quint wasn't the only one personally invested. Plus, she wanted to be the one to help Quint move on with his life after Tessa. She wanted to help give him the closure he needed to pick up the pieces of his life again.

"Okay," she said. "I'm all in with you, Quint."

The look he gave said she'd caught him off guard.

"What? Did you think I was going to walk away and leave you hanging?" she said, faking being offended in dramatic fashion. The mood needed to be lightened if they were going to continue to work together.

Quint laughed, then winced.

"Don't strain yourself," she teased, lifting up her coffee cup.

"I can probably still do legwork," he said. "If I don't move something, I'll lose my mind sitting around all day."

"We should head into the living room. Start with walking and see how the bleeding goes?" she offered.

"That's probably a good idea." His lips curled into a smirk.

"I know. Patience has never been your forte unless it directly relates to a case," she quipped.

"I can't deny that," he stated, setting down his mug on the table before slowly standing.

"You start bleeding and we dial it back," she warned.

"Yes, ma'am," he said with that same heart-melting smirk. There was something incredibly sexy about the way Quint smiled.

"Why don't you lean some of your weight on me until the room stops spinning," she instructed.

"How do you know the room is spinning?" He put an arm around her shoulder.

"I can see it in your eyes, Casey." She gave him "the look." Part of her wanted to argue for him to go back to bed and heal. The part that grew up with four brothers said the more she pushed a stubborn person like Quint, the more he would push back. He needed to walk around and test out his body a little bit to see where he stood. He wouldn't be able to figure that out lying in a bed. And he didn't have to tell her any of that for her to know what he was doing sitting in the kitchen instead.

"What was that look for?" he asked.

"You seem to forget I grew up with a bunch of brothers and a grandfather," she stated, regretting the statement as soon as it left her mouth. She sounded like a jerk reminding him of the lonely childhood he'd had in comparison, being the only child of a single mother who worked long hours to make ends meet.

Quint took a couple of steps and then leaned heavily on her. She wrapped her arm around his midsection to keep him from falling over and managed to touch a sore spot. He winced and grunted.

"Sorry," she said.

"Don't be," he countered, grabbing on to the doorjamb. "I have to push through this and get a true gauge of what I can do."

"A day makes a big difference when it comes to healing injuries, in my experience," she said.

"When have you been hurt?" he asked.

"Growing up with four brothers?" she quipped. "Every couple of days it seems like. I've fractured two fingers, my left wrist and my clavicle." She flashed eyes at him. "Don't ask."

"Scout's honor," he said, the spark in his eyes returning for the first time since she'd seen him in this condition.

"We both know you were never a Scout," she teased.

"You're not wrong there." He smiled as he took another step.

"Then there was the summer I spent in a cast because I broke my arm right when I fell off the tire swing," she continued, distracting him with her story so he would hopefully not focus on how much pain he was in. "Witnesses agree that I was pushed, but Finn argues it to this day."

"Out of curiosity, what did Finn think he was doing?" Quint made it to the hallway.

"He swears he was pushing the swing to make it go faster and his hands slipped," she said. "We all know he wanted me off the swing."

"Somehow, I'm sure you didn't let him get away with that," Quint said with a laugh that made every muscle in his torso tense up.

"No, but then my mom got mad at me because she said

I hit him out of spite," she said, thinking her rocky relationship with her mother went as far back as she could remember.

"Was she right?" he asked.

"Probably," she said, bursting out laughing at the thought. "I wasn't exactly a saint in my childhood, but he started it." She heard how that sounded and laughed again.

"I'm not touching that statement with a ten-foot pole. No drawing up sides here," he said.

"Come to think of it, Finn and I used to fight the most," she continued.

"Too close in age?" he asked.

"Probably," she said. "But now he fights fires and our mother couldn't be prouder of him."

They made it to the living room, where Lucas held up his cell. "The marshal just pulled into the driveway."

The driveway was rear-entry, meaning all the houses on this block had their garage doors at the back of the house. It was daylight outside. A sharpshooter could hit them from a good distance on a clear day like today. There were no houses behind them, just a brick wall enclosing the neighborhood and a busy street on the other side of it.

"Are you good?" Ree whispered to Quint.

He nodded before grabbing on to the wall for support. As much as he didn't want to acknowledge it, he would be a liability in a fight right now. But she'd seen bigger healing miracles and figured she'd give him another day to rest and then they'd have a better idea of where he was.

"I'll get A and B," Ree said. The Ivans were inside the second bedroom with the door closed in order to give them privacy. Besides, they didn't have any information that could help the case. Talking to them was fruitless.

They were assets to be kept safe and delivered to WITSEC in exchange for information from Axel Ivan.

Ree knocked on the door, then opened it. "Time to go."

Ariana was curled up in her mother's lap. Laurie was stroking her daughter's hair.

"What if we changed our mind and don't want to cooperate?" Laurie asked.

Ree stepped inside the room and closed the door behind her. She moved to the foot of the bed and perched on the edge. "Mind if I ask why?"

The teen whimpered quietly in her mother's arms.

"We've had a change of heart about going along with this." Laurie waved her arms in the air.

"Do you remember what happened in your neighborhood yesterday?" Ree asked.

"I've had a chance to think things over and this isn't the kind of life I want to lead. Always hiding. Running like scared chickens with their heads cut off," Laurie continued as Ariana turned up the tears. "Look at what this is doing to my daughter. She didn't ask for any of this and neither did I."

Ree didn't think this was the exact moment to point out Laurie had, in fact, signed up for this very thing—a husband in jail and a life in hiding. Saying these things out loud wouldn't get her what she wanted or needed—cooperation.

"Let's think this through, Laurie," Ree said in as calm a voice as she could muster. "What happens now if I let you walk out that door?"

"You would do that?" Laurie's surprise would be funny if it wasn't so frustrating. The woman seemed clueless.

"If you refuse to cooperate then you two are the local police's problem, not mine." Ree folded her arms over her chest. Playing a little hardball might work to shock Laurie back to reality.

"What does that mean?" Laurie's eyebrows furrowed.

"Exactly what it sounds like. You walk out the front door and I don't ever see you again," Ree said.

Those words caused Ariana to perk up. She looked up at her mother, big tears spilling down her cheeks. Teenagers sure seemed to know how to pour on the drama and tug at their mother's heartstrings. Growing up with all boys, tears didn't work in the Sheppard household. Ree wouldn't know how to turn hers on. But she had a serious problem sitting a few feet away from her on the bed. Without their cooperation, the investigation died right here. So it was up to her to convince them to stick to the plan.

Chapter Seven

"Mama." There was so much hope and pleading in Ariana's eyes.

"We need to think this through carefully, Ari," Laurie said to her daughter.

Ree was still a little shocked there was anything to think about. "You leave protective custody and there'll be a dozen others coming for you."

Laurie covered her daughter's ears as Ariana buried her head in her mother's arms again. "Please. Not in front of my baby."

This also didn't seem like the time to point out that Ariana was no baby. She was a high-school freshman, which made her around fourteen years old despite looking more mature for her age.

"I'm sorry to be so blunt, Laurie. But I take her life very seriously." Ree figured she needed to take a different approach to get through to these two. "And if I don't inform you of what's likely to happen when you leave without protection, I wouldn't be doing my job. In WITSEC, you'll get the fresh start you need."

The sound of those last words sent Laurie's "baby" into a crying jag. There was only one reason a girl would break down to that degree—a boyfriend.

"I promise you that whoever is in your daughter's life isn't worth risking death for," Ree continued.

The crying ramped up, but Laurie was mulling over the facts. Ree had hit on the teen's reason for working on her mother.

"It's her life, too," Laurie stated with a shrug. "You see how all this is affecting her."

Ree had a suspicion the teen was used to using tears to get what she wanted. It seemed to be working if her mother was considering backing out of WITSEC.

"I have a US Marshal in the house who is expecting to escort both of you to another safe house, where—"

"I can't live in a place like this, Mama," the teen cried in dramatic fashion.

"Do you want to die in a town house?" Ree asked, being as blunt as she could be. The teen needed discipline, not coddling. The best part about Ree's childhood was that she hadn't been sheltered from life, good or bad. Granted, losing her father at such a young age and being brought up in a houseful of testosterone no doubt marked her childhood in a different way. Ree's mother might have wanted a daughter who wore bows in her hair but she would never have tolerated a child who cried to get her way.

On the ranch, everyone had pitched in to clean and do laundry. The boys weren't spared housework and she'd learned to drive the riding lawnmower on her twelfth birthday. Big or small, all ranches operated the same in terms of everyone having to do their part. Big families were no different. The fact that she'd grown up in a big family on a small ranch kept her doubly grounded.

Ariana went all in with the tears.

Laurie started rocking her "baby" and trying to soothe her.

"I know how difficult this must be for both of you.

You've been whisked out of your home on a moment's notice and not allowed to bring anything with you but the clothes on your backs. I promise you'll be reunited with a few essentials once you're settled down in a new location," Ree explained.

Crybaby turned it up another notch. How much louder could this teen get? Probably loud enough to get what she wanted. Laurie's face twisted in confusion and what looked like frustration about their predicament.

"It'll be hard at first," Ree continued. "But we're working it out where you'll be able to see your husband on a regular basis."

Laurie perked up over this news.

"I haven't been allowed to visit my Axel in months," she said.

"Your husband asked for these provisions for you and his little girl because he knows the kind of people who want him to keep quiet," Ree continued, figuring she'd struck a nerve. "He claims these same people murdered someone in prison. Do you really believe you and Ariana can go up against them and survive?"

The teen's crying slowed to a whimper with an occasional hiccup.

"Axel is behind bars. How will we ever be safe?" Laurie asked.

"That's a good question," Ree stated. "I'm certain the marshal in the next room can detail out a plan. His agency has been protecting witnesses and their families for a very long time. It's what they specialize in and they are very good at what they do."

"What will happen to my husband?" Laurie asked. At least she seemed concerned about his welfare in all this. Ree was beginning to wonder if the only thing Laurie cared about was her "baby."

"He has already been moved to a different facility and once you're settled, he'll be relocated closer to the two of you so you can see him while he finishes out his sentence rather than go on trial for a crime he didn't commit," Ree said. "I'm not certain all the details of the deal he's asking for but I wouldn't be surprised if a reduced sentence was one of the sticking points."

Laurie looked up and to the left. Ree was getting through to the woman.

"It might be hard at first, but you guys will make new friends while you wait for your husband's release," Ree continued. "Then the three of you will be together again in a new life—a legitimate life where he doesn't have to look over his shoulder to see if his past has caught up with him."

"We'll get new identities?" Laurie asked.

"And so will he," Ree confirmed.

"Mama, we're in love," Ariana whined. "What kind of life do I have without him?"

"You would trade your father for a boyfriend?" Laurie's voice took a different tone now. It reeked of disapproval and the importance of loyalty.

"That's not what I said," Ariana complained.

"Listen to me," Laurie said. "This family means everything to me. We have a chance to be reunited with your father and live together again. Is that something you're willing to trade for a boy?"

Ariana sniffled a couple of times, but her eyes were dry. She might be spoiled and used to getting her way, but she also seemed to realize when she'd overstepped a boundary.

Laurie raised her eyes to meet Ree's.

"You can guarantee I'll see my husband?" she asked.

"I think we both know there are no guarantees in

life," Ree said. "Except the fact your allowance will be cut off now that your husband is turning against his former employers."

Laurie's eyes widened.

"Did I forget to mention that earlier?" Ree asked. "Because they'll cut you off financially so quick your head will spin."

Ariana slumped at this news, as though there was a balloon in her chest that had suddenly deflated.

"And that's if they allow you to live, which I sincerely doubt. They will kill you both to get revenge on Axel, who, by the way, asked for nothing for himself except to get to watch his daughter graduate from high school." Ree capitalized on their attention. "Should I send word that you have decided not to follow his wishes to keep you both safe?"

A knock at the door interrupted them. Lucas stuck his head inside.

"The marshal said he doesn't have all day," Lucas said.

"What will it be, ladies?" Ree put the question out there. Now, she had to hope she'd been convincing.

QUINT LEANED AGAINST the wall as Ree led Axel Ivan's family to the living room. Marshal Rodgers has been personally vetted by Bjorn, a reassuring fact. The guy was tall and solidly built.

"Thank you for coming," Ree said to the marshal after shaking hands. No introductions were made with the Ivans. None were necessary. They would be receiving new identities soon enough, anyway. "These are the assets you've been made aware of."

Marshal Rodgers gave a quick nod. "If you ladies will follow me out the back, we'll be on our way."

Mrs. Ivan took in a deep breath, tightening her hold

around her daughter. The younger Ivan's face was buried in her mother's arms as they walked out. Mrs. Ivan shot a look at Ree that Quint couldn't quite pinpoint. He crossed his arms over his chest and shifted his gaze to the carpet so as not to make the duo any more uncomfortable.

Ree walked them out the back door and to the garage, disappearing from view when she entered the small hallway that held a washer-and-dryer combo. She returned a few minutes later as the garage door closed.

"What was that all about?" he asked.

"Standing up, I see," she quipped.

"Yes, and you didn't answer my question," he continued.

"They balked about going into WITSEC. I had to talk them into it," she said. "Everything happened so fast back at the town house. I'm guessing they finally had a chance to process and it scared the hell out of them both."

"These things usually involve the opposite sex," he pointed out.

"True enough in this case," she said. "The teenager didn't want to leave her boyfriend. You know what it's like at that age."

"Can't say that I do," he stated. He'd never had a traditional childhood with two parents and gated communities.

"At first, I was afraid Laurie had someone else in her life. I'm not convinced it's untrue, but she seems to be choosing her husband for now," she said.

"He's been away for a couple of years and she was all done up with clothes, hair and makeup," he observed.

"My thoughts exactly when I first saw her. If she's having an affair, the daughter doesn't know," she said. "In the end, Laurie chose her family."

"And we get to fulfill our side of the bargain," Quint said.

Ree nodded.

"Is the interview with Axel set up for tomorrow morning?" he asked.

"I believe so," she stated.

"Do we have a location?" he asked.

"A vehicle will show up at some point tonight with instructions tucked underneath the driver's seat, according to Grappell," she informed him.

"How very Bond of him," Quint joked. He needed to lighten the tension and cracking a joke took his mind off the pain every time he breathed.

"Looks like we have a full day ahead of us," Ree said, quirking an eyebrow as she walked past him. "If that's the best you have, it's going to be a long one."

Ree was out of earshot by the time he came back with a snappy response. He was definitely off his game and had the battle scars to prove it. With nothing to do until early tomorrow morning, he made a couple of loops around the living room and kitchen area before easing down on the sofa, where he put his head back and took a power nap.

He woke to the sounds of *click-click-clack* in the background. Slowly, he brought his hand up to his head and pinched the bridge of his nose. Waiting was torture, but even Quint realized he was in no condition to take anyone on in a physical fight. He also realized he wouldn't exactly be the quickest person right now. All he could count on was a rapid-fire trigger finger. Putting a bullet in someone always was and always would be a last resort. Not only was he bound by a code to uphold the law, but he also believed in it one hundred percent.

Quint blinked a few times. Pain caused his vision to blur. He shook his head. Big mistake there. The movement served to remind him of the headache forming right between his eyes. Since he refused to take any real pain medication, he figured popping a couple ibuprofen would take the edge off enough for him to think a little more clearly.

Normally, a good workout would wipe away at least some of his stress. The point between his shoulder blades felt like someone was stabbing him with a needle. Since push-ups were out of the question, he forced himself to stand up and walk around the room a couple of times. Going outside might be a nice change of scenery, but he would draw attention in his condition.

He glanced around, looking for Ree. She was in the adjacent dining room, sitting across the table from Lucas, who was studying his laptop screen. She had her cell phone out and was typing. Her thumbs moved like lightning.

Seeing her sit with Lucas sent a jolt of jealousy ripping through Quint. After their last conversation, he figured being jealous wasn't productive. They were in a weird place in their relationship where he couldn't move forward or backward. Kissing Ree, making love to her, had been right up there with the best experiences of his life. He'd heard people talk about having a connection with someone like no other and thought it was trying too hard to make something out of thin air. Attraction was a physical response to someone's looks.

Then, he'd met Ree. There was much more to her than physical beauty. Although, she had that, too. There was a whole lot more to her than intelligence. Although, she had that in spades. And she was an amazing agent—right up there with the best. The connection he had with her, that intangible thing that was almost impossible to explain, was off the charts.

Quint didn't deserve the kind of happiness he could

have with Ree. Where was Tessa's happiness? Where was her future? Gone. Erased. Dead.

This damn case might be the death of him, too.

Chapter Eight

"Everything okay?" Ree asked Quint as she watched him pace out of the corner of her eye.

"Sure" was the noncommittal response.

Ree shrugged her shoulders and went back to typing an email to Grappell, trying to get any information out of him she possibly could. It would be helpful if she knew what part of Texas they would be driving to so she could prepare. "Do they have any clothes here besides what's already on your back?"

"Not much." Quint made another lap around the living room. He was still moving slowly but this was an improvement. He was up and around, which was a good sign. She should have known a person as tough as Quint would push himself. Since she would most likely do the same thing if the situation was reversed, she couldn't criticize him.

Tapping her toe on the tile flooring, she waited for a response from Grappell.

"A vehicle has driven by the front of the house for the third time now. I'm watching it from the camera," Lucas said, looking up from his laptop and locking gazes with Ree. "This last time, they slowed down."

Ree bit back a curse.

"I didn't do a body check with the teenager like I

should have to see if she had a cell phone on her," Ree stated. "I didn't see anything in her hands, so I assumed she'd set it down somewhere inside her house."

"She might have had pockets that weren't easily seen," Lucas said.

"Either way, we're sitting ducks in this house now. We have to move," Ree stated.

"We can take the Jeep in the garage," Lucas said, closing his laptop and tucking it underneath his arm. "I'll give you guys a ride wherever you want to go."

"Let's go," Ree stated, figuring they didn't have much time before the vehicle returned. Her gaze immediately flew to Quint. "Are you good? Do you need help?"

"Never better," he quipped as he beat feet toward her. "Wallet's still in my pocket, so I won't be leaving anything behind."

"Good." Ree moved to his side and helped him toward the hallway leading to the garage.

On the way out, she saw Lucas open a trap door and pull out a case that probably contained weapons.

"What about Chelsea?" she asked.

"She's the one who texted me to take a look at the cameras," Lucas said as he tucked the case that was the size of a decent piece of luggage in the very back of the bright orange Jeep. His Gap T-shirt, cotton shorts and flip-flops were a perfect cover for someone she imagined would drive such a vehicle. There was a Hook 'em Horns bumper sticker on the front of the vehicle. Lucas fit the description of a University of Texas at Austin graduate to a T.

Ree called shotgun, then helped Quint ease into the back seat. Once he was strapped in, settled and armed, she claimed the passenger side.

"Be ready for anything when I hit this button," Lucas said, motioning toward the garage-door release.

"What kind of vehicle am I looking for?" Ree palmed a Glock that had been provided to her when she'd first arrived. She kept the barrel low in the event a neighbor was watching or patrolling the alley out back. Although, this safe house was forever blown at this point. The place would be cleaned out and on the market as arranged by desk-job agents.

"A silver Buick," he stated.

A second later, the button was pushed. The timing couldn't have been worse as the Buick crept along the alley, stopping and blocking them in. The glint of metal had Ree and Lucas both reaching for the button to close the garage door.

As it went down, Quint aimed and fired a shot. "Got a tire and maybe a few extra minutes."

He was already climbing out of the back seat and grimacing with pain that the movement had caused. Ree quickly followed.

"What if you two stay in here and I run around the building?" she asked as an idea took shape. "Get the Jeep out of the garage and onto the street, where I'll join you."

"Okay," Lucas said. "Go."

Quint's face muscles tensed and she knew he would want to argue.

"There's no time, Quint. Get back inside the vehicle and stick with the plan. I'll back them off. They won't expect me to come from around the house," she stated.

He gave a resigned nod before climbing into the passenger seat. His movement was labored and slow. They both knew he would end up shot, or worse, if he tried to trade places.

Ree threaded her way to the master bedroom, where

she opened a window and then climbed out. The hem of her shirt caught on the sill when she jumped. She heard the sound of ripping but would deal with that later.

The door in the eight-foot wooden privacy fence Texans were known for in these parts was locked, so she had to scale it using the Japanese boxwood. Branches jabbed her ankles and calves as she struggled to find her footing.

She scaled the fence, feeling every splinter lodging in her hands and arms. She threw one leg over, then the other, and momentum carried her over the wall. She landed hard on the dry, spiky grass.

Ree popped up to her feet and ran with her Glock out front. The few seconds it took to point and shoot if she didn't have her weapon at the ready could mean the difference between life and death. It was Law Enforcement 101.

The only sound was the hum of the Buick's engine idling in the alleyway behind the home. The driver was waiting. He was about to get a surprise.

The gate leading to the driveway was unlocked. Ree lifted the metal hook and then used her shoulder to keep the gate from closing all the way again. *One. Two. Three.*

She jabbed the door with her shoulder. It swung open. She took aim at the Buick's driver.

The guy had on reflective shades. Since it was lighter outside than inside the Buick, she couldn't get a good look at his face. The only details she could make out were his dark hair and an oval-shaped face. The description narrowed it down to most of the male population in North Texas.

As she squeezed the trigger, the tires spun out and he ducked. The smell of burning rubber lit her nostrils on fire as the Buick jolted forward and out of sight. The garage door slowly opened and then she hopped in the back of the vehicle. Head down, she was ready to fire again. The noise would no doubt draw attention to them.

Lucas bolted out in the opposite direction as Quint stayed on a cell phone. It must belong to Lucas because Quint's had gone missing and a replacement hadn't shown up yet. Ree scanned the area, ready and willing to shoot if their lives were threatened.

She faintly heard Quint providing details of the house's location and the color of the Buick. With a major road behind them, it would be all too easy for him to disappear into traffic. North Dallas was no stranger to traffic jams throughout the day. Even midday, the road was thick with cars as they merged onto Webb Chapel Road.

"Where to?" Lucas finally asked after making a few cuts and unexpected turns. He zipped through traffic with the ease of a native driver. She was used to driving in traffic but never developed a taste for it having grown up in the country.

"Can you get us to Waco?" she asked.

"Don't see why not," Lucas said.

Ree slumped in her seat after buckling the seat belt. "I'll make sure we have a ride from there."

Waco would get her closer to home. For reasons she couldn't explain, she needed to see her house.

BEING INJURED DURING a hot investigation made Quint want to put his fist through a wall.

The ride to Waco was quiet as Ree checked in with Grappell and gave him an update. He arranged for a vehicle to be waiting for them at the parking lot of the $266 million football stadium at Baylor University.

McLane Stadium itself was a sight. It sat on the north bank of the Brazos River, and spectators could arrive by boat.

"Ever been to a game here?" Lucas asked.

"No. You?" Quint asked as the Jeep came to a stop in a parking spot in front of a Chevy Blazer. The vehicle would blend in nicely with drivers on the highway.

"Once, in August, a few years back," Lucas said.

"The season opener?" Quint asked. He kept track of a few football programs and Baylor University was one of them. Although, it seemed like Alabama's Crimson Tide was an unstoppable force in the game.

"Yup," Lucas said. "Scored tickets through my father, who used to be the special-teams coach."

"Lucky," Quint said, remembering the historic landslide win over SMU.

"It was a great game," Lucas said.

"Did you come in by boat?" Quint asked.

"No, but that would have been epic." Lucas rocked his head and smiled. "Good memories."

"That's about all we can expect in this life, right?" Quint said, wondering where the sudden bout of wistfulness had come from. Had it come out of talking about Tessa earlier with Lucas? For the first time, the memories didn't cut a deeper hole in his heart. The difference was having Ree around. Her presence was a balm on his broken soul. Why couldn't he just go ahead and take the next step with her?

"End of the line," Lucas said. "It's been great working with you both."

"Same with you," Quint said.

"You did great work back there with the unsubs," Lucas said to Ree. "And you saved both of our lives in the driveway. I appreciate it."

"Nothing you wouldn't do for me," Ree said, brushing off the compliment. She always did that a little too quickly.

"Ree is one of the best I've ever had the privilege to work with," Quint said.

"You two are good together," Lucas stated. "It's easy to see."

"A good partnership is built on mutual trust and respect," Ree said quickly. A little too quickly to cover up the fact there'd been more to their relationship than work. Lucas had picked up on it earlier. If he hadn't, he wouldn't be a very observant agent and not someone Quint would feel comfortable working with in the future.

"Yeah," Lucas agreed loosely. His tone said he wouldn't push the issue. "Take care. Both of you."

"Same to you and Chelsea," Ree said.

Quint made his way over to the driver's side and shook Lucas's hand while Ree moved to the Chevy.

"I'd appreciate it if you'd leave the personal stuff out of the case file," Quint said quietly.

"Wouldn't think of adding it," Lucas said, giving Quint a look that said he understood what was really being said.

Quint didn't want anyone to discuss his and Ree's relationship, work or otherwise. He didn't want her name coming up at the proverbial water cooler. In short, he wanted to protect her professional reputation.

"You're a good agent, Lucas," Quint said. "I hope to work with you again someday."

"That means a lot," Lucas responded. "If you need anything, give me a shout. The agency knows how to find me at pretty much all times."

"I swear they put a GPS tracker in all of us during orientation," Quint quipped, grateful for the lighter conversation.

"Take care of her," Lucas said. "It's obvious to anyone with eyes that she cares a great deal about you, man. Someone like Ree doesn't come around often."

"I will," Quint promised. "And I hear you."

The statement made Quint realize he wasn't the only one interested in her. It seemed Lucas had noticed her, too. Maybe Quint's earlier jealousy wasn't so far-fetched after all.

The sun was blazing by the time Lucas pulled away. Quint had a headache to match. Ree had gone to the back tire on the driver's side to retrieve the key.

"Where are we headed?" he asked, because it was clear she had a destination in mind.

"I need to go home," she said, giving him a look that told him not to argue.

"Let's go home then," he stated without hesitation.

"I let Grappell know. He said we'd be safe to get to our next destination by ten o'clock tomorrow," she said as she climbed into the driver's seat. "Do you need a hand up?"

"No," he replied. "I got this."

The pain was real as he reached for the handle and pulled himself up while taking a step on the stair that came out as soon as he opened the door. At least Grappell had sprung for a deluxe model. Quint would give him that.

"Any chance you have ibuprofen at your house?" Quint asked after a while.

"That, and coffee," she said, ramping up the speed on the highway.

"Mind if I lean back while you drive?" he asked, figuring he could get in a catnap so he'd be fresh by the time they got to her house. *Fresh* was a relative term considering he hadn't showered in the past twenty-four hours.

"Go for it," she said with a shrug.

He couldn't quite pinpoint what had changed in her

during the last couple of hours. They'd been in rough spots before and gotten out just fine. They'd been shaken up before and she'd kept her eye on the prize. Granted, they were technically in between assignments at the moment. Going home and freshening up was probably a good idea. They'd lost everything they'd had with them, anyway.

At her place, they could regroup and maybe get in a full eight hours of sleep before heading out to wherever Axel was being transported. All Quint knew was they'd delivered the wife and kid. Their part of the deal was done. There was no reason for Axel to withhold names now.

That was Quint's last thought before he dozed off. By the time he woke, Ree was gently shaking him by the shoulder.

"Hey, sleepyhead. We're here," she said. She'd managed to park, turn off the vehicle and come around to the passenger side without disturbing him. That must be some kind of record. It also spoke to the injuries Quint had racked up. He never slept so deeply that the slightest noise didn't wake him.

He'd needed the sleep, though.

"That was fast," he teased.

"Easy for you to say." She rolled her eyes and smiled. The day had been long already and it was barely dinnertime.

Quint forced himself out of the Chevy and followed her to the front door. "Did Grappell give you any idea where we'll be going tomorrow morning for the meeting?"

"None. They struck a deal to release Axel now that someone came forward to corroborate his story, so they are working out the details of what that will look like," she said, unlocking and opening her door. The lights were on, so she held a hand up.

Quint pulled the borrowed Glock out of his holster, ready to clear the place. Neither spoke as they moved with precision through the living room, weapons leading the way. After the living room, dining room and kitchen were cleared, Ree led him to the hallway. She took two steps in and stopped.

The bathroom door was cracked open. Apparently, this wasn't something that normally happened at Ree's house. She put up a fisted hand as a warning.

Quint took in a slow breath, wondering if this day was about to get a whole lot worse.

Chapter Nine

Ree's finger hovered over the trigger mechanism. This seemed to be turning into one of those days. Hell, this case was turning into one of those cases that never seemed to end and kept getting worse. If she didn't care so much about Quint, she would have pulled out. It had bad juju all over it and she should probably run as far away as possible.

Sticking with the case was the only way to ensure Quint would be all right. She couldn't let him be assigned a random partner who wouldn't understand him because he wouldn't abandon her, either, when times got tough.

The wood flooring creaked right before the bathroom door opened and Zoey yelled, "Surprise!"

Ree blew out a sharp breath as she considered just how close Zoey had come to having her head blown off.

"Sorry." Zoey's big brown eyes widened as fear seemed to strike a physical blow. She was holding the cutest golden retriever puppy in her arms. "I got a dog."

"Where are you parked?" Ree asked, trying to shake out of the fog. Zoey York was a young woman Ree had met during the Greenlight bust. She'd been caught up in a bad relationship that nearly cost her everything. Ree was able to convince Zoey to get help in a women's shelter in Austin.

Quint had lowered his weapon and placed a hand on her shoulder. His touch was reassuring despite the fact she didn't want it to be.

"You scared me to death," Zoey said, her shoulders dropping as she walked straight up to Ree and brought her into a hug.

"I didn't know you were here," Ree said, hoping she and Quint hadn't just given away the fact they worked in law enforcement.

"You asked about my car. I parked around back because I wanted to surprise you," Zoey said.

"How'd you get in?" Ree asked, then realized this wasn't the first time Zoey had broken in somewhere. The eighteen-year-old had slipped into the cabin during Quint and Ree's first case in Cricket Creek, Texas.

"I let myself in," Zoey said with a smile. She had a mischievous twinkle in her eyes. "Hi, Quint."

"How long have you been here?" Ree asked, turning tail and walking into the living room. The others followed.

"Twenty minutes," Zoey said.

"Why aren't you still at the shelter?" Ree asked, motioning toward the small round dining table adjacent to the kitchen.

"I'm out on furlough and I didn't have any place to go, so…"

"Don't mind me. I need a shower," Quint said.

"What happened to you?" Zoey looked him up and down.

"I got into a motorcycle accident," he said.

"Oh, no." Zoey's face morphed to concern.

"I'll be fine," Quint reassured her. "You two catch up while I get cleaned up."

"How did you find this place?" Ree asked, hoping

their cover wasn't blown. Zoey would believe that she and Quint were newlyweds. She also just realized Quint wasn't wearing the boot that had also been part of their cover story. Although, weeks had passed since the first case and he could technically be out of the boot by now.

"You sent flowers. Thank you, by the way." Zoey shrugged. She really was a resourceful young person. "I met a genius hacker in Austin and she got the address from the florist's database."

"Remind me never to be on your bad side," Ree teased.

"You couldn't be," Zoey said so fast and with innocence that tugged at Ree's heart.

"How are you doing? Really?" Ree asked, moving to the coffee machine. She'd hoped for a few hours of rest but seeing Zoey again was providing a different kind of moral boost.

Zoey had gotten herself involved in an abusive relationship. One of the best things that had come out of the Cricket Creek bust was that Ree had convinced Zoey to go to a women's shelter in Austin.

"It's only been a few weeks, so this is going to sound stupid, but I can already feel a difference," Zoey said, her brown eyes lighting up when she spoke. "Week one, I was a hot mess. The second week wasn't much better, but then something clicked inside me around the third week that asked what kind of person I wanted to be and what kind of relationship I wanted to be in. I'd honestly never asked myself those questions before."

"Did you find answers?" Ree asked, going about fixing the coffee.

"Yes. I want to be like you," Zoey said. Her answer pretty much melted Ree's heart. Zoey was a good and decent young woman who deserved more than the hand she'd been dealt in life, with a mother who'd ditched her daughter. There'd been no one to care about Zoey, and she'd gotten mixed up with the wrong person.

"That's quite a compliment," Ree said. They were racking up today. "One I appreciate very much."

Zoey practically beamed as Ree poured two cups of coffee and brought one over. She set it down on the table in front of Zoey.

"I'd like to be more like you, too," Ree admitted.

Zoey's face twisted up in confusion.

"You're smart and kind. You're a really good person who is working hard to better yourself," Ree stated. "Plus, you really know how to break into a place."

Zoey laughed.

Ree also made a mental note to get an alarm system installed. She'd never really thought about one before, since she'd lived in the country. Most folks kept their doors unlocked and their vehicles running when they popped out to the store for a quick errand. The thought of an alarm was the last thing on Ree's mind despite working a job most would consider dangerous.

Thankfully, there wasn't a whole lot of agency paraphernalia lying around. Ree had decorated with a few random snapshots of her and her brothers. Her mother was in a picture or two with Ree's father before their world had been turned upside down by his death. And then there was a picture of Ree's grandfather, whom she adored. She'd been worried about him while in Houston and the worry turned out to be for nothing. He was fine, same as always.

It occurred to Ree the jig might be up on the marriage front, considering Quint didn't have any clothes hanging in the closet and Zoey struck Ree as the type who might snoop around if she got bored. However, there had to be something of one of her brothers around.

And then she realized what she had. A smile turned up the corners of her lips when she held up a finger and said she'd be right back.

Ree made a beeline for her master bedroom closet. Voila! There it was, folded and on top of the vintage dresser inside her walk-in. Overalls made from denim no less. She grabbed them, along with a T-shirt and boxers she'd washed after her brother had taken a fall in the mud while helping her install gutters six months ago.

She knocked on the bathroom door before walking inside. The water was running and the outline of Quint's strong frame came through the white curtain.

"I found clothes for you to wear since I realized you don't have anything here. I don't think Zoey is on to us but she will be if she realizes you don't have clothes in the same house you're supposed to live in," Ree said. She heard her own voice and tried to clear the frog in her throat.

The spigot squeaked before the water turned off. Suddenly Ree wasn't laughing. Instead, her heart raced as her pulse kicked up a few notches. Quint ripped open the curtain and stood there with a towel wrapped around his waist, wad of Saran wrap in his hand. Beads of water rolled down a muscled chest and onto a bandaged stomach. She set down the folded clothing on the counter and backed out of the room.

"Thank you," Quint said, drying his hair with a different towel. Lucky towels, she thought.

"I'll just be in the other room if you need anything else," she said, thinking how easy it was to lean into her attraction to Quint and how hard reality was when it slapped her in the face.

Before he could answer or she could say anything she

might regret, she turned and headed back to the living room, where Zoey waited.

QUINT STOOD THERE, drying off, forcing his thoughts away from Ree and back onto the case. There was at least a slight chance Axel's wife and daughter might renege on their promise to go into WITSEC. He wouldn't rest easy until they got the information from Axel as promised and it checked out.

Hunger pangs had him moving a little faster than his injuries would have liked, but the smell of food wafting down the hallway made him realize how long it had been since he'd eaten.

Quint picked up the denim overalls and shook his head. This would have to do even though it would make him look like Farmer Brown. At least the items were clean. The T-shirt wasn't bad. It fit a little tight, but he could make do. The boxers were a little snug as well, but clean trumped fitted or anything else right now.

As he dressed, he checked his bandages. They seemed to be holding despite the shower. He wasn't looking forward to changing them considering the hairs on his chest would be yanked out along with the tape holding him together.

The sleep on the way over made a dent in how Quint was feeling. If he could just cocoon for a couple of days, he'd be good to go. Since they didn't have the luxury, he'd do what he could.

Overalls on, he headed down the hallway and to the kitchen. He heard the low hum of conversation and the lighthearted laughter Ree deserved. He was beginning to feel like he was bringing nothing but destruction and sorrow to Ree's life.

Quint stopped himself right there. Ree was a solid

agent. He would put her skills up against the best and she would come out on top. She'd chosen this life, this job. And yet, he couldn't deny there was something different about her now. From the day he'd met her on the first case to now, there'd been a subtle shift and he couldn't quite put his finger on what had caused it.

"What's cooking?" he said as he came around and into view.

"Pizza," Ree said. "I have one with the works on now and there's a barbecue-chicken one up next. Take your pick."

A bell dinged and he assumed it meant the pizza was done cooking.

"I'll take the first available," he quipped before catching Zoey eyeing him up and down. She was savvy and would have questions. This time, he didn't have any easy explanations, so he decided to avoid any potential landmine topics altogether.

Ree had three plates stacked by the pizza cooker sitting on the counter. She sliced the pizza before placing the second one in the fancy cooker with a rotating heating element. He had an oven and a microwave at his place. Those were the only two places any cooking or heating got done. He could admit to mostly heating. Ree, he'd noticed, had all kinds of small appliances. She had a blender on the countertop for one. And a toaster. She definitely had more than two pans in her cupboard.

She portioned out three slices on each plate as he joined her.

"I can take these two," he said, picking up his and Zoey's plates.

"Okay," she said. "I'll grab drinks."

"Nothing but water for me," he said. "And I'll grab my own."

When he turned, he caught Zoey staring at them with her mouth open.

"What?" he asked as he brought over the two plates.

"Nothing." She shrugged before fixing her gaze on the plate in front of her. "I've just never seen that before."

"Never seen what?" he asked, taking a seat at the cozy table.

"A man help around the kitchen," she said as her cheeks turned three shades of red from embarrassment. She stroked the puppy in her lap double time.

"Everyone should pitch in," he stated, picking up a hot slice and then quickly setting it back down. "I grew up with a single mother. My dad ditched us before I had a chance to get to know him. My head wasn't on straight for a long time and I gave her hell, which I'm not proud of to this day. When I finally woke up to what a jerk I was being, I figured it was up to me to find ways to make her life easier, not harder. After that, I paid attention in school and brought my grades up. I stopped getting in fights and hanging around with the wrong crowd. And I didn't wait for her to ask me to take out the trash or help set the table."

A hint of a smile crossed the young woman's face.

"That's nice," she said. "The part about you deciding to help out."

"It's what I should have done all along but didn't," he said.

"Where is your mother now?" Zoey asked, picking up a slice as Ree joined them.

"She passed away years ago," he said before getting hit with a surprising bout of melancholy. He could be honest with himself enough to admit he still missed her. It was worse some days more than others. He could only hope his mother was looking after Tessa and her baby in a better place.

Although they'd never met, he had always believed his mother would have gotten along well with Tessa. And she would have loved Ree. Quint stopped himself right there before he let himself go down that road.

"I'm sorry," Zoey said. "That must have been hard on you since the two of you were so close."

He nodded.

"At least she got to see her son turn his life around," he said. "I think that's all she wanted in the end. Just to see me doing well and being a decent human being."

Zoey smiled but it didn't reach her eyes.

"My mom ditched like your dad," she said after taking a bite of pizza. "It's probably for the best."

The pain in her voice nearly gutted him. She was too young to be all alone with no one to help guide her. He needed to change the subject before he got angry at Zoey's lot in life.

"What's her name?" He motioned toward the dog in her lap.

"I haven't decided yet," she said, perking up considerably. "Let me know if you have any ideas."

"Maggie," he said.

Zoey wrinkled her forehead. "No. It doesn't fit."

"Dixie?"

She shook her head.

"Marley?" he continued, unfazed.

"Too sad," she quickly countered.

"You're probably right about that one," he laughed before taking another bite. "Molly?"

"What's up with all these names that begin with the letter *M*?" Zoey asked.

"Piper?" he continued.

Zoey thought about that one for a long moment before nixing it, too.

"Your food is getting cold," Ree scolded.

The three of them sitting here like this, bantering back and forth about names, caused an ache to form in Quint's chest. Out of the blue, he wondered what it would be like to sit here with his and Ree's kid and a dog.

Chapter Ten

"Pixie."

Ree laughed at how determined Quint seemed to be to find the perfect name for Zoey's dog. Her cell buzzed, indicating a text coming through. She excused herself and went over to the coffee table, where she remembered last setting it down.

The message was from Agent Grappell. There was an address along with confirmation of the meetup time. She looked up the address on the map feature and saw that it was a residence on Lake Travis in Austin and not a jail. Interesting. The only reason she could think of was that it would be too dangerous to keep Axel locked up in any institution. Dumitru's reach was shocking if that was true. Then again, Bjorn might not want to take any chances. She could be dotting every *i* and crossing every *t*. He was also going to testify against someone in law enforcement who killed a prisoner.

Axel was in a no-win situation. At least he would be reunited with his wife and daughter in the process.

Sitting at the table with Quint, Zoey and the dog had put a different image in her thoughts. She'd locked gazes with Quint at one point and, for a split second, could have sworn he was thinking the exact same thing. But kids and a dog weren't something she'd ever seen herself wanting. What had changed?

Ree could admit to feeling a certain emptiness in her life. The fact her mother constantly seemed eager to push Ree's buttons made her want to run in the opposite direction. She sighed and then rejoined the other two at the table.

"Ruby?" Quint asked.

Zoey laughed and held the puppy even closer to her chest. "I just don't see her as a Ruby. You know?"

"Sandy?" he continued.

"How about Red?" Zoey said with the excitement of a six-year-old on Christmas morning.

"I mean if you want a plain name that's more of a description than anything else…fine." Quint crossed his arms over his chest and made a pouty face.

Ree was probably just exhausted, but she broke out into a stomach-busting laugh. The kind that made her double over and went on so long her cheeks actually hurt. How long had it been since she'd really laughed?

In that moment, she realized she had some thinking to do about her life, her next steps and her future. If the thought of having a dog made her happy, she should go for it. Would she miss going undercover? Living on the edge?

This job was the only thing she'd known. She'd gone to work for the ATF immediately out of college. She'd only ever wanted to work in law enforcement and had never considered any other possibility. At thirty-six, she was also starting to realize there were other things in life she'd given up in order to have the career she'd wanted.

Looking at Red made her heart hurt. She could see a puppy running around on her small property, constantly by her side. A flash of a kiddo sitting in a high chair, dropping pieces of food as scraps and laughing furiously when the dog snapped them up.

This seemed like a good time to remind herself near-death experiences had a way of causing a person to reexamine life choices. This wasn't the first time she'd reevaluated going all in with her career and leaving almost no room for anything else. It was just the first time the idea had any teeth to it.

After two pizzas were inhaled, the trio took the dog out back for a walk. Ree arranged for her brother Shane to take care of having an alarm installed while she was in Austin the following morning. The faster she got that extra layer of protection, the better, as far as she was concerned. There was something particularly creepy about this case. It was probably the prison murders and the fact they were having to take so many precautions with Axel.

If Zoey could get inside Ree's home, someone else could, too. Shane texted back that he could get her remote monitoring with the ability to turn the alarm on and off with her smartphone. The idea appealed even more. Technology was a miracle when it wasn't being a pain in the backside. She couldn't imagine living without her cell phone. The thought of being away from it even for a few hours gave her anxiety. She had no idea how Quint was surviving.

The walk around her property had done her good. Now, Quint sat on the grass, playing with Red. Zoey looked more like her age than Ree had ever seen. Pride welled up in her chest at the progress Zoey was making in her life. Being able to help someone like her was a rewarding part of the job.

Strangely, there was less helping in that sense and more locking bad guys away so they couldn't hurt anyone else. Knowing her efforts protected people like Zoey gave her a deep sense of pride. The only problem was how easy it became to lose sight of what was important when she constantly dealt with the dark side of humanity.

Watching Zoey, Ree realized she wanted to work more with young people like her. People who'd had a bad draw in the form of parents. There were too many folks who didn't have a person in the world who seemed to care about them.

The urge to do more about it struck. Ree would let the idea sit for a minute and see if it gained any steam.

Zoey pushed up to standing and gathered her puppy in her arms. "I have to drive back now. There's a ten-o'clock curfew."

"The shelter is okay with you having Red?" Ree asked. She had been wanting to foster a puppy for when Zoey left the shelter and got established on her own somewhere but didn't have time.

"I got it okayed by my case worker," she said with a smile. It was good to see her happy. She really was a sweetheart. *Bad break*, Ree thought.

Despite her constant conflicts with her mother, Ree could honestly say she never doubted the woman loved her. Ree also had brothers and a grandfather who would do anything for her. She glanced at Zoey and then Quint. He'd had a mother who loved him, at least. He'd had someone who believed in him and became a father figure. Families weren't always created by birth. She thought about the sister-brother love Quint and Tessa had shared and how that bond was still very much alive even though Tessa was gone. Some families came from the heart instead.

"It's really good to see you, Zoey." Ree hugged the puppy and young woman in one fell swoop.

Quint managed to stand up on his own with some effort. It took him a second and pain was written all over his face, but he smiled and winked in acknowledgment of his progress.

"Drive safe on your way back to Austin," Ree said as Zoey climbed in her two-door blue hatchback.

Ree stuck out her hand.

"Hand me your phone," she said.

Zoey gave a confused look but complied with the request.

"I'm putting my number in here," Ree stated as she tapped away at the screen. "The next time you want to visit, make sure you text first in case I'm not home. I have an alarm company coming tomorrow and you won't be able to break in any longer."

Ree handed over the cell when she was done.

"Will do," Zoey said, looking like a scolded teenager. Red bounced around in his box in the passenger seat. "Simmer down, Red."

"Let Ree know if you need anything, Zoey," Quint said. "I mean it."

"Stop by if you're ever in Austin," Zoey said.

"You know we will," Ree said. "I texted myself using your phone so I have your number now, too."

Zoey cranked up the engine with a wide smile. There was something different about her that was hard to pinpoint. There was a spark in her eyes now.

Had Ree lost the spark in hers?

"BED" WAS ALL Quint said as he watched Zoey take off, her blue hatchback disappearing around the bend.

"I was thinking the same thing," Ree admitted. "You've already showered, so you're ahead of the game."

"What was the text about earlier?" Quint asked.

"Grappell was confirming the time for the meetup and he sent an address in Austin," she stated.

"Doesn't look like we'll be dropping by to see Zoey on this trip," Quint said, taking her hand and tugging her inside the house. He locked up behind them as Ree cleared the dishes from the table. The two worked in comfortable silence. Neither of them needed to fill the air with words, plus Quint didn't have the energy to do a whole lot of talking, anyway.

"This is the second time she's broken in somewhere we were staying," Ree said when they met at the mouth of the hallway. "And this time, it was my house."

"You weren't kidding about the alarm, were you?" he asked.

"No. I can't be caught off guard like that again," she stated. "Zoey reminded me that my place is vulnerable and it shouldn't be."

Quint nodded.

"Where do you want me?" he asked, motioning toward the hallway.

"Since I'm repainting my guest bedroom and it's a mess right now, you'll have to sleep with me in the master," she said, a sexy red blush crawling up her neck.

"I can make do on the sofa if that's better," he offered if it would make her more comfortable.

"You'll sleep a whole lot better on my bed. It's comfortable and you're way too big to fit on my sofa. Be real, Quint." Ree rolled her eyes and then laughed. "I'm slap-happy. I'm probably not going to make a whole lot of sense from here on out. But I have an extra toothbrush still in its wrapper in my medicine cabinet that you're welcome to have."

"Already beat you to that one," he said. "I couldn't stand my breath and thought it was criminal to force it on you and Zoey."

Ree laughed again before straightening up. "I'm going to take a shower. My bedroom has blackout curtains. You're welcome to close them."

"I like to know when the sun comes up, if that's all right with you," he said.

"Same. I used to use them a long time ago and then stopped because I felt like I was in a cave and had no idea when it was night or day," she stated, then pointed toward the master before heading that way.

Quint went around the place, double-checking window locks and then doors. When Ree's home was safely secured, he made a beeline for the master bath. Ignoring the fact Ree was naked behind the curtain, he brushed his teeth before hitting the sack. His eyes were barely closed when he conked out…

An alarm shrieked. Quint bolted upright. The sun peeking through the slats of the miniblinds told him it was time to be awake.

Ree absently reached over and tapped at the alarm, no doubt trying to find the snooze button. He moved around to her side of the bed and turned off the noise instead. She groaned. "Time to get up already?"

"We had a solid ten hours of sleep," he said quietly, liking the fact she'd been curled up next to him in bed all night. He cursed himself for not bringing in the suitcase. What was wrong with him? Ree was the only person he'd ever wanted to bring a suitcase to and yet he'd stopped himself.

Before he chewed on that again, he figured the least he could do was make coffee before she got out of bed.

Thankfully, he'd peeled himself out of those overalls last night. The boxers might be a little bit tight but the seams weren't busting out. He wished he hadn't left the suitcase in his vehicle for more than one reason.

As Quint fumbled around looking for coffee supplies, he heard a key being inserted into the lock in the living room.

"Hey, sis." Shane's voice was unmistakable. And since he was in the living room, there was no way Quint was getting out of being caught in his underwear in the kitchen.

Since he didn't want to surprise Shane, Quint cleared his throat. "She's in the bedroom. I'm making coffee. How about a cup?"

"Quint?" Shane didn't bother to hide his shock.

"It's me," Quint confirmed.

"I thought the alarm contractor might have beaten me here," Shane said in exacerbation as he rounded the corner, then stopped cold in his tracks. He gave Quint a once-over before taking a step back.

"My clothes are in the next room," Quint said, pouring a cup of fresh brew. "Coffee?"

"Thanks," Shane said, taking the offering but looking mighty unsure of this situation.

"We're working a case together and I got into a fight," Quint stated as he poured his own cup and one for Ree.

"I hope the other guy looks worse," Shane quipped. They both laughed. It was to relieve some of the awkward tension of Shane walking into his sister's house to find a man in her kitchen who was barely dressed.

The alarm in the master blared again.

"I'll just take this to Ree and throw on some pants," Quint said.

"Sounds like a plan." Shane turned toward the window as Quint walked past.

Ree was wrestling with the alarm clock when Quint returned.

"Hey, you might want to get up seeing as how your brother is here." Quint looked around for the overalls he'd shed last night before climbing in bed.

"Shane is here?" Ree sat right up after hearing that news.

"He's in the kitchen, drinking coffee," Quint said, taking a sip of fresh brew before setting his mug on top of the dresser. He located the overalls and pulled them on, thinking he should have thrown his clothes in the wash yesterday. He'd been preoccupied nursing his injuries.

"What did he say?" Ree asked, throwing covers off and scrambling out of bed.

"That he was going outside to get his shotgun," Quint joked.

Ree's expression was priceless. The moment of shock before she realized he was jerking her chain was worth the pain that came with laughing.

"For that, I'm not giving your other clothes back," she stated.

"Even though I brought coffee?" he asked, motioning toward the mug he'd set next to her side of the bed on the nightstand.

"Have I told you how much I love you?" Ree's expression dropped the instant those words left her mouth. She immediately started backtracking. "I wasn't saying that I—"

"Don't worry about it," he interjected. "It's just an expression. I knew what you meant."

"That's a relief," she said before taking a sip of coffee.

She lifted the mug in the air afterward. "Remind me not to talk before I've had a sufficient amount of caffeine in the future, will you?"

Quint wasn't so sure he wanted to take that bargain. Hearing the words *I love you* come out of Ree's mouth had caused his chest to squeeze.

Chapter Eleven

Ree threw on clothes, brushed her teeth and polished off her first cup of coffee for the day before deciding to face her brother. She'd packed an overnight bag while Quint had been asleep last night, so she brought that out to the living room and set it next to the door before getting a yogurt from the fridge.

Thankfully, Shane was outside with the alarm-company contractor. She wanted to slip out the door and head to Austin without having a big conversation with her brother about something she couldn't exactly define. Her relationship with Quint was professional only. Everything else between them was complicated and she didn't know how to define it, let alone explain it to someone else.

So when Quint was fed, caffeinated and dressed before Shane came back inside, she was relieved.

"Ready?" she asked. "We'll be late if we don't get out of here right now."

"Don't you want to speak to Shane?" Quint asked.

"No," she said quickly. A little too quickly?

Ree shook her head and then grabbed her overnight bag. She slipped the strap over her shoulder. "Bjorn approved a clothing allowance for you since you can't exactly wear the same outfit every day you borrowed from the safe house, but, fair warning, she didn't give a whole lot." She cracked a smile at the thought of him shopping in a thrift store. "We could probably hit an army surplus store on the way to Austin."

"Funny," he said, heading toward the door with a piece of toast in his hand. "We'll be able to stop off at my place after the meetup."

"You don't live far from Austin?" she asked.

He shook his head. "New Braunfels area."

"Okay then," she said. "Shall we see what Axel Ivan has to say?"

"After all the trouble we went through to ensure his wife and daughter are safe, he'd better have something we can use," Quint muttered under his breath.

Ree couldn't agree more. Axel's family had been a handful and his teenager had most likely been responsible for ruining a safe-house location in the process. Teens and their phones. Ree understood how lost she'd feel without hers. And yet, if it came down to life or death, she'd have no problem ditching her cell.

Leading the way outside, she ducked when Shane tried to wave her over.

"Gotta run," she shouted as she tossed her overnight bag in the back seat before climbing into the driver's seat of the Chevy.

Shane looked a little constipated, like he had a whole lot to say and the words were backed up.

"I'll call you later," she said, then closed the door and started the engine.

"You're sure getting out of Dodge a little fast," Quint stated as he eased into the passenger seat.

"My brother walked in on you in my kitchen wearing nothing but boxers that didn't leave a whole lot to the imagination," she said as she stomped on the gas pedal.

"What do *you* think he wants to talk to me about? It sure isn't the alarm system."

"Oh," Quint said.

"'Oh' is right," she agreed before navigating onto the main road and then the highway. The steady hum of tires on pavement was the only noise in the vehicle on the way to the meetup.

"Where exactly are we headed again?" Quint asked, breaking the silence.

"It's a house overlooking Lake Travis," she said. "I mapped it out earlier and the turnoff is easy to miss. It comes not long after a corner store and is basically vertical for a quarter of a mile."

"I can drive if it's a problem for you," he offered.

"Thanks, but you seem to keep forgetting that I grew up with four brothers who kept me on my toes," she said. "Plus, we're still in the heat of Texas. It's not like there will be ice or anything to worry about."

"True."

Ree continued the drive in silence until they passed the corner store. "There's the road we're looking for. If you can call it that."

It wasn't even a paved road so she was grateful for the SUV. There was only one way to get up that hill, and that was to go for it. Hesitate and she'd lose traction. It was a whole lot like driving on ice in that respect. She had to move at a slow and steady pace.

Gravel spewed underneath tires as she snaked up the trail. She was never more thankful than when the road leveled off and resembled something like tar. She didn't realize how stressed she'd been until she glanced at the rearview mirror and saw beads of sweat on her forehead.

Thankful that was over, she finished the drive and parked in the driveway of the safe house. There had to be cameras in the trees on the way up to the home. No one could drive a vehicle up here and go undetected.

"Let's do this," Quint said, seeming eager to get out of the Chevy.

Before they exited the vehicle, a man in a dark suit walked out. His tie was undone and he had an earpiece.

"My name is Marshal Hamlin." He immediately stuck his hand in between him and Quint, who happened to be closest to the door. Quint eased the rest of the way out of the SUV and took the offering.

"I'm Agent Casey and this is my partner Agent Shepperd," Quint said.

Hamlin met Ree in front of the SUV for a vigorous shake. After exchanging pleasantries, his face morphed into a serious expression. "As you both know, the implications in this case make it more sensitive than most."

"We're aware," Ree said.

"I'll have to check your IDs and pat you down. No weapons are allowed inside," Hamlin continued.

Ree didn't like the sound of that, but she could see where a criminal could take advantage of an armed agent if they lost focus. She wouldn't argue and shot a look at Quint when he started to. WITSEC was the US Marshals Service territory. It wasn't her and Quint's place to question their protocol.

Quint pulled out his wallet and showed his license. Ree did the same. When Hamlin had checked both, inspecting them like he was a customs agent and they were trying to get back in the country, he nodded.

"I apologize for any inconvenience," he said, motioning for them to put their hands on the hood of the Chevy.

"I'll save you the trouble," Ree stated. "I'm armed." She pulled her Glock out of the holster underneath her armpit and placed it under the seat of the Chevy. Quint did the same with his weapon.

"I still have to pat you down," Hamlin informed them.

Ree put out her hands and positioned her legs three feet apart. Quint followed suit but the look on his face told her phone calls were going to be made after they walked out of this house.

QUINT OPENED THE door for Ree, needing something to do with his hands besides throw a punch at the arrogant agent who'd just patted down him and Ree. Hamlin had known to expect them and, no doubt, had personally watched them drive up the road on camera. He'd probably also used facial-recognition software to ensure it was truly them. The pat-down was wholly unnecessary in Quint's book. Hamlin was flexing, saying he was in charge.

Since all Quint needed from Axel was a name and a trail to follow, he brushed off his frustration.

"Thank you," Ree said as she crossed over the threshold.

He gave a quick nod and could see she was reading him. She would also realize his laser focus was engaged. Following her inside, the hallway was dark despite the time. They'd been punctual, too, arriving at 9:53 a.m. The dark wood flooring extended down a set of five steps where the room opened up to what might look like a small art gallery. Two crushed-velvet sofas faced each other, acting as the center point of the room. The walls had dim lights illuminating various pieces of artwork, most of which was centered around photographs of nature and trees.

Another set of five stairs down and the rather large rectangular dining room seated a dozen folks. There was half the number currently engaged in conversation. Coffee mugs in a neat line. The entire home was positioned to take advantage of the wall of windows and the view of treetops perched above the lake.

The place looked like something out of *Architectural Digest* magazine. It might not be Quint's personal taste, but it was a piece of art. This was by far the fanciest safe house Quint had ever seen and he wondered what kind of favors had been called in to get this place. He also couldn't help wondering who owned the place.

As the trio made their way toward the table, a few glances came their way. No one seemed to be bothered by their presence or feel threatened. But then Hamlin did a decent job of screening as annoying as the man could be.

A person who had his back to the room was large-framed enough to be Axel. His dark hair was cut short, curling just above the collar. He wore a crisp white tailored shirt.

Ree and Quint joined the small group at the table after a quick introduction by Hamlin. Other than Axel, there were five agents present. There were three males, plus Hamlin, and two females, representing three agencies. Now Quint understood why Axel wasn't in prison. He was giving up names, dates and locations. He had to be in order to have this many law-enforcement personnel in one room ready and waiting to interview him.

"Now that the final two agents are here, why don't you start from the beginning and tell everyone what happened in the prison yard that day," one of the male agents sitting at the head of the table said.

Hamlin immediately disappeared once they sat.

"Once this meeting is done, I'll be reunited with my family?" Axel asked as he took a seat.

"We've gone over this before, sir," the lead agent said.

"The answer is still the same. Give us enough information and you'll get to be with your family again. The three of you will then leave with Marshal Hamlin."

Axel nodded. He was a large man with the kind of build people referred to as big-boned. His short haircut did little to veil an oversize forehead. His large nose hooked and he had the kind of pockmarked skin that revealed he'd struggled with acne in his teenage years. Still, there was a particular refinement about the way he sat there, in his tailored shirt and black slacks, hands folded on top of the table.

Would he give Quint and Ree the information they needed?

Chapter Twelve

Ree leaned back in her chair with her back facing the incredible view of treetops and the lake beyond. She crossed her arms over her chest and studied Axel Ivan. After meeting his wife and daughter, she tried to fit the puzzle pieces together. She thought about the possibility of Laurie Ivan having an affair while her husband was incarcerated. The man sitting across the table wasn't the type to take an affair lightly.

For Laurie's sake, she hoped Axel never found out.

"It went down like this," Axel said, the grip on his hands tightening. "Correction Officer Ricky Barns came to my cell one night. He stood on the other side of the bars and tapped his billy club against the metal until I woke up. It was the middle of the night." He shrugged. "I'm not sure exactly what time but it was pitch-black outside."

He glanced at the faces around the table. Was he gauging whether or not each agent believed him so far?

"He mumbled something about it being my unlucky day," Axel continued when no one spoke. "I asked him what he was talking about but all he said was that my number had come up. He threw me for a loop because on the inside certain groups look out for their own. You know what I mean?"

A few heads nodded. One of the agents was recording

the session. Others nursed cups of coffee as they studied Axel. Everyone at the table was getting a read on the man and she hoped they would exchange notes at the end of the interview.

"Sure," the lead agent said.

"So I couldn't figure out what the hell Ricky—"

Axel looked around like he'd just given out the secret recipe to Coke. When he was satisfied no one seemed upset by the familiarity of using the officer's first name, he kept going. "The man says something that stuck with me next. He said he was unlucky, too. Said we were two unlucky bastards." Axel stopped like he needed a minute before continuing. "Then he walks off like I'm supposed to know what any of that means."

"And what did it mean?" the lead agent asked.

"That I was going down for murder and Ricky was the one who got tagged to do it," Axel said as a thin sheen of sweat covered his Frankenstein-like forehead. His pulse seemed to kick up a few notches at recounting the story and he shifted positions in his seat, as if he was suddenly uncomfortable.

"How do you know it was Officer Barns who killed the victim?" the lead agent continued.

"I stayed up after his visit and tried to figure out what he meant," Axel admitted. "When I tried to go back to sleep, my eyes wouldn't stay shut. After that, I paid attention when Officer Barns interacted with anyone."

"The victim was brought out of solitary confinement," the lead agent reminded him.

"Which explains why I'd never seen the dude before," Axel said. "I'd swear on my mother's grave, rest her soul."

"So you didn't know the victim?" the lead agent asked.

"No, sir," Axel replied without hesitation. "Never met him or seen him before."

"Where were you when the victim was brought to the yard?" the lead agent asked.

"I was outside, working out," Axel said. His muscled arms were probably as thick as Ree's thighs. To get arms like those, he had to work out more than a few times a week. "I was on the bench, lifting, when my spotter says, 'Hey, would you look at that?'"

"If you were on the bench, how would you have seen what was happening?" the lead agent asked.

"My spotter," Axel stated, as plain as the nose on his face. "The next thing I heard from him was 'Oh, hell, Ricky is behind him.'"

"Why didn't your spotter come forward?" the lead agent asked.

"He didn't want to end up in a box six feet under for snitching. Inmates take that seriously," Axel informed them. "By the time I sat up, I saw Ricky strangle this guy a couple of feet behind the basket while a game of three-on-three took place. No one stopped, looked, or tried to stop Ricky. Like I said, it's best to mind your own business on the inside. Next thing I know, I'm being hauled in to speak to the warden and I'm being told I'll never make parole." Axel threw up his hands. "There wasn't a thing I could do about it, either."

He issued a sharp sigh.

"They own you when you're inside," he explained. "And if they don't, your crew on the outside does. The people I worked for have long fingers, if you know what I mean. It's not the first time someone died after word spread that they were going to talk to the feds. In fact, it's considered the kiss of death where I come from."

"And who is it you work for on the outside?" the lead agent asked.

Axel leaned forward, then back. He wiped his hands

on his pants at the thighs, like he was trying to sop up sweat. Even with his life on the line, it didn't seem to be easy to give up names.

"Who would want the victim dead?" the agent pressed as Marshal Hamlin re-entered the room, and then stood next to the door.

"I give you this information and I get to see my wife and daughter, right?" Axel asked.

Ree figured this wasn't the time to mention the fact his family had considered walking away to stay in a life that wouldn't include him any longer.

"That would be Vadik Gajov." Axel's face went as white as a sheet when he said the name. It was information that could place a bounty on his head.

Ree glanced over at Quint. His hands were fisted, his lips thinned, and every muscle in his face tensed.

"He is the right hand to someone by the name of Dumitru," Axel continued after another sharp sigh. He had to know this was the point of no return. Then again, after they tried to frame him for murder, he had nothing left to lose.

"How do we get to Vadik?" Quint asked, drawing a disapproving sideways glance from the lead agent. The man looked like a real stiff.

This was the information they'd come for. No one should be surprised that Quint was eager to get down to brass tacks.

"I have a contact for you," Axel said quietly. "Her name is Giselle and she'll be friends with your female agent, not you. The operation is run out of Dallas. Giselle can get you invited to a party. She's risking a lot without knowing you're law enforcement, but she'll help you get in when I tell her to. Once there, it's up to you."

"Who is this Giselle and what is her contact information?" the lead agent asked, but Axel looked directly at Ree.

"She'll work with you," he said. "Hand me your phone."

Ree did despite the grunt from the lead agent. Once the contact information was secured in her phone, Quint stood up.

"We've gotten what we came for," he stated.

"I need one more thing," Axel interjected as the lead agent fired off a text. Marshal Hamlin came to the table, moving at a decent clip. From the corner of Ree's eye, she saw Quint's hand twitch and start to make a move for his empty holster.

"Yeah?" Quint asked. "What's that?"

"Protection for Giselle," Axel stated, like he had the power to call the shots. It was an interesting shift, but there was something about the look in his eyes that said this was a nonnegotiable point. Did he want Quint to kiss a ring after this exchange?

"I'm going to need the contact information," the lead agent said, but no one was listening to him anymore.

"I'll tell her to walk away when you reach out to her otherwise," Axel stated. The threat was interesting considering he wasn't exactly in a position to make more demands. Unless he had other information these agencies wanted. Ree understood wanting to protect an asset. She went to great lengths to ensure the people who came forward and trusted her didn't suffer. Crime might pay but the bill was sometimes an informant's life.

"Agent Casey is hardly in charge here," the lead agent protested.

"Why is that so important to you?" Quint asked Axel. "Your family is…"

The reason Axel was so emphatic seemed to dawn on

Quint at the same moment it did on Ree. The two had been having an affair.

"Can I ask who she is to you?" Quint asked. They both seemed to realize Axel meant business. He protected the people he loved and he wouldn't want to expose Giselle without giving her a way out of the lifestyle.

"She's family" was all he said. Then he crossed his arms over his chest. He was telling them to make their move.

"I want the contact information," the lead agent said for the third time.

Quint stood there for a long moment like he was contemplating his next move carefully. He'd burned a few bridges in this room and had to know it.

Ree typed out a text to Agent Grappell with the request to secure WITSEC for one more person connected to the case. She tapped the toe of her shoe on the tile flooring while waiting for a response. Two minutes of silence preceded a response. Done.

"Got it," Ree said to Quint.

He looked to Axel. "She'll be offered WITSEC but I can't guarantee that she'll take it."

"She will," Axel said, looking pretty confident. His expression softened when he looked at Quint and said, "Thank you."

"You're welcome," Quint responded. His gaze shifted to the lead agent. "As far as the contact information goes, you'll read it in my report." He turned toward Ree. "Are you ready to go, Agent Sheppard?"

"Thought you'd never ask." Ree was already making her way around the table when Marshal Hamlin blocked their access to the stairs.

"You can call my boss. You can request an investigation into my actions here today. And you can raise hell about me not playing well in the sandbox," Quint growled through clenched teeth. "But if you block my exit, I'll have no problem forcibly removing you."

Axel smirked.

QUINT STOOD IN front of Marshal Hamlin, daring the man to make a move. They'd gotten what they needed to move forward with their investigation. This dog-and-pony show was no longer any use to them. And after the way they'd been treated so far, he wasn't particularly interested in playing nice-nice.

Ree stood beside him, her fingers dancing across the screen of her phone at a record pace. She would most likely be requesting assistance from Bjorn. The concerned wrinkle in her forehead was meant for him. He'd bet money on the fact she wasn't stressed about whether or not he could remove the smug look from Hamlin's face. The wrinkle had appeared the minute she heard the one name that would skyrocket Quint's blood pressure—Dumitru.

Vadik was close to the source. He worked out of Dallas. Giselle could get Quint and Ree inside the man's apartment. Done deal. There was no reason for Quint to hang around. He didn't care about Officer Barns, except to say he had been unlucky. He wouldn't have an out like Axel. Even then, he was going to have to look over his shoulder for the rest of his natural life. Axel knew it. Ree knew it. Quint knew it.

But what choice did the man have? He could go down for a crime he didn't commit and very likely be sentenced to death. Or he could give up information, grab his family and go into Witness Protection for the rest of his life. And it would be a lifelong commitment to their new identities. Tough going considering he had a typical teenager who would have too much access to social media. One slip and she could give away their location. It was clear to anyone paying attention that Axel Ivan loved his family above all else.

If Axel committed himself to whatever new identity he and his family would receive they would have a real shot in life, a second chance to get it right and live on the good side of the law. Quint wished the man luck in his new life.

“Step aside or your boss will get a call from ours.” Ree hoisted the text message up to Hamlin’s face, stopping within an inch of the screen smacking him right in the nose.

He blinked and took a quick step backward. Quint couldn’t wipe the smirk off his face. Ree was a force to be reckoned with and she backed down from no one when she was in the right. Quint almost laughed because she didn’t relent when she wasn’t right, either. His partner had a stubborn streak a mile long.

Hamlin glanced at the screen before swatting it away and stepping aside. “Be my guest.”

“Your hospitality has been much appreciated,” Quint said, not bothering to hide his sarcasm. “I’ll be sure to request to work with you again real soon on another case.”

“Door’s tricky,” Hamlin said. “Sometimes it can hit you right in the backside as you exit. I’d be careful if I was you.”

The thinly veiled threat made no difference to Quint. Working with other agencies after Tessa’s death held no appeal. He needed to figure out a way to keep Bjorn from assigning him to task forces again. This macho, territorial show was for the birds.

Ree led the way out as Quint grabbed the door from her.

“Better watch that one,” she quipped as she navigated

to the door and then stepped outside into the muggy air. "I hear it has a mind of its own."

Quint chuckled as he walked outside. He felt a whole lot better once he returned his weapon to its holster. Ree's facial muscles relaxed as she did the same before taking the driver's seat.

"Should I take your phone while you drive so I can work out arrangements in Dallas with Grappell?" Quint asked as he struggled with the seat belt. Twisting his body was not a good move if he wanted to stay out of mind-numbing pain.

"I slipped the phone onto my chair and called him with the phone on mute both ways," she stated as she fired up the engine. There was more than a hint of pride in her voice.

"Good idea," he said, duly impressed by his partner. He reached over and touched the back of her hand. The familiar electrical current ran through him at the point of contact.

"I'll point us toward Dallas and somewhere along the three-to-four-hour drive, Grappell will start hitting my phone with instructions," Ree said. "Are you hungry? Because I could definitely eat."

"We can stop off on the way. It'll give Grappell more time to work out the details," he said. He fished in his pocket for the folded-up piece of paper with the tree on it. "Mind if I use this pen?" He motioned toward the one on the dashboard.

"Go for it," she said. "I didn't even realize it was there."

Quint grabbed the pen as she navigated down the steep incline toward a road that didn't feel like the first drop on a roller coaster. He smoothed the paper out flat on his thigh as he bent over. He made a new branch between

Constantin and Dumitru. On the branch, he wrote Vadik's name. He drew a line from Vadik to Dumitru and wrote *right-hand man.* Off to the side in a cloud all on its own, he jotted down the name Giselle. He drew a couple of circles around her name.

"Do you want to stop off at Czech Stop on the way?" Ree asked. This was a gas station, convenience store, and authentic Czech deli rolled into one.

"That can't be a serious question," he quipped.

"I can almost taste a fruit kolache right now," she said with a little mewl of pleasure.

Quint's mind snapped to the last time he'd heard a sound like that from her and an ache welled up inside of him so fast he almost didn't know what to do with it. They were going into a dangerous situation and Quint knew, without a doubt, he would put his life on the line in a heartbeat if it meant bringing justice to Tessa's killer. Dumitru didn't have to be the one to put the bullet in her to be responsible for her death. The jerk didn't deserve to live. He didn't deserve to be the one to have a family and a long life, or any of the things Tessa had been robbed of.

At some point a while later, Ree pulled off the highway. He realized they'd made their exit and he was shocked at how hours could feel like minutes when he was lost in thought. A couple of minutes later, she was parking. Her cell buzzed and she checked the screen before they got out.

"It's our boss," she said, handing over the cell.

"Meet you inside?" he asked.

Ree nodded before exiting the vehicle. She paused as she closed the door like she needed reassurance it was okay to leave him alone on the phone with Bjorn.

"I'll be right in," he said before answering.

"What the hell did you just do, Agent Casey?" Bjorn's

voice had the kind of calm that was like looking at the surface of a lake, placid on top while the real danger lurked underneath.

Chapter Thirteen

Ree stood in line, ordered a dozen fruit kolaches and twin cups of coffee, and paid with no sign of Quint. Her own stress levels climbed at what Bjorn might be saying to Quint right now. There was always a possibility he could get pulled from the case—even he had to realize it. The thought of working with a new partner sent the equivalent of a lead ball spiraling through her stomach.

Taking the box of goodies and balancing the coffee cups, she turned around and got a glimpse of Quint in conversation with Bjorn. It wasn't good. Even from here, she could see a vein bulging in his forehead.

With a deep breath, Ree walked outside and to the passenger window. Quint rolled it down immediately and took the box, then the coffees, as she handed them over one at a time. She reclaimed the driver's seat to the sounds of Bjorn's heated dressing-down.

Trying not to focus on what was blasting through her cell, she turned on the engine and navigated back onto the highway. The hum of the road helped drown out Bjorn's screaming. Ree tensed, listening for the moment Bjorn told Quint she was removing him from the case altogether.

Shock of all shocks, Bjorn ended the call saying she needed a full report of what happened and what was said because she didn't appreciate another agency being disrespectful to her agents. Bjorn was the equivalent of an older sibling in that sense. Someone who could dish it out to a younger sibling, but no one else was allowed to.

"That was brutal," she finally said to Quint after he took a couple sips of his coffee.

"I've had worse," he said with a half-smile. He opened the box and held out a kolache, which she managed to eat while driving. "She approved the request for WITSEC, which seemed to matter a whole lot to Axel."

"Think Axel and Giselle were having an affair?" she asked, but already had formed her own opinion on that one.

"Of course, and it had to have started long before he went in," he quickly responded. "I'm not sure if I'm disgusted or respect him."

"Same," she said. The man was cheating on his wife, breaking his marriage vows. But then, he was stepping up and protecting someone who obviously meant a great deal to him. Did he love her? Who knew? The idea he didn't want to throw her under the bus made him seem almost like a decent human being.

In all Ree's years in law enforcement, she'd come to realize everyone had a story. It was rare for someone to come from a good upbringing and turn to crime. She'd seen it but it wasn't the norm. Robbery, jealousy and vengeance were the three main motives behind almost all murders. Committing to a life of crime, a world on the edge of what was considered normal society, was a different ballgame. There, folks typically joined to feel a sense of community or belonging. Crime syndicates replaced traditional families. Some were generational and grew up in neighborhoods controlled by gangs or crime rings. In those cases, going into a life of crime was normalized.

Being part of a family was something Ree understood. There was a need to fit in, belong. Her mother never seemed to catch on to the fact Ree had a need to be her own person. For some reason the girlie gene skipped over her despite her mother's best attempts to force her into wearing hair bows when she was little.

The highway narrowed and road construction was a bear on this stretch, but Ree kept herself from spilling the yummy jelly of her fruit kolache on her blouse. Quint's silence said he realized there would be a reckoning with Bjorn. He seemed to be walking a tightrope. The thought of doing any of this without him caused Ree's chest to squeeze.

"Try not to get yourself kicked off this team, okay?" Ree wasn't sure why she said that out loud, except to say that work wouldn't be the same without Quint. Tracking Dumitru wouldn't be the same without him, either. This was his case and she was along for the ride. The reality of getting one step closer to the ultimate target sat in the silence between them.

"I'll do my best, Ree." There was anguish and resignation in his voice. Another emotion was present too. Regret?

Her cell started buzzing, indicating multiple texts coming in.

"Do you mind?" she asked, motioning toward the noise-maker.

He picked up her phone and started reading. The first text was the address of their new apartment. The second told them their new cover was husband and wife.

"Your alarm system is installed and Shane set it up with the password you requested," Quint finally said.

"That's good news," she stated. "No more surprises.

I loved seeing Zoey but it creeped me out that she was able to get inside my home so easily."

"Living out in the country makes it easy to let your guard down," he stated.

"I won't be doing that anymore," she quickly countered. He shot a look like he was asking if she was still talking about the alarm system at her home?

"You're twenty-nine in this scenario," Quint continued. "And a new wardrobe will be waiting for you at the apartment. Agent Grappell said you shouldn't freak out and Bjorn thinks you can pull off the look."

"That's not reassuring," she stated.

Quint seemed amused by all this. "Turns out, we're a partying couple. I supposedly came from Houston and work odd jobs. The story is that I used to come from money but got cut off when I blew through my inheritance at twenty-five years old. Now, I've been 'freelancing,' doing whatever work needs to be done. I've been a bouncer at a high-end nightclub and had to leave Houston for Dallas to find better quality work."

"You're kind of a loser," Ree teased. "I'm not so certain I want to be in a relationship with someone who doesn't have their act together."

"You happen to be one of those party girls who never seems to have a job but always has money and is always dressed to the nines," he continued, the smirk growing.

"Great. Now I don't even know what I am," she said. There was no doubt she could act the part. That was the basis of undercover work. She could throw on concealer and lipstick, and make herself appear younger. In reality, she wouldn't go back in time for anything. For the first time in her life, she felt like she was finally starting to figure a few things out about herself, outside of who she wanted to be at work.

Ree had been fighting so hard against her mother's image of what she should be that she'd forgotten to look inside herself and decide those things for herself.

"And who are you in this scenario?" she asked.

"I've just been released from prison on a trafficking charge. We're originally from Texas but had been living in Seattle. We're home now for a fresh start," he said.

"I'm guessing Giselle knows people in Seattle," Ree mused.

"It's where she's from," he stated. "And there's something else you should know."

The statement got her attention.

"Giselle has a four-year-old son," Quint informed her.

"Axel?" she asked.

"He's been in jail for the last three years, so I'd put my money on him being the father," Quint stated.

"Certainly explains his insistence on taking care of her," she said. "Wonder why he didn't mention the kid."

"He wasn't ready to tell the other agents in the room," he said.

"They would use it against him," she realized. "Plus, they have direct contact with his wife right now."

"He can't afford for his wife to find out about Giselle," he concluded.

"That would make for serious trouble at home," she agreed. "But I was almost certain Laurie was having an affair when she hesitated to go into WITSEC. At first, I believed she was second-guessing taking her daughter away from everything and everyone she knew and loved, but there was more to it."

"Isn't there always more to the story than meets the eye?" Quint asked.

Ree could say the same about their partnership. Not

knowing where they stood, being in limbo, was the worst. At least the case was moving forward now.

QUINT FOCUSED ON the messages as they came in rather than let his mind wander over his last comment. Ree had gotten quiet and he didn't want to get inside his head about what that indicated.

At least he was going to get to do the heavy lifting with Vadik. She would basically play the role of arm candy while he infiltrated. The switch was comforting as they got closer to the evil that had caused Tessa's death. Her baby had been on his mind a great deal lately. Shaking off the anger that came with going down that trail, he refocused on the phone.

"Looks like I'll have a new wardrobe waiting as well as a new car," he stated.

"What will you be driving?" she asked.

"A BMW convertible 4 series in skyscraper-gray metallic," he said. Not bad.

"The appearance of a once-wealthy life of crime. Stinks that you aren't much of a convertible person," she stated.

"When did I ever say that?" he asked.

She laughed and he realized she was teasing.

"Besides, it's part of the cover story. Apparently, after being locked up, I need the open air," he said.

"How long have you been inside?" she asked, figuring they needed to get their stories straight.

"Three years," he continued. "We bottomed out our savings on appeals and finally got a judge to listen. So the story is that I'm in need of work and looking to sell the BMW to keep us going. The apartment where we live belongs to Jenn and Raul, who are out of the country right now."

"What's our last names?" she asked.

"You're Ree Parker-Matthews and I'm Quint Matthews," he stated.

She repeated their names a couple of times. "Got it."

Ree was one of those people who possessed a unique ability to hear something once, repeat it a couple of times and lock it in. Then again, she was one of the sharpest agents he'd ever worked with, no disrespect meant to Tessa's memory.

"What else?" she asked.

"You've been getting by living with your sister and her family for the last three years and couldn't wait to get out of Seattle after my release," he stated.

"A sister?" she balked and that caused him to laugh.

"You really wouldn't know what to do with one of those, would you?" he teased.

"I'll do my best to sell the lie but it's too bad they didn't give me a brother to work with instead," she said. "Brothers, I know."

"Pretend you grew up braiding each other's hair and singing into hairbrushes or something," he quipped.

Ree fake-gagged. "No. Sorry. Can't. My sister will be the marriage-and-family type, while I couldn't stand that noose around my neck. I'm a party girl, remember? I can always say my sister was practically a puritan and we weren't close. That should help."

"We can use the same story about our first date as before," he stated.

"Right. That means we met in Austin," she said.

"I was passing through and stopped off to hear a band," he continued.

"Black Pistol Fire," she immediately stated.

"I like that band, too," he stated.

"They have an interesting bluesy rock-'n'-roll quality, right?" she asked.

"There's something soulful and edgy about their work," he agreed, surprised at the revelation of their music tastes being so similar. He should know these things about Ree instead of how quick she was with a Glock or how capable she was in an altercation. It was strange not to know the basics about someone he'd fallen for. And, yes, Quint could admit to himself their attraction was something far deeper than infatuation.

There was no one else he would want having his back on this investigation and yet her presence made things somewhat problematic. His feelings for her complicated the situation. He was losing his objectivity and some of the burning fire he felt to nail the bastard responsible for Tessa's death was flickering out.

Dumitru belonged behind bars. No one would deny it. Quint needed to be the one to watch the jerk be handcuffed. Better yet, let him be the one who slapped the metal bracelets on the guy.

Tessa and her baby deserved Quint's full attention. She would do no less for him if the situation had been reversed and he was the one six feet under. Recalling the image of Tessa in that hospital bed, lying there lifeless, fueled his anger.

"What happened just now, Quint?" Ree asked, breaking through the fog of his heavy thoughts. "Where did you go?"

"Nowhere," he lied. "It's nothing. I was just trying to memorize the details of our undercover operation. That's all."

Ree sat quietly for a few long moments that seemed to stretch on.

"We were talking about music," he said. "Austin."

She nodded.

"Our first 'date' at the pizza place," he continued.

"Uh-huh," she said absently.

More of that silence sat between them.

"Quint..." she began.

"Yes."

"Don't ever lie to me again," she said simply.

His pulse kicked up a couple of notches. She could read him a little too well and that might backfire in the heat of the moment, when he had to make a critical decision. He could only hope it wouldn't come to that.

Chapter Fourteen

Disappointment sat heavy on Ree's shoulders. When it came to her relationship with Quint, it was always one step forward, two steps back. The push and pull of her attraction to Quint was like fighting against gravity. It was exhausting to say the least. Every attempt to shut it off failed.

Ree wasn't trying hard enough. This man would surely break her heart.

The final minutes of the drive to Dallas were spent with Quint giving her directions from the map feature of her cell phone. The thirty-story high-rise at 350 North Paul Street had all the trappings of a new build.

"What's our floor?" Ree asked, praying it wouldn't be above the tenth floor. She never had been one for heights, preferring to keep her feet on the ground.

"Twenty-seventh," he said, glancing over at her. He did a double take. "What's wrong?"

"Nothing," she lied. "Why?"

"You don't like the setup?" he asked.

"Have I mentioned that I don't love heights?"

"I don't believe you have." He seemed caught off guard by the news.

"I'm not invincible, you know," she stated defensively. "And I'm pretty good at hiding it."

"I'll contact Grappell and see if we can get a lower floor." His gaze shifted back to the screen.

"Don't worry about it. I'll adjust," she stated.

"It's no trouble to ask," he said, but he stopped mid-text. They both knew setting up an apartment on such short notice was nothing short of a miracle.

"I'm serious, Quint. I'll figure it out. Besides, we might not even be here long enough for it to matter," she said. It was true. No one knew for certain how quickly a case would go, but the last two seemed to fly by. "We have an in with Vadik by someone inside his circle. It shouldn't be too hard to gather enough evidence to put the man behind bars."

"He's Dumitru's right hand," Quint said. "He won't roll over on him easily. There's a reason he's the guy's second in command."

"I understand that," Ree agreed. "Which is all the more reason we will need to get in and get out. If we give him and his people time, they'll ferret us out. They'll poke around in our backgrounds. The initial meeting and being brought in by someone on the inside will only get us so far."

"Agreed," he said.

"In my experience, and I'm sure the same applies to you, the higher up you go in a crime ring, the faster you want to get in and get out," she stated.

"I'm in this for the long haul, Ree. You already know that. I'll be here for as long as it takes." His grip tightened around her cell phone until his knuckles turned white.

"I am, too, Quint. You're not doing this alone," she reassured him.

He nodded, but she could already see the wheels turning.

"Promise me you won't go off half-cocked, Quint."

The statement seemed to hit home.

"You're my partner, Ree. But if there's a chance to protect you, I'll take it," he said without any hint of apology.

"The best way to protect me is to keep me informed of your every move," she said, and meant it. "No one cares about putting Dumitru behind bars more than you."

Quint nodded.

"Which means we have to keep playing this tight," she said. "We've gotten this far by working together."

"I know," he replied.

Ree was first to exit the vehicle. Quint took his time getting out, looking like he needed a minute to grease the squeaky wheels. She checked the space where the BMW should be parked. Found it. Although she wasn't much of a convertible person, she had to admit it was a beauty.

"The keys are inside the apartment and the door is unlocked. Everything should be waiting in an envelope on the kitchen counter," Quint said, joining her. He stretched out his arms and yawned. They'd been inside a vehicle for the better part of a day having started early this morning. The saying *feeling like they'd been in a car all day* applied here.

Her own back was sore and she'd long lost feeling in her behind. A walk would do them both some good. There was an ominous feeling sitting heavy on her chest at the thought of crossing the threshold of apartment 2705. One she tried to shake off.

"Do you want to scout the area with me before we head up?" she asked. There'd been a twentysomething guy standing across the street, arms folded, looking like he was trying not to get caught watching their building.

"I need to stretch my legs, too," he said. "Did you see Green Shirt?"

The guy had had on a bright green Polo shirt.

"I was just thinking about him," she admitted. "He could be stalking someone."

"In that loud shirt?" Quint asked. "Maybe."

"Sometimes the best way to blend in is to be loud," she remarked as they started walking.

The block around the apartment teemed with cars. A few of those standup scooters zipped by with mostly young people hanging on to the handlebars. The apartment building sat in the heart of Dallas and was walking distance to quite a few major attractions. The American Airlines Center was nearby, as well as a Dallas favorite, House of Blues. The Dallas Museum of Art wasn't far and neither was Reunion Tower. Katy Trail was easily accessible. There were restaurants along the street. She took note of the location of Highways 75 and I-35. Escape routes were always good to have on hand.

After gaining her bearings, they made the walk back to the building. Dallas wasn't known for its skyscrapers so it would always be easy to find the place. Green Shirt had taken a seat and was playing drums on a set of plastic paint tubs from Home Depot that had been turned upside down. She had to admit, he wasn't bad.

There were two options for heading to the apartment, the main elevators or service elevator. She opted for the latter. Double glass doors led the way into a lobby that resembled another art gallery. This one, as opposed to the Austin house, seemed to let all the light in. Light wood floors. Light walls. Light pictures.

Apartment 2705 was just as impressive.

"You are about to experience six hundred and ninety-four feet of luxury living," Quint said with a wink as he opened the door for her.

"How do you know how many square feet our apartment is?" She must have given quite the look as she walked by because he laughed.

"I looked it up once Grappell gave me the address. Wanted to know what we were getting into," he said, wiggling his eyebrows. The conversation might be lighter now, but the tension between them was still thick. Ree hated it.

She blew out a breath as she walked by, and couldn't help but crack a small smile.

"I, for one, can't wait to see what my new wardrobe looks like," she quipped, figuring there would be more figure-flattering clothes hanging inside. Grappell really had pulled off a miracle getting them this place. It was beautiful, with its smoky, gray velvet couch and coordinating cream-colored fuzzy chairs nestled around a glass end table. The view out the window was amazing even though Ree wouldn't get close enough to truly enjoy it. There was an industrial-looking glass-and-metal dining table with seating for six. It was small and cozy. A man Quint's size would have a time getting comfortable in the midcentury modern forest-green chairs, but she'd seen him make do in her small dinette area. There were two barstools in front of a short counter that separated rooms while still giving an open-concept feel. The kitchen might be on the small side but the cabinets were sleek and the appliances chef-grade. That had always been the irony of urban living. People wanted expensive, high-end kitchens but rarely ever cooked in them. A surprising addition to the kitchen was an under-counter wine fridge. *Nice touch.*

The bedroom was exactly what she expected. One king-size bed in a room that had just enough walking room around it to fit Quint. There were twin nightstands, made of mirrors and steel, and fuzzy throw pillows on the bed. The colors were gray, forest-green and cream. The scheme made it all the way into the master bath.

"At least we can both fit on the bed," she murmured when Quint walked past her. They had to turn sideways for him to pass her in the hallway. Apparently, these luxury apartments had a type, and it wasn't Quint.

"There's a plus," Quint said and there was something low and hungry in his voice that caused all kinds of electrical currents to ripple through her. They were like a livewire at this point, sizzling and curling, causing her stomach to drop.

The air in the room was charged, too, and an ache welled up like a squall inside Ree. The need to touch Quint, to feel his skin against hers, was its own force. They'd made love in Houston and it had been the best of her life. Was there any going back after?

They were stuck somewhere between going all in and taking the plunge to really be together and a dedication to their jobs that reminded them how unprofessional it would be to continue their relationship while on a case.

Ree cleared her throat and walked away, figuring putting some space between them would be a good idea. She located the large yellow envelope on the counter. It wasn't hard to find in a room of gray, green and cream colors. She'd been too distracted by the window earlier to notice it.

She opened the package and emptied the contents onto the counter, where place mats were set up for two. This must be the breakfast bar. At least she had her cell phone and a laptop. There was a cell inside marked with Quint's name on it. Good. He needed a new one after losing his.

Quint joined her a few minutes later.

"The shower in this place is the best part," he said. "Did you check out the closet yet?"

"I didn't have the stomach for it," she admitted with a small smile.

"My new cell?" He picked up the piece of technology after she nodded. He checked the contacts with her standing there, scrolling through fake friends until he stopped at her name, Ree Parker-Matthews. Maybe her new identity could quash her attraction to her partner.

"When this case is over, we need to sit down and have a conversation about us."

"I know," he said with a tone of voice that sounded defeated.

It caused her chest to tighten and a sense of dread to wash over her.

QUINT KNEW REE was right about talking. Nothing in him wanted to sit down with her and break her heart. Hell, he didn't want to break his own heart and the thought of being without her, even for a few minutes, caused an ache like he'd never known.

They were coworkers and terrific partners. He and Tessa used to joke that relationships came and went but a good partnership was forever. Everyone in Quint's life had been temporary. His mother had died too young. His mentor had had a family of his own to keep him busy.

There'd been relationships but none that could measure up to hanging out with his best friend. And now Tessa was gone, too, through no fault of her own. She hadn't wanted to check out at such a young age, especially while pregnant.

A strange thought struck. Did the father of Tessa's baby even know she was gone? The jerk who'd walked away and told her that he didn't want to have anything to do with her or the baby didn't deserve to know what had happened. And yet, a nagging piece of Quint wondered if the guy should know.

The tricky part would be figuring out who he was. Tessa had been tight-lipped. At her funeral, he'd scanned every male face present, searching for some kind of emotion that would give him away. Guilt. Remorse.

If the father of Tessa's baby had been there, Quint hadn't seen him. Another thought struck. Knowing Tessa, she might have not wanted the guy in her or the baby's life. Was it possible she'd made up the part about telling him and him rejecting her?

Quint shook off the thought. There was no way she would lie to him. Right? *Lie* might be a strong word. She'd been known to fudge the truth from time to time. Tessa believed in the gray area, whereas Quint saw things more in black and white. She'd remarked once or twice that he was too literal.

Was he taking liberties now? Had he found the gray area that he wasn't convinced had existed in the past? Everyone had a breaking point, he thought. And he'd always told himself that once he found his, it would be time to get out of law enforcement.

Standing in the breakfast nook, looking at Ree now, he couldn't help but wonder if this was it. Without a doubt, he realized he would do whatever it took to bring down Dumitru. He could chalk it up to the name of justice and probably convince a jury. The problem was facing himself after. How would he do that?

"Are you hungry?" he asked.

"Starving," she said. "The kolaches were amazing but basically too much sugar to hold me for long."

"I could order pizza or walk outside and see what options we have," he said.

She picked up her cell and showed him the screen.

"Or you could just Yelp something and save yourself the walk."

"I need to clear my head," he said. "A walk would do me good."

Ree nodded. Then she locked gazes with him.

"After being around Zoey last night, I've decided to get a dog," she stated with the kind of certainty that told him this was a new development to her, too.

"Lots of animals need good homes at the pound," he said, staring at her. Did that mean what he thought? She was considering a change in career. There was something present in her eyes that said this wasn't a good time to ask. So he made a mental note and then tucked his cell inside his jeans pocket.

His mind had been bouncing around from thinking about Tessa, to wondering how far he would go to find and nail Dumitru. Before Ree had entered the picture, avenging Tessa's death had been the only thing he'd thought about. There'd been no clear division between right and wrong. Now, he was starting to question himself.

Before Ree, he hadn't given much thought to his future. Now, all he could think about was being with her when she picked out her damn dog. When did that happen? More of the guilt washed over him when he thought about how much he wanted to kiss those pink lips of hers, too.

This seemed like a good time to head downstairs, get some food and see if Green Shirt was still there.

Chapter Fifteen

Ree didn't care what kind of food she got as long as she ate something soon. She checked the fridge after Quint left. It was bare. Not even a gallon of milk or coffee. She would need to remedy that immediately. She'd never survive without coffee in the morning. There was something about spending a day driving that made her extra tired and her muscles felt like they'd been coiled for the ride up. She stretched out her arms and rolled her shoulders as a text came in.

There were only two things she needed more than air—a shower and a bed, in exactly that order.

The message was from Agent Grappell. Giselle is coming over—get ready.

Ree bit back a curse. She checked to ensure Quint was on the group chat. Thankfully, he was. She made a beeline for the bedroom. The undercover show was about to start and she was dressed way too conservatively to sell her new identity. She also needed to take off her jacket and shoulder holster. Those were dead giveaways.

As she passed a mirror, she also realized there was work to do to her face. There had better be makeup in that bathroom if they wanted her to look younger. Concealer and a bright-colored lipstick at the very least.

The clothes in the closet would be considered scandalous in most circles. Ree slipped on a black minidress that she would not be caught dead in under normal circumstances. The spiked heels with red soles made her tall enough to stand eye-to-eye with Quint. Well, almost.

In the bathroom, there was a basket full of makeup. Thankfully, Grappell seemed to have pulled her records from past assignments because the colors worked with her fiery red hair and green eyes. She let out a yelp when she saw the highlighter brand of makeup she couldn't afford to buy under normal circumstances. Grappell had arranged for her to have the good stuff, too. Too bad she couldn't take any of this home with her when this case was over.

Would it ever be truly over? Not if Dumitru disappeared. Not for Quint.

For his sake, she hoped to be able to break into the inner circle and get in with Vadik. It was a strange thing to wish for because the move would also put Quint's life in danger. There were cases and then there were *cases*. This definitely qualified as the latter. The relentless quality, the torture in Quint's eyes when he thought he was getting closer would never allow him to be at peace until Dumitru was behind bars.

Would it work? She couldn't help but wonder because those things wouldn't bring Tessa back. Her ghost would haunt Quint forever. Ree was beginning to see it so clearly now.

Looking in the mirror, she realized she needed to do something with her hair. There was a curling iron, so she plugged it in. The thing heated up fast. Before she knew it, she'd put a few long, loose curls in her hair. The middle part wasn't something she loved, but it seemed to be the craze, so she went with it.

To finish off the look, she found a glossy lip color

that was a deep brown with gold undertones. The name was Consensual. There was a thought, she joked as she opened the round tin before dabbing her finger inside. She tapped the color on her lips before rubbing her lips together to even out the color. *Hey, kid. Not too bad.*

Of course, the "kid" days were long over for her, but she figured this look might convince others she was still in her twenties. This was the rare time having a baby face paid off. Plus, her fair skin had made it impossible to tan in the summer, so she never tried. Now, she was realizing it was more of a gift than a curse because the overly tanned bunch from high school was starting to look a little bit like beef jerky in their pictures on social media. Speaking of which, she sent a text to Grappell reminding him to set up accounts for them under their new identities.

He immediately responded that their social imprint was being worked on. This was the tricky part about a case that came together fast. Creating a believable social-media trail took time and resources.

She made a mental note to bring cookies into the office for Grappell the next time she was in. Having someone like him on the desk made everything else possible. It didn't hurt that she was working on a high-profile case. Even though Dumitru hadn't been the one to pull the trigger, the whole department wanted to see him go down after Tessa's death.

Another text came through that sent her pulse through the roof. Giselle was in the building heading up. Ree slid her holster and Glock in between the mattresses, figuring she'd find a better hiding spot later when she had more time.

Quint texted that he was on his way with pizza and a

bottle of wine. This didn't seem like the time to mention they were out of coffee and milk.

She shelved the thought and headed into the kitchen to fill a water glass. A couple of deep breaths on the way and her nerves relaxed a few more notches. An adrenaline spike right before a case went undercover was normal. Deep breaths helped. So did thinking about her family and reminding herself that she would see them again.

Speaking of which, her grandfather wasn't getting any younger. Being on the job made seeing him on the regular a challenge. She missed playing Spicy Uno with him despite his ridiculous rules meant to liven up the game. He looked for all her weaknesses in order to give her more cards, especially the one where no one could talk if a six was played.

By some miracle she wouldn't dare question, Quint made it inside the apartment before Giselle got there.

"How?" she asked but all he did was kiss her. The kiss sent warmth swirling through her and caused all kinds of carnal desires to swim in her head. He pulled back first.

"What was that for?" she asked.

"We're out of practice," he stated. "Plus, I figured us being a couple would be more believable if some of your lipstick rubbed off on me. I've supposedly been in prison for three years and that means I wouldn't be able to keep my hands off you."

"Go change," she said ushering him toward the master and trying to shake off the remnants of that kiss. Her stomach plummeted at his last comment.

As she opened the cabinet to pull out a few plates, a soft knock on the door sounded. Ree walked over, gave herself one last pep talk and then opened the door.

Giselle was the opposite of Laurie. The younger woman had curly blond hair that ran halfway down her back. She was dressed in a crop top and jeans that highlighted a tanned, toned midsection. The woman spent time at the gym. She would regret all that sun later, Ree said to herself.

"Hi," Ree said, ratcheting her voice up several octaves. "Come in."

The twentysomething ducked her shoulders and smiled. "You're friends with Axel?"

"That's right," Ree stated. "But not *friends*, if you know what I mean. We just know each other. In fact, he knows my husband better. I'm Ree Matthews, by the way."

If the last minute was any indication, Ree's cheeks were going to be sore later from smiling so much.

Giselle stepped inside and looked around.

"Nice apartment," she said.

"It belongs to a friend," Ree admitted. "Have you eaten? My husband just brought home pizza and a bottle of wine."

"I could take a slice," Giselle said with an ear-to-ear smile. She was clearly out of her comfort zone and must have cared for Axel a whole lot to trust him this much. Unless…

Did Giselle think she was here for some kind of threesome? The thought was a face slap. Was the young woman for hire? Was that how she knew Axel?

"Make yourself comfortable," Ree said, motioning toward the table. Giselle had the kind of slight frame that would make the dining chairs look roomy. It was difficult to believe a baby had ever been inside that body. She'd certainly bounced back. Although, to be fair, the kid was four years old and that would have made her in her early twenties when she'd had him. "How did you meet Axel?"

Giselle perched on one of the stools before taking off

her cross-body bag and hooking it on the back of the chair. She had the kind of annoyingly shiny hair Ree would have killed for in her youth.

"Um, you know, through people," she said, being cautious with information.

At this rate, they wouldn't get anything useful out of her. Then again, she was about to put her life on the line to give them an in with Vadik's people. It was obvious she knew the position she was being put in.

"Where was your husband locked up?" Giselle asked.

"Seattle," Ree said, dodging the question and hoping she could get away with it. They hadn't discussed where he'd been in prison.

QUINT WALKED OUT in time to hear Ree give a pat answer. She gave a quick glance at him, indicating she would appreciate a save. He walked right over to their guest and introduced himself. "You must be Giselle."

"That's right," she said, smiling. Giselle was younger than he expected her to be.

He could admit there was a certain beauty to her, but she was nowhere near on the same scale as Ree. One look at her nearly knocked him over.

"How long have you known Axel?" Giselle asked.

"On and off for five years or so," Quint stated, moving around to the kitchen.

"How about a glass of wine?" Ree asked. "I'm afraid we just got to town and don't have anything else around unless you want water from the tap."

"Wine is good," Giselle stated.

"You got it," Quint said, shooing Ree out of the kitchen after giving her a kiss that left his own lips burning. It might have been for show, but he'd been wanting to do that all day.

Giselle's smile said she approved of the two of them being waited on.

"Axel says I should vouch for you," Giselle admitted.

"I'd appreciate a good word as long as it doesn't put you in a tight spot," Quint said, playing it cool. Sounding too eager was the kiss of death in situations like these.

"No, I'm good. Axel wouldn't ask me to bring you in if he didn't trust you. I trust his judgment," Giselle said. "I just thought we should get to know a little more about each other before we head to the party tonight."

"Tonight?" Quint asked before he could reel the question back in.

"We have time for you to eat your pizza," she said quickly. "Can't have anyone showing up on an empty stomach."

Quint opened the wine and poured three glasses, figuring Ree needed one after hearing the news they would be up later tonight than planned. It was good, though. There was no time like the present and he'd waited long enough for a break. Some cases shot right out of the gate while others lagged, taking time. Now that there was action, this one seemed ready for the express train.

He set down the glasses on the counter and then plated the slices. After passing out the plates, he picked up his own and ate. Talking slowed, which meant everyone was hungry.

Giselle pulled her cell out of her purse after she'd polished off the last bite. She set it down on the counter. "I should probably get your contact info while I'm thinking about it."

"Oh, good. Right," Ree stated.

"I meant Quint's," Giselle clarified. There was something worldly about her, like she was someone who knew the ropes and partied most nights. It wasn't the motherly image he expected from Axel's mistress. Then again, his wife was with their daughter. The three of them were a "traditional" family, whereas Giselle was something on the side. Quint wondered if there were others like her and her son for Axel.

Speaking of which, the photo on her screensaver was of a little dark-haired boy who resembled his father.

"This must be your son," Ree stated. "Axel talked about him."

"He did?" Giselle sounded surprised and a little bit proud.

"Yes, of course," Ree said. "Your son is adorable."

"He stays with my sister," Giselle said, her shoulders slumping forward, looking deflated. "But Axel always makes sure Axel Junior has everything he needs."

"I'm sure he does," Quint said. "I know how proud he is of his boy."

The comment seemed to win favor with Giselle, who brought up her pictures and scrolled through a few.

"He hasn't been able to spend much time with his daddy, but they're two peas in a pod," she said, showing Axel holding his son as an infant. She looked to Ree. "Do you have kids?"

"Me? No," she said quickly. "Not with Quint locked up for the past few years. I had a scare when he first went in, but it turned out to be a false positive."

"Oh, I'm sorry," Giselle said sympathetically. She reached over and touched Ree's hand. "That must have been hard."

"I think it turned out for the best," Ree said. "I was already living with my sister in Seattle. I would have wanted Quint to see our kid take its first steps and do all that stuff kids do."

Giselle took a long pull of wine.

"Axel has missed out on a lot while locked up. Laurie gets all the visitation days, so I haven't been able to see him since he went in," Giselle admitted.

"That must be hard," Ree said with as much sympathy as it looked like she could muster.

"It's been okay," she said, sitting up a little straighter. "He said things will be different now that he's being released. He said Axel Junior and me will be together and that I shouldn't worry."

Quint nodded, thinking the faster he got in and got evidence, the better, now that Axel had turned state's witness. Vadik would surely come after Giselle the minute word got out and there was no way to know when that would happen.

The other question looming was whether or not these arrests would spook Dumitru into heading back overseas until everything cooled. The only thing they had working in their favor was the man's ego. If he believed himself to be untouchable, his arrogance could be his downfall.

This close, Quint could almost taste the victory. *A bad sign*, he thought. Their recent successes might be making him feel foolproof. The old saying *pride comes before the fall* came to mind.

"I'll have to bring Ree into the party first and then check to see if it's okay if her husband can come," Giselle stated. "It's a lot easier to bring a chick into Vadik's apartment than a dude."

Quint's blood pressure shot up a few notches but he managed a calm smile.

"You really can't be too careful these days," Quint said, knowing full well if he seemed too interested he might tip her off. No matter how much she loved Axel, she might not go along with the plan if she knew she was working an undercover sting operation. Her life was on the line and that wasn't something Quint took lightly. Knowing she was a single mother hit home. Despite her partying ways, there was something in her tone when she spoke about Axel and their son that convinced Quint she would much rather be part of a family than stay in this life.

Choices were a strange thing. When Quint was younger and in near-constant trouble, he'd told himself that he didn't have a choice. Everyone around him walked on the wrong side of the law, save for his mother, whom he barely saw. And then Officer Jazzy had come along at just the right time in Quint's life. The school liaison officer showed an interest in Quint's life and helped him realize circumstances didn't determine a life, choices did.

The lesson hadn't come easy or been developed overnight, but once Quint realized the power he had over his own choices, rather than allowing his environment to take the wheel, he knew he was ready to make changes. He designed his life and his career from there. He had everything he thought he'd ever wanted. *Except the right person to share it with*, the annoying voice in the back of his mind reminded him. Now, the thought of putting her at risk for his revenge sat heavy on his chest.

Chapter Sixteen

Ree could already get a read on Giselle. Her son was important to her even though he didn't live with her. Kids in general seemed important, too. Ree had made a couple of slips when talking about kids. Giselle's son not living with her seemed like a big deal. The fact that Axel said they would be reunited soon sent up a few alarms. He'd negotiated for WITSEC for his mistress and their love child. Clearly, no one had told her about that part of the bargain. Was that a total surprise? Not as much as it should be.

Quint entered his cell-phone number into Giselle's contacts. The act shouldn't bother Ree and yet seeing him giving out his number to someone so young and pretty caused a surprising reaction. She needed to get over it and fast, now that the case was growing legs.

"What time is the party?" Ree asked.

"It starts at seven thirty." Giselle checked the time on her phone. "Or maybe I should say *started*."

The time was quarter to eight. Ree stifled a yawn, figuring she could fall asleep right there on the stool if no one would notice. Since she couldn't get away with that, she took a sip of wine and gave herself a mental headshake. Having food in her stomach only made her more tired. Coffee would wake her up better than wine.

"We should probably get going. Vadik likes chicks there early." Giselle tucked her phone inside her purse and stood up.

"How far is his place from here?" Ree asked.

"It's only two blocks," Giselle stated. "We should be able to walk it fine."

"If it comes up, I have a BMW I'm thinking about selling," Quint stated.

"You love that car, hon," Ree interjected, playing the sympathetic wife.

"I love you more and we need the money." He walked over and hauled her against his chest, reaching around to squeeze her bottom. The familiarity between them helped them sell the lie they were together and Giselle wouldn't expect to be around the kind of guy who held back from taking what he wanted.

The move seemed to work. Giselle blushed before excusing herself and waiting at the door. It also bought a few seconds of privacy.

"I'll be close if you need me," Quint whispered in her ear.

Ree didn't have to push up to her tiptoes in these heels. She planted a kiss on Quint that made her own bones melt. She'd missed this between them. Being a married couple while undercover felt like the most natural thing once they got over the initial hump of getting to know each other. Working side by side without being in constant physical contact since their last case ended seemed strange to her now.

After another steamy kiss, Ree headed toward the front door. Giselle's hand was on the knob and she was absently scrolling on her cell phone when Ree walked over. The clicking of her heels on the tile flooring gave Giselle a heads-up.

"Let's go," Ree said to a smiling Giselle.

"Fair warning," Giselle stated. "Vadik has a thing for redheads."

"Good to know," Ree said. "I'm taken, by the way."

"Just make sure you know that," Giselle stated, heading toward the elevator bank. "Vadik can be convincing when he really wants to be and I've seen more than a few couples break up over him."

"I'm solid with Quint," Ree stated. "What about you?"

"Oh, I'm not his type and I'm with one of his people," she said. "He and Axel go way back."

Ree wondered how far because she was also worried Vadik was the one who'd sent the Acura driver to do away with Laurie and Ariana. Although, someone might have been getting to them in order to hold them over Axel's head. It was impossible to know if they were meant to be kidnapped or murdered at this point.

Ree made a mental note to read the report tonight. It was possible something had been found inside the Acura that might clue them in. Her nerves tingled at the thought of going into Vadik's apartment so soon. A whole lot had happened in the last few days. Introducing a new person right now was risky.

Were they moving too fast?

"Vadik can be a little handsy at first. If you get to meet him tonight, that is," Giselle said. "I'm sure you know how to handle dudes like him."

"Sure can," Ree said, thinking she'd like to drop him to the mat if he tried anything with her. Playing a helpless party girl made her want to vomit. It was so the opposite of Ree's natural personality. She tucked in all her tomboy tendencies for the time being. *Unnatural*, she thought.

Thankfully, these cases didn't last forever. She would die in these heels and the skirt was already riding up, giving all the people on the street a bird's-eye view of her long legs. She could only hope nothing was hanging out. Resisting the urge to reach around to her backside and check, she asked, "How about you? How did you meet Axel?"

"At one of Vadik's parties," Giselle said as a blush overtook her cheeks. "I'm originally from Mexia. Do you know where that is?"

"I sure do." Ree knew exactly where it was—about an hour and twenty minutes south of Dallas and east of Waco. There was no viable public transportation between Dallas and Mexia except by car. "Did you like living in a small town?"

"No. I hated it. There was never anything to do and my childhood was boring," Giselle stated. "I worked at the DQ in high school before dropping out."

"What brought you to Dallas?" Ree asked.

"Are you kidding? I would have been willing to move anywhere else to get away from Mexia," Giselle said.

Ree didn't agree. She loved the quiet of a small town. The peacefulness and the way neighbors still knew each other. She loved being part of a community. Although, to be fair, with her work schedule she hadn't been to a town fair or tree-lighting ceremony since she could remember. College?

"But I had a friend moving here who said we could work as waitresses in a strip club on Harry Hines," Giselle stated. "My friend met one of his guys and soon after we were invited to one of these parties. That's how I met Axel."

What a family man, Ree thought wryly.

"We hit it off right away and he convinced Vadik to hire me to work his parties as a cocktail waitress so we could spend more time together," she said. Again, she blushed. It was clear the woman had deep feelings for Axel.

"What a sweetie," Ree said, forcing the sarcasm out of her tone.

"I know. Right?" Giselle agreed, turning a darker shade of crimson.

They turned the corner at the end of two blocks. "This is it. This is Vadik's building."

The all-glass structure looked like something out of a futuristic movie.

"He's on thirty-three. The penthouse," Giselle said. "When I'm in there—" she pointed toward the sky "—I go by Gigi."

"Got it," Ree said, her body involuntarily shivering at the thought of being that high in the air. "I'm just Ree no matter where I am." It was true. She always used her real first name when she was undercover. It reduced her chances of making a mistake and giving out the wrong name straight out of the gate. Nothing was perfect, though. It also made it easier to keep going with her real last name.

"Cool," Giselle said as they entered the building. The outside might look futuristic, but the inside was a cool chic that resembled a high-end hotel. There was a concierge waiting behind an all-glass counter. He immediately started to come around to greet them until his gaze landed on Giselle. He simply nodded and returned to his spot, looking down like he'd just witnessed a mob crime and knew better than to stare.

The Italian marbled tile had probably been flown over piece by piece. Ree had thought her building was nice until she stepped inside this one. The sound of their heels clicking on the flooring echoed across a massive lobby. There was an abundance of seating and no one taking advantage of it. There was also a table with a rather large glass water server on the back wall with enough small clear cups to hydrate a small army.

The glass elevators weren't Ree's favorite. She sucked in a breath and grabbed on to Giselle's arm.

"They're freaky, right?" Giselle stated. She had the glamour of a party girl but there was still a hint of her small-town accent. "These elevators, I mean."

"I'm not a fan of heights," Ree admitted, trying not to dig her nails into Giselle's flesh. "Sorry."

"Don't be," Giselle said. "Whatever helps get you through is all right by me."

As the elevator dinged, indicating their arrival on the penthouse floor, Giselle grabbed a pill bottle out of her purse. "Do you want one?"

They stepped out of the elevator and the doors immediately closed behind them.

"What is that?" Ree asked. She didn't know what she was being offered based on the bottle's label. People went to great lengths to camouflage their drugs in the simplest of containers.

"It's a muscle relaxer," Giselle stated. "It's pretty lightweight so you'll still be able to drink at the party. Takes the edge off, if you know what I mean."

"The last time I took one of those, I almost passed out after two glasses of wine," Ree lied.

"Better not do that." Giselle closed her hand around the pair of white pills. She dry-swallowed them. "The dudes who come through can pretty much get away with anything they want. They walk past and want to pat you on the tail, and they get to as long as you're not claimed by somebody else. Even then, if he's not in the room some dudes might take advantage. We aren't allowed to complain, get sloppy, or hang all over someone who isn't in to it."

All Ree could think was how the Me Too movement seemed to have slipped past these jerks.

"So it's basically like all the parties I've been to in the past but in a better building," Ree quipped, trying to build some camaraderie.

Giselle rolled her eyes, blew out a breath and smiled. "Seriously. Crappy, right?"

"I've been to worse places with a whole lot worse people," Ree stated. In all honestly, she had, too.

"Same," Giselle said with another eye roll. She pulled a key out of her purse. "Only VIPs get these. We'll walk in and head straight to the kitchen. Just follow me and you'll be fine."

Ree touched Giselle's arm.

"Do I look okay?" She shouldn't be nervous but she couldn't help it and it was easy enough to play it off as party jitters.

"You? You're amazing," Giselle said with a hint of admiration. "Don't even worry about it. Everyone will love you."

"I hope you're right," she said. She always got a burst of adrenaline and was hit with doubts right before walking into a risky situation. Normally, it energized her and kept her sharp. Fear kept her alert.

This time, a sense of dread filled her, along with the very real thought she might not walk out of here again. She had no place to put a backup weapon and no way to communicate with Quint other than a cell phone.

But this was her job and she'd complete this mission no matter the cost.

Chapter Seventeen

Giselle unlocked the door, tucked the key back inside a small pocket in her purse and walked in like she belonged. Ree followed suit, taking in the massive corner room with two walls of windows. The views here were even more incredible than at her place. There was land as far as the eye could see. The room was shaped like a square and she had to take two steps down to enter the space. Twin couches faced each other and there was enough seating around both for a dozen or more people to gather. To the right of the room was a glass bar complete with a bartender. There was a hallway she assumed led to the kitchen, but it was tucked away off to one side. Another hallway on the opposite side must have led to bedrooms.

The second that her and Giselle stepped inside, they were patted down by two men in suits who looked like they should be in a *Godfather* movie and not here in Dallas. One requested she open her purse. She did, so he could look inside. He felt around for a secret lining.

Vadik was thorough. She would give him that. And had a decent decorator.

Everything in the space was black, white and gray. Modern was the best way to describe it and nothing looked especially comfortable, like a sofa she could sink into and watch a movie. But then, she highly doubted movie premieres were the purpose of this room. In fact, she didn't see a screen anywhere.

Ree followed Giselle into the kitchen as a few heads turned toward them. There was a sea of average-looking men who were dressed nicely. The women in the room were the real showstoppers. Not a surprise given the fact that Vadik seemed like a class-A chauvinist based on what Giselle had just said in the hall.

Arresting a jerk like that always gave Ree an extra boost of pride. It felt good to take another womanizer off the street before he could pass on his ideology to the next generation of young men. Doing so was infinitely trickier from behind bars.

In the kitchen, more folks stood around talking, much the same as in the living room. There were a few couples and then others who weren't so clearly matched up standing around. Another make-Ree-puke fact was the ratio of men to women. To say the scales were tipped to more women was an understatement. The number of females didn't double the number of males, but it came close.

"Nice night, Gigi," one of the men Ree recognized from the Wanted database said to Giselle. He walked up and slung his arm around her like she was his possession. His name was Sylvester Keeting, but his nickname was Sly as an homage to the actor in the Rocky Balboa movies.

"Hey, Sly," Giselle, calm as anyone could be, remarked. It was clear to Ree the woman loved Axel, so this had to feel slimy to her. "How's Angie?"

"Good. Home with the kids," he said. Based on the slurring of his words, he was already a little bit drunk.

"Tell her I'm real sorry to hear about her mother,"

Giselle said, strategically shrugging out of Sly's grip as she made a move for the cheese platter.

"How have you been?" Sly continued, not bothered by the attempt to duck out of his grip. He simply dropped his hand and squeezed her bottom.

"Real good lately," she said, keeping her voice even. To a drunk, she would seem compliant. To anyone half-way sober, they would feel the chill rolling off her in palpable waves. "Have you seen him?"

Sly took a step to the side. He seemed to sober up when she mentioned *him.* She could only mean one person—Vadik.

"Last I heard, he was on the patio with Gorge," Sly said, his tone suddenly far more serious than it had been. Good to know all she had to do was mention *him* and the men seemed to stand up a little straighter. They might be given a free pass to sexually harass women but there seemed to be lines even they wouldn't cross.

"Do you know what they were talking about?" she asked.

"None of my business," Sly said. He was five feet ten inches. Slicked-black hair and a large nose made him resemble the Italian from the movie, except that was where the similarities ended. Rocky's character might be a thug, but he stood up for the little guy. He collected debts for guys like Vadik because he didn't want to starve, not because he was a jerk who enjoyed torturing others. Sly was wanted for human trafficking. Not exactly a stand-up guy. He turned his attention on Ree. "Who is the red-head over here?"

"I'm Ree," she said, smiling as she twirled a strand of hair in her finger to flirt a little bit. Did it make her stomach turn? Yes. It was necessary to do her job.

She made another mental note to check out Sly's rap

sheet later while she read the report on the Acura driver. This was one of those times she wished she'd been able to fix some kind of communication device on herself so she could send information back to Quint more easily. Excusing herself to go to the bathroom would draw attention.

Strangely, no female was on her phone, unlike pretty much everywhere Ree went outside of this apartment. It was odd how dependent everyone had become on those devices that were practically glued to their hands.

The guys did whatever they pleased. One stood in the corner of the room looking out a window while on his cell. He spoke quietly, so she couldn't pick up what he was saying. There was a low hum of conversation along with a Frank Sinatra song playing in the background.

Vadik must consider himself a renaissance man. Interesting, she thought as Sly sidled over next to her. He tucked an errant strand of hair behind her ear and, once again, her stomach turned.

"She hasn't met *him* yet," Giselle warned.

Those words were all that was required for Sly to bring his hand back, as though he'd just touched a hot stove. There must be an approval required for interaction. She would thank Vadik later, once he was wearing handcuffs.

Sly worked his way around the granite island, nibbling and watching as Giselle poured a couple of glasses of wine then handed one over. She clinked glasses with Ree and said, "Bottom's up."

Ree took a long pull off the wine. "There's a bar in the other room."

"It's for the men. Vadik doesn't think it's ladylike for a chick to stand at the bar," Giselle explained. "He keeps wine back here for us."

"Let me guess, he doesn't think it's proper for a woman to drink anything else," Ree mused.

Giselle nodded.

The double standard would normally frustrate Ree to no end. She could throw back a shot as well as any one of her brothers despite not being a big drinker. Her brothers had always joked it was their Irish heritage that gave her such a high tolerance. She'd thank her DNA later.

"Give me a minute, will you?" Giselle asked. For reasons Ree couldn't explain, the thought distressed her. The ominous feeling she'd had at the door returned and she couldn't for the life of her figure out why.

"Sure. Go ahead." Ree tried not to notice the grin on Sly's face at having her alone in the kitchen.

Cell Phone Guy ended his call about the time Giselle made her exit. She was most likely going to speak to Vadik about Ree being here and hopefully lay the groundwork for Quint to work for the organization like Axel did, thereby infiltrating the organization and ultimately leading him to Dumitru. She took note of the fact Axel had asked them to keep quiet about the WITSEC part of the deal. He didn't want her to be told about it until arrests were made. The decision hinted toward him possibly not trusting her enough to keep the secret.

"What's your name?" Cell Phone Guy asked.

"Ree," she responded. "What's yours?"

"Cedric," he said as he walked over. "What happened to Gigi?"

"She went to talk to Vadik about me, I guess," Ree admitted.

"Must be your first time here then," Cedric said as Sly made his exit. There were others in the room. A couple standing by the fridge who should probably be in one of the bedrooms instead of out in the open. Their hands were all over each other. A mistress? This seemed to be the place.

On her way in, Ree hadn't seen a whole lot of women who looked like they'd had kids. Then again, Giselle was tiny. No evidence of carrying Axel's baby on her slight frame. Ree wasn't sure what she thought a mother looked like, but Giselle didn't match that description, either. She had her own sister-in-law to compare everyone to. Evelyn was the ultimate in home and heart. She baked from scratch and cooked most every day. Evelyn loved being pregnant and said she'd never felt better than when she was carrying a baby. More evidence that Ree wasn't cut out for that kind of life.

Except that since meeting Quint she could see herself married with kids. But not so she could stay home and bake every day. She would be more like the reheat in the microwave kind of mom.

Ree shook off the thought. The notion she was considering what kind of parent she would be was a foreign one. It should make her uncomfortable but felt like the most natural thing with a partner like Quint.

Being honest with herself, she could admit he was special to her.

Giselle reappeared and walked straight over to Ree, taking her by the hand and making eyes at her that said *follow my lead.* Ree didn't seem to have a choice as Giselle did an immediate about-face, walking them in the direction from where she'd come a few seconds ago. She didn't stop until they reached the open double doors that led out to an expansive balcony. The three-quarters wall keeping her from falling down thirty-three stories was made of a concrete-and-stone mix.

Stepping outside, this was the moment Ree prayed the engineer who'd built this building knew what he was doing and that she wouldn't plummet to her death. There were quite a few people out here already and she had no idea if there was a weight tipping point that would bring the structure crashing down with her and everyone else along with it.

Taking a deep breath meant to fortify herself, she kept walking, careful not to look to her left. Instead, she focused her gaze on the concrete flooring. When Giselle stopped, Ree looked up.

The man standing in front of them had dark hair and slate-gray eyes. He stood with his arms folded, like he was inspecting her, deciding if she made the cut. There was something about his scrutiny that made her feel like she wanted to put on a sweater.

Then, he smiled and gave a slight nod. Giselle seemed to breathe a sigh of relief before giving him Ree's hand. The move only contributed to the awkwardness of the meeting.

"This is Ree," she said.

He gave another show of white, crooked teeth. In the animal kingdom, this would be reason for worry. Humans might view the act differently but it had the effect on Ree of the wildlife version.

Vadik was five-nine to five-ten, no more or less, which was average for elsewhere but not in Texas. Here, he was on the short side.

"Ree's husband is in the market to sell his BMW," Giselle stated as Vadik took his time perusing Ree.

She wanted to go home and take a shower after he was finished. He seemed pleased with her appearance and this seemed like a good time to remind herself she'd passed muster. This would give her access to the inner circle and she would remember the look on his face when she busted him, which would hopefully be soon. There was no telling how quickly word about Axel would get out and his mistress would go down right along with him.

Now that Ree thought about it, she wondered why that hadn't happened already. Speed Runner had been sent to pick up the wife and teen, or murder them. The jury was still out since Ree hadn't had a chance to read Grappell's report—a report that should be uploaded by now.

"I haven't seen you before. Where did you come from?" Vadik finally said in a thick Eastern European accent.

"I've been living in Seattle with my sister while my husband was locked up," Ree said, disengaging her hand from Vadik's the second she thought she could get away with it.

A mix of emotions passed behind his eyes in a flicker. Surprise. Jealousy. Desire. Had she just made herself a challenge in his eyes? A chauvinist like him would see her refusal of an advance in that light.

"Where is he now?" Vadik glanced around.

"At home. We just moved a couple of blocks away," Ree stated.

"Why is he selling his car?" Vadik asked.

Ree could slip in the poor-us line and tell him they needed the money. Except it was too obvious and, in her opinion, too pushy coming from her. Instead, she shrugged. "You know men and their cars. They love them one day and the next they want something new." She fluttered her eyelashes at him, then added, "Not unlike the relationship they have with their women."

"I can't imagine a man ever getting tired of you," Vadik said before turning his attention toward a man to his left.

Realizing she'd been excused, she walked away. No, *walked* wasn't nearly close enough to what she did. It was more like a saunter that was meant to draw attention to her backside and the gentle sway of her hips.

After standing at the kitchen island and slowly sipping her wine for half an hour while fighting off the exhaustion of the day, someone came up behind her and took her by the arm. She turned in time to meet Vadik at eye level.

"If your husband is looking for work, I might have something for him," Vadik said.

"I can ask if he'd be interested," she said, trying her best to act nonchalant.

"He is," the man responded with a threatening look.

Ree stood up a little straighter. "I'll text him right now to come meet you."

Vadik nodded, and then retreated to the balcony along with his entourage of four men in suits. Bodyguards? Then a twentysomething woman done up in a miniskirt and a shirt that was missing the bottom half appeared. Abs on full display, the woman could barely walk on the heels that were more like stilts.

The second she got close to Vadik, he snaked his arm around her waist and pulled her against his body without missing a beat in his conversation. As Ree texted the okay to Quint, the man on the patio ignored the woman plastered against him. The term *arm candy* came to mind. Again, Ree's body involuntarily shivered at the thought of being treated like an afterthought. She literally would rather be single for the rest of her life than settle. Besides, she'd done all right for herself alone.

She'd worked, saved and bought a home that she loved. She had a career and, more importantly, a reason to get out of bed every morning. She had an exciting job even if the shine was starting to wear off the dangerous side. And she planned to get a puppy, especially after spending time with Zoey's. Ree was smart. She could figure out how to manage her job and care for a dog. She had family to count on. One of her brothers would watch Fido—or whatever its name was—if she asked.

And so what if she was suddenly starting to notice she hadn't been in a long-term relationship for far too many years? It wasn't like meeting new people had been high on her priority list lately.

Another hand on her arm caused her to suck in a sharp breath.

"Sorry," Giselle said. She smiled from ear to ear. "Looks like your husband is in."

Ree nodded and returned the smile but with less enthusiasm. Quint was in. Now, the real danger began.

Chapter Eighteen

Quint waited for twenty minutes before leaving the apartment and then took his time walking the couple of blocks to Vadik's building, suppressing the urge to bolt right over after receiving the text from Ree. Eagerness reeked of desperation.

He texted Ree the minute the elevator doors closed. She and Giselle met him at the top.

Quint brought Ree into an intimate embrace before kissing her. He turned his attention toward Giselle and thanked her for mentioning him to Vadik.

"I don't think he's interested in the car," Giselle said on a sigh.

"Work is good," he quickly stated.

She nodded before leading them inside the apartment, where Quint was immediately searched. Once he was given the green light, Giselle walked him to the balcony, took Ree's hand from his and excused them both.

Vadik's gray eyes met Quint's. He could tell a whole lot about a person by looking into their eyes. There was a cruelty in his that spoke of pure evil. Vadik gave a slight nod and two men who'd been standing huddled together near the balcony entrance came toward Quint.

"Come with us," one of the guys said.

Quint was walked out a side door by the kitchen and

onto the service elevator, where a third man stood holding open the door. He had on a suit and black, shiny shoes Quint would expect to see worn with a tuxedo.

No one asked if he wanted to go, but if he didn't, it was clear he would be escorted out forcefully. Not exactly a good sign.

"I'm Quint," he said to Shiny Shoes, who popped up his chin in response.

"Chef," he said and Quint probably didn't want to know where the nickname originated from. "Over there is Keith and next to him is Samuel."

The color of the evening seemed to be black. Chef had on a black mock turtleneck and dark slacks. Keith wore black slacks with a black-and-white checkered shirt that looked to be a size too small. His arms bulged, as though his muscles might break through the material restraining them. Then there was Samuel. He had on silvery gray slacks with a black cotton button-down shirt. Keith had a thick neck and looked like someone who'd just walked off a rugby pitch, whereas Samuel had more of a lean, runner's build. He looked wiry, like the kind of guy who could surprise a person with his strength. Then, there was Chef. Black on him did little to hide his big stomach. It was large and round, and what most people would refer to as a beer belly, or beer baby depending.

Quint himself had on an all-black ensemble. His black button-down shirt was shinier than the others'. His slacks were off-the-rack, while theirs had a tailored quality. Maybe they shared the same guy, or Vadik liked the people surrounding him to look a certain way. It was the illusion of class, since any one of the men upstairs, or in this elevator, would probably rip off a person's head at Vadik's command.

"Where are we headed, fellas?" Quint asked as an uneasy feeling settled over him. Ree was upstairs and there was no way to get a message to her.

"Phone. Wallet. Keys." Chef held out his hands, beggar-style.

Quint emptied his pockets. While Ree was at the party, he'd secured their home just in case. If these guys took him back to his own apartment to search it, they would be covered. Being caught off guard earlier had clearly rattled Ree. She'd pulled it together and looked the part by the time he'd returned with the pizza, but she'd had very little in the way of advance notice.

The foursome left the service elevator and walked into an alley. Keith picked up a rock and tossed it at the light over the door, shattering it. They were plunged into darkness.

"I heard you got picked up by Dallas PD a couple of days ago," Chef said. "What the hell were you doing in North Dallas?"

"Helping out a friend," Quint said. There would be a record of his arrest and he hadn't played the ATF agent card on purpose. He was undercover and didn't want to blow it.

"Who do you really work for?" Chef said.

A light came on. One of those flashlight apps on a cell phone. Quint squinted against the near-blinding light.

"No one," he said. He barely got the words out when the first punch landed. He bent forward and dropped to his knees. He muttered a string of curses as pain ripped through him.

"You don't want to tell us?" Chef said.

Another blow came. This time, striking his shoulder. Quint grunted and blew out a couple of sharp breaths in succession, trying to slow the agony.

"I can't," he stated. "I went freelance. Got a message

to pick up a chick and her teenage daughter. Apparently, I wasn't the only one. Cops came and I ended up getting arrested along with another guy. That's all I know."

"How'd you pick up the assignment?" Chef pressed, agitation in his voice.

"A blind call on the internet," Quint confessed right before the toe of a hard shoe drilled into his thigh.

For a split second, he thought about fighting back. Everything inside him wanted to take these men out. Permanently. A second kick was the heel of a shoe to his kidneys. That one dropped him onto the pavement. Quint curled in a ball to protect his vital organs as Keith and Samuel gave him their best. The blows were felt much more on top of his previous injury. His vision blurred and the room started to spin from pain.

"Stop," Chef finally said.

Now, everything hurt. There wasn't a part of his body that wasn't screaming in pain.

A few extra punches came before Chef seemed to put his body in between Keith and Samuel. No doubt about it, these were Vadik's henchmen.

"You need a hand up?" Chef asked.

"No. I got it," Quint immediately said. His pride wouldn't allow for it unless it was absolutely necessary for the case. It wasn't, and there was no way in hell he was taking a hand from one of these bastards. Slowly, he managed to sit up. His head was spinning, and for a second, he thought he might black out.

"Go up," Chef ordered his cohorts in a surprise move.

Keith and Samuel didn't say a whole lot. They seemed to speak with their fists and the message was loud and clear—don't betray Vadik. They were letting Quint know his life depended on it.

The light disappeared and then a few seconds later,

the door opened and closed. One of the guys put a rock in the way, keeping the door cracked for Chef.

"You need something?" Chef asked.

Quint grunted.

"I got into a scuffle and then ended up stabbed before I got arrested," Quint said in between grunts. "But I'm fine."

"Yeah, you sound like it," Chef said with a chuckle. He seemed to respect Quint's honesty. "The boss likes for people to know what they're getting into before he gives them a job. Not a lot of people pass the test, if you know what I mean."

"Did I?" Quint could already feel himself bleeding through his shirt. Dammit.

"I think so," Chef said. "Now, I'll give you a hand up if you need one but I gotta get back upstairs."

"Nope. I said I got this and I do." With great effort, Quint got to his feet. He took two steps and had to grab on to the wall to stay upright. "If I wasn't already banged up, those two wouldn't have been able to do this much damage."

Chef held the door open and smiled. "For some reason, I believe you."

GISELLE CAUGHT REE's attention and glared at her. She made a face to go along with it.

Ree twisted her hands together and forced herself to stop pacing in the kitchen. She pressed flat palms against the cool granite. She took in a couple of slow breaths before picking up her wineglass and taking another pull.

The back door opened and two of the men who'd escorted Quint outside walked in. They made a beeline for the balcony, where Vadik was in lip-lock with Disco Skirt. He had her up against the railing, both hands to either side of her, trapping her. What was he afraid of? She couldn't exactly run away unless she jumped.

Ree's pulse kicked up a few notches when she saw one of the guys tug at the other one's sleeve. He nodded back to the kitchen, where they went to the sink and washed blood off their hands. One shook out his hand like it still burned from punching someone. Where was Quint?

Giselle started toward Ree when the back door opened again. This time, a big guy walked inside with Quint following. He looked to be in bad shape. His shirt was blood-soaked and there was no sign of him bruising on his knuckles.

He walked straight over to Ree and kissed her. The move, she noticed, also allowed him to lean on her without looking like he was about to collapse. He was showing strength but she could see that he was about to drop.

"We have to go, Gigi," she said to Giselle. "We'll come back another time."

"Let me walk you out," Giselle said.

"No, thanks," Ree countered. "We know the way to the door. We'll be fine."

"Call me later," Giselle said, more than a hint of concern in her voice.

"I will," Ree stated. She let Quint throw a possessive arm around her as they walked to the door and out to the elevator. The minute the doors closed, he slumped onto the railing. "What happened to you?"

"They asked about the arrest," he groaned.

"They must have someone watching out at Dallas PD," she said.

He nodded but looked ready to pass out.

"Hold on," she said to him as she helped hoist him up so he could walk out of the elevator, through the lobby and out the front door.

The two blocks to their apartment felt like it took forever to walk. She let him lean on her as she shielded the blood from view. He left a few bright red dots on the sidewalk as they journeyed back.

Once inside, he slumped to the floor with his back against the door. Ree immediately jumped into action, texting Grappell to send a doctor and then searching for anything she could use to clean up Quint and stop the bleeding.

"Stay with me, Quint," she said, tapping his cheek as his head rolled from side to side. "You're going to be okay. Got it?"

He didn't respond and she hoped it was because he was conserving energy and not because he was losing consciousness. She couldn't take off his shirt fast enough. Her fingers fumbled with the buttons. Her hands trembled as adrenaline faded. The bandage below his ribs was soaked in blood. What had those animals done to him?

Her skin crawled at the memory of Vadik's hands on her. This was so much worse.

Yes, she was going to enjoy locking that jerk and his cohorts behind bars and throwing away the key. But Quint needed to live long enough to see it happen. Longer than that to be with her and figure out where this thing that kept growing between them would decide to take them.

Ree peeled the bandage off his left side. His hands came up to hers and his eyes blinked open as he winced. He curled forward.

"I'm sorry," Ree said quietly. "I don't mean to hurt you. I need to get something to stop the bleeding."

She hopped up to her feet and bolted into the bathroom. After retrieving a couple of clean hand towels, she hurried back to a slumped-over Quint. His skin had an ashen quality that sent her stress levels soaring.

"You're going to be fine," she said, mostly for her own benefit even though she hoped he could hear her.

His slight nod said he was hanging in there.

"A doctor is on the way," she reassured him. "I have to stop the bleeding, and this might hurt. Stay strong for me, okay?"

Without waiting for a response, she folded a hand towel and pressed it against his wound. Quint sat bolt upright. If he was feeling pain, he was still alive. She took it as a promising sign even though she hated hurting him.

A knock at the door came at the same time as a text. This must be the doctor. Thank heaven they were in a major city. She'd been on assignments in the country where there wasn't a doctor on standby.

A quick peek through the peephole confirmed her suspicions. She eased Quint away from the door and then opened it. Her cell started buzzing like crazy and she figured it was Grappell trying to get ahold of her to get a status update on Quint.

"Come on in, Doctor," she said, glancing at the name stitched above the pocket of his lab coat. Ramirez.

At this point, Quint was lying on his side, curled up. She could only imagine the beating he'd taken once he'd left the penthouse. At least the two of them hadn't been made. The case wasn't a total loss, even though she couldn't imagine going back there.

End of the line?

It might very well be for Quint. His injuries looked severe before the beating. Now? She couldn't imagine how the man could keep going. He'd barely made it this far and had lost a lot of blood. He'd barely made it to their apartment before sliding down the door and settling onto the floor.

Dr. Ramirez went right to work as Ree washed the blood off her hands and then checked her cell phone. The messages coming in weren't from Grappell at all. They were from Bjorn.

If she told their boss what was really happening with Quint, she would remove him from the case. Backing out now would do enormous damage after the progress they'd made. Being honest with their boss would erase all the hard work Quint had done up to this point.

If only there was a way to ask him what he wanted her to do about Bjorn. Talking to their boss without him felt like going behind his back. Doing so would damage the trust they'd built.

Should she risk everything between them personally and do it for the sake of the case?

Chapter Nineteen

For the next forty-eight hours, Quint was in and out of consciousness. Most of the time was a blur, except that he remembered being taken out of the apartment on a gurney and then returned in a wheelchair. Every time he opened his eyes, Ree was there, just as she was now as she sat staring out the window.

"I had a nightmare that I got in a fight," he said. His voice seemed to catch her off guard.

"Quint. You're awake," she said, immediately moving to his side. She perched on the bed and took his hand in hers.

"I'm still kicking." He made a move to sit up and concern wrinkled her forehead. She wore a weary expression, like someone who had been to hell and back from worry.

"Good. I happen to like you that way," she said with a forced smile. It didn't reach her eyes but he was grateful for the attempt. The news from the doctor must not have been great over the last few days.

"I was out for two days," he said, easing up to sitting.

"How do you know?" she asked.

"I counted the number of times the sun went down," he stated. He was surprisingly not thirsty but had a tacky taste in his mouth. Right. He hadn't brushed his teeth in all that time.

"Can I get you anything?" she asked. "The doctor had me order power bars in case you woke up hungry."

"One might be nice but I can't put anything in my mouth until I brush my teeth," he admitted. He made a move to get up and the room started spinning.

"You might want to slow down there, mister," she warned, her tone lighter now but still cautious.

"Where's the fun in that?" he quipped.

"At least your sense of humor is intact," she responded. "Hold on. I'll get a toothbrush."

Ree disappeared into the bathroom and then came back with supplies. "You get started brushing and I'll grab a bowl along with a cup of water."

"You might be an angel," he said.

"Hold on to that thought." She disappeared again, returning at the same time he started brushing. Her timing had always been spot-on. She set the bowl on his lap and held on to the water cup.

Brushing his teeth made him feel like he might have died and gone to heaven. It was always the little things he took for granted every day that seemed so huge when they were taken away. Once he'd thoroughly rinsed, he tugged Ree toward him.

"What?" The concern wrinkle came back.

"Okay if I kiss you?" he asked and his stomach tied in knots, as if he was suddenly in high school asking out the prom queen.

"I'd like that a lot," she said, leaning into him until their lips gently touched. She pulled back quickly. "I don't want to hurt you."

"Thank you for taking care of me, Ree."

She smiled.

"Let me get something for you to eat," she said, brushing right past his thank-you.

"I mean it, Ree. You're an amazing person and partner. I hit the jackpot with you and I can't imagine doing this with anyone else," he said in all honesty.

A mix of emotions passed behind those emerald eyes.

"What is it?" he asked, picking up on something. She was hiding information. And it immediately dawned on him what it was. "Is Bjorn pulling you from the case?"

"Me?" she asked. "No."

Before he could ask another question, she held up a hand and hurried out of the room. By the time she returned ten minutes later, the smell of fresh-brewed coffee had him sitting all the way up.

Ree set two mugs on the nightstand and then produced a couple of power bars.

"They taste a little bit like mud, but a lot of protein is packed in there," she said, taking a seat and peeling open hers.

"Could be worse," he said, then locked gazes with her. "Tell me. How much worse is it for me?"

Ree issued a sharp sigh.

"Bjorn wants you off the case," she admitted.

"I should have seen that coming," he said. "How long do I have to convince her or is the paperwork already in process?"

"It was, but I managed to hold her at bay once you got a text that said you're needed for a job in two days," she said.

"And Bjorn went for it?" He had to admit that he was more than a little surprised.

"Not at first, but I convinced her that you'd made a lot of progress with Vadik in a short amount of time. Giselle said so, too. I used it to push an agenda that I knew you wanted. But that isn't to say I feel good about doing it, Quint."

A storm clouded those green eyes.

"If you could have seen what you looked like when I got you home…" She stopped speaking and just stared at the rim of the coffee cup she picked up. It wasn't like Ree to cry, but he suspected tears were the reason she tucked her chin to her chest and refused to look at him directly.

"I'm fine now," he said. "The food and caffeine will help."

"I just don't know if continuing on the case right now is the best idea," she said on a shrug.

"Thank you for not agreeing with Bjorn." If she had, he wouldn't be in this room right now. He'd be in the hospital, and then would eventually be released after a medical evaluation only to find himself sitting at a desk for another six months or longer. "You're right about the progress. We'd lose ground if we pulled out of the case now. Who knows when we'll get this close again?"

"Is it worth your life, though?"

There was a time not all that long ago when he would have answered a resounding yes. Quint had gone to sleep thinking about how much he'd let down Tessa and her baby, and woken up missing his best friend so badly he ached. Some people would have said the two of them should have gotten married. There were worse things in a marriage than to be best friends. He'd offered, half-jokingly, when she'd told him about the pregnancy. He'd almost convinced her that everyone would just believe the child was his, anyway, considering their closeness wasn't exactly a secret.

Tessa had touched his hand and told him that she could never allow him to settle for her when he would never love her. And then something in her eyes—something he'd chalked up to pregnancy hormones at the time—had made him believe she might have crossed an emotional line and fallen for him.

She'd whipped out all the lines, like he deserved better and that he would find someone he couldn't live without some day. He'd told her, honestly, that he didn't want to live without her.

They both knew they weren't talking about the same kind of love. He'd explained that he did love her and there was no one he'd rather spend a Sunday afternoon with watching a game or going for a hike. She'd smiled—and that smile still haunted him—and told him how much she appreciated his friendship.

Tessa knew that he would do anything for her and that kid, even if it meant living the rest of his life with someone he loved but wasn't *in love* with. Quint had reached a point in life where he didn't believe he was capable. He'd dated a whole lot of people without finding the magic Tessa seemed so certain was out there waiting for him. Half of him believed if he hadn't found it by now, he never would. So he'd made the marriage offer.

Now, looking at Ree, he realized what he'd been missing all these years. But he had a responsibility to Tessa and her baby that would eat him alive if he tried to walk away from this case.

"I have to see this thing through," he said to Ree. He could only hope she understood his reasoning.

"OKAY," REE SAID. This wasn't the time to try to unpack everything bottling up inside her when it came to Quint Casey and his need for revenge. "I'll let Bjorn know you're good to keeping working."

"She'll trust your opinion," Quint said, taking a bite of the power bar.

"I know." She had so many mixed feelings about making the recommendation for him to continue. The thing she kept coming back to was wondering what she would do if the shoe was on the other foot. What if Shane or Finn, or one of her other brothers, had been killed by one of these bastards?

Ree would go to the ends of the earth to lock up the person responsible. So she couldn't fault Quint, but it was hard to be in love with him. She picked up her mug and took a sip of coffee. With her free hand, she reached for his. He threaded their fingers together.

"Thank you for sticking with me on this case," he said quietly.

"I'm not going to lie and say it's easy by any stretch of the imagination," she responded honestly. "But I have two days to get you in good enough shape to pick up where we left off a couple of nights ago. And I plan to do everything in my power to ensure you can get the evidence we need for a bust."

An emotion flickered behind Quint's eyes that she couldn't immediately read. And then it dawned on her.

"You don't care about putting Vadik behind bars, do you?" she asked.

"Not if it would scare away Dumitru," he admitted after a long pause.

"Think about what you might be doing," she said to Quint.

"I've had nothing but time to think," he stated. "The low-level guys can go down. It happens a lot because they are on the front lines. If I take Vadik down before getting to Dumitru, he'll spook."

"We'll go after him, Quint. We'll lock him up and throw away the key," Ree said. "But we have to eliminate each level of threat."

"I don't agree on this one, Ree," he said and then abruptly changed the subject. "What do you know about the Acura guy?"

She stared at him for a long moment, not exactly ready to move on but also realizing when a battle wasn't worth fighting.

After taking a deep breath, she started in. "I looked at the file. The name on his ID was Timothy Challan. He has ties to Christian Moffo, who has loose ties with Vadik."

Quint nodded.

"Do you know where the jeans I had on are?" he asked.

"As a matter of fact, I do." She set down her coffee mug and retrieved what he was actually looking for—the folded-up piece of paper he kept inside his pocket. She grabbed a pen before he asked, knowing full well he wanted to jot down the new name and link on the tree he'd created.

She handed over the paper and pen before reclaiming her seat. As expected, he made the note.

"How are you feeling?" she asked, really looking at him. His coloring was coming back and he had a whole lot more life in his expression than in the last forty-eight hours.

"I've been better," he quipped, leaning back against the headboard. He lifted his mug. "This is a huge help. Otherwise, I feel like I've been run over by a Mack truck."

"You kind of were," she said with a slow exhale.

"Chef," he said, drawing a few lines from Vadik's name. He wrote the names Keith and Samuel underneath Chef's.

"He must be fairly high up if he's calling the shots," she said.

"I'm guessing the other night was an initiation if they already reached out to give me work," he said.

"I figured," she admitted.

"What's your impression of Vadik?" he asked.

"Other than being a dirty criminal who also happens to be a chauvinist pig?" She arched an eyebrow. "There isn't much to like about him."

"He's slick," Quint said. "It'll be hard to get evidence against him because I doubt he gets his hands dirty at his level."

Ree nodded her agreement. "He has an entourage around him at all times from what I can tell. Giselle is afraid of him and also seems to have a healthy respect for him."

"What about her? Is she trustworthy?" he asked.

"She seems loyal to Axel, but who really knows," she said. "I would trust any one of these people about as much as I can throw them and she hasn't exactly stopped by to see if you are okay or check on me."

"Challan had duct tape and rope in the Acura," she said, circling back to their earlier conversation.

"Pretty much makes him guilty as sin," he stated.

"He wasn't able to get to Axel's family, but they were able to get him on attempted murder charges with your statement," she said.

Quint nodded.

At full strength, she had no doubt he could take on any one of these jerks. Injured? She worried.

"What do you think about the two of us taking off for a few days? Maybe a week?" she asked. "We could always say I had to go back to Seattle to see my sister."

He shook his head. She figured he wouldn't agree but it had been worth a shot.

"Is he out?" he asked. "Challan?"

"We lucked out because he was out on parole, so he'll be locked up for a long time," she said. "He's out of the picture for a while."

"Good. I don't need to run in to him again or have him on the outside looking for me," he stated. "In fact, now that I'm thinking about it, Chef mentioned something about me being in jail while Keith and Samuel took a baseball bat to me."

Now it was Ree's turn to wince.

"It only felt like one," he said with a smirk. "I'm pretty sure they only kicked and punched me."

"You couldn't fight back," she said. "It wasn't fair."

"Initiations never are," he stated. "At first, I was afraid they'd made me. But then I realized I had to strap on for the ride. If I'd fought back, they probably would have killed me and then dropped me in the Trinity River."

"In your condition, you wouldn't have been able to do much damage to them, anyway," she said on a sigh.

"We got through it." He threaded their fingers again. Then he brought the back of her hand up to his lips and pressed a tender kiss there.

Her stomach dropped and her chest squeezed. It would be so easy to go down that road again with Quint. The same question haunted her: where would it lead?

Chapter Twenty

Two days of nothing but food, rest and the gym had Quint raring to go. The assignment came down from Chef and meant he'd be working side by side with Keith and Samuel. Not exactly a warm and fuzzy thought after the beating in the alley, but he'd take the progress toward Vadik and, ultimately, Dumitru.

"I wish I could be there," Ree said as Quint shrugged into a black T-shirt. His all-dark outfit would fade into the background.

"Believe me, I'd like it if you had my back rather than Keith or Samuel, but that's not an option here," he stated.

"On some level, I do know that," she replied. "You'll be wearing a wire and I'll be around as soon as I can get away from the party."

Vadik was stuck in the Dark Ages when it came to how to treat the opposite sex. He seemed to believe women were nothing more than arm candy meant to give him something pretty to look at.

"Shame you can't fake a headache," he said, attaching the safety pin that was actually a listening device to the inside of his shirt.

"I noticed Security at the penthouse door barely patted Giselle down the first time I was there," Ree stated. "Once you're in, they probably get more lax."

"Still, be careful," he said. "If they see the earpiece disguised as an earring—"

"That's not going in until I'm out of there," she said, putting her hands up in the surrender position. "Did Chef give you any idea of where you might be headed?"

"No." Quint shook his head. "All I know is that we'll be responsible for 'product' that will be brought to an empty warehouse in the warehouse district until it's loaded and onto its next destination. That's pretty much all I'm being told right now."

"A babysitting job," she said.

"I imagine we'll be helping unload and then load. They must change vehicles while in transit," he continued.

"Makes sense. Moving the product to a different vehicle every so often would lessen the chances of getting caught," she said. "The trucks only have to weigh in at certain intervals. What happens in between is impossible to track."

"Exactly right. We've seen it before. It's slow and methodical," he stated.

"Which also makes me believe it's a large load," she said.

"I can't help but wonder if some of it isn't going to be offloaded here in the Dallas area," he added.

"This is a big market for weapons," she said. "Despite being able to buy a gun easily in the state."

"We all know they want to get around a paper trail," he said with another nod.

"That's just what this city needs. More weapons that can't be traced back to an individual," she said on a sigh.

Quint finished buttoning the last button of his shirt and then locked gazes with Ree, who was sitting on the bathroom counter, facing him.

"This is as good as it gets," he said, motioning toward his reflection in the mirror.

"Looks pretty great from where I sit," she quipped, and her cheeks turned a few shades of red. "The shirt. It's nice. That's what I mean."

Quint leaned a little closer until his lips pressed against hers. For the last two days, neither one of them brought up their relationship status, or where they thought it was going. They were important questions and they deserved answers. For now, it was nice just to spend time together. He'd missed holding her at night and waking up with her hair spilled out across the pillow. He'd missed her warm body tangled with his. And he'd missed the easy way they had with each other. Neither had to work for conversation. In fact, Quint had never considered himself the chatty type until Ree. Color him shocked that he had a hard time sleeping at night because he wanted to hear more about her childhood. Growing up with four brothers, she had stories. No matter how much she tried to convince him otherwise, it was easy to see how much she loved every single one of them.

"I could stay here all night," he said, his lips moving against hers.

"We've covered that ground, mister. Back to work," she teased, leaning back until she rested against the mirror.

"In case I didn't tell you earlier, you're beautiful," he said.

The blush came back.

"I'm pretty sure you already said that half a dozen times tonight," she said with a smile that threatened to break down all of his defenses. "And yet it never gets old."

"Good. Because I plan to say it a whole lot more," he

said as his phone buzzed in the next room. "We should probably head out."

She nodded.

"I see how these top criminals live and, sometimes—no, all the time—think the good guys should definitely get paid more than we do," Ree said, pushing off the counter. The sleek black silk bodysuit hugged her curves and showed off long legs. She had on a jade necklace that brought out the green in her eyes and caused his heart to detonate. "For instance, take Vadik living in the penthouse. That has to cost a pretty penny."

"I'm sure it does." Quint flicked off the bathroom light as they exited and moved toward the living room/kitchen area.

"Funny thing is, you couldn't pay me to live in a penthouse downtown no matter how great Dallas might be for some," she said. "I couldn't be happier than when I'm home, sitting outside with a cup of coffee in the morning as the sun's coming up. There's no better view than watching the sun rise above the trees to the east on my property."

"You have a beautiful home, Ree. You found a piece of paradise here on earth and bought it with your own money," he said. "You should be very proud of what you've accomplished."

She stopped and planted a kiss on his lips at the door.

"Thank you, Quint," she said. "You're the first person to say those words to me."

"I'm sure your family means them, too," he said. "It's easy to see how much they love you."

"My brothers and grandfather? Yes. My mother—"

"Just doesn't know how to show it," he interrupted. "She leads with her worry when she should tell you what an amazing woman you are." She needed to know the truth. He'd seen a whole lot of love in the form of concern from her mother. Was she going about their relationship the wrong way? Absolutely. He wouldn't defend her there. And yet it was easy to see just how tight the family was. And her mother wouldn't worry at all if she didn't come from a place of caring.

Ree caught his gaze. "My brother Shane has been telling me the same thing for years. Why is it so hard to believe?"

"I think you have to look inside yourself for the answer to that question," he said to her.

"She has been so critical of me," she stated.

"There's no excuse for it," he agreed. "It undermines all the love she has for you."

Ree concurred, then pressed a tender kiss to his lips.

"Thank you for not defending her or hating her. Most seem to fall into one camp or the other," she said. "There hasn't been a whole lot of middle ground when it comes to mine and my mother's relationship."

"Family is complicated," he said with a shrug. "I'm the last one to known how to handle them."

"They can be a handful but I wouldn't trade any one of them for the world," she said with a smile that cracked more of his defenses.

"They're lucky to have you," he said, then whispered, "And so am I."

She must not have heard him because she pulled back and said, "It's party time."

THE WALK TO the penthouse was short and quiet. Ree knew she would be hooked into Quint the entire time with the earring and yet being physically away from each other was going to be hard. What if he needed backup? It was just the two of them on this fact-finding mission.

The last place she wanted to be was at the penthouse with Vadik when the real work was being done in the field by Quint. It gave her a new appreciation for what Quint must have been feeling on their last two cases, when she had to work as first a waitress in a restaurant/bar and then at a popular Houston nightspot for the well-off. Those undercover assignments had led them to this point.

Ree was uncomfortable walking around in these heels, and she was grumpy. At least she would be able to listen to Quint the entire time he was gone.

Giselle met them both at the front door of Vadik's building. She gave each a quick hug, then said, "Chef is expecting you around back. He said you'd know where to meet him."

Quint nodded before giving Ree a kiss that threatened to melt all her defenses. She was having a difficult enough time thinking about when this case would end and she would go back to her normal life.

A thought struck her, out of the blue. She was done with undercover work. Ree set it aside. She'd been contemplating whether or not she wanted to stay on the job recently. What surprised her was the finality of it. A decision had been made and now it was just about working out the details, the timing, and what she planned to do next.

This career path had played out for her and it was time to make some hard decisions. She had some money saved. Could she take time off to figure out her next move?

Ree shelved the thought and grabbed Giselle's arm.

"We should probably get upstairs," she said, shaking off a foreboding feeling that suddenly came over her. It was a heavy gray cloud that showed up on a perfect day, hovering over her and thickening the air around her, making it hard to breathe.

"How is he really feeling?" Giselle asked.

"It wouldn't matter," she responded. "He needs the work so he was going to be here no matter what."

Ree held on to Giselle for the elevator ride to the penthouse, keeping her eyes squeezed shut for most of it. Being in the city reminded her how deeply she wished she was home instead. A few deep breaths later and the elevator dinged. Thankfully.

She opened her eyes and practically jumped out. From the corner of her eye, she caught Giselle smiling.

"I'll never get used to heights," Ree admitted.

"We all have something to get over, right?" Giselle said. She squeezed Ree's hand. "You did great."

After walking inside and being patted down, Ree was escorted to the balcony. *Great.* She did realize being near Vadik would make it easier to figure out how to get to Dumitru. The faster she could hand over the information to Quint, the quicker this whole nightmare would end.

Vadik nodded to her escort. Giselle walked Ree over to him.

"Thank you, Gigi," he said and Giselle seemed to take the hint she was supposed to exit the area.

She retreated with a quick glance at Ree.

There were two men standing with Vadik and three others leaning on the wall or sitting on a chair. Twice as many women milled around, looking like accessories.

"Come closer," Vadik said to Ree.

She did.

"I owe you an apology," he began, surprising her with the line of thought.

"Why is that?" she asked, cocking an eyebrow.

"My associates became a little too enthusiastic the

other night," he said. She glanced down at his fingers, which were braided in front of him, and imagined all the blood on those hands.

Through her earpiece, she heard the low hum of a vehicle's engine on what sounded like a highway. There was music playing in the background, too, some kind of rap.

"He was pretty banged-up," she agreed. "Said he tripped on the way downstairs."

Vadik's eyes widened and he clamped his mouth shut. He must not have been expecting a response like that one. "I'm afraid my guys might have helped him along when they should have stopped him from hitting the ground."

"He's feeling better now," she said nonchalantly, throwing in a shrug for effect. He seemed to be buying her routine. Violence was part of the deal in a life of crime. Initiations could be brutal and sometimes led to death. As far as she was concerned, Quint had made it out alive and therefore was successful. The fact that she'd had to wear ridiculously tight and form-fitting clothing on their last two assignments paled in comparison to what he'd been through two days ago. The other problem was that he was now in a weakened state. Fighting back would be that much more difficult.

That she hadn't heard him speak after the initial greeting with Keith and Samuel didn't help. At least he had his phone with him. On it was an encrypted tracking app that no one would be able to detect. Once Quint got home, they could pull it up and retrace the trail. It would make it easier for Quint so he could focus on what was happening with Keith and Samuel rather than worry about memorizing landmarks. Although, knowing Quint, he was doing that, too.

"That's good to hear," Vadik said. She could tell he was feeling her out. There was no way to tell if she'd truly passed or not. If she made a mistake on her end, it could cost Quint's life. Being on this side of the equation and out of the direct action was even more stressful than she realized.

Giselle reappeared. Vadik nodded.

Ree could only hope it meant she'd done okay.

Chapter Twenty-One

The vehicle stopped in front of a warehouse on the outskirts of Dallas. Quint had only been in the SUV for twenty-three minutes, according to his cell phone, from the time they left downtown Dallas to reaching their destination to the north. Much to his surprise, they'd pulled into the back of a jewelry import shop on Harry Hines Boulevard.

"We have a shipment coming in and we have to sit on it for a while," Keith said.

Quint involuntarily fisted his hands, wishing he could throw a few punches to get Keith and Samuel back for the other night. Forcing his fingers to open again, he tucked his cell inside his pocket and exited the white Suburban. It was already dark outside. The sun had just descended. And yet, it was still hot enough to make him sweat through his button-down.

"We'll just throw the assets in the back here, like usual." Samuel unlocked the back door of the warehouse-style building.

He flipped on a light and the three of them filed in. This looked like a regular office area. A wall of shelves caught Quint's eye. This area should be larger. He took note and followed Keith and Samuel.

"This door here leads to the showroom," Keith said.

He tried the handle and opened it a crack. "We keep it closed while we're working back here so no one can see us from the front window."

"Got it," Quint stated.

"Bathroom is over here." Keith pointed to another closed door. "And this is where we keep the assets." He walked over to the shelves and moved a stack of books. He punched in a code and the shelves came toward him.

Quint stood at the mouth of the room. There were three mattresses scattered on the floor. A commode and sink gave the place a prison feel. It hit him immediately there was a whole lot more than gunrunning going on in there. Could be fugitives. Hiding them with guns could keep them underground for long periods.

But his mind snapped to a different place when he saw a box of toys in the corner. Human trafficking. These were the most difficult cases. He didn't need to have children of his own to feel sick at the thought of young girls being sold into the sex trade. It was almost incomprehensible to him that crimes like that occurred in the twentieth-first century, except experience had taught him the trade was alive, well and prospering.

Still made him want to vomit.

"Make yourself at home," Keith said. "We might be here a while."

"Is this driver good?" Quint asked.

"We don't get into that side of the business," Keith said, exchanging a look with Samuel.

"Hey, I just got out. I need to make sure I'm not working with amateur hour here," Quint protested. "I go back in and I'm not seeing my wife in a very long time."

"Don't worry about her," Keith said with a whistle. "I'll keep her warm until you get out."

"I hate to break the news to you but if I go down,

there's a real good chance the three of us go down together," Quint said, acting nonplussed even though he really wanted to put his fist through Keith's crooked teeth.

"The driver better check out," Keith said. "But I don't have any control over that side of the business."

The idea of going to jail didn't seem to sit well with Keith. Good. Because the bastard was going down if Quint had anything to say about it. And he did. There was circumstantial evidence here. Not enough to put Keith away.

The sound of a truck pulling up to the back got Keith off the internet, where he'd been going back and forth between watching preseason football and finding a new place to live. Apparently, he was in the market for a two-bedroom apartment somewhere downtown that was close to Vadik but not in the same building. For one, he said he couldn't afford it. The other reason was that he didn't want to run in to Vadik downstairs at the gym. Work was one thing, Keith had explained. He liked to keep his personal life separate.

Quint couldn't wait to find out exactly what kind of shipment they were receiving. Until a frightened-looking young girl was hustled into the room. She couldn't have been more than eleven or twelve years old. She was followed by another kid close to her age. Then another. The small room filled with half a dozen girls in a matter of minutes.

Next came the weapons. There were five four-by-eight-foot crates. All locked. All set inside the room with the girls, giving them even less room. The first girl had the biggest pair of round, scared eyes—eyes that looked like they were ready to pop out of her head. She was in so much shock that she didn't speak, most likely couldn't if she'd tried. Everything seemed to be happening around her instead of to her. She'd checked out mentally and emotionally in a big way.

Quint knew right then, without a doubt, he couldn't let this girl be sold into a system that caused his stomach to churn just thinking about it. Even if it meant losing the trail to Dumitru. Tessa would not want Quint to allow these children to be treated and sold like pieces of furniture, as if their lives had no value. She would be disappointed in him if he didn't do everything he could to put a stop to this transaction.

Which meant pulling a bust way before he'd intended. Quint cursed underneath his breath. The kid with the bug eyes and stringy blond hair would haunt him. He'd planned on holding off on initiating a bust so he could use Vadik to get closer to Dumitru. A bust this soon would ruin his chances. And yet, it couldn't be helped. He would schedule a raid. It was the only choice.

"Get food and feed the assets," Keith said.

It took everything inside Quint not to correct Keith by saying, *do you mean the little girls?* Rage boiled inside his veins that someone could be so callous when talking about children.

There were five girls with varying shades of dark hair, and the blonde. For some reason, she hit him the hardest. Was it because she looked like a miniature version of Tessa? Or did he imagine Tessa's baby might look like the kid?

More of that rage filled him and it took all his willpower to calm down before he was noticed. He helped carry in the last crate as Samuel sat on the desk chair, spinning around like an eight-year-old, eating an apple. The fruit was probably meant for the kids.

Keith checked his cell phone. He cursed as he closed and locked the back door.

"What's wrong? Is the next truck going to be late with pickup?" Samuel asked.

Quint knew better than to say a word. First of all, his anger was bubbling dangerously close to the surface. He couldn't allow it to spill over, and there was only so much he could take. This seemed like a good time to remind himself of the jail time coming for these guys, and that he and Ree would save these kids so they could be reunited with their families.

The blond girl had dirt on her face and a tattered bow in her hair. It was an image he wouldn't soon forget.

Quint knew full well the trail to Dumitru might stop right here, so he looked at the young girl one more time. She drew back under his scrutiny. He wanted to offer some reassurance to her and the others. He wanted to let them know he wasn't there to hurt them. That he was the good guy. And he wanted to tell them he would find their families if it was the last thing he ever did. But they were in shock. A couple of them had huddled together, clinging to each other as if their lives depended on it. Trauma could do that to someone. His heart went out to these kiddos. They'd clearly been through more than any kid this age should have to go through.

Keith stared at his phone.

"One of the clients is trying to back out of the sale," Keith said. "We need to pay him a visit."

"I'll grab the tire iron." Samuel rubbed his hands together.

Quint tensed before forcing himself to breathe. He relaxed his shoulders.

"You wait here with the merch," Keith said to him. "We'll handle this."

"Who is it this time?" Samuel asked.

"A judge in Plano," Keith stated. "Chef is sending the address."

So far, Quint could link human and weapons trafficking to Vadik's business. But any lawyer worth his salt would be able to get Vadik off the hook by saying he wasn't aware of what was happening with his business.

"Stick around and make sure these are ready to go," Keith said, motioning toward the kids.

"Will do, chief," Quint said. He managed to get out the words without gritting his teeth.

Despite knowing he would get these kids to safety, he couldn't say a word to any of them. Not yet. Not after the ordeal they'd been through. They might not believe him, anyway. Who knew what had been promised to them, or the manner in which they'd been separated from their families?

The minute Keith and Samuel were out of the building, he moved to the fridge. There were stacks of Lunchables inside, along with juice boxes. He started passing them out as the kids huddled together on one of the mattresses.

One thing was certain—Vadik was pure evil. The jewelry import shop made for an easy way to launder money. The North Dallas location made for an easy hub to move product throughout the country. Merchandise could split three ways from here.

After handing out food, he gave them drinks. There were water bottles in the fridge as well, so he passed those out.

"If anyone needs to use the restroom, there's a better one out here," he said, wishing he could call Ree. If his mouth moved while talking toward the wire and he wasn't in conversation with anyone, suspicion could be raised. There could be a camera hidden somewhere in the place. He had to play it cool. Being obvious about looking for it would only tip off Vadik's guys. Chef could be watching. He seemed to be in charge.

Quint coughed into his elbow, covering his mouth. In the few seconds it happened, he said, "Send the troops. Watch for Keith and Samuel. Nail all those bastards."

He could only hope she'd heard him. And now, all he could do was wait for Keith and Samuel to return.

REE HAD LOST contact with Quint. Fear gripped her that Keith and Samuel might have taken him somewhere to kill him this time. Vadik didn't give her the impression he was any the wiser about their undercover status. But he was slick.

Since she'd heard background noise earlier, she assumed the electronic devices had been working. It was possible Quint was in an area that cut off reception. They were using cell towers, just like with a phone.

"How long have you been together?" Giselle asked Ree as they munched on snacks at the granite island.

"Eight years," Ree said, figuring they'd be busted if someone was on the other side asking Quint the same questions. "How about you and Axel?"

"Almost five years," she said.

Ree wondered if half the reason Axel cheated on his wife was to get a boy. Some guys were in to that macho stuff and this crowd seemed ripe for that particular brand of old-fashioned thinking.

Where was Quint?

She wanted to check her phone to see if location was a problem, but couldn't with Chef in this room. While Quint was healing, he'd told her every detail about the incident from a few nights ago. He probably wasn't strong enough to be out there doing whatever it was they had him doing.

Ree was seriously whipping herself into a frenzy.

"Relax," Giselle said quietly. "He'll be back." With her back to Chef, she made eyes at Ree.

This probably wasn't the time to point out the fact Giselle couldn't possibly know if that was true. Being nervous wasn't going to help.

"You're right," Ree said. "It's just he spent two days in bed after the last time he left with those two. And he was back before now."

"Initiations are hard. A whole lot don't come back to the penthouse after the first night," Giselle explained. "But your guy did. And now he'll be part of the crew. It might take time but he can work his way up. There's a real career here."

Ree smiled and nodded. Giselle seemed to have bought in to the whole nine yards. She'd gone in hook, line and sinker. Now, Ree questioned whether or not Giselle would leave once her part was done and WITSEC showed. She seemed married to this life. The best hope to go along with Axel's wishes was the possibility of getting her son back. It had been clear she loved him and didn't want him to stay at her sister's. But then, she'd also gotten used to the freedom that came with not having him around.

As much as Ree didn't want to admit it, not everyone could be saved. A person had to want it and Giselle looked mighty comfortable here at the penthouse. "Do you come here every night?"

"Mostly." Giselle lifted a shoulder like she was more than a little put off by the question.

"Just wondering what my life might have just changed to," Ree said. She walked over to Giselle and took her arm. "It's amazing here."

"I know. Right?" Giselle's enthusiasm was back.

"What should we do next?" Ree asked, hoping there

was something going on to kill the time until Quint returned or enough time had passed for her to go home. She had no idea what the courtesy wait limit was or if Quint would be coming back tonight at all.

"We could get a room," Giselle said and gave a look that Ree recognized as being hit on.

She immediately withdrew her hand from Giselle's. The act of touching clearly didn't mean the same thing to Giselle that it did to Ree. On Ree's side, it was innocent contact. Maybe to Giselle, being with a woman didn't feel like cheating.

"Or we could grab a glass of wine and eat a little more," Ree offered.

Giselle gave a nod of disappointment. She looked defeated.

"I'm sorry if I gave you the wrong impression," Ree said. "Quint and me have barely been back together after not seeing each other in a few years. It wouldn't seem right for me to be with you while he's out there trying to rebuild our life."

Ree hoped the explanation would float because she'd come up with it on the fly.

"Right. Makes sense," Giselle said, sounding a little less hurt by the rejection.

When did dating and being in relationships get so complicated? All Ree wanted at this point was someone to come home to every night. Someone like Quint, whom she couldn't wait to see so she could share all the good news. And someone who had broad enough shoulders to lean on when times got tough. She fully expected the support to be a two-way street, too.

Quint's voice came through. Ree toyed with the strap of her purse as she listened. Was he asking for help?

Chapter Twenty-Two

An hour passed. Then another. Finally, a vehicle pulled in the back. Quint hoped it was Keith and Samuel, but he prepared himself to see pretty much anything walk through the door. The voices on the other side belonged to them, and he breathed a sigh of relief.

Again, he coughed so he could send the signal for help.

The kids had settled down, clinging to each other as sleep eventually tugged them under. The little blonde sat in front of the pack, legs and arms folded, with her shoulders hunched forward as she played with the seam of a well-used blanket.

Quint's heart squeezed at the fact this little girl who should be out playing kickball, or with her Barbie dolls, was in a defensive position, ready to fight. Her arms were spindly, so she wouldn't be able to do much. But her small size didn't seem to matter to her. She sat there as though on point.

Keith came inside first, followed by Samuel.

"Did you get it taken care of?" Quint asked them.

Keith nodded. When Quint looked down at Samuel's right fist, he saw blood. The first thing Samuel did was walk to the bathroom. The sink turned on next. Quint cursed at the fact that evidence was being washed down the drain.

It was okay, he reminded himself. A good forensic tech would be able to corroborate Quint's story. There would be blood in the Suburban, enough DNA to retrace the steps and confirm what had happened. A judge in Plano had been beaten up. He would either call in sick tomorrow or show up battered and bruised.

Samuel was relentless once he locked on. The guy seemed to derive a sick pleasure from beating someone to a pulp. If Chef hadn't been there to intervene, Quint had no idea how far the man would have gone with him the other night. Too far?

The next thing Quint knew, the back door opened and something was tossed inside. Smoke started filling the room. Samuel cursed.

"It's a raid," he shouted and then started coughing.

"What do we do with the merch?" Quint said to Samuel.

"Do whatever the hell you want. It's every man for himself right now," Samuel said before climbing onto the desk. He pushed open one of the squares in the ceiling as Quint heard the littles in the next room start to cough.

"Vadik won't appreciate losing his merchandise," Quint said, knowing full well the team would have thrown a listening device inside along with the smoke bomb.

He pulled his shirt up over his nose and mouth to breathe as Keith joined Samuel on the desk. The guy hoisted himself up and into the opening in the ceiling. Keith quickly followed. Then, Samuel's head popped through the opening.

"Are you coming, man?" he asked.

"I'll find another way out," he said. "Go on."

There was no way he was leaving the kids inside alone.

Plus, he needed to break away from Keith and Samuel if he was going to have a chance to get away.

"Keys," he said to Samuel. A set came flying through the opening.

"Good luck, man," Samuel said, seeming to have a new respect for Quint.

"You, too." It literally hurt Quint to say that. The last thing he wanted was for Samuel or Keith to get away. Law enforcement should be waiting outside at all possible exits. But even if they escaped, their DNA was all over the place.

The next thing he knew, something was being poured out of the opening. And then he heard the strike of a match. A second later, he saw the flames.

Quint cursed as he realized Keith and Samuel were torching the place.

Now, he really had to get the kids out. He bolted across the room, using the cloth of his shirt to cover his mouth and nose as best he could. He kicked the can toward the front of the room, in the opposite direction of the door he intended to walk through.

"Come on," he said, rounding up the half-dozen kids. "We have to get out of here."

Bug Eyes stared at him in disbelief but she did exactly as he said, gathering up the others to make sure they followed directions.

"Let's go," he urged, realizing the place could really go up at any second.

Through flames, he led the kids to the back door.

"You guys go out first, okay?" he urged.

They formed a semicircle around him. There were agents waiting at the other side of the back door, as expected. Quint put his hands in the air and squatted down so he would be at eye level with the kids if they were facing him.

They fanned out and the little girl stepped forward as though speaking for all of them. When Quint saw his chance, he bolted to the left. The alley in general was dark. He was fit and a fast runner. Granted, he was in a weakened state. These agents didn't know him from Adam, and would arrest him if he was caught because they either weren't aware of his undercover status or wouldn't blow his cover. Either way, he had to make a move now or risk exposure.

The problem with arrest was that he would go to jail alongside Samuel and Keith. Quint would come out and have to disappear. He'd have to hide his face for years because he would be viewed as rolling over in jail. No one would be released with evidence this strong against him.

Quint's lungs burned and his ribs hurt but he pumped his arms and legs as fast as they would go. An agent had broken off from the group at the door and given chase, as expected.

The kids had acted as human shields, allowing for Quint's exit. At least the kids were in safe hands now.

Quint tripped and nearly did a face-plant. He scrambled up onto all fours and then to his feet. Adrenaline was the only reason he was still moving at this point. The pain would set in later. At least the kids were going home.

He dipped right and then left, pushing his way into a bar and a throng of people. Quint took an accidental elbow to the ribs as he weaved in and out of people around the bar. Thump. Thump. Thump. The bass vibrated through him as he crossed the small but packed dance floor.

Since running through the back and out the door would be expected, he made a circle and then exited out the front. His plan worked and he was free from the agent who'd been chasing him. He immediately unbuttoned his shirt, took it off and threw it inside a nearby dumpster. The agent believed he was chasing a guy in a black button-down. The initial visual was a strong one. Immediately changing his look would buy him time.

Music thumped from the row of dive bars on Harry Hines. A guy was dressed in black leather. Quint walked up to the tall shirtless, suspender-wearing blond guy.

"Any chance you'd be willing to sell your hat?" Quint asked, pulling out his wallet. "I have two hundred dollars."

"Sold," the blond said. He took off the black faux leather captain's hat and handed it over with an ear-to-ear grin.

"Thank you." Quint handed over the money.

"I feel like I should be thanking you," the guy quipped, waving the two Benjamins in the air. "You know I bought that for twelve ninety-nine. Right?"

"I'd be happy to take some of my money back," Quint stated after putting on the hat. He stepped a little closer to the group as a squad car rolled past. The cops were no doubt looking for him.

"Not tonight," the man stated. "But if you come inside with us, the first round is on me."

The cop car kept going, shining a light in between buildings.

"I'm good," Quint stated, cutting through the group and walking in the opposite direction of the squad car.

REE STOOD AT the island, nibbling on fruit, cheese and crackers while praying for word from Quint. She started picking up occasional street noises in her earpiece and then could have sworn she'd heard clubbing music.

Ever since the rejection, Giselle had kept her distance. Ree had lost track of the woman and figured she might have found someone to go into "a room" with after hitting up Ree.

Chef had been in the kitchen most of the evening as well. Was that how he'd earned his nickname? And then cell phones started going off. A buzz of activity began, causing panic to well up inside her.

The next thing she knew, Chef was being summoned out on the balcony. Giselle appeared. Her lipstick was a little bit smeared and her hair a bit messy. From all appearances, she'd gone into a room with someone.

"What's going on?" Ree asked in a whisper.

"From the looks of it, there's been a raid," Giselle informed her. She made eyes at Ree, who took in a deep breath.

"I don't want to lose him again. He just got out," she said, using her cover to explain why tears sprang to her eyes. "They'll throw away the key this time."

"It'll be okay," Giselle stated. "We don't know what happened yet. There's no reason to panic. Stay calm."

It sounded like Giselle was trying to convince herself.

"If he got away, he won't come here. There's no way he would draw attention to Vadik," Ree said. "He would, however, go home. I need to go."

"Not right now, you don't," Giselle warned. There was something in her voice that rooted Ree to her spot. A threat?

"You're right. It would look bad if I got caught leaving the building. I'm sure the feds are watching," she said. "Seeing if anyone panics."

"They're always around somewhere, lurking," Giselle stated and a whole different side to her started shining through. This evening had been filled with surprises, twists and turns. Ree couldn't wait to get the hell away from this penthouse.

Right now, all she could think of was Quint's safety.

If he got arrested, there'd be no explaining why he was released. Neither of them would be able to show their faces around this crowd again. For Ree, the idea was appealing. She'd made a decision to wrap up her undercover career in favor of sleeping in her own bed seven nights a week. Zoey and the puppy had tugged at a heartstring Ree didn't realize was there. Change was good. Right? She was pushing forty years old. A number that caused plenty of people to rethink their strategy in life. Two of her older brothers had already hit the number, gotten married and started families. Finn, the youngest and closest in age to Ree, was in a long-term relationship. His fortieth was around the corner.

What was it about birthdays that ended with zeroes that had people feeling like they should be at a certain point in life?

"Jail would be the end of us," Ree continued, picking up the earlier thread. "I wouldn't make it through another stint and he'd be going away for much longer this time."

"You might surprise yourself. It's crazy what you'll do for love," Giselle said, pouring herself a fresh glass of wine. "Want one?"

"Why not," Ree stated. She'd been nursing the same drink all evening without taking more than two sips. She'd set it down somewhere and one of the arm-candy ladies had gone behind her and cleaned it up. Besides, she needed to look like she fit in and Giselle was drinking. Plus, it would give her something to do with her hands.

Giselle poured another glass and handed it over. Ree took a long pull before setting the glass on the granite.

Chef appeared in the doorway. His gaze was locked on to Ree and his expression told her bad news was coming.

Chapter Twenty-Three

"There have been two arrests," Chef stated. "And Vadik's workplace went up in flames."

"Do we have names?" Ree immediately asked.

Chef shook his head.

And then it dawned on her someone might have perished in the fire. "Did everyone get out of the building?"

"It seems so, but we can't be certain yet," Chef stated.

Ree picked up her wineglass and took another long pull. More than anything else, she wanted to go home. Leave here and she might seem too eager. Plus, she could miss out on information. But every fiber of her being wanted her to walk out that door and either head home or go for a drive to check the area. Quint could be lying in a ditch somewhere for all she knew.

Returning the glass to its spot, she wrung her hands together.

"Have you heard from your man?" Chef asked. At least, the recent turn of events gave her a reason to check her cell phone.

She pulled her phone from her purse and checked the screen. Her heart gave an audible thud when there was nothing from Quint. She shook her head.

"You'll let us know if anything changes," he said, but it was more statement than question.

"I will," she said to Chef as Giselle moved beside Ree and then linked their arms. Ree must have shot a warning look because Giselle shrugged and made eyes that said she wasn't trying to hit on Ree.

Good. Because dating sure had become confusing. Ree took this as another sign she'd been out of the swing of things far too long. The thought of turning forty alone was enough to make her realize change was needed.

Right now, all she wanted to focus on was getting Quint home safely. The thought of leaving her job and finding a new career was gaining momentum, sounding better and better every time she thought about it.

And the first person she wanted to bounce the idea off of was Quint. The thought of never seeing him again threatened to pull her under and toss her around at the bottom of the ocean. Waiting was hard. Not knowing was hard. Being without Quint was hard.

A half hour passed with her standing at the island. The men inside hovered around Vadik. Ree knew an agent would be here at some point. After all, the jewelry import store that had been set on fire belonged to Vadik.

"I should probably head home," Ree finally said to Giselle when another fifteen minutes passed.

"It's probably good that we haven't heard anything yet," Giselle said with a smile that didn't reach her eyes. Did this bring back memories of when Axel was busted?

Speaking of which, Giselle would be going into witness protection soon with her son. It was odd knowing someone's life was about to change forever when they were oblivious. After the invitation to grab a room plus seeing how much Giselle seemed to fit right in here at the penthouse, Ree again questioned whether or not the woman would accept the offer.

"I guess," Ree finally answered. "I want to go just in

case he shows up there. There's no telling what shape he'll be in and he must have lost his cell phone or I would have heard from him by now."

Giselle nodded as panic mounted inside Ree. For once, she didn't have to hide it and it felt good to be her authentic self for a change.

"Will you tell Chef that I left and that I'll let you know if I hear from him?" Ree asked, figuring she could sneak out by using the service elevator. She didn't want to think about what had happened the last time Quint had exited in the same manner. At least she would be alone.

"Sure," Giselle said with a look of sympathy. She, of all people, could relate to her boyfriend ending up in jail, or worse. Looking closer, Giselle's eyes had a dullness to them that said she'd been in this position before and realized she wouldn't always walk away from it.

"Stop over at the apartment when you think it's safe. Okay?" Ree asked. She needed to check in with Grappell before she told Giselle the real reason Axel had her bring Ree and Quint into the fold. There was something small and lost about the young woman now. Ree had a real weakness for those who had no one to look out for them in life.

"I promise to," Giselle stated with a forced-looking smile.

Ree could practically see the wheels turning in Giselle's mind. Was she concerned about being locked up, away from her son? Did this scenario remind her of the time Axel was busted? Ree had no idea what the young woman was thinking. All she knew for certain was that she needed to get home and check in with Grappell. Sticking around here was getting her nowhere. At the apartment, she could find out what the agents knew.

"Thanks," Ree said to Giselle before slipping out the back. She tapped her toe on the tile flooring, waiting for the elevator. It took its sweet time but finally made it. The trip down was quick. She exited into the alleyway where Quint had taken a beating a couple of nights ago. A cold chill raced down her back at the thought of what had happened as she made her way out of the alley and onto the street.

Ree barely made it to the opposite sidewalk as three vehicles she recognized as belonging to federal agents came roaring up. There were two SUVs and a white minivan. Three teams flooded the sidewalk, and all members wore navy blue windbreakers with their alphabet letters running across the back and another set on the sleeve.

Ree discreetly slipped her cell out of her purse as she made a beeline toward her apartment, keeping her head down the whole time. Being recognized by one of the agents wouldn't be ideal. Plus, the timing of her exit would cast her under suspicion with Vadik, and possibly get Quint killed. She managed to fire off a warning text about the bust to Giselle without drawing attention to herself by the agents.

A team entered the building as one positioned themselves in front. A third headed toward the alley. There must be solid evidence against Vadik. A link to the building wouldn't be enough to bring out this many teams unless Grappell had been able to arrange a warrant.

The buzz of her cell sent her heart rate soaring. She checked the screen and saw a response from Giselle. They must have crossed paths with their communication. Ree read the message. Apparently, a third person had been arrested in connection with the raid. Since three guys left together, that meant Quint was in jail.

This wasn't the worst-case scenario that had been running through Ree's head, because it meant he was still alive. She wouldn't exactly celebrate, though, because it also meant Quint had to pull out of the hunt for justice for Tessa. Dumitru and his people wouldn't have anything to do with Quint now. The fact he was released from jail would signal to them that he must have given up information in return for a plea deal.

On the one hand, relief washed over Ree that the case was coming to a close.

However, for Quint's sanity, she wished he'd gotten the closure he needed in order to put Tessa and her baby's deaths behind him. This way, he would always be haunted. It was a no-win situation now.

The thought of not seeing Quint when she entered the apartment weighed heavily on her mind. She wanted to see he was safe and alive with her own two eyes. *It was over*, she repeated.

Their apartment was no longer needed. Ree would go inside, take a shower and pack up her few belongings. She didn't want to leave Dallas without Quint, so she planned to stick around until his release. They could brief another team and let someone else find a way in. Quint wasn't the only one who wanted justice for Tessa.

Walking into their building, the weight on her chest pressed harder. The elevator ride was short this time. She slowly took her key out of her purse. The minute she unlocked the door, it opened.

Ree's heart took a hit at seeing Quint standing there. He quickly ushered her inside, closed the door behind her before engaging the lock, and then hauled her against his chest.

"What? How?" She blinked a couple of times, unable to trust her own eyes as she looped her arms around his neck and ran her fingers through the back of his hair. The move caused her breasts to press against a brick-wall chest.

"I'm here."

"Who is in jail then?" she asked. "Giselle said a third person has been arrested."

"A stand-in who has my ID and is being paid well for an acting job," he stated. "I just got word on the raid at Vadik's penthouse. He's been arrested, too."

"How?" she asked, amazed by his quick thinking.

"I'd rather kiss you than answer work questions right now," he stated a moment before her lips found his.

Their mouths moved together in a perfect dance. Her pulse climbed as something as simple as taking in air suddenly became less of a priority. Her head swam in the fog that was Quint Casey and she realized in that moment just how lost she was in his arms. Lost in the best possible way. In a way that made her want to stay there longer and just be.

When she pulled back, she admitted, "I love you, Quint. That might be too fast and I have no idea if you're ready to hear it, but wondering if something had happened to you made me realize just how important you are to me."

His arms tightened around her. Her body was flush with his. He leaned down as his lips almost grazed her ear. He whispered, "I love you, Ree. I've been wanting to say those words for days without knowing how or if you wanted to hear them after the way I showed up at your house."

This time, their kisses were tender, loving and long.

"There's no question I'm in love with you, Quint." She pulled back enough to catch his gaze and hold on to it. "What do we do about it?"

"I don't need a trial run," he started. "All I need is a U-Haul truck and space cleared out at your place for a few of my things. I want to move in together, Ree." He got down on one knee. "And I want you to marry me."

When he looked up at her, tears filled her eyes and her heart detonated.

"Marriage is a big step, Quint," she said, barely able to take in enough air to fill her lungs.

"Are you scared? We can wait. *I* can wait," he said.

"We've waited long enough," she stated with a certainty she'd never known. "I'm in love with you and I want to spend the rest of our lives together."

"Does that mean I can bring my U-Haul?" he asked with a smile that melted all of her resolve.

"It means I'll go with you to pick it up," she said, tugging him to his feet. "But I have one condition."

"Name it," he said without hesitation.

"I want a puppy," she said, unable to stop smiling. Quint was here. He was hers. And they were pledging to spend the rest of their lives together.

"As long as you say yes to marrying me you can have anything you want," he said with a smile.

"Yes," she said. "I'll marry you, Quint Casey. I'll be your wife. Your real wife."

Quint stood up and claimed her lips one more time. This time, Ree knew she'd found home.

BAGS WERE PACKED at Quint's place, and he was about to turn out the lights at the apartment before heading to Ree's house. *Their* house, he corrected. Quint needed to get used to the idea because Ree was the best thing that had ever happened to him and there was no way he was letting her get away after she'd said she loved him. He'd been searching for the right way to tell her the same thing.

Axel had been reunited with his family and sent to a long-term safehouse. Someone was heading over to pick up Giselle and offer WITSEC. And the girls Vadik and his crew were trafficking had been reunited with their families. Their trauma was unthinkable and healing would take time. But every single one of them was home, safe in their own beds.

"Let me get this straight. Someone is posing as you in jail right now and Bjorn is working out the details," Ree stated as they stood at the door.

"That's right," Quint confirmed. "The case is dead, so there's no reason for me to stick around any longer."

"I'm sorry, Quint. I know how important it is to you to be the one to bring Dumitru down," Ree said.

"As long as he goes down, I'll be happy," he said, but they both knew that wasn't entirely true. He'd wanted to be the one to slap cuffs on the bastard responsible. And now, would Dumitru ever trust Quint enough to get anywhere near him?

His cell buzzed. Quint checked the screen.

Get rid of Vadik. Come see me when it's done and you're out. Dumitru

The text from Agent Grappell shocked Quint. The desk agent explained this message had been written in a note handed to Quint's stand-in by a prison guard. The message would need to be authenticated before a plan could be developed, but this meant he was still in the game.

"What is it?" Ree asked as another text came in.

Quint checked the screen to find another message

from Grappell. If Quint was moving up to work with Dumitru, the offer to Giselle needed to be put on hold.

"Nothing. I'll tell you in the car," he said. Now, he just had to figure out a way to tell his bride-to-be this wasn't over. At least, not for him.

* * * * *

CLOSING IN ON THE COWBOY

CARLA CASSIDY

Chapter One

Johnny King breathed deeply of the fresh spring scent of the pasture. The grass had turned to green once again, and all the trees were sporting new leaves after a long, cold winter.

The April afternoon sun was warm on his shoulders as he leisurely rode his horse along the fence line that separated the King property from the Blacks' ranch.

There was nothing he loved more than checking on the huge herd of cattle that had made the King ranch one of the most successful in the entire state of Kansas.

Normally his father would be riding alongside him, but the sudden death of the man who had been mayor had warranted a special election, and Big John King had thrown his hat into the ring. The election was due to take place in five weeks, and so right now all of his father's time and energy was being spent trying to get the lead against the two other men running for the office.

As far as Johnny was concerned, his father was the sure winner. John King was a powerhouse businessman who not only ran the very successful cattle business but also had financial interests in half the stores in town. Beyond that, he was a humble man, who was well-liked and respected in the small Kansas town of Coyote Creek.

Johnny now emptied his head of all thoughts of his father and the election and urged his horse, Lady, to go faster. He always liked a swift run along the fence line from a tall, thick oak tree in the pasture to an old, abandoned wagon on the Black property in the distance. He gave Lady free rein to run while he lowered his head to make sure his black cowboy hat stayed put on his head.

It was only as he approached the old wagon that he reined her in and slowed to a walk. It was also only as he came closer to the wagon that he saw a pair of long, shapely feminine legs poking out of the wagon and propped up with bare feet on the edge of the wooden bench seat.

They were sexy legs that he instantly recognized. Chelsea. He barely had time to process that she was here in front of him when she sat up and her unusual, nearly neon-green eyes widened in surprise. "Johnny," she said.

"Chelsea, I… I didn't know you were back in town." He steeled himself for the rush of emotions that raged through him at the unexpected sight of her.

It helped somewhat that she didn't look quite the same as she had five years before when she'd left here for a new life in New York City. At that time, she'd left Coyote Creek with a headful of dreams and his raw, hurting heart.

"I've been back for about a week now, but I've been sticking pretty close to home."

"On vacation?" he asked.

She shook her head. Her pale blond hair sparkled

in the sunshine as she gazed at him soberly. "I'm back home to stay." She looked at someplace in the distance.

He was surprised, and yet he wasn't. Her fall from grace as a top model had been very public and covered by tabloids and a variety of news media.

In her first year in New York, she had been discovered and proclaimed the new It Girl in the runway modeling world. Her long hair had been cut off for a short, edgy cut that emphasized her large eyes and high cheekbones.

She'd always been slender, but now clad in a pair of jean shorts and a tight navy blue T-shirt, she looked far too thin and fragile. Once again, he fought against a surge of unwanted emotions.

He never wanted to care about her again. There had been a time when he'd been crazy-mad in love with her. He'd wanted to marry her and have babies with her. He'd dreamed of the life they would build here, and he'd believed she shared in those dreams.

She'd destroyed his love for her when she'd given him back his engagement ring and had basically told him he just wasn't enough for her. There was no way his heart would ever be open to her again.

"Did Melinda come home with you as well?" he asked. When Chelsea had left for New York, her best friend Melinda Wells had gone along with her.

"Yes, Melinda came home with me," she replied.

"So, you're staying with your mother?" he asked. She nodded positively. "I'm sure she's glad to have you back home."

Chelsea released a small, dry laugh. "You know Stella. It's hard to know from moment to moment how she feels. One minute she's happy I'm home, and the next she's telling me what a big loser I am."

He winced. He knew Stella Black could be extremely mean-spirited behind closed doors while being a pillar of society in Coyote Creek. "I'm sorry if she's giving you a hard time," he replied.

Chelsea shrugged. "I'm used to it. So, how have you been?"

There were so many things he wanted to say to her. He wanted to tell her how deeply she'd hurt him when she'd broken off their engagement. He wanted her to know that it had taken him a very long time to get over that pain and the absence of her in his life.

More importantly he wanted to ask her if leaving him and all the love he'd had to offer her had really been worth it. Had she thought about him at all after she'd left? Had she missed him at all?

And yet he didn't want to know. Nor did he want to reveal to her the depth of his pain when she had left him. "Things are good. Lately I've been staying really busy here at the ranch with my dad otherwise occupied."

"I heard he was running for mayor." She laid the book she held in her hand to the side and sat up straighter. A light breeze blew a fragrance of lilacs and vanilla to him. It was a familiar scent, one that she had always worn, and one that had always stirred a wealth of desire inside him.

"Yeah. He's deep in the campaigning right now," Johnny replied, trying to ignore how her scent still had the ability to affect him.

"How's your mother?"

"She's been through the wringer, but finally the cancer is behind her, and she's looking forward to the future."

"She had cancer?" Chelsea appeared stricken.

"Breast cancer, twice. She's undergone radiation, chemo and finally a double mastectomy. She's still a bit fragile, but she's doing okay and taking it one day at a time."

"Please tell her I asked about her," she said, a touch of sadness in her voice. At one time Chelsea and Johnny's mother, Margaret, had been very close. Of course, that had all changed when Chelsea had called off the engagement and left town.

"I'll tell her." He shifted positions in the saddle. "So, what are your plans now that you're back in town?"

"My only plan at the moment is to move out of my mother's house and into someplace else as soon as possible. Other than that, I don't know what comes next for me. I'm just taking some time for myself right now." Her eyes darkened with what appeared to be haunted shadows.

An awkward silence grew between them. For him it held the weight of a thousand words unsaid…and a hundred questions he wanted to ask her but wouldn't.

"How's your brother?" he finally asked.

A quick smile curved her lips. "Jacob is good. I'm hoping he's planning on moving back here soon."

"Is he still a policeman?"

"Yeah, he's still on the Kansas City police force. I'm trying to talk him into applying for a position in the police department here."

Chelsea's brother was thirty-four, five years older than Johnny and eight years older than Chelsea. He'd left Coyote Creek soon after graduating from high school and hadn't been back since.

"I'm sure he'd make a good addition to our police force," Johnny said. "Well, I'd better get moving. I guess I'll see you around town." He pulled the reins to turn away.

"Johnny…"

He turned around to face her once again. Before she could speak again a gunshot boomed. Immediately a scream rent the air. Every nerve and muscle in Johnny's body tensed. He knew that scream. It was his mother. Another gunshot cracked, and the screaming continued.

Johnny whirled Lady around and took off galloping toward the house. His heart beat frantically, and the taste of fear filled his mouth. Who had shot a gun, and why was his mother screaming? Had she somehow accidentally been shot?

As the large ranch house came into view, horror swept through him at the scene of utter chaos. His mother stood in the middle of the driveway, with Johnny's younger brother Luke obviously trying to move her toward the safety of the house.

His sister, Ashley was just stepping out of the front door. "Ashley, stay inside," Johnny yelled as he dismounted his horse and pulled his gun from his holster. He hit the ground. Thankfully, Luke managed to get their mother into the house, although Johnny could still hear her hysterical sobs.

Now he saw why she had screamed. Big John King lay sprawled on his back in the driveway between the house and the garage. Johnny began to crawl on the ground toward his father, unsure if more bullets would fly.

"Hang on, Dad. I'm coming," he yelled. He crawled as fast as he could go, scared out of his mind because his dad hadn't moved or responded to him in any way.

What had happened here? Who had shot his father, and how badly was he wounded? A million thoughts raced through his head in the moments it took him to reach his father's side.

His father was vibrant and bigger than life. He had always seemed invincible. He was the head of the family, the man in charge of keeping the King ranch one of the most profitable ranches in a four-state area. He was the man who had taught Johnny everything he knew.

But when Johnny reached his father's side, his horror only increased. Big John's chest was covered in blood. "Dad… Dad!" Johnny cried out. He pressed his hands on the bleeding wound, not knowing what else to do.

"Johnny," Luke yelled to him from the house.

"Call 9-1-1. We need an ambulance and the sheriff right away," Johnny yelled back.

"Already done," Luke replied.

"Just hang on, Dad. I'm right here with you." Johnny grabbed his father's hand and squeezed it tightly. "Do you hear me, Dad? I'm right here."

The sound of a siren filled the air. It should have given Johnny an enormous sense of relief, but it didn't. He already knew it was too late. A sharp pang of grief pierced through him, along with an overwhelming sense of rage.

His father was dead. Big John King had been murdered by somebody, and Johnny wouldn't stop until he found the person responsible.

THE MURDER OF cattle baron John King was the biggest scandal to hit the small town of Coyote Creek since Annie Harris had shot her husband in the butt while he was making love to his mistress in their marital bed.

As Chelsea Black dressed to attend the funeral for John, her head was filled with myriad thoughts and emotions. This was the first time she would be making an appearance in public since returning home.

If she knew the people of this small town as well as she thought she did, then most of them would know about her skyrocket climb to fame in the modeling world in New York…and her disastrous fall in disgrace.

There was a part of her that would like to skip the funeral and remain hidden away from everyone here in her childhood bedroom. But there was a much bigger part of her that wanted—that needed—to be there the way the King family had always been there for her over the years. Her need to pay her respects outweighed the knowledge that she would be fodder for the gossipers in town.

John King had shown her the kind of paternal love she'd never had since her father hadn't stuck around to raise her and had been completely absent from her life.

Margaret had known that Stella could be a harsh, critical mother to Chelsea, and while Margaret had never said a single word against her mother, Margaret had always been warm and loving and supportive of Chelsea.

Chelsea had become friends with Ashley and Luke

King. She'd found the youngest King sibling, Caleb, to be a strange kid who had grown into a strange adult.

And then there was Johnny. She'd fallen in love with him when she was thirteen years old and he was sixteen. It was when she was sixteen that he'd told her he was crazy about her too, but he wouldn't date her or have any real relationship with her until she turned eighteen.

Still, they had spent many stolen hours together just talking every day after school or when he was finished doing his daily chores on the ranch. When she was eighteen, they had officially begun to date.

She released a deep sigh as she pulled on the only black dress she had in her closet. Seeing Johnny again had stirred all kinds of emotions…ones she'd tried to forget over the last five years.

It didn't matter what she might still feel where Johnny was concerned. She knew she'd hurt him terribly when she'd broken off their engagement and had left town. He'd probably spent the last five years hating her for what she had done to him.

"Chelsea, are you about ready to go?" Chelsea's mother knocked rapidly on the bedroom door. "We don't want to be late."

Chelsea gave a last look in her dresser mirror and then opened her door. "I'm ready."

Stella Black was a very attractive woman. Although she was only fifty-eight years old, her blond hair had turned a beautiful silver shade that was a perfect foil to her blue-green eyes.

Those eyes now gazed at Chelsea from head to toe, and her upper lip slowly curled up. Chelsea steeled herself. The upper-lip curl was never a good sign.

"That dress is far too short and tight. It might have been appropriate in New York City, but it's absolutely not appropriate for Coyote Creek. And I can't believe you allowed somebody to cut your hair into that choppy, ridiculous style."

"Are you finished?" Chelsea asked with a sigh. "This is the only black dress I own. Besides, everyone in town will have something to say about what I wear and how I look. After all, I was a top model who ruined my career with drugs and also had a variety of undiagnosed mental illness issues."

A wealth of bitterness rose up in the back of her throat. The tabloids had been brutal to her, as had the people who were supposed to have had her back. The only person who had tried to clean up the bad press with the truth had been Melinda. Chelsea's best friend since third grade, Melinda had worked as Chelsea's secretary and press person after she had begun her successful modeling journey.

"Don't even bring that up to me," her mother replied curtly. "I can't wait for your brother to move back here. He has never given me any trouble." She released an audible, disapproving sigh. "Let's just go. I told you I don't want to be late."

Minutes later Stella was behind the wheel of the car, and Chelsea sat in the passenger seat as they headed toward the Coyote Creek Cemetery.

Nerves fluttered through Chelsea. This would be her first public outing since she'd arrived home and she couldn't believe it was to John's funeral. Who had killed him? So far, according to all the news sources she'd seen and heard, there didn't seem to be any leads in the case.

She could almost feel sorry for police chief Lane Caldwell. The pressure on him to solve the murder would be huge. Not only from a lot of people in town but also from the influential King family and their equally influential friends as well.

As they drew closer to the cemetery, thoughts of Johnny filled her head once again. She hadn't seen him again since the day of the murder, but she knew Big John's death had assuredly shattered him.

Johnny had always idolized his father, and as he'd gotten older the two had been not only father and son but best friends as well. She couldn't think of anything that might have changed that close relationship in the past five years.

She knew Johnny would not only be heartbroken about his father's death but also filled with a burning desire to find the guilty party.

If she had made a different decision years ago, then she would have been by Johnny's side today. She would have held him tightly as he grieved. She would have loved him through the trauma.

Who would be holding him tonight when the funeral was over and all the people went home? For all she knew, he was married and had a family by now. She couldn't begrudge him that. She hoped he had found love after she'd left him. It didn't matter that the very idea of him with another woman tugged at her heart more than a little bit.

The cemetery parking lot was full, and an attendant guided Stella to a spot in a grassy area among dozens of other cars. "This will be the biggest social event we've seen here in Coyote Creek in years," Stella said as she shut off the car engine. "Everybody who is anybody will be here."

Chelsea bit her tongue. She certainly didn't view a funeral as a social event. But her mother saw every outing as an opportunity to remind people that she, as president of the Ladies' League and a friend of City Hall, was a powerful woman who should be respected and revered.

As the two women got out of the car and headed toward the crowd gathered in and around a large white tent, Chelsea steeled herself for the scrutiny that would be on her, a scrutiny she hoped wouldn't detract from the King family and the solemn ceremony that had brought everyone together.

Rather than stand at the back of the crowd, her mother grabbed her arm and wove her way around people until they were beneath the tent. Chelsea would have much preferred to stand at the back as she was aware of the stares and whispers that followed in her wake. But when she tried to pull away from Stella, she merely tightened her grip on Chelsea's arm.

The King family stood together and appeared to make a protective circle around frail-looking Margaret…except for Johnny. He stood slightly separate from the others. His features were expressionless, except for his blue eyes. They simmered with what appeared to be a combination of both deep grief and rich rage.

Why did he not have anyone standing next to him…a wife or a girlfriend, supporting him through this dark time? He looked stoic and so all alone. Despite the time that had gone by, her heart ached for him.

His gaze suddenly caught hers. For several long moments their gazes remained locked, and in the depths of his eyes she thought she saw a whisper of the man who had once loved her. There was a softness there only for a minute, and then it was gone, making her wonder if she'd only imagined it.

At that time Pastor Jim Jeffries began the eulogy. The graveside service was fairly short, and afterward Stella insisted they go to the King ranch to show their support as intimate friends of the family.

By that time all Chelsea wanted was to go back home and hide in her room. She'd had enough of the whispering, the raised brows and furtive glances she knew she'd garnered.

She'd tugged at the hemline of her dress, wishing for another inch or two in length as she'd kept her gaze mostly focused on the ground or on the trees in the distance. And now she would be in a smaller group of people at the King ranch.

She hoped Melinda would be at the ranch. She'd seen her friend at the funeral, but the two had been too far apart to speak to each other. In fact, Chelsea hadn't spoken to Melinda since the two of them had come back home.

As Stella drove up to the King house, Chelsea regarded it curiously. She was oddly pleased that it still looked like it had five years ago. It was an impressive place, a huge rambling ranch with a wraparound porch.

Chelsea knew there were seven bedrooms, five bathrooms and a formal dining room along with a huge great room and kitchen. It was the biggest house in Coyote Creek and decorated beautifully.

Yet despite its beauty, there was a warmth inside that instantly made people feel welcome. This had been Chelsea's home away from home when she'd been growing up, and there were many happy memories within its walls.

Stella parked, and together the two got out of the car and headed for the front door. They were greeted there by Robert Martin, fellow rancher and good friend of the King family.

"Robert," Stella said, and the two of them briefly hugged.

"Chelsea, it's nice to see you back in town," Robert said. "Although with this mess, it's a terrible time to be here."

Robert was in his midsixties. He was a tall, slightly burly man with a gentle smile. He'd been a widower for years, and Chelsea had always believed he had a secret crush on her mother. In any case, he'd always been kind to Chelsea.

"Thank you, Robert," she replied.

He looked back at Stella. "The family isn't back here yet, but there are several others in the great room and kitchen."

"Then we'll just head in there," Stella replied.

In the kitchen several women bustled around setting up trays of food to carry to the dining-room table. Stella began to help them while she waved Chelsea to a chair in the corner of the kitchen. Chelsea would have insisted on helping but knew she would only get in the other women's way.

Minutes later the King family arrived home. Chelsea got up and walked into the great room where Margaret was seated in one of the cranberry wing-backed chairs. Johnny stood on one side of her and Luke on the other, two sober-faced sentries of protection.

Chelsea's only desire at the moment was to offer support and love to the woman who had been like a second mom to her. However, she wasn't sure how Margaret would receive her. After all, Chelsea was the woman who had broken her son's heart five years before.

Before Chelsea got all the way to her, Margaret stood and opened her arms to her. Unexpected tears blurred Chelsea's vision as she felt Margaret's arms surrounding her. The tears became soft sobs as the two women hugged long and hard. Margaret had always been a small woman, but now she felt achingly fragile.

"Margaret, I'm so sorry for your loss," Chelsea managed to get out between sobs as the two finally separated. "I can't even believe this has happened."

Margaret's lower lip trembled. "None of us can believe this has happened. But it's so good to see you again, Chelsea. You need to come over and eat some of my cheddar mashed potatoes and put a little meat on your bones." She offered Chelsea a small, sad smile. "You always loved my mashed potatoes."

Chelsea quickly swiped at her tears and returned Margaret's smile. "Yes, I did, and you know I've always loved you."

At that moment several other people descended on Margaret, and Chelsea moved away. Aware of more stares and whispers following her, she stepped outside and walked around the porch to the side of the house where there were two wicker chairs with a small glass-topped table between them.

She sank down in one of the chairs and tried to get hold of her emotions. She hadn't meant to cry, but seeing Margaret again, knowing how much the older woman had loved and adored her husband, had nearly undone Chelsea.

She closed her eyes and raised her face to the warm sun. She had no idea how long Stella intended to stay, but Chelsea was ready to go home. She'd paid her respects to Margaret, and that was all that was important.

She wasn't sure how long she'd sat there before she sensed somebody nearby. She opened her eyes to see Johnny standing at the porch railing with his back toward her.

"Johnny," she said softly. He turned to look at her. His eyes were dark and unfathomable, and his features were taut with tension. "Johnny… I'm so sorry about your dad."

He gave a curt nod of his head.

"Does the sheriff have any clues as to who might have done this?" she asked.

He released a deep sigh. "Not yet, but sooner or later we'll catch the person responsible." His eyes flashed with anger. "And whoever it is, he better hope the sheriff gets to him before I do." His hands tightened into fists at his sides and then relaxed. "I'm rather surprised to see you here."

"Why wouldn't I be here? You know how much I always loved your family…how much I loved your father." Her voice broke as she once again found herself swallowing against the deep emotion that threatened to overwhelm her.

It was an emotion not only wrought from the death of Big John but also from the regrets that filled her heart with a heaviness, the regret of losing five years here.

"So, how are you all getting along?" she asked.

He shoved his hands in his suit-pants pockets and shrugged. "It depends on what time you ask. Mom is alternating between trying to stay strong and completely falling apart. Luke is quieter than I've ever seen him, and Ashley is stifling her own grief in an effort to be strong for Mom. As for Caleb…who knows how he's dealing? He hasn't been around much since the murder."

"I'm just so sorry, Johnny," she said again.

"Thanks." Again, their gazes met and held for several long moments, and in the blue depths of his eyes she once again thought she saw a softness.

She'd always thought Johnny was one of the handsomest men in town, and the past five years hadn't changed that. His black, shiny hair was on the shaggy side, but that didn't detract from his strong, bold features or the sapphire shine of his eyes.

Now, she believed that he at almost thirty years old was even more handsome than he'd been at twenty-five. There was a new maturity to his features that only made him more attractive.

The black suit he wore only enhanced his attractiveness, the jacket fitting perfectly on his big, broad shoulders, and the trousers hanging nicely on his long, muscular legs.

There had always been a spark with him, a heady pull toward him, and she was surprised to realize the spark was still there for her. In this moment she couldn't believe she'd turned her back and walked away from this man and the love she'd known he'd had for her.

"So, what happens now for all of you?" she asked.

"Nothing much changes except I'll be running the ranch instead of my father. Actually, Dad left meticulous instructions in the event that anything happened to him. So, Luke and I will continue to work here."

"What about Ashley and Caleb? What are they up to these days?" She hesitated a moment and then continued. "I'm sorry if I'm asking too many questions. I'm just trying to play catch-up, but maybe this isn't the time or place to do that."

"You're fine," he replied. "Ashley now owns a trinket-and-dress shop in town, and Caleb…well, nobody is ever sure what he's doing. He's still into painting, but nobody has seen any of his work."

"Are you all still living here?" Once again there were so many things she wanted to say to him, but now definitely wasn't the time or place for those kinds of things. There might never be a time for her to speak her heart to him.

"After doing a bunch of renovations, I'm now living in the foreman's cabin. Luke has built a house on the property down by the old pond. Ashley has a house in town but has moved back in here temporarily, and Caleb still lives here."

"What kind of renovations have you done to the foreman's cabin?" Oh, how well she remembered that place! Many times in the past the two of them had met there to spend intimate, alone time together. Just thinking about those passionate trysts evoked a sweet heat to rush through her. Was he remembering those moments too?

"I completely gutted the place except for the fireplace. The kitchen is now updated, and I added a second bedroom," he said.

"Oh, that sounds nice." Once again, their gazes met each other's and held for a long, breathless moment. Was it possible there might be a chance that he'd forgive her for what she had done to him in the past? Was it possible they could reignite the love they had once had for each other and share a beautiful future together?

"Darling…there you are." An attractive brunette rounded the corner and moved to Johnny's side, dousing any hope Chelsea might have momentarily entertained about a future with Johnny.

Chapter Two

It was a beautiful Tuesday morning when Johnny and Luke got into Johnny's truck and headed away from the King ranch. "I can't believe everything is greening up and blooming already," Luke said.

"Yeah, let's just hope the spring storms stay away from us," Johnny replied.

"They rarely do," Luke replied.

"Then let's just hope if the storms find us, they aren't too bad this year." Johnny glanced over at his brother. Luke had been unusually quiet since their father's murder. In fact, he'd been quiet and yet he'd also been negative, which wasn't like him at all.

The two fell silent for the remainder of the fifteen-minute drive to Coyote Creek proper. Although the town was small, it had a thriving downtown. Along Main Street there was a two-block run of businesses that were kept healthy by the support of the town's people.

Johnny once again glanced at his brother. With only a year between them, the two brothers were very close, although there had been a lot of competitiveness when they were growing up. Luke had always been content just being a ranch hand, but Johnny was hoping he'd step up now and take on more responsibility.

However, ranch business wasn't what had brought the two into town today. The funeral had been two days ago, and chief of police Lane Caldwell hadn't come to see them with any updates on the investigation since a couple of days before the funeral. And what they all wanted, what they all needed right now was answers as to who had committed the murder.

The Coyote Creek Police Station was in a long brick building. The building held not only Lane's and his men's offices but on one side was a tattoo shop and on the other side was his sister's store. Her store was closed for now, but he knew eventually she'd need to get back to her real life.

Actually, they were all going to have to find a new normal. His father's death had changed and would change things in ways he had yet to even consider.

He shoved everything out of his mind as he pulled into a parking space in front of the station and turned off his engine.

"Let's do it," Luke said.

Together the two of them got out of the truck. Johnny pushed open the police-station door with Luke at his heels. Henrietta Benson sat behind the reception desk, where she had sat for as long as Johnny could remember.

"Good morning, Henrietta," Johnny said.

"Johnny, Luke." She greeted them with a smile.

"Hi, Henrietta. Is he in?" Johnny asked.

"He is." She pushed a button that unlocked the door between the public and the officers. Johnny and Luke entered a long hallway. Lane's office was the first doorway on the right.

As they walked in, Lane looked up from whatever he'd been reading, and his eyes widened. He half stood, but Johnny waved him back down.

"Hi, Lane. We just thought we'd drop in to see where you are in the investigation," Johnny said. He and Luke sat in the two chairs in front of the desk. Johnny hoped that subtly signaled to the lawman that they weren't going away without some answers.

Lane leaned back in his chair and released a deep sigh. "I wish I had something concrete to tell you. All we really know at this time is somebody was on the Black property and fired those two shots, and whoever it was, he was a damned good marksman. Both bullets slammed into your father's chest."

"Being a good marksman describes most every man in town," Luke said with obvious frustration in his voice.

"Almost everyone in town knew that my father was going to win the mayoral race. Have you talked to Wayne and Joe?" Johnny asked, referencing Wayne Bridges and Joe Daniels, the two men who had also been running for mayor against Big John. "Those two definitely had a motive to get rid of Dad."

"I've conducted an initial interview with them both, and now we're working to confirm their alibis," Lane replied.

"And what are their alibis?" Johnny asked. He knew both men had been highly competitive about the race, and just before the murder Wayne had begun nasty rumors and innuendos against Big John. However, the mudslinging hadn't stuck. Most everyone in town knew the truth about John's character, which was exemplary.

"Wayne was home with his wife, Martha, and she corroborated his alibi."

"Martha Bridges is as ambitious as they come. She'd lie in a heartbeat to protect Wayne," Johnny scoffed. "And what about Joe?"

"Joe claims he was out in his field at the time of the murder." Lane sat back up straight in his chair. "His ranch foreman confirmed that he was there."

"Who else have you spoken to? I know most of the people in this town liked my father, but I also know he made some enemies along the way," Johnny said.

"My men and I are in the process of working down the list of names you gave me right before the funeral."

"We know the shooter was on the Black property. Have you been able to locate specifically where the shooter stood?" Luke asked, his blue eyes darker than usual as he stared at Lane. It was an obvious sign that Luke was frustrated, as was Johnny.

"We have not. As you know that's a huge piece of property, and even knowing how far a rifle can shoot and the trajectory of the bullets doesn't narrow down the location much. We've walked the field in an effort to find anything left behind by the killer, but we found nothing, including shell casings." Lane shook his head. "I'm sorry, but at this point in the investigation, I don't have any more information for you. You know I'll keep you posted as the work continues."

Johnny released a deep sigh and stood, and Luke followed his lead by getting to his feet as well. "We need answers, Lane," Johnny said. "If you and your officers can't get them for us, then we'll work to get them for ourselves."

Lane got out of his chair, a deep frown cutting across his broad forehead. "Now, you know you need to leave the investigating to me. The last thing I need is for the two of you going off half-cocked and potentially ruining a case against the perpetrator. It's only been a week. We just need more time."

Johnny bit back a deep sigh of frustration. He knew he was probably being unreasonable in demanding answers after only seven days, but he wanted to know who had killed his father and why.

"Just keep us in the loop, Lane," he finally said.

"You know I will," the lawman returned.

"Well, that was a big waste of time," Luke said the moment they stepped out of the building.

"You've got that right," Johnny agreed. They both got back into the truck to head back home.

"As much as I want to know the who, I definitely want to know the why," Johnny said. "What would make somebody want to kill Dad?"

"My money is on Wayne. You know how badly he wants to win the mayoral seat, and Dad was in his way," Luke said.

"I just find it hard to believe anyone would commit murder over the mayoral position in a small town in Kansas," Johnny replied.

"Maybe he has bigger political aspirations, and becoming mayor is just the first step," Luke said.

"Maybe."

The two fell silent for several minutes. Luke cleared his voice. "Okay, I'm going to say something that's been on my mind and probably on yours as well…something that feels rather taboo."

Johnny shot his brother a curious glance. "Taboo? What are you talking about?"

"Caleb," Luke replied.

Johnny released the deep sigh that felt as if it had been trapped deep in his chest since his father's murder. "Surely you don't think Caleb shot Dad." There was no question that their younger brother had issues, but Johnny couldn't imagine him being a killer.

"I don't think Caleb would shoot Dad when he was sober, but who knows what condition he might have been in at the time? You know he drinks too much and God knows what kinds of drugs he takes. Nobody saw him until hours after the murder, and when Lane questioned him, he couldn't even say exactly where he had been when Dad was shot. And he and Dad had a huge fight the night before the murder." The words shot out of Luke with the force of an enormous internal pressure.

"A fight? I didn't know anything about a fight they had," Johnny said in surprise.

"Yeah, I didn't mention it to you before because I figured you had enough on your hands with executing Dad's will," Luke admitted.

"So, when exactly did this fight happen?"

"It was after dinner. You had already left to go back to your place, and I was just hanging around before going back to my house."

"Do you know what it was about?" Johnny's head reeled with this new information.

"Caleb wanted Dad to loan him money to open a storefront in town to sell his paintings, and Dad told him he needed to get out of the hayloft and off his artistic behind and do some work around the ranch before he'd even think about giving Caleb any money."

"How did Caleb react?" Johnny's hands tightened on the steering wheel as a new tension pressed hard inside his chest.

"He threw one of his usual temper tantrums. He said he hated Dad, who had never really loved him…yada yada," Luke said. "Caleb finally stormed out of the house."

"I should probably take this information to Lane," Johnny said reluctantly.

"Or not," Luke replied. "Maybe we keep this information under wraps for a bit and you and I investigate our brother. I don't want to throw Caleb under the bus without real evidence."

"That sounds good to me," Johnny instantly agreed. Besides, he found it almost impossible to believe that his youngest brother had killed his father in cold blood.

Johnny pulled up in front of his cabin, cut the engine and then turned in his seat to look at Luke. "What's on your agenda for today?"

"I thought I'd take Rod and Justin and head out to the south pasture to fix that fencing so we can get some cattle back in that area," Luke said.

Rod Jackson and Justin Albertson were two of the five ranch hands that lived in private rooms in the barn's hayloft. The rooms were as nice as some apartments, with each small unit having a bathroom complete with a shower.

"What's your plan for the rest of the afternoon?" Luke asked as the two got out of the truck.

"I think I'll take a quick ride on Lady, and then I've got a ton of paperwork waiting for me in the cabin."

"Anything I can help with?" Luke asked.

"No, it's still stuff I'm dealing with since Dad's death. Eventually I'll get to the end of it all." Johnny had been shocked by the amount of administrative tasks that had to be done upon a death, especially with all the business dealings his father had.

"Then I'll see you at dinner tonight." Luke waved and headed toward the barn. Since his father's death, all the siblings had been eating their evening meal together in the big house with their mother. Margaret was a strong woman, but she'd just been slowly recuperating from her bout with cancer, and being hit with Big John's death had nearly broken her.

Johnny headed for the stables, telling himself he needed a quick ride to clear his head, but deep down inside he knew there was another reason for it. It was just about this time of the day when he'd ridden out and found Chelsea reading in the old wagon. He wasn't sure why he wanted to see her again. He certainly didn't want to get involved with her in any way.

As he saddled up Lady, he thought about seeing Chelsea at the funeral. There was no question that she'd looked sexy as hell in her short little black dress and with her dramatic hairstyle.

Despite the somber occasion, he'd instantly been filled with all kinds of unexpected memories of making love to her. There had been a time when he'd been positively addicted to her. Kissing her had always dizzied his senses, and the feel of her body pressed against his had been beyond wonderful. Hell, he'd even loved the very smell of her skin.

His addiction to her had gone far beyond the physical. The sound of her laughter had intoxicated him. A simple smile from her had once had the ability to create a well of happiness inside him. She had been the first thing on his mind when he'd awakened in the mornings and the last thing he'd thought about before going to sleep.

Of course, all those feelings had died five years ago when she'd turned her back on him and taken off for New York. He felt nothing for her now except a bit of curiosity about her time in the big city. At least, that's what he told himself, but as he approached the old wagon and saw her sitting there, curiosity didn't account for the sweet heat that suddenly rushed through him.

SHE HEARD HIM COMING, and she couldn't help the way her heartbeat quickened. Since the funeral, Chelsea had tried to put all thoughts of Johnny out of her head. She'd been shocked to realize that he was in a relationship with Tanya Brooks, a girl who had bullied Chelsea all through high school, and a woman who had been instrumental in Chelsea's decision to leave town.

Of course, none of that mattered now. Besides, she was certain that Johnny still hated her for what she'd done to him. Even though he'd been pleasant to her, that didn't mean there was a chance in hell for them to pick up where they had left off.

He'd moved on, as he should have, and no matter how many regrets she had for the choices she had made, it didn't change where they were in the here and now.

He came into view, looking as hot as ever on the back of his horse and with a black cowboy hat riding his head at a cocky angle.

Despite everything, she couldn't help the smile that curved her lips at the sight of him. She set aside the book she'd been reading as he pulled up in front of the wagon.

"Hi, Johnny," she said, pleased that her voice held none of the emotions that raced inside her. His black T-shirt stretched taut across his broad shoulders, and she knew he would smell like sunshine and the clean-scented cologne he'd always worn.

"Hey, Chelsea. Nice day to be outside."

"I love sitting out here to read. It's so peaceful and pleasant."

"It won't be too long before it will get too hot to sit outside," he replied.

"I'm hoping by then I'll be in my own place," she replied. "I've been looking, but there doesn't seem to be much available right now, at least not that I can find. What I'd really like is to rent or buy a house instead of living in an apartment."

"Do you have somebody helping you look? I know there are several empty houses in town, but I don't know who they belong to or if they would be an option for renting," he said. "If you want, I could check them out for you."

"Oh, I wouldn't want to impose," she protested.

"It's not an imposition if I offer," he returned with a smile.

"Then I would really appreciate it," she replied, trying to stanch the warmth that swept through her with his smile. Johnny had a beautiful smile.

He gave her a quick nod. "And I appreciated you showing up for the funeral."

"I wouldn't have missed it. Johnny, my heart just breaks for your family," Chelsea said with a wealth of emotion.

He looked off in the distance and then returned his gaze to her. "Thanks, Chelsea. I have to admit, it's been tough."

"I can't even imagine."

They fell silent for a few long moments. Once again it was a charged silence. "So, how long have you been dating Tanya?" she asked, then cursed herself. "I'm sorry. That's really none of my business."

He shrugged his broad shoulders. "It's no big secret. Tanya and I having been hanging out together for the last couple of months, although it isn't anything real serious right now."

His saddle creaked as he shifted his weight. "I know there was a time when Tanya wasn't very nice to you, but she's changed, Chelsea. She's kind and highly respected for her work with charities. She's a teacher, and the kids and parents really love her. I think you'll like her now."

When hell freezes over, Chelsea thought to herself. It was difficult to even think about forgiving the person who had made Chelsea's high-school years a complete nightmare. In any case, Chelsea couldn't imagine any reason for the two women to ever hang out together.

"That's nice to hear," she replied.

Again, an awkward silence descended. She stared off

in the distance, where the old two-story house where she'd grown up was visible. That structure had never felt like home.

The Kings' house had been home, with Margaret always bustling in the kitchen and the sound of laughter ringing out and Johnny's blue eyes gazing at her with love.

Many evenings when she'd been growing up, she could be found at the Kings' place enjoying the loving atmosphere that was lacking in her own home.

"Maybe you'd like to come over this evening to check out all the renovations I made to the foreman's cabin," he said.

She looked back at him in surprise. "I'd love to see the changes you've made."

"Then why don't you come by around seven this evening. Does that work for you?" he asked.

"Let me check my social calendar," she said jokingly. "Oh, looks like I'm free tonight." She smiled at him, and when he returned her smile, her heart warmed with myriad old emotions. His smile had always made her feel as if she was the only woman in the world, but she reminded herself that it was no longer hers to cherish.

"Then I'll see you this evening," he said. He reached up and readjusted his hat on his head and then turned his horse around and headed back toward the King home.

For the rest of the afternoon, Chelsea tried to tamp down her crazy emotions where the visit to Johnny's house was concerned. She shouldn't have taken him up on his invitation. There was no reason for her to see where he now lived. However, there was no question that she was curious about his life since she'd left him.

Was he curious about her life in the last five years? Or had he read the salacious tabloids and believed that she'd become a drug addict who had self-destructed, that she'd blown all her money on dope and had come home broke and scorned by the people who had once believed in her? Or maybe he believed that she had mental issues.

Or did he simply not care what had happened to her while she'd been gone? She was surprised he'd invited her to see the cabin and that he was being kind to her. She didn't deserve that after what she had done to him.

Perhaps he wasn't as affected by her leaving as she thought he'd been. Maybe soon after she'd left he'd realized he really wasn't in love with her and her breaking up with him had been a huge relief.

She shoved all these thoughts out of her head as she got ready for the evening. When she was finished dressing and applying her makeup, she looked at her reflection in the mirror.

The jeans fit tight on her long, thin legs, and the long-sleeved pink blouse hung below her hips and was slightly too large for her. She'd kept her makeup to a minimum…just mascara and lip gloss.

Bug-eyed skinny legs. That's what Tanya and her mean girlfriends had called Chelsea all through high school. *Alien creature*, they'd said with disdain. They'd had even worse names for her, and she'd never known exactly why she'd been chosen to be the girl scorned by them. She had a feeling it had to do with the fact that the handsome, popular Johnny King only had eyes for her.

As she went downstairs to leave the house, she wondered if Tanya would be at the cabin with Johnny. If so, then Chelsea would be nice and polite. She didn't have to like the woman to be civil.

"Where are you sneaking off to?" Stella sat on the overstuffed sofa in the living room with a magazine open in her lap.

Chelsea laughed. "If I was sneaking out, then I would have gone out my bedroom window and shimmied down the big oak tree like I did when I was a teenager."

"Where are you off to?" Stella asked testily.

"Johnny invited me over to see what he's done to the old foreman's cabin."

Stella put her magazine to the side and looked at Chelsea with interest. "Is it possible you two will get back together?" Stella didn't wait for Chelsea to answer but instead continued. "You were a fool to walk away from him in the first place. I'll never understand why you did that. It would be an honor for you to be a King."

"A reconciliation between us is out of the question," Chelsea said firmly. "So, get that thought right out of your mind."

"With Big John dead now, Johnny will be one of the most powerful people in the county. It would be a great move to merge our two families together."

"That has nothing to do with me. And in any case, he's dating Tanya Brooks."

Stella sneered. "That twit wouldn't stand a chance if you decided to go after Johnny."

"I'm not interested in going after Johnny. I'm not interested in dating anyone right now. We're just being friendly with each other. Now, I don't know when I'll be home, so don't wait up for me."

A moment later Chelsea stepped out the back door and into the cool, spring evening air. The only thing she carried with her was her cell phone, although she had nobody to call, and certainly nobody was calling her these days. Still, she figured she'd use the cell phone flashlight to help her get home after dark.

Not only did she want a place to live, but eventually she also needed to get herself a car. But even if she had one, she probably would have still walked to Johnny's cabin.

It had been years since she'd made the trek from her home to the old foreman's cabin, but her feet remembered the way without thought.

The cabin had been a favorite place for her to meet Johnny when they'd been young and wanted to be alone. At that time the structure had been sound, with a stone fireplace, a working bathroom and a living room and bedroom.

However, there had been no furniture, and several of the windows had been broken. There was no electricity, and mice had considered it a fine place to live. But she and Johnny hadn't cared about any shortcomings in the place.

Johnny had made a bed with hay beneath a thick blanket, and with a flashlight playing on the wall, they had spent hours there not only making love but also talking and planning their future together.

That was then…and this was now.

Twilight was falling, painting the landscape in shades

of deep golds and purples. A half-moon spilled down a silvery light from the cloudless skies.

She'd always loved the smell of the pasture in the spring. It was the fragrance of sweet grass and a lingering hint of sunshine. It smelled of rich earth and wildflowers. It was the comforting scent of home.

She passed old outbuildings on her mother's property and then climbed a fence onto the King pasture. There were more outbuildings and thick-trunked trees and brush.

She hadn't gone too far when the hair on the nape of her neck rose, and she thought she heard footsteps behind her. She whirled around but saw nothing and nobody. Even though she didn't really need it, she flipped on her flashlight and shone it all around.

Nothing. She turned back around, turned off her flashlight and continued, laughing at her own jumpiness. And yet she couldn't shake the feeling that somebody was watching her as she hurried toward the cabin.

When it came into view, a small gasp escaped her. The place was at least three times larger than it had been before. The front of it looked homey with a covered porch that held two wicker rocking chairs and a planter colorful with pink and red flowers.

The closer she got, the more nervous she became, and she wasn't sure why. She and Johnny had known each other since they were kids, so what was there to be nervous about?

A rustling came from someplace behind her, and her nerves suddenly became about something much different than spending time with Johnny. She'd been a little bit on edge since coming home.

During her last year in New York, she had garnered the attention of a couple of rabid, scary fans. Even though it was highly unlikely that one of them had followed her here, an irrational fear filled her head.

More rustling sounded. She had no idea whether it was man or beast, but she wasn't going to turn around to find out. Fear torched through her. Her heart pounded loudly, deafening her to anything else, and her throat squeezed tight.

She raced as fast as she could the last few yards to the cabin and then knocked frantically on the door. When Johnny opened the door, she threw herself into his arms.

Chapter Three

"Whoa!" Johnny's arms automatically wound around Chelsea, and he held her trembling body tight against his own. "Chelsea…what's wrong? What's going on?"

She released a small laugh and quickly stepped out of his embrace. "Nothing is wrong… I—I'm so embarrassed. I just heard a lot of rustling noises on the way here, and I managed to freak myself out."

"There's a big old fox that wanders around this time of the night. That's probably what you heard." His body still retained the imprint of hers, even though he'd only held her for mere seconds. Her scent surrounded him, that lilac-and-vanilla fragrance that always stirred him.

He took a step back from her and opened his door wide enough to allow her entry. She stepped into the living room and instantly stopped, her gaze going around the room. "Oh, Johnny, this is beautiful."

A sense of pride filled him as he followed her gaze. Rich thick light gray carpeting covered what had once been rough plank flooring. The stone fireplace had been scrubbed clean to showcase the beauty of the natural rocks, and a thick wooden mantel held his flat-screen television.

An upholstered black sofa was flanked by smoked-glass end tables, and a matching coffee table stood before it. A black recliner completed the furnishings.

"I can't even believe this is the same place," she said.

"Come on, I'll give you the full tour," he replied. The kitchen had been updated with granite countertops and up-to-date appliances, and the small bedroom where they had once spent so many hours together had been transformed into a state-of-the-art office.

There were still times when he sat at his desk and thought he caught a whiff of her perfume lingering in the air. Before any of those memories could drag him back, he took her into the room he had built on.

It was a huge bedroom with a skylight in the ceiling. The king-size bed was covered with a navy spread, and there was nothing better than staring up at the stars as he drifted off to sleep. There was also a full bathroom, complete with a Jacuzzi tub and a shower.

"Johnny, it's absolutely breathtaking." She turned and looked at him. "You've transformed this place from a run-down old foreman's cabin into a beautiful home. You must be very proud of yourself."

"I am," he admitted and then gestured her toward the sofa in the living room. "Have a seat. Would you like something to drink? Some iced tea or a soda? Or perhaps a glass of wine?" He wasn't sure if offering her alcohol was even appropriate, given what he'd read in the tabloids about her.

"Actually, I'd love a glass of wine," she replied.

"Red or white? I have both." As she sank down on the sofa, he moved to the kitchen area. She looked beautiful tonight. The pink blouse enhanced her green eyes and blond hair and brought a light pink glow to her face. He could admire her without becoming emotional involved with her, he told himself firmly.

"White would be great," she replied.

He poured her glass of wine and took it to her and then went back and poured a glass for himself and grabbed a platter of sliced cheese and salami and crackers that he'd prepared minutes before she'd arrived.

He returned to the sofa and sat next to her, trying to ignore the evocative scent of her that drifted his way. "I made some phone calls this afternoon and found three houses that are empty here in town. Two are for sale, and one is for rent," he said.

"Thank you for finding out for me what's available. When can I see them?"

"If you want, I can take you to see all three of them tomorrow afternoon," he offered. Someplace in the back of his mind he wondered what in the hell he was doing.

Yet he also had a feeling why he was offering to spend some time with Chelsea. She was an easy distraction from the anger that gnawed at him over his father's murder, from the grief that clawed at his insides as he tried to keep his family together.

"Johnny, I'm sure you have much better things to do than escort me around town looking at houses," she protested.

"Chelsea, I'd be glad to take you to see them. Why don't I pick you up around one? Will that work for you?"

"Well, yes, but..."

"No *but*s," he replied.

She flashed him a smile that took him back to a place and time when she'd been his girl and all was right with the world. He cleared his throat and broke eye contact with her.

"Okay, thank you. But tell me about this place. It must have taken you a long time to get it like this," she said.

"It took me the better part of four years working on it nights and weekends to get it just the way I wanted it." There was no reason to tell her that it was the pain of losing her that had made him work so hard. He'd needed a project to focus on to keep his thoughts off her after she'd left him.

"Your hard work certainly shows. I especially love the skylight in the bedroom." She smiled again. This time it appeared to be a bittersweet smile. "We always did like looking at the stars together."

Once again, he steeled himself for a new rush of emotions that fired through him. "I'll bet it was hard to see the stars at night in New York City."

She picked up a cracker and nibbled on it as she shook her head and then finally replied. "I lost sight of the stars while I was gone." She shook her head slightly again and then leaned back into the sofa cushion. "So, tell me what's happened while I've been gone. Are you still in touch with all the kids from high school?"

"Most of them. Sarah Crawley and Mick Kendall got married soon after you left town."

Chelsea laughed. "That girl chased him shamelessly all through high school. She was crazy in love with that guy. I even rode with her a couple of times past his house to see if she could just catch a glimpse of him before going to bed. I guess Mick got tired of being chased and finally let her catch him."

"They seem really happy together. They have a little boy, and she's pregnant again." He fought against a quick wave of wistfulness. He'd thought by this time he'd be married and have a couple of children.

"Good for them. Tell me more about who is with who and what's happened since I've been gone."

For the next two hours they ate crackers and cheese and talked about what had happened in town over the last half decade. They laughed together as he related some of the more ridiculous things that had occurred in the small town…like when old man Leroy Simmons had gotten mad at his wife for not making his breakfast. Leroy had stormed into the café but had been in such a rage, he'd forgotten to put his pants on before leaving home.

He had always loved the sound of Chelsea's laughter. It was a tinkling, melodious sound that was not only pleasant on the ears but also contagious. He found himself searching for stories that he knew would make her laugh. They had always shared the same sense of humor.

Coyote Creek was a town that loved a party. There had been spring flings and Octoberfest celebrations that she had missed, and he tried to tell her the highlights of them all.

"I should probably head home," she finally said. It was just after nine. She stood, and he also got up from the sofa.

He walked with her to the front door, and she turned to face him. "It was nice visiting with you, Johnny. I've really enjoyed myself."

"I've enjoyed it too. I'll see you tomorrow at one so we can see about finding you a place to live."

As they moved closer to the door, she suddenly stood so close to him he could feel the heat from her body radiating out to his. He could smell the dizzying scent of her that had always stirred him.

All evening he had tried to ignore the slow burn of desire that she stoked inside him. But now he stood so close to her, and her lips were right in front of him, looking so achingly kissable.

Her eyes sparked brighter, and she leaned toward him just a bit. Oh, it was so damned tempting… But he stepped back and grabbed the doorknob, effectively breaking the moment. "Are you sure you're okay to get home?" he asked and opened the door. "I could always drive you back."

She smiled. "Johnny, I've made this journey from my house to yours and back a million times in the past. Now that I know there's a big old fox making all the rustling noises, I'll be just fine."

"Then I'll see you tomorrow at one," he said.

"Thanks, Johnny. Good night."

"Good night, Chelsea." He watched as she turned on the flashlight feature of her phone and then took off walking. He finally closed the door and walked over to the coffee table to clear the glasses and the remains of the cheese and crackers platter.

As he cleaned up, his mind whirled a million miles a minute, all with thoughts of Chelsea. He hated to admit to himself that she still had an enormous power over him.

It wasn't just the desire to make love to her again, it was a desire to hold her when she was sad and to make her laugh whenever possible.

It was the desire to know all her secrets and to share his with her. She had not only been his lover in the past, she'd been his best friend.

Had she had somebody like that in New York? Had there been a man there who had stood beside her? Supported her through her troubles? Had there been a man in her life who had loved her as much as he had?

He'd seen a couple of publicity photos of her on the arm of some actor. Had he been her lover? Had he been the one who had loved and supported her? And had she loved him back?

He finished the cleanup and then sank back down on the sofa. He had to stay away from her. She was dangerous to his well-being and the peace of mind he'd finally found without her.

He had a feeling it would be so easy for him to fall in love with her all over again. He hadn't been enough for her before, and there was no reason to believe he would be now. Besides, he didn't believe that she was really here to stay permanently, no matter what she said.

He'd keep his word and show her the houses tomorrow, but after that he would go back to his life, and she could get on with building her life without him.

As Chelsea slowly made her way toward her home in the distance, her thoughts were on Johnny. It had felt good to spend time with him again. She always felt safe and warm when she was in his presence. With him, she'd always felt like she was home.

A deep sadness swept over her as regrets once again weighed heavily on her heart. She wasn't sure why Johnny was being so nice to her, but she suspected she'd never have a chance to have more than a casual friendship with him.

She would never feel his lips on hers again or know the safety of his big strong arms around her. She would never again know the sweet slide of his naked body against her own.

And it was all her own fault. She could have been married to him, but she'd chosen another path. It had been a necessary move for her, and she didn't regret her personal journey, but she regretted that the cost of her own growth had been her relationship with Johnny.

She jumped as she heard a rustling noise behind her.

She turned around and used her light to look behind her. The light didn't do much to penetrate the darkness more than a few inches in front of her. Seeing nothing, a small, nervous laugh escaped her. That darned fox was going to give her a heart attack.

Once again, she forged forward, but the hair on the back of her neck rose as she again got the feeling of somehow being watched. She'd never been afraid of the dark before but, at the moment, she was more than a little bit creeped out.

More rustling filled the otherwise-silent night, and this time it was a loud noise that definitely sounded bigger than a fox running through the brush. She turned around and froze in horror.

Crashing through the brush and rushing toward her was a person dressed all in black. A ski mask covered the person's head, and he was swinging a scythe back and forth in a threatening manner.

The figure was like something out of a horror movie. Chelsea stumbled backward, terror cutting through her.

Her brain sputtered, trying to make sense of what was happening. What…? Who…?

Her momentary inertia broke, and she turned and ran for home. Panicked sobs filled her throat, and her chest squeezed tight, making it impossible for her to scream.

Whish...whish...whish. The sound of the scythe slicing through the air just behind her absolutely petrified her. Oh, God, why was this happening? Who was this madman chasing her? She raced as fast as she could in an effort to stay ahead of the threatening person.

Her side ached, and her lungs burned. She threw a quick glance over her shoulder. The person was still coming. The scythe was still swinging. Oh, God, she had to run faster, faster! She couldn't let the person catch her.

She stumbled, slamming into the ground. Her phone crashed out of her hand, and the flashlight immediately shut off. Panicked and sobbing, completely out of breath, she still managed to quickly get to her feet and continue running as fast as she'd ever run in her life.

Whish...whish...whish. The scythe created the sound of death just behind her. Even as she ran, she couldn't believe this was happening to her. Who was the nightmare boogeyman who was chasing her…and why?

When she finally reached the back door of her house, she yanked it open, raced inside, locked the door and then slammed her back against it. She bent over, feeling nauseous as she tried to catch her breath.

She drew several deep, long breaths and then finally straightened up and moved the curtain aside on the door to peer outside. The moonlight shone down on the yard, and there was nobody there. No indication at all of the person who had chased her through the fields.

She leaned with her back against the door once again, frantically looking around the kitchen. What had just happened? Oh, God, what should she do? Fear still caused her to tremble uncontrollably.

Stella was one of those early-to-bed and early-to-rise kind of people. She would be sound asleep. Besides, what could Stella do? Her gaze fell on the landline that Stella insisted they keep.

Call the police, a voice screamed in her head. She went over to the phone and picked up the receiver, but before she could dial, visions of the tabloid headlines screamed in her head.

Half the people in town probably thought she was a drug addict, and the other half probably believed she was mentally unstable. If she called Lane, would he really believe that a dark figure in a ski mask had chased her through the darkness wielding a scythe?

Or would he believe she had suffered some sort of a drug-induced hallucination? Would he believe she'd had a mental break with reality? She could just imagine the snickers and knowing glances that would follow her tomorrow if she called Lane. Heck, she could barely believe what had just happened.

A new sob escaped her, and she dropped her hand from the phone. *But it really happened*, a voice cried inside her. She wasn't mentally unstable, but a crazy person had chased her. And what would have happened if she'd been caught? Had the intent been to scare her half to death? Then it had succeeded. But what if the intent had been worse?

An icy chill trickled down her spine and pooled in the pit of her stomach. If things had been different, the first person she would have called would have been Johnny, but she didn't even have his phone number anymore. And in any case, she had no right to call him.

She remained in the center of the kitchen, a hand stuffed in her mouth to stanch the deep, retching sobs of terror that continued to work through her. She looked out the window once again, and still seeing nobody, she finally made her way upstairs to her bedroom.

Once there, she changed out of her clothes and into a nightshirt. She crawled into her bed and curled up into a fetal ball. Over and over, the visions of the scythe-swinging madman shot through her mind, making her shiver and cry.

She remained awake long into the night, her ears pricked for any sound that didn't belong. Would the person break into the house and hurt her? Had the person really gone away or was he waiting until the night deepened to make another move? Her heart continued to beat too quickly and fear iced through her. At some point she had fallen asleep and into nightmares that kept her tossing and turning.

Finally early-morning sun woke her. Even though she was still exhausted from the lack of any real sleep, she dragged herself out of bed and directly into a hot shower.

As she stood beneath the pelting spray, she found herself thinking about the hours she had spent with Johnny before the night had been hijacked by horror.

He'd transformed the old cabin into a beautiful place to call home. If she hadn't made the choices she had years before, then that beautiful cabin would have been her home too.

There was no question that despite the years that had passed, in spite of all the experiences she'd had, she still had a wealth of love for Johnny in her heart.

He was the only lover she had ever known, and even now the idea of making love with anyone else was somehow repugnant. There had been many nights when she'd been alone in her East Side apartment in New York and she'd thought of him. There had been many times when she'd wanted to call him and share what was happening in her life, when she'd wanted to know what was happening in his.

Was he being nice to her now because he still had love for her in his heart? Was it possible they could reconcile after all this time and after what she'd done to him years before?

Maybe he was in love with Tanya now. Certainly, Tanya was a beautiful woman, and he'd spoken of her with great admiration. Chelsea would never step on Tanya's toes where Johnny was concerned, even though she owed Tanya no respect for the way she and her group of mean girl friends had treated Chelsea over the years.

No matter how she tried to distract herself with the pleasant evening she'd spent with Johnny, the horror of being chased intruded into her thoughts.

When she was dressed for the day she headed downstairs, where her mother sat at the kitchen table with a cup of coffee and the morning newspaper before her.

"You're up early," Stella said without looking up from the paper.

"I didn't sleep very well, so when I saw the sun shining through the window I just decided to get up." Chelsea walked over to the counter, poured herself a cup of coffee and then sat at the table across from her mother.

"How did things go last night with Johnny?" Her mother picked up her coffee cup and peered at Chelsea over the rim.

"It was fine. He did an amazing amount of work on the cabin and turned it into a beautiful place." Chelsea wrapped her fingers around the warmth of her cup as she thought again about the night before. "It was scarcely recognizable from the little run-down cabin it had been."

"Did you tell him how stupid you had been to leave him?" Stella asked.

"We didn't talk about the past. We just visited for a little while."

"Any indication that he's still interested in you?"

"Mom, I told you before that Johnny and I aren't getting back together, so please leave it alone," Chelsea said.

Stella returned her attention back to the paper. For the next few minutes Chelsea drank her coffee and tried to get up her nerve to tell Stella what had happened to her on the way home from Johnny's place.

She drew a deep breath and released it slowly. "The reason I didn't sleep well last night is that something frightening happened when I was walking home last night."

Once again Stella gazed at her over the top of her cup. "Something frightening?"

"You're not going to believe this, but as I was walking home somebody dressed all in black and wearing a ski mask chased me with a scythe." The words exploded out of her on a single breath.

Stella slowly lowered her coffee cup to the table as she stared at Chelsea. Her upper lip curled and her gaze hardened. "I hope you didn't call Lane and bother him with such nonsense. Honestly, Chelsea, if you're taking some sort of drugs, then you need to stop it right now. If this is some sort of a wild ploy for attention, then you need to grow up. I'm running for mayor, and I won't have you bring me down with this kind of ridiculousness."

Her mother's words lashed at her, making her sorry she'd said anything at all. "Don't worry, I didn't call Lane. But it really happened. Somebody really chased me. I'm not on drugs, and I didn't just make it up."

Chelsea got up from the table and went out the back door. Once there she sank down on the stoop and fought against the tears that threatened to fall. She should have known not to turn to her mother for support or comfort.

How she wished her brother was here right now! Jacob had always been a buffer between Stella and her. He would have believed Chelsea's tale, and he would be concerned about it…concerned about her.

She stared out toward the King place. She wasn't taking drugs. She had never taken any drugs. She hadn't made it up. Somebody had chased her last night with a scythe. Dammit, it had really happened.

She had no idea how long she sat there, feeling more alone than she'd ever felt in her life. She finally pulled herself up and put her self-pity away.

The first thing she wanted to do this morning was try

to find her cell phone. Hopefully it hadn't been picked up by the person who had chased her or broken into pieces. She had a general idea where she had fallen and dropped it, so she now headed in that direction. She had no fear with the bright sun overhead.

She was glad she hadn't called Lane the night before. His response probably would have been just like her mother's, and the last thing she wanted was to be the topic of more gossip in the town.

Still, she couldn't help but wonder who had chased her and why. Who had wanted to terrorize her? Who had wanted to harm her? There was no question in her mind that if that person had caught her, she would have been badly hurt or killed. Thank God she had managed to run faster than her pursuer.

As she reached the part of the pasture where she thought she'd dropped her phone, she began running her feet through the thick grass, her concentration focused on the ground. The phone had a pink sparkly case, so it shouldn't be that difficult to see among the fresh, spring grass.

"What are you doing out here, Chelsea?"

She squeaked a surprise at Johnny's deep voice. She looked up to see him coming toward her. The sun shone on his dark hair and it was impossible not to notice the broadness of his shoulders beneath his white T-shirt. His worn jeans fit him to perfection.

Would her heart leap in her chest at any handsome man who looked so great, or was it just Johnny who made her heart quicken at his mere appearance?

"Chelsea?" He looked at her quizzically. "What are you doing?"

"I…uh…dropped my phone last night on the way back home from your place, and I'm looking for it." She averted her gaze from his.

"You dropped your phone? How did that happen?"

"Yeah…uh… I was running, and I tripped and fell, and it flew out of my hand."

She felt his gaze remain on her intently. "Why were you running?" he asked. "You know it's never a good idea to run through a pasture in the dark. There are exposed roots and burrows and all kinds of things that can trip you up. Why were you running?"

"Uh… I don't know." The last thing she wanted was for Johnny to think she was crazy or on drugs too.

"Chelsea, look at me." He waited until she met his gaze again. "You know better than to run through a pasture in the dark, so why were you running? And why didn't you just pick up your phone after you dropped it?"

"I was running because I was being chased." She hadn't intended on telling him what had happened, but the words fell out of her. "I was being chased by somebody dressed all in black and wearing a ski mask and swinging a scythe. The person chased me, Johnny. I'm not on drugs, and I didn't make it up. It happened. It really happened."

The words exploded out of her fast and furiously, and hot tears filled her eyes. The terror that she'd felt the night before once again speared through her.

Then Johnny's big, strong arms were around her, holding her as she trembled and wept. God, she'd needed somebody to hold her. She'd desperately needed someone to tell her it was going to be okay and she was safe.

Even after her tears stopped, she remained in his

embrace for several long moments. The scent of his fresh cologne soothed her. The feel of his body against hers quieted the fear that had momentarily been overwhelming.

She finally stepped away from him. "I'm sorry. I didn't mean to do that."

"Chelsea, I need you to tell me again what happened." A deep frown cut across his forehead.

She told him again, more slowly this time, about the person who had chased her. "I truly believe if he'd caught me, I would have been hurt or killed. Johnny, no matter what the tabloids speculated about me, they were wrong. I wasn't doing drugs while I was in New York. I didn't hallucinate this person, and despite my mother thinking I made all this up for attention, I didn't. It really happened, and it was terrifying."

"We need to call Lane," he said and pulled his cell phone from his pocket.

She placed her hand over his on the phone. "Are you sure you want to do that? He probably won't believe me."

Once again Johnny gazed at her intently. "Chelsea, I believe you, and Lane will believe me."

"I hope so," she replied fervently and dropped her hand back to her side.

She stared out over the field as Johnny made the call to Lane and asked him to come to his place. Nerves jangled in her veins.

Either Lane would believe her and Johnny, or this would merely add to the notion that she was on drugs and either crazy or she was seeking attention.

Meanwhile, if the person had meant to kill her the

night before, then he had been unsuccessful. How soon before he tried to do it again? Where would the next threat come from?

Chapter Four

As they waited for Lane to arrive, they both looked for her cell phone. Johnny's head reeled with what Chelsea had told him. Despite the fact that her story sounded outlandish, he believed her. Besides, he'd spent the whole evening with her and knew she hadn't been on any drugs and she'd only had one glass of wine. He also believed her when she said the tabloids had been wrong about her.

Chelsea had never been a liar, and despite what her mother thought, he'd never known Chelsea to be an attention-seeker. If she told him this had happened, then he believed her.

While he was highly concerned about what had happened to her, he wondered if it was really somebody trying to hurt him, or his family.

Had the person somehow mistaken Chelsea for Ashley? Was it possible the person had hoped to take out another King family member? Or had they known it was Chelsea and that in hurting her it would also hurt Johnny?

It was just an odd and very troubling thing to have

happen right on the heels of his father's murder. Was it possible somebody was targeting his whole family?

These were definitely questions he intended to bounce off Lane when he arrived. They finally found Chelsea's cell phone. It appeared to be in good condition; however, the battery was dead.

They had just walked back to his cabin when Lane's car appeared. Within minutes, the three of them were seated in Johnny's living room and Chelsea was telling the police chief what had happened to her the night before.

"Could you tell if it was a man or a woman?" Lane asked when Chelsea was finished.

She frowned and slowly shook her head. "I have no idea. All I can tell you is he was definitely scary. I guess I just assumed it was a man considering how he swung the scythe. I'm sorry. I only got a brief glimpse of him because I was busy running."

"Did he say anything to you?" Lane asked.

Once again, she shook her head. "No. He didn't make a sound, which just made it all creepier."

Johnny sat next to her on the sofa and fought with his desire to put his arm around her and pull her close. At the moment her eyes were haunted with the revisit of the events of the night before and her body trembled slightly.

"Is there anything else you can tell me about the person?" Lane asked.

Chelsea released a deep sigh. "I'm sorry—no. Again, I was too busy running from him to notice much of anything. All I could hear was the sound of the scythe being swung just behind me, and I was afraid at any moment I'd be sliced with it."

"If you think of anything else, call me." Lane got up from the chair.

"I'll walk you out," Johnny said to Lane. "I'll be right back," he told Chelsea.

"Do you believe this story?" Lane asked the minute the two of them were outside.

"I do," Johnny replied firmly. "Remember, I've known Chelsea for years, and last night she wasn't impaired by any drugs. What I'd like to know is if the person was after Chelsea specifically or whether this was an attempt to hurt my family." He told Lane about the thoughts he'd entertained on the matter while looking for Chelsea's phone.

"I'd say at this point it doesn't matter what his motive was," Lane said as a deep frown cut across his forehead. "Is it possible he used your scythe? Because maybe I can pull some fingerprints off it."

"I don't even own a scythe," Johnny replied.

"I'll do my best to try to find the person, but without any more of a description, it's going to be difficult," Lane admitted. "I'll inform you if I learn anything."

Johnny didn't waste his breath asking about his father's case. He knew if Lane had any new information, he would have told him.

Once Lane was back in his car, Johnny returned to the cabin. "Tell me the truth, did he believe me?" Chelsea immediately asked.

"Of course he did," Johnny replied. "You should have called me last night and told me what had happened."

"I don't have your phone number," she replied.

He looked at her in surprise. "It's the same number it's always been."

"Oh, I just assumed you'd changed it…uh…before, I mean after…" Her voice trailed off.

He had never considered changing his number after she'd left Coyote Creek. There had been a part of him that had hoped she would call him, that she would miss talking to him. But she'd never called. "Do you still have it?"

She nodded affirmatively and then stood. "I need to get out of your hair now."

"Chelsea, if anything like this happens to you again, I want you to call me immediately," he said. "I'll drive you home," he added, not wanting her to take the walk through the pasture alone again.

"That's really not necessary. I'm not afraid as long as the sun is shining."

"But there's no reason for you to walk back if I can drive you," he countered. She might not be afraid in the sunlight, but he knew very well evil could come in the daytime. His father had been shot on a beautiful, cloudless day.

Minutes later they were in his truck, and he was headed to the Black house. "Are we still on for this afternoon?" he asked.

"As far as I'm concerned we are, but it's up to you. I've already taken up most of your morning. Maybe you need the afternoon to catch up."

"No. Besides, I know how eager you are to find a place, so we're still on for one o'clock." He pulled up in front of the two-story house.

"Thanks, Johnny. I'll be ready."

He watched as she walked up to her front door, and once again countless questions flew through his head. Who had donned a ski mask and chased her through the pasture swinging a scythe? And why? Who had murdered his father, and why?

The questions continued to plague him until he pulled back up in front of the Black house. Chelsea flew out the door, a vision in white capris and a yellow blouse. Between the blouse and her bright smile, she looked like a ray of sunshine.

"I'm so excited," she said as she got into the passenger seat. "I can't wait to view these places and see if one of them will be my future home."

"The first one I'm taking you to is the rental. It's the nicest of the three," he said.

As they headed into town, they engaged in small talk. One of the things he had always admired about Chelsea was her ability to compartmentalize. When her mother yelled and said horrible things about her, she would tell Johnny about it and then was able to quickly move past it.

Now, it was obvious she'd put the night's horror behind her and was totally invested in the potential of finding a place to live.

He pulled up in front of the attractive ranch house for rent. "Oh, it's nice," she said. The house was painted a light brown with darker brown shutters. A flowerbed was full of petunias, and the lawn was perfectly manicured.

A few moments later Johnny put in the combination that would open the lockbox and provide a key. They stepped into a nice-sized living room with what appeared to be new beige carpeting and freshly painted walls.

"It's a very nice place," she said after they'd walked through. "But I was really hoping to buy a house, and in any case this one just doesn't speak to me."

He'd been sure she'd choose to move in here where the house was in perfect move-in condition and the monthly rent was on the low side.

"Okay. Then let's go see the next one," he replied.

The next house was a two-story. There was a wraparound porch with an unsteady railing that needed repairs, and the house could use a coat of paint.

"This one is owned by the bank," he said as he unlocked the door. "It's been empty for about a year."

They walked into a large living room with a fireplace on one wall. The walls also needed fresh paint. He followed her as she went into the kitchen and then climbed the stairs to the second floor.

He remained at the top of the stairs as she checked out the three bedrooms and the bathroom. She came out of the master bedroom and practically danced down the hall toward him.

"Oh, Johnny, I love this house. There's even a big tree outside the master-bedroom window that reminds me of the one outside my bedroom in Mom's house."

Her eyes sparkled with excitement, and when she reached him she wrapped her arms around his neck and kissed him on the cheek.

He froze, the familiar feel of her in his arms shooting a swift, unexpected desire through him. Thankfully she stepped back from him before he could do something stupid like capture her lips with his.

"There's no need to show me the last house. This is the one I want. I love everything about this one. I can totally see myself here," she said.

They headed back downstairs and went outside to his truck. "Are you sure this is what you want?" he said before starting his engine. "This place is going to require some work."

"That's okay. It's mostly just cosmetic stuff. Surely there's a handyman here in town I can hire to take care of things."

Johnny started the truck. "Jeb Taylor is a reputable handyman. I'll give you his phone number, and I also need to give you the phone number of my contact at the bank who can help you with the house."

"Oh, I'm so excited. I can't wait to be in that house and out of my mother's place," she said. "Although, I have to be honest, staying with Stella has been so stressful I was ready to find an empty rabbit burrow and move in there."

He smiled. "Thank goodness it didn't come to that. I'm just glad you found something you like." He could still feel the heated imprint of her lips against his cheek. She was still in his blood, but now that he had fulfilled his promise to take her to see potential places for her to live, he intended to walk away from her.

It was time he got back to his own life…a life without Chelsea in it. It was also time for her to build whatever life she wanted.

Despite the fact that she intended to buy the house, he still wasn't convinced she'd stick around. Coyote Creek would be a pretty boring place after the excitement and bright lights of New York City. How long before she longed for the city that never slept?

In any case, she'd broken his heart once, and there was no way he was giving her a chance to do it again.

When they reached Stella's place, he gave her the phone numbers she needed, and they said their goodbyes. As he drove home she remained in his thoughts.

He had a feeling there was a part of him that would always love Chelsea. She'd been his first lover, and for a long time he'd believed she would be his wife and the mother of his children.

There was no question that her return to town had shaken him up, stirring old memories of passion and love. He'd finally gotten to a place where he'd moved past her, but seeing her and spending time with her again had thrown him off his game. But it was time he shoved memories of Chelsea away.

Once he went back to the ranch, he busied himself with the chores he had missed that morning, and then it was time to go inside for dinner with his family.

As the King family all came together for the evening meal, the head-of-table chair remained empty. It was an emptiness that screamed inside Johnny. It was a cry of pain, of anger and grief, over his father's absence.

Dinner was provided by a woman Big John had hired when his wife had first gotten ill. Nellie Maddox was in her midsixties and lived in one of the spare rooms in the house. She was a great cook and provided all three meals for the King family.

Tonight, she had made a feast of fried chicken, baked beans and coleslaw. There was also a Jell-O salad and golden corn bread with honey butter.

As they ate, Johnny tried to engage each of them in conversation. Luke appeared to be deep in his own head, not eager for any small talk directed at him.

Ashley was also unusually quiet, answering questions in one or two words. Caleb appeared to be in his own head too. But that wasn't unusual for him. Finally, there was their mother. Margaret looked drawn and tired and still appeared achingly fragile.

When the meal was over, Johnny walked to his cabin, his thoughts troubled. Somebody had murdered his father, and law enforcement didn't have a clue as to the criminal. Somebody had chased Chelsea across the pasture wielding a scythe. And he felt like his family was falling apart.

He knew his father would expect him to keep the family going, but right now they didn't feel like a family at all. They all appeared to be on separate islands with no way to bring them all together.

Right now his father would be disappointed in him for not being able to accomplish that. Big John had always stressed the importance of the family.

God, he missed his dad. Every day when doing the chores, he longed for his dad's voice, longed to hear his deep, raucous laughter. He missed the conversations they'd shared, talks where his dad had always imparted some nugget of wisdom to him.

For the most part Johnny had few male friends. It had always been enough to have his father and Luke as his best friends. But his dad was now gone, and Luke had become distant, and Johnny realized he was lonely for the male bonds he'd had with both of them.

His dark and troubling thoughts continued to plague

him throughout the evening. When darkness came and bedtime rolled around, he realized he was too restless to settle in.

Instead of getting into bed and waiting for sleep to come, he stepped outside with the idea of walking around, in the hopes of tiring himself out.

The night was dark, but the moon reflected light with no clouds to hinder it. Night insects clicked and whirred with their songs as he headed up the path that would take him to the barn.

He walked slowly, trying to tell himself that he needed to let go of the things he couldn't control. He had no control over the investigation Lane was conducting into his father's death and now Chelsea's attacker.

He also had little control over how his family members were dealing with Big John's death. He could only hope with more time and with his continued steadying support, they would all come back together again, stronger than ever.

He reached the side of the barn and leaned with his back against the wood. He stared up at the stars overhead and wondered what Chelsea was doing tonight.

Had she called the bank and made the arrangements to buy the house? Could she even get a mortgage without having a job? He frowned. It was none of his business and not his problem, he reminded himself.

He needed to call Tanya and set up a date with her for the coming weekend. Even though he wasn't in love with her, he did enjoy seeing her and spending time with her occasionally. He felt no pressure from her to deepen their relationship, which was good.

He had a feeling he would never love another woman

like he had loved Chelsea. She had imprinted so deep in his heart there wasn't room for another woman…at least, not yet.

Maybe someday there would be room for somebody else. He wanted that. He wanted a woman who would be his best friend, who would always have his back and would love him deeply.

He wanted a woman he could love deeply, one who he would protect with his life and would give him the family he longed to have. So far, the only woman who had ever filled all his wants and needs had been Chelsea. There had to be another woman out there for him. He'd just have to be patient until she came along.

With a deep sigh he started to head back to his cabin, but something caught his eye…movement in the pasture. He narrowed his eyes and realized it was a man walking across the landscape.

Who in the hell would be in his pasture at this time of night? Visions of somebody chasing Chelsea filled his head. Was it the same person? Why would anyone be out here?

Adrenaline flooded through his veins. He took off, half-running after the person. He ran as quietly as possible, but when he drew closer the person must have heard him approaching. The trespasser threw a glance over his shoulder, and then he started to run.

Johnny hadn't gotten a good enough look to be able to identify the interloper, but he raced as fast as he could in an effort to catch him.

"Hey…stop," Johnny yelled. Not only was it suspicious for a person to be out here but it was even more suspicious that he was running in an effort not to be caught.

Dammit, normally Johnny would wear a gun when he was outside, but he'd been so distracted tonight he'd neglected to grab it before leaving his cabin. While he would never shoot a man in the back, he would have fired a warning shot that might have stopped the man in his tracks.

Unfortunately, he didn't have his gun. He ran as fast as he could, his breaths coming in labored gasps as he was determined to catch the person.

He began to gain on the man, and he pushed himself even harder. Knowing it was possible this was the same perp that had tormented and threatened Chelsea, he was damned and determined that the creep wasn't going to get away.

He finally got close enough to lunge at the person. He hit him in the shoulders, and they both went down to the ground. "Okay…okay," the man said and allowed Johnny to pull him to his feet.

It was then Johnny recognized him. "Leroy Hicks… what in the hell are you doing out here on my property?"

Leroy was a small man with pinched features and a long nose that gave him a face that resembled a weasel. Six months ago he'd worked as a foreman for Big John, but he had been fired for misappropriation of funds and for being drunk on the job on numerous occasions.

Two things quickly flew through Johnny's head. The first was that right at this moment Leroy reeked of alcohol. The second was that he hadn't thought about Leroy when he'd given his list of potential suspects to Lane.

"I was visiting with Caleb," Leroy replied defensively. "Last I heard, visiting a friend wasn't against the law."

"Why didn't you leave by the main entrance? What are you doing trekking across the pasture?"

Leroy shrugged. "Stella hired me a week ago, so I've been living in her foreman's cabin, and the easiest way to get from Caleb's place to mine is through the pasture."

Why on earth would Caleb be interested in getting together with a lowlife like Leroy, a man their father had fired and who had wished all kinds of bad things on Big John and his ranch?

"Why don't we go have a little chat with Caleb," Johnny said, unsure he believed the man about visiting with his youngest brother.

Leroy shrugged again. "Fine with me."

The two men began the walk back to the Kings' barn. They walked in silence, but Johnny's head was filled with suppositions and possibilities.

Was Leroy the person who had chased Chelsea? Certainly Leroy knew that harming her would ultimately hurt Johnny. When Big John had fired the man, Leroy had vowed vengeance on the King family.

Johnny couldn't believe he'd forgotten all about Leroy when he'd made his list of potential suspects for Lane. First thing tomorrow morning he'd call Lane to add the former foreman to the list.

They finally reached the barn. Bales of hay rose up on one side of the large structure. There were four rooms on the second floor that were occupied by four of the men who worked for the ranch. Caleb's room was on the first floor.

Johnny strode to the door and knocked rapidly. There

was no answer. He knocked once again. "Okay, okay, I'm coming," Caleb's voice rang out.

A moment later Caleb opened his door. The smell of pot and booze drifted through the doorway. Caleb stared at Johnny and Leroy. "What's going on?"

"I caught Leroy out in our pasture, and he said he'd been visiting you," Johnny said.

"He was." Caleb narrowed his eyes. "Is that a problem? Are you trying to tell me who I can or can't be friends with, Johnny? That's something Dad always tried to do. But now Dad is dead, and I don't have to listen to him anymore. He doesn't get to ride my back anymore. I definitely don't have to listen to you about anything, including who my friends are."

Johnny nearly stumbled backward beneath his brother's venomous tone. He drew in a deep breath and released it. "You are a grown man, Caleb. You can certainly pick your own friends. I just wanted to confirm that Leroy had been here with you."

"Yeah, he was here. We've become good friends," Caleb replied with a lift of his chin. "He likes my artwork and believes I have a lot of talent. So, are you done with me now?" Before Johnny could reply Caleb slammed his door shut.

Johnny turned to Leroy. "I'm sorry I bothered you, but I suggest in the future you come and go from the main entrance of the ranch. Skulking around in the dark in the pasture isn't a good idea. It could get you shot."

"Got it," Leroy replied. Together the two men left the barn, and Johnny watched as Leroy headed down the path that would lead him to the driveway.

Johnny frowned as he watched Leroy go. Was it possible he was the man who had chased Chelsea the night before? Yes, it was possible.

He was definitely shocked that his brother was friendly with Leroy. Equally as shocking was Caleb's brief diatribe. As Johnny walked back to his cabin, his head felt like it was going to explode with all the disturbing thoughts whirling around.

Along with the things that were already bothering him he now had a bigger, darker thought in his head. He hadn't really considered it a viable option when Luke had brought it up, but it now felt far more possible.

On top of all the other troubling thoughts that weighed heavily on his mind, he now had a deeper, darker question adding to his burden.

Had Caleb killed his father? Was Johnny's brother a cold-blooded killer? The possibility seemed much stronger now and shot a new cold dread into the pit of Johnny's stomach.

Chapter Five

It had been ten days since Johnny had shown Chelsea this house, and the past ten days had been a flurry of activity. She had bought the house, a surprisingly easy process due to the fact that she'd paid cash for it and hadn't needed to apply for a mortgage.

She'd immediately hired Jeb Taylor, an affable man in his midfifties who had a shiny bald head and beautiful green eyes. He'd gone to work on painting all the rooms on the lower level. He worked hard and fast. He wasn't much of a talker, but he did great work.

When the painting on the lower level was finished, Chelsea had bought new furniture for the entire house, and tonight she was welcoming her very first houseguest.

She now checked on the cheese enchiladas to make sure they were cooking nicely. She stirred the rice and then began to pour tortilla chips into a bowl.

Except for the brief sighting at John's funeral, she hadn't really seen Melinda since the two had left New York and returned to Coyote Creek. However, she had heard through the grapevine that Melinda was back with the boyfriend she'd dated before she'd left town.

Chelsea hoped her friend was happy. Melinda had supported the two of them when they'd first arrived in the big city. She'd gone to work at a deli a block away from the tiny West Side apartment they'd rented. While Chelsea had been hitting the sidewalks looking for a modeling agency who would take her on, Melinda had worked fifty-and sixty-hour weeks to pay the bills.

When Chelsea hit it big, she had rented a nice apartment on the East Side for herself and one for Melinda. She'd put Melinda on her payroll, and she no longer needed to work in the deli.

Chelsea shook her head with a smile. She and Melinda had eaten mac and cheese for months before Chelsea had begun to make money.

At least tonight there was no mac and cheese on the menu. Chelsea had chosen a cheerful yellow dish set, and with the chips and salsa in bright red bowls the table looked quite festive.

She checked her watch and scurried up the stairs to get dressed and put on a little makeup before Melinda arrived. Her bedroom was only half-painted, and since it was Saturday, Jeb wouldn't be back until Monday to continue the work.

She removed the housedress she'd worn all day and changed into a pair of jeans and a navy blue blouse. After lightly applying cosmetics, she went back down the stairs.

Once in the living room she plumped the pink and yellow throw pillows on the white sofa. The end tables held lamps that most people would describe as *blingy*, and the coffee table held a beautiful candle arrangement.

The space had started to truly feel like home. The

only thing missing was somebody for her to share it with. A vision of Johnny filled her head.

She'd heard and seen nothing of him in the past ten days, although he'd never been far from her thoughts. Every time he popped into her mind, she consciously tried to shove him out. It was obvious he had no intention of pursuing any kind of a relationship with her, nor did she really expect him to.

There would always be a sadness in her heart where he was concerned. She would always regret leaving him all those years ago, even though it had been necessary at the time. Now she just had to live with her choice. He was living the life he'd been leading before she'd returned to town, and she had to figure out what her life was going to be like moving forward.

Before she could get too much deeper into her thoughts, her doorbell rang. She reached the front door and pulled it open, then smiled at the dark-haired, slightly plump woman who had been her best friend for years.

"Melinda, come on in." Chelsea opened the door wider to allow Melinda entry, and the two hugged.

"Oh my goodness, Chels, I can't believe how nice you've made it in here," Melinda exclaimed as she looked around the living room. "Everything smells so new."

Chelsea laughed. "That's because everything is new."

"I would have known this was your place just by peeking in the window," Melinda said.

"How?" Chelsea asked.

Melinda laughed. "Who else in Coyote Creek would have pink throw pillows on their sofa?"

Chelsea grinned at her friend. “Come on into the kitchen. I’ve got dinner ready and your favorite brand of tequila waiting for you.”

Melinda followed Chelsea where she motioned her guest to the kitchen table. “Sit and enjoy the chips and salsa, and I’ll pour you a tequila shot.”

“Sounds good to me.” For the next few minutes, the two women drank their shots, ate chips and caught up with each other.

“I heard you and Roger were back together,” Chelsea said. Melinda and Roger Simmons had been a couple before Melinda had left Coyote Creek with Chelsea.

“Yeah, I couldn’t believe it when he showed up at my parents’ house to see me. I figured he’d probably got married while I was gone, but he told me he’d just been waiting and hoping that I’d wind up back here. It all just seemed easy and natural. It was as if the last five years didn’t happen.”

“That’s so sweet. I always said that Roger is the nicest man in Coyote Creek,” Chelsea said.

“He is a real sweetheart,” Melinda agreed.

“Are you ready to settle down with him?” While in New York and once Melinda had become Chelsea’s secretary and publicity person, she had become quite the party girl. While Chelsea stayed home night after night all alone, Melinda was out at bars and parties almost every night. Chelsea’s name had gotten Melinda into a lot of posh parties.

She now smiled at Chelsea. “I think all my wild days are finally behind me, so yes, I’m ready to settle down with Roger.”

“Then I’m happy for you.” Chelsea stood. “Now,

I've got some cheese enchiladas and Mexican rice that I made just for you."

"Ah, you know how much I love your enchiladas."

Chelsea pulled the meal out of the oven and set the dish in the middle of the table. She then put the rice in a serving bowl and added it to the table.

"So, what's going on with you and Johnny?" Melinda asked as they filled their plates.

"Absolutely nothing is going on with us. He was very kind and helped me find this place, but I haven't seen or heard from him since."

"I was wondering, because Roger and I saw him out Saturday night at the café with Tanya Brooks. Roger told me they'd been dating for a while."

"Yeah, I knew he was seeing her," Chelsea replied and tried to ignore the swift pang in her heart.

"That's got to really chap your hide," Melissa said. "She and her friends were so crappy and hateful to you for so many years."

"Johnny told me she's changed, that she's really nice and kind and well-respected now."

Melinda snorted. "That's a load of cow manure. A leopard doesn't change its spots, and you'll never convince me that Tanya has changed her personality. She's always had a big core of hatefulness inside her, and she and her friends were positively cruel to you."

Chelsea shrugged. "I guess she's Johnny's problem now." A tiny spear once again shot through her heart. Of all the people Johnny could be dating, why did it have to be a woman who had been so mean to her?

"I heard some news about your mother this morning. She's running for mayor?"

Chelsea released a deep sigh. "Yes, she is."

"How is good old Stella doing?"

"You know Stella. As long as it's all about her she's happy. She decided to run for mayor after Big John King's murder."

Melinda's brown eyes widened. "What's up with that? Does Lane have any clue as to who is responsible?"

"Last I heard he had no clue." Chelsea hesitated a moment and then told Melinda about the wild chase through the pasture from Johnny's place.

"Oh, my God, girl! That must have been absolutely terrifying." Melinda reached across the table, grabbed Chelsea's hand and squeezed it tightly. "Thank God you managed to get away."

"It was more than terrifying." A cold shiver threatened to walk up Chelsea's spine at the memory. "I truly thought I was going to die."

"Why didn't you call me and tell me about this right after it happened?"

"Oh, Melinda. Everything seemed to go by in a whirlwind. Johnny had me call Lane to investigate the incident, and then I bought this place and there was so much work to do."

"That's okay, I forgive you, and I'm here now." Melinda served herself another enchilada. "Do you miss New York at all?"

"Not one bit," Chelsea replied truthfully. "You know I was ready to come home long before I was cast out."

"I just didn't understand it. You were riding so high. You had the whole world at your feet."

"Not without paying a heavy price," Chelsea countered. "It was definitely a wild ride," she added.

Melinda laughed. "It was that. Remember those nights when we thought it was a real treat to add a little hamburger to our mac and cheese?"

Chelsea laughed. "I was just remembering those mac-and-cheese nights earlier."

They finished eating and then moved into the living room for more girl talk. Melinda had been out in town more than Chelsea, so she had heard all the latest gossip, which she happily shared with Chelsea.

The two laughed as they reminisced about both their time in the big city and their years in high school. Chelsea had spent many sleepovers at Melinda's house where the two had plotted revenge on Tanya and her friends. They had been ridiculous, over-the-top revenge plots that had never been acted on, but at the time it had been fun to talk about.

At eleven o'clock Melinda called it a night. "We have to get together again soon. Maybe one night later in the week we can go to the Red Barn and drink a little and kick up our heels," she said as Chelsea walked her to the front door. "Roger can be our designated driver, and it would be good for you to get out socially."

The Red Barn was a popular bar and dance hall on the outskirts of town. "That sounds like a plan. I know I need to get out a little more often. I haven't even had a meal in the café yet."

"You definitely need to get out and see who is on the market. We've got to find you a nice, sexy boyfriend."

Chelsea laughed. "Maybe before I get a new boyfriend I need to figure out what I want to do as far as a job is concerned."

"Ah, you can't fool me. I know you banked all the money you made as a top model. With the low cost of living here, you probably will never have to work again," Melinda replied.

"I need a job for my own peace of mind. I need to feel productive. It really has nothing to do with money," Chelsea replied. She opened the door where outside the night's darkness was broken up by a nearby streetlight.

"Call me, and we'll set up a night later this week or next week to go out," Melinda said as the two hugged.

Minutes later Chelsea closed and locked her front door and then returned to the kitchen to clean up the dinner dishes and take care of the leftovers.

As she worked, a smile curved her lips. She always felt good after spending time with Melinda. Melinda was bright and funny and had always had Chelsea's back. She had a wicked sense of humor and had always been able to make Chelsea laugh.

Although going out to the Red Barn wasn't really Chelsea's thing, she knew it would be far too easy for her to become a hermit here in her home.

She'd thought about approaching Ashley about a job in her shop. When Chelsea had been at the grocery store the day before, she'd seen that the store had reopened.

The idea of working there was more appealing than sacking groceries or working as a waitress. However, she didn't want to ride on the fact that she'd once been Ashley's brother's fiancée.

The last thing she wanted was for Ashley to somehow feel obligated to give Chelsea a job. Chelsea believed she'd know if Ashley might hire her out of some kind of pity, and that was the last thing Chelsea wanted.

She finished clearing the dishes, and with the leftovers safely stored in the fridge, she finally made her way upstairs. The master bedroom was half-painted a creamy beige, and she had chosen contemporary furniture that included a makeup vanity. At the moment the furniture was all shoved toward the center of the room to aid Jeb's painting.

She now sat at the vanity to take off her makeup. Once it was removed, she stared at her reflection. She had made the mistake of taking on and believing Tanya's words…that she was ugly and strange-looking.

Johnny had always made her feel beautiful, but deep down she hadn't really believed him. It had taken five years for Chelsea to finally embrace her appearance, to reach an inner peace she'd desperately needed. It had been her personal journey and one she'd needed to leave Johnny and Coyote Creek behind to attain.

She got up from the vanity and opened a drawer to retrieve her nightshirt. Stifling a yawn, she changed into the thigh-high cotton garment and then got into bed.

She'd been so busy over the last week and a half she now felt completely exhausted. She curled up beneath her sheets and almost immediately fell asleep.

She jolted wide awake and shot upright, her heart racing a million beats a minute. What? What was going on? What had suddenly awakened her in a flight-or-fight state of mind?

Had it been a bad dream that had jerked her awake? If so, she didn't remember anything about it. Then she heard it. A tinkling of something coming from downstairs.

What was that noise? She hadn't really been in the house long enough to be familiar with all the sounds it might make in the night. Was it some strange water trickle through the pipes? Did a neighbor have a wind chime hanging in a tree that was clinking in a breeze?

The noise halted for a moment and then resumed. Chelsea slid out of bed and grabbed her cell phone off the nightstand. She turned on the flashlight feature and slowly walked down the stairs, her heart still pounding fast and furiously.

She was halfway down the stairs when she realized the noise was the sound of breaking glass. She turned off the flashlight as the moon drifting into the windows made enough light for her to see.

The noise seemed to be coming from the kitchen, and she headed there. The minute she entered the room she saw him…the same dark figure wearing a ski mask and breaking the panels of glass near the doorknob in her back door.

She screamed, and the figure looked up. Pure hated glared from the person's eyes. She screamed again and then remembered she had her cell phone in her hand. She quickly punched in the emergency number, but when she looked up again the figure was gone.

As she told the dispatcher her name and address, she grabbed the biggest, sharpest knife from the butcher block on the countertop and held it tightly in her trembling hand.

Where had he gone? Had he moved to another window someplace else in the house? Where? She tried to listen to see if she could hear breaking glass anywhere else, but all she could hear was the frantic beat of her heart pounding in her head and the panicked gasps of terror that escaped her.

What if he managed to break in before help arrived? The kitchen clock read 2:00. Nothing good happened at this time of the morning. If she hadn't heard that first tinkle of glass and awakened, what would have happened to her?

Would he have entered the house and silently crept up the stairs to her bedroom? Would he have raped her? Killed her? Oh, God, what was taking so long for the police to get here?

She clutched the knife tightly and prayed she wouldn't have to use it, but she would definitely do so to save her own life. In the other hand she still held her phone. Johnny. He had told her to call him if anything like this happened again.

She hesitated a moment and then punched in his number. He answered on the second ring, his voice husky with sleep. "Johnny," she said and then burst into tears.

"CHELSEA, WHAT'S GOING ON?" Johnny clutched his cell phone to his ear and at the same time he sat up and turned on the lamp on his nightstand.

"That man…that man is here. He tried to b-break in." The words came amid sobs. "He…he was at my back d-door and breaking the gl-glass to get in."

"Hang up and call Lane," he instructed as he got out of bed.

"I…already called, but n-nobody is here yet."

Johnny could hear the abject terror in her voice, and an icy fear shot through him. "Where are you now?"

"I'm in the kitchen."

"Get to the bathroom and lock yourself in. Do you hear me? Lock yourself in the bathroom, and I'll be there as quickly as I can," he instructed.

"Please hurry. I don't know where he is now, and I'm so scared."

"Just get to the bathroom. Lock the door, and don't open it for anyone but me or the police." He hung up and quickly dressed. He then strapped on his gun and left his cabin. Any residual sleepiness he might have felt was instantly gone, replaced by a sharp edge of tension that tightened his chest.

It took him only moments to get into his truck and head into town. As he drove his mind worked overtime. First and foremost, he prayed that she had done what he told her to and was now locked behind another door.

If this was the same person who had chased her through the pasture, then it had nothing to do with his family and everything to do with Chelsea.

Who was after her and why? As far as he knew, she hadn't had any issues with anyone. The way he'd heard it, she'd scarcely been out of her house since buying it. So, the same questions repeated in his head…who was after her and why?

He drove as fast as he possibly could without getting reckless. The terror in her voice had frightened him. What was happening now? Had the man managed to get inside the house? Was she being attacked right this very minute? Or had the police finally shown up?

She was all alone with a madman attempting to break into her house. Again he hoped she had done what he'd told her and locked herself in the bathroom. At least that would be one more barrier for the intruder to get through if he did get into the house.

When he turned the corner of her street, he breathed a deep sigh of relief as he saw two patrol cars, with their red and blue lights swirling, parked in her driveway. Hopefully they had gotten there in time to catch the culprit and save Chelsea from any harm.

He parked against the curb and then jumped out of his truck and raced toward the house. The front door was open, and when he walked in, he saw Chelsea seated on the sofa looking small and vulnerable in a hot-pink nightshirt. Lane and two other officers were standing by.

The minute Chelsea saw him she flew off the sofa and into his arms, sobs racking her body. "Shhh," he soothed her as he patted her back. "It's okay… You're safe now." As she continued to cry, he shot a helpless look at Lane, who shrugged back at him.

She cried for several long moments and then finally pulled herself together, although her body still trembled as he continued to hold her.

Finally, she stepped out of his arms and returned to her seat on the sofa. "Somebody tried to break in through her back door," Lane said before Johnny could ask.

"It was the same person who chased me through the pasture," Chelsea said. "He hates me. Whoever it is hates me and wants me dead."

"Have you had any problems with anyone here in town?" Lane asked her.

"No…nobody. I've kept a pretty low profile since I've been back here," she replied in a trembly voice.

"Can you think of anyone who might have a reason to hurt you?" Lane asked.

Chelsea shook her head. "No, no one." She looked searchingly at Johnny and then back at Lane. "I don't know why this is happening. I wish somebody could tell me why this is happening to me. I've racked my brain trying to figure out the who and the why."

Johnny walked over and sank down on the sofa beside her as Lane continued to question her. "And you saw no identifying features on the person."

"None. He had on a ski mask and was wearing dark clothes," she replied.

"When he reached through the window, what was the color of his skin?" Lane continued.

"He was wearing gloves. I didn't see any of his skin."

Even though Johnny was several inches away from her, he could still feel the tremors of her body. Tears clung to her incredibly long eyelashes, and her face was as pale as he'd ever seen it.

A surge of protectiveness rose up inside him, along with a healthy dose of anger. He wanted to find the person who was tormenting her and beat the man's face in. He also wanted to pull Chelsea tight against him and hold her until her tremors of fear halted. However, he remained where he was as Lane continued to question her.

Lane was a good lawman, but no matter how good he was he couldn't find a bad guy without any clues, and so far it sounded like there were none at all.

Since the perp had worn gloves, then there would be no fingerprints. Since he'd worn a ski mask, there would be no physical description. How was Lane supposed to catch a ghost who struck at night and left no evidence behind? And who on earth would want to hurt Chelsea?

"What about back in New York? Was there anyone there who was giving you trouble?" Lane asked.

She frowned. "Actually there were two people I had to get a restraining order against," she said, surprising Johnny. "I'm not sure if either of them was truly dangerous, but they were definitely super-fan stalkers that made me frightened."

"What are their names?" Lane asked.

"Jerry Walkins and Dixie Sampson."

As Lane gathered more information on those two people, another thought suddenly flittered through Johnny's brain. Surely it wasn't possible. "Chelsea? Is it possible the attacker was a woman?" he asked.

She looked at him in surprise. "I guess anything is possible. Why would you ask that?"

"I just figured if we could rule out a woman being responsible, then it would make the investigation easier for Lane," he replied.

She frowned and looked at Lane. "I'm sorry. I don't know if it was a man or a woman. I don't know if he was black or white or green." Her voice rose with a touch of hysteria. "I don't know who or why or anything."

"Chelsea, it's important that you tell me if you think of anyone you might have accidentally offended or hurt," Lane said. "Maybe before you left town you said or did something to hurt somebody, and now that you've returned to town they want to make you pay."

"The only person I hurt before I left town was

Johnny." She looked at him now, her eyes filled with guilt and what appeared to be regret.

"I'm certainly not the bad guy here," he protested.

"I didn't mean that," Chelsea replied hurriedly. "My point is that before I left here I don't believe I hurt or angered anyone except you, and I know you would never do anything like this to me."

Lane put his small notebook into his back pocket. "My guys have cleared the area and didn't see anyone lurking around the house or in the general neighborhood. Whoever it is, he's probably done for the night. Unfortunately, you'll need to replace some glass in your back door."

"I'll help her with that," Johnny said and got up from the sofa.

"Chelsea, I'll be in touch," Lane said. The two other patrol officers left, and then Johnny stepped outside with Lane.

"Well, I think we now know that the chase across your pasture was about Chelsea and not your family," Lane said when the two men stepped out into the darkness of night. "And I have serious doubts that somebody followed her here from New York. I would have noticed a new face in town."

"I agree. This might sound crazy, but maybe you should check out Tanya for this," Johnny said.

From the light of the streetlamp, Johnny saw the surprise that flittered across Lane's face. "Tanya…really? You think this might be some sort of a jealousy issue?"

"Hell if I know, but it's possible Tanya might see Chelsea as some sort of a rival. The two never really got along in the past. I can't see Tanya doing something like this, but I also can't think of anyone else who might have a motive to hurt Chelsea."

"I'll check her out," Lane said. "And in the meantime, call me if you think of anything else."

"Will do." Johnny watched as the chief headed to his car, and then he went back inside where Chelsea was still on the sofa. "I'm going to go into the kitchen and check things out."

Chelsea nodded, and he went in to see what the person had done. The door had panes of glass, and two of them had been broken in the effort to reach in and unlock the door.

A slight chill walked up his spine. If Chelsea hadn't awakened when she had, the person would have been inside the house. He didn't even want to think about what might have happened.

There was no way he would believe that this person didn't mean to harm Chelsea. It would have been so damned easy to overtake her while she was sleeping. Another chill swept through him.

He returned to the living room and sank back down next to Chelsea. He was grateful to see that some of the color had returned to her face, although her eyes were still filled with more than a little bit of fear.

"Are you doing okay now?" he asked, even though he knew she wasn't.

"Yes…no… I just don't understand any of this," she replied in obvious frustration. "I have no idea why this is happening to me. Who hates me enough to do these things to me?"

"I wish I had an answer to give you. Do you have anything around here I can use to board up the door with?"

She frowned. "There might be something out in the shed in the back. Jeb has brought in a few supplies to fix the porch, and I think there was already some scrap pieces of wood in there when I moved in."

"I'll go check it out. Do you have a flashlight?"

"There's one under the kitchen sink." She got up from the sofa, and together they returned to the kitchen. When she saw the door, tears once again welled up in her eyes.

Johnny couldn't help but respond. He pulled her into his arms once again. "Don't cry, Chelsea. The good news is you're safe now."

"Yeah, but the bad news is the person is still somewhere out there," she replied.

"And tomorrow you'll go out and buy some extra locks. You also might consider contacting Charlie Harrison down at the feed store. He carries and installs a line of home alarm systems." He released her and got the large flashlight out from beneath the sink. "I'll be back in just a few minutes."

"I'll just stand right here and wait for you."

He opened the door, stepped outside and then clicked on the flashlight's high beam while she moved to stand on the threshold.

He shone the flashlight to the left and then the right as he headed toward the large shed in the back. Back and forth he checked out the surroundings. He saw nothing to give him pause. He almost hoped he'd see somebody hiding in the night shadows. More than anything he wanted to find the person responsible for Chelsea's terror-filled eyes and her fearful cries.

Once inside the shed he found a piece of scrap plywood big enough to cover over the broken windowpanes. Now, he hoped she had a hammer and some nails.

He found what he needed in a large bucket of tools Jeb had left behind, and it took him only minutes to hammer the plywood into place while she swept up all the broken glass. "Now nobody is getting through here," he said to Chelsea when he was finished.

"I'm still so afraid." She wrapped her arms around herself and hesitated a long moment and then spoke again. "Johnny, I know it's a lot to ask, but would you consider staying with me for the rest of the night? Please? I wouldn't ask if I wasn't so freaked out."

Her eyes pleaded with him, and she looked so small and fragile he couldn't help but say yes even as warning bells rang in the back of his mind.

He'd spent the last ten days staying away from her, not wanting to care deeply about her ever again. But there was no way he'd walk away from her now when she was so frightened and needed somebody…needed him to make her feel safe through the rest of the night.

"Okay, I'll stay," he told her.

"Thank you, Johnny. I really appreciate it."

Minutes later Johnny went around the house, checking to make sure all doors and windows were closed and locked up tight, and then he followed her up the stairs to her bedroom.

"Sorry about the mess," she said. "Jeb has been working in here."

"It's fine. At this time of the early morning, the most important thing now is getting some sleep," he replied.

She nodded and crawled into bed while he took off his gun belt and his shirt and then shucked his jeans, leaving him clad only in his boxers.

He got into bed next to her, and she immediately curled herself against his side. It felt only natural that his arm would wrap around her as she cuddled closer against him. "Thank you, Johnny," she murmured sleepily. "I feel so much better with you here next to me."

"Just go to sleep," he returned softly. It didn't take long until her slow, deep breathing let him know she'd fallen asleep. He wasn't so lucky.

Each point of contact where their skin met felt fevered. The familiar scent of her evoked memories of making love to her, and those memories tormented him.

While there had been a few women he had slept with since she'd left town, Tanya wasn't one of them. He enjoyed her company, but he didn't have a sense of deep desire for her.

There had only ever been one woman he'd had deep desire for, and that was the woman curled up next to him, her soft breathing warming the base of his throat. Even now, not wanting to feel anything for her, he couldn't help the sweeping passion, the deep caring that rose up inside him for her.

Of course, he didn't love her. He refused to ever love her again, but that didn't stop him from wanting her. But he didn't intend to ever return there with her. He instinctively knew that to act on his physical desire for her would give her the wrong message. There was no future for them together. She had to know that he would never put his heart on the line for her again.

He consciously slowed his breathing and watched the shadow of the tree outside her window dance along the ceiling. Finally, he fell asleep and into sweet dreams of Chelsea.

Chapter Six

Chelsea awoke slowly. She was wrapped in warmth, spooned against Johnny's body. His arm was thrown across her waist and his even breathing whispered against her nape.

Oh, how she had missed this. How she had missed him. The moment he had walked into her house last night, she'd felt safe and protected, like it was right for him to be here with her.

She was so grateful he'd agreed to stay with her overnight. Despite the terror she'd experienced earlier in the night, she had slept soundly and peacefully in his arms. She knew if he hadn't been there, she would have gotten no sleep at all. She'd always slept peacefully in Johnny's arms.

She now slowly extricated herself from his embrace and turned over, grateful that her movements hadn't awakened him. With a faint glow of morning sneaking in around her curtains, she stared at his features.

Even in sleep and with a five-o'clock shadow dusting his lower jaw, he looked beautiful and strong. His brow was smooth, and his brown eyelashes were dark, thick and long. His sexy mouth was relaxed, and all she could think about was kissing him.

She didn't know how long she had been looking at him when his eyes suddenly opened and he was looking back at her. In the depths of his eyes was a flame that instantly lit a fire deep inside her. "Johnny." His name fell from her lips on a whisper of want…of need and she placed a hand on his chest.

"Chelsea," he whispered back. He looked still half-asleep as his arms reached out to pull her closer to him.

And then her lips were on his in a kiss that erased any other thoughts from her head. There was just Johnny and his sexy lips stoking the heat inside her even hotter.

His hands began to move up and down her back in slow caresses that half stole her breath away. This was where she belonged, in Johnny's big, strong arms. This was where she had always belonged.

He deepened the kiss, his tongue swirling erotically with hers. It felt wonderfully comfortable and familiar and yet exciting and different. It had been so long since she'd been kissed by him, so long since she'd been held in his arms.

For five years she'd longed for him. For five long years she'd yearned for him. It hadn't been just this she had missed. She'd ached for the conversations they used to have about both serious and silly things. She'd wanted to hear his deep laughter and for five years had only imagined it in her mind.

His hands now moved to her breasts. Even through the cotton material of her nightshirt, his touch caused electrical currents to zing through her, and her nipples rose eagerly.

She sat up and pulled her nightshirt over her head, leaving her clad only in a pair of wispy pink panties. She then crawled on top of him. His hands immediately covered her breasts once again. Warm and slightly calloused, his hands not only cupped her but also teased and tormented her turgid peaks.

She could feel his erection beneath her. He was fully aroused, and that only turned her on more. He had to feel the same way about her that she did about him. Surely he forgave her for the past and knew they belonged together from this amazing moment forward.

She moved her hips against him, and he moaned deep in his throat. She leaned over and kissed him at the base of his throat. She then licked and kissed up his neck to just behind his ear.

He moaned again. God, she loved the sound of his pleasure. He pulled her down, and their lips reconnected in a kiss of desperate need and sweet, hot desire. Within moments his boxers and her panties were off, and they were skin-to-skin.

He lifted her up and positioned her to take him in. She knew he'd always liked her to be on the top, and as she eased down on him, she released a low moan. For a moment she didn't move as she waited for her body to adjust to his length. He filled her up in an exquisite way.

Then she moved, raising herself up and then sinking back down on him. He hissed his pleasure, and his eyes burned into hers. She felt as if he was making love to her with his eyes, those blue eyes that appeared to be looking into her very soul.

He placed his hands on either side of her, and she

leaned forward and popped her hips faster, pleasuring herself at the same time she pleasured him.

"Chelsea." He whispered her name with tremendous emotion, the single word filled with desire and love.

"Johnny, my sweet Johnny," she whispered back. Her body was filled with him, as was her mind. There was nothing but him and her and this moment.

Her climax was suddenly on her, shooting wave after wave of intense fulfillment through her. At the same time he moaned her name again and then groaned with his own release.

She collapsed on top of him, gasping with breathless joy. He too was winded for several minutes. When her breathing finally returned to normal, she remained on his chest.

The room was quiet except for the soft tapping of tree limbs against her window. "I can't believe you found a house with a big tree outside your bedroom window."

She laughed softly. "If it wasn't for that big tree outside my bedroom window while I was growing up, I wouldn't have been able to sneak out to meet you."

"Have you climbed down the one here yet?" he asked.

"Not yet. Want to do it with me?" She raised her head to look at him.

"I know you've got to be teasing me because you know I don't do heights," he replied.

She smiled. "I'm definitely teasing you." She straightened up and smiled down at him.

"I know what you want now," she said.

"And what would that be?" he asked.

"Some of my super special French toast with a big side of bacon," she replied.

"You really don't have to cook for me, Chelsea," he protested.

"Of course I don't have to, but I really want to," she replied. "I know you always liked my French toast. Please let me make it for you as a thank-you for staying here with me last night."

He smiled up at her. "Okay, go knock yourself out."

She crawled off him, grabbed clothes out of her closet and then headed for the bathroom. A few minutes later she went down the stairs to the kitchen. She refused to allow the sight of her back door boarded up to spoil the happiness that flooded through her veins in this moment.

Her body still felt warm from Johnny's, and her heart was filled with the knowledge that he still wanted her… that he must still love her. She put the coffee on to brew, then grabbed a frying pan and got the bacon going.

Everything had happened so quickly. Their passion had been like a sweeping wildfire that had raged quickly out of control. That's how it had always been between them, and she was happy that nothing about that had changed.

She knew Johnny would probably leave once he ate. She couldn't expect him to hang around all day. He had ranch business to get back to, and she needed to head to the feed store and talk to Charlie Harrison about getting a security system. But right now the sun was shining, and she wanted to keep this happiness she felt about her relationship with Johnny going.

By the time the bacon was finished frying and she'd

pulled out her griddle to make the French toast, Johnny joined her in the kitchen. Although he was clad in the same clothes, she could tell he'd taken a shower. He smelled fresh and clean, and his hair was damp and shiny.

She wished she had known he was going to shower. She would have loved to join him and wind up in bed once again for another bout of lovemaking.

"Sit down and I'll pour you a cup of coffee," she said.

He sank down at the table. "I didn't get a chance to tell you last night, but I can't believe how you've pulled this place together so quickly."

"It's been with a lot of help from Jeb. Thanks for giving me his contact information. He's fast but thorough, and I'm really pleased with his work so far." She carried a cup of coffee to him and then went back to the counter to finish up the French toast.

There had been many mornings in their past when he would show up at her mother's back door, and Chelsea would pull him inside and make him breakfast. This felt natural; it felt so right for her to be cooking him the morning meal once again.

As she worked, they talked about the house, not only the things she'd already accomplished but the things she still wanted to do.

While they ate breakfast, she was grateful that the conversation remained light and neither of them spoke about the events from the night before that had brought him here with her. She didn't even want to think about the terror she'd felt when she'd seen the intruder at her back door.

"I'll help you with the dishes," he said once the meal was finished.

"You don't have to do that," she protested.

"I always helped clean up after breakfast so we didn't leave a mess for your mother to be upset about," he replied.

She smiled ruefully. "Even when we left the kitchen spotless, she always found something to complain about."

He rose and grabbed their plates as she got up and reached for the syrup and butter in the center of the table. He fell silent as they worked to clean up the kitchen.

"I've got to get back to the ranch," he said when they were finished with the work and they went into the living room. "But before I go, we need to have a talk. Why don't we sit for a minute?"

"Okay." She sat on the sofa, her heart suddenly beating too fast. He looked so serious. What did he want to talk about now?

He sat next to her, a frown appearing across his forehead. "Chelsea, I'm not lying when I say making love to you again was wonderful, but it was wrong."

"Wrong? What was wrong about it? Johnny, being back in your arms was positively magical."

He winced. "I'm sorry, but it shouldn't have happened, and it won't happen again. I don't want to give you the wrong idea, Chelsea. We had our time together, and it ended five years ago. We didn't work out, and our time is over. I'm just not willing to try it again."

She stared at him as each one of his words chipped away at her happiness and stabbed her through her heart. She still loved him but also realized she couldn't make him love her again. Given their past and the way she had left him, it was no wonder he wasn't willing to try again.

"Making love with you once certainly didn't make me think we were going to have a relationship." She said the lie around the large lump in her throat. "Don't worry, Johnny. I don't expect anything from you."

Relief smoothed out his frown, and he stood. "Thanks, Chelsea. I just needed to know that we're on the same page." He smiled at her. "Nevertheless, I certainly want you to contact me if anything else happens with whoever is after you."

She got up from the sofa, and together they walked to the front door. "Even though it's Sunday, I'm assuming I can talk to Charlie Harrison this afternoon about putting in a security system here."

"Good, that will certainly give me some peace of mind." He reached up and ran his hand down her cheek, and she couldn't help but turn into the caress. "I care about you, Chelsea," he said softly. "I'll always care about you, and I want to be here for you as a friend." He dropped his hand back to his side.

She forced her lips to turn up in a smile. "Thanks, Johnny, I appreciate that. I can always use another friend." She unlocked the door and opened it.

"Keep in touch, and I'll see you around," he said.

"Bye, Johnny." She watched as he walked down her sidewalk to his truck parked by the curb, then she closed and relocked the door and returned to the sofa.

She sank down, grabbed one of the throw pillows and held it tightly against her aching chest. She'd thought...

she'd assumed…she'd just hoped that what they had just shared in bed meant they were back to where they had been before she'd left town.

She'd been foolish to believe that a passionate roll in bed would fix her relationship with him. She should have known it was much more complicated than that. She'd been stupid to believe that he would want to get back together with her.

Trying to hold in the tears that suddenly burned hot at her eyes, she mentally kicked herself for being upset. Yet she was upset. She felt as if the rug had been pulled out from under her. Until this very moment, she hadn't realized how much she'd wanted to be loved by Johnny again.

He wanted to be here for her as a friend. Had any woman in love ever heard worse words? She lost the battle with her tears, and they began to trek down her cheeks as the reality of her situation pounded in her head.

And the reality was she loved a man who would never love her back and she had a person who appeared to want her dead.

JOHNNY MENTALLY KICKED himself as he got into his truck to head home from Chelsea's house. He chastised himself for being so weak where Chelsea was concerned.

He'd known the moment he'd opened his eyes that she wanted to make love to him. He'd recognized the hunger in her eyes as he'd seen it a thousand times in their past.

There was no question that in that moment she had

stirred a white-hot desire in him. What he should have done was immediately get out of bed and head home.

Instead, he'd given in to his own desire. And it had been just as wonderful, just as magical, as it had always been with her. Maybe someplace in the back of his mind, he'd hoped it wouldn't be as good as he remembered. But that hadn't been the case.

Her lips had tasted like they always had, of exciting first love and hot summer caresses. She had tasted of cold snuggly nights and the hope of love forever more.

Holding her in his arms again had been like a dream come true. She'd fit so neatly against him, like she always had. For the past five years he had tried to forget the passion he'd always had for her, but making love to her again had only reminded him of his wild and deep desire for her.

And the minute she had placed his breakfast on the table before him, he'd realized she wanted to get back with him, that she wanted to go back to when they were together and happy. He'd seen it in the shine of her eyes, in the soft smiles that had curved her lips.

He knew he'd hurt her. Despite her brave face, he'd seen the signs on her features. He should take pleasure in that, given how badly she had hurt him in the past, but he didn't. He was surprised to realize that the very last thing he would ever want to do was hurt Chelsea, no matter what had happened in their past.

He had shared some of the best moments of his life with her. She knew him better than anyone else on this earth knew him. She knew he had an irrational fear of heights and that he dreamed of having a big family.

She knew that he'd wet his pants in the third grade, and instead of telling anyone, he had run out of the classroom and all the way home. He'd hidden in the barn until his father had found him. She knew things he'd never shared with anyone else.

Now he knew how important it was that he stay away from her. Because he had no desire to go back in time and rekindle a relationship with her, the kindest thing he could do for her and for himself was stay out of her life.

He hoped Lane figured out who was after her. He also hoped Lane would figure out who killed his father, but at the moment, the most imminent danger was to Chelsea.

Minutes later when he pulled up in front of his cabin, he was surprised to see Luke sitting in one of the chairs outside his front door.

"Hey, brother. What's up?" he asked when he got out of his truck.

"You tell me what's up," Luke said, a slightly hostile tone to his voice.

Johnny got his house key out and frowned at his brother. "What's chapping your hide this morning?"

Luke looked left and then right and then got up from the chair. "Let's talk inside."

The two men entered the cabin, and Johnny gestured his brother to the sofa while he sank down in his recliner. "What's going on with you this morning?"

Luke leaned forward and drummed his fingers briefly on the top of the coffee table. From the time Luke was a young boy he'd always been a tapper when he was nervous or upset.

"The real question is what's going on with you this morning?" Luke said with a raised brow.

"What are you talking about?" Johnny asked in confusion.

"I knew when she came back to town she'd be a major distraction for you. I'm assuming that's where you were last night…with her." Luke didn't even try to hide his irritation.

Johnny released a dry laugh. "I haven't had to explain my whereabouts to anybody for a very long time. But yes, I was with Chelsea." Johnny went on to explain the call he'd received from her in the middle of the night and what had happened.

When he was finished, Luke looked a bit contrite. "I'm sorry she's going through something like that. Does Lane have any ideas who might be after her?"

Johnny shook his head. "None."

"Lane is batting zero right now with figuring out what's going on in this town." A simmering anger was back in Luke's voice. "I just don't want you to get all caught up in Chelsea and forget that somebody killed Dad."

"First of all, I'm not about to forget that Dad was murdered, and second, you don't have to worry about me getting 'all caught up in Chelsea' because I don't intend to have a relationship with her. But if I did decide to date her, then it wouldn't be any of your business," Johnny replied firmly.

Luke flushed. "Johnny, it's been almost a month, and we aren't any closer to getting answers about his murder. I'm just so damned frustrated. I feel like each day that passes without answers is a dishonor to Dad."

"What do you suggest we do, Luke?"

Luke ran a hand through his shaggy dark hair and a deep frown creased his forehead. "I think it's time we start our own investigation."

"I've given Lane every name of anyone I could think of who might have a motive. I even told him to look at Caleb. What else can we do?"

"I still think it was either Wayne Bridges or Joe Daniels who did it. Both of them were running against Dad in the mayoral race, and they both knew Dad was beating them by a lot."

"I agree, but how do we investigate them better than Lane already has?"

"I don't know," Luke admitted. His eyes held a torment that Johnny had never seen there before. "I just feel like I need to do something."

"Luke, the best thing we can do right now is leave the investigation to Lane and his staff. We have a ranch to run here, and I need you to be focused on being my right-hand man."

Luke nodded slowly, the frown still running across his face. "I just feel like I'm letting down Dad by not doing anything more."

"You aren't letting down Dad," Johnny countered. "If we let the ranch business fall apart, then we'd be letting him down."

Luke drew a deep breath and released it. "I know you're right. And speaking of that, I guess I'll get back to the chores." He got up from the sofa and Johnny stood as well.

When they reached the door, Johnny patted his brother on the back. "We're all hurting, Luke, but we need to leave things to Lane and his officers and wait for justice to be served."

"My biggest fear is that we aren't going to ever get any answers. We'll never know who killed him, and the murderer will still be walking the streets of our town."

"Yeah, that's my fear too," Johnny admitted as the two stepped outside. "Just don't get too deep into your head, Luke. You know you've always had a tendency to do that."

"I know." Luke flashed him a quick grin. "Sorry if I ruined your morning with all this."

Johnny returned his smile. "Hey, no harm, no foul. Come on, I'll walk with you to the stable, and we can take a ride together through the cattle."

"Sounds good to me."

The brothers saddled up and rode together for an hour and a half, talking about pasture grass and the general health of the cattle and checking water troughs to make sure they were all full.

Then they parted ways. Johnny headed back to the cabin to check inventory and cut payroll checks for the men who worked for them, and Luke rode on to check the condition of some of the farther pastures.

It took Johnny most of the afternoon to write checks and contact suppliers to order various items that the ranch needed. It took longer than usual because thoughts of Chelsea kept intruding in his mind.

Had she contacted Charlie about a security system? Had she installed more locks on her doors? He couldn't help but be concerned about her after what had happened the night before. No matter how many times he told himself she wasn't his problem, he couldn't stop worrying about her.

He finally knocked off work to have dinner with his family. Caleb didn't show up, nor did Ashley, who was working late at her store. It was a quiet meal with just his mother, Luke and himself.

As he was walking back to his cabin he saw Caleb standing just outside the barn with Leroy and deep in conversation. They were near two fifty-gallon drums that held special feed for a couple of the horses. Once again, he wondered what the two had in common. It was definitely an odd friendship as far as Johnny was concerned, but just like his relationship with Chelsea wasn't any of Luke's business, Caleb's friendship wasn't any of Johnny's business.

The minute he got back into the cabin, he picked up the phone and called Tanya. "Hi, Johnny." Her voice was warm and welcoming.

"Hey, Tanya. How are you doing?"

"I'm just finishing up some lesson plans for school tomorrow," she replied. Tanya was a third-grade teacher at the local elementary school. "What are you doing?"

"I've spent most of the day doing paperwork," he replied.

"Ugh. Don't you hate wasting a beautiful spring day with admin?"

"I do, but it's a necessary evil. I was actually wondering if this Friday night you'd like to have dinner with me at the café and then head to the Red Barn for a little two-stepping?"

"Sounds like a perfect way to end a week. I'd love to go with you," she replied.

"Great, why don't I pick you up around six?"

"That will be just fine. Anything else new?" she asked.

He immediately wondered if she'd heard he'd spent the night at Chelsea's place. It would only take one person driving by and seeing his truck parked there early this morning for word to get back to Tanya.

He decided to tell her the truth, minus the intimate details that really weren't anyone's business. He wasn't sleeping with Tanya, so he hadn't broken any sacred trust. They also had never talked about theirs being a monogamous dating relationship.

Still, he told her about the attempted break-in there and that he'd spent the night, although he didn't tell her he'd passed it in Chelsea's bed.

"Oh my goodness, that's terrible," Tanya said when he was finished. "I'm just glad she's okay."

It was obvious from her surprise at the news that Lane hadn't spoken to her yet. "She should be just fine," he said. "She planned on getting extra locks today and finding out about a security system."

"That's good. Still, it's hard to believe those things are even necessary in Coyote Creek. Do the police know who's responsible?"

"Lane had no idea last night, and I haven't heard anything more from him today. It's really not my issue," he replied firmly, as if trying to convince himself of that fact.

"Well, I hope Lane finds the bad guy."

"Me too, but that's between Chelsea and Lane. So, we're all set for Friday night?"

"Definitely. I look forward to it."

They said their goodbyes, and then Johnny took off his gun belt and settled into his chair to relax and watch some television.

His call to Tanya had been an attempt to get Chelsea out of his mind. It didn't work as well as he'd hoped. Thoughts of Chelsea and what they had shared continued to run through his brain.

He must have dozed off, for the sound of gunshots jerked him awake and out of his chair. What the hell? As more gunfire boomed, he grabbed his gun from the holster and headed for the front door.

He must have dozed longer than he'd thought, as deep twilight had fallen. Still, he was able to see Caleb and Leroy pinned behind the gallon drums by gunfire coming from two, possibly three, men in the distance.

He saw Leroy returning fire, but he knew Caleb probably didn't have a weapon with him. He rarely carried a gun even when he was out and about the ranch. Johnny slid out his cabin door.

As the men in the field continued to shoot toward Caleb and Leroy, Johnny began shooting toward them. Luke appeared next to Johnny and added his firepower to Johnny's.

The men in the distance suddenly disappeared, and the night went still. "What is going on?" Luke asked, breaking the silence that had descended.

"Hell if I know. I heard the gunshots and came out here to see what was going on. Maybe Caleb can fill us in." With one eye on the place where the shooters had been, Johnny walked hurriedly to the barn with Luke by his side.

Caleb and Leroy stepped out from behind the drums.

"Thanks for the help," Leroy said with a cautious look toward the field.

"Either of you two want to fill us in on what's going on?" Johnny asked, his gaze going from Leroy to Caleb.

"We don't know," Caleb replied. "We were just hanging around out here, and all of a sudden those men appeared and started shooting at us."

"Did you recognize any of them?" Luke asked.

"Yeah, did you know who they were?" Johnny added.

Leroy and Caleb exchanged quick glances. "I have no idea who they were," Caleb replied.

"I didn't recognize any of them. It all happened too fast," Leroy said.

Johnny frowned, unsure if he believed them or not. "Have you two had trouble with anyone? Offended somebody?"

"Not me," Caleb said quickly. "I haven't even left the ranch in the last couple of weeks."

"I haven't had any trouble with anyone either. I've been keeping my nose to the grindstone at the Blacks' during the day and hanging out here with Caleb in the evenings," Leroy said.

"And you're positive you didn't recognize any of them," Johnny pressed.

The two men looked at each other and then back at Johnny. Both of them indicated they had no idea who the men were, but Johnny didn't believe them. There had to be a reason that somebody had been shooting at them.

Or had this been an attempt to take out another member of the King family?

"I'm going to drive up there and see if I can find anything that might give us a clue about them," Johnny said.

"I'll go with you," Luke replied.

"Do you think this was an attack on our family?" Luke asked minutes later when they were in Johnny's truck and headed toward the area where the men had been when they'd been firing their guns.

"Maybe," Johnny said. "I suppose it's possible that whoever shot Dad isn't done with us yet. However, I got the feeling Leroy and Caleb weren't telling us the whole truth about not knowing who the men were."

"The real question is what mess the two of them might be in," Luke said.

"I honestly don't know what to think about this," Johnny admitted.

He drove as far as he could into the field and then parked the truck, and the two brothers got out and walked to where Johnny thought the men had stood shooting. With the aid of powerful flashlights from Johnny's cabin, they began to scan the area.

Johnny shone his light in the distance where trees crowded together and the brush was thick and tangled. This was a field they didn't use because of the rise and fall of the land and the heavy woods.

Seeing nothing amiss, he continued his search on the ground. "The grass is trampled in patterns that could only be made by horses," he said.

"So, whoever it was, they rode in," Luke replied.

"It looks like it." Johnny tightened his hand around his flashlight. Was this really just another attack on his family, or was Caleb harboring secrets…dark secrets that could potentially get them all killed?

Chapter Seven

It had been another busy week for Chelsea. She'd bought herself a car, a midsize Ford that was bright red and had low mileage. She'd spent a day driving around on country roads, making turns left and right to familiarize herself after five years of not driving any kind of a vehicle.

It was Friday, and tonight she was going to the Red Barn with Melinda and Roger, although she'd insisted that she would meet the couple at the local bar. She knew they'd want to stay much later than she did so it was important she have her own set of wheels to come home in when she'd had enough of the loud music and socializing.

However, that was later tonight. Before the night's activity, her mother was coming over for lunch. It would be the first time her mother would be visiting her here, and Chelsea wanted everything to be perfect.

She checked the table, pleased with the fresh flower arrangement she'd bought earlier in the day. The water glasses were spotless, and her yellow dishes with the yellow-and-white-checkered cloth napkins looked cheerful and bright.

The chicken salad was in the refrigerator, ready to

be placed on the croissant rolls, and a large green salad awaited drizzling with homemade green goddess dressing. There was also cherry cheesecake from her mother's favorite bakery in town for dessert.

Jeb had continued to work on the house. He'd finished up the painting in her bedroom, and she had set him to work on the porch steps and railing before painting more inside. He'd finished the work on them late last night. He had three more rooms to paint upstairs, and then the entire outside of the house.

Charlie Harrison had sent several men to her place to install a security system, so she now felt safe in her own home. It had been a good week except for one thing… the absence of Johnny.

Even though she knew she needed to get over him, that there was no path forward for her with him, it was difficult to do. While her head had gotten his message loud and clear, her heart still refused to let go.

However, she couldn't think about him now, not with her mother arriving within minutes. She did one last run-through to make sure everything was dusted and clean, and by that time her mother was knocking on her door.

"Hi, come in," Chelsea greeted her mother with a smile.

"The place is a bit of an eyesore," Stella said with a frown.

"Jeb will be painting it all in the next couple of days," Chelsea replied. "Why don't you have a seat on the sofa so we can visit for a while. It seems like it has been forever since I've seen or talked to you." Chelsea gestured toward the sofa.

"Can't we just get right to lunch? I have a lot of things to do today, and I shouldn't be taking this time off as it is," Stella asked.

"Of course. Then come on into the kitchen. It will just take me a matter of minutes to get the meal on the table." Chelsea led her mother into the kitchen where Stella sat and gazed around. Chelsea got busy pulling things out of the fridge.

"It looks good in here," Stella said. "The fresh flowers on the table are a nice touch."

"Thanks. I thought you might enjoy them." Chelsea dressed the salad and then placed it on the table and then quickly put together the chicken croissants. After filling their glasses with ice and water, she then sat down across from her mother.

"Word on the street is you're definitely in position to become the next mayor," Chelsea said.

"Big John King had a good platform, and by me espousing the same values and goals he had for this town, I'm capturing the votes that would have gone to him."

"Maybe as mayor you can do something to help find his killer," Chelsea said.

"That would be nice, wouldn't it? I heard through the grapevine that you had a little excitement here too. Somebody tried to break in?"

"It was the same man who chased me through the pasture," Chelsea said.

Stella's nostrils thinned, and her lip curled up. "I'm sure whoever tried to break in here was hoping to get a stash of new items knowing that you'd just moved in."

"Maybe," Chelsea replied. The last thing she wanted was to get into an argument with her mother about what had happened. But Chelsea knew that the man trying to break in hadn't wanted any stash of new items. He'd wanted to hurt her…possibly kill her.

"Well, there's only a couple more weeks before the election. What all do you have planned to assure your success?" Chelsea asked, knowing her mother loved to talk about herself.

Stella lit up, and for the rest of the meal she talked about town-hall meetings and campaign gatherings and what she intended to do as mayor of the small town.

Once Stella was finished eating, she rose and headed for the front door. Chelsea had bagged up the cheesecake as her mother was taking the dessert with her. "Thank you for the meal. It was quite good, I must say. And I'll really enjoy the cheesecake later this evening."

"I'm so glad you enjoyed the meal," Chelsea replied.

"I'm glad it looks like you're settling in here nicely. Now, if you could just find a man for yourself."

Chelsea smiled. "I could say the same thing to you."

"I have never needed a man in my life, but you're weak, Chelsea. And you're young. You need a man to give me some grandbabies. I still can't believe you screwed things up so badly with Johnny."

"I guess Johnny wasn't written in the stars for me," Chelsea replied and couldn't help the sadness that laced her voice.

"Ah, I hear the regret in your voice. Unfortunately, we all have to live with the consequences of the choices we make in life. For me, my one regret was sleeping with your father. I knew he was no good, but he was a handsome, smooth-talking devil, and I let down my guard. Then the moment I told him I was pregnant, he ran for the hills or back to hell where he belonged."

It was a story Chelsea had heard for most of her life, and she believed it was at the root of why her mother didn't really love her.

Stella had been married to Jacob's father, but when Jacob was just a baby, Greg Black had died in a tragic farm accident. Stella had loved Greg, and she adored their son, but there had been far less love for the little girl whose father had abandoned her mother.

After Stella left, Chelsea cleaned up the kitchen and then went upstairs for a short nap before the night out. She awoke at five thirty, ate a leftover chicken croissant and then headed back upstairs to start getting ready for the night. She was meeting Melinda and Roger at seven in front of the popular bar.

The Red Barn was strictly casual, so Chelsea pulled on a pair of jeans and a fitted red blouse that hung just off her shoulders. She put her makeup on a little heavier, adding color to her cheeks and then focusing on her eyes.

When she was ready, it was time to go. She grabbed her house keys and set the alarm, then headed toward her car in the driveway.

As she drove toward the outskirts of town where the bar was located, she found herself thinking about the lunch with her mother. It had gone far better than Chelsea had expected. Maybe with Chelsea living separately but in the same town with her mother, they could build a new and better relationship. Chelsea certainly hoped so. She'd always longed for a loving relationship with her mother.

However, Chelsea wasn't weak, and she certainly didn't need a man to complete her. She had gone through some of the worst days of her life at the end of her stay in New York, and she'd gone through it all alone.

Needing a man and wanting one were two different things. She wanted Johnny, but she didn't need him. She wanted him, and he didn't want her.

She released a deep sigh. Maybe she'd meet somebody tonight who would spark her interest, somebody who would be interested in getting to know her. It would be nice to have somebody to share a meal with or spend an evening with.

As she drove, she told herself she needed to be open to meeting new people and reacquainting herself with others. She'd always been so wound up with Johnny she had never given other men in town a second look.

When she pulled up, the parking lot was already filling up. She saw Roger's truck and pulled into the empty space next to it. Melinda waved at her from Roger's passenger window.

They got out of their vehicles, and Melinda grabbed Chelsea's arm. "I was afraid you wouldn't come," she said.

"Well, I'm here," Chelsea replied. As she looked toward the large building with neon beer signs flashing in the windows, a wave of nervousness struck her.

She hadn't put herself out there in such a public forum since she'd returned to Coyote Creek. Would people believe the press that had excoriated her? Would they believe she was a drug addict who had self-destructed? Or a woman with mental issues? Would she be treated like a pariah? Would nobody be interested in approaching her?

"Come on, Chelsea. You'll be just fine," Melinda said as if she'd read Chelsea's mind.

"We're here for you," Roger added.

"Thanks. You're right, I'll be just fine," Chelsea replied firmly in an attempt to assure not only them but herself.

"Then let's get inside and get a table." Melinda headed toward the entrance with Chelsea and Roger trailing behind. Stepping inside the dim interior was like walking into another universe.

The air smelled of booze and greasy bar food, and the music piping in overhead was loud as peanut shells on the floor crunched underfoot.

Melinda led them to an empty table next to the large dance floor where several couples were already two-stepping to the country tune.

"What do you want to drink?" Roger asked her.

"Just a diet cola for me," Chelsea said.

"Nonsense," Melinda immediately said to Roger. "Get her a margarita, frozen like mine."

Chelsea started to protest but then decided to let Melinda have her way. Besides, it wouldn't hurt for Chelsea to have one drink while it was so early in the evening.

By the time Roger returned from the long bar on one side of the room, the place had grown more crowded. A blond man approached their table. He looked familiar to Chelsea, but his name escaped her.

"Chelsea." He greeted her with a wide, pleasant smile.

"Hi, Adam," Roger said, and instantly Chelsea remembered: Adam Pearson. He'd been in her high-school class and had always been nice to her.

"Hey, Adam," she now said. "How's it going?"

"Good, and it's great to see you back in town again. Would you take a turn on the dance floor with me?"

Chelsea hesitated for a long moment, and then Melinda unceremoniously pushed her off her chair. "She would love to dance with you, Adam," Melinda said.

Chelsea laughed. "I guess we're going to dance."

She and Adam moved to the large dance floor and began to dance to the rock music playing now. Adam was a good dancer, and Chelsea felt herself letting loose a bit.

"You know, I had a major crush on you in high school," he said to her as they walked back to her table.

"Really? I never knew that," she replied in surprise.

"A lot of guys were crushing on you back then, but nobody ever approached you because everybody was afraid of Johnny, and it was obvious you two were a strong couple," he said.

"Well, that was then, and this is now," she replied.

"So, if I was to work up the nerve to ask you out to dinner at the café one evening, would you be interested?" he asked.

"I don't know. I guess you'll have to work up the nerve to ask me and then we'll see," she replied. God, she was being flirtatious. She'd never flirted with anyone but Johnny. They exchanged numbers, and then Adam left her at the table and headed across the room to the bar.

"You could do much worse," Melinda said.

"Yeah, Adam is a good guy," Roger added.

But he isn't Johnny, a little voice whispered in her head. "I'm open to getting to know him better," Chelsea finally replied.

"That's my girl," Melinda exclaimed.

Over the next half an hour, Chelsea was surprised by how many men invited her to dance with them. She exchanged numbers with several of them, hoping that maybe she could move on from Johnny. She had to open herself up in order to possibly have a new love.

As the night went on, she and Melinda and Roger shared a lot of laughs. Chelsea finished her drink and then ordered a diet cola, knowing another alcoholic drink might make her too buzzed to drive home safely.

She was surprised by how much fun she was having, and then he walked in, Johnny with Tanya by his side, and Chelsea's heart plummeted to the ground.

HE SAW HER almost immediately. Chelsea looked totally hot in her tight jeans and the red blouse that exposed her beautiful shoulders. Dammit, he couldn't help the way his heart leaped at the sight of her.

Tanya must have seen her too, for she grabbed Johnny's arm and held tight. He smiled down at the dark-haired woman. "Let's find a table, and I'll get our drinks," he said, raising his voice to be heard over the loud music.

It took only minutes to wind through the crowd and claim one of the few empty tables that were left. Unfortunately, the table gave him a perfect view of Chelsea and her friends at their table.

He got Tanya settled in and then wove his way back toward the bar. He was greeted by friends and acquaintances on his way. When he got to the bar, he ordered himself a whiskey on the rocks, and for Tanya he ordered a gin and tonic with a twist of lime. He'd been dating Tanya long enough to know what she liked.

Once he returned to the table, he pulled Tanya out on the dance floor. The fast-paced music couldn't get Chelsea out of his head. Even when the music slowed and Tanya was dancing close to him, it did nothing but make him remember all the times he had danced with Chelsea.

What the hell was wrong with him? He hadn't been able to get Chelsea out of his mind since they had made love again. Even now, memories of the two of them kept crashing through his head.

He saw Chelsea was dancing with Adam Pearson. Adam was a nice guy, but he was all wrong for her. Chelsea needed somebody who would challenge her mentally with stimulating conversation, somebody who was as passionate about things as she was. She needed somebody who shared the same quirky sense of humor. She needed somebody like him.

At that very moment he realized he needed to stop seeing Tanya. It was unfair of him to continue to date her knowing there was never going to be any kind of a future with her. He enjoyed her company, but he wasn't going to marry her. He was wasting her time, and that wasn't right.

He didn't know if there was any kind of a future with Chelsea, but she felt like unfinished business, and he wouldn't have complete closure where she was concerned unless he finished that business once and for all.

However, he needed to have the difficult conversation with Tanya tonight. Now that he realized she would never be his person, it seemed important he break it off with her as soon as possible. The last thing he wanted to do was keep her from finding a real love that would lead to marriage and children.

He knew the minute Chelsea left the bar, for she seemed to take all the color, all the vibrancy of the place, with her. She'd left alone, which made him ridiculously happy.

Melinda and Roger left soon after Chelsea. He and Tanya stayed another hour or so. Thankfully Tanya had only had the one alcoholic drink, so her mind should be clear for the conversation he'd have with her when he took her home.

All too soon he was pulling up in front of her attractive ranch house, and a ball of dread hung heavy in his stomach. He really should have done this long before now, and it had nothing to do with Chelsea returning to Coyote Creek.

"Want to come in for a nightcap?" Tanya asked when he cut his engine.

Several times after going out he ended the night with a drink at her place. He definitely didn't want to have his conversation with her in the car. He respected her far more than that.

"Okay, I'll come in for a few minutes," he replied.

Tanya lived in a modest ranch-style house a block off Main Street. Her living room was decorated in earth tones, making it feel warm and welcoming. Once inside he declined the offer of another drink, and together they sat on the sofa.

"It was a fun evening. As always, thank you, Johnny,"

she said with a smile. It was a smile he knew he was about to knock off her lips.

"We need to talk, Tanya." Sure enough her smile instantly disappeared.

"You look quite serious," she observed.

"Tanya, I've really enjoyed the time we've spent together," he began. "But I'm sorry. I don't see our relationship proceeding any deeper, and dating me is really just a waste of your time."

Her brown eyes appeared to grow darker as she stared at him for a long moment. "It's her, isn't it?" A bitter laugh escaped her. "Of course it's her. I knew when she showed up back here in town she would ruin everything for us."

"This isn't about Chelsea and me, it is about us," he replied. "It's about me. I value your friendship, Tanya. But I don't see you as a romantic partner. I just don't have those kinds of feelings for you."

"Ah, so you're friend-zoning me." She raised one of her eyebrows and gazed at him with a hint of coldness in her eyes. "Have you slept with her yet?"

"That's really none of your business," he replied softly. "I'm sorry if I've hurt you. That was never my intention. I'd hoped that my feelings for you would move beyond caring about you into loving you, but that hasn't happened, and I don't believe it will."

Her gaze still held his, although she was utterly silent.

"Like I said, I'm really sorry, Tanya. I shouldn't have led you on for as long as I did."

"You're absolutely pathetic, Johnny," she said derisively. "You're still whipped over a woman who left you virtually at the altar. Chelsea is probably laughing over how easily she's wrapped you around her finger all over again."

Johnny winced and stood. "Tanya, I'd at least hoped we could still remain friends."

"Well, that's certainly not going to happen," she replied curtly. "You don't deserve my friendship."

"Then I'm sorry about that too," he said.

"Yeah, you're a sorry excuse of a man," she retorted. "You're a weasel, Johnny. I'm better for you than she will ever be. She's nothing but a joke, and you're an even bigger joke."

He headed for the door, refusing to sit and listen to her belittling words any longer. "Then I'll just say good-night now, and I'll see you around."

"Don't let the door hit you on your backside," she replied, the sarcasm still rife in her voice.

Johnny stepped out into the dark of the night and released a deep sigh. He knew he'd hurt Tanya, and he felt badly for that. Still, he'd been shocked by the vitriol in her voice, by the way she had responded to him. But he also felt a huge sense of relief.

With or without Chelsea being back in town, his breakup with Tanya would have happened anyway. He'd dated Tanya long enough to know he was never going to fall in love with her, and Tanya had mentioned several times that she was looking forward to marriage and having children. And he knew he wasn't the man to give those things to her. He would never be.

He headed for his truck in her driveway, and once inside, replayed Tanya's words. She'd had a tone he'd never heard from her before. It had been sarcastic and mocking and had completely shocked him.

Maybe he hadn't been all wrong to bring Tanya into Lane's sights. It had been obvious by her words and questions that she was extremely jealous of Chelsea. Had that jealousy driven Tanya to want to hurt Chelsea?

As thoughts of Tanya left his mind, visions of Chelsea appeared. He wished he could have shared a slow dance with her tonight. He'd always loved dancing with her. They moved perfectly together to the music, and he had loved the way her body always melded into his own.

She would lean her head into the crook of his neck, and her arms would wind around his neck, and her evocative scent would surround him. He would completely lose himself to the music and to her.

He snapped out of his memories of dancing with Chelsea and pulled away from Tanya's home. Instead of heading back to his ranch, he drove the streets of the small town, hoping to empty his head before going home and going to bed.

His father had loved not only their ranch but also this town where he'd been born and raised like his father before him. Big John had been the person people in Coyote Creek came to for advice, for personal and business loans and support. Johnny hadn't known just how many people in town his father had helped until the murder.

As Johnny leisurely drove down Main Street, he slowed down at each of the stores he knew his father had helped in one way or another. His father had encouraged everyone to shop local and keep their small-town economy strong.

God, he missed his dad. Every day he had a moment of wanting to talk to him, and then he'd remember that he could never talk to him again. The loss would pierce through his heart all over again. His dad would never see him get married or enjoy the grandchildren Johnny would have eventually given him.

It made him so angry that they still had no answers as to who had killed Big John. Dammit, somehow… someway Lane had to solve this murder. Johnny and the rest of his family deserved to know who had done it and why.

Had the murder really been because of a mayoral seat? Or had it had something to do with his father's business dealings? Or, worse than either of those two scenarios, had it been at the hands of his own flesh and blood, a son who had resented his father and had never felt loved by him?

He shoved these dark and troubling thoughts out of his head, knowing he'd never get to sleep tonight if he dwelled on them.

He finally turned down the street where Chelsea lived. He'd been surprised to see how much she'd gotten done the last time he was there. He wasn't surprised that she'd surrounded herself with vivid colors and textures. That's the way he'd always seen Chelsea…as bright colors and different textures and happiness.

As he drew closer to her house, he frowned. Something was in her yard. A sign of some kind. Maybe a poster for her mother's campaign? He'd begun to see them all around town. He pulled closer to the curb, and with the aid of his headlights he saw that it was no kind of campaign sign.

Despite the warmth of the night his blood chilled. The sign read A DEAD WOMAN LIVES HERE… BUT SHE WON'T BE LIVING HERE FOR LONG. THIS DEAD WOMAN WILL BE BURIED SOON. It was a nasty piece of work, obviously meant to terrorize and horrify Chelsea once again.

He could only assume she hadn't seen the sign yet, and as far as he was concerned, she wasn't going to see it. He parked, got out of his truck and strode across the lawn to the sign. He ripped it out of the ground and threw it in the bed of his pickup.

Although he wasn't ready to talk to Chelsea yet, he wanted to make sure she was okay, given the threat of the sign. Her living room light was on and so he crept across the lawn and peeked inside the slightly open blinds.

He breathed a sigh of relief as he saw her sitting on her sofa. She was clad in a nightshirt and was reading a book. She was safe and sound and that's all he cared about. He left the window and strode back to his truck.

Usually on a Friday night Lane was on duty until the bar closed at three, so Johnny drove directly to the police station. Once there, he parked the truck, grabbed the sign and headed inside.

He found Lane leaning over the front desk and chatting with the night receptionist and dispatcher, Walt Eaton. Walt was far beyond retirement years, but nobody knew exactly how old he really was. His hair was completely gray, but his blue eyes snapped with a youthfulness and a keen intelligence.

"Now, that doesn't look like a happy face, Chief, does

it?" Walt said. He moved his wheelchair back from the desk. "What's up, Johnny boy?"

Walt had been a deputy and a ranch worker for years. He was a well-known face around the community and had been an especially good friend of Johnny's father. A ranch accident with a tractor had partially paralyzed Walt in his lower limbs, but he was just as feisty as he'd always been.

"Hey, Walt. Lane." Johnny greeted the two and then turned the sign around so the two men could read it.

Walt released a low whistle. "Now, that's some piece of disgusting."

"I'm assuming Chelsea didn't see this, otherwise she'd be here with you," Lane said.

"I'm assuming she didn't see it either. I was on my way home from Tanya's and happened to drive by Chelsea's and found it in her yard. If at all possible, I'd like to keep this just between the three of us," Johnny said. "It's just meant to further terrorize her, and there's really no reason to let her know it was there."

"You know me, Johnny." Walt raised his fingers to his mouth and made a locking motion. "Tick a lock. Nobody will hear anything about this from me."

"Thanks, Walt. I appreciate it." Johnny knew the older man was as good as his word.

"I'm sure as hell not going to tell anyone unless I'm questioning somebody about it. I agree that there's no reason to frighten Chelsea even more than she's already been."

Lane frowned and stared at the sign once again. "It's written all in block letters which is going to make it more difficult to find the author, and I imagine it's written with plain red marker, also nearly impossible to trace."

Lane sighed in obvious frustration. "I've never felt less like a good lawman than in the past month or so. I haven't been able to find your father's killer, and I'm no closer to identifying Chelsea's attacker than the morning she told me about being chased through your pasture."

"Don't beat yourself up too much, Lane. You can only do what's humanly possible in both situations," Johnny said.

"If I find out who killed your daddy, I'll personally get out of this chariot and kick his ass from here to next week," Walt said fervently. "I miss that man, even though he used to beat me so badly in poker I was ashamed to show my face the next day."

A small laugh escaped Johnny. "Thanks, Walt."

"What worries me at the moment is the boldness of leaving this sign," Lane said. "It's announcing that a murder is intended and the potential killer is apparently feeling very confident."

"I'm assuming she got a security system put in?" Johnny asked for confirmation.

"She did. If there's a breach in either her doors or windows, it rings through straight to me and to the dispatcher's desk," Lane replied.

"That should keep her safe as long as she stays in her house," Johnny said with relief. "And I'll be sure to remind her that she needs to stay focused on her surroundings whenever she goes out anywhere."

"Maybe if we're lucky, something will break loose in both cases over the next couple of days," Lane said.

Johnny hoped so. He couldn't really move past his father's death until he had the answers he needed, and he would never be able to live with himself if something horrible happened to Chelsea. But right now that seemed like a very real possibility.

Chapter Eight

Chelsea had no plans to leave her house today. Jeb had called her earlier to tell her he wasn't feeling well and wouldn't be coming in to work. That gave her the perfect excuse to pull on an old pair of jogging shorts and a faded tank top and just chill for the day without seeing anyone.

If she was perfectly honest with herself she would admit that she was licking her wounds after seeing Johnny and Tanya together the night before. It had upset her more than she cared to admit. But she had to get used to it, and she positively had to get over him.

It was strange. She'd just assumed when she returned here Johnny would be lost to her. She'd just figured he'd have moved on, might be married and a family man. However, when she'd come back and found him single, when he'd been so kind to her and when he'd made love to her, she'd truly believed they were destined to be together once again. Now she had to readjust her thinking all over again.

She also had to admit that she'd enjoyed the night out at the Red Barn. As she carried her cup of coffee into her living room and settled in on her sofa, she thought about the night before.

It had been fun to cut loose with Melinda again and see some of the people she'd gone to school with. She'd ended up exchanging numbers with four different guys. They weren't Johnny, but nobody would ever fill the space in her heart that he had.

The standout of the men had been Adam Pearson. She'd ended up dancing with him a couple of times the night before, and if he called to ask her out, she supposed she might go out with him.

Realizing she was sick of thinking about it all, she turned on the television for some mind-numbing entertainment, and for the next hour she merely relaxed and sipped her coffee.

When she'd finished her cup, she paused the television and then headed back into the kitchen for a refill. She had just settled back on the sofa again when her doorbell rang.

Who could it be? Surely none of the men would just casually drop by for a chat so early on a Saturday morning and without calling first.

She jumped back up and approached the front door. Before she looked out the peephole, she ran a hand down her old, comfortable clothes and then through her hair which she'd barely brushed that morning.

She finally looked through the door, and her heart immediately quickened its pace. Johnny. What on earth was he doing here? She turned off the alarm and opened the door. Oh, he looked so handsome in his worn jeans and a blue T-shirt that did absolutely amazing things to his beautiful crystal-blue eyes.

"Hi, Chelsea… Can I come in?"

"Sure." As he moved past her, she caught a whiff of his fresh-scented cologne, and her heartbeat went even faster at the familiar scent. "Uh…would you like a cup of coffee?" she asked.

"That sounds great," he replied. "Do you have time to talk to me?"

"As you can see, I wasn't planning on going anywhere, so I've got all the time in the world. Let me just get your coffee." As he sank down on the sofa she went back into the kitchen.

Jeez, she should have put on better clothes and a little makeup this morning. The last person she'd expected to see this morning was Johnny. Why was he here? She poured a cup for him and then carried it into the living room and set it on the coffee table in front of him.

"Thanks," he said.

She sank down at the opposite end from him and looked at him expectedly. She couldn't begin to guess why he was here or what he might need to talk to her about.

"I was surprised to see you last night at the Red Barn," he said as he picked up the coffee cup.

"Melinda forced me to get out of the house and enjoy a little social time," she replied. "I have to admit I really enjoyed being out and kicking up my heels a little bit."

"I'm glad you enjoyed yourself. You looked really pretty in that red blouse."

"Thank you." A flutter of warmth washed through her at his compliment. "Did you and Tanya have a good time?" she asked even as the thought of the two together hurt her heart.

"It was okay. When we got back to her house, I told her I wouldn't be dating her anymore."

"Oh… Why?" Chelsea's heart renewed its quickened pace. "From what I understood, the two of you had been dating for some time."

"We had been, but I realized last night the relationship wasn't going anywhere and never would. I just saw her as a friend to pass time with, and I thought that it really wasn't fair to her, so I told her we wouldn't be going out together anymore."

"Oh," Chelsea repeated, unsure what to say. She watched him take a sip of the coffee and then place his cup back on the table top. "Uh, how did she take it?"

"Surprisingly badly. I saw a bit of her ugly side when I told her," he replied. "Actually, I was surprised by her unpleasantness."

Chelsea kept her mouth shut tight, even though there was a part of her that wanted to shout *I told you so*. He took another drink, and then an awkward silence ensued.

He finally looked around and then gazed at her with a smile. "The place looks really good, Chelsea." He held the eye contact with her for another long moment and then averted his gaze.

"Thanks." What, exactly, was going on here? Had he just stopped over to compliment her decorating style? Or to tell her he broke up with Tanya? "Johnny, what are you doing here?" she finally asked when the silence had gone on between them for too long.

He leaned back against the sofa and raced a hand through his thick hair and then stared at her intently. "Chelsea, I need some answers."

"Answers? About what?"

"About what happened five years ago. About why I wasn't enough for you. Why didn't I hear about your dreams to become a model in New York before the day you broke up with me and left town? I mean, did I somehow miss something, Chelsea?" His eyes held a shimmer of pain as he held her gaze.

Each word he said broke her heart. She'd never wanted him to think that he had been somehow lacking. Rather, she had been the one who had been lacking in self-worth. She had been the one who had been so broken.

"Oh, Johnny." She moved closer to him on the sofa. "It wasn't about you. It was never about you. It was about me being enough for me. Or, actually, about me not being enough for myself."

She got up, finding it difficult to stay seated and go back to that troubling time in her life. "I shared so many things with you, Johnny." She moved to the other side of the coffee table and began to pace back and forth. "I shared my dreams and my hopes, my passion and love. But there were some things I didn't share with you… things I kept deep inside."

Johnny leaned forward, confusion radiating from his eyes. "Things like what? Tell me, Chelsea. Help me to understand what happened with us."

She stopped moving and forced herself to go back in time. "I was never enough for my mother, and she reminded me of that every day. I know we used to joke about Stella, but you have no idea how much her lack of support or love hurt me, how much it played in my mind. I mean, if my own mother couldn't love me, then how could anyone else?"

"Oh, Chelsea…baby." He started to rise, but she put up her hand to keep him in place. He needed to hear all of it to understand why she had left him.

"Then there was the constant belittling by Tanya and her mean girlfriends. Every day I was told I was ugly and crazy-looking with my big eyes and skinny legs. I was told I looked like an alien or an insect." She paused, her emotions suddenly threatening to overtake her.

She drew several deep breaths, released them slowly and then continued. "I was also told over and over again that you were dating me out of pity and that the only way I was keeping you was by having wild sex with you. And that was only happening because you probably put a paper bag over my head so you didn't have to look at me."

"Surely you didn't believe any of that," Johnny exclaimed.

She frowned. "When you hear things like that over and over again, it tends to get deep into your head, into your very soul."

"They were bullying you." There was a touch of anger in Johnny's voice. "I knew some of those girls weren't nice to you, but I didn't know the full extent of it. Chelsea, you should have come to me. You should have told me more about it."

"They were pretty careful about not being too mean to me in front of you, but when you weren't around all bets were off. And I didn't tell you because I was embarrassed and ashamed." She began to pace again. "Anyway, on the day I broke up with you, I'd gotten a particularly nasty note telling me how ugly I was and how unworthy I was to be with you. It finally broke me." Tears blurred her vision.

She swiped her cheeks where the hot tears had fallen. "I had to get away from here. I had to get away to figure out who I really was away from the constant noise of Tanya and her friends, away from my critical mother."

Johnny got up and walked over to her. When he reached her, he wrapped his arms around her and gazed intently into her eyes. "You should have told me all this. You should have told me about your insecurities."

She shook her head. "Johnny, don't you understand? You couldn't fix me. No matter how much you told me you loved me, I had to get away and fix myself." She stepped out of his embrace.

"But you must have felt some vindication. You became a top model. People described you as *hauntingly beautiful* and *dramatically gorgeous*." She looked at him in surprise. "I followed your career, Chelsea, and you proved all those mean girls wrong."

"It's funny, I didn't find my self-worth on a runway or through being a model. I found it in the quiet moments I spent alone in my apartment. I spent hours in self-reflection and deciding what was important to me and what was not. I realized it didn't matter what other people thought about my looks. All that was important was how I felt about myself, and I realized I was okay with me."

She turned and walked back to the sofa and flopped down. He quickly joined her there, sitting right at her side. "I wasn't worthy of your love, Johnny, only because I had to discover my own worth."

"So, what really happened to bring you back here?" he asked.

She knew he was asking about the drug rumors that had plagued her in the tabloids after her infamous fall from a runway. "I'd already decided I wanted to come back here, but I was under contract with my agent, and I intended to finish that out and then move back."

She changed positions as a new rush of emotion swept through her. "It was Fashion Week, and I'd been chosen to walk in a high-profile designer's show. That day when I fell off the runway, I had gotten up that morning not feeling well. I'd been on a four-hundred-calorie-a-day diet for three weeks in order to lose ten more pounds that my agent insisted on, which I needed to do to fit in the dresses I was going to wear. Anyway, I felt a bit light-headed, but knew the show must go on."

Once again a wave of emotion threatened to overwhelm her. She swallowed hard against it. "By the time I got ready to walk the runway, I was dizzy and on the verge of being disoriented, and in the middle of my walk, I passed out and fell. I woke up in the hospital where I was told that I was half-starved and severely dehydrated."

Once again, she took several deep breaths and let them out slowly. "And that's when the rumors began."

"About you being on drugs," Johnny said softly.

She nodded. "About me doing drugs and having severe mental issues. I have my suspicions about who started those vicious rumors. There was another model. Her model name is Verda. Verda and I seemed to always be pitted against each other when it came to jobs. Usually, I got the jobs over her. I know she hated me, and she was very ambitious, and I believe she started the rumors to get me out. Melinda, as my publicity person, tried her best to fight against the rumors, but in the end nothing she did worked. My agent dropped me, so once I made arrangements to get out of the two apartment leases, I was free to come home."

"Are you going to miss New York?" he asked. "Is there a chance you'll go back to modeling again?"

"No chance whatsoever. My time there was never about the modeling. I know it sounds cliché or like a cop-out, but it was about me finding me, and I did that." She smiled at him. "I don't give a damn if every person in this town thinks I'm ugly. I don't need anyone to define me or try to demean me. I define myself, and I like who I am."

"I'm glad you got what you needed, Chelsea." He hesitated and then asked, "Did you ever think of me while you were gone?"

"Oh, Johnny, I thought about you every night." She leaned forward and stroked her fingers down the side of his beloved face. "I thought about you all day long, and every night I fell asleep with thoughts of you playing in my mind. But I knew I'd hurt you terribly, and I just figured I'd blown it with you. I expected to come back here and find you married and with a child or two."

"But I saw photos of you out with that actor, and the articles talked about the two of you being madly in love," he said.

She dropped her hand from his face. "Anthony Winchester. The dates were strictly for publicity. Anthony was an arrogant little twit who I found repulsive, but my agent set up the dates in hopes of jump-starting his career. It was always you, Johnny. There has never been anyone else for me."

Her heart trembled in her chest as she held his gaze. She had bared her very soul to him, and there was nothing else she could say.

He frowned and cast his gaze to the wall beside her. When he looked at her once again, his eyes held a sadness that pierced her to her very soul.

In her need to find herself, had she forever lost him? She'd always assumed that had been the price she paid. He'd confirmed that fact after he'd slept with her, but a small hope had ignited in her chest when he'd shown up on her doorstep today. But the sadness she saw on his features doused that optimism.

"I'm just sad that we lost five years together," he finally said.

"I am too," she replied. "When I left here, I never dreamed I'd be away so long. I never dreamed I'd become a model in such demand, and for a while life and time got away from me," she replied.

"Chelsea, it's always been you and only you. I tried like hell to move on from you, but in five years I couldn't."

He leaned toward her. "I want to try it again, Chelsea. Obviously, the timing wasn't right for us before. God help me, but I want to see if we can get it right this time."

He leaned forward and captured her lips in a kiss that shot a sweet warmth through her. It was a kiss that filled her with hope and possibility, even as a small voice whispered inside that it was just possible he might be playing with her heart to get revenge for her breaking his heart years ago.

JOHNNY WALKED OUT of Chelsea's house with the imprint of her lips still warm on his. Even though they had already had sex since she'd been back, they had both agreed to take things slowly this time, and so they were going out to dinner together the next night.

He hadn't known about all the deeply emotional issues she'd been battling years ago, and it somehow hurt that she hadn't been able to share that with him then. He still wasn't sure he trusted a hundred percent that she could be happy here in Coyote Creek. He wasn't totally certain she could be completely happy with him and his quiet ranch life.

There was that little piece of his heart he couldn't quite give to her because he couldn't quite believe she'd be here long-term…to be his forever. And he wanted forever with her.

He was glad he hadn't told her about the sign in her yard, although before he'd left, he'd reminded her that she had to be careful whenever she went out of her house until her would-be attacker was in jail.

When he'd handed the sign over to Lane, before he'd left the police station, the chief had told him he'd checked out both the stalkers Chelsea had mentioned, and both people had been ruled out as suspects. According to the NYPD, one of their officers had checked them out, and both were still in New York and had not traveled recently.

Johnny was therefore back to knowing that her assailant was somebody here in town. Tanya? After having that talk with Tanya on Friday night, he found it much more plausible that it could be her.

While he didn't believe Tanya would really harm anyone, he could see her tormenting Chelsea, especially since she'd shown him a different side of herself the last time he'd spoken to her.

He couldn't believe how truly hateful Tanya and her girlfriends had been to Chelsea all through school. When she'd related to him all the hurtful things they had said to her, his heart had absolutely ached for her.

He had a much better understanding now of the forces that had driven her away from him and from Coyote Creek. And while he wished she had been able to discover her love for herself here in town with him at her side, that simply hadn't been the way it had played out.

Still, his mind returned to the real question at hand. If it wasn't Tanya who was terrorizing Chelsea, then who? Was there some man in town who had harbored a secret rage against Chelsea? Maybe Adam Pearson? Johnny knew Adam as a nice guy, but it had been obvious in the bar that he was interested in Chelsea.

Adam had never married, and as far as Johnny knew he hadn't dated much. Had Adam been obsessed with Chelsea since high school? Had he been angry that he hadn't managed to garner any interest from her?

Johnny mentally shook his head. If he was so good at investigating, he would have solved his father's murder by now. What he really needed to do was get back to the ranch business and leave the investigating to Lane and his force.

Throughout the rest of the afternoon and the next

day, all he could think about was having dinner with Chelsea. He realized she wasn't the same rather-fragile young woman who had left Coyote Creek five years ago. She had a new confidence that shone from her eyes, an attitude he found very sexy.

Their relationship would now be different than it had been before. They both had changed and grown over the years apart, and he was eager to explore the changes and see if their relationship was as strong as it had been before the time and distance.

He knew that he was possibly setting himself up for a new heartache where she was concerned. But he'd never be able to truly move on unless he took this one last chance with her. However, he still intended to hold back some pieces of his heart, just in case she took off on him once again.

The next evening when he picked her up for dinner, it was difficult to think about holding back anything. Before he could get out of his pickup, she flew out of her front door with a big smile on her face.

"Hi," she said as she got into his truck.

"Hi, yourself," he replied with a smile of his own. "You look beautiful," he added. She wore a green blouse exactly the color of her eyes and a pair of white capris. White earrings dangled from her ears, and her blond hair sparkled brightly in the sunshine.

"Thanks," she replied. "You clean up real nice too."

He laughed. He hadn't exactly dressed up for dinner at the café. He wore jeans and a button-down, short-sleeved blue shirt. "Thanks. I hope you're hungry."

"I'm absolutely starving. What's the special on Sunday nights?"

"Hot turkey sandwiches with mashed potatoes and gravy and a side of corn casserole and cranberry salad," he replied. As always the scent of her was familiar and enchanting. She smelled like lilacs and sunshine… She smelled like home.

"I'm not sure what I'm going to get, but it's definitely going to include some mashed potatoes," she replied.

"That's good. It wouldn't hurt you to put on some weight." He flashed her a quick glance. "Did I just offend you?"

"No, not at all. I know I'm too thin, and I'm eager to eat my way back to a healthier weight. After starving myself for the last five years, I dream about milkshakes and french fries and chocolate cake and ice cream."

"And here I thought all you ever dreamed about was me," he replied teasingly.

"Oh, yeah, that too." Her eyes sparkled brightly, and then she suddenly frowned. "Are you expecting trouble tonight?"

He knew she was talking about the fact that he had on his holster and gun. "No, not at all. But since my father's murder, I've been wearing my gun most of the time when I go out," he replied, not wanting to worry her about her own situation.

It was true that he'd taken to wearing his gun whenever he came into town since his father's murder, but now he wore it for a second reason…to protect Chelsea. Nobody was going to harm her as long as she was with him.

Thankfully she didn't press the issue. They had some small talk on the drive to the café. He told her about things on the ranch, and she talked about her quiet day and what she'd watched on television.

Sunday nights the café was always packed, and tonight was no exception. They had to park a block and a half away and walk, but the evening was pleasant, and as he grabbed her hand with his, a swell of deep contentment filled him. The only thing that would have made his life better was if he'd been pushing a stroller with their child in it. But he was getting way ahead of himself.

He didn't quite trust her yet. Despite the conversation they'd shared the day before, he still wasn't a hundred percent sure she was truly here to stay. It was going to take time for him to really be all in with her.

But he wasn't letting any doubts ruin this evening with her. She looked amazing, and despite all the weight that was on his shoulders, a lightness had descended on him the moment Chelsea had climbed into his truck.

They entered the café, and his ears were assaulted by the sounds of happy chatter and laughter and the clink of silverware. The aromas were mouthwatering: warm bread and a variety of meats cooking and sugary treats.

For a moment they stood just inside the door as he looked around for an empty booth or table. He spied an open booth toward the back and led her to it.

They settled in and opened the menus. "Oh my gosh, everything looks so good," Chelsea said.

"Feel free to order whatever your heart desires," he replied.

"What are you having?"

"A steak and a baked potato," he replied without hesitation. "They actually grill a really good steak here."

"I think I'm having the special." She closed the menu. "And chocolate cake for dessert. Does Rosie still own this place?"

"She does." Rosie Graham was a tiny woman who, according to the rumors, ran the café with an iron fist. Even though she had a bit of a temper, she cooked great food and baked like an angel.

"Oh, good. Then I know the cake will be awesome," Chelsea replied.

Their waitress arrived and took their orders, and while they waited for their food they talked about the mild weather that might be broken in the next couple of days with some spring storms in the forecast. He knew she hated storms, but they were a part of living in the Midwest.

They also chatted about who she'd seen at the Red Door and various people they'd gone to school with. By that time the waitress had arrived with their orders.

For the next few minutes, they were silent as they ate. He loved watching her eat with such gusto. Tanya had always picked at her food and left more on the plate than she ate.

Thoughts of Tanya brought up concerns about the person who was after Chelsea. Was it really possible that jealousy had driven Tanya to attempt the attacks on Chelsea? At least Johnny knew when Chelsea was out with him she was safe, and that's why he'd worn his gun tonight.

They lingered over dessert and coffee. True to her word, she ate a large piece of cake with ice cream and then leaned back against the booth and released a huge satisfied sigh. "I'm totally stuffed," she said.

"Good," he replied. "Ready to take a walk back to my truck?"

She grinned. "I feel like I need to take a four-mile walk to work off some of this food."

"Well, I'm not up for that," he returned with a smile of his own. "A walk to the truck will have to do." He motioned to the waitress to bring the check.

Minutes later they headed to the exit. They nearly bumped into Wayne Bridges and his wife and several other people who were coming in with him.

Johnny immediately stiffened as he eyed the man who had been running against his father for mayor. Wayne was definitely at the top of the suspect list.

He was a big man with a barrel chest, and hearing him laughing with his friends shot a jagged arrow of grief through Johnny.

If he'd killed Big John and Johnny got evidence of that, he would make sure the man never laughed again.

Chapter Nine

Police chief Lane Caldwell pulled into his driveway, parked and turned off his car. It was just after eleven, and as he got out of his vehicle, a bolt of lightning split the dark skies overhead. A moment later a rumble of thunder sounded.

The wind whipped around him as he hurried to his front door. As he unlocked it, the first raindrops began to fall. The stormy weather definitely was a perfect reflection of his mood.

He stepped into the living room where a lamp in the corner created a soft glow. Despite his mood, he smiled. Rebecca never forgot to turn on the light for him.

As he turned off the lamp, lightning slashed through the darkness followed by a crash of thunder. He walked down the hallway to the master bedroom where Rebecca was sitting up in bed with a book in her lap.

When he saw her a calmness filled him. Her long, brown hair fell around her shoulders and her heart-shaped face was one he never tired of looking at. Unfortunately, they had wanted children but had not been able to have any, but they'd always had each other. When she saw him she put her book on the nightstand next to her.

"I figured you'd be asleep by now," he said to her.

"Really? The storm overhead isn't exactly making lullaby music right now," she replied. She watched as he took off his gun belt and placed it on the top of the chest of drawers. He then sank down on the edge of the bed with a deep sigh.

"You're later tonight than usual for a Wednesday night," she said as he took off his shoes and socks.

"Yeah, I was about ready to come home earlier, but then a call came in from Hannah. Jackson was all liquored up and being combative with her. I headed over there, and it took me about an hour to finally get the man in bed." He stood to finish undressing.

Hannah Elder and her husband, Jackson, were fixtures around town. They were both in their seventies and got along really well until Jackson decided to get his nose in the sauce.

"Just what you need with everything else on your mind."

He nodded as a deep weariness swept over him. He shucked down to his boxers and then went into the adjoining bathroom to wash his face and brush his teeth before bed.

When he was finished, he stared at his reflection in the mirror. He was forty years old, but at the moment he looked like he was closer to fifty.

He frowned and shut off the bathroom light and then returned to the bedroom. He slid into bed, and immediately Rebecca reached for his hand.

"Talk to me, honey," she said softly. After twenty years of marriage, she knew him and all his moods quite well. Tonight, his utter defeat was profound. She squeezed his hand, and her soft blue eyes gazed at him lovingly.

He released a deep sigh. "Maybe it's time I retired."

A small laugh escaped her. "Honey, you're way too young to even think about retiring."

"Then maybe I need to resign and get a job flipping burgers or sweeping floors," he replied.

Once again Rebecca laughed. "You were born to be a law officer. It's the job you always wanted, so what's really going on with you tonight, Lane?"

He released another deep sigh. "I don't know. I'm just feeling more than a bit defeated tonight."

"Are you talking about John King's murder?"

He nodded. "That, and whoever is after Chelsea."

"You can only do what you can do, Lane. You're a good sheriff, a thorough and intelligent man. What exactly happened today that threw you for a loop? What's different today from yesterday?"

"Aside from the fact that I haven't been able to solve these crimes and another day has passed?" He released her hand and instead raked his hand through his hair. "I got a call from the governor this afternoon. You know he and Big John were good friends. Anyway, the governor wanted to know if I was any closer to finding John's killer, and I had to confess to him that the case has stalled."

"Oh, honey, I know that must have been difficult for you." Rain began to pelt against the window as the storm continued to rage. It seemed somehow appropriate that they would be talking about murder and mayhem on a dark and stormy night. "I know Johnny mentioned that he wanted you to look at Caleb for the crime. Have you interviewed him again?"

"I have. He told me when the murder occurred, he was in a field taking pictures of things he wanted to paint."

"Do you believe him?"

"I do. He's a strange man. Maybe I'm missing something, but I just can't see him killing his own father. I feel it in my gut that Wayne is behind the murder. Unfortunately, my gut instinct isn't enough to bring him in for an arrest."

Rebecca straightened up. "Do you really think Wayne actually pulled the trigger?"

Lane had thought about that question for some time now. "I don't think Wayne would actually get his hands dirty. He's got a couple of ranch hands who are fiercely loyal to him. One of them, Peter Jeffries, has won a number of marksmanship medals. He's a deadeye with a rifle. I think he's the one who actually pulled the trigger, and I think he was probably paid a handsome price for doing it. But so far there's no sign of any money exchanged between the two."

"If Wayne or one of his minions really killed John because John was set to become the next mayor, then you better warn Stella Black, because right now it looks like she's beating the pants off the competition," Rebecca said.

"I already spoke to her about it. I told her she needed to watch her back, and since then I've noticed that when she's out and about town, she has a couple of her ranch hands with her as obvious protection."

"As far as John's murder, I believe sooner or later

somebody is going to get drunk and say too much, and the killer will be exposed."

"That would be nice," Lane replied.

"As far as Chelsea is concerned, sooner or later the perp will overplay his hand, and he'll be exposed as well."

"Aren't you the optimist tonight?" Lane said with a weary smile at her.

"I just believe good will always overcome evil. I also know that secrets are hard to keep in this town. Eventually you'll get the bad guys in jail. I have complete faith in you, Lane."

He leaned forward and kissed the woman who had been and still was his lover, his partner and his best friend. "I love you, my sweet Becky."

She placed her hand on his cheek, her gaze soft. "And I love you, my sweet Lane." She dropped her hand from his face, "Now, what you need to do is get some sleep. You've been working long hours, and I know how exhausted you've been."

"I am tired," he admitted.

"It sounds like the storm is passing, and hopefully you'll have good dreams and deep rest," she replied. "Ready for the light to go out?"

"Ready."

A half an hour later Lane remained wide awake, a million thoughts chasing sleep away. The governor's call to him today had added immeasurable pressure on him. He had no idea if Johnny was behind the call or not. It didn't really matter.

The call was a reminder of just how powerful the

King family was, and if they decided to use that power against Lane, they could oust him from office.

Still, Rebecca was right. He could only do what he could do, and right now the odds were stacked against him. He had a murderer running loose in his town, and another would-be killer plotting against Chelsea.

How soon before the person plotting against Chelsea made another move? How soon before that person was successful in killing her?

How long before John's murderer decided somebody else needed to die? How emboldened would he be, given he'd already gotten away with killing somebody?

Lane finally fell asleep and into dreams of faceless shooters and ski-masked monsters.

CHELSEA GOT OUT of her car and nervously ran her hand down her navy skirt. She hoped the navy-and-white blouse coupled with the skirt she had on gave her a professional look. For the first time in a long time, she was going to apply for a real job.

It didn't matter that she was applying for a job in Johnny's sister's store. She was still nervous about it. In the past week she'd given a lot of thought as to what she wanted to do with her life.

She knew working in Ashley's store would be fun. The store contained a variety of beautiful knickknacks and candles, lovely costume jewelry and a small rack of colorful dresses. It was the kind of place she'd love to work.

She hadn't told Johnny she was applying for a job with his sister. She didn't want him to put in a good word for her, and she definitely didn't want Ashley to feel any pressure to hire her.

Smoothing her skirt one last time, Chelsea walked into the store. A tiny bell tinkled to announce her arrival. The air inside smelled pleasantly of fresh spring flowers and ocean waters.

"Hi, Chelsea," Ashley greeted her from a chair behind the glass counter that displayed the jewelry and held a cash register on top.

"Hi, Ashley," Chelsea replied.

Ashley moved from behind the counter, a smile on her lips as she approached where Chelsea stood just inside the door. "Is there anything specific you're looking for today that I can help you with?"

"A job?"

Ashley looked at her in surprise. "Are you serious?"

"Dead serious. I'd love to work here, Ashley. I love what you sell, and I could seriously sell all the items with enthusiasm to shoppers." Chelsea shut her mouth, aware that maybe she was coming on too strong.

"Why don't you come on back to my office where we can sit and chat." Ashley led the way to the back of the store and through a beaded curtain.

Ashley's so-called office consisted of two folding chairs set up amid boxes of inventory. Ashley sat on one and gestured Chelsea to the other.

"Ashley, I certainly don't want you to feel any pressure about this just because I'm back together with Johnny," Chelsea said hurriedly.

"Thanks, Chelsea. I appreciate that." Ashley frowned thoughtfully. "Actually, you approaching me about this now is perfect timing. It's been just me running this shop since I opened it, but I've been working twelve-hour days, and I don't have time for anything else. Since Dad's death I really need to spend more time with my mom, and I've been considering hiring somebody here to help me out."

"Ashley, I'd be available to work whatever hours you need me to," Chelsea replied.

"Okay, then. You're hired."

"I am?" A wave of excitement swept through Chelsea. "That was way easier than I expected."

Ashley laughed. "You just happen to be the right person who showed up at the right time."

"I promise you won't regret hiring me. I'm reliable, and I'll work hard for you."

Her new boss smiled. "Why don't you come in tomorrow morning about nine, and I'll train you on the register, then we can talk about your hours."

Chelsea jumped up from the chair. "Thanks, Ashley. I'll see you at nine tomorrow."

Ashley got up, and together the two women headed back toward the front door. "By the way, how are things going with you and Johnny?" Ashley asked.

"Good. We're still taking things slow and learning how we've each changed in the last five years," Chelsea replied.

Ashley held her gaze for a long moment. "Just don't break his heart again, Chelsea."

"I'm all in with him, Ashley. I love him with all my heart. I've always loved him, and I'm hoping he will be my happily-ever-after."

Ashley held her gaze for another long moment and

then nodded as if satisfied by what she saw. "I'm hoping that too."

"Thanks. I'll see you in the morning." Chelsea walked out to cloudy skies, but she felt as if the sun was shining in her heart.

Things were going well with Johnny, and she had landed a job she was looking forward to performing. When she got into the car, her first thought was to call Johnny and tell him about her new job, but she decided to wait. He was coming over for dinner, and she'd tell him then.

The past week she'd seen Johnny twice, although they had talked on the phone every evening before bedtime. She would have loved to be in his bed each night, but he had been serious about taking things slowly.

There had been no more lovemaking between them. Instead they spent their time together talking about both silly and serious topics. They were learning things about each other…things that had changed about themselves during the time they had been apart.

Nothing she'd learned about Johnny had changed her mind about him. He was still the man she loved… would always love. She wanted to marry him and be his wife. She wanted to give him babies and build a family with him.

But Johnny hadn't offered to give her engagement ring back. She sensed that he was holding back, and that scared her more than a little bit. She'd told Ashley the truth: she was all in with Johnny. She always had been, despite the difficult choice she'd made years ago.

She just wasn't sure if he was all in on her. She couldn't blame him for being a bit wary, given what she'd done to him years ago. All she could do was keep on telling him that he was the one and only for her and that she would love him through eternity. Hopefully he'd quickly come to believe that she was his forever.

She arrived at her house, which was now newly painted an attractive light gray with darker gray shutters at all the windows. She immediately headed for the kitchen.

Tonight, she was showing Johnny her love for him by cooking one of his favorite meals. She knew he loved his mother's spaghetti and meatball recipe, so the day before she'd called Margaret to get the recipe.

Right now, she needed to get the tomato sauce cooking and then add the meatballs in to cook with the sauce. Thankfully it was relatively early so she'd have it all ready by six o'clock when Johnny was set to arrive.

Forty-five minutes later she dropped the last meatball into the simmering sauce. She then made herself a cup of coffee and sank down at the table. Her gaze automatically went to the back door, where the plywood still covered the broken windowpanes. She should have had the door fixed by now, but for some reason she'd been reluctant to do so. The plywood was a reminder she needed to be careful when she was out and about and when she was home alone.

Thankfully, nothing frightening had happened since that night. She hoped that whoever hated her was over it now and any threat against her was gone. Still, she intended to remain vigilant. Certainly, the alarm system made her sleep more easily at night and feel safe whenever she was in the house.

She jumped as her phone rang. She picked it up to

see that the caller identification said *A. Pearson*. "Hi, Adam," she said when she answered.

"Hey, Chelsea. How are things going with you?" His voice was deep and friendly.

"Good. What about you?"

"Life has been good. I'm staying busy at my office. You know I sell insurance…have my own agency now."

"No, I didn't know that. Congratulations on having your own agency," she replied.

"Thanks. Anyway, life has been going good, but it would be much better if you would go out with me this Friday night. Maybe have some dinner at the café and then kick up our heels at the Red Barn." He laughed. "I'm calling because I finally got up the nerve to ask you out."

"Oh, Adam. I'm so sorry, but Johnny and I are back together."

There was a moment of silence, and then he laughed again. "Wow, that certainly happened fast. I guess that means I'm out in the cold once again." His voice sounded less friendly now.

"What do you mean by *out in the cold once again*?" she asked curiously.

"All through high school I kept waiting for a blip in your relationship with Johnny so I could get a chance to go out with you."

"Really," she replied in stunned surprise.

"Yeah. I told you the other night at the Red Barn that I had a major crush on you back then. I meant what I said. Oh, well, I guess Johnny wins again."

"I'm so sorry, Adam. I hope you find the woman who is perfect for you."

"Yeah, thanks. I'll see you around." He didn't wait for her reply before hanging up.

Chelsea set her cell phone back on the table. She'd definitely found the brief conversation a bit troubling. Was it possible Adam had resented her all through high school? Was it possible his resentment had grown through the years and he hated her so much now he'd come after her? It sounded crazy, but murders had happened for lesser motives.

Was Adam her stalker? A shiver suddenly walked up her spine. If so, had she just given him another reason to hate her…to want to kill her?

JOHNNY PULLED UP in front of Chelsea's house, and a sweet rush of anticipation swept through him. It had been a couple days since he'd seen her. The storms that had blown through a couple of days ago had partially ripped down a tin-roofed outbuilding, and since that time he and two of his ranch hands had been working late into the evenings to fix the building.

If he followed his heart, he would tell her to sell her house and move in with him. But his head still wasn't all in with her. He still had doubts about her being happy here after the glamorous way she'd lived in New York City. He just wished he could convince himself she was truly here to stay. He didn't even know for sure what would have to happen for him to give her the last pieces of his heart.

He was adamant that they take things slowly. While he would have gladly taken her to bed and made love to her night after night, he wanted to keep their sexual relationship out of it for now. It was easy to love Chelsea when they were making love, but he wanted to make sure their relationship was much deeper than the physical pull they had toward each other.

He got out of the truck and a moment later knocked on the door. She answered with a wide smile that instantly warmed his heart. "Come on in," she said invitingly.

"Hmm, something smells really good," he said as he stepped inside.

"It's one of your favorites. Spaghetti and meatballs. I even called your mother yesterday to get the recipe."

"You did?" He grinned at her. "Mom actually gave you her secret recipe?"

"She did, and I followed it to a T. Come sit down. Let's chat a bit before we eat," she said.

He sat on the sofa next to her. As always, she looked beautiful clad in a pair of jeans and a green-and-white-striped blouse. Her green eyes sparkled brightly as she faced him. "Guess what."

"What?" he replied.

"I got a job today."

He looked at her in surprise. "Really? Where?"

"I start tomorrow morning at your sister's shop."

"How did that come about?" He was happy she had gotten a job. He didn't think it was healthy for anyone to sit around day after day with nothing to do. He believed it was important that people worked, no matter what kind of work it was. It promoted a sense of pride and confidence.

"I went in to talk to her this morning and walked out with the job." She looked at him proudly. "And I don't think it had anything to do with the fact that you and I are back together."

"That's great, Chelsea, and Ashley wouldn't have hired you if she didn't think you'd be an asset, family ties be damned."

Her smile grew thoughtful. "I'm also kind of thinking about starting a blog."

"A blog about what?" he asked curiously. He didn't know that much about social media things other than online banking and paying bills.

"I was thinking about it being a kind of cautionary tale about the modeling world. Letting young girls know that compromising their health isn't an option and things like that. I'd like to educate young women on what is acceptable and what is not."

Once again, he looked at her in surprise. "I think that would be a great thing for you to do."

"I'll probably get some haters, but I'm prepared for that," she continued.

He reached out and took one of her hands in his. "Well, you can believe that I'm going to be one of your biggest fans."

She smiled and squeezed his hand then released it. "Then let's move into the kitchen, and I'll feed my biggest fan."

Minutes later they were at the table. She'd not only made the spaghetti and meatballs but also a salad and garlic bread. As they ate she continued to talk about her excitement about starting the job with Ashley and the blog. He then told her about the wind damage that had taken down some branches and the tin on the outbuilding.

"You may have some more wind damage to contend

with before this week is over," she said. "There are more storms in the forecast."

"Yeah, that's what I've heard. This is working up to be one of the stormiest springs that I can remember," he replied.

"You'll want all this rain back about July or August when everything is dry and burning up."

He laughed. "You're right about that."

"Still, I'm not looking forward to more storms." She shivered. "Thunder still makes me afraid." She laughed then. "I guess I'm just a big baby."

"You're my baby," he replied, winning one of the smiles from her that made him believe everything was right in the world.

"You know, back to speaking about jobs, the biggest job I'm most looking forward to is that of being a mom," she said.

"Are you still thinking two children…a boy and a girl?" he asked.

"That's always what our plan was."

"Well, my plan has changed," he said.

Instantly a sliver of apprehension danced into her eyes. "Changed how?" she asked.

"I'm thinking I'd like to have two boys and two girls."

She laughed. "And why don't we throw in a set of triplets while we're at it?"

"Works for me," he replied with a grin.

They remained at the table after eating, laughing about some of the more ridiculous plans they had made when they'd been young and in love, including living in a tent if they couldn't afford a house.

The mood remained light and fun until they were cleaning up the dishes and she told him about her conversation with Adam Pearson.

When she finished, his stomach was tied in a knot as he considered what she'd told him. Adam Pearson? Was it possible he was her perp? Had he secretly harbored a resentment toward her that had exploded out of control when she'd come back to town?

Adam had never married and only rarely dated. Was that because he'd had some sort of an obsessive love for Chelsea? While the man had always been affable to Johnny, who knew what dark secrets he might hold in his mind? And was one of those secrets his obsessive love turned to abject hatred of Chelsea?

If Johnny found out Adam was behind the terrorizing of Chelsea, he would give him a beatdown that the man would never forget. Then he would turn him over to Lane to make sure he was prosecuted to the fullest extent of the law.

Chapter Ten

At promptly nine o'clock the next morning, Chelsea walked into Ashley's shop, Bling and Things. There was a display table when customers first walked in showcasing new items that had arrived in the shop. Once past the display table, the store was divided into four long aisles of fare for sale. Across the back of the store was a rack for clothing and accessories.

Ashley greeted her with a big smile. Today Chelsea's new boss looked particularly pretty with her long black hair pulled into a high, stylish ponytail that showed off her high cheekbones and bright blue eyes.

"There's nothing I love more than people who show up on time," she said.

"I've always believed it's the height of rudeness to be late and make somebody else wait," Chelsea replied.

"You're speaking my language now," Ashley replied with a laugh.

For the next two hours she taught Chelsea how to work the register, how the inventory was stored and then told her to wander around the store and familiarize herself with all the items for sale.

Chelsea wandered the aisles and racks and took notes

about the various things, not only for selling but also making a separate list of things she'd like to buy for herself.

It was about noon when Ashley handed her a schedule of her work days and hours. Chelsea was pleased to see it was a mix of morning and evening hours, although she had a feeling Johnny was going to give her a hard time about the evening hours as long as her stalker was still on the loose.

But she was being careful. Every time she went outside, she checked her surroundings to make sure nobody was lurking nearby. She carried pepper spray in her purse, and she now thought it was possible that Adam was the person who had chased her through the field and tried to break into her house, so she was definitely keeping an eye out for him.

While Chelsea was still in the shop, two women came in, and Ashley asked Chelsea to take care of them. One of the women wandered around the store and then left without making a purchase. The second woman bought a lovely silver vase, and Chelsea successfully rang up the sale.

When the woman left, the shop was quiet. "Ashley, are you dating anyone?" Chelsea asked curiously.

"Nobody in particular. I'm still waiting for my knight in shining armor," she replied.

"In this town you're more likely to find a dusty cowboy wearing jeans," Chelsea said with a laugh.

"That's okay. I'm looking for a man like my brothers. Johnny and Luke are good men with fairly fierce facades and gentle souls. They have good values and morals, and that's what I want in a man."

"You don't have to explain to me why you'd want to find somebody like them. I don't know about Luke, but I know Johnny is my knight in shining armor. He always has been and always will be."

"Johnny told me about the issues you've been having. Aren't you terrified?"

"Not so much now that I have a home security system installed."

"But what about when you aren't at home?" Ashley's blue eyes were wide.

"I'm being careful and watching my surroundings. Besides, I'm not going to live my life like a hermit and never leave my house just because some creep is after me."

"Do you have any idea who is after you?" Ashley's eyes grew even wider.

Chelsea thought about mentioning Adam but then decided not to. She wasn't sure he was her boogeyman, and it wouldn't be prudent to throw his name out there without any real evidence against him. "I have some suspicions, but I really don't know who it is for sure."

"Have you considered that it might be Tanya? I know she was really hateful to you in the past, and she was really into Johnny. He dropped her pretty fast after he learned you were back in town."

"That might be, but I considered her, and I just can't see her taking any jealousy issues she might have with me this far. I can't see her chasing me across a pasture or swinging a scythe."

Ashley narrowed her gaze. "I wouldn't put anything past that woman. I couldn't stand her when Johnny was dating her. She was dismissive and rude to me when he wasn't around."

Chelsea laughed. "Welcome to my world."

"I tried to tell him how nasty she was, but he thought I was being overly sensitive." Ashley reached out and took one of Chelsea's hands in hers. "I'm so glad you're back, Chelsea, and I'm so happy you and Johnny have found your way back together again. You've always been family."

"Stop it, or you're going to make me cry," Chelsea said with a strangled laugh.

Ashley laughed and released her hand. "That's the last thing I want."

"Still, I really appreciate the sentiment, Ashley. I've always felt like part of your family. Even while I was away I wanted to be back in your home with your mom fussing in the kitchen and your dad doling out words of wisdom from his armchair." Chelsea's heart clutched at thoughts of Big John. "Oh, Ashley, I can't imagine how much you must miss him."

"I was his princess, and he was my hero," Ashley said, her blue eyes misting with the threat of tears. "It just happened so fast. One minute he was here, and the next minute he was gone, but now I'm particularly worried about both Johnny and Luke."

"Why?" Chelsea asked in surprise. "I mean, I know they are grieving, but that's only natural."

"I worry about Johnny because he is trying to be the be-all and end-all for everyone. He's not only carrying the weight of the ranch business but also trying to hold the family together. Luke worries me even more."

"How so?"

Ashley frowned. "I've never seen him as intense as he is right now. He's so angry about Dad's murder, and he's not healing in any way. I'm worried that in his absolute need to find out who killed Dad, he's going to do something stupid and get himself in trouble."

"Have you talked to Johnny about him?" Chelsea asked.

Ashley shook her head. "No, because I don't want to add to Johnny's burdens right now. I'm just hoping that with more time, Luke will calm down and not go chasing after trouble."

"I'm sure Lane is doing everything he can to find the murderer."

"I'm sure he is too. I just wish there were more clues or some evidence pointing to the guilty person."

Their conversation was halted by two women coming into the shop. "You're good to go for today, Chelsea," Ashley said. "Just be careful when you're out and about."

As Ashley greeted the customers, Chelsea slid out of the door.

Dark clouds had rolled in overhead, usurping the sunshine with a semidarkness. True to what she and Johnny had talked about the night before, the forecast was for a stormy afternoon and an even stormier night.

She'd always had a bit of fear where storms were concerned. She'd been afraid of the thunder and lightning since she was a little girl with nobody to soothe or calm her fears.

She had only run to her mother's bed once in fear of a storm, and Stella had told her to stop being a big baby and had sent her back to her room. Chelsea had been about five years old at the time. She had never sought comfort from her mother again.

At least it hadn't started to rain yet, she thought as she hurried to her car. She had no plans to see Johnny tonight. He was setting the pace in this new relationship, but it was way too slow as far as she was concerned.

However, she refused to push him where their relationship was concerned, especially after talking with Ashley. She'd never want to be an additional burden on Johnny. She wanted to be his support, his quiet and soft place to fall.

She still couldn't believe she was getting a second chance with him, that after so many years apart they had found each other again. She wasn't about to blow it up by rushing him in any way. Still, she longed to have her engagement ring back on her finger and to have that ultimate commitment from him.

Heck, she didn't even know if he still had the beautiful diamond ring he had given to her before. For all she knew he'd sold it or lost it or thrown it in the trash after she had given it back to him. She wouldn't have blamed him if he'd gotten rid of it.

At least it would be a perfect afternoon and evening to play around with the idea of a blog. She could lock the doors, put on some jammin' music and play around with a ring light and the blogging equipment she'd received in the mail the day before.

It was going to be a stormy night, but she'd be safe and sound and enjoying the evening all by herself.

"I'M THINKING ABOUT adding a horse-breeding business," Johnny said to Luke. The two men were seated in Johnny's living room. A preternatural darkness had fallen with the thickening of storm clouds. Even though it was only six thirty in the evening, Johnny had turned on the lamps on either side of the sofa to battle the encroaching darkness.

"What?" Luke asked. It was obvious he had been distracted since he'd come to Johnny's cabin after dinner.

Johnny repeated himself and then added, "And I'm hoping you'll take the helm of this new endeavor. What do you think about it?"

Luke frowned thoughtfully. "I know Dad had talked about starting a horse-breeding program before he…before he died…before he was murdered. I guess I might be up for something like that."

"Great. I've done some research, and I'll email what I have to you, but there's a lot more research that needs to be done. Once you have a plan together, we'll sit down with Mom and Caleb and Ashley and take a family vote on moving forward with the new project."

"Caleb sure as hell won't care what we do with the ranch as long as he gets enough allowance to buy new canvas and paint and booze," Luke replied. "And Ashley completely trusts us when it comes to the ranch business."

"True, but we've always made decisions as a family," Johnny said. "We need to get their approval for spending money on purebred horses, and we'll need to add on to the stables, among a bunch of other things."

Luke got up from the sofa and began to pace in front of Johnny's recliner. "You do realize the more time that passes, the less of a chance Lane is going to find the murderer. It's basically become a cold case."

Johnny released a small sigh. He'd hoped by giving Luke the horse program it would give him something else to think about. Luke was being eaten alive by his grief and rage, and Johnny didn't know how to help him.

"Luke, we might never know who killed him," Johnny finally said.

Luke's gaze burned into Johnny's. "I can't accept that. I can't live like that. Somebody has got to pay for this."

"Luke, we all miss him, and I want somebody arrested for the murder as much as you do. But you can't let this eat you up. You need to figure out how to let go of some of your anger and move on."

"I'll let it go when Lane arrests somebody for the crime. In the meantime, I intend to do a little sleuthing on my own. I really believe Wayne Bridges is behind it, and I think one of his ranch hands actually pulled the trigger. I'm not sure which one did it, but I'm going to find out."

Johnny got out of his chair, and at the same time a rumble of thunder sounded in the distance. "Luke, don't do anything foolish. I need you here on the ranch and not in a jail cell for harassing somebody."

"Don't worry about me, Johnny. I can do some investigating without harassing anyone. I'm not about to get arrested for trying to find my father's killer." It thundered once again as if to punctuate his words.

"I'd better get to my place before it really starts storming," Luke added and headed for the front door.

Johnny walked with him, and as Luke opened the door, Johnny grabbed him by the arm. "Luke, you've got to let some of this go and get back to living your life. I need your time and energy focused on this horse program."

"I hear you," Luke replied and pulled away from Johnny. "Don't worry about me, brother."

"I care about you, and it hurts me to see you in so much pain."

Luke reached out and patted his older sibling on the shoulder. "I love you too, bro. Send me the stuff you have about breeding programs, and I'll do more research and get back to you with a plan for going forward."

With that, Luke stepped outside and headed to his own place. Johnny watched him go and then returned to his chair, and when he sat down a deep sigh escaped him.

Over the last week, he'd seen Luke wind himself tighter and tighter. Johnny had always planned on expanding the business by getting into horse breeding, but he'd intended to do it sometime in the future.

He'd changed his mind and decided to explore it right now hoping it would be a distraction for Luke from his all-consuming grief. However, Luke wasn't the only person Johnny was concerned about. Caleb was drinking and, Johnny suspected, drugging more than ever before.

Johnny didn't believe Leroy Hicks was a good influence on his youngest brother, and he still had the feeling that somehow the two were up to no good.

Johnny had tried several times in the last week to engage with Caleb. He'd asked if he could see some of Caleb's paintings, but Caleb had told him no.

"I'm preparing for a sidewalk sale," Caleb had said. "And I don't want anyone to see my work right now.

It will all be on display very soon. Besides, nobody in this family has ever been interested in what I was doing before."

"Who is sponsoring this sidewalk sale?" Johnny had asked.

"Nobody. I'm setting it up on the empty lot between the feed store and the post office."

"Don't you need a permit or something like that?"

Caleb had smiled slyly. "I'm a King. Nobody would dare shut me down. I don't need some stupid permit."

All Johnny could hope for was that Caleb would be successful and sell lots of paintings. It would certainly be good for his self-esteem, and maybe it would help him really turn his life around.

As the thunder boomed overhead, Johnny picked up his cell phone and called Chelsea. She answered on the first ring. "Hi, Johnny."

Just the sound of her voice lightened his mood more than a little bit. "What are you doing?"

"I've been playing around with this blog idea. For the last hour I've been trying to take a decent selfie to put on a web page. I've always had people photograph me. I never learned the fine art of a selfie."

"It can't be that hard. Just point the camera at your face and click a picture," he replied.

"In the point-and-clicks I've taken so far, my nose looks too big or my ears look like Dumbo's. My smiles make me look either like a madwoman who escaped from an asylum or so vacuous it's pathetic. I know everyone is supposed to have a good side, but so far I can't find mine on either side."

He laughed. "Baby, I'm sure in every photo you take you're absolutely beautiful."

"Spoken like a truly good boyfriend," she replied.

"Sounds like you're being too hard on yourself."

"Maybe," she replied dubiously.

Once again thunder rumbled. "It's going to be stormy tonight," he said.

"I know, but I'll be all right. I'm a big girl now, and maybe if the lightning illuminates my bedroom just right, I'll manage to get a good selfie."

Once again, he laughed, pleased that she sounded so strong and so charming at the same time. "I hope that happens for you. Maybe tomorrow we can go out to dinner at the café and you can show me your perfect selfie shot."

"That sounds like a plan," she replied. "If I manage to get a good one by then."

"I'll pick you up around six o'clock. Does that work for you?"

"Yeah. Tomorrow morning I'm working from nine until two, so I've got my evening free."

"Chelsea, I love that you're taking steps to have a good life here," he replied. Each step she took gave him more and more confidence that she wasn't going to take off and run from Coyote Creek again.

"That's my goal. I want a great life here with you, Johnny. I don't want to depend on you. I like that I have a job and that I'm building a bit of a life separate from you. I think it's important for me to have something just for myself. I think it's healthy for both of us."

He smiled into the phone. "I agree."

"I don't just want to be Johnny's girlfriend or Johnny's wife. I need to have an identity that's all my own. You're Johnny King, the cattle baron, and now I'll be Chelsea, that girl who works in Ashley's shop."

He laughed once again. "Ah, Chelsea. I knew you would cheer me up."

"Did you need cheering up?" she asked with obvious concern in her tone. "What's going on, Johnny?"

"Oh, it's nothing. I'm just a little bit concerned about Luke," he admitted.

"Ashley mentioned the same thing when I saw her this morning," Chelsea said.

For the next few minutes Johnny talked about his worries about both of his brothers.

"Johnny, you can't take on the burdens of the world. You can't heal them. That's something only they can do for themselves."

"Thanks, Chelsea. I guess I needed to hear that." They spoke for a few more minutes, and then he finally bade Chelsea good-night. The minute he hung up the phone he looked forward to talking to her again, to seeing her.

He knew she was just waiting for him to ask her to marry him again. He got up out of his chair and walked into his office. Built into the wall next to his desk was a safe. He crouched in front of it and spun the combination lock and then opened it.

Inside was important paperwork for the plot of land where his cabin was located, deeded to him by his father and mother, among other things. Far in the back, beneath all the papers, was a small velvet box.

He pulled it out and opened it, exposing the two-and-a-half-carat diamond in an elaborate gold setting.

At the time he'd given Chelsea the ring, he'd believed they would be together always. The day she had given the ring back to him had been one of the worst days in his life.

Was he ready to give her the ring back? Was he ready to reinvest with his whole heart and soul into the dreams they had once shared? That they might share again?

He just wasn't sure.

Chapter Eleven

It was almost nine o'clock, and the full brunt of the storm had just begun to rage overhead. The wind whipped the tree outside her bedroom window, making the branches tap…tap…tap on the glass. Amid the taps of the tree, rain slashed down.

Lightning slashed the skies, and thunder boomed overhead. Chelsea tried to ignore the storm even as her heartbeat raced a little faster.

She told herself nothing happening outside could hurt her. Instead of focusing on the storm, she continued to research how to build a web site and blog.

One thing she had definitely learned over the last few hours: building a professional-looking web page was way beyond her pay grade. She'd spent the last hour researching people who built them for a living.

She finally settled on two people who looked interesting and wrote down their names and contact information. She intended to contact them both first thing in the morning about building her web site.

She wanted to see what each of them would bring to the table, then she could make her final decision as to who would work for her. And if those two didn't work out, then she could do some more research. At least she'd finally managed to get a decent selfie.

The night was now complete. She'd spoken to Johnny, and she'd worked hard, and now she was hoping that the storm would pass quickly so she could get a good night's sleep.

She changed into a black nightshirt that had stars and the moon across the front and then stood in front of her closet to pick out her clothes for the next morning.

She knew it was important for her to look professional for working in the shop. She wanted to look classy, yet trendy, to reflect the ambience of the place. She finally pulled out a pair of white slacks with a red-and-white tri-cut blouse and bold red earrings.

A loud banging came from someplace downstairs. Her heart leaped into her throat. What was it? Had a shutter come loose in the wind? Was somebody trying to get in? The alarm hadn't gone off.

She walked halfway down the stairs and realized the banging was somebody at her front door. Who on earth would be here at this time of night and in the middle of a storm?

She hurried to the door and peered outside. With a gasp of surprise, she quickly unarmed the alarm and unlocked and opened the door. "Melinda, what on earth are you doing here?" She grabbed her friend's arm and yanked her through the door. Melinda's oversize purse smacked into the wall as she reeled inside. Chelsea locked the door and set the alarm, then turned back to Melinda.

"Oh my gosh, you're soaking wet. Wait there and let me go get you a towel." Chelsea quickly ran into the guest bathroom just off the living room and grabbed a thick fluffy towel, then hurried back to Melinda whose dark hair had curled up to make her look like a bedraggled poodle.

"Thanks." Melinda took the towel from her and dried her hair and then ran the towel down her shoulders. She then handed the towel back to Chelsea, who returned it to the bathroom.

By that time Melinda had parked herself on the sofa. "What are you doing here at this time of night in this kind of weather?" Chelsea asked as she sank down next to her friend.

"I couldn't wait until morning to tell you." Melinda's brown eyes sparkled brightly.

"To tell me what?" Chelsea asked.

"To tell you this." She thrust her hand out, exposing a diamond ring. "I'm engaged," she squealed.

Chelsea squealed back, and the two hugged each other. "Wait. This calls for a champagne toast," Chelsea said. "I'll be right back."

Chelsea ran into the kitchen to the cabinet that held her liquor. She tried to always keep champagne for any special occasions that might come along. And this was definitely one of them.

She carried the bottle and two crystal stemmed glasses back into the living room. "Ta-da," she said as she managed to open the bottle with a pop but no spray. She poured the two glasses and handed one to Melinda.

"To you and Roger and love forever more," she said.

"I'll drink to that," Melinda said with a girlish giggle.

The two clinked their glasses together, sipped the drink and then Chelsea set her glass on the coffee table.

"Now, tell me all about it. How did Roger ask you?" Chelsea asked.

Lightning flashed outside the window, and the thunder boomed loudly. "It was so sweet," Melinda said. "We had dinner at the café like we usually do when we go out. Normally Roger is pretty laid back when we eat out. But tonight, he ate fast and encouraged me to eat quickly as well. I thought maybe he was eager to get rid of me."

"Did you tell him that you were upset?"

"When we were finished with our meals, I told him how I was feeling, that I felt like he was rushing the time with me, and it was hurting my feelings. He immediately apologized and said we'd linger over coffee and dessert. So, I ordered my usual, a piece of strawberry cream cake, and when it came the ring was on the top of it. Suddenly Robert fell to one knee right there in the café, and he asked me to marry him. When I said yes, everyone in the place stood up and cheered."

"Oh my gosh, how exciting! You must be thrilled. Girl, I'm so very happy for you," Chelsea said and leaned over to hug Melinda once again. "Have you set a date yet?" She straightened up again.

"Yeah, September 15."

"This September?" Chelsea asked in surprise. "That doesn't give you much time."

Melinda nodded. "It's just going to be a small affair. Roger doesn't want a huge ceremony that costs us a fortune. He'd much rather we save the money so we can buy a house, and I agree with him."

"Still, you want a nice ceremony. Hopefully it will

be the only wedding you get, and you and Roger will live happily ever after."

Melinda laughed. "Trust me, I only intend to have this one wedding and stay happily married forever. Now, I have a question to ask you. I'd like you to be my only bridesmaid."

Chelsea's heart swelled with happiness. "Oh, Melinda, I'd be honored to be your bridesmaid."

"You know we swore we'd be in each other's weddings when we were about fourteen years old," Melinda reminded her.

"And we elaborately planned our weddings before we were old enough to even know how to kiss a boy. Have you thought about what colors you want?"

For the next thirty minutes or so, as the storm continued to rage overhead, the two talked about the wedding. Chelsea was thrilled for her friend, but she couldn't help but wish she was also planning her own wedding.

Still, it was fun to talk about Melinda's special day. They talked about dresses and food, flowers and music. They laughed together as the ideas grew more outrageous and over-the-top.

Finally, Melinda stood. "I've taken up enough of your time. I've got to get home."

"Melinda, it's still storming out. Why don't you wait a while…or better yet you could stay in my spare room overnight and go home in the morning," Chelsea replied. "I'll even make you breakfast."

"No, I'm good. Thanks for the offer, but I like to sleep in my own bed. Besides, a little rain certainly won't hurt me."

Together the two women walked to the front door.

"Oh, wait," Melinda said before Chelsea could unarm the security and open the door. "I have something for you. It's a special gift."

"For me?" Chelsea asked, wondering what Melinda might have for her.

Melinda reached into her oversize bag and withdrew a hatchet. In one quick movement, before Chelsea could absorb what was happening, Melinda swung the hatchet at her, catching her on her upper arm.

The sharpness of the blade sliced through Chelsea's skin. She gasped in pain at the same time she stumbled back from Melinda. "What are you doing?" she screamed. "W-why did you do that?"

Melinda's eyes narrowed, and she took a step toward Chelsea. "Because I want to see you hurt. I want to see you bleed before I kill you."

Chelsea gasped. "Are you crazy? What's wrong with you? Melinda, if this is some sort of a joke, then you need to stop." Chelsea's arm burned as warm blood ran down it. Her breaths came in pants as she looked at her friend in stunned surprise.

"Oh, Chelsea, trust me. This is no joke." Melinda's face twisted into an expression of hatred that Chelsea had never seen before. "You've already escaped me twice, but you won't this time."

Melinda remained several feet away from where Chelsea stood. A new shock raced through Chelsea. Melinda? It had been Melinda who had chased her through the field with the scythe? She was the person who had tried to break into Chelsea's house?

Chelsea's heart raced a million beats a minute. "You?

It was all you? But why? Melinda, I'm your friend." Chelsea clasped her hand over her bleeding wound.

"And you totally ruined my life," Melinda screamed, her features displaying a rage Chelsea had never seen before. Melinda raised the hatchet again, and Chelsea took another step backward.

"How did I ruin your life?" Chelsea screamed back, her body poised in fight-or-flight mode.

"By not eating, you stupid bitch. By not taking care of yourself and falling off a damned runway. I had it made in New York. As long as you were doing well, I was living the good life." Melinda's entire body shook with her fury.

"I was living in a great apartment and going to all the A-list parties. I was meeting handsome, sexy men and living the life I deserved, and then you ruined everything. You ruined everything for me!"

"You could have stayed in New York," Chelsea replied fervently.

"What, and gone back to breaking my back working in a deli? No way. You were my ticket to the good life, but without you there was no such thing for me. You ruined it all!" Melinda released a bloodcurdling scream and then rushed toward Chelsea.

Chelsea grabbed the lamp off the end table and threw it at Melinda, but the delicate blingy item merely glanced off her body.

Chelsea frantically looked around for something she could use for her defense. Seeing nothing and with Melinda quickly advancing on her, Chelsea turned and ran to the staircase.

She screamed as Melinda swung the hatchet, barely

missing her. The blade hit the wall with a loud thud. "Did you really think I wanted to come back to this stupid little town? Did you really believe I'd be happy marrying some pasty-face farm boy?" The hatchet smashed into the wall again.

Chelsea ran up the stairs as fast as she could, sobs of terror ripping up her throat. She couldn't believe this was happening. She and Melinda had been friends since third grade. How could she come after Chelsea like this now? To add to the madness, the thunder and lightning continued outside as if to match the mayhem that was occurring inside.

Melinda was like a wild animal at her heels. Chelsea screamed as the hatchet caught her in the back of her calf. Thank God it was another glancing blow, but that didn't stop the excruciating pain that roared through her.

Oh, God…oh, God… She had to get someplace safe, but where? She was certain nobody knew Melinda was here. The police weren't going to magically appear to save her. She was all on her own.

She limped as fast as possible and reached the top of the stairs, then whirled around and kicked Melinda as hard as she could in the chest.

The woman reeled backward, flailing her arms for balance. Chelsea hoped Melinda fell, but she didn't stick around to find out. She turned and limped down the hallway.

At least her bedroom door had a lock on it. If she could just get there, it would buy her some time. Besides, her phone was there. She could call for help.

Her arm screamed with pain, and her leg was pure agony as blood poured out of the wound and onto the wooden floor. Sobs continued to rip through her as her mind tried to grapple with everything that had happened so far.

Melinda really wanted to kill her. It was so hard to believe that she had been the one who had chased Chelsea that night in the field. It was equally difficult to believe it had been Melinda trying to break into her house in the middle of the night with the intention to kill her.

Chelsea felt as if she was in a dream, but there was no waking up from this nightmare. She never suspected that Melinda was her boogeyman, nor had anyone else suspected the woman.

This is happening. This is really happening, a voice screamed inside her head. She wasn't on drugs, and she wasn't crazy. This was real!

Chelsea reached her bedroom and slammed the door shut and locked it. She leaned with her back against it in an effort to catch her breath.

She looked down at her leg. It was still bleeding pretty badly, as was her arm. She squeezed her eyes tightly closed and drew in deep breaths in an effort to get past the pain that seared through her.

"Hey, Chelsea." Melinda's voice came from the other side of the door. "I'm sorry. All this was really meant to be a joke. I never intended to actually hit you with the hatchet. I'm so sorry if I hurt you. I was really just trying to be funny. Why don't you open the door and let me help you clean up your wounds?"

"I don't need your help," Chelsea replied. She knew Melinda was lying. There was no way this was a joke, and there was no way Chelsea was just going to unlock her door and invite the monster into her bedroom.

"You're going to need help when the police arrest you," Chelsea added.

Melinda crashed into the door on the other side. "You might as well open the door, Chelsea. There's no place for you to run. There's no place for you to hide. This is really going to happen, Chelsea. You are going to die a grisly, painful death, and I'm going to laugh as I chop you into pieces."

Deep shudders shot up and down Chelsea's body. For a moment she couldn't move, her terror momentarily keeping her frozen in place. Melinda hit the door with so much force the hatchet splintered the wood. Chelsea screamed and moved away from it. Melinda slammed into it again, the blade of the tool breaking through a second time.

Chelsea's mental inertia snapped. She ran to the nightstand where her phone was. She grabbed it and punched Johnny's number. He answered on the first ring, but before she could say anything to him, Melinda hit the door again and Chelsea realized within seconds the enraged Melinda would be inside the bedroom.

And then what? The bathroom off her bedroom didn't have a lock on the door, and in any case that would just prolong the inevitable. She screamed again as the hole in her bedroom door continued to get bigger with each blow Melinda delivered.

Chelsea quickly gazed around the room, seeking a weapon that could counter a hatchet. There was nothing. She was virtually at Melinda's mercy, and the crazed woman had no mercy to give.

Chelsea's gaze shot to the window. Outside the storm

still raged, and Melinda was only seconds away from breaking into the bedroom.

Chelsea ran to the window and threw it open. She had two choices. Stay inside and be killed, or take her chances outside.

Stay inside, or go out into a tall tree she had never climbed with lightning striking all around.

New sobs escaped her as she went out the window.

Chapter Twelve

Johnny held his phone in his hand. The call had come from Chelsea, but it must have been a butt-dial, for she wasn't on the phone.

Still, the sounds he heard were hard to discern. There was a loud banging, and as he was trying to figure out what she could be doing at this time of night, he heard her scream. The sound shot chills up his spine.

When she screamed again, utter terror was in the sound. He leaped out of bed. Chelsea was in trouble. The words screamed in his head. He yanked on his jeans and pulled on a white T-shirt. He then grabbed his gun and his truck keys and raced for the door.

Minutes later he was in his truck and headed into town. His heart beat a million beats a minute as a thousand questions whirled in his head.

If somebody had broken in, then why hadn't her security system worked? He hadn't heard an alarm screeching in the phone call. He still had the phone on the call from her, and his phone was on the passenger seat next to him.

He heard another scream, and his blood chilled.

Lightning slashed across the sky, followed by a boom of thunder that seemed to shake the very earth.

"You can't escape from me," a voice screamed. "I'm going to chop you into pieces and feed you to the pigs."

That voice… Melinda? Melinda wanted to kill Chelsea? Confusion roared through his head. What the hell was happening? Melinda and Chelsea had been best friends since they were young girls. They had gone to New York together, and Johnny knew from conversations he'd had with Chelsea that she had taken very good care of Melinda once she had started making money.

Thoughts warred in his mind, but at the moment his biggest worry was the fact that he could no longer hear Chelsea. And that scared the hell out of him. What was happening? He had no idea what was going on, but he knew it was vital that he get to her as soon as possible.

Rain pelted his windshield, lowering visibility and slowing his speed. His chest squeezed tight with fear. Whatever was going on, he had to get to Chelsea in time to make sure she wasn't harmed. Any other option was unthinkable.

The rain turned to pebbles of hail, further impeding his speed. Dammit. It was as if the weather was against him…against Chelsea.

He picked up the phone again and still not hearing Chelsea, he made the difficult decision to hang up. He immediately called Lane.

The chief answered on the second ring. "Lane, you need to get to Chelsea's house as soon as possible. She's in danger and needs help right now."

"I'm on my way." Lane disconnected.

Johnny was grateful Lane hadn't hung on the phone

asking questions. Right now every second counted. He winced as a lightning flash nearly blinded him.

It was bad enough that Chelsea was afraid of storms, but as he replayed Melinda's words, he couldn't imagine what Chelsea was going through.

Too late. It couldn't be too late. For her…for them. As he reached the town, despite the hail, he increased his speed. He took the corner near Chelsea's house and fishtailed out. He quickly corrected and roared on down the street.

There was no police presence at her house yet. He pulled his truck to a halt in front of her place and then jumped out. The hail changed back to rain, and above the storm sounds, he immediately heard the vague sound of Chelsea screaming.

He raced up to the front door and grabbed the doorknob. It was locked. He cocked his head and listened. It sounded like Chelsea's screams were coming from outside the house. He stepped back, and that's when he saw her.

She was high up in the tree, clinging onto a branch while somebody—he assumed Melinda—slashed out of the window with a hatchet. The wind buffeted the tree, and the branch she clung to swayed back and forth.

Dear God, just looking up to where she was in the tall tree gave him a faint sense of vertigo. "Chelsea," he yelled to be heard above the storm. He quickly wiped a hand down his face as the rain made it difficult for him to see.

A strike of lightning lit up her face as she looked down. He'd never seen such terror. Her features were taut, and her eyes were wide pools of sheer fear. "Johnny," she cried.

"It's okay, baby. I'm here, and I'm not going to allow her to hurt you." But worry shot through him. Where was Melinda now? She had disappeared from the window.

At that same moment, sirens sounded in the distance. The last thing he wanted Chelsea to do was go back in the window of the house where Melinda might be waiting for her.

"Chelsea, honey, can you come down the tree?"

"I can't. Johnny, I'm… I'm too afraid." She screamed as the thunder crashed overhead. She was wound so tight around the tree trunk, it looked as if she was a part of the bark.

Lane's car, followed by two more patrol cars, roared down the street, sirens blaring and lights flashing. As they pulled up in front of Chelsea's house, they cut the sirens.

Lane jumped out of his vehicle and three more officers got out of theirs, and they all ran toward Johnny. "It's Melinda Wells. She tried to kill Chelsea," Johnny said quickly. "I don't know where she is right now. The last I saw, she was inside the house at Chelsea's bedroom window. The front door is locked, and so far, the house alarm hasn't gone off."

The words tumbled from him fast and furiously as he kept his gaze up on Chelsea. "Do you have this handled?" Lane asked as he, too, looked up at Chelsea.

"I'm working on it," Johnny replied.

Chelsea's house alarm began to ring, indicating a breach in the security. "Around back," Lane yelled to his deputies. They all raced around the side of the house, leaving Johnny to try to get Chelsea down from the tree.

The rain had changed to a fine mist, and Johnny was desperate to have Chelsea safe and in his arms. "Chelsea, you can come down now. You're safe."

"Johnny, I'm so afraid. I—I need you to help me." Her words came out with deep sobs.

"Chelsea, pretend you're climbing down the tree to come and meet me at the cabin," he replied.

"I… I can't, Johnny. I really need you to help me down," she cried.

Her need battled with Johnny's fear of heights. Her need of him won out. Thankfully, the tree appeared to be perfect for climbing. "I'm coming, Chelsea," he yelled up and then grabbed a limb and pulled himself up.

As he moved higher in the tree, a sense of dizziness shot off inside him again. When he was halfway up to where she was, he made the mistake of looking down.

His chest tightened, and nausea welled up inside him. He closed his eyes as he clung tight to the tree trunk. The limb beneath his feet swayed with the wind, and he froze.

"Johnny, please help me."

Her voice sliced through his irrational fear. He opened his eyes and looked up. He could do this. He could do this for her. He grabbed the next limb and pulled himself higher.

He continued to climb until he reached the branch just beneath her. It was then he saw the big, bleeding gash in her leg, and any fear he might have entertained about climbing the tree fled beneath his worry for her and a new rage toward Melinda.

"Baby, I'm right here," he said. He needed to get her out of the tree and to the emergency room as soon as possible. The wound in her leg was dripping blood. Who knew how much blood she had already lost?

He stepped up to the limb where she stood and wrapped an arm around her. He realized her arm also had a nasty bleeding wound. Dear God, where else might she be hurt?

"Chelsea, we need to get you down and to the hospital. You can climb down."

"No, I can't," she cried.

"Yes, you can," he countered firmly. "Remember how you used to climb down the tree outside your mother's house to sneak out to see me? This is the same thing. Chelsea, you can climb down this tree with me."

"Okay," she replied tearfully. "With you, Johnny, I can do it."

"Then let's go." He kept his gaze focused on her as he began to work his way back down the tree.

Slowly they climbed down together. The storm was moving out, the thunder more distant than it had been. By the time they reached the ground, Lane was waiting for them. "She must have gone out the back door, but so far, we haven't been able to locate her."

"You take care of getting her in custody. I'm getting Chelsea to the hospital." Johnny didn't wait for a reply. He swept Chelsea up into his arms. Her arms encircled his neck, and she buried her face into his shoulder and began to weep.

He carried her to his truck, opened the door and gently placed her on the passenger seat. He then closed the door and hurried around to his door.

Before he got there, Chelsea screamed and jerked forward. Melinda hung over the back seat, attempting to grab her. She must have slipped the view of the officers and managed to hide in his truck. Johnny yanked on the driver's-side door. Locked.

He didn't wait for his key to automatically unlock the door, instead he grabbed his gun and swung the butt of it as hard as possible against the window.

The window shattered. He reached in and unlocked the door. Everything only took seconds. Chelsea was screaming and battling with Melinda over the seat.

"Die, you bitch!" Melinda growled and tried to swing her hatchet at Chelsea's head.

Johnny yanked open the back door and reached in and grabbed hold of Melinda. She became a kicking, spitting, scratching hellcat, fighting Johnny to stay in the truck.

"I want her to die," she screamed.

"Not on my watch," Johnny replied. He grabbed the arm with the hatchet and with all his might yanked her out of the truck. He threw her to the ground and then seized the hatchet from her grasp. Lane rushed over to help him, and together they got her to her feet so Lane could handcuff her.

"I'll take her from here," Lane said above Melinda's screams and curses.

Johnny hurried back to his truck where he closed the back door and then got into the driver's seat. Chelsea had quieted. She was no longer screaming or crying.

She merely slumped in the seat with her eyes closed. Johnny eyed her worriedly.

"She'll never be able to hurt you again, honey. Lane is taking her straight to jail," he said. Chelsea merely nodded.

He put his truck into Drive and pulled away from the curb. The wounds on her leg and arm were still bleeding, and when he glanced at her, her face was as pale as he'd ever seen it. He suddenly realized she wasn't out of the woods yet. With this frightening thought in mind, he stepped on the gas, frantic to get her to the hospital as quickly as possible.

Minutes later he pulled up in front of the emergency entrance and frantically honked his horn. Two orderlies rushed outside, and Johnny got out. "We need a wheelchair," he cried.

One of the orderlies rushed back toward the hospital and the other one opened the passenger door. Johnny rushed around the truck. "She has a hatchet wound to her leg and arm, and I'm not sure what else."

Chelsea opened her eyes. "Thank you, Johnny. I love you so very much." Her eyes drifted closed again.

For the first time Johnny's abject fear for her roared through his head and heart. He fought back the overwhelming emotions that flooded through him as he helped to get her loaded into the wheelchair.

"I love you too," he shouted as the orderly wheeled her toward the building. "Do you hear me, Chelsea? I love you too."

A sense of helplessness swept through him as he watched them disappear into the hospital. Had he gotten to her in time? The little hospital in Coyote Creek didn't have a specialized trauma unit. Would it have what she needed?

He got back into his truck and pulled it into a regular parking place, then headed to the small emergency waiting room.

Adrienne Alexander was the night receptionist on duty. Johnny checked in with her and then sat in one of the cheap green plastic chairs to wait for a doctor to come out and let him know how Chelsea was doing.

He had so many questions about what had happened. Why had Melinda gone after Chelsea? What might cause a friend to turn into a killing machine? With a hatchet, no less. Once again fear torched through him, tightening his chest and bringing a mist of tears to his eyes.

The minutes ticked by, and the longer it took, the more desperate Johnny felt. What was taking so long? Why hadn't a doctor come out to talk to him yet? Had there been more wounds than had been visible?

Chelsea had to be okay. She just had to be. Their love story couldn't end like this. Not like this with terror and blood and…death.

CHELSEA CAME TO SLOWLY. When she opened her eyes, she immediately knew she was in the hospital, but for several long moments she didn't remember why.

Faint sun crept over the horizon, indicating to her that it was morning. She frowned. Wasn't it storming? She remembered the thunder and lightning.

Then it all slammed back into her brain. The storm… and Melinda. Melinda had tried to kill her. The very idea still didn't seem real.

But it had really happened. She wasn't crazy or on drugs. Melinda had really attacked her with a hatchet. She squeezed her eyes tightly closed. Not only had Melinda hurt her leg and her arm, she'd ripped into Chelsea's very heart.

Melinda had been the friend who had helped Chelsea get through her painful high-school years. She'd been the person who had known all of Chelsea's secrets and desires, and she thought she'd known all of Melinda's too.

But she'd been wrong. She hadn't believed Tanya had an evil soul, yet she had never seen the total rottenness in her own best friend. And it felt like such a deep betrayal.

Her leg ached, as did her arm. She raised her arm up to look at the area where Melinda had sliced her, but it was covered in a long bandage.

Her thoughts were all scattered. She hoped Melinda went to prison for a very long time. Chelsea certainly never wanted to see the woman again. She also hoped she never found herself in the top of a tree during a thunderstorm again. As she remembered the booming, deafening thunder and the sizzle of nearby lightning, a chill shot through her body.

The chill immediately warmed. Johnny had climbed the tree for her. The awe of that moment sat with her and brought with it a wave of warmth.

She knew how frightened he was of heights. He'd been scared of heights since he was a kid. Yet somehow he'd managed to set that aside and climb up a tree to help her get down.

Her heart swelled with love for him. Thank God he'd

arrived last night when he had. Thank God the police had shown up when they had. If nobody had come in time…she'd be dead right now.

She'd love to see Johnny, but she knew he'd have chores to do. He knew she was safe, and he'd probably come to see her sometime this afternoon.

With that thought in mind, she drifted back to sleep. About an hour later she was awakened by Carrie Carlson, a cute young nurse with dark hair and blue-violet eyes. "I'm sorry to wake you," she said to Chelsea. "I need to take your vitals."

"It's okay. I was ready to wake up anyway."

"Let me get your temperature first."

Carrie quickly went through her routine and then smiled with a gentleness at Chelsea. "How are you feeling this morning?"

"Good, except for the pain in my arm and leg," Chelsea admitted.

"On a scale of one to ten, ten being the worse pain you've ever had, where are you?" Carrie asked.

Chelsea frowned. "Maybe about a seven."

"I'll speak to the doctor about giving you some pain medication. In any case, he should be in to speak to you in just a little while."

"Thanks," Chelsea replied.

Minutes later Carrie was back with pain meds that she put into Chelsea's IV, and some minutes after that, Chelsea dozed off.

She was awakened by the doctor coming in. She was pleased to see it was Dr. Michael Morris. The gray-haired man with his warm brown eyes had been Chelsea's doctor through most of her life.

"Chelsea, how are you feeling this morning?" he asked.

"Better now that I got a little pain medication in me," she replied. "So, tell me the damage."

"I don't know how much you remember from last night when you were brought in. You were in shock and had lost a lot of blood, and then there were the wounds on your arm and leg."

He paused and pulled a chair up closer to her bed and sat. His eyes emoted great empathy. "The first thing we did was give you a tetanus shot. Your arm took twenty-two stitches. Thankfully it appeared to be a glancing wound that didn't go into any muscle or nerves beneath the skin."

She winced. "And what about my leg?"

"Unfortunately, that was a little more complicated. We had to do some internal stitching as the wound was deeper. Externally you have fifty-four stitches. I tried to do them small and neat, hoping the scar you'll have won't look too bad. But it will be significant."

"I'm alive, and that's all I really care about. When can I bust out of this joint?"

"I'm pumping you full of good antibiotics today. As long as your vitals stay fine, you could possibly go home later this afternoon."

"That would be terrific," she replied.

However, as the hours went by, the idea of going back to her house grew more and more repugnant. She knew there was damage to the wall going up the stairs, and her bedroom door was smashed to pieces.

Everywhere she looked in the house there would be memories of a madwoman chasing her with a hatchet in an effort to kill her. Hopefully those memories would fade once the damage was repaired and some time had passed.

She dozed off again, and this time when she opened her eyes, Johnny was in the chair next to her bed. As she gazed at him, all the horrifying emotions from the night before rose up inside her.

Chapter Thirteen

Johnny saw the wealth of emotions that crossed Chelsea's features, and the fear and the pain as her eyes misted with tears and her lower lip began to tremble.

Before he could respond to her she laughed, and the tears in her eyes disappeared instead of running down her cheeks. "Johnny, you climbed a tree for me," she said.

He smiled at her. "I did, although don't think I'm going to do that all the time now."

Her smile immediately faltered and shadows darkened her eyes. "I hope you never, ever have to do that again for me."

He reached out and took her hand in his. "How are you feeling? Are you in a lot of pain?"

"The pain isn't too bad right now. They gave me some medication a while ago, and it took the edge off it. Have you talked to Dr. Morris?"

"I spoke to him just a few minutes ago. He's writing up the orders to let you go. Are you ready to go home?"

She hesitated several long moments and then nodded. "Sure, I'm ready."

However, it was obvious by her hesitation that she

wasn't. "Are you wanting to stay here longer, maybe so they can continue to ease your pain with meds?"

She drew in a deep breath and released it on a shuddery sigh. "No, it's not that. I know my leg and my arm are going to hurt, and I can handle the pain. It's just that…that…the house… She destroyed it, Johnny."

"I was actually going to suggest that you come home with me, and tomorrow we can get Jeb to work on fixing what she wrecked," he said.

"Really? Are you sure you wouldn't mind?" Her eyes instantly brightened at his suggestion.

He squeezed her hand tightly. "Chelsea, I promise you I won't mind. I'd love to have you stay with me. Besides, it's doctor's orders. He doesn't want you up and around on that leg for a while."

She frowned. "We'll need to go by my house and get some clothes and things."

"I'll let Lane know because I imagine your house is a crime scene right now. Has he been here to talk to you yet?"

She shook her head. "I haven't spoken to anyone today except the doctor and a couple of the nurses."

Johnny knew sooner or later Lane would need to get a statement from her, and he knew that would be difficult for her. If he had his way, he would take her memories of Melinda and the night before away from her and put them someplace where they couldn't hurt her ever again.

He'd wanted to be here first thing this morning, but when he'd called the doctor for an update, he'd indicated that she was sleeping. Not wanting to interfere with her getting her rest, he'd waited until now to come to see her.

And he was ready to take her home with him.

His sleep had been haunted by terrible nightmares. They had been dreams where Melinda had killed Chelsea and he'd watched, frozen in place and unable to do anything about it. That nightmare had ended only for another one to unfold. In that one, Chelsea was up in the tree and couldn't get down. The lightning hit all around the tree, and Johnny knew it was just a matter of time before a killer electrical current zapped through the tree…and Chelsea. Yet he couldn't climb the tree to help her down.

All he wanted to do tonight was hold her in his arms to assure himself she was really and truly okay. "Johnny, I can't tell you how much I love you," she now said.

Before he could reply, the nurse walked in. He recognized her as Emily Timmons, who they had both gone to high school with.

"Hi, Chelsea, Johnny," she said with a bright smile. "I'm here to get you out of this place," she said to the patient.

"That sounds good to me," Chelsea replied.

Johnny released her hand as Emily set up a tray and grabbed fresh bandages from a shelf. "The first thing I'm going to do is remove your IV," Emily said. It took her only moments to get rid of the line.

"And now I'm going to change your bandages so you go home with clean ones," Emily continued. Carefully, she removed the one on Chelsea's arm.

When Johnny saw the row of stitches, his stomach tightened. Melinda was lucky to be in Lane's custody.

Otherwise, Johnny didn't know what he might have done to the woman.

Emily changed the bandage and then moved down to take care of Chelsea's leg. When she exposed the long line of stitches, Johnny once again felt a rage directed at the woman who had attacked Chelsea.

This wound was much bigger…much uglier than the one on her arm. It was obvious from Chelsea's stunned look at it that this was the first time she'd seen it.

Tears sprang to her eyes, but she quickly swiped them away and then released a shaky laugh. "Well, I guess it's official. There's definitely no more modeling in my future."

Her words chilled a place deep in Johnny's heart. He didn't want Chelsea by default. He didn't want her to choose him because her option of returning to modeling was over. He wanted her to choose him because she loved him more than modeling and more than the spotlight and city life. He wanted her to want him more than anything else, and now he wouldn't know if he was really just her second choice for happiness.

She was finally bandaged up and had a prescription for pain pills in her hand, and Emily helped her into a wheelchair. She was going home in the nightgown she'd been wearing the night before. "I'll go ahead and pull my truck up out front," Johnny said.

He hurried out of the hospital and to his truck. The early evening was clear with no signs of the storm that had blown through the night before.

Last night he'd been ready to ask her again to marry him. He'd been ready to give the ring back to her.

But now, he felt himself mentally taking a step back from her.

She definitely would need help through her recuperation. Her doctor's orders had been for her to stay off her feet for a couple of weeks. He certainly intended to be here for her while she got better, and in that time he needed to figure out if they were really meant to be together forever.

Once Chelsea was settled into his truck, he made a stop to pick up her pain meds, and then they stopped at her place where Lane allowed him to go in and get some clothes for her. By the time they arrived at the cabin, he could tell that she was hurting and tired.

He picked her up and carried her into the cabin and gently placed her on the sofa. "Sit tight, and I'll get you a blanket and a pain tablet."

"Thank you, Johnny. I don't know what I'd do without you," she replied with a tired smile.

"Right now you don't have to know," he replied.

Minutes later she was snuggled beneath a soft blanket, and Johnny sat in his recliner and watched her sleep. His love for her nearly overwhelmed him. He'd loved her since he was seventeen. He didn't know how to love anyone else. He'd never really wanted to love anyone else. She was in his heart and in his very soul.

The question was: Did she love him in the same way, or was he her second choice? Was she now defaulting to him because, as she said, modeling was now out of the question?

CHELSEA HAD BEEN at Johnny's place for almost a week. The day after she'd come here she'd set Jeb to work on repairing the damage to her house, but what she really wanted was for Johnny to tell her to sell the place and make a forever home here with him at the cabin.

However, she felt a distance from him, a strange detachment that had her feeling less confident of where their relationship was going. Each night she slept in his arms, in his bed under the stars. He'd made no attempt to make love to her, and she was beginning to wonder if his love for her had somehow changed.

Had the craziness and drama of Melinda put him off? Lane had come by on her second day at Johnny's to get her statement. Johnny had sat next to her as she'd relived the horror of that night. But was he over it? Was he over her?

Each morning he made sure she'd eaten breakfast and had everything she might need at her fingertips before he left for work. He stopped and checked in with her at noon and then returned for the day at around six.

She was now seated in the kitchen, waiting for his arrival home. She usually sat there and watched him make dinner, and he talked about things around the ranch, and she caught him up on what television shows she'd watched during the day.

Ashley had been very supportive and understanding about her not working in the store until the doctor completely released Chelsea and she was feeling better. Ashley had promised Chelsea that the job would still be hers when she was ready.

She now looked up with a smile as Johnny came in through the back door. "Hey, handsome," she said.

He flashed her a quick smile. "Hey, beautiful," he replied. "How was your day?"

"Fine, although I can't wait to get all these stitches out. They're starting to itch."

"Right now, those stitches are holding you together. Don't hurry the healing process." He walked over to the sink and washed his hands, then moved to the refrigerator and took out a package of hamburger. "I figured I'd fry us up a couple of burgers for dinner."

"Sounds good to me. Once I get these stitches out I can start cooking meals for you. Of course, once I get better, I'll be back at my own place."

She waited for him to protest her words. She waited for him to tell her that he wanted her here in the cabin with him forever. When that didn't happen a wave of apprehension shot through her.

She'd thought they were on the same page, that they were building a stronger, deeper relationship with each day that passed and that very quickly she'd be by his side every day and every night.

"Johnny, is everything all right?" she asked once he had the hamburger patties in the skillet.

"Sure. Why do you ask?" He sat in the chair across from her.

"You've just felt a little distant since I've been here." She searched his features. "I know it's been difficult to take care of me along with everything else you have on your plate."

He flashed her a quick smile. "Taking care of you is the least of my problems."

"What can I do to help with the other problems?" she asked.

"If you could catch the person who murdered my

father, that would go a long way in solving some of the other issues."

"Oh, Johnny." She covered one of his hands with hers. "I wish I could do that for you."

He turned his hand over so he held hers, and for a long moment their gazes locked. Myriad emotions chased across the blue depths of his…sadness and a touch of anger and something else…something she couldn't quite identify.

He pulled his hand away and stood. "I need to flip these burgers."

She watched as he took care of the cooking and then pulled out a fat tomato, a head of lettuce and several slices of cheese from the fridge.

"Can I help?" she asked.

"No, I've got this."

He said no more as he finished preparing the evening meal. As they ate, she tried to make conversation with him, but he remained quiet and obviously distant.

It scared her. Was he having doubts where she was concerned? Did he see her now as damaged goods? Was his love for her waning? She'd always wanted to be Johnny's girl. She'd wanted to be his forever girl, and she'd thought that was what he wanted too. Now she wasn't so sure anymore.

It was a quiet meal, and when it was finished while he cleared the dishes she went back to the sofa. She'd felt like having a second chance with Johnny had been a gift from Heaven, but now she wasn't so sure. Maybe fate had only been laughing at her.

Johnny came into the living room and sat in his chair,

although he didn't recline it. Instead, he once again held her gaze for a long moment.

"Chelsea, I've been doing a lot of thinking over the past few days," he said.

"Thinking about what?" She tried to read him, but his features gave nothing away.

"About us."

Her stomach churned with tension, and her heart began to race. "What about us?"

"I wasn't sure I wanted to be your default. I didn't want to be the one you chose because your injury took modeling away from you, but I've realized now I'll take you however I can get you."

To her surprise, he fell to one knee and pulled the ring he'd given her once before out of his pocket. "Will you marry me, Chelsea? Will you marry me and make me the happiest man on the face of the earth?"

Her initial joy was tempered by his words. "Johnny, you aren't my default. I'm not choosing you because modeling is now out of the question. It was out of the question the moment you told me you wanted to try again with me."

She got up from the sofa, took his hand and tugged him to his feet. "Johnny, I love you. You're my first choice in love. There has never been anything or anyone I love more than you."

His features relaxed and softened, and his eyes gazed at her with the love that had always made her feel as if she was home. She wound her arms around his neck. "Johnny, I thought I lost you once, and I never want to lose you again. Yes, I'll marry you, and that would have been my answer if you'd asked me before I got all these stitches."

She might have said more, but at that moment his lips took hers in a kiss that spoke of love and passion and commitment. When the kiss stopped, he slid the ring on her finger.

"I've loved you forever, Chelsea, and I will continue to love you through eternity. I want to marry you and have babies with you and build our lives here together." His eyes, those beautiful eyes of his, gazed at her with love.

This was really happening. She wasn't crazy and she wasn't on drugs. This beautiful moment with Johnny was really happening, and a voice whispered happiness into her heart.

"Yes, please." She looked up at him with all the love she had in her heart. "When can we start?"

He laughed. "We might have to wait a little bit for our wedding, but we can start making babies as soon as you feel better."

"I'm feeling better right now," she replied half-breathlessly.

Without warning he scooped her up in his arms and carried her toward the bedroom. But she knew he was carrying her to her future.

She knew with her Johnny it was going to be a future filled with laughter and passion and everlasting love.

Epilogue

Johnny stepped out of the cabin and into the waning light of day. Chelsea was sleeping in his bed with his ring on her finger, and for the moment a wealth of happiness filled his heart.

The girl he'd grown up loving was the woman he would love until the end of time. He knew she felt the same way. He refused to allow any doubts about her loving him to enter his mind. He'd decided in the past three days that even if he only had her in his life for a day or a month it was worth it.

However, he knew in his heart they were going to be together forever. He'd known it since he'd been a boy. She was his person, and he knew he was hers.

She was going to be the mother of his children, and he knew she'd be awesome at the job. He couldn't wait to start building a family with her.

He looked in the distance and frowned as he saw Leroy and Caleb outside the barn. He still believed his brother and the ranch hand had secrets. He just didn't know if their secrets had anything to do with his father's murder.

Then there was his worry about Luke. His younger

brother seemed to be holding on to his sanity by a thread, and Johnny feared what might happen if that connection broke.

Finally, there was the fact that nobody had been arrested for his father's murder. Lane had admitted to him earlier that day that the case had gone completely cold, and he had no real suspect in mind.

Johnny couldn't stand the fact that his dad's murderer was walking around free in town. He hoped like hell Caleb had nothing to do with their father's death and that he could find a way to walk Luke through his anger and grief. Only time would tell.

In the meantime, he had a warm, loving woman in his bed, and the stars had begun to shine overhead. It was time for Johnny to get into bed and enjoy both of those things.

* * * * *

JOIN US ON SOCIAL MEDIA!

Stay up to date with our latest releases, author news and gossip, special offers and discounts, and all the behind-the-scenes action from Mills & Boon...

millsandboon

millsandboonuk

millsandboon

It might just be true love...

MILLS & BOON MEDICAL

Pulse-Racing Passion

Set your pulse racing with dedicated, delectable doctors in the high-pressure world of medicine, where emotions run high and passion, comfort and love are the best medicine.

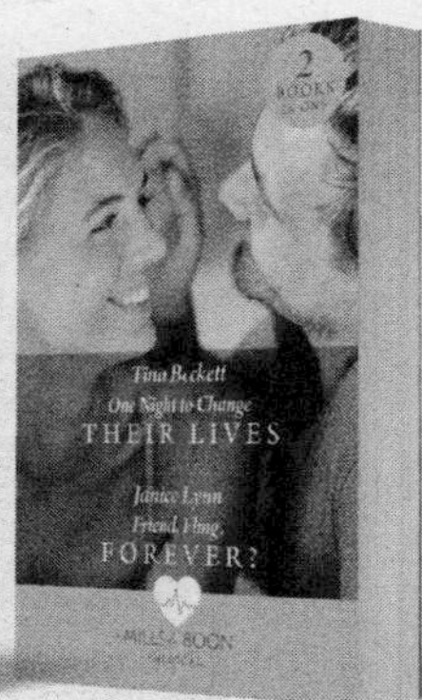

ight Medical stories published every month, find them all at:

millsandboon.co.uk

USA TODAY bestselling author **Debbie Herbert** writes paranormal romance novels reflecting her belief that love, like magic, casts its own spell of enchantment. She's always been fascinated by magic, romance and gothic stories. Married and living in Alabama, she roots for the Crimson Tide football team. Her eldest son, like many of her characters, has autism. Her youngest son is in the US Army. A past Maggie Award finalist in both young adult and paranormal romance, she's a member of the Georgia Romance Writers of America.

Kimberly Van Meter wrote her first book at sixteen and finally achieved publication in December 2006. She has written for various Mills & Boon lines. She and her husband of seventeen years have three children, three cats, and always a houseful of friends, family and fun.

Also by Debbie Herbert

Appalachian Prey
Appalachian Abduction
Unmasking the Shadow Man
Murder in the Shallows
Bayou Shadow Hunter
Bayou Shadow Protector
Bayou Wolf
Siren's Secret
Siren's Treasure
Siren's Call

Also by Kimberly Van Meter

Soldier for Hire
Soldier Protector
The Sniper
The Agent's Surrender
Moving Target
Deep Cover
The Killer You Know
Like One of the Family
Playing the Part
Something to Believe In

APPALACHIAN PERIL

DEBBIE HERBERT

COLTON'S AMNESIA TARGET

KIMBERLY VAN METER

MILLS & BOON

First Published in Great Britain 2020
by Mills & Boon, an imprint of HarperCollins*Publishers*
1 London Bridge Street, London, SE1 9GF

Special thanks and acknowledgement are given to Kimberly Van Meter for her contribution to *The Coltons of Kansas* series.

ISBN: 978-0-263-28044-9

0820

MIX
Paper from
responsible sources
FSC™ C007454

This book is produced from independently certified FSC™ paper to ensure responsible forest management.

For more information visit: www.harpercollins.co.uk/green

Printed and bound in Spain
by CPI, Barcelona

APPALACHIAN PERIL

DEBBIE HERBERT

As always, to my husband, Tim;
my sons, Byron and Jacob;
and my father, J.W. Gainey.
Much love to you all!

Chapter One

He'd found her. Again.

The chill churning Beth's insides had nothing to do with the biting Appalachian wind and everything to do with the letter in her hand. She wanted to fling it into the snow, let the white paper blend and melt into the icy flakes coating the mansion's lawn. But curiosity and a sense of self-preservation would not allow her to act so foolish. She looked up from the stack of mail in her hand and scanned the area.

Nothing marred the pristine white landscape of the exclusive Falling Rock community. Stately homes banked the lanes of the gated subdivision, and smoke curled from the chimneys of several houses. On the surface, all was cozy, civilized and well contained.

Was he watching her now? Delighting in her fear? Beth inhaled the frigid air and braced her shoulders. She wouldn't give him the satisfaction. This was a dangerous game the recently released convict played. If he'd meant physical harm, he'd already had the opportunity to do so in Boston when he broke into her condo.

She closed the mailbox lid and strolled up the driveway, even curled her lips in the semblance of a smile—just in case he was watching from the safety of the woods that lined the mountain's ridge. *Take that, Lam-*

bert. At last she reached the front door, and her numb fingers fumbled at the doorknob for a moment before she pushed her way inside.

The warmth enveloped Beth as she locked the door behind her and leaned against it, her knees suddenly no more substantial than pudding. The pile of letters slipped from her fingers and dropped to the marble floor.

Movement flickered at the end of the long hallway. Cynthia passed by, wearing black pants and an eggplant-colored cashmere sweater that was a perfect foil for her brown hair highlighted with caramel streaks. How could anyone look so good so soon after waking? Beth sighed as she removed a striped knitted hat, her hair still wet from an early-morning shower. She hung up her coat on the antique hall tree, kicked off her shoes and picked up the fallen mail, placing her letter at the back. No need to worry Cynthia about that. This was her problem.

"Morning," Beth called as she entered the den and sank onto the leather sofa across from the fireplace. Abbie had already lit a fire, and the oak logs crackled and hissed, releasing a smoky, woodsy aroma.

"Morning. Would you like Abbie to bring you a cup of coffee?" Cynthia asked. "She's in the kitchen making it now."

Beth resisted a rueful smile. Cynthia fell naturally into the hostess role, but in fact, this house belonged to *Beth* now, not her stepmother. What was Cynthia even doing there? Usually she preferred to stay in Atlanta, close to her son. Beth picked up the mug on the end table beside her. "No coffee. I already have green tea."

"So healthy you are." Cynthia shot her an indulgent smile. "You and your herbal teas. Is that what's popular in Boston with the young crowd? As for me, I need a strong dose of caffeine."

Beth tucked her stockinged feet beneath her and sipped the tea, wishing it were a Bloody Mary. Anything to take the edge off the unease rippling down her spine. Was Lambert out there now? How much longer would he hound her? Hadn't she suffered enough for, according to the convict, the so-called sins of her father?

"Beth? Beth!" Cynthia leaned in front of her, waving a hand in front of her face. "What's wrong with you?"

"N-nothing," she lied.

Cynthia's smooth forehead creased, and she straightened. "I was talking to you, and you stared out the window looking, well, frightened."

Cynthia might be on the self-absorbed side, but she was observant. Too observant. Beth wiggled her toes, considering how much to divulge.

Cynthia eased into a nearby chair. "Go on. Tell me. I'll help if I can."

She'd always been that way. A buffer between Beth and her stern father. Judge Wynngate had remained aloof and unapproachable to his only child right up until his death seven months ago. The chance for a proper father-daughter reconciliation was over.

"I had a bit of trouble in Boston," she admitted. "Somebody had been following me, even broke into my condo once."

"That's terrible." Cynthia drew back, placing a bejeweled hand with well-manicured nails against her chest. "Did the police catch the intruder?"

Beth shook her head, inwardly wincing as she recalled the cop's skepticism when she'd told him about the strange intrusion. "I'm not even sure they believed me when I reported the break-in."

"That doesn't make sense. Why wouldn't they?"

"Because nothing was stolen. My stuff had been rearranged, though. My journal and papers were taken from my bedroom and laid open on the kitchen table."

Cynthia gasped. "Why, that's—"

"Here's your coffee. One cream, no sugar."

Abbie placed the steaming mug on the table and gazed at Beth, her freckled face paler than normal and her brown eyes wide with concern. So she'd overheard.

"Thank you, Abigail."

At Cynthia's dismissive tone, Abbie hurried from the room, avoiding meeting Beth's eyes, which were filled with a silent apology for her stepmother's terse manner. Cynthia affixed her sharp gaze on Beth. "Go on."

Beth realized she wanted—no, *needed*—to talk to someone about her fear. Someone who'd take her seriously. And didn't her stepmother deserve to know about the continued slander Lambert had flung against her dad, Cynthia's late husband? She drew a deep breath and plunged ahead.

"The thing is, just a couple days before that happened, I'd received a threatening letter that said I have to pay for my father's corruption."

"Corruption?" Cynthia's lipsticked mouth fell open. "What's that supposed to mean? Edward was aboveboard in every way."

"I don't know. That's all the note said. I immediately suspected it was written by Dorsey Lambert."

Cynthia's face scrunched in displeasure. "I'd hoped to never hear that name again."

They fell silent, remembering the troublesome case of the drug dealer who'd been led from Judge Wyngate's courtroom, defiant and screaming about corruption in the justice system. Specifically, against the honored judge himself. Lambert had vowed revenge and her father had taken the matter so seriously that he'd installed an elaborate security system for their Atlanta estate. Too bad he hadn't done the same for this house in the North Georgia mountains.

"At least the Boston police checked out that lead for me," she said at last. "Turns out Dorsey Lambert was released from prison only two weeks ago."

"Did they question him?"

"Not personally. They contacted Atlanta PD, who went to the address Lambert provided the Georgia Department of Corrections. His mother vouched for him. Said he was living with her, working a steady job and completely off drugs."

"Of course she did," Cynthia said with an elegant lift of her chin. "What mother wouldn't provide an alibi for her child?"

"Exactly." Beth stared at her stepmother, wondering if Cynthia remembered doing much the same for her son, Aiden. Cynthia's protection of Aiden had come at Beth's expense, and her father had sided with his wife. The entire incident had created a distance from her dad that was never bridged before his death.

Old news. Let it go. Beth drew a deep breath. "Anyway, after getting that note I returned to the Boston PD to report the latest incident, and they kind of gave me the brush-off. Had me fill out a report and said they'd look into the matter." Beth stopped, flushing as she remembered how the cop on duty had lifted his eyebrows as she'd relayed what happened. He clearly thought she'd been spooked by an admittedly creepy letter and was making mountains of molehills.

"You should have told me earlier. I can make a few

phone calls and have the Boston police prodded to do a thorough investigation."

Beth had considered it, of course. But winter break from her art teaching job had been around the corner, and she'd hoped it would all blow over by the time she returned. Her fingers tapped the pile of mail. Clearly, matters had not blown over with Lambert.

Cynthia's gaze dropped to the mail. "What's the matter? Did you get another letter?"

Sighing, Beth picked it up and stared at the envelope, which was postmarked Atlanta and had no return mailing information. Her name and address were printed in a standard computer font. She turned it over and picked at the edge.

"Shouldn't you be wearing gloves?"

"Too late now." Beth ripped it open, then frowned at the tiny scraps of paper littering the bottom.

"What is it?" Cynthia asked, leaning forward.

"I'm not sure." She emptied the bits of paper on the coffee table and spread them out. The small pieces had crisp edges, as though they'd been precisely cut with scissors or some other sharp tool. They were black and white and gray with printed text on the back, obviously clipped from a newspaper. She tried to arrange the text in some logical order but failed. Next, she arranged the scraps on the reverse side and gazed down at the jagged newspaper photo that emerged. Fear fizzed the nape of her neck.

She recognized the photograph. It had been shot at one of the few charitable events she'd attended with her father three years earlier. The judge was seated at a head table, Cynthia and her son, Aiden, on his right, and Beth at his immediate left. Her father held a wineglass in the air, proposing a toast to the guests and thanking them for their attendance.

In the midst of the varying shades of pixilated gray, a red marker circled Beth's body, and in the center of her chest was a red dot.

A lethal target mark.

"Oh my God," Cynthia said. With a loud thud, she set her coffee mug on the table. "I'll call Sheriff Sampson to come here at once. I really wished you had put on gloves like I asked."

"Me, too," she murmured, eyes fixed on the angry red dot.

An unexpected, warm pressure landed on her right shoulder, and Beth jumped to her feet. Twisting around, she half expected to find Lambert had sneaked in and was upon them. Instead, she faced Abbie's troubled eyes.

"Who would do something like this?" Abbie breathed, pressing her hands to her cheeks.

"I can only think of one person."

"Call the sheriff's office," Cynthia said crisply into her cell phone. It instantly obeyed her voice command, and the digital ring buzzed through the den.

"We could just go down to the station," Beth pointed out. If the local officers were anything like the Boston PD, they wouldn't find this latest letter an emergency worthy of their immediate attention.

Cynthia waved an impatient hand, phone pressed to an ear. "I'd like to speak to Harlan Sampson," she demanded.

She and Abbie exchanged a look. How like her stepmother to go straight to the top of the chain. "This is Mrs. Cynthia Wynngate of Falling Rock. It's a matter of the utmost importance."

It was a familiar tone that both embarrassed and irritated Beth. Still, she had to admit that Cynthia's air of confident privilege was one that certainly got results.

"What do you mean he's not in? I need to speak with him at once." Her lips pursed. "A conference, you say? When will he be back?" Pause. "Then send out your next highest-ranking officer. I'll explain when he gets here. The address is 2331 Apple Orchard Lane."

Cynthia tapped a button, then dropped the phone on the sofa. "We should expect them in the next fifteen minutes or so. Abbie, make more coffee and heat up those cheese Danish rolls in the refrigerator."

Abbie slowly returned to the kitchen, casting troubled glances over her shoulder.

Cynthia retrieved her phone, aimed it at the macabre cut-up puzzle and snapped a photo. "The officer will collect this for evidence. Figured it wouldn't hurt for us to keep a backup photo. You can't be too careful. Do you have a copy of the first letter?"

"The Boston PD kept it."

She gave a quick nod, already in her familiar take-charge mode. "We'll have Harlan contact them and coordinate an investigation."

"You really think they'll do anything?" Beth asked doubtfully.

"Of course. I contributed to Harlan's reelection campaign. If nothing else, he'll investigate as a favor to me."

A new worry nagged at Beth. What if they sent Officer Armstrong over to the house? No, no. Surely not. Cynthia had asked for the next in line to the sheriff. Hopefully, that person wasn't Armstrong. Could she really be that unlucky? Hadn't her morning been bad enough?

She stared out the patio door with its panoramic view

of the Appalachian Mountains. Snow brushed the tips and limbs of the trees and cleanly blanketed the ground.

Except for the large footprints originating at the edge of the woods and ending at their back porch.

Chapter Two

Sammy sighed as he finished his grits, slapped the cash on the counter and took a final gulp of iced tea. Yeah, he was a cop, so he should have been drinking the proverbial coffee and eating doughnuts. Call him a rebel.

"Trouble?" Jack asked, collecting the money and stuffing it in the till.

"Nah. Just duty calling. Catch you later."

He strolled to the cruiser, refusing to acknowledge the slight ping he'd experienced when the dispatcher had given him the name and address. No big deal, he told himself as he drove the short distance from Lavender to Blood Mountain. No need to think Mrs. Wynngate's stepdaughter would be visiting. No reason to believe there was danger brewing.

He waved to the security guard at the gate and breezed into the Falling Rock community with its rows of manicured homes. Blood Mountain was only half the size of its neighbor and sparsely inhabited except for this one exclusive subdivision. When people like Cynthia Wynngate called, they expected immediate attention, no matter the problem. He'd heard that Mrs. Wynngate's husband had died many) months ago. At least he wouldn't be stepping into a domestic disturbance situation. Those were the worst.

He knew exactly which showcase house belonged to the Wynngates, even if he hadn't been there in years. Sammy parked in the semicircular brick driveway and strode to the door, automatically surveying the area and cataloging details.

The Massachusetts license plate on the sleek BMW was the first sign of trouble.

Cynthia Wynngate's cold welcome at the door—"What took you so long to get here?"—was the second sign.

The final confirmation of trouble was the woman pacing the den. Pewter eyes, cool as gunmetal, slammed into him—she was clearly as unhappy to see him as he was to cross paths with her again. A younger girl he didn't recognize stood in the corner of the room, polishing a cherry hutch, trying to act inconspicuous but watching everything from the corner of her eyes.

Mrs. Wynngate didn't bother with introductions. He'd met her a few times over the years at local charity events and political fund-raisers. Not that she'd remember him. He was a law enforcement officer, a guy with a badge who served a function if she ever needed his service. Nothing more. She waved a hand at the coffee table as she sank onto a sofa. "Beth, tell him what's going on."

Beth uncrossed her arms and reluctantly made her way over, pointing at scraps of paper littering the table. "This came in the mail today."

He took a seat and peered down. "What is this? A cut-up old newspaper photo?"

Beth leaned over him, and he inhaled the clean scent of shampoo and talcum powder. A sudden, inexplicable urge to pull her into his lap and inhale her sweet freshness nearly overwhelmed him. *Stop it. Concentrate on the job.*

"Yes," she answered. "The photo's from many years ago. And that red dot is where he marked my chest."

The crimson ink made the hairs on his forearms rise. Why would anyone want to harm Beth? Perhaps it had been a particularly bad breakup with a boyfriend. Or an encounter with a guy who'd harbored hidden stalker behavior. "Any idea who might have sent this?"

"Dorsey Lambert," Beth answered at once. "He threatened retaliation against Dad when he was sentenced twelve years back."

His forehead creased. The name didn't ring a bell. "But that was a long time ago. How can you be so sure—"

"They released him two weeks ago. Within days, I got a letter in Boston saying I'd have to pay for my father's corruption."

Mrs. Wynngate made a ticking noise of disgust as she rose from her seat and signaled to the young girl by the hutch. "Such a ridiculous accusation. Abbie, see if the officer would like coffee or refreshments."

Sammy flashed a quick smile in the girl's direction and held up a hand. "No, thanks," he told her, returning his attention to the photograph.

A disgruntled ex-con. Should be easy enough to track down the guy and have him questioned. He was obviously trying to scare Beth, but odds were he'd never take action. Often, these kinds of cowardly threats amounted to nothing more than bluster. But he'd definitely investigate. If this Lambert guy was released on parole rather than end-of-sentence, then he'd report the threats to Lambert's parole officer and have his parole revoked.

"I'll check this out," he promised Beth.

"Hope that means more than a phone call to the Georgia Department of Corrections," she said stiffly. "Because that's all the Boston PD did for me."

"I told you I'd follow up. As soon as I have information, I'll call you."

The skeptical look on her face made him want to groan. Of course she had no reason to trust him, of all people. She opened her mouth, no doubt to utter some sharp retort, but her stepmother interrupted.

"Tell him about the footprints," Cynthia said.

Footprints? That was definitely more foreboding than anonymous mail. It meant danger was close by. It meant someone intended harm.

With a sigh, Beth strolled to the French doors overlooking the backyard. "Right there," she said. "They start at the tree line by the back of the property and come all the way to the patio."

A Peeping Tom, perhaps? Yet he couldn't disregard the coincidence of them appearing on the same day as the letter. He eyed the prints. Large and wide, probably from a male.

"Tell you what. I'll snap some close-up photos of these prints and follow them out to the woods. Take a look around. I'll be back shortly to collect that mail as evidence. In the meantime, don't touch it anymore, okay? The fewer fingerprints on it, the better."

"Of course," she muttered, and he had the feeling she was barely able to refrain from rolling her eyes.

Sammy stepped outside and withdrew his cell phone, then bent on one knee and observed the footprint. About a man's size thirteen, he guessed. It wasn't much to go on. The snow was so light that no identifying shoe treads remained, only the outline of the shoe and the dark earth beneath the dusting of snow. He snapped several photos, then followed the tracks to the woods.

At the woods' edge, a *whish* sounded from behind, and he spun around.

"I wanted to see if you found anything." Beth stood before him, a stubborn set to her heart-shaped face.

It was an expression he'd witnessed several times before.

"Not a good idea. Better get back to the house, just in case. Those tracks were fresh."

"I'd rather not. And this is our property, after all. I have a right to know if anyone's trespassing."

"You also have the right to get hurt if someone's still out here," he retorted.

She said nothing, merely crossed her arms over her chest and lifted her chin a fraction. Clearly, she didn't intend to listen to reason. Especially not coming from him. He shrugged. Whoever had been here had surely seen him pull up in the sheriff's department cruiser and had hightailed it out. "Suit yourself. But stay behind me and keep quiet."

Surprisingly, she complied. He carefully picked his way through dead vines, leafless shrubs and evergreen trees, eyes peeled for any sign of broken twigs or an object left behind. But the snow hadn't drifted down past the heavy canopy of the treetops, and there were no tracks evident, only mounds of seemingly undisturbed pine needles and twigs. Only ten feet into the woods, the ground dropped off sharply along the ridge forming Blood Mountain.

Sammy scanned the area. From here, he could view the dirt road below and the much larger Lavender Mountain, which loomed across from them. There was no evidence that anyone had recently tromped through these woods, and the unpaved road below sported an untouched sprinkling of snow. Whoever had been at the Wynngate estate was either still hiding somewhere in the thick woods, or he'd parked an ATV farther down the dirt road, well out of their sight. He stood silent for several minutes, trying to make out any unnatural rustling or spot anything out of the ordinary in the green, brown, gray and white landscape.

Nothing.

"He's gone," Beth whispered, stepping beside him.

"Appears that way. Soon as I leave here, I'll get the department's ATV and drive down the dirt road. See if there're any recent road tracks."

"You will?"

Again with the skeptical tone in her voice. "If I say I'm going to do something, I do it."

She nodded, started to turn away and then faced him again. "Thank you."

Must have killed her to say that. She clearly still held a grudge. He followed her back to the house, and just as Beth was about to reach for the patio door to reenter the den, he decided to try, one last time, to explain about that night so many years ago. He tapped her shoulder for attention and let his hand drop when she faced him.

"Look, Beth. Hear me out. I'm sorry for what happened back then. It wasn't fair that you were left taking all the blame that night for a situation that had clearly grown out of your control."

Her mouth pursed in a tight line. "Damn right it wasn't fair. The house was packed with people, and I was probably the only person in it not drinking or smoking pot."

"It was filled with *underage* people at *your* house,"

he reminded her. “And we found traces of heavier drugs. Not just marijuana.”

“But I knew nothing about that. I didn’t even know most of those people or where they came from. I was only seventeen, and somehow, a small party while my parents were away turned into something I couldn’t control.”

“I understood that, even as a rookie cop. But I had no—”

“I needed your help. If you understood the situation, then why the hell did you have to arrest me?”

The question hung between them.

Again he tried to explain. “Like I said, I was a rookie. My partner was an experienced patrol officer, and I was only a few weeks into my probationary period. He took the hard-nosed approach, and I had no choice in the matter.”

He remembered Beth’s panicked eyes that night, her tear-streaked face as she’d opened the door and let them into the house where the party raged uncontrollably. “Thank God you’re here,” she’d said. “I can’t find Aiden anywhere.”

She’d recognized him that night. He and her brother had played baseball together in the Lavender Mountain Youth League every summer for years. They’d been close friends up until high school, when Aiden had run with a different set of friends that were more into parties than sports, and they’d drifted away from each other.

“You have no idea how that arrest affected me.” Beth crossed her arms and bit her lip, as though regretting that admission.

“It wasn’t fair that everything came down on you,” he admitted.

Sammy had no doubt Aiden was responsible for the

wild crowd that evening. Yet the Golden Boy had managed to escape the debacle with no arrest record to mar his future career as a criminal attorney. Actually, everyone had gone free, save Beth. The herd of partygoers had stampeded out the back door, leaving behind all the drugs and alcohol. The quiet mountain subdivision had roared with the sound of their vehicles hastily exiting the premises.

"Forget it," she said at last, her back stiffening.

"I would, but apparently you can't," he said. "I was only doing my job that night. I hope you understand."

She gave a grudging nod. "I can appreciate that. I just wish…that you'd been able to intervene on my behalf. I was scared and unsure what to do."

That had been obvious. But Sergeant Thomas had been unmoved, ordering Sammy to handcuff Beth and place her in the cruiser.

"Did you really try to soften the older cop, or did you blindly follow orders?" Beth asked.

And there was the crux of the matter. He'd voiced his opinion, but once the sergeant shot down his objection, he'd kept his mouth shut. If he'd had it to do all over again, Sammy liked to think he'd have acted differently, have insisted that Aiden be held responsible for what had happened in that house.

He cleared his throat, about to defend himself once more, when he spotted movement within the house. Cynthia Wynngate emerged from the hallway into the den, rolling a large piece of luggage across the gleaming walnut floor.

"Does your stepmother have plans to go somewhere?" he asked.

Beth frowned and pushed open the door. "Not that I'm aware of."

They reentered the warmth of the spacious living room, where Abbie collected used coffee cups.

"Where are you going?" Beth asked Cynthia.

"Back to Atlanta. I couldn't possibly stay here after all this."

Actually, that wouldn't be a bad idea, Sammy mulled. If they left for the city, they might be safer in a new location that wasn't so isolated.

Mrs. Wynngate turned to Abbie. "I left your paycheck on the mantel. I won't be needing your services again until all this is cleared up." Her gaze flickered to where they stood by the door. "Beth, be careful about keeping the house locked tight. Officer—" her eyes scrunched as she peered at his ID badge "—Officer Armstrong. Can your department be sure to patrol by the house and keep surveillance on it? So many neighbors have already vacated their homes during the off season, and I don't want any trouble."

He blinked at the elegant woman before him. Was she really going to leave Beth behind and not even offer her the option of returning to Atlanta with her? Apparently, her only concern seemed to be for the house itself. What kind of person left another to face danger alone? Especially a family member?

Abbie spoke up. "I'll stay with you if you'd like, Beth."

"That would be great, Abbie," she said softly. "Thank you."

Mrs. Wynngate frowned. "But she's no longer in my employ."

"Abbie and I will work something out," Beth said.

He marveled at Beth's composure. Did she not even see how she'd been so coldly dismissed by her stepmother? That Cynthia had even made it clear she wasn't footing the bill for Abbie's sleepover? Or maybe this was all par for the course, and Beth expected nothing from the woman.

Strange family.

Chapter Three

Something was…not quite right.

Beth snapped from the void of sleep to alertness. Slivers of moonbeams jabbed through the blind's slats, etching vertical patterns against an onyx darkness. Although the house was silent, she was sure there had been a noise. A click of a latch, perhaps…a brief metallic ping that had no place in the dead of night.

She hardly dared move, her right hand tightly bunching a mound of down comforter as she eased into a sitting position. Seconds passed, then several minutes, the only noise a loud whooshing of her unsteady breath.

Her mind scrambled for an explanation. Maybe Abbie had awakened and gone to the bathroom down the hall, locking the door behind her. Yes, that made sense. All this business with Dorsey Lambert had troubled her so deeply that it had invaded her dreams. Yet Beth remained upright in bed, waiting for the bathroom door to creak open.

It didn't.

Cautiously, she swung her legs over the side of the bed and gently lowered her feet to the floor. Without flipping on a light, she unplugged her cell phone from the charger at her nightstand and walked to the door, her bare toes plunging into the plush carpet. Her hand grasped the doorknob, turned it ever so slowly, and then pushed the door open an inch. Just as deliberately as she'd turned the knob clockwise to open it, she released it counterclockwise and peered down the hallway.

No splinter of light shone beneath the bathroom door.

The large windows of the den's cathedral ceiling provided enough illumination to inch forward. She continued down the hallway toward the guest room at the end of the hall where Abbie was staying. At the girl's door, Beth raised a hand to knock, then hesitated. How foolish she'd look if she awakened Abbie for no reason.

Kerthunk.

Beth jumped at the sound that had emanated one story below. Her father's old study. It sounded as though one of the books had tumbled from the shelf onto the hardwood flooring. The first logical explanation that came to mind was that some nimble feline had accidently knocked over a heavy object.

Too bad Cynthia didn't have a cat.

She swallowed hard past the lump in her throat, not wanting to acknowledge the other logical conclusion: someone was in the house. Indecision tore at her. Should she call the cops and barricade herself and Abbie in the guest room, or try to figure out what the hell was going on?

The unmistakable rustling of papers from below prompted her to immediate action. She opened the bedroom door and hurried to the bed.

Abbie wasn't there.

Confusion spiked her mind. Had she entered the wrong guest room? No, the girl's overnight bag was on the dresser. So where was Abbie? Beth put a hand on her chest and willed her racing heart to slow. Now was the time for level thinking.

Perhaps Abbie was the one in the study. She'd gotten up in the middle of the night and, unable to sleep, had gone downstairs to read or watch television. She could have gone in Dad's study to get a book, accidentally bumped against the desk and knocked something over.

Beth almost smiled with relief. Still, she kept her phone on with speed dial at the ready in case there was a more sinister explanation. She almost hadn't let Sammy put his number in her phone, but he'd appeared unwilling to leave until she allowed him to do so. And she'd wanted him to go. His presence unnerved her.

Careful to make no noise, she returned to the hallway and made her way to the winding staircase leading to the den. At the bottom of the stairs, she picked her way through the den and the kitchen. Sure enough, the study door was cracked open several inches, and dim light spilled from the lamp on Dad's desk.

She'd been right. Pleased with her logic, Beth opened her mouth to call out a greeting to Abbie, but the words died in her throat.

A man wearing jeans and a black hoodie was rifling through the file cabinet.

Not. Abbie.

He jerked a handful of papers out of a file and thrust them under the lamp, studying their contents. The intruder wore black gloves—and that detail terrified her more than the hoodie drawn tightly about his face.

She tried not to make a sound as she again picked her way back through the kitchen and then the den. Where the hell was Abbie? Beth ran up the stairs, hoping the carpet muffled her footsteps. At the top of the stairs, she paused. She didn't dare dial Sammy, afraid the intruder would hear her speak. Instead, she shot Sammy a text: There's someone in my house.

She hit Send, and then immediately typed a second one: Hurry.

She watched until the gray bar on the text screen read Sent and then Delivered. Good. She'd follow up with a phone call once she'd locked herself in her room. But before she even reached the bedroom door, the phone vibrated in her palm. Beth waited until she was safely tucked into her room before reading the message.

On my way. Lock yourself in your room. Don't open it for anyone but me.

Thank heavens he'd responded so quickly so late at night. Yeah, she could lock herself up. But what about Abbie? She couldn't leave her to fend for herself. Beth wished she had Abbie's phone number to warn her of the danger. A sudden thought clutched at her heart: Had the intruder tied and gagged Abbie? The longer the silence, the more convinced Beth grew that it must be the case.

She padded to the window and peered through the slats. Abbie's car was still in the driveway. The girl was in as much or more danger as she was. No way Beth would cower in her room and let Abbie come to any harm. What if the intruder decided to kill her when he'd finished his business?

Before losing her courage, Beth again tiptoed out of her room. She'd grab the poker by the fireplace as a makeshift weapon. Dad used to keep a firearm in his bedroom, but she doubted Cynthia still had it. She'd always claimed that having the gun made her nervous.

Slowly, slowly, *slowly* Beth descended the stairs, vigilant for any noise or shifting patterns in the darkness. Another faint rustling of papers came from the study. At least she knew where the man was. Hastily, she scurried to the fireplace and clasped the poker. The cold, hard metal in her palms allayed her fear only an iota. If the man had a gun, the poker was useless. Still, it was better than nothing if he tried to rush at her.

She surveyed the den, seeking a bound and gagged Abbie, but the sofa and chairs were empty, and there were no signs of a struggle. Beth walked softly out of the room and went on to check the downstairs bedrooms, bathrooms and dining room. Nothing, nothing and nothing.

How much longer until Sammy arrived?

Could she have missed seeing Abbie somewhere in the kitchen? If Abbie were lucky, she'd have seen or heard the intruder and slipped outside to the patio, probably caught unawares without a phone or car keys. Even now, she might be out in the cold, shivering and frightened. First, Beth would check the kitchen, and then proceed outside.

A murmur emanated from the study, and her heart slammed in her ribs. Was the man talking to himself? More murmurs, an exchange of different pitches in the low warble of the voices.

There were *two* of them.

Her hands convulsed against the poker, and her eyes flicked around the den. A swish of fabric sounded as someone moved toward the kitchen. Whoever he was, his steps were deliberate and unhurried. She glanced over her shoulder, eyeing the distance between where she stood and the comparative safety of the hallway. It seemed to stretch as long as a football field.

No time to retreat. Beth ducked behind the sofa and prayed they were heading for the back door and leaving as quietly as they had entered.

Her nose prickled—the involuntary tingling of an

oncoming sneeze. No! Not now. Fear danced in her gut. She splayed a hand across her nose and mouth, trying to suppress the telltale reflex. A muffled explosion escaped her mouth.

The fabric swishing stopped.

"What's that?" one of the men asked, his voice so near that horror chilled every inch of her flesh.

"Someone there?" another man called out.

Elliptical beams of headlights and a dizzying blue strobe pierced the glass panels lining the front door. Judging by the profusion of colors, more than one cop car had arrived at the scene.

"Damn it!"

"Let's get outta here!"

The two men raced toward the back patio and jerked open the French doors, flinging them aside. Glass exploded with a crash. Shards rained down with a loud, scattered tinkling, and a cool burst of air swept through the room, chilling her arms.

She was going to live through this nightmare. Now to find Abbie. Beth rose, still clutching the poker. "Abbie?" she called. "It's safe now. Where are you?"

A high-pitched cry exploded through the open patio door. Abbie was alive.

Beth ran forward. "Abbie? You all right?"

Abbie ran in the door, her red hair sprinkled with snow and her arms clasped around her waist. Blood dribbled from a cut in her forehead, and she shivered violently.

"They hurt you!" Beth cried. She grabbed a woolen afghan from the sofa and draped it over Abbie's shoulders. "You must be freezing. You're safe now. Let the cops in the front door while I lock the patio doors."

Outside, the stygian atmosphere wholly absorbed

any sight of the trespassers. The intruders' dark clothing had allowed them to slip into the black velvet of the night. Hastily, she pulled the door shut and fastened the lock. More glass splintered and crashed to the floor. One good kick and the whole glass door would completely shatter. Hardly did any good to secure it shut, but maybe it would buy a few seconds' time if the intruders returned and had to kick the remaining glass.

"Beth! Are you okay?"

She swiveled at Sammy's shout, surprised at its underlying sound of concern.

"We're good," she called.

He entered the den, his eyes immediately fixating on her face. She pointed at the door. "They ran outside."

Footsteps trampled in the hallway as more officers entered. Sirens blared, signaling that more were on the way. Beth rubbed her arms, suddenly conscious she was clad in an old T-shirt and pajama bottoms.

Sammy stood beside her, draped a blanket over her shoulders and wordlessly guided her to the sofa. Abbie was already seated nearby, speaking with an officer.

His kind brown eyes calmed her as he waited, letting her catch her breath. Old memories suddenly resurfaced. Instead of seeing Sammy as an emblem of the great divide in her life that had spiraled her fortune downward, Beth remembered her teenage crush on him. He was Aiden's close friend, several years older and totally out of reach. During their summers at Blood Mountain, she'd attended every baseball game he and Aiden played, secretly thrilling at his muscular physique in uniform, the speed with which he ran bases, the skill and power with which he batted.

The house suddenly blazed with swirling blue lights from every window. Out back, a floodlight flicked on and illuminated the yard all the way to the mountain ridge. The rooms buzzed with the cackle of two-way radios and men shouting orders as they spread through the house, guns drawn. Beth dropped her gaze from Sammy, pushing the memories away. “Thanks for getting here so quickly.”

“I told you to call whenever you needed me. I’m glad you did.”

She looked back up, studying the gentle and determined set of his face. The chaos surrounding them melted away, and only his dark eyes remained. For the first time all day, she felt warm and safe.

Until he opened his mouth.

“How well do you know this Abbie girl?”

She shrugged, surprised at the question. “Well enough, I guess. She’s worked two or three years for Cynthia, and we’ve talked a bit during my brief visits. She works part-time here and goes to community college. Why? What about her?”

“Do you even know her last name?”

Sheepish, Beth glanced down at her bare feet. “Honestly, no. But what does that matter? She’s always—”

“It matters plenty,” he cut in, his tone rough with suspicion.

Beth gave Abbie a quick glance. The girl’s forehead was already beginning to swell and bruise. Someone had handed her a tissue, and she blotted at the trickle of blood still seeping from her wound. Beth already sensed Sammy’s answer, but she had to ask anyway. “What’s Abbie’s last name?” she whispered.

“It’s Lambert.”

Chapter Four

"Lambert?" Beth's body recoiled in surprise.

Pretty much his reaction when he'd checked up on the girl this afternoon. "Actually, it's her maiden name. But yeah."

"She doesn't look old enough to be married." Beth studied Abbie from across the room.

"Married at seventeen, divorced at twenty-one. Legal name is Abigail Lambert Fenton."

"I had no idea. Cynthia couldn't have known that either when she hired her."

"To be fair, Lambert's a common name in these hills. Dorsey was originally from Ellijay, only thirty miles from here. Man's got plenty of extended family in the area."

"Seems I ran straight into the lion's den," Beth said with a snort. "Should have stayed in Boston."

"Could be her relationship to Dorsey is distant, and this is all a coincidence." Not that Sammy believed that for a minute. Abbie Fenton was probably involved up to her freckled little neck in this mischief. With any luck, he'd put a stop to it all this evening. No more threats and break-ins.

"She seemed so nice." Hurt chased across Beth's eyes.

"You know what they say. Got to watch those quiet

ones," he said, attempting a smile to alleviate her worry. "Woman even volunteered to stay the night with you. Call me jaded, but that rang an alarm in my mind. I'd intended to come back this morning and have a chat with her. Imagine my surprise when I got your text."

Beth's gray eyes widened. "You don't think she had anything to do with those intruders, do you? I mean, she's hurt."

"A superficial cut on the forehead. Could be self-induced. And at first glance, I see no signs of forced entry. Officers are checking all the windows and doors as we speak."

"Surely you don't think… Are you saying Abbie *let* them in?"

"We're not ruling anything out at this point. Now tell me everything that happened tonight. What first alerted you—"

Beth shoved the chair from beneath her and strode to where Abbie sat with an officer. The woman's mouth opened in surprise when she spotted Beth headed her way. Abbie's eyes hardened, and she stiffly drew up her slight frame, clearly signaling she expected a confrontation and was prepared to dig in her heels.

"Did you let those men in my house?" Beth asked, voice tight with anger.

A sullen Abigail lifted her chin and refused to respond. She looked older now, a certain sternness in her features that hadn't been there earlier. Officer Graham raised a quizzical brow at Sammy.

Quickly, Sammy rushed to Beth's side. "Let us ask the questions," he admonished.

Beth ignored him. "Well, did you?" she persisted. "Why? What do they want?"

Abbie kept her face averted, eyes focused on the patio door, her mouth set in a grim twist.

Sammy took Beth's elbow and steered her to the kitchen. Beth still wasn't through. "How could you do such a thing?" she called over her shoulder. "We trusted you!"

"Let Officer Graham ask the questions and do his job. In the meantime, I want a statement from you."

"Can I at least put on a sweater and start coffee?" she grumbled.

"Be my guest." There was no hurry. He'd stay here all night if necessary. He wouldn't rest until the intruders had been found and Abbie had confessed to her role in tonight's invasion. More important, he wouldn't leave Beth alone in this house until he knew she was safe.

She hurried from the kitchen, nearly colliding with Officer Markwell. Both officers watched as she slipped from the room.

"No signs of forced entry anywhere," Markwell reported without preamble. "No open or broken windows, no damaged doors and no footprints around the sides of the house. Point of entry appears to be the patio door, where we found several sets of footprints leading to the woods at the back of the property."

"No damage to the patio door locks?" he asked.

"None."

The two-way radio at his belt crackled, and the voice of Officer Lipscomb cut in. "No sign yet of anyone on the property. Heading to the road below to see if there are any tracks."

"Ten-four," he answered before turning to Markwell. "Sweep through every room. Make sure they're empty and mark any signs of disturbance."

Markwell left, and Sammy stared at Abbie. Her lips

were pinched together, and her chin lifted in stubborn defiance. She was going to be a tough nut to crack.

Beth reentered the kitchen wearing a long, loose cardigan sweater. She'd also donned a pair of thick woolen socks. Without sparing him a glance, she poured water into the coffee maker. "Want a cup?" she asked, her back to him.

"No, but I'll take a soda if you've got one."

"In the fridge. Help yourself."

He got out a can and opened it, taking a long swallow as he watched Beth. Her hands trembled as she pressed the machine's buttons. Now that the shock had worn off, the reality of what had happened was settling in. He'd seen it many times before.

"We won't leave until we're sure your place is locked up tight," he assured her. "And we'll keep a patrol outside, too."

She looked up, and her lips trembled before she offered a tight smile. "Thank you. Really. I don't know what might have happened if you hadn't arrived so quickly."

For the first time in ages, Beth gazed at him without a trace of acrimony. The air between them crackled with an electrical charge, one not caused by animosity. That was certainly new.

The aroma of coffee filled the air, and she jerked her gaze away, busying herself with retrieving a cup from the cabinet. After she'd fortified her nerves with the brew, he'd walk with Beth to the downstairs study and ask her to check for any missing items.

What had those men been after? This went way beyond the scare tactics of menacing mail. And if it had been a robbery, they would have gone after electronics or searched for jewelry and money. Beth's purse hung on the back of one of the kitchen chairs, apparently undisturbed.

"Check your bag," he said. "See if anything's missing."

Beth gasped and went to her purse. "Didn't even think of that." After riffling through it and opening her wallet, she shook her head. "Everything's here—my credit cards, cash and driver's license."

No simple burglary, then. Of course, he'd known that anyway because of Abbie's obvious connection with the Lambert clan. But what had they been after? Again, his gaze drifted to the recalcitrant, unremorseful Abigail. Doubtful she was going to volunteer any information.

Did she and other members of Dorsey's disreputable family really believe that Judge Wynngate had been corrupt? Had they planned tonight's invasion to search for evidence to back their wild claims?

It was the only explanation that made sense. As Beth sipped coffee, he strolled to the kitchen window, watching snowflakes sift quietly to the ground. Had the men found what they'd come to collect? Would they return? If they did, it would be incredibly stupid, but no one said criminals possessed the brightest brains.

Returning would be a grave mistake on their part. There'd be no more Abbie to silently open the door and allow them easy access. Still, he should probably convince Beth that she wasn't safe here, that the best thing she could do was return to Boston as soon as possible. At the very least, she needed to spend the rest of her visit with her stepmother in Atlanta—whether Cynthia Wynngate wanted her there or not.

Sammy quashed the small dash of disappointment that arose at the prospect of Beth leaving. She intrigued him, even all those years ago when she'd sat in the stands watching him and Aiden playing baseball. But their age difference had seemed too great then, and she was his friend's sister, after all. Back then, Aiden's friendship had been important to him. Aiden…a solution popped into his mind.

"Maybe it's time you paid a visit to Aiden," he suggested. "At least until we've made an arrest and it's safe to return. How long were you planning to stay on vacation, anyway?"

She lifted a shoulder and let it drop. "No idea. I like to play things by ear. Keep it fluid. I'm free until after the New Year, when classes start up again. I teach art to middle schoolers."

Aiden had mentioned that Beth had an "artsy" job teaching children. He'd said it with a smile that Sammy couldn't decipher, either proud of his sister's occupation or indulgent in a patronizing way.

"So what about visiting your brother?" he asked again, aware she'd sidestepped the question.

She lifted the cup to her lips and took a small sip before answering. "Maybe."

He didn't push. His peripheral vision picked up Officer Graham motioning to him. Sammy started in his direction, and Graham met him halfway.

"The suspect's refusing to answer questions. How about I take her to the station?"

A change of environment might loosen her tongue, especially when faced with the chill starkness of an interrogation room. Members of the Lambert family were no strangers to a jail's ambience, but perhaps Abbie was young enough never to have witnessed it outside of family visitation days. Being questioned and held in a cell didn't compare to the inmate guest experience.

"Yep. Get her out of here," he told Graham. "And don't release her unless you check with me first."

Graham returned to the den, took Abbie by the arm and guided her toward the foyer. She pointedly kept her face averted to avoid Sammy's gaze. Or Beth's. Either way, Sammy took it as a sign of guilt. If Abbie were innocent, she'd be pleading her case to Beth.

"Glad she's gone," Beth muttered. "I hope to never see her again."

"You won't have to. Next time, Cynthia needs to be more thorough in hiring help."

"Agreed." Beth set down her cup. "Ready to take my statement?"

"First, let's go to your dad's office. Take a good look around and see if anything's missing."

Beth tugged the sweater and gave a brisk nod. Wordlessly, she strode past him, and he followed her through the main floor and then down one level to the study.

The room was brightly lit from an overhead fixture as well as a lamp atop a huge mahogany desk. Two matching mahogany file cabinets, most of the drawers hanging open, banked a side wall. Behind the desk, legal tomes crammed a floor-to-ceiling bookcase. A steady, studious office with an old-fashioned vibe. All befitting a judge.

Several files were scattered across the desk's gleaming surface, along with an open laptop. Papers littered the floor where the intruders had dropped them in their haste to leave. Without touching the papers, Sammy leaned down to peer at the words. Seemed to be court records of various convicted felons. He put on a pair of plastic gloves, and with the tip of a finger, he turned the computer to face him. The screen was black. He tapped the keyboard, and a desktop wallpaper featuring the Atlanta federal courthouse sprang to life. In the center of the monitor was:

Edward Preston Wynngate III

Invalid Password. Try again.

The intruders hadn't cracked the code, so they weren't dealing with experienced hackers. Sammy wondered if they'd planned on stealing the laptop to investigate further, but the unexpected arrival of the cops had interrupted their plan. "Do you know your father's password?" he asked Beth.

She shook her head. "Sorry. He was a reserved man and preferred we not even enter his office while he was working. Said it disturbed his concentration." Her eyes scanned the room. "Actually, he didn't like people coming in even when he wasn't at work."

"Why?"

"He was very meticulous. Probably afraid we'd mess everything up."

Sammy could think of another reason. One that had to do with keeping secrets. "To your knowledge, does Cynthia ever use this computer?"

"I doubt it. She prefers to do everything either on her phone or tablet."

Then Mrs. Wynngate should have no objections to them temporarily confiscating the laptop and having a computer forensic expert review its contents. The sooner they got to the bottom of what Dorsey Lambert was seeking, the safer the Wynngate family would be. Sammy made a mental note to call her first thing in the morning.

"Take a good look around," he urged Beth. "Anything valuable your father kept down here?"

"Not that I'm aware of. But like I said, it isn't a place I entered very often."

He skirted around to the back of the desk and opened

a few drawers. Nothing but standard office supplies, neatly arranged and stacked.

His mind flashed to his infrequent meetings with the judge over the years. The man had been physically fit for his age and pleasant enough. But something about his rigid stance, even in the comfort of his home, and his meticulous formality had been off-putting to Sammy—as though with a glance, the judge had taken stock of Sammy's blue-collar background and had merely tolerated him as Aiden's temporary buddy in the weeks they lived at Falling Rock each summer.

Beth sank onto the desk chair and groaned, placing her head in her hands. "What do these lunatic Lamberts want?"

Proof. The answer sprang into his mind fully formed, pure and simple. They must believe Lambert was unfairly sentenced and were out to avenge the family name. Had there been anything shady behind the conviction on the judge's end? He'd question Beth as tactfully as possible.

"Any possibility your father might be involved in something unethical?"

Her head snapped up, and she glared. "Dad was beyond reproach. The most ethical person you'd ever meet. You could even describe him as unyielding when it came to his principles. Maybe too rigid."

Her eyes grew unfocused as she strummed her fingers on the polished mahogany. Obviously, her thoughts had drifted away from the present situation. Sammy could well imagine the judge as a stern, remote father who imposed a strict code of justice. He'd never particularly cared for the guy, but he pushed aside his personal feelings. Had Judge Wynngate truly been on the take or involved in criminal activity?

Dorsey Lambert sure held a grudge against the man. He'd have a talk with him and ask what he, or his family, believed the judge might have in his office and why they'd sent Beth threatening mail. Bad enough she'd been the one left holding the bag when Aiden and his buddies had disappeared from that ill-fated party years ago. Hadn't she already suffered enough for a family member's transgression?

He wouldn't let it happen again.

"Do you have somewhere to stay tonight?" Sammy asked, breaking her reverie. "A friend you can stay with? At the very least, you could drive to Atlanta and stay with Aiden for the time being. I'm sure he—"

"I'm not calling him at this time of night," she answered stiffly. Clearly, Beth was still rankled over his earlier remark about her father.

"I don't want to leave you alone here with the broken door."

She rose and brushed past him. "Of course I won't stay here tonight. I'll go to a motel until I figure out what to do in the morning."

"Good plan. I'll drive you over."

Her gray eyes bore into him. "You've done enough. I'm perfectly capable of driving myself."

Seems when it came to Beth Wynngate, he just couldn't win.

Chapter Five

Sammy's question about her father's integrity pricked Beth's heart like barbed wire. If he'd known her father, he'd never doubt the man's honesty and rigid moral code. Her spoon clanked so loudly against her cup she was surprised other customers at the coffee shop didn't glance her way.

Bells tinkled, and a gust of cold air whipped through the room as the door opened. Lilah Sampson walked in, golden curls enveloping her in an angelic aura. People craned their necks to catch a glimpse of her, their eyes softening and mouths involuntarily upturning at the fresh cheerfulness she naturally bestowed upon everyone. Lilah scanned the shop and then waved at Beth, hurrying over to her table.

"Hey, Beth! It's good to see you again." Lilah gave her a quick embrace, her pregnant belly bumping into Beth's abs. Lilah released her and awkwardly dropped onto the opposite chair, hands gripping the table for balance.

"You look so happy. And healthy," Beth said. Pregnancy certainly agreed with her old friend.

"I'm both of the above," Lilah agreed. "Although sometimes I wonder how I'm ever going to take care of a new baby when Ellie is a little hellion."

"How old is she again? Two? Three?"

"Almost four years old." Lilah extracted her cell phone from her purse. "Just one quick picture, I promise."

Dutifully, Beth cooed over the photo of the blue-eyed blonde—which was easy to do, as Ellie was an adorable mini version of her mother. "Here," she said, pushing the plate of doughnuts toward Lilah. "Chocolate frosting with sprinkles."

"My fave. I shouldn't, but I can never say no to them. Especially now." Lilah picked up a doughnut, brought it halfway to her mouth and then stopped. She set it back down, her face tight with concern. "The smell of chocolate in this place must have scrambled my brains. How are you? I mean, I know what happened at your place yesterday."

"Figured Harlan would fill you in." As sheriff, her husband had a pulse on everything that went down in Elmore County.

"I wish he'd told me last night instead of waiting until this morning. Why didn't you call? You know you can stay with me until you need to go back to Boston."

She loved her old friend but staying with her for more than a day or two was out of the question. Lilah kept busy enough with her own family and work without an additional burden. "I stayed at a motel last night. I'll probably go visit Aiden a few days. But first, I want to oversee getting the patio doors fixed this afternoon. Cynthia would have a fit if she knew they were busted."

Lilah's eyes flashed confusion. "You mean she doesn't know about the break-in yet? Thought you would have called her immediately."

"There was no point worrying her so late in the evening. Nothing was stolen. Guess I should run it by her, though, if Sammy hasn't already told her about it. Cynthia needs to be careful not to hire any more Lamberts."

Lilah shrugged, and her mouth ticked upward in a wan smile. "The Lamberts are the only family whose name has a worse reputation around here than the Tedders."

The Tedders were infamous moonshiners and outlaws. Their penchant for crime had even become national news four years earlier. Still, as far as Beth was concerned, Lilah's brush with a serial killer in her family was worse than her own scare the previous night. "But you're not a Tedder anymore," Beth reminded her. "You're a Sampson."

"Ha! As if anyone in Lavender Mountain's going to forget my maiden name." But Lilah smiled and took a bite of her doughnut as though she couldn't care less about other people's opinions. Harlan Sampson might not be Beth's cup of tea, but he made Lilah happy, and that was all that mattered.

"Bet Cynthia hasn't forgotten my background," Lilah said with a roll of her eyes.

Beth's stepmother had never approved of her friendship with, as she put it, "that Tedder girl." But surprisingly, her father had overruled his wife, saying that Beth needed a friend during the summers spent at Blood Mountain. And Lilah had been a true friend. Their friendship had remained strong even after Beth had been exiled to a private school for troubled rich kids. Beth would never forget Lilah's kindness, especially since her former friends at the elite Atlanta academy where she'd attended high school regarded her as a social pariah. She'd never heard from any of them again.

"The important people in our lives don't care about our past," Beth reminded Lilah. A current of understanding bolted through the short distance between them. If they lived to be a hundred, they'd always have this bond.

Lilah bit into the doughnut again and momentarily closed her eyes, apparently blissed out on sugar. Guilt nibbled in Beth's stomach. She hadn't invited Lilah over for a casual chat. Best to just ask the favor and get it over with. "How much did Harlan tell you about last night?" she asked.

Lilah's eyes flew open. "Everything," she admitted. "Hope you don't mind. He knows we're close, and I'd want to hear it from him before anyone else."

"Even about…the possible motive behind the break-in?" Sammy's question about her father still stung.

"Yeah," Lilah nodded. "They have to explore every angle and ask the tough questions. Part of the job."

Beth tamped down her reluctance to ask for the favor. Was she as bad as Cynthia, expecting to get preferential treatment because of her social status? No, she decided. This was merely a request from one friend to another. Cynthia wouldn't ask—she'd demand. She wasn't anything like her stepmother. Beth went out of her way not to flaunt her name or her money. Her only motive in asking the favor was to keep Sammy at arm's length. Besides questioning her father's character, he brought up too many memories and made her uncomfortable. She drew a deep breath and then blurted, "Is there any way Harlan can oversee the investigation?"

"You mean, instead of Sammy?"

"Exactly."

Lilah cocked her head to the side. "Harlan's involved in a big case right now with the Georgia Bureau of Investigation. It eats up all his time."

Disappointment seeped into her. At least she'd tried.

"What's the problem?" Lilah asked. "Sammy's his right-hand man. Besides, have you met Sammy's partner, Charlotte?"

"No. She wasn't there last night."

"Well, Charlotte's great. She used to work for the Atlanta PD and has lots of experience. They'll get to the bottom of the case."

A wry voice beside them cut through their conversation. "Thanks for the vote of confidence."

Beth almost jumped at the sight of the officer who glared down at her, clutching a white bag of pastries. The buttons of her brown uniform blouse stretched tightly across her heavily pregnant belly, threatening to pop open at any moment. Her red hair was pulled back in a ponytail, and her eyes stared accusingly at Beth.

"You don't get to decide which officer investigates which case," the fierce redhead said stiffly.

Lilah quickly tried to defuse the situation. "Beth, this is my sister-in-law, Charlotte. Sammy's partner." She flashed a placating smile at Charlotte. "We were just talking about the break-in."

But Charlotte ignored Lilah and kept her gaze directed at Beth. She read the woman's name badge: C. Tedder. What rotten luck that she happened to be walking by at the exact moment she'd asked Lilah for a favor. Beth had forgotten how frequently this kind of chance encounter could occur in a small town.

"I assure you that your case will receive due diligence on our part," Officer Tedder said in a clipped voice.

"Good to know," Beth muttered.

"You have any complaint with the way we're conducting our investigation?"

The woman was relentless. Determined to put her in her place. "Not yet," she mumbled.

"Charlotte and Sammy are the best," Lilah said easily. "What flavor doughnuts did you get?" she asked her sister-in-law in an obvious attempt to change the subject.

Charlotte answered, keeping her gaze affixed on Beth, "Lemon custard."

A sour treat for a sour cop. But Beth didn't dare say it aloud. At last Charlotte broke eye contact and regarded Lilah. The stern set of her jaw softened as she gave her a small nod. With a start, Beth realized the woman was actually pretty when she wasn't being such a hard-ass.

"See you at dinner this evening?" the woman asked. "James plans to grill steaks."

"Wouldn't miss it."

With one final glare in Beth's direction, Charlotte eased away from their table.

"Whew." Beth let out a sigh as she watched Charlotte exit the building. "I'm not winning friends and influencing people today, am I?" she joked.

Lilah merely laughed. "She'll get over it. Maybe we can all have lunch together one day."

She'd as soon have dental surgery than endure a meal with Officer Tedder. But it was too late to do any good, so Beth kept her mouth shut. No need to alienate anyone else affiliated with the sheriff's office. Poor James. What must it be like for Lilah's brother, married to a woman like that? Beth sighed, resigned now to having Sammy and Charlotte as the investigators of record. She wouldn't be around much longer, anyway, so no big deal. Might as well enjoy time with her friend while she had the opportunity. The rest of her get-together with Lilah was pleasant, as Beth put the encounter with Charlotte behind her.

Thirty minutes later, bundled against the winter chill, Beth returned to her car. She kept her head bent low, away from the full force of the biting wind. A pair of large men's boots beneath two tall columns of denim suddenly appeared in her view, and she moved to the right to get out of the way.

A large hand clamped on her right forearm. Startled, she stared up at a giant of a man. He glared, blue eyes lasering through the frosty air. Thick red hair curled out beneath his knitted hat, and a scarf covered his chin and mouth. A muffled, guttural sound tried to escape the woolen scarf.

"What are you doing? Let go of me," she snapped, trying to snatch her arm from his grasp. He tightened it several degrees. Even through the thick coat, his fingers dug painfully into her flesh. Where was grumpy Officer Charlotte Tedder when she actually needed her? Beth scanned the practically vacant street. Nowhere, evidently. *Figures.*

The stranger lowered his scarf and growled. "You owe us."

What the hell did that mean? Was he a bill collector? All her bills were paid. Maybe he had her confused with someone else. "Are you a car repossesser or something? You must be mistaken. Now let go of me before I start screaming."

"Ain't no mistake, Elizabeth Jane Wynngate. Pay us back the fifty grand, and we'll go away."

"Fifty grand?" She practically snorted in derision. "Let me just get my checkbook out of my purse." His demand ricocheted in her brain. "Wait a minute. *Us?* Who is *us*?" And then she understood.

"That's right," he nodded, evidently seeing the light dawn in her eyes.

"Are you Dorsey in the flesh or another family member ordered to harass me?" She'd guess family member. From what she'd seen in the news media years ago, Dorsey had been a short, thin man with skinny wrists and ankles. His prison uniform practically fell off his small frame as he'd been led from a Department of Corrections van into a federal court building.

Her father's courtroom.

"We only want what's due us," he said gruffly. "Play fair."

"Your due for what? You think it's fair to intimidate me into giving you my money? Extortion's a serious crime. I'm not paying a dime just to get you off my back. Leave me alone before I call the cops on you."

The fingers on her arm loosened. With his free hand, the man dug into his coat pocket and pulled out a slip of paper. "Get the cash. By tomorrow evening. Then call this number, and we'll come collect." With a gloved hand, he thrust the paper into her palm. "Don't be stupid. The number goes to a burner phone. And no matter where you go, remember, we're watching you."

He pivoted and, with surprising speed for a man his size, hurried down the alley adjoining the coffee shop and an antique store. Beth glanced down at his large footprints in the snow. Was he one of the same men who'd been sneaking around their property? Maybe he was even one of the masked intruders who'd eluded the law last evening.

Anger overcame her fear. Perhaps if she followed him, she could get his car tag or another clue for the police to find him and bring him in for questioning. Quickly, she raced to her car and started the engine.

If she hurried, there was a chance she could make it around the block and onto the street running parallel before he got away. Beth accelerated from the curb, thankful that the streets were practically empty. At the stop sign twenty yards ahead, she barely slowed as she turned right and then took an immediate left.

Ahead, she spotted the Lambert family member hopping into a rusty pickup truck and speeding off as fast as the old engine allowed. Without stopping to examine the risk, Beth hit the accelerator on her sleek sports car. If it came to a speed race, she'd be the clear winner. If nothing else, she had the make and model of his vehicle now. But if she could draw a little closer, she'd get the real prize—a tag number.

Beth pulled up Sammy's number on her Bluetooth dashboard and punched the button. It rang over and over. His deep, disembodied voice sounded. "Sorry, I'm unable to come to the phone right now. At the tone, please leave a message, or if this is an emergency, please call 911."

She smashed a palm on the dashboard. Where the hell was he? She didn't let up on the gas as the truck she followed left town and turned onto a county road, its wheels screeching in the haste to put distance between them. They both began their ascent up Lavender Mountain. The road narrowed and twisted up the steep incline.

Finally, *finally* the voice recording ended with a loud, drawn-out beep.

"Sammy? It's me. Beth. I was harassed in town today by someone sent by Dorsey. I'm following his truck now. It's a rusted-out blue Ford. And the tag number is…" She squinted her eyes. The sun reflecting off the white snow was almost blinding. "It's GA 9—"

A cannonade sound erupted, followed by a steep drop on the right side of her car. Her vehicle swerved, and she gripped the steering wheel, praying she didn't spin out of control down the side of the mountain. The entire right side of her car swiped the flimsy guardrail, the metal screech ringing in her ears. At the last possible second, Beth righted the vehicle's course. A sharp pain bulldozed down her back at the whiplash movement. What had she run over that had flattened her tire and caused so much damage? The truck driver leaned out of the open window on the driver's side and leveled a shotgun.

Oh, hell. That explained everything. The first shot had blown out a tire. Was she the next target?

Beth slumped beneath the dashboard and hit the brakes. Her car skidded on the icy road.

Boom.

The BMW dropped a foot on the left side. The man had shot out her other front tire. She couldn't stay behind the dashboard any longer with her car spinning out of control. Death could as easily come from a crash off the mountain as a bullet. Beth rose up and managed to bring her car to a complete stop. The muscle pull in her back spasmed, and she caught her breath, forcing her lungs to take in oxygen more slowly and shallowly.

The blue truck rounded a bend in the road and passed out of sight. She supposed she should be thankful he didn't hop out of the truck with his shotgun and approach. But he wasn't trying to kill her. Not yet, anyway. He—they—wanted her money, and that meant keeping her alive.

But what if he came back anyway? This could be a chance to kidnap her and force her to withdraw money from an ATM or write a check. She needed the cops.

Beth inserted the car key into the lock, but it wouldn't turn. Something had jammed the ignition. Okay, then. Her car was dead, but she still had her cell phone to call for help.

Only…where had it gone? Frantically, her gaze roamed the floorboards, but it wasn't there. She reached behind her to pat her seat, but the movement shot another burst of pain through her spine. She groaned, more in frustration than from the hurt. The phone had to be there somewhere. Steeling herself, she gingerly scooted forward, then extended her arm backward, but her hand only brushed against the smooth leather seats. She really didn't want to do this, but the alternative was to remain where she was—a sitting duck if the man returned. For all she knew, he might have collected one or two more of his family to come kidnap her and do Lord knows what.

Cautiously she reached a hand under the driver's seat. She gasped; a sharp knife of pain shot through her as her back protested the movement. Her vision went dark, and she collapsed forward. Deep, deep breaths. Her sight might have forsaken her, but she could hear the wind in the trees, the far-off sound of cars in town. She'd read once that your hearing was the last thing to go before unconsciousness. Unfortunately, she now knew it to be true.

Everything's going to be all right, she repeated to herself like a mantra. Someone was bound to be along this road shortly. They'd call the police. Sammy would find her. And probably be furious that she'd been so foolish as to chase after a man who'd threatened her. She deserved a scolding, too, not that she'd admit such a thing.

And then she heard it. The roar of a vehicle approaching. The direction the noise came from was in front of her, which meant the person was descending the mountain. It wasn't someone from town climbing back up. The abrupt squeal of brakes rang out, and then a door opened and slammed shut.

Blood pounded in her ears, and she hardly dared try to lift her head and open her eyes. Good chance that whoever approached might be her tormentor and not her savior. Heavy footsteps crunched through snow and came to an abrupt halt by her car. She feared that if she opened her eyes, she'd find an enemy within a couple of feet of where she slumped, easy prey for the taking.

Chapter Six

From the corner of his eyes, Sammy caught Charlotte waving at him. He pushed away from his desk and crossed the aisle where she sat, phone glued to an ear. *Lambert*, she mouthed.

He plopped into the metal chair beside his partner, eavesdropping. He'd tried several times that morning to make contact with the forwarding phone number on file for Dorsey Lambert. No one had answered his call, and despite his repeated message that it was urgent they speak, they hadn't bothered to call back, either.

"Yes, Mrs. Lambert. Good to hear your son's found a job and is staying out of trouble," Charlotte said in her most soothing tone. She flashed him a wink. "There's no problem that a simple conversation with Dorsey wouldn't clear up. When do you expect him home this evening?"

A long pause.

"I promise we're not out to fling him back in jail if he's staying clean. We've got a little matter in Elmore County that we believe he can help us with, that's all."

Charlotte held up crossed fingers at him, and he returned the gesture. With any luck, they'd get answers from the ex-convict tonight.

"Seven o'clock tonight is perfect. Yes, ma'am. And thank you."

She hung up the phone and gave a satisfied smirk. "Mama Lambert is convinced her son is a new man. Prison reformed his sorry ass."

Sadly, he shared her cynical outlook. He'd seen the recidivism rates on felons, and recent circumstances had done nothing to make him believe Dorsey Lambert was going to prove an exception to those abysmal statistics.

Charlotte's two-way radio emitted a loud crackle, and she unclipped it from her belt. Sammy glanced down at the desk blotter and read the scribbled address for Rayna Clementine Lambert. Ellijay would be a short trip. He'd contact Sheriff Roby in Gilmer County beforehand as a professional courtesy.

"Ten-ten at the Flight Club," Charlotte announced abruptly, standing and then quickly heading to the station exit.

"This early in the day?" He shook his head as he leaped to his feet and followed on her heels. "Where's Graham and Markwell? They can take this call."

He didn't say what he was really thinking. If he did, Charlotte would give him a good blistering for trying to protect her. Despite starting maternity leave in a couple of weeks, she refused to ask for special accommodations and insisted on carrying out business as usual. Her husband, James, had given up trying to convince her to take the temporary desk job Sammy had offered.

Despite her stubbornness, Sammy had to admit she was the best partner he'd ever had. He worried she wouldn't want to return to the job after her maternity leave was over, but she'd assured him otherwise.

With an efficiency born of a long working relationship, Charlotte proceeded to the driver's side of the cruiser—it was her turn to drive—while he slipped into the passenger seat. She flicked on the blue lights, and they pulled out of the station.

"Who you reckon it's going to be this time?" he asked. "The Halbert brothers?"

"My money's on Ike Johnson starting up trouble again."

"Usual bet?" he asked.

"You're on."

She sped through the main street intersection and onto the county road heading south. The Flight Club was less than two miles down the road, an ugly concrete square of a building with a dirt parking lot always filled with worse-for-the-wear vehicles, no matter the time of day or night.

A roll of unease rumbled through his gut as they pulled up to the building, the way it always did whenever he caught sight of the run-down bar. As a teenager, he'd spent way too many evenings here coaxing his inebriated father to get in his car so he could drive him home.

Before they exited the cruiser, two men tumbled out the front door, each grabbing a shirtful of the other as they dragged their fight outside. Bert Fierra, the club's owner and bartender, stood in the doorway, scowling at the men.

"The Halbert brothers," Sammy said to Charlotte as they approached the fighters. "You owe me. I'll take Hank while you take Charlie."

She shot him a suspicious look. Charlie was the smaller of the two brothers. Lucky for him, there was no time for her to argue that she was capable of taking on the bigger guy.

Within minutes, they had the two separated, hands

cuffed behind their backs and inside the cruiser. Both were too drunk to offer much resistance. As was their habit, the two brothers quickly made up and were contrite by the time they'd reached the station and been placed in lockup.

"Not only do you owe me a six-pack of soda, you get to handle the paperwork," he told Charlotte smugly once they returned to their desks.

"I can finish it in half the time it takes you," she bragged.

"Then you should file the incident reports every time."

"You wish."

"A guy can try." Sammy chuckled as he slid into his seat. "We make a good team."

She slid him a sly glance. "Too bad Beth Wynngate doesn't appreciate our awesomeness."

His amusement melted. "What do you mean?"

"Overheard her talking to Lilah this morning at the doughnut shop. Seems she wants to pull the friendship card and get Harlan to take over the case."

Surprise, then resentment, flushed over him. "Did she say why?"

"Isn't it obvious? She must hold our investigative skills in low regard."

Either that, or Beth was still put out that he'd questioned the judge's possible involvement in something unethical or illegal. "What did Lilah say?"

"Basically, that Harlan was too busy at the moment and that she should trust us."

"Bet that thrilled her." If Beth was anything like Cynthia, she'd keep demanding until she had her way. Sammy tried to let the insult roll off his shoulders, but found it surprisingly difficult.

He dug his cell phone from his jacket pocket and laid it on the desk. Missed call. Voice mail message lit up the screen. In the bustle of taking in the Halberts, he hadn't noticed the phone ringing. He tapped Play on the voice mail app, and Beth's voice, tinny with excitement and fear, spilled into his ears. His chest tightened as he listened and then nearly burst at the unmistakable crack of a bullet erupting. Had Lambert found her? Or had he sent a hit man? Tires squealed on the road. The message played on in eerie silence for thirty seconds before the recording ended.

"Damn it!" He slammed his hand on the desk. What had happened? Where was she now? He checked the time of the recording: 10:18 a.m., almost ten minutes since she'd dialed.

Charlotte quirked a brow. "What's up?"

"Check with the dispatcher. See what calls have come through in the last fifteen minutes."

Charlotte grabbed her phone while he dialed her number. Beth's cell phone rang three times before switching to voice mail. He dialed again. And again. He dug the cruiser keys from his pocket. If nothing else, he'd drive out toward Falling Rock to see if there'd been any accidents. If she were alone and injured, or in grave peril, he had to find her. At once.

"A ten-fifty-two call came in less than a minute ago," Charlotte announced. "Fuller's en route."

An ambulance request? Sammy raced to the front door as Charlotte followed at his heels, passing along more information.

"Address given was County Road 190, about a third the way up Lavender Mountain. A citizen reported a green BMW Z3 blocking the road. A woman was slumped over the dashboard and unresponsive."

Beth's car. The tightness in his chest twisted deeper, squeezing his lungs. Had she been shot? Sammy's mind whirled as he got in their cruiser, Charlotte beside him, and peeled out of the station and toward the accident scene.

"What's going on?" Charlotte asked.

He nodded at his cell phone on the console. "Play the last voice mail."

Charlotte did. Again the crack of a bullet and squealing tires ripped into him, doubling his tension.

At last they turned onto the county road. A police sedan was ahead of them, lights flashing and siren blaring. Sammy hit the gas until he nearly overtook Officer Fuller responding to the call. From behind, the wail of an ambulance sounded.

"Don't get us wrecked trying to assist Fuller," Charlotte warned. "You're no good to Beth hurt."

But he could think of nothing except Beth needing him at once. If Lambert had managed to get to her, this was his fault. He should have protected her. Insisted that she get away from the area and go into hiding.

Fuller came to an abrupt stop, and Sammy slammed on his brakes, jumping out of the vehicle the moment he slipped the gear into Park. He ran past Officer Fuller, nearly falling on the slick, snowy road in his haste. The nose of Beth's BMW sloped downward, the front two tires completely depleted of air.

Her head and shoulders were slumped over the steering wheel, and her long brown hair hung down, veiling her face. In spite of all the chaotic sirens and lights, Beth wasn't moving. Sammy rapped his knuckles at the driver's-side windows before flinging open the door.

"Beth! What happened?"

No blood was visible on her body or in the car's interior, from where he stood. No apparent bullet wound. This was a good sign. His chest and lungs loosened a notch. Careful not to move her body in case of a neck or back injury, Sammy smoothed back her hair. Beth groaned and leaned back into the seat. Blood poured from a gash on her forehead. Her eyes flickered open, confusion clouding the gray irises. "Sammy?" she whispered, so softly he barely heard her.

"An ambulance is on the way. How badly are you hurt?"

She lifted an unsteady hand to her injured temple and frowned. "I… I'm not sure. Not too bad?"

The EMTs would be there in a moment. "Can you tell me what happened?"

"He shot at me."

"Who?"

"Don't know his name." She straightened and licked her lips. Color returned to her face as she apparently rose from the fog of unconsciousness. "I tried to call you."

"Right. I got your voice mail. Describe the man who harassed you. What exactly did he say?"

"Big giant of a guy with red hair who demanded I pay him fifty grand. He gave me a piece of paper with a phone number to call when I got the money together. When he left, I tried to follow him—"

"Damn it, Beth," he muttered.

"Coming through!" an EMT shouted by his elbow.

Their time was up. "Anything else you remember about the guy or the truck he drove?" he asked quickly.

"No."

Sammy nodded. "We're on it. If you think of something later, call me." He started to turn away, but Beth caught his arm. "Did you remember something?"

"I just wanted to say..." She offered a wan smile. "We should stop meeting like this."

Sammy stared at her dumbly before he realized Beth was making a joke.

Brad Pelling, an EMT he'd met many times, squeezed between him and Beth. "Got to do our job," he explained apologetically, feeling the pulse at Beth's neck.

"Of course." Sammy watched as Brad questioned Beth and continued taking her vital signs.

"She's fine." Charlotte moved to his side and searched his face, her eyes much too sharp and knowing. "Seems you are unusually focused on this particular victim."

"We've known each other for years. Her brother used to be a good friend." He gave a casual shrug but knew his partner wasn't fooled. What was his deal when it came to Beth Wynngate? As he'd explained to Charlotte, she was merely an old friend's little sister. Nothing more or less.

But as Brad and another EMT pulled out a stretcher and laid Beth on it, he swallowed hard past a thick lump in his throat.

"Go with them and stay with Beth," Charlotte quietly urged. "I'll run what I can on the information she provided and ask around to see if there were any witnesses. If I come up with anything, I'll ring you."

He was torn between wanting to leap into the case and find who'd hurt Beth, and a desire to stay with her until she was released from the hospital.

"You know the hospital is unlikely to keep her overnight, even for a concussion," Charlotte said. "We need to consider how to protect her from another attack when they let her go."

That settled the matter. He forked over the cruiser

keys. "Call me if you get any leads. After Beth is somewhere safe, I'll head to Atlanta and pay Lambert a surprise visit."

"Sounds like a plan. This situation with the Lambert family needs to be handled quickly before someone is seriously hurt or killed. Be careful."

"You, too." Bad enough he hadn't protected Beth—he didn't need an injured partner on his conscience, as well. James Tedder, Charlotte's husband, was his best friend, and he'd be damned if James's wife and their future baby suffered because he'd overlooked a hidden danger.

Chapter Seven

Beth fought the effects of the prescription painkiller and anti-inflammatory pills the hospital had administered. At least she'd talked them into giving her only a mild dosage. She'd need all her wits for the coming interview. Sammy didn't know it yet, but she was going to confront Dorsey Lambert. No way she'd miss the opportunity to get answers.

The rolling hills of North Georgia gave way to the crowded metro Atlanta area with its skyscrapers and traffic. Lots of traffic. Gingerly, she touched the bandage by her temple.

"Your head starting to hurt?" Sammy asked.

"No." She shrugged and relented at his raised brows. "Well, maybe a little. I consider myself lucky not to have a concussion." She quickly rushed to change the subject. If she wanted to see Dorsey, she couldn't let Sammy harp on her injuries. He'd use it as an excuse to exclude her access. It'd been hard enough convincing him to let her go with him to Atlanta. "Does the traffic bother you?"

"It doesn't thrill me."

Sammy wasn't in the best of moods. En route, he'd contacted the Atlanta PD to provide backup while he questioned the suspect. They'd responded that there were no available officers and wouldn't be for several hours—if then. Sammy had told her that he'd almost turned around but decided the risk of her getting hurt again was greater than the danger of facing the man alone.

She covertly studied his profile. Sammy Armstrong was like a bad-luck charm that showed up at some of the worst moments in her life—the teenage arrest, the break-in at her house, and today's mess. But maybe it was good luck instead of bad, even the arrest. If he and his partner hadn't broken up the party when they did, the aftermath might have been even worse for her.

Sammy turned onto I-20, and a couple of miles later, they were driving through East Atlanta Village with its older homes, quirky shops and even an urban llama farm nestled less than a mile from the interstate mayhem. It was unlike the other parts of Atlanta Beth was used to. Their old family home, which Cynthia still occupied, was in Sandy Springs, which sported an old-money vibe with scenic mansions sprawled along single-lane roads. Aiden favored the affluent Buckhead area and lived in a high-rise condo near his law practice. Beth appreciated their different styles, but as for herself, she enjoyed the SoWa section in the South End of Boston, which served as a mecca of the arts.

Sammy pulled into the driveway of a modest ranch-style home with an old Plymouth Duster parked out front. He shut off the engine and then frowned when he caught her undoing her seat belt. "No way. You stay locked in here. It shouldn't take me long. Chances are he's not living here with his mother, anyway. Probably only listed her address to provide an answer on the Corrections release form."

"I'm not seeing her alone. I'm with an armed law enforcement officer. I couldn't possibly be any safer."

Lines creased on his forehead. "But—"

"No *buts.*" Before he could answer, she hopped out of the car and shut the door. She offered him a breezy smile and sauntered toward the porch walkway.

Sammy exited the vehicle and let out a sigh that she guessed could be heard all the way down the street. "You let me do all the talking. I'll explain your presence as a recently hired detective. She'll assume you're in training. Agreed?"

"Of course," she assured him. *Unless I have a burning question for Lambert that you don't ask him yourself.* "Want me to stand at the back door in case he's home and tries to make a run for it?"

The look he threw her was so stern she instantly realized her mistake. "Just kidding," she offered. Quickly, she scooted up the porch steps in case he changed his mind. Sammy moved in front of her and rapped at the door.

A game show played on the TV until someone inside suddenly muted it. "Who's there?" called a raspy voice that could have been male or female.

"Elmore County Sheriff's Department."

Silence.

The peephole darkened briefly, and then the door flung open. A woman stood before them in a floral muumuu. Unkempt gray hair floated past her shoulders, and she sported the lip wrinkles associated with a long-term cigarette smoker. "You ain't got no jurisdiction in Fulton County," she pointed out in a gravelly voice. "What do you want?"

"Mrs. Rayna Lambert? We'd like a word with you

about your son, Dorsey. You told Detective Tedder this morning that he lives with you at this address?"

"Like I told that woman, he ain't here," she offered unhelpfully. "He's at work down at the Coca Cola plant. Won't be home for hours."

"I'd like his cell phone number. I can meet him at the plant. Won't take but a few minutes of his time."

Rayna spat out a series of numbers that Sammy punched in his own phone. Beth peered past the woman's bulky frame and into the den, which was surprisingly well furnished and neat. Mrs. Lambert took more care with her housekeeping than she did her personal appearance. From the den, she had a view of the kitchen and a hallway that led to more rooms and a back door. A flash of red hair poked from one of the hallway rooms. The man had a gaunt, pale face with eyes focused on where they stood on the porch. He had the intent furtiveness of a hunted animal assessing danger. He caught her stare, and his eyes widened. Before she could alert Sammy, the man bolted from the room and sprinted to the back door.

"Hey, he's here!" she said, tugging on Sammy's jacket. "He's making a run for the back!"

"Halt," he called out, trying to push past Rayna Lambert's hulking frame. "We just have a few questions."

"Guess he don't want to talk to you," she said without a trace of humor in her flat voice.

Sammy flew down the steps. "Get in the car," he ordered.

Like hell. Beth waited until he'd sped past the corner of the house before she ran after him.

Magnolia trees haphazardly dotted the large backyard, but enough snow lay on the ground to show Lambert's footprints leading straight to the neighbor's abutting property. Lambert was thin and lithe and had the adrenaline rush of the hunted as he scaled the privacy fence and disappeared from her sight. Sammy was close behind, and he also quickly climbed over.

Unlike Aiden, she'd never been the athletic type, preferring the solitary pursuit of painting while he went to ball practice. Scaling a six-foot fence was not in her wheelhouse, especially after being banged up in the car. Instead, she sped to the side of the property, arriving in time to watch as Sammy pursued Lambert down the tree-lined street and then around the bend in the road.

Should she call 911? She tapped the cell phone in her back pocket but decided Sammy might not appreciate her interference. It might be best to let him either apprehend Dorsey on his own or make arrangements to return later with a police officer. But retreat to the cruiser? Beth slowly turned around, facing Rayna, who stood rooted on the back porch, hands crossed over her chest, watching the drama with a stone-faced expression.

Dorsey might have given them the slip, but his mother hadn't. She slowly walked toward her, as though Rayna were a wild animal who'd balk at the slightest provocation and retreat into her lair. But the Lambert matriarch was made of sterner stuff than that. She eyed Beth dead-on and never flinched a muscle, even though her son was running from the law, even though she was clad only in a thin housedress in the frigid cold—cold for Atlanta, that was—and even though a stranger approached.

Beth stopped at the edge of the back porch, staring into the woman's implacable face. "Why?" she asked simply.

Rayna pulled a pack of cigarettes and a lighter from the pocket of her dress, expertly cupped her hands over her mouth to shield the flame from the wind, and lit up. She drew heavily and then exhaled a noxious cloud of gray smoke. "Why what?" she asked abruptly.

"Why is your son out to get me?"

"First of all, I don't even know who the hell you are."

"Beth Wynngate."

"Ah." The pale eyes flickered. "You must be related to Judge Edward Wynngate." She spat out the name as though she'd accidentally swallowed a morsel of something putrid.

Beth squared her shoulders, unashamed to claim the familial connection. "His daughter."

Rayna cast disapproving eyes over her from head to toe, and Beth was conscious of how she must appear to the older woman—a tasteful Berber knitted cap with matching scarf, diamond studs discreetly gleaming on her earlobes, a wool coat of the finest quality, tailored trousers and designer boots. And there was also the little matter of the bandage over her right temple.

"Go on," Rayna urged. "What's Dorsey done got himself into?"

"I've been threatened. Several times." She touched the bandage. "Most recently this morning. Your son seems to hold some kind of grudge against my father—who died seven months ago, by the way."

If she'd expected sympathy, she'd have been disappointed. Rayna's features didn't soften for an instant.

"Anyway, a man confronted me this morning, saying I needed to fork over fifty thousand dollars to make all this go away."

"But it weren't Dorsey."

"No. But it has to be someone he sent, probably a member of the family, judging by the red hair."

"Sounds like a pretty flimsy connection to me."

She didn't want to give away any specific information to this woman, so she merely stated the obvious. "Oh yeah? Then why'd your son run from us?"

"He's an ex-convict. Why wouldn't his first instinct be to run from the cops? He never wants to be behind bars again." She drew on the cigarette. "I don't want that for him, either."

"Then work with us. If Dorsey isn't behind this, he can clear his name."

"Like you'd believe anything he'd say."

"Can you just get him to leave me alone?" she asked, burying her pride. "I haven't done anything to him. Whatever grudge he had with my father, that's in the past. The man's dead, and his sentencing was always fair and within the bounds of the law. This vendetta is ridiculous."

"Poor little rich girl. Daddy's dead, and here you stand, looking like a million bucks. Must have inherited a nice bundle."

Beth said nothing. What was the point in denial?

Rayna tilted her head back and blew out a series of spiral smoke rings. "I'll tell you this much," she said at last. "Dorsey may be a lot of things. Bad things. But he ain't gonna rough up no woman. And he certainly ain't a killer."

Delusional mother. "Maybe you don't know him as well as you think you do. And what about the rest of the family?"

Rayna tossed the cigarette in the snow, snuffing it out. "I'll speak to him."

"Thank you." A modicum of relief swept through her. Even if Sammy couldn't catch up to Dorsey, perhaps some good had come out of this trip.

"I ain't doin' it for you, missy." Rayna started to turn away. "Now get the hell off my property."

What are you going to do if I refuse, call the cops? But of course, Beth didn't say it aloud. No point in antagonizing the woman and calling her out over an idle threat. Rayna retreated inside, and the door slammed shut.

Beth hunched forward, bracing against a chilly gust of wind. Where was Sammy? Was he okay? Dorsey's small build wouldn't match up well with Sammy's fit, muscular body, but a cornered rat might prove dangerous. If she had the cruiser keys, she could search the neighborhood. She was just lucky he'd left it unlocked for her.

She looked over her shoulder, but there was no sign of either man. Might as well wait in the warm car rather than stand out here in the cold, her very presence ticking off Rayna Lambert, a possible ally. And even if she didn't want to admit it to Sammy, her head and back ached from the wreck. She'd been lucky the guardrails had held and that her car hadn't crashed down the mountain. Just imagining being trapped inside the twisted metal heap as it flipped and landed in the hollow below made her knees weak.

Once in the cruiser, Beth leaned back in the seat and closed her eyes, willing herself to relax and have faith that Sammy knew what he was doing and was in no danger. They'd caught Dorsey unawares, so it was unlikely he had a weapon on him as he'd raced from the house. Actually, he'd been wearing a T-shirt and long johns, and he'd been barefoot. A distinct disadvantage against Sammy. She hoped that helped make up for Sammy's lack of knowledge about the layout of the neighborhood, but she pictured Dorsey slunk below the foundation of someone's house, curled into a tight ball like a stray animal hiding.

The car door suddenly slung open, and she jumped in her seat. Her heart jackhammered against her ribs until she saw it was Sammy.

Alone.

"He got away, huh?" she asked. "Figures. He's like a pesky rodent scurrying out of trouble."

"I'd say more than pesky," he answered, pointing at her injury.

Sammy started the car, and they rolled away. A slight lift of the curtain at the front of the house told Beth that Dorsey's mother had been keeping a close watch. Her son would slither back home soon enough.

"Are you going to contact the Atlanta PD again and update them?"

"Already did." His jaw was tight and his hands white-knuckled as they gripped the steering wheel. "I knew I should have waited until they had an officer available."

"You couldn't have known if Dorsey would even be home tonight," she pointed out. "Are we going to drive around the neighborhood and see if he's around?"

"We can. The local cops agreed to put out a BOLO. Maybe they'll capture him."

He circled around the block and then widened the search to another neighborhood in the direction Dorsey had run.

"Could be he's got friends or relatives close by that've already taken him in. But the good news is that Rayna Lambert agreed to see if she could talk some sense into her son."

Sammy snorted. "Don't count on that happening. Apple doesn't usually fall far from the tree."

Let him be cynical. Beth believed Rayna would try.

After all, she was his mother, and it was obvious that if Dorsey didn't stop pursuing her, this wouldn't end well for him. "Time will tell," she said in a you'll-see tone.

"This is pointless," Sammy said at last, running a hand through his dark hair. "Now to figure out what to do with you."

"What do you mean?"

"You're obviously not safe in Blood Mountain. While we're in Atlanta, maybe you should pay your stepmother a visit. Surely you can stay with her until Lambert is apprehended."

The too-casual way Sammy threw out the suggestion didn't fool her. She had the sneaking suspicion this had been his intent all along in coming to Atlanta—to dump her off on Cynthia. Her stepmother would hate that even more than she would.

"No way. I'll take my chances back home."

"Home? Meaning…you're going back to Boston?"

"Blood Mountain." Strange that she considered it home rather than her dad's old house in Sandy Springs or her apartment in Boston.

He frowned. "Then stay with Aiden."

"He's still out of town."

Sammy pulled onto the interstate, his fingers tapping out a beat against the dashboard. "There has to be a safe place for you somewhere." He cleared his throat, as if uncomfortable with what he was about to say. "Would you consider staying with me? I have a guest room." His voice was no-nonsense, but she detected a note of tension in it, as if afraid of her answer.

"Nope. That's not happening. I can't imagine your boss would cotton to that idea, either."

"Harlan's a friend. Speaking of which, Charlotte

mentioned you could stay with Lilah, if being with me bothers you so much."

"Lilah's busy. I wouldn't feel right imposing. Not when her baby's due any moment."

"Stubborn," he mumbled, shifting in his seat.

"I heard that." She wasn't offended, though, especially considering that it was the truth. She'd lived too long in places where she wasn't truly wanted. Once she'd left high school, she'd sworn she'd never again be a millstone around another person's neck.

"There's always Boston." Her heart wasn't in the suggestion, though, since it had proven unsafe once before. But it would put distance between her and the Lamberts.

"That's no good. You were followed up there."

"True. But I think Rayna can put a stop to Dorsey's stalking."

"Don't kid yourself on that score." He shot her a hooded glance. "Is the thought of staying with me so disagreeable? Are you worried about what people will say?"

"It's not that."

"Then what is it?"

"I won't put anyone else in danger again."

"I can take care of myself while I protect you. For crying out loud, Beth. I'm a cop."

"Out of the question," she insisted.

Sammy shook his head and mouthed the word *stubborn.*

She was refusing for his own good, even if he couldn't see it. His offer was tempting. But no matter how easily Sammy shrugged off the impropriety, it wouldn't look good for him professionally to have her, a targeted victim, living in his home. So the problem remained. Where could she stay, besides possibly a string of impersonal hotels, where no Lambert would find her? Someplace where her presence wouldn't be a danger to her host?

A fully formed image blasted into her mind—a small but comfortable cabin near Lavender Mountain's peak. Her dad's former hunting cabin was so isolated that she doubted anyone else even knew of its existence.

If she couldn't hide out there in the wilds, then no place was safe.

Chapter Eight

"I don't like it," Sammy said as he finally spotted the tiny lodge almost hidden from sight. Although the oak trees and shrubs were bare, the wooden structure melded seamlessly behind a copse of evergreen pines, and snow covered its roof.

"You haven't even been inside yet. Give it a chance," Beth said.

His Jeep jostled as he hit a pothole. The dirt road had become so overgrown from a long period of no travelers that tree branches arching from each side of the embankment met in the middle to form a gnarled, brown tunnel. Limbs scratched the sides of his vehicle; the metal frame rubbing dead wood sounded like a knife scraping against a plate. His forearms momentarily goose-bumped at the high-octave screech.

"Jeep's going to need a paint job before this is over," he grumbled.

She grinned back at him. "Jeeps are made for off-road use. The scratches will give it character."

He couldn't help returning the grin. With every mile they'd put between them and Atlanta, Beth had visibly relaxed. He didn't share her confidence that the danger was past, but he took heart that she seemed to have forgiven him for daring to question her father's integrity.

Unless absolutely necessary, he wouldn't tread again in that emotional quagmire.

He pulled the vehicle as close as possible to the cabin, but they still had to trudge a good twenty yards with all the supplies they'd picked up in town after he'd swapped out the cruiser for his own vehicle. Quickly, they hauled their stash inside, hoping to get everything unloaded and a fire started before the sun set. Already the shadows lengthened, birds flocked noisily to find their night's resting place, and the air grew chillier. Night fell quickly in the mountains, and with the darkness came an almost unsettling quiet.

Sammy paused in his work, a pile of firewood in his arms, and surveyed the land. How many years had it been since he and Harlan and James had spent a weekend hunting? Too many. His friends were busy with their own families now, and the realization briefly pinched his heart. *It's understandable. They've moved on.* Once their children were older, they'd probably be able to get away for an occasional all-guy trip. As for himself, the whole marriage-and-kiddos thing held no appeal. He'd seen how much a bad marriage could devastate a man. His dad had been proof of that.

A loud clatter erupted from the cabin, and his heart hammered. He dropped the pile of wood and raced inside. Had the cabin been booby-trapped? A string tied to a shotgun trigger or trip wires set to an explosive? The Lambert men were rugged mountain folks with little regard for the law and notorious for holding grudges. If they knew of the cabin and had gotten there first…

Beth stood in the kitchen, arms akimbo, staring at the dozens of food cans rolling around the rough pine floor. She held up a brown sack with a torn bottom by way of explanation.

He huffed out a breath of relief, almost laughing at his imagination.

"Didn't mean to scare you," she said.

"Are you sure no one outside of your family knows about this place?"

"How many times do I have to assure you? I'm positive no one else has seen this place, not even hikers or hunters. It's isolated, yes, but that's an advantage. No one knows about it. It's private property. I doubt Cynthia and Aiden even come here. Aiden only bothered with it when he wanted to throw parties far away from parental eyes."

Sammy bent down and helped her pick up the strewn cans. "Still can't believe Judge Wynngate liked to hunt. Didn't picture him as an outdoors kind of guy."

"Dad grew up in the North Carolina mountains. That's why he bought the house at Falling Rock and then built this cabin as his own private retreat. His job dictated he live in a big city, but he enjoyed time in nature."

He caught the wistful note in her voice. "I also had the impression that you and your father weren't all that close."

"Not since I was a little girl," she admitted. "When Mom died of cancer, a part of my dad seemed to wither away, even after he married Cynthia a few years later. And once I became a teenager...well, things changed between us."

Sammy was well aware of the wedge her arrest had driven between Beth and her family—an arrest he was partially responsible for making. "I remember your mom. Nice lady."

Beth's gray eyes brightened. "You do?"

"Yep. I do."

A charged silence fell between them, and he was intensely aware of the closeness of her body, the soft floral scent that was always a part of Beth. With just the two of them alone inside the cozy cabin, it seemed they were isolated from the rest of the world.

He stepped backward, breaking the spell. Protecting Beth was his job, and he'd better remember that fact. "I'll get the rest of the stuff in before it gets too dark."

"Right," she quickly agreed, her cheeks flushed pink. "Lots to do before I get settled in."

"Before *we* get settled in," he corrected.

"I already told you, I'm fine out here. Perfectly safe. No need—"

"I'm staying," he insisted. "At least for tonight."

Actually, he planned to stay with her until he got word that the Atlanta PD had Lambert in custody. But he'd fight that battle with Beth later. One day at a time. And who knew? By tomorrow, Dorsey Lambert indeed might be locked away.

Outside, Sammy inhaled the bracing winter air. *This is business only*, he reminded himself. *Get a grip.* He brought in the rest of the boxes from the Jeep. Amazing how much stuff you needed to bring along, even for a short visit. Once all was unloaded, he set to work building a fire. It didn't take long for the small interior to be filled with its warmth and the pleasant scent of burning oak.

"Your gourmet meal awaits," Beth said, carrying their take-out food on a tray into the living area. She'd placed the Mexican fast-food dishes on plates and filled two glasses with soda. They sat across from one another as they ate, Beth on a chair she'd pulled over to the coffee table, while he sprawled on the leather sofa. He dipped a tortilla chip into the salsa bowl and pointed at the canvas frame she'd set in the corner of the room. A sheet draped the front. "What are you working on?"

"A snowscape of Blood Mountain."

"May I see?"

Color rose on her cheeks. "It's not finished yet. Since there's no television up here, I figured I'd pass the time painting. Maybe start a few new ones."

She didn't feel comfortable sharing her work with him. "I suppose most artists don't like showing their works in progress. I can respect that. As someone who has zippo artistic talent, I have to say that I admire seeing it in others," he said.

The blue specks in her dove-gray eyes shimmered as she silently regarded him. "You have an interest in the arts?"

"Who doesn't?" he countered with a shrug. "I may not have access to local museums like you do in Boston, but I can still appreciate beauty. I just get mine from a different source. Like walking through the woods or driving around mountain roads with panoramic views of Appalachia."

"Touché," she said, lifting her glass of soda in a mock toast and taking a swallow. "I wish my family had half as much appreciation for art as you do. They see my painting as dabbling. A hobby. And the art classes I teach middle graders? It's not a distinguished enough career for their respect. They act embarrassed when their friends ask what I do in Boston."

Sammy wasn't surprised. Cynthia Wynngate appeared the sort to only care about social prestige, and Aiden had adopted his mother's attitude over the years. He and Aiden had drifted apart soon after Aiden started college. Sammy heard his former friend spent summers hanging out in the city with new buddies, tossing around money without limits. On the few occasions Sammy had run into Aiden, there had been a subtle change in the way Aiden treated him. Without sports, they'd discovered they had no common interests, and even short conversations became awkward.

"I'm sorry," he said. "I hope their attitude doesn't upset you. It's their problem, not yours."

A genuine smile lit her face. "It doesn't bother me. Not much, anyway. Besides, I only see them once or twice a year. No big deal."

He hoped that was true.

She gestured at the canvas frame. "You can look, if you'd like."

"You're sure?"

"Yes. Just don't expect Van Gogh or something."

He stood and crossed the room, but she remained seated. Carefully, he lifted the sheet and stared at the painting. A plumage of white, yellow, pink and coral clouds drifted over the mountains dotted green with pine and espresso-colored oak trees, their branches glinting with ice. Old Man Brooks's abandoned red barn adorned the right corner of the canvas. The wide swath of snow blanketing the ground reflected the sky's multicolored palette.

Sammy stared at it for long moments before speaking. He felt like he could step into that scene of crisp pastoral elegance. "It's beautiful," he said simply, then turned to look her in the eyes.

"You mean it?" She rose and sauntered toward him. "It still needs a few finishing touches."

"I mean it."

"Thanks, Sammy." Her breathy voice was close by his side, and he swallowed hard. He scanned a couple more paintings, all in various stages of completion, all alive with pastel washes of color. He knew little of art, but he recognized talent when he saw it. Beth had it. Looking at her work was unexpectedly intimate, as though by viewing her art, he glimpsed something of her soul and how she perceived the beauty in the world. Slowly, he faced her.

Firelight flickered golden on her face, neck and arms. Thin strands of cinnamon highlights streaked her sleek sable hair, and Beth's understated beauty made his breath hitch. As it had been earlier in the kitchen, everything seemed to still. There was only the two of them, alone, with the fireplace crackling in the background. His gaze drifted to her lips. Just one taste. What was the harm? Her mouth parted, and she almost imperceptibly leaned into him. This was it. This was the moment. Sammy bowed his head and pressed his lips to hers. They were as warm and intoxicating as he'd imagined.

He lost himself in the softness of her lips. This was where he was always meant to be. As though the kiss had been inevitable from the moment he saw her again, looking shaken by the threatening letter but determined to get to the bottom of the matter.

Aiden's little sister all grown up.

A barred owl screeched nearby, invading his senses, which had grown thick and heavy with passion. He clasped his hands under her forearms and pulled away. He was supposed to be there to protect Beth, not make love to her. "This isn't a good idea."

Beth stared at him wide-eyed, one hand drifting up to touch her lips. Confusion, then hurt, and at last, resignation flashed across her face. "You're probably right."

Part of him wished she'd protested, but a saner inner voice assured him he'd done the right thing. They returned to dinner and went to bed early, Beth retiring to the one bedroom on the other side of the kitchen while he lay on the sofa under a woolen blanket. For hours he stared into the fireplace as the flames crackled, and then the logs dwindled to blazing orange embers. Had pulling away from Beth been a mistake? The longer he lay awake, the less confident he became of his decision. There were so many reasons not to get involved with her—it would be unprofessional; she lived hundreds of miles away; she resented him for arresting her years ago; and the Wynngates were in a different social league. The distance between them and the reasons to keep it that way seemed impenetrable.

Yet he couldn't deny that their kiss had shaken him to his core.

DAWN FILTERED THROUGH the small window of the cabin. Beth huddled deeper beneath the quilt, reluctant to leave the lazy warmth of the featherbed. And getting up meant facing Sammy, who'd delivered a mind-blowing kiss only to reject her moments later.

But what a kiss.

Somehow she'd have to pretend it had never happened and just get on with the day. Surely he didn't plan to hang around too long? She'd have to convince him there was no danger so far into the woods. She'd be careful to keep the doors locked, her shotgun loaded and at the ready. After all, this was her cabin, and she got to decide who had permission to come and go. Being alone was what she needed. Without the distraction of television and the internet, she'd absorb herself with painting, and when she tired of that, she'd curl up in bed with a good book. Plan made, she pulled on jeans and a sweatshirt and headed to the kitchen.

Sammy was already up. He sat on the edge of the sofa, drinking his usual morning drink of soda, and raised his head at her approach. His jaw had an unshaven shadow that looked sexy as hell.

"Good morning," she called out airily. "I'm up. You should head on back to work now."

"I'm not leaving."

"Doesn't your partner need you?"

"Not as much as you do."

"Don't be ridiculous. I'll lock the door behind you. Any sign of trouble, I'll call 911." She nodded at the shotgun above the fireplace. "And don't forget I have a weapon." Beth turned her back on him and rummaged through the cooler for an orange juice pack. "Did you ever call Cynthia about the break-in?"

"Yep. And got her permission to have a tech guy search your dad's computer." He took a seat at the kitchen table and eyed her curiously. "Your stepmother didn't tell you?"

"She called early yesterday morning, but I was talking to Lilah at the time. The right moment to call her back just didn't happen. Too much going on."

Understatement of the year. Luckily, Sammy didn't bother pointing out that now was as good a time as any. She'd call Cynthia back later today, once she was alone and not so frazzled. Beth sat across from Sammy at the table, then picked up a small metal cylinder that hadn't been there last night. "What's this?"

"Pepper spray. Keep it clipped on a belt or a loop on your jeans. It's police-strength and has a range of ten feet."

She eyed it warily. "I'm afraid I'll hurt myself more than the criminal I'm aiming at. How's it work?"

"It's easy. I'll show you."

Sammy demonstrated how to rotate the trigger to the fire position.

"What if I accidently spray myself?"

"You won't."

"Okay. If it makes you feel better." She looped the canister onto her jeans, privately resolving to take it off the moment he finally left.

"Have you ever shot a pistol?"

"No, but Dad taught me to use the shotgun."

"I can teach you—"

"No, thanks. I'm good."

"Then I insist you at least let me teach you a few self-defense moves."

She started to object, then closed her mouth, remembering the tall stranger from yesterday looming over her. "Not a bad idea."

"How sore is your back?"

"Surprisingly good. No headache, either."

"Great." He slammed both hands on the table. "Grab your jacket, and let's get to work."

"Can't we do it in the den?"

"Not enough space."

"Fine," she muttered, grabbing her designer jacket.

Sammy paused in the doorway and cocked his head toward the fireplace mantel, where the shotgun hung. "That thing loaded?"

"Yes."

"I'll test it and make sure it's in running order. Bring it along with that box of extra shells on the sofa."

Beth picked up the items and followed him out the door. How long could it take? Fifteen, maybe twenty minutes tops, and then she'd have the cabin to herself.

They trudged through the snow a good distance

to get to a clearing wide enough to test the shotgun. "This'll do," he said at last.

She handed him the gun, and he checked the barrel. Satisfied, he lifted it to his shoulder and shot off a round. Even though she expected it, the blast in the forest silence made her jump. It'd been over a decade since she'd come out here with Dad and shot cans off a fallen tree log for target practice. Back before their falling-out over the party.

"Your turn."

She took the shotgun, steeled her legs in anticipation of the kickback and fired off a round. It felt good. No one would find her out here in the boonies, but if worse came to worst, she wouldn't hesitate to protect herself. She raised the gun in one hand. "Who needs self-defense moves when you've got this?"

"Can't carry it with you everywhere, every moment."

Beth carefully set the shotgun against a tree, resigned to another lesson. "Show me what I need to learn."

Sammy shrugged out of his jacket and tossed it on the ground. "First demonstration. Say your attacker approaches you from the front and grabs your arm." He clamped his hand down on her right forearm and regarded her sternly. "How would you try to escape this hold?"

"Kick you in the nuts?" she guessed.

"Wrong. He'd see it coming and block it." Sammy placed her left fist on his hand that was clutching her arm. "Now point your left elbow up, and then slice down with every muscle in your core."

She tried, but Sammy held fast.

"Give it all you've got," he urged. "Muscle and weight."

It took several attempts, but to her surprise, the move worked to free her from Sammy's grip.

"Good job. Now let's try a different scenario. Let's say someone grabs you from behind and places his arms around your waist."

Sammy moved behind her and held her tight in his arms. His hard body pressed against her back, and heat flared through her. The memory of last night's kiss fueled her awareness of him. If she turned her head an inch to one side, her lips would land on his chin, and then his mouth would seek hers, and—

His arms clenched tighter around her abs and squeezed. "Pay attention," he said, his voice harsh and deep in her ears.

The warm rush of his breath sent shivers down to her core. How could she possibly concentrate when her mind was thick with the possibilities of the two of them kissing? With great effort, she shook off the images playing in her head. "I'm listening," she said. "What do I do next?"

"Grab my arms and then pull yourself in."

"Like this?" she asked, holding tight to his arms.

"That's it. Now swing your hips to one side and make a fist."

Surprisingly, she felt his hold give way, and she held up her fist. "Now what?"

"If this was an attacker, you'd strike his groin with that fist. Hard as you can."

"That should buy me a few seconds," she remarked dryly.

"Use that time to run. If you're out in public, scream as loudly as you can." He frowned. "Next time I'm at the office, I'll get you a whistle."

Beth stepped away from him, glad to put a little distance between them. "Thanks. I'll keep these moves in mind."

He looked at her in surprise. "We're not nearly through yet."

"We aren't?"

"I've got a couple more moves to show you, and then you're going to practice until your reactions become automatic. Otherwise, you won't remember any of this if an attacker comes at you with no warning."

Sweat trickled down her neck and chest, despite the cold air and snow. Beth shrugged out of her coat as Sammy had done earlier. Over and over, they rehearsed her reactions for every eventuality, whether she was attacked from the front or behind.

"Remember the key vulnerable areas—eyes, nose, throat and groin," he kept reminding her. "Use your head and stay aware of your surroundings. If an attacker aims a gun at you, then run away in a zigzag pattern while seeking shelter."

Forty-five minutes later, Beth's body dripped head to toe with sweat, and she was panting. But she was prepared. "I'm feeling pretty badass," she said with a cocky grin.

Sammy didn't return the smile, still intent on drilling home his message. He made a sudden lunge for her, and she raised her fists by her face, ready to fight. Again and again Sammy came at her, and she fended him off. At last he broke away and gave an approving nod. "I think you've got it. One last thing. If you have no choice but to fight back, commit to it and never hesitate to hit as hard as you can." His eyes darkened. "If you do get overpowered, fake compliance, and then strike again or run at the first opportunity."

"Got it," she said. Beth had never felt more competent. If someone did try to take her by force, she'd at least put up a good fight.

Chapter Nine

"So how come you never got married?"

Sammy nearly choked on the vegetable soup they ate for dinner in front of the fireplace.

A flash of worry flickered in Beth's eyes. "Or are you?"

"Wh-what?" he stammered, clearing his throat. His eyes watered, and he hastily swallowed iced tea.

"You okay there?" Beth placed her hand between his shoulder blades and patted.

"What in the world brought on that question?"

She shrugged. "Why not? I mean, we're stuck out here together. Nothing else to do but talk."

He quirked a brow at her. He could think of plenty of things to do besides talking. If she noticed his amusement, she pretended otherwise.

"Well, are you?" she prodded.

"I'm not married, although I was engaged once." He hadn't thought of Emily in years.

"How long ago? What happened?"

"Years ago."

Beth's gray eyes remained pinned on him.

"She dumped me for another guy."

Her mouth rounded in an O of surprise and sympathy flooded her face. "That's horrible. I'm so sorry that—"

Sammy held up a hand. “It was my fault. She kept pressuring me to set a date and I wasn’t ready. Frankly, getting engaged had been a mistake from the beginning. It was a decision I later regretted.”

“Why? Did you fall out of love? Realize she wasn’t the right woman for you?”

More like cold feet. Actually, that had been more than half of the problem. Sammy moved his bowl to the side and faced Beth where she sat opposite him. They were both cross-legged on the floor, casually dining in front of the fireplace—the only warm spot in the cabin. He could give a short nod to her questions, because Beth was partly right, but he wanted honesty between them.

“The idea of tying myself down forever to one woman and raising kids scared the hell out of me,” he admitted. “Judging by my parents’ marriage, it’s a miserable way to live. Guess you’ve heard stories about my dad. It’s a small town.”

Her forehead creased, and she bit her lip. “You’re almost a decade older than me so it’s not like we ran in the same circles. But it seems like I did overhear that he had a drinking problem.”

“Stone-cold alcoholic.” Sammy drew a deep breath and decided to rip the bandage off as it were. “Mom ran off with my high school math teacher when I was a junior. Even though the marriage had never been great, it broke Dad. He started drinking heavily.”

Sammy kept his face averted, not wanting to see the sympathy in Beth’s eyes. He believed in letting the past stay buried and rarely mentioned either of his parents.

“That must have been horrible for you as a teenager. I had no idea. You always seemed so happy and cheerful when I saw you with Aiden.”

All an act. Sports had been a lifesaver in his teenage

years. While Dad spent most of his free time at local bars, playing ball had given him an activity to focus on instead of sitting alone in a dark and cold house waiting for parents who'd both deserted him—in mind if not in body.

"It wasn't that big of a deal," he lied.

Beth's hands closed over his fists. He hadn't even realized he'd clenched his hands into hard knots, or that his body was wound up tight as a swollen tick. Not until the warm softness of Beth's fingers caressed his knuckles, bathing him with light.

"Of course it was a big deal," she murmured. She squeezed his hands and let go. "Do you regret letting her get away?"

"Who?" he asked, confused at the question.

"Your ex-fiancée."

"Emily?" He chuckled. "Not at all. I run into her from time to time. She's happily married with two boys. I'm glad for her. It's what she always wanted. What about you?" Turnabout was fair play.

"Me?"

"Why aren't you married?" That was the real mystery. A woman with her looks, brains and talent must have been hotly pursued.

"Guess the right guy hasn't come along yet. I've had a few close relationships but..." Her voice trailed off.

"I call bullshit."

Instead of taking offense, Beth laughed. "You might say I fundamentally distrust most people. That doesn't make for strong, lasting relationships."

"You trusted Rayna Lambert yesterday."

"Maybe I just wanted to believe there was an easy way out of this mess. That a mom can appeal to her son's basic decency and set everything right."

"That outcome's highly doubtful."

"True."

She turned her head toward the hearth and he watched the play of fire glow on her elegant features. "You seem to trust me," he ventured.

"Also true."

Perhaps she'd had no choice but to do so. "You can, you know," he said gently. "Trust me, that is. I won't let anyone hurt you."

"You can't make a promise like that."

"I just did."

She fixed her attention on him again. "This—" she swept the room with her hand "—is only a brief respite, not a fun getaway in the woods, much as I try to pretend that it is."

"There's plenty going on behind the scenes while we hide out. Charlotte's working on the case, and the Atlanta PD will eventually pick Lambert up now that he's on their radar. Until Lambert's accounted for, this is our best option." He cocked his head to the side and studied Beth. "Is it so bad being stuck with me?"

"Of course not. Only it feels like my entire life's on hold. It's frustrating. I came down to visit friends and family and instead I'm burrowed underground like a mole."

"Not for long." At least, he hoped that was the case. This morning, Charlotte had informed him that Judge Wynngate's computer hard drive was sent to a tech specialist in Atlanta, but that she'd been unable to place a priority on the task. A stalking case in Appalachia didn't rank high in their opinion. To be fair, they had murders and kidnapping cases that rightly took precedent. There was never enough manpower to investigate every potential crime risk.

"Some visit," she mumbled.

Visit. Meaning she'd be leaving soon. He'd managed to keep pushing that bit of reality from his mind. Getting too close to Beth would be a mistake.

So why did his arms reach for her, draw her close into an embrace? He rested his head on the top of her scalp, inhaling the clean scent of shampoo. Her hair was silky and warm against his cheek. She wiggled closer into him. Side by side they watched the flames in the fireplace leap and play in the darkness. Night came early in the mountain woods and it lay thick around them. With no neighbors and no electricity, the only light outside came from moonbeams reflecting on the pristine snowy ground.

He rained down kisses, starting at the top of her scalp, and then trailing the side of her face. Beth turned into him, her lips seeking his own. His tongue sought hers and she moaned softly as her arms wrapped behind his neck, urging him closer—deeper.

She could be gone tomorrow. Sammy tamped down the thought as her fingers traced the nape of his neck and then stroked his hair. *This can never last.* Damn that incessant, rational voice in his brain that fired off warning missiles.

Beth climbed into his lap and straddled him, never breaking their kiss. His pulse skyrocketed, and a fever of need coursed through his body. *She'll only leave you.*

That got his attention. The thought triggered his dad's often-repeated words about how women always left you high and dry and to never trust them.

Sammy broke off the kiss, cupping Beth's chin in his hands. Her eyes were graphite-dark and clouded with passion and her lips were swollen and moist. How could he possibly say *no* to this magic between them?

He couldn't.

And he was experienced enough to know this was more than a physical reaction. Blended with the raw passion was tenderness and awe. His heart was in so much trouble.

Abruptly, Beth stood and then pulled her sweater and T-shirt over her head. Her long, dark hair wildly tumbled around her pale shoulders. His throat went dry as she locked her gaze with his and unhooked her bra. The sight of her semi-naked body took his breath away. Sammy couldn't even speak. Instead, he held out his hand. Beth took it and she kneeled in front of him. Impatiently he pulled loose and stripped out of his T-shirt and then his jeans. Her eyes devoured him as he shed everything and stood before her, his need evident.

And then he was beside her, lying on the soft rug, their bodies pressed against each other. Who cared about tomorrow when tonight was so entrancing? For now there was only the heat of the fire on their nude bodies, the heat of bare skin brushing against bare skin, and the heat of need bubbling inside him like a fiery cauldron.

Much, much later, Sammy drifted in the twilight between sleep and wakefulness as Beth lay sound asleep beside him. He tucked the quilt she'd brought from the bedroom around her shoulders and smiled as she sighed and snuggled closer into the warmth of his body. A peaceful, contented drowsiness lazed through him.

Right now, holding Beth after a night of lovemaking had to be a top ten moment in his life. Scratch that, top five at least. Maybe even the best moment he'd ever experienced… Quickly, Sammy eradicated the thought. The sexual afterglow had clouded his perspective. There was no need to rank or analyze what he was feeling.

Just enjoy this time while it lasts. Determined to follow his own advice, Sammy yawned and succumbed to the lethargy.

Through the fog of sleep, a slight noise pricked his awareness. Sammy mentally swatted at it, annoyed at the disruption, and drifted back into a doze. A slight flicker of light disturbed the inky darkness behind his eyelids. A slight crackling erupted from the silence, probably the dying flames consuming the last of the oak. Come morning, he'd add more wood to the fire.

Crunch.

Sammy's eyes popped open, alertness splashing over him like icy water. His body tensed, ready to spring into action. A quick glance assured him Beth still slept undisturbed by his side. He waited, as still as a cat ready to pounce.

Crunch, crunch and then *crunch, crunch.* The sound of advancing footsteps muffled in the snow.

Someone had found them.

This was bad. There'd been no noise or oncoming headlights from a car. No phone communication from the outside world warning of an emergency visit. It had to be Lambert or one of his men. Sammy eased the blanket off while his eyes searched the dark room. The fireplace embers provided just enough light to locate his pistol set on the mantel. Slowly, he rose and grabbed it, the cold metal gripped in his palm reassuring. Beth turned restlessly, pulling the quilt up until it almost covered her face.

He pondered the wisdom of waking her. The advantage would be that she'd be his backup, armed with a shotgun. The disadvantage would be that in waking Beth, he'd startle her, and she'd make a noise, alerting whoever was out there that they were awake and onto them. Swiftly, he decided to rouse her. He couldn't very well leave her alone and vulnerable while he searched out the danger.

Noiselessly, he kneeled and placed a hand on her shoulder. No response. He gave her shoulder a little shake. Her eyes flew open in alarm, then softened when she focused on him. Keeping his gun in his right hand, Sammy lifted the index finger of his opposite hand and pressed it against his puckered lips.

Hush.

Her eyes widened with fear, but she nodded understanding. He pointed at his gun and then to the fireplace. *Get your shotgun.* Nimbly, she tossed aside the quilt and rose. They both had on sweats they'd donned before falling asleep in the chilly cabin. He saw her scoop up her cell phone and shove it into a pocket as she went to the mantel. When she held the shotgun, he raised a palm toward her. *Stay here.*

Beth violently shook her head *no*. He glared at her and she returned his gaze with equal determination. Seemed he had a backup after all.

Sammy leaned into her and whispered in her ear. "Someone's out there. I'm going outside."

Beth nodded and whispered, "Let's go."

"Stay behind me."

He walked to the door and disengaged the lock. A barely audible click sounded before he slid the metal bolts to the side. Fighting an instinct to fling open the door and run wildly into the dark, Sammy turned the knob, conscious of Beth's soft breathing behind him and the warmth of her body pressed against his back. He released the pistol's safety mechanism.

Frosty air bombarded him, and his bare feet sank into snow. Thank heavens it'd been so cold that he and

Beth had put on clothes before falling asleep in front of the fire. They'd saved precious time.

Impossible to see more than a few feet ahead, but there was no sign of anyone and no car in sight. Had he imagined the noise? Could it have been an animal rather than a human? Slowly, he advanced to the side of the cabin, Beth at his back with her shotgun at the ready.

An explosion of shattered glass broke the night's eerie silence. Sammy ran toward the back of the cabin, gun raised. The shadows shifted, and he made out a large figure running toward the tree line that bordered the county road. The bedroom window was broken.

"Halt!" he shouted. The figure kept running. No way he could see well enough to land a shot, but Sammy fired his pistol in the air, hoping it would scare the man into surrender.

It did not.

Sammy gave chase, his mind racing as fast as his feet running in the freezing snow. Had the attacker heard them approach? Why hadn't he entered the cabin through the broken window. Unless…

He reached out an arm for Beth, relieved when he made contact with the solid strength of her body. "Get down!"

An explosion shook the ground at his feet as he dropped to his knees and then laid his body above Beth's. His ears rang with the sound of an incendiary pipe bomb exploding. Fire billowed from the cabin, illuminating the sky like lightning. Debris flew through the wind—wood, glass and ash. The snow reflected the giant leaping flames, giving the impression of molten lava spilling on the ground.

Sammy tore his eyes from the horrific damage and

scanned the area, eyes peeled for any sight of the attacker returning or any accomplices lurking nearby.

From up the road, the beam of car headlights cut through the darkness.

"They're getting away!" Beth said, pushing him off and scrambling to her feet. "We've got to stop them."

She ran toward the cabin, and he caught up to her, tugging at her arm. "Hurry," she urged. "Get the car keys. We can't let them escape."

"I'll get them. You wait here."

"I can help you search."

"Too dangerous."

Without waiting for an argument, he ran past her. Sammy pulled off his T-shirt and covered his mouth and nose. At the gaping door, precariously tilted to the right, he blinked against the plumes of ash and smoke. His keys, cell phone and two-way radio were located on the far left end of the den on the coffee table they'd pushed against the wall last night so they could sleep in front of the fire. Among other things they'd done there. If they hadn't made love and slept together, if Beth had slept in the bedroom as she had the previous night, she'd be dead.

A chill racked his body—one that had nothing to do with winter. His professional training kicked in. *Deal with that later; there's work to be done.* He sucked in a chest full of air and entered the smoky cabin. Acrid fumes assaulted his nose and eyes. Blinking wildly, he put one hand along the wall to move forward without becoming disoriented by the thick curtain of smoke. Sammy crouched low and tried to ignore the heat emanating from the blistered wood that burned his hand and feet.

Even though he tried not to take deep breaths, smoke

filled his lungs and he coughed, struggling for oxygen. The hair on his arms bristled painfully from the heat. Fire roared and crackled and pieces of wood haphazardly fell from the ceiling.

Just a few more steps.

Pain shot through the arch of his right foot as a large glass shard cut through flesh. Sammy kept going. He had no choice; they had to pursue whoever had tried to kill them. This might be their only chance to capture the bastard.

He felt the edge of the coffee table before he saw it. Would the radio and phones already be destroyed by heat and smoke? They were fiery in his palms, but he pocketed the items. Where were those damn keys? He brushed the surface of the table, scorching the bare skin of his right forearm. Nothing. They must have fallen on the floor. Still keeping one hand in contact with the wall, he got on all fours and swept his free hand along the floor until they brushed against jagged metal.

Feeling victorious, he stuffed them in his pocket and started to rise back up on his feet. His head bumped against something solid. The easel clattered to the ground.

Beth's paintings! Her stunning, elegant snowscapes.

Violent coughing seized his lungs. *Get out*, brain and body urged. But he couldn't let Beth's art burn to smithereens. All that work, all that beauty. He slid his left foot over until it thumped against the wall, his anchor in the sea of flames and smoke, and then he gathered the canvases that had fallen to the ground, praying that the thick cloth she'd thrown over the paintings had kept her work from being destroyed.

A large beam fell from the ceiling, landing only a foot from where he stood. It was past time to get the hell out of the cabin. Sammy sprinted toward the door, enduring the gauntlet of the hot floor littered with broken glass. At last he hobbled outside and gulped crisp mountain air down his parched lungs. Snow numbed the bottoms of his burning feet that were laced with gashes.

He thrust the paintings into Beth's arms and turned back to make a mad dash for their jackets and shoes, but the singed door frame buckled, and the overhead wooden strip of the frame dangled precariously in the opening.

Barefoot it was.

And there was no time to waste if they wanted to catch a killer.

Chapter Ten

Beth gaped as Sammy shoved her oil paintings into her arms. She hadn't given them a moment's thought. After all, how many had she painted over the years? Dozens and dozens. And although painting was her profession—one of the ways she made a living, along with teaching art—no one would ever believe her work so valuable that they would risk death by fire to save them.

Not her father, who, though proud, had viewed her "hobby" with an indulgence she'd found more condescending than appreciative,

Not Cynthia, who filtered everything and everybody through the lens of their monetary value.

Not Aiden, who mostly regarded the world from the same perspective as his mother, mixed with an intellectual vigor that her father had favored and encouraged.

If Mom had lived, Beth felt certain she would have understood and appreciated her daughter's artistic success, modest though it was. Mom had always insisted on Beth receiving art lessons and had proudly displayed her childhood drawings. But Mom had died a long, long time ago and Beth still missed her love and encouragement. Since a young teen, she'd felt like a misunderstood, undervalued changeling in the Wynngate family.

And then there was Sammy. The man who had arrested her as a teenager. The man she'd blamed for over a decade for exiling her from her family. She'd misjudged him as uncaring, arrogant.

Beth forgot the horrific explosion, the burning cabin her father had loved, the chill seeping in her bones and bare feet, and the knowledge that someone was trying to kill her. There was only Sammy, covered with ash and grime, rescuing her canvases as though Dad's cabin was a museum on fire and her work was Van Gogh's.

She couldn't move. Couldn't speak past the pinch in her heart.

"Let's go!" Sammy ran past her, limping and still coughing violently.

Beth blinked away the hot tears that had unexpectedly arisen. "You're hurt. I'll drive."

Without argument, Sammy dug in his jeans pocket and tossed her the keys. Beth tossed her paintings in the back seat, got in and started the motor. It took a couple of seconds to find the light switch on the dashboard panel and get her bearings with a strange vehicle, then the Jeep lurched forward as she hit the accelerator. She bounced in her seat as they crossed over the uneven land of the small clearing and then onto a dirt road. Only one way out of here and then onto the main road.

She had to catch up to the bomber. If they didn't, she could never feel safe again. Each attack grew more aggressive. Next time, she might not escape with her life. How the hell had he found them out here? Was it Dorsey? Sammy had been right. Rayna had no influence on her son—either that, or she hadn't even tried to get through to him.

"Maybe I should have wired that fifty thousand dollars," she said, finding and switching to bright lights. "Or tried to promise them I would get them the money somehow. If I had, they might not have come after me tonight."

"Hell, no! You can't deal with criminals that way." Sammy fiddled with a dial and a blast of welcome heat fanned her chilled body. "It's a game you'd never win."

Snow silently whirled through the wind. Pine trees crowded the road alongside of the Jeep. They made it to the paved county road. In the distance, she caught the elliptical beam of headlights rounding a curve. The attacker was heading north.

Beth stayed focused on the twin rays of headlights ahead, steadily gaining on the bomber. Did he know they were in pursuit? She barely registered Sammy's ongoing radio conversation as he called in their location and requested backup. The static stop-and-go talking provided a comforting backdrop of noise as she sped down the lonely stretch of pavement in the moonlight.

Miles flew past, and although she seemed to be gaining on the vehicle ahead, it stayed frustratingly out of eyesight. She wanted that tag number. She wanted an arrest. She wanted this ordeal to be over. Tonight. Not only for herself, but for her family and for Sammy. No one in her circle was safe.

The county road began to twist as they headed back up the mountain and the elevation rose. With every turn and climb, the wind howled stronger. The snow seemed to swirl faster, and the trees flashed by at an alarming rate. But Beth drove on, jaw clenched with determination even as her fingers painfully clenched the steering wheel. Her bare feet vibrated with the rumble of the Jeep's engine as it strained under the demanding conditions.

Ahead, she caught a glimpse of a yellow Dodge truck. A little closer and they'd have the tag number.

But her jubilation was short-lived as the truck turned sharply onto GA 180—Georgia's own deadly version of the Tail of the Dragon roadway. Bad enough during the day when motorcyclists and other thrill seekers often raced down it. But on a snowy winter night? Despite the continued blast of the heater, her whole body began to tremble.

"We don't have to chase him down the mountain," Sammy said. "If we're lucky, one of our cops might get here in time to put up a roadblock."

If they were lucky. Right now, she didn't feel like Lady Luck was on her side. "I'm not quitting," she told Sammy.

"Want me to drive?"

"There's no time to switch places. We could lose him." Before she could change her mind, Beth turned the Jeep onto GA 180. At least she knew what to expect—a road as narrow as the width of a driveway with miles of blind turns and steep elevation changes. As a teenager, she'd driven down it a time or two, only to prove to Aiden that she wasn't a chicken. Whoever they were pursuing must also be a local to even attempt the ride.

She began the descent down the Tail of the Dragon. At the first blind turn, the Jeep's tires skidded on a sudden icy patch and the vehicle slid several feet to the very edge of the bank. Beth's heart beat painfully against her ribs, even after she righted course and prepared for the next turn.

"Careful there," Sammy said tightly. "Didn't know your real name was Mrs. Mario Andretti."

"Who?"

"Andretti. A legendary race car driver."

Beth slowed a fraction. The only worse outcome than

the bomber escaping them would be if she crashed the Jeep. Multiple wooden cross memorials alongside the road were a silent testament to the danger.

The yellow truck ahead didn't slow. Seemed the bomber was more desperate to escape them than they were to capture him and demand answers. At the next sharp curve, the truck veered so close to the edge of the cliff that it clipped the guardrail. The sound of tire squeals and grinding metal screamed through the snowy gales.

Down, down she drove, frustrated at the growing distance between the Jeep and the truck but too cautious to try and gain on it again.

"You're doing a great job," Sammy said softly. "We're over the halfway point down now. It's almost over."

"It won't be over until we get—"

Another squeal of tires filled the air—long and shrill. The truck's driver must have lost control of his vehicle. Beth tapped on the brakes, not knowing what to expect when she emerged from the blind curve. If the driver had crashed into the mountain wall on the right, his truck might be flung back onto the middle of the road, a deadly obstruction for their oncoming Jeep.

She rounded the bend—to see her worst fear come true. The truck slammed into the mountain with a deafening crash. Sparks mingled with snow and metal debris flew through the air like firecracker missiles.

"Look out!" Sammy shouted.

This was no time for mere brake-tapping. "Hold tight," she warned, slamming her foot on the brake, arms clenched to the steering wheel in a death grip as she braced for possible impact.

The truck spun out of control and back toward the

guardrail. More grinding of metal on metal ensued and an unmistakable human wail of terror rent the air.

The Jeep grounded to a sudden halt, in time for front-row viewing to a nightmare. The truck toppled over the rail, flipping once before disappearing into darkness. But she heard the crash from the bottom of the mountain as it landed once, then twice, and finally a third time. With each thunderous clap of the tumbling truck, Beth winced. Sammy was back on the two-way radio, barking out their location and requesting an ambulance. Again her body shook so hard that her teeth began to chatter. Sammy flung an arm over her shoulders and squeezed her tight. The solid strength of his arms comforted her and warmed the chilly despair that had momentarily overtaken her body.

"You did great, Beth. I couldn't have asked for a better partner tonight. Help's on the way."

Before she could do more than nod in reply, an explosion blasted from below. Tall flames burst high in a column of orange flares. Sirens wailed in the distance. Sammy flung open the passenger door.

"What are you doing?" she cried in surprise. "You can't go out there. You're not even wearing shoes!"

Sammy's gaze flicked to the back seat and he leaned over, plucking a towel and a jacket from a gym bag. He hastily pulled out the larger shards in his feet, then wrapped each item on a foot for makeshift shoes. "Keep the headlights pointed straight ahead," he instructed. "They know we're here by mile marker eight. I'm just going to stand by the edge of the road and take a quick look."

The door shut behind him and she watched as he picked his way through the haphazardly strewn metal wreckage. A compulsion to see the burning truck overcame her common sense. She opened the Jeep door and Sammy spun around.

"Don't come out here. There's glass everywhere."

"I want to see."

He shook his head and then crossed over to her. "Okay. Just for a minute," he said, putting an arm under her thighs and then lifting her out of the vehicle. She leaned into his solid warmth as the mountain wind whipped around them. He only took a few steps before stopping, mere inches from the smashed-in guardrail.

The twisted metal hull of the truck was engulfed by flames. Black plumes of smoke spiraled among the fire. For the second time tonight, the smell of gasoline permeated the air. But now the acrid scent of scorched rubber mixed with the fuel. The Tail of the Dragon was breathing fire tonight as it claimed yet another victim.

"He couldn't have survived," she whispered.

"No," he grimly agreed. "So much for that lead."

His harsh words weighed on her. "But won't you be able to discover who that man was? Or at least who owned the truck?"

"We will."

"Then we'll be closer to an answer."

Blue lights and sirens snaked up the mountain. Sammy carried her back to the Jeep, and she waited inside as he met with law enforcement officers. EMTs scrambled from an ambulance with stretchers and headed down the mountain. Firefighters joined them and somehow the dark corner of the mountain was flooded with light in all directions as emergency responders set to work. Sammy emerged from the crowd of people and returned to the Jeep, an EMT by his side.

"You need to go with Adam," Sammy told her gently. "He'll take you to the Elmore Community Hospital.

You need to be checked for shock and to make sure you don't have any serious wounds."

"Wounds?" she asked blankly.

"You're covered with cuts," he explained.

She glanced down, surprised at the number of bloody scratches crisscrossing her arms and legs. "How..."

"When the bomb went off, debris flew everywhere. You've been too pumped with adrenaline to notice."

"What about you? You've been limping. Did you burn your feet in the fire?"

"I'll be fine—"

"What's this?" A deep voice interrupted. "Are you injured, Sammy?" Sheriff Harlan Sampson suddenly stood beside them, frowning and surveying them with his hands on his hips.

"It's not bad, mostly a gash on one foot," Sammy said, obviously trying to minimize the injury.

Harlan cocked his head toward the ambulance. "Go get it looked at."

"But you need my report and—"

"That can wait. We have enough information for tonight. We'll get your car down the mountain for you." Harlan glanced at her thoughtfully. "Besides, someone needs to watch out for Ms. Wynngate at the hospital. My wife would never forgive me if something happened to her friend."

His manner was not unkind, but Beth suddenly felt a crushing weight on her chest. She'd placed his officer in danger. Harlan most likely would love to see her hightail it back to Boston, far away from his department's responsibility. Far away from Lilah. Not that she couldn't understand his feelings. Danger followed wherever she roamed, no matter how far or remote the location.

She followed Sammy into the back of another officer's cruiser, which rushed them to the hospital. Sammy's foot required stitches and by the time they were fully examined and cleaned up, dawn streaked the sky. Even though the adrenaline had left her body, she felt oddly restless and not in the least tired.

Lilah burst through the examination room, carrying several large plastic bags. She dropped them to the floor and enveloped Beth in a bear hug. "Are you okay? Harlan told me what happened." Lilah stepped back and appraised her. "You look horrible."

"Why, thank you," Beth said, attempting a smile.

"You know what I mean." Lilah retrieved one of the fallen bags and handed it to her. "I brought clean clothes for you." She shoved the other bag at Sammy. "And for you. I believe you and Harlan are about the same size, so these should fit."

"I can't wait to change out of these stinky clothes," Beth said, wondering if the stench of smoke would ever leave her nostrils.

"Ditto," Sammy echoed, hobbling over to the men's room to change.

Lilah followed her into the ladies' bathroom. "So what's the game plan now? You and Sammy should come stay with us until all this mess blows over."

Beth's gaze involuntarily slid to Lilah's pregnant belly. Much as she would enjoy staying at Lilah's, she couldn't put her friend in danger. "I've worked it out already. Aiden returned early from his trip and insisted I come stay with him a few days until Lambert's locked up."

After the abysmal failure of the remote cabin to keep her safe, the busy high-rise condo bustling with people felt infinitely more secure. At least someone would hear her scream if Lambert attacked.

Lilah stuffed the smoke-ruined clothes in an empty plastic bag as Beth changed into jeans and a sweater. "I'll wash these for you," Lilah offered.

"Those old things? Don't bother. Just dump them in the trash can."

Lilah pulled a pair of sneakers and slippers from the bag. "My shoes might be a size too small for you, if I remember right. If nothing else, you can wear these bedroom slippers and stop somewhere on the way to buy a new pair of shoes."

Beth didn't even try the sneakers, opting for the warm, furry slippers. "Thanks, Lilah. I'll return everything to you later."

Lilah waved a dismissive hand. "Is Sammy driving you to Aiden's place?"

"Your husband made sure his car was brought to the hospital. And Sammy insisted on taking me."

"Might be a good idea." Lilah shook her head and held open the bathroom door. "Still can't get over that they tried to kill you."

"They?" Beth's brow furrowed. Lilah must be speaking of the Lambert family in general.

"Yeah. Those two whose bodies the cops found last night. They'd been flung a good distance from the truck."

It hadn't even occurred to her there would be more than the lone driver behind the attack. "So one of them threw the pipe bomb while another waited in a getaway truck?"

"That's what Harlan speculates."

It felt as though a cold ice cube suddenly slivered down her spine. The whole thing had been so…premeditated. "Wonder if one of the men was the same guy who threatened me in town yesterday."

"Maybe. I wouldn't put anything past Marty Upshaw."

Beth stepped into the brightly lit hospital hallway. Now that she'd donned fresh clothes, the scent of smoke was replaced by an antiseptic zing in the air. "And who did the other body belong to?"

Lilah's brows rose. "You haven't heard yet?"

A knot of dread formed in her stomach. Judging by Lilah's reaction, this person might have been someone she'd known. "Who?" she whispered.

"Abbie Fenton."

Chapter Eleven

Sammy stepped off the elevator, Beth's suitcases in each of his hands. It had been quick work gathering her clothes and toiletries from the Wynngate house before the short drive to Atlanta. He followed her down a long hallway in Aiden's condo building, impressed that even this utilitarian part of the building had a luxurious feel, with chandeliers, plush carpeting and a view of downtown from floor-to-ceiling windows that banked both ends of the hall. Beth, of course, paid it no mind as she strode to Aiden's door and rang the bell.

Unease niggled the back of his mind. With all the danger and forced intimacy between them, he'd pushed away the realization of how different their social statuses were. A blue-collar man like himself would be a real step down in the world inhabited by the Wynngates and others with their wealth.

Steps sounded from the opposite side of the door and he wondered how his old friend would greet him. It'd been at least four or five years since they'd last met. The encounter had felt awkward for Sammy and he suspected it had for Aiden, as well. After only a minute of reminiscing on old times, he'd found himself floundering in the conversation. There was no longer a common ground between them.

The door flung open, and Aiden filled the doorway with his tall, charismatic presence, throwing Sammy a grin as he hugged Beth in welcome. "You always bring the excitement when you visit us," he teased.

"Sure you don't mind me crashing a few days?"

"Don't be silly. 'Course not." Aiden thrust out his hand to Sammy. "How you doing, buddy?"

"Fine," he answered, as though he and Beth hadn't been through hell all last night.

Aiden opened the door all the way and gestured them inside. The industrial, minimalistic feel of the place struck Sammy as coldly formal. Everything was gray or dull white. The room would be much improved if Beth's colorful paintings graced the stark walls. Odd that her brother didn't display any of them, but he supposed everyone should be allowed to live with their own tastes in their own home. Beth stood beside him and leaned into him, resting her head against his chest. He slung an arm over her shoulder and gave her a reassuring squeeze. The worst was over. Now they needed to rest and recoup.

If Aiden wondered about the connection between his sister and old friend, he didn't remark on it. "You both must be dead on your feet," he said. "Come on in and sit down."

"That's okay. I should be going—"

"Nonsense."

Beth pleaded with her eyes. "You should rest before driving back to Lavender Mountain. Maybe even take a nap?"

"Good idea," Aiden said approvingly. "I have a couple of empty guest rooms. Stay as long as you want."

"No, I really need to get some paperwork done today," he argued. Not to mention there were so many angles he wanted to follow up on. With any luck, Charlotte might have unearthed something useful in the investigation. He could use a bit of good news right about now.

"At least sit down and drink some coffee," Beth urged.

Aiden clapped his hands together. "Excellent idea. I have an espresso machine that makes a mean cup of joe."

Of course he did. Sammy would have preferred a soda, but he gave Aiden a nod. "Sounds good."

Beth lifted the two suitcases sitting by the doorway. "If you don't mind, I'm going to take a quick shower."

He needed one, as well, but he'd wait until he got home. Sammy followed Aiden into the kitchen with its broad expanse of marble countertops and stainless steel appliances. "Nice place," he commented.

"Isn't it?" Aiden agreed with an appreciative smile. "And you should see the gym and pool downstairs. We even have an indoor racquetball court." He beamed with pride as he ground fresh coffee beans and then emptied them into a complicated-looking machine. "There's even a five-star restaurant on the lobby level that delivers room service on nights I'm too beat to cook or go out. Best of all, my office is less than a quarter mile away. So convenient."

"Must be nice," he offered, watching as Aiden fussed with the espresso maker and retrieved glass cups from a cabinet. From the bank of windows over the sink, he could see a line of cars inching forward on the bypass. Good thing Aiden lived so close to his law firm. Otherwise, the commute would be a bitch.

No thanks. He'd take the slow pace of Lavender Mountain any day. Frowning, Sammy eyed the button-down shirt and tailored gray pants Aiden wore. "Are you going back to work today? I thought you were still on vacation."

"Vacation?" He barked out a laugh. "Is that what Beth told you? I've been on a business trip. No rest when you're the boss. But don't worry, I can work here at home the next few days while y'all get this situation sorted. Any idea when they might arrest Lambert?"

Aiden filled both their cups and pointed at the cream and sugar by the machine.

"Atlanta PD has an APB out on him. Could be any minute now."

Aiden shook his head. "Can't imagine why anyone would want to hurt my sister. Are the Lamberts trying to kidnap Beth and hold her for ransom? Is that the theory?"

"Maybe." If Beth hadn't volunteered more information, he certainly wouldn't. Sammy sipped the coffee. For all the elegant preparation and presentation, it tasted like any old cup of black coffee. Maybe his taste buds, like his life in general, lacked sophistication.

"She'll be safe with me, although we might drive each other up the wall if we're home alone together all day every day." Aiden chuckled. "Between us, Beth can be pretty flaky. If you know what I mean."

He frowned. "No, I don't know what you mean. She seems extremely levelheaded to me. Brave, too."

"Oh, sure, sure," Aiden said placatingly. "But you don't know her as well as I do. She's a typical artist. Kind of moody and always has her head in the clouds. It's cute at first, but it wears thin after a while."

"In what way?" Sammy asked, unable to keep the sharp edge out of his voice.

"Don't get me wrong, she's my sister and I love her

of course, but she can be overly dramatic. Not to mention a bit spoiled, too. The judge sent her to the finest schools and left her a substantial inheritance. And what does she have to show for it? A job teaching art to middle schoolers." He gave a smug snicker.

"There's nothing wrong with the teaching profession. And Beth happens to be a highly talented painter."

Aiden sipped his coffee and then set it down. "She's a dilettante. By now, she should be seeing someone in our crowd or going to graduate school and learning a real profession."

Anger burned his cheeks and the nape of his neck. Could Aiden have been more obvious in his disapproval of his and Beth's attraction? With one broad stroke, he'd managed to insult Beth as a flighty no-talent hack and himself as a poor, unacceptable match for a member of the Wynngate family.

"Maybe what Beth wants isn't the same as what you believe she needs," Sammy said, striving to keep his anger in check. "And give her a little credit. Beth is a smart, talented and capable woman who makes her own decisions."

Aiden frowned. "You misunderstand what I'm saying. I'm only—"

A sharp voice sounded from behind. "Your message was unmistakable." Beth glared at her brother, pushing back a lock of wet hair from her face. "Nice to know your real opinion of me—an overly dramatic, spoiled dilettante."

"You're twisting my words," he protested. "And how long have you been eavesdropping?

"I'm repeating exactly what you said. And I couldn't help but overhear as I walked over."

"C'mon, Beth, I'm sorry. Don't be so sensitive. I didn't mean anything by it."

A bitter laugh escaped her mouth. "Of course you meant something by it. And you insulted Sammy, too. Apologize to him."

Although gratified at Beth's quick defense, Sammy didn't want to cause trouble between her and her brother. "It's okay," he said quickly.

Aiden's face flushed crimson and he didn't spare Sammy a glance. "You're making a big deal out of nothing," he insisted.

"You implied he was unsuitable. Not good enough for a Wynngate."

"I didn't say that." Again Aiden refused to look him in the eye.

"Bad enough you put me down, but I'm not going to stand by and let you do the same with my friends. At least Sammy hasn't come to me with his hands out, asking to borrow money."

"I asked if you wanted to invest in my new law firm. Not to borrow." Aiden carefully set his coffee cup on the counter. "There's a big difference. It's not like you don't have the money."

Sammy started to ease out of the kitchen. This was family business and he didn't belong.

"And I gladly lent you thousands of dollars," Beth said, her voice calmer now. "This isn't about the money. It's about respect."

Aiden held up his hands, palms out. "You're right. I don't want to argue. Sammy, don't leave. Seems I owe you an apology. No offense, okay?"

"Sure," Sammy said, not believing for a second that Aiden was sincere, but to ease Beth's feelings. She'd been through enough the last few days without him contributing to this sibling conflict. So what if Aiden looked down his patrician nose at him? He really didn't give a damn. Their friendship had been over for years.

"See? Sammy's fine. And I promise, you'll get your money back within the year. With interest."

Sammy cleared his throat. "Guess I'll be heading down the road. Thanks for letting Beth stay with you a few days, Aiden."

"My pleasure—"

"I'm not staying." Beth strode out of the kitchen and headed for the door.

Aiden trailed after her. "But—I thought you needed a safe place to stay."

Sammy sighed. He couldn't blame Beth for not wanting to hide out here. But where could she go now that was safe? She'd already refused to stay with him, and her stepmother obviously didn't want Beth at her place or Beth would have gone there.

Beth snatched her bags from one of the bedrooms and reemerged with her face still set in stony resolve, Aiden at her heels and trying to convince her not to leave. Sammy held the door open and Beth faced her brother one last time. "We'll talk later. I'm too upset right now. Bye, Aiden."

Sammy gave a quick nod to the chagrined Aiden and they silently proceeded to the elevator. Once the doors closed behind them, Beth gave him a rueful smile. "Sorry you had to see that. It was ugly, wasn't it?"

"A little. Can't say I blame you for walking out, but now we have to figure out our next move. Have you changed your mind about staying with me in Lavender Mountain? I can provide 24/7 police protection."

"No. I won't put you in that kind of danger. Plus,

there's too many eyes in that town. Word would get around where I'm staying."

"Let me decide about the risk. My main concern is your protection. I don't want anything to happen to you."

Chapter Twelve

Sammy's worry about her safety thawed the chill in her heart left from Aiden's harsh words. But then, how much was merely professional concern on his part? Couldn't look good on a deputy sheriff's record to have someone hurt while under his protection. Beth shook off the depressing thought, her usual optimism starting to surface. A good breakfast and a few hours' sleep in her favorite hotel was in order.

"This is it," she announced. "Pull up to the lobby entrance and let's spring for valet service."

"Fancy," Sammy commented as he whipped the Jeep to the door.

The downtown W Hotel gleamed like a skyscraper diamond in the morning sunshine—all glass and chrome, a tall beacon promising warmth and comfort. It was her favorite place to stay in the city. On annual home visits, she often opted to stay at the W in a private suite instead of with family. That way she, Cynthia and Aiden didn't get into each other's hair too much.

With quick and courteous efficiency, they were ushered into the studio suite she preferred. The corner room featured floor-to-ceiling windows that offered stunning views of Atlanta. The energy of the city was also captured in the vibrant turquoise-and-magenta color scheme that clicked with her artist's eye.

"This is amazing," Sammy said, surveying the room. The dazed, appreciative expression on his face spoke volumes. Luxury suites probably weren't much on his radar, living as he did on a deputy sheriff's salary. She hoped she hadn't made him uncomfortable. Perhaps this wasn't the best choice after Aiden's so-recent snobby remarks. Although she'd inherited a substantial amount of money from her parents, she wasn't one to flaunt her wealth. But after everything they'd been through last night, she wanted to treat them both to the very best.

Beth flopped onto the king-size bed and sought to put him at ease. "I hope you love it here as much as I do. It's 'old-fashioned Southern hospitality meets modern chic meets artistic flair.'"

"I suppose this room will be okay," he remarked dryly. "Although I could do without the hot-pink blanket and pillows."

"Think of it as a rich shade of magenta, not pink."

"Tell it to my hormones. My testosterone level dropped the moment I saw it."

Beth laughed and sprang to her feet. "Let's order room service for breakfast and then catch a nap."

"I really should head back to the station. Harlan will be expecting a report by the end of the day."

"Harlan would expect you to rest and then do whatever you have to do. Besides, you can order a laptop brought here from the hotel's business center and email a report. No need to drive all the way back to Lavender Mountain."

"They would do that?" he asked in surprise.

"Of course. Welcome to the twenty-first century."

"The technology isn't what surprised me. I'm talking about the service. You don't get that at the local motel chains I use."

She searched his face for a hint of rancor but, to her relief, found none. Treating Sammy to the very best was going to be fun. In short order, they were seated at the window table and dining on a brunch of shrimp and grits, fried green tomatoes and bacon biscuits. The coziness felt extra intimate as they watched office workers and shoppers crowding the streets below under a light dusting of snow.

Once their hunger was sated, a different physical appetite was aroused. His eyes blazed across the table at her as he slowly set his fork down. Wordlessly, Sammy took her hand and led her to bed. That large luscious bed with its soft mattress—a stark contrast to the hard floor of the cabin where they'd made love last night. Not that she was complaining. She'd always treasure the memory of discovering the feel of his strong, sleek body and the taste of his mouth as the fireplace crackled in the background.

Beth never imagined it possible but making love to Sammy the second time around was even more exciting than the first. He kissed and touched her in just the right places, already an expert on her sensual desires. Need welled in her, frantic and desperate until at last he entered her. She met each thrust with wild abandon. Pleasure at last ripped through her and she held on to him as the tremors subsided. Only then did he allow his own orgasm and she marveled at what a skillful and tender lover Sammy was.

The long, sleepless hours finally caught up to her. Beth closed her eyes and snuggled into Sammy's warm arms, drifting into welcome slumber.

A cell phone rang, jarring her out of sleep. The illusion of safety and isolation from the rest of the world lifted in an instant. Sammy rolled away from her and picked the phone up off the nightstand.

"Armstrong, here." A pause and then he sat up, all business. "You've got him? I'll be right down."

"What is it?" she asked breathlessly. "Has Lambert been found?"

"Found and arrested. Atlanta PD are holding him at their midtown station." Sammy slid out of bed and picked up his clothes lying on the floor. "Can't wait to interrogate the little bastard."

Beth got out of bed and snatched up her clothes, as well. "I'll go with you."

"No need. Go back to sleep. I could be gone for hours." He quickly began dressing.

She paused, about to pull her T-shirt over her head. "Are you sure?"

"Positive." He grinned and drew her in for a brief, fierce kiss. "You're safe now," he proclaimed. "We're shutting Lambert and the rest of his family down. It's finally over, Beth."

Just that quickly. It was almost hard to take in. "Safe," she echoed. "I like the sound of that."

Sammy grabbed his jacket. "Let's celebrate when I get back. Anywhere you want to go." He gestured at the windows. Already, lights twinkled in the gathering dusk. "The city's finest dining and entertainment. You decide."

"Perfect."

With a quick wave, he left, and the door shut behind him, only to open a second later. "Dead bolt the lock behind me."

"Thought I was safe," she said with a laugh.

"Can't be too careful."

Once a cop, always a cop. Although Beth couldn't say she minded his attention and concern. She'd lived alone too long not to appreciate the caring behind the admonitions. Dutifully, she crossed to the door and secured the lock. Turning around, she faced the rumpled bed where they'd just made love. Should she crawl back in and catch more sleep?

The idea had no appeal. She was too excited to go back to sleep. At the windows, she glimpsed the valet bringing around the Jeep and the slight limp in Sammy's step where he'd had stitches. He drove off and she sighed, wishing she'd insisted on going with him. Although, what good would that do? She wasn't a cop and they wouldn't let her listen in on the interrogation. She'd be stuck sitting in the dismal precinct atmosphere for at least a couple of hours sipping bad coffee and munching vending machine potato chips.

Beth sat in a turquoise-and-pink chair by the window and gazed at the view. The blue-top dome of the Polaris lounge caught her eye. Instantly, her mouth watered with the remembered taste of the peach frozen daiquiri they were famous for making. The place had its own bee garden to harvest honey for their handcrafted libations. Plus, the domed restaurant atop the Hyatt Regency rotated, offering spectacular views of Atlanta at night. Sammy might get a kick out of the fresh vegetables grown on their rooftop garden.

Decision made, Beth called and made a reservation. If Sammy had time tomorrow, they could extend their celebration and spend the day at the Georgia Aquarium. She glanced at the time on her cell phone, noting that only twenty minutes had passed since Sammy left. She paced the room, wondering what Dorsey Lambert was telling the police. Would he rat out members of his family he'd recruited to help him? She thought of Abbie. So young to have died. The violence of the truck crash played out in her mind—the sound of it as it flipped and rolled down rocky mountain terrain and then burst into flames. In a way, the sights and sounds of the crash made her cringe as much as the exploding pipe bomb in the cabin. At least that disaster had been unexpected. They'd never seen it coming. But that icy race down the Tail of the Dragon had seemed to go on for hours and hours.

At last she managed to rest for a while in the comfortable chair, even dozing a little as she waited for Sammy's return. She didn't know how long she conked out but eventually she roused, blinking her eyes fast to reorient herself.

From the hallway, an elevator door pinged open and shut. It was a busy time of day for guests to head out for cocktails and dinner. More footsteps shuffled outside and then came to an abrupt halt by her room. Beneath the door slat, a pair of dark men's shoes blocked the hall light. The lock jiggled. Her heart hammered, and her throat went dry.

A drunken businessman mistaking her room for his?

A sharp rap hammered the door. Beth didn't move. Didn't speak. Maybe whoever was out there would realize his mistake and just go away.

Another loud knock. *You're safe now*, Sammy had said. She'd known it was too good to be true.

Beth grabbed her cell phone and punched in 9-1-1 with trembling fingers. If whoever was out there tried to break down the door, she'd hit the call button.

"Beth?" a deep voice called out. "Beth, are you in there?"

"Wh-who is it?" she asked, a hand at her throat.

"It's me, Aiden. Come to apologize. Let me in."

Aiden. A tsunami of relief swooshed through her body and her knees threatened to buckle. She grabbed onto a chair to keep from falling to the floor. Drawing a deep breath, she hurried to the door and flung it open. Aiden grinned down, holding up a bottle of merlot. "I knew you'd be at this place. Figured I'd bribe you to let me in with your favorite wine."

She gave a weak laugh. "You scared the hell out of me. Come on in."

Aiden sauntered inside and surveyed the room. "Nice digs. You always liked this place. Where's Sammy?"

"At the police station." She shut the door and reset the dead bolt. "They called not thirty minutes ago saying they had Dorsey Lambert in custody. Sammy will be back before too long."

"They've got Lambert? That's fantastic news! Let's have a drink and toast an excellent bit of police work."

"You didn't have to come bearing gifts," she admonished, though secretly glad for the company.

Aiden set to work, gathering two crystal glasses from the kitchenette and setting them on the table. He popped the cork and began to pour.

"I'll join you in a second," she said.

Beth scurried into the bathroom and winced at her reflection. As she suspected, the mussed hair and streaked mascara made it appear as though she'd just rolled out of bed—after being thoroughly pleasured by a lover. Which she was. But she didn't need to parade that fact in front of her brother, because…just *eww*, he was her brother. Hastily, she brushed her hair and swiped at the makeup under her eyes. Much better.

When she returned to the table, Aiden was already seated, drinking wine. He gestured to the other poured glass and she gratefully sipped. The merlot was smooth and flavorful but a bit on the dry side, with the faintest afternote of bitter. Still, it was delicious and just what she needed after the last few harrowing days. If only Sammy was here to join them, the evening would be perfect.

"You've been through a hell of an ordeal, haven't you?" Aiden's dark brown eyes were warm with concern. "And then I heaped more trouble on you when you came to me for help. I was way out of line. I'm really sorry. Forgive me?"

"Of course." And she meant it. The Aiden seated across from her was her brother of old, his refreshing tenderness a quality that always helped brush over Cynthia's sometimes cutting indifference.

Aiden glanced at his expensive watch. "How long before Sammy returns? An hour? Two hours?"

"Two at the most. I'm hoping he'll be back within the hour."

"Heading home when he returns?"

"Nope. Going out to celebrate. Come with us for cocktails and dinner at the Polaris."

"Maybe."

"Anything wrong?" she asked. "You seem on edge this evening."

"No, no. Everything's fine. Matter of fact, I've got some good news, too."

More good news. Tonight was certainly her lucky night. Everything was nicely turning around. "Tell me."

Aiden raised his glass. "Drink up first."

Beth took another long sip. "Now what's up?"

"My firm's finally in the black. We got a large civil suit settlement and several more excellent prospects lined up. Wynngate LLC is starting to attract prominent customers."

Beth flushed with pride that her family's name was being honored by her stepbrother's firm. Dad had adopted Aiden when he married Cynthia and Aiden had always aspired to follow in his footsteps. "That's great. I'm so proud of you, Aiden. I knew you'd make a success of it."

When he'd first approached her six months ago to invest in his new criminal defense law firm, she'd had a few misgivings. Particularly when she heard the office would be in a new, swanky building situated in the trendy Buckhead area of the city. "Takes money to make money," Aiden had assured her. And spent money he had. Her brother was always wining and dining potential clients, but it looked as though the hard work was finally paying off.

Aiden raised his glass and pointedly looked at hers. Beth obligingly took another swallow.

"Best of all," he continued, "I should be able to repay you—with interest—by the first of the year."

Beth tried not to show her relief, afraid Aiden would take it as a lack of faith in his abilities. But more than the money, she wanted their sibling relationship unencumbered by awkwardness over the loan.

He clinked his glass with hers and they toasted his good fortune. Aiden picked up the merlot bottle and refilled her glass.

"I'm not sure I should have another," she protested. "My heart's set on a peach daiquiri later."

"Lighten up," he said with a laugh. "You deserve this. And I certainly don't want to drink alone."

A second glass of wine never hurt anybody. Beth shrugged and took another sip from the full glass. Already, her body seemed to be floating and her head swam. With shaking hands, she carefully set the goblet on the table, oddly mesmerized by the shimmer of the crimson liquid under the lamp.

"No more for me," she stated with an uneasy laugh.

"Well, you're no fun. I bought this merlot just for you."

"Doesn't mean I can drink it all in one sitting."

"That's my Beth. Always were a bit of a spoilsport. Never one to party hard like me and my friends."

And yet, she was the one who had paid the price years ago when his friends had left her high and dry at the party when the cops arrived.

"I thought you artsy types were supposed to have a more live-and-let-live lifestyle."

Was his tone faintly mocking or was the alcohol screwing with her judgment? "Those stories of wild artists are mainly a myth."

"So you consider yourself an artist and not a middle school teacher?"

Again his words seemed laced with a trace of superiority. "We can't all be hotshot lawyers and judges," she countered.

"You're right. It takes a particular intellect to succeed in those fields."

Beth swallowed an angry retort. Aiden couldn't help being a bit of a snob, considering he was raised by Cynthia. She rose to her feet and then quickly grabbed the table to keep from losing balance. Wine had never affected her so quickly before. Drinking on an empty stomach didn't agree with her. "Thanks for bringing the wine, Aiden, but I think I need to take a little nap before Sammy comes back."

Aiden chuckled. "It's catching up to you, huh?"

No point denying it. "Yes." She gestured to the door. "We'll talk later. Congratulations again on your firm's success."

"This wasn't much of a celebration. Tell you what, let's you and me go on over to the Polaris. Sammy can join us when he finishes business."

"I don't feel like going out."

"You need food," he said firmly. "How long since you've eaten?"

She thought through the fog clouding her mind. "Not since a late breakfast."

"There you go then. The Polaris is only a few blocks away. You can walk off the effect of the drink and eat dinner. You don't want Sammy to see you sloppy drunk, do you? What would he think?"

"I suppose you have a point," she said with a longing glance at the bed.

Aiden took her arm, leading her to the door. "I'll get a taxi. Trust me, going out to eat is just what you need."

With a sigh, she looked around for her purse, then spotted it on the nightstand. "Let me get my purse."

"No need. This is my treat."

"If you're sure—"

"Least I can do after all you've done for me. I couldn't ask for a better sister. It was my lucky day when Mom married your dad."

Aiden unlocked the door and she stumbled into the hallway. The floor felt uneven and her stomach rumbled. "I feel sick. Maybe I better—"

"No." His grip on her arm seemed to tighten.

"But—"

Instead of slowing down to accommodate her wobbly feet, Aiden quickened his pace and they walked past the elevators.

Beth frowned and tried to sort what was happening. “Why aren’t we getting on the elevator?”

“We’ll take the stairs.”

“But why?”

“You need to walk, sis. You’re right—that wine went straight to your head. Besides, I can’t be seen with you stumbling around in public. What if I ran into an important client or a colleague?”

Heat rose in her cheeks. “Going out was your idea.” She tried to jerk her arm free, but Aiden tightened his grip even more.

“Don’t be so sensitive,” he chided. “I’m doing this for you, not me.”

They reached the end of the hallway. Beth dug in her feet at the exit stairwell door. “I’ve changed my mind.”

He tugged at her elbow, his jaw set stubbornly. “Too late for that.”

Chapter Thirteen

Sammy entered the interrogation room, noting that it looked almost identical to the one in Elmore County. He suspected every such room at any police station looked much the same—windowless, dreary colors, cheap linoleum floors and no furniture except for a table and couple of metal chairs.

Dorsey Lambert sat slumped in a chair, scowling at the gouged surface of the table. He didn't raise his head when Sammy entered. A uniformed cop rose and nodded as he exited the room. "He's all yours."

Sammy took a seat across from Lambert, who stubbornly refused to face him. He waited, sweating him out. A full minute rolled by before the suspect met his gaze. "Who are you supposed to be?" he demanded, evidently expecting to see someone in a cop uniform or a detective with a suit sporting a badge.

"You don't remember me? I chased you a good three or four blocks when you bolted from your mom's home."

Recognition sparked in Lambert's unnaturally intense blue eyes. He scrubbed at his jaw, speckled with auburn stubble. The man was skinny and, as Sammy recalled, rather on the short side. But he carried himself like a mean yard dog itching for a fight and no doubt he could probably hold his own with most men twice his size. Sammy tried to think back on the height of the pipe bomb suspect who'd run away. Could there have been a third person there that night that they didn't know about? But Sammy couldn't recall anything concrete about the suspect that had tossed the bomb; it had been too dark and too brief an encounter to hazard a guess on the man's size.

"Are you the reason I'm here?" Lambert groused, lazing back in his chair. "Whatcha want with me?"

"You know why."

"No, I don't."

"Haven't you spoken with your mother?"

Lambert suddenly leaned forward and practically growled. "Leave Momma and my kin outta this."

Interesting to note the suspect felt such loyalty. "So it's okay for you and your family to terrorize a woman but then not man up when the law finally catches up to you?"

"Man up? That what you call snitching on your own family? 'Cause that ain't happening."

"I'm not here to debate semantics with you." At Lambert's blank look, he leveled him with a grim smile. "Let me put it another way. Either you cooperate, or I'll be questioning your mother every day until you confess."

Lambert sprang to his feet, chest puffed out. Sammy also rose and stared him down, daring the man to strike.

The door opened. "Need any backup?" a uniformed cop asked.

Dorsey's eyes darted nervously; he knew he was trapped.

"That's okay. I think we're ready to have a civilized conversation now, aren't we, Lambert?"

Dorsey didn't respond but slumped back down in his chair. Sammy also took a seat and tried a new tactic.

"Two cousins of yours—Abbie Fenton and Marty Upshaw—are already dead. Do you really want more lives wasted? Let's end this. Right here, right now."

Dorsey's mouth twisted. "End it? You mean arrest me for only trying to get what's due me." His voice oozed with bitterness. "Ain't that always the way, though? Rich man gets away with everything while people like me and my family are the ones who suffer."

Sammy picked up on his earlier statement. "What do you mean by trying to get what you're due?"

"Judge Wynngate was dirty. Everyone knew it. With the right amount of money, you could buy an innocent verdict or get your jail time cut in half."

"Why should I believe you?"

"Why would I lie about it? I paid fifty thousand bucks and what did that bastard do for me?"

Sammy stared back at him impassively, waiting for Lambert to continue. Dorsey slammed his hand on the table. "Nothing! He did nothing. Wynngate took my money and then gave me the maximum sentence possible. All I wanted was to get my money back. That kind of money don't mean nothing to some rich bitch like his daughter. She should give it back to me."

Sammy grabbed a fistful of Lambert's flannel shirt. "Don't you dare call her that." Conscious he was being watched, Sammy reluctantly let go. "Beth Wynngate has nothing to do with her father's so-called crimes."

"Yeah, but she inherited his dirty money, now, didn't she? I seen it in the papers after he died. She got nearly all of it. All I ask is that she give back what's rightfully due me and my family. Scraping together that money was a real hardship on us. And while I was in prison, I couldn't hold down a job and help out my momma.

Without my paycheck, she lives off a measly government check that don't cover all she needs."

Regular paycheck? Dorsey Lambert was a known drug dealer, not a stalwart employee earning an honest income, but Sammy let that go for now.

"I fail to see how killing Beth Wynngate is going to get your money returned to you."

Dorsey's eyes widened, and his jaw slackened. "Kill her? Ain't nobody trying to kill her."

"Don't lie to me! Why else were Marty and Abbie out there when the cabin exploded?"

Confusion clouded his eyes. "What cabin explosion?"

Sammy narrowed his eyes at him. Dorsey appeared surprised, but ex-cons were often good actors. His department hadn't reported the arson crime to the newspapers so the few Lavender Mountain locals who knew the fire department had been called out didn't know what had caused the fire.

"I know about the high-speed chase. Weren't no mention in the papers about a cabin exploding. We ain't got nothing to do with that."

"You saying your cousin Marty didn't have anything to do with it?"

"No, sir." Some of Dorsey's defiant bravado faded. "I admit they were out there keeping watch on Wynngate. I told them to wait for an opportunity when she was alone and then lean on her again about the money. Last time I talked to them, they'd followed y'all out to the cabin. Figured you'd return to work the next day and Wynngate would be alone at the cabin. The perfect opportunity to squeeze her for the money."

Sammy's blood chilled at the thought of Beth being alone in the woods and "squeezed" for money. "Let's back everything up a minute. Tell me more about your claim of paying off Judge Wynngate."

Dorsey shrugged. "Everybody knew he could be bought."

"You got any proof you paid him this money?"

"No," he admitted, his voice souring again. "I didn't pay him directly. I paid one of his collectors. Cash. Just as I was told to do."

"Who took your money?"

A cagey look came over his face. "Don't know his name."

"You're lying. You expect me to believe you paid a stranger fifty thousand in cash?" Dorsey wasn't the sharpest tool in the shed, but he did appear to have some street smarts.

"I did. I swear it's true. Some buddies of mine got time shaved off their sentences doin' the same thing."

"And how do you know this collector didn't just pocket the money and never forwarded it to the judge?"

"He paid him," Dorsey insisted. "Just my bad luck that federal heat was coming down on the judge not long after he took my money. The middleman told me I'd have to wait it out a few months. If Wynngate gave me a light sentence, it could be viewed in a negative light for the judge. The feds were looking for a pattern. Guy told me that when the heat died down, the judge would lighten my sentence on appeal."

First thing he needed to check was Lambert's claim of a federal investigation on the judge. He'd see if Harlan could use his contacts to find out unofficially. That should prove much faster than a formal inquiry.

Dorsey kicked at the empty chair beside him in disgust. "Then the bastard up and dies on me. Can you believe that crap? All that money wasted."

"Forget about the money. It's gone and you'll never get it back. You've already done your time. It's over. Think of the future. Now you're looking at a bigger mess. Attempted murder."

Dorsey threw up his hands, eyes wide with panic. "I wasn't anywhere near that cabin. I've been here in Atlanta at my mom's house. Didn't even know about the explosion until you told me five minutes ago."

"Yet you readily admit you had family members there that night, working for you."

"They didn't do it! I know them. They wouldn't kill nobody."

"Why should I believe a word you're telling me?"

"Ask around. Check with the feds about my story. Look, man, all I wanted was my money back. I ain't never killed anybody and don't plan on starting now."

Sammy steepled his fingers and regarded Dorsey's pleading eyes. "So you say. But greed and revenge are powerful motives for murder. I'd say both of those factors are at play in your head."

"I didn't do it!" He kicked at the chair again.

"If you're not guilty we'll find out soon enough. But your admission about involving your cousins in a scheme to extort money from Beth Wynngate is pretty damning. It places them right at the scene of the crime."

"That don't prove nothing. You can't keep me here."

"Of course we can. You've technically broken parole."

Dorsey squeezed his eyes shut and crinkled his nose, evidently regretting his words. He crossed his arms over his chest. "I want a lawyer."

Of course he did. Sammy nodded and rose. "Don't even think about asking anyone else in your family to come after Beth Wynngate. If you do, I'll make sure you're so old by the next time you get out of prison that you'll go directly into a nursing home to live out whatever's left of your sorry life."

"I ain't messin' with her no more. You have my word," Dorsey said, surprising him. Then again, a man would say anything to avoid returning to prison.

As though reading his mind, Dorsey spoke once more. "Like you said, the past is the past. My money's gone. Best I can hope for now is to live out my days in peace. Try to be an honest man."

Sammy walked to the door, but Dorsey hadn't finished speaking his mind.

"Sounds like someone's trying to kill that girl, but it ain't me."

THE ATLANTA TRAFFIC was heavy. Sammy kept hitting redial on his phone, but Beth didn't answer. With every failed ring, his unease grew. Surely she hadn't already gone out on the town on her own. And not while there were so many unanswered questions. Hell, they still bore the scars from last night's attempt on her life. Impatiently, he began weaving his way through the clogged lanes as fast as possible. At the hotel, he left the Jeep parked at the main entrance. "Back in a moment," he told the startled valet drivers.

Sammy raced through the lobby and entered the elevator, punching the button for the thirty-third floor. When the elevator door opened, he pushed through and scanned the hallway. To his left, he took in the sight of a man and a woman about to enter the exit stairwell. Relief washed over him.

"Where are y'all going?" he called out to Aiden and Beth, rushing over to them. "I've been trying to call."

Something was off. Beth looked disgruntled and

wobbly all at once. Aiden's eyes flashed with an annoyance that was replaced so quickly with his usual effervescent charm that Sammy wondered if he'd seen it in the first place. And after the scene at his condo earlier, why the hell had he come around? That must account for the frustration in Beth's eyes. She was still upset over his remarks a few hours ago.

"We were going to go out for a drink at the Polaris, but Beth changed her mind," Aiden said smoothly. "She decided to wait for your return. Tells me you're planning a celebration this evening."

Sammy glanced at Beth. She placed a hand on her forehead and shot him a rueful smile. "I might have to take a rain check on the celebration dinner. Aiden brought over some merlot and it's hit my system like a ton of bricks."

Aiden chuckled. "Seems my sister can't hold her liquor."

That didn't sound like Beth to overdrink. It seemed out of character. "The celebration can wait," he said.

"Sounds good. Guess I'll head on back home." Aiden extended a hand to Sammy. "We'll do it another night?"

"Sure. I'll call you."

"Great. Catch you later." Aiden raised an arm at the stairwell door. "Guess I'll take the stairs and burn some calories."

Beth started back toward their room and stumbled. He grabbed her elbow to keep her from falling. "Easy now."

She drew a deep breath. "Thanks. I can't believe how dizzy I am."

"If you're dizzy, why in hell were y'all going to take the stairs instead of the elevator?"

She grimaced. "Seems that in my present condition, Aiden was afraid I'd embarrass him in the lobby."

"Then he shouldn't have taken you out. Period. Besides, you'd have been in public with him anyway at the Polaris."

Beth shook her head, as if to clear mental cobwebs. "Right. Who knows what he was thinking? I love my brother, but sometimes he befuddles me."

"What was he doing here? Apologizing again?"

"Yep. Showed up with a bottle of merlot and a hangdog expression." She gave a soft chuckle. "I can't stay angry with him when he pulls that."

For the second time that day, unease prickled down his back and he slowed his steps. Beth cocked her head to the side and smiled. "What's the matter? Somebody step on your grave?"

He tamped down the apprehension. Beth was here with him, a little tipsy, but they were both intact. A small miracle considering last night's attack. This was still a cause for celebration. Maybe he should wait until tomorrow to tell her of Dorsey's claims. After all, the ex-con could be lying. And she'd been so angry at him when the intruder had entered her house and he'd asked if the judge might have had some secret. He and Harlan would investigate his allegations about her father. If they were true, then Beth would be the first person he told.

Inside their room, he led her to the bed and propped her up with pillows. "I'll call room service and we'll have dinner by candlelight right here. No need to go out."

"Perfect," she agreed with a grin. "Just don't order celebratory champagne. I'm not up for it."

Neither was he, matter of fact. Thanks to Dorsey

Lambert. A small corner of his mind remained disquieted. The case still didn't feel over.

Not yet.

Chapter Fourteen

Beth glowed with contentment as she gazed around her Falling Rock home. In only two days, Cynthia had arrived and taken charge of the holiday decorations. A twelve-foot-high balsam fir in the den was lit with twinkling lights and the fireplace mantel decorated with fresh garland and cinnamon-scented pine cones. In every room, even the bathrooms, Cynthia had set out scented candles and holiday figurines. Beth had to hand it to her stepmother; she was a whiz at creating a warm, cozy atmosphere at Christmas, right down to the aroma of freshly baked gingerbread and cookies. Her nesting instincts at this time of year contrasted with her usual social activities of superficial cocktail parties.

The oven alarm dinged. “Pull out that pan for me, hon,” Cynthia called out, elbow-deep in a new batch of cookie dough.

Beth retrieved the lightly browned chocolate chip cookies and set them on the cooling rack. Much as she was enjoying the domestic bonding with Cynthia, a small part of her remained hurt that she’d cut out on Beth last week after the first sign of trouble. Of course, she hadn’t expected Cynthia to stay in the house, but it rankled that her stepmother hadn’t even offered to have her as a guest at her Atlanta home until the danger had passed.

At least she was thankful that the threat had been removed. Nothing suspicious had happened since Dorsey Lambert's arrest. Even though he'd been released yesterday, Beth hadn't received even a hang-up call or any hint she was being followed. The only matter casting a tinge of sadness today was the thought of returning to Boston next week. How much did Sammy care that she'd be leaving? They'd been almost inseparable the last few days. When he wasn't at work, he spent all his free time with her. The thought of their returning to their normal lives living hundreds of miles apart made her heart pinch.

As though she'd conjured Sammy from sheer willpower, his Jeep pulled into the circular driveway.

"You should fill a tin with cookies for him," Cynthia suggested. Beth shook her head in bemusement. Since arriving, Cynthia had been friendly with Sammy instead of acting formal and vaguely condescending. Beth wasn't naive enough to think she actually approved of her choice in boyfriends, but her stepmother probably figured there was no harm in their temporary relationship. Beth would be leaving soon enough.

She strode to the front door and flung it open, determined to enjoy whatever time was left with Sammy.

He didn't return her welcoming smile.

Now what? "Is it Lambert? Has he done something?" she asked, holding the door open.

He entered, glancing into the kitchen where Cynthia hummed along with a Christmas carol as she continued baking. "We need to talk. Somewhere private."

Must be serious. "Downstairs, then."

Only when they were seated in the recreation room

did he lean forward and speak. "When I interviewed Lambert earlier this week he claimed that he paid a middleman to have your father reduce his drug sentence."

"That's absurd," she scoffed, raising her voice. "What a piece of—"

"Don't shoot the messenger."

Beth gritted her teeth. "Go on. What else did he lie about?"

"As I was saying, Lambert claimed to have paid fifty thousand dollars for your father to lighten his sentence. He started harassing you in the hopes of getting his money back. He had two family members, he wouldn't name names, search your father's study that night, seeking proof of payment."

"What good would that do? Even if there was, it's not like he could enter a store and show a receipt to return merchandise and get his money returned."

"I'm sure he believed you'd do anything to protect your father's reputation, including paying him off."

"Blackmail," she said grimly. "Not that I would ever have agreed to such a thing."

"No doubt Lambert wouldn't be satisfied with merely getting his money back."

"He'd start asking for interest, then payment for the pain and suffering of being incarcerated. It would never end." She observed Sammy's set face more closely. "But Lambert's claim is nothing new. What else did he say?"

"That federal authorities were investigating your dad several months before he died."

Beth couldn't speak right away, and she bit the inside of her mouth to stop the involuntary tremble of her lips. "You wouldn't be telling me this if you didn't think it was true."

He nodded. "I checked it out. Your father was under

investigation after numerous allegations that he accepted bribes."

"Go on," she whispered at his pause, expecting the worst.

"There appeared to be some validity to the claims, but they dropped the investigation upon his death."

"I see." She pictured the last time she'd seen her father, in the hospital ICU unit after triple bypass surgery. Had the stress of an investigation contributed to his heart attack? Sammy took her hand and gave it a squeeze.

"But it's possible Dad was innocent," she insisted. "I mean, they didn't actually declare him guilty of any crime."

"Anything's possible."

Beth blinked back tears. Sammy was just being kind. More than likely, her dad had been involved in shady business. He drew a nice salary as a federal judge, but they'd enjoyed a very luxurious lifestyle—expensive schools, oversea travels, gorgeous homes. Perhaps, in hindsight, that had been a bit of a stretch based on his salary. But she'd always attributed the wealth to his smart investments and side businesses.

With a sinking heart, she remembered one odd fact that had struck her after Dad died and the will had been probated. He'd owned several companies, but four months prior to his death, he'd liquidated them all. At the time, she'd wondered if he'd done so because he had a premonition of his deteriorating health and wanted to simplify his financial affairs.

"Does Cynthia know about that investigation?" she asked.

"You know her better than I do. What do you think?"

Beth considered her own question. She hadn't been

living nearby to see them regularly while all this had been going on, but she didn't recall anything that would lead her to believe Cynthia was aware of possible impending doom. There had been no whispered conversations, or sudden talks of Dad retiring early. Nothing to indicate they were anything but settled and happy in their comfortable life.

"I don't think Cynthia knows anything," she said slowly.

"I don't know what?"

They both whipped their heads around. Cynthia stood halfway down the carpeted stairs, an oven mitt in one hand and a tray of cookies in the other.

Beth stood and ran a hand through her hair. "I didn't hear you coming."

"Obviously." Her stepmother gazed back and forth between them. "What's going on?"

Sammy shot her a sideways look that said, "This is up to you."

"Maybe I should tell her. I mean, if Lambert came after me for money, she might be in danger, too."

"Danger?" Cynthia slowly made her way down the steps and laid the cookies on a coffee table. "Tell me what's going on. I thought Lambert had been arrested."

"He's already been released. You better sit down for this." Beth gestured toward the couch and they sat, Sammy across from them. "You know Sammy interviewed Dorsey Lambert earlier this week and he claimed to have paid Dad for a lighter sentence."

Cynthia's lips pressed together for an instant. Her face reddened, and she removed the mitt from her hand, smacking it down on the sofa. "He's nothing but a liar. Surely you don't believe him, do you?"

Sammy cleared his throat. "Actually, there was an

ongoing federal investigation prior to your husband's death. Were you aware of that?"

Cynthia's mouth parted in astonishment. "Investigation? Are you sure?"

"Yes, ma'am. I personally spoke with the federal officer overseeing it."

"Why, I—I don't know what to say. Edward never said a word to me." Cynthia cast her a bewildered glance. "Beth?"

"He didn't say anything to me, either."

Cynthia leaped to her feet. "I refuse to believe any of this nonsense. Lambert and other convicts are just scumbags. The dregs of society. They'll say anything to cause trouble."

Sammy pulled out his cell phone. "Be that as it may, take a look at this latest mug shot of Dorsey Lambert. Wouldn't hurt for you to be aware of his appearance, so you can be on the lookout."

Cynthia gave it a quick glance, her lips curled in a sneer. "He looks thoroughly disreputable. I can't believe you'd entertain him, or others like him, for one minute. Do you really think my husband could have done such a despicable thing?

Sammy tucked the cell phone back in his pocket. "I don't know, ma'am. We might never know the full truth given his untimely death."

"I know the truth. You didn't know him like I did. Like *we* knew him. How dare you come in my home and besmirch Edward's name?"

"Sammy's only doing his job," Beth said, gently patting Cynthia's arm. "He's not accusing Dad. He came here to warn us."

"Fine. I've been warned." Cynthia stood and lifted

her chin at Sammy. "Now I want you to leave my house. And Christmas Eve dinner tomorrow night? Forget it."

Beth's face flamed with heat. It was one thing for her stepmother to assume that superior air with her, but she wouldn't tolerate it being aimed at someone she cared about. Sammy started to rise, apparently unruffled at Cynthia's outburst, but Beth gestured for him to stay seated.

"Actually, Cynthia, if you want to get technical about it, this is my house. Dad left this place to me and the Atlanta home to you. So Sammy is staying and he's having dinner with us tomorrow, too."

Cynthia's haughty mien crumbled in an instant. She opened her mouth to speak, and then clamped it shut. Tears pooled in her eyes.

Damn. She hadn't meant to hurt her feelings; she'd only wanted to stop her from trying to order Sammy around. Cynthia spun on her heel and headed to the stairs.

"Wait a minute, I'm sorry," Beth began. But Cynthia held up a palm, warding off her apology. She disappeared from sight, and seconds later the door slammed shut behind her.

Sammy gave a low whistle. "Didn't mean to cause trouble for you. Is it always this tense between the two of you?"

"Without Dad as a buffer—yes. It's not like we have a whole lot in common. Things are better when Aiden's around. He keeps the conversation going and smooths out any friction. Thank heavens he's coming in tomorrow and staying over the weekend."

"You know, you're always welcome to spend the holiday with my family," he offered. "It's a large, boisterous household when we all get together. There's my uncle and his bunch, and several cousins and their kids. Always plenty of commotion and conversation," Sammy said with a grin. "It may make you want to come running back here for a little peace and quiet."

No, what it sounded like was a loving family who enjoyed getting together. Would they really appreciate an outsider horning in on their celebration? "I'm already spending Christmas Day with you at your dad's. Don't want to overstay my welcome."

"You won't be." He hugged her and planted a quick kiss on her forehead. She rested the side of her face against the crisp cotton fabric of his uniform shirt, inhaling the clean linen smell mixed with a hint of a leathery aftershave. Her dismay at Cynthia's outburst seeped out of her body. She'd work things out with her stepmother. They always had before. She could suck it up a few more days until Cynthia returned to Atlanta and she to Boston.

Boston.

She pulled Sammy to her a little tighter, wanting to savor every possible moment they were together.

"You okay?" he asked in a husky voice that sent shivers—the good kind—down her back.

Beth pasted on a bright smile. "Fine. Guess you need to get back to work, huh?"

He held her shoulders, gazing deep into her eyes. "I have a few things to check on, but if you need me, I'm all yours."

"No, you should go. I'll talk to Cynthia now."

It took a few minutes to reassure him all was well, but at last she waved at him from the doorway as he drove off. Cynthia was nowhere in sight. Beth walked through the kitchen, noting that the oven had been turned off and all the baking supplies put away. Cynthia wasn't in the dining room or den, either. Had she been so upset that she'd packed up her things and left?

She opened the door and peeked into the garage. Cynthia's silver Town Car was still there. Perhaps she'd retired to her bedroom, unwilling to face her. She should apologize for sounding so harsh. Beneath her somewhat icy exterior, Cynthia was an emotional woman.

As she passed by the French doors in the den, a movement from outside froze her midstride. A camo-colored ATV motored by the edge of the woods. On her property.

Anger infused her body and without thinking, she hurried to the door and opened it. "Hey," she called out. "What are you doing?"

The driver braked and stared at her for an instant. He was tall and wore a large brown parka. A black ski cap covered his head, but strings of long red hair peeked out.

Not Dorsey, but he could definitely be a member of the Lambert clan. Her breath caught, and she hastily stepped back inside. In a burst of engine pedal-hitting-metal noise, the man drove the ATV into the woods and out of sight.

But not out of mind. Beth slammed the door shut and locked it, remembering how recently two men had broken into her home and destroyed the previous door. She placed a hand on her heart, feeling it pound inside her rib cage. Should she call Sammy? Grab Cynthia and insist they leave at once and spend the holidays in Atlanta?

In the end, she did neither. *Probably only a hunter scouting locations*, she told herself. *Or somebody just bored and out for a ride.* It wouldn't be the first time they'd seen people along the tree line of Blood Mountain. ATV riding was a popular activity in the area.

Beth rubbed her arms, relieved she wasn't alone in

the house. There was safety in numbers. Maybe she should give Aiden a call and see if he could come earlier than originally planned. It would soothe Cynthia and lighten the mood. Impulsively, she lifted the receiver of the landline to call him.

"I miss you so much, baby. I hate we're so far apart."

Oops. Cynthia was already on the line. She must have wanted Aiden to come home earlier, as well. Beth started to hang up the phone when an unfamiliar, deep voice spoke.

"Ditch the family. It's been a year. Bad enough we had to sneak around when your husband was alive. But now?"

Surprise rooted Beth to the spot, hand gripped on the phone that she held to an ear. Who the hell was this man? Cynthia was a cheater. Had Dad discovered this before he died?

"Just a little longer, sweetheart," her stepmother murmured. "If we're seen together too soon, people might start to wonder how long we've been a thing."

"I don't give a damn what people think and neither—"

"And from there, some might even speculate how convenient it was for us that Edward died while I was having an affair. After all, I did end up collecting some of his money in the will."

Beth held her breath and an ominous chill ghosted across her flesh. She could hardly reconcile the grief-stricken Cynthia at her father's funeral with this woman speaking so casually to her lover about the will. She hoped Dad had never suspected. That until the very end he'd been happily married and blissfully ignorant of his wife's deceit.

"You should have gotten *all* the money," the mystery man groused.

Cynthia laughed. A high-pitched artificial sound that grated on Beth's ears. "I couldn't agree more. But what's done is done. I had no idea I wouldn't collect everything. If I'd known seven months earlier that Edward would leave Beth most of his estate, then I would have done things differently."

Things? What things? What had her stepmother done?

"Did you hear something on the line?" Cynthia asked sharply.

Beth bit her lip and wildly glanced around the room. If she hung up now, they'd definitely hear a click as the call disconnected. She raised a shaky hand to her mouth to stifle any betraying gasp.

"Nope. You're paranoid," the man said, barking out a small chuckle. "Always worried others will discover your little secrets. Why the hell did you call me on the landline anyway?"

"I forgot to charge my cell phone battery last night. Anyway, I should get off the phone, just to be safe. I'll call you later tonight."

"Come home soon," he said.

The line went dead. Beth immediately placed the phone back on the receiver. *That's what you get when you eavesdrop on people*, she heard her father's reproving voice scold in her mind. *It will never be anything good.* But it wasn't like she'd meant to listen in on a private conversation. Not really. Not until the conversation had taken such a dark, twisty path. Then she'd been hooked and there was no going back.

The scent of chocolate and caramelized sugar suddenly turned cloyingly sweet. The air felt oppressively hot and humid from all the residual heat still radiating from the oven.

She had to get out of there. She couldn't face Cynthia. Not now. Not until she'd worked out everything she'd overheard. Beth scrambled through a kitchen drawer, searching for pen and paper. She'd leave Cynthia a note that she'd gone out for a bit.

A door screeched open upstairs. Cynthia was coming.

Floorboards creaked, and footsteps started down the hallway, then onto the stairs leading to the den. Strange to think of all the times she'd ever spent with Cynthia and now the idea of being alone with her filled her with disgust and anxiety. Beth desperately snatched her purse from the counter and stole a quick glance up.

Cynthia stood at the top of the stairs, looking cool and composed again, a slight smile curving her lips. As though she hadn't stormed out of the recreation room ten minutes ago. As though she hadn't been on the phone with the lover she'd been cheating with while married. As though she bore no ill feelings for her stepdaughter.

A lie. Everything about her was a lie.

Beth rushed to the foyer and pulled on a coat.

"Where are you going?" Cynthia asked.

"Out." Beth didn't dare glance her way, afraid her emotions would be written all over her face.

"Listen, don't go. I want to apologize for losing my temper. Of course, Sammy was only doing his job. He's always welcome here."

A jolt of irritation pricked through Beth's nervousness. How many times did she have to remind Cynthia this was *her* home, not her stepmother's. And it was *her* decision who came and went.

"Good to know," Beth commented wryly.

"You're still upset."

"Of course I am." Beth unlocked the dead bolt and buttoned her coat. "I need to run to the store. Be back later."

Cynthia reached her and ran a hand through Beth's errant locks. It took all of her willpower not to cringe from the woman's touch.

"Okay. I hope you realize I was only upset because of the slur to your father's name."

As if you care, Beth wanted to scream. Had Cynthia ever really loved her father? Or had it always been about the money from day one? Another one of those mysteries she'd probably never learn the answer to.

Without responding, Beth hurried out the door and into the cool, bracing air. After the stifling hot kitchen, the fresh winter breeze was as refreshing as a gulp of iced tea in the heat of a Georgia summer. She felt Cynthia's assessing eyes upon her as she opened the rental car door and slipped inside. Thank goodness Lilah had been so thoughtful to arrange a rental for her to use temporarily.

Her mind swirled, recalling every word of the overheard conversation.

Always worried others will discover your little secrets...

How convenient it was for us that Edward died while I was having an affair...

If I'd known seven months earlier that he'd leave Beth half of his estate, then I would have done things differently.

The more she ruminated, the more sinister the implications grew. Could Cynthia have played a part in her father's death? Perhaps his heart attack was brought on by the shock of discovering her affair. She had to concede that if that were the case, his heart probably wasn't in good condition to begin with.

How could Cynthia have betrayed him like this? Dad had rescued her from a minimum-wage job as a nurse's aide where she'd struggled to make ends meet for herself and her young son, Aiden. Dad had given her everything—a beautiful home, a first-class education for her son, a lifestyle that included travel and security—and all his love and loyalty.

The security guard at the gate waved at her as she passed through. Not that he'd done much good when her house had been broken into the first time. It was way too easy to access the Falling Rock houses via the woods at the back of the subdivision.

Beth shook her head as she left the gated community. What was she doing driving out of her own neighborhood? Instead of fleeing, she should have booted Cynthia out of the house. It had been such a shock to learn of her deceit that her first instinct had been to get away until she was more in control of her feelings. To hell with that. Next opportunity to turn around, she'd take it.

She started down the narrow mountain road and tapped the brakes as she came to the first bend. Nothing. She pressed her foot down until the pedal jammed against the floorboard. The car only gathered speed as it began its descent.

Panic bore down her, squeezing her chest with dread and fear. The car sped faster with every turn. To keep from going over the edge of the mountain, she had to drive in the middle of the road. If someone else came around a curve, they were both toast.

Be calm. Think.

She was already over halfway down. An S curve

loomed about fifty feet ahead—bad news—but the good news was that the side of the road broadened at the curve's end. If she could just manage this last curve, she could pull over onto flat land and hope that the car would eventually stop in the wide plain before she crashed into a tree.

If, if, if.

But there was no time to speculate on her chance of survival. She desperately jerked one way on the steering wheel, then the opposite, trying to keep the vehicle from either veering off the mountain or crashing against its rocky side.

This was it. The last bend in the curve. She only had seconds to exit off the road and into flat terrain. Beth yanked at the steering wheel and the car bounced as it traversed the bumpy field. But at least she was losing speed and not endangering anyone else's life. Too soon, the open field ended, and trees jutted the landscape. She was headed straight on to a collision with a copse of pine trees.

Should she open the door and try to roll away from the car's path? Or would she risk injury by staying in the car and jerking the wheel in time to either avoid the tree or have it only hit the rear?

Beth opted to remain in the car. She gripped the steering wheel and twisted it. Her muscles tensed, anticipating impact.

Bang!

Metal crashed against bark and the car fishtailed. She held on to the steering wheel, praying that the force of the collision didn't send her body flying through the front window. Her torso strained against the seat belt. An explosion of sound and force slammed into her consciousness, so powerful her teeth rattled.

The world went white. It was as though she'd been thrown into a blinding snowstorm, so thick that it smothered, choking out the rest of the universe. Only this snow scalded. She breathed in hot fumes of dust. Beth struggled to understand what was happening.

The ivory veil abruptly dropped. She blinked. Dazedly, she glanced down and noted a deflated bag and broken sunglasses on her lap. How did they get there? Pale yellow smoke curled up from the bag and a film of dust coated the dashboard.

The dashboard…she was seated in an unmoving car. How strange. She looked out the shattered window and took in the snowy field and green pines. Where was she? Beth pulled at the door handle, but it was jammed shut. She was trapped.

Yet the idea didn't fill her with alarm. The observation merely floated through her mind like a cloud on a windy day. Again, she glanced down and saw her purse on the passenger floorboard, its contents spilled. The black screen of the cell phone seemed to blink at her as it caught a gleam of sunlight.

She undid her seat belt and leaned over to collect it, wincing as her banged-up muscles protested the movement. The solid weight of it in her palm brought her slowly back into focus, grounding her to the present reality. She'd driven off the road and hit a tree.

The moment of blankness and scalding heat she'd felt was from where the deployed airbag had punched her upper torso. In the dashboard mirror she saw several abrasions to her face and chest.

But she was alive.

And then she remembered the suddenly defective brakes. The terrifying sensation of being at the mercy of four tons of metal careening down a mountain. Had it been a freak accident or had someone tampered with them? Someone who wanted her dead. Someone named Dorsey Lambert.

Fear sharpened her dull senses and she spun her head left to right, searching for anyone lying in wait. To her immense relief, she appeared to be utterly alone. Beth turned off the sputtering engine and punched in Sammy's number.

He answered almost immediately, and she filled him in on the situation.

"I'll be right there," he assured her. "I'll send an ambulance, too. Just to make sure you're really okay."

Beth huddled deeper into her coat, the outside chill beginning to seep inside the idle, smashed car.

"You need me to call James to come pick you up? Or I could give you a ride home."

She shook her head. "I can drive myself home. See you in the morning."

He watched as she slowly made her way to the lobby, wondering if the baby had decided to make an early appearance. Wouldn't surprise him if James called in the morning announcing the arrival of a baby. It was times like this that reminded Sammy just how alone in the world he'd become over the years. One by one, all of his closest friends had gotten married and most were now raising children.

Sammy mentally shrugged off the disquieting thought. He had plenty of time to muse on his life choices later. Right now, he needed to solve this puzzle of Aiden and his contact with Raden. Aiden was a criminal attorney now, so it was possible Raden was a client. Could there be more to it than just an attorney-client relationship, though?

Could Aiden be responsible for any of the attempts on Beth's life? The question went round and round in his mind. Sammy stood and paced the office, ruminating over dark, dangerous possibilities.

At least Beth was protected for the moment. It had taken lots of persuading, but she'd agreed to spend the night with Lilah. Harlan's place was as good as a safe house. By morning, Cynthia would be ousted from the Falling Rock home and kicked back to Atlanta.

With something of a shock, he realized night had crept up on him. Most of the downtown shops were closed and under the yellow streetlamp beams. The only people out and about were a few coming and going from the diner.

His computer dinged, signaling an incoming email.

He hurried back to his desk and saw he had missed several messages. He opened the first one and scanned the bank records he'd requested. Thankfully, he was able to access them because of the ongoing criminal probe of Raden. The numbers confirmed why Aiden had sought a loan from Beth. Both his personal and business accounts had bounced checks and had huge outstanding credit card balances from extravagant expenditures and high rent.

Next, Sammy turned to the message from his friend at the Elmore County Courthouse. After scrolling through pages of legalese he found the bottom line—Judge Wynngate had left seventy percent of his estate to Beth and thirty percent to his wife. It wasn't unusual to see children inherit the majority of an estate upon a person's second marriage, but Cynthia might not have viewed the terms in such a light. Perhaps she was determined to gain the rest of the inheritance she believed rightly belonged to her and not Beth? And if she was, she might have recruited her son in the effort.

He mopped his face with a hand and sighed. Beth's accidental discovery of Cynthia talking to her lover might have saved her life. His thoughts went deeper, darker. Did Cynthia have anything to do with her husband's unexpected heart attack? He made a note to check the hospital records in the morning before that office closed for the holiday and speak with the attending physician of record. Not much hope that would reveal anything, though. If there'd been any suspicion of foul play there would have been an autopsy and the sheriff's department would have been asked to investigate.

With no more avenues to explore, Sammy gazed out the window, absently tapping his pencil on the desktop. He briefly considered dropping by Harlan's place and asking Beth to spend the night with him instead. *No.* He was being selfish and paranoid. She'd looked so tired and haggard when he'd driven her there from the hospital after the wreck, Lilah's fierce nurturing mode had kicked in. She'd immediately embraced Beth and led her inside, fussing over her. Once Beth was seated, Lilah had immediately placed a pillow behind her back, pulled a blanket over her legs, and demanded Beth rest while she cooked a pot of chicken and dumplings.

For all he knew, Beth might have taken one of the prescribed pain pills and already be peacefully dozing.

No, tomorrow morning would be soon enough to see Beth and explore the possibility that the person, or persons, who wanted her dead might be the very ones closest to home.

Chapter Sixteen

After a nap and a home-cooked family meal, Beth at last felt better. Her automobile accident and the conversation she'd overheard earlier had unsettled her. Instead of being afraid, though, she was angry. Furious, actually. And she didn't want to wait until tomorrow morning to have a much-needed conversation with Cynthia. The sooner she got that woman out of her home, the better.

As she fumed over what to do, she reached out to her stepbrother, her hand clenched around her cell as she spoke.

"Did you know about this?" she asked, her voice filled with rage after she told Aiden of his mother's affair.

"Calm down, sis. I suspected something. I'm headed to the house, and maybe we should talk to her together. Find out what's really going on. We can present a united front," he suggested.

Relieved he was willing to help, Beth quickly agreed. She'd feel more in the holiday spirit if she settled this with her stepmother first.

Despite Lilah objection's, Beth drove her rental car back to Falling Rock and pulled into the drive. A quick glance into the garage window showed it was empty.

Had Cynthia left of her own accord, sensing that Beth was angry and onto her? So much the better.

Beth unlocked the door and entered her home, feeling a mixture of both relief and disappointment. She'd been all set to light into her stepmother and demand an explanation for her appalling behavior. But instead, she wandered aimlessly in the quiet house. The kitchen still smelled of fresh baked cookies and the Christmas tree twinkled in the gathering darkness. She marched upstairs and peeked in her stepmother's bedroom.

Cynthia had cleared out. The bed was made and the closets empty.

Beth strolled to the window and looked out over the yard. Snow blanketed the ground. The beauty of the scene made her fingers itch to capture the play of light and shadow in the twilight. Well, why not? It would give her something to do as well as quiet the unease that twisted her gut as she waited for Aiden to arrive. She'd already called him to tell him he needn't come because Cynthia was gone, but he said he was on his way and to just head to bed if she was tired. They still had things to discuss, he'd told her. Quickly, she gathered her painting materials and set to work.

Over two hours later, she'd finished the small painting and regarded it with satisfaction. Beth stood and stretched, contemplating taking another pain pill before bedtime. Ultimately, she decided plain aspirin would suffice. She'd go to bed early, as Aiden had suggested, and call Sammy first thing to tell him she'd had a change of heart and would love to spend Christmas Eve with him and his family. Mind made up, she donned pajamas and slipped into bed. It had probably been for the best she'd not had a confrontation with Cynthia this evening. Tomorrow, she'd be able to talk to her in a more civilized manner. For her father's sake, she'd be polite—but barely. As far as she was concerned, any relationship with her stepmother was officially over. And as for Aiden—the jury was still out. This past week had not brought out the best in her stepbrother. Maybe she'd always been too giving in their relationship, as well. Always the one to forgive and forget. She was glad he'd offered to confront Cynthia together, but she still wondered what his true motives were.

Beth punched at the pillow and rolled over, struggling to find a comfortable position and quiet her mind. Again she recalled the terror of hurtling down the mountain in a car without brakes and the phone conversation she'd overheard—the little innuendos that sent spider-crawls of suspicion skittering down her spine.

Headlight beams pierced the darkness of her bedroom and the sound of a car motor interrupted the night's silence. A spark of involuntary fear paralyzed her for a moment before she pulled back the bedspread and hurried to the window. Keeping cover behind the curtain, she watched from a small slit of windowpane as the familiar dark blue sedan stopped on the driveway. Aiden sprang from the vehicle, a bottle, presumably liquor, tucked between one arm and his waist.

Too bad it hadn't been Sammy. She wasn't sure she had the energy to deal with Aiden so late in the evening. Had her brother spoken with Cynthia already? Or had her stepmother given him some sob story—that Beth had possibly overheard a conversation and misunderstood everything?

Briefly, she considered ignoring his arrival. No, she couldn't be that rude. With a sigh, Beth turned on the lamp, grabbed her robe from the foot of the bed and donned slippers. Two piercing chimes buzzed through the house as she hurried down to the main level. Already, her back and shoulders ached and protested her sudden movement. The tumble down the mountain earlier had left her body feeling slightly battered.

She flung open the door as Aiden jabbed it yet a third time.

"I'm here," she said irritably. Cold wind slapped against her body and she hugged her waist, belting the robe tighter.

Aiden pretended not to notice her cranky mood. "Where's the party?" he said with a laugh, holding up a bottle of wine. "It's not even eleven yet."

"Guess you didn't hear about my car wreck." Beth stepped aside, allowing him entrance. She'd not told him about it.

Alarm slackened his jaw and his eyes quickly scanned her body. "Oh my God! Are you okay?"

"By some miracle, I'm only sore."

"You've got scratches on your forehead. What happened? How bad was the wreck?" Aiden hung his jacket on the coat rack and followed her into the den. "And where's Mom? She never came back?"

"She never did. I thought you might have tried to reach her to find out what her side of the story was."

"No. Thought we'd talk first. Damn, sounds like you've had a rough day all around. And I haven't helped things barging in here so late at night. Sorry, hon." Aiden gestured toward the sofa. "Sit down and put your feet up. I want to hear all about it. But first, I'll pour us a glass of bourbon."

She shook her head, then groaned at the jolt of pain in her right temple. "Better not. I took a pain pill earlier today."

"What does it matter? Just a few sips before heading to bed. It won't hurt anything."

"I'd rather not. Didn't work out for me so well last time I drank."

A dark shadow crossed his face. Did Aiden have a drinking problem? Did it make him feel better about his alcohol issue if he wasn't drinking alone? She started to give in, then stopped herself. No, it was high time she put her needs before what her family wanted and right now she didn't want a nightcap.

Aiden sighed. "Okay, okay, spoilsport. How about a cup of tea, then?"

"Great idea," she conceded. "I'll show you—"

"I know where everything is. You just relax. I'll take care of you."

That sounded wonderful. Beth sank against the couch cushions and smiled. "Not going to argue with you. I could use a little pampering after the day I've had."

"Poor kid. Be right back."

Beth glanced out the window as Aiden rumbled around in the kitchen. The night was so peaceful, so beautiful. She actually found herself looking forward to Christmas. Without Cynthia underfoot, it'd be less stressful. It would be fun meeting Sammy's family and then later she and Aiden could chill out here at home watching a couple movies and microwaving popcorn. It'd be like the old days.

Maybe Sammy wouldn't mind if Aiden had dinner with his family, as well. She'd ask him in the morning.

The kettle whistle blew and moments later Aiden appeared with a mug. "Two sugars and a splash of cream, right?"

"You got it."

He placed the mug in her hand and the heat warmed her chilled fingers. Steam spiraled upward, and she inhaled the slightly citrus aroma of the Earl Grey. It made her think of lemon orchards in the middle of winter.

"So where's your boyfriend tonight?" Aiden asked, kicking back in the recliner with a highball glass filled with bourbon and ice.

"Working late." Beth sipped her tea. *Hmm.* The taste was slightly off. Aiden must have accidently only used one packet of sugar instead of two.

"Problem?" he asked.

"Nothing," she hastened to reassure him, taking another swallow. He'd driven all the way from Atlanta and must be tired. She certainly wasn't some diva who insisted on perfection and expected others to wait on her hand and foot. "Want to have dinner tomorrow with Sammy's family? We can come back here afterward for movies and popcorn." Beth frowned. "But I guess Cynthia expects you to be with her tomorrow night?"

He lifted and dropped a shoulder. "We'll play it by ear. Right now, all I can think about is this evening. Tomorrow will take care of itself. We can work things out."

Typical Aiden. Always had been one to live in the moment. She'd wondered if law school and his new career would make him more cautious, less spontaneous. Apparently, it had not. He took a long swallow of bourbon and she studied his tight face. Despite his casual words and laissez-faire attitude, he didn't seem quite himself. Maybe he was as upset as she was about Cynthia's disloyalty. "Are you really happy in your job?"

"Couldn't be happier. Why?"

"I don't know," she said, cautiously picking her words. "You seem a bit wound up this visit. Under stress."

He snorted. "How would you even know what it feels like to be under stress? Teaching nine-year-olds how to finger-paint is hardly what anyone would call stressful. Besides, you're loaded. Born with a silver spoon, you lucky bitch."

Aiden said the words with a laugh, but they were too harsh for normal sibling teasing. Something more was at play here. She'd had no idea he resented her inheritance so much. After all, Aiden had been left a generous stipend in her father's will and she was Dad's only biological child. Not to mention some of the inherited money had come from her mother.

"Maybe you need to slow down with the drinking," she said. "Your jealousy is showing. Not a good look for you, brother. I think I'll go to bed after all. We'll talk in the morning about Cynthia. My mind's too much in a fog right now."

"No, no, you're right. I was out of line there. It's just that I've been under a lot of pressure at work trying to make a go of my new firm. Go on and finish your tea."

Beth started to rise and then shrugged. It was practically Christmas. She didn't want to argue. It wasn't like she was living with her brother, or even anywhere near him for that matter. Wasn't that what families did when thrown together for the holidays? Try to get along for the brief period of time they had with each other? She swallowed her annoyance and took a large gulp of the cooled tea. The sooner she finished, the sooner she could get to bed and end this conversation. And having Aiden in the house was comforting, what with all the break-ins and threats from Lambert and his family. In the morning, they'd decide what to do about Cynthia.

"More tea?" he asked when she set down her cup and started to rise.

"Any more caffeine and I might not sleep tonight." A rush of dizziness assaulted her as she stood, and Beth grasped the sofa arm and closed her eyes, willing the room to stop spinning.

"Feeling a bit woozy, little sister?" Aiden's voice was singsongy and chirpy. As though he found her unsteadiness amusing.

"A bit."

His hand grasped her forearm. "Good."

Good? What was that supposed to mean? Beth's eyes flew open and she stared at him.

The Aiden who stared back was a stranger. Dead eyes, a lifted chin and a curled upper lip made him appear cold and disdainful. As though…as though he hated her.

"I've got something I want you to sign." He dragged her toward the kitchen, fingers cruelly kneading into her flesh.

Beth fought down the sudden wave of fear. This was Aiden, her brother. He could be a giant jerk, but he meant her no harm. He couldn't realize how his own strength made his grip painful. On the kitchen island, a mound of paperwork lay on the counter, a pen splayed across the top sheet. They hadn't been there before.

"Let go of me. Can't this wait until morning?"

He roughly planted her at the edge of the counter. "Do it now."

She gaped at him, startled at the mean edge in his voice. "What's wrong with you?"

"Just do as you're told. It will go easier for you."

Beth glanced down at the top sheet of the paper. The text seemed to squiggle and squirm. "I—I can't read it. What do you want me to sign?"

"Doesn't matter. Now do it."

Beth picked up the pen with shaking fingers and licked her lips. *Concentrate.* Something was very, very wrong here. She hunched over the counter and squinted her eyes. Several words and phrases leaped into coherent form. It was a legal document of some sorts: *Being of sound mind and body, bequeath to Aiden Lyle Wyngate, my legal heir, seventy-five percent of all my assets, in the event of my death.*

My death.

The full import of the words fell on Beth like a knockout punch to the gut. At least it had the effect of snapping the mental lethargy that had clouded her mind. Aiden applied a deeper, bruising pressure on her forearm. "Sign it."

"Why are you doing this?" she asked, searching his dark eyes for a spark of human warmth. But his eyes were a vacuum, a black abyss of implacable hatred and determination.

He sneered. "Isn't it obvious?"

Her fingers grasped the pen and held on to it as though it were an anchor. Her mind skittered around the source of its greatest fear and then accepted the monstrosity.

Her brother wanted to murder her for money. He'd not rushed to her side to offer comfort and counsel about Cynthia. She'd be willing to bet that he'd invented some ruse to his mother to ensure that she didn't return here today. He'd been planning on showing up all along. To get rid of her.

She'd deal with the horror of that fact later. For now, she had to keep Aiden talking, to understand every nuance of his plan. "You drugged me," she accused. "What did you put in that tea?"

"A little something to make you drowsy." He grinned, as though mentally congratulating his own cleverness.

"But…why?"

"C'mon, Beth. You aren't the brightest bulb in the pack, but you aren't totally stupid. Do I have to spell it out for you? Fine, then."

He leaned forward, his face inches from her own. The scent of bourbon on his breath made her eyes water. "I want your money. I hate people like you. So entitled. Blissfully ignorant of what it's like in the real world."

"You—you hate me?" Memories rushed past her with cyclone speed—Aiden driving her to get ice cream in the summers before she had a driver's license, Aiden teasing her about past boyfriends, Aiden who always could lighten the tension in the house with his jokes and easy manner.

He released his grip on her arm and gave a slow clap. "Now you're catching on."

"What did I ever do to you?" Beth slowly sidled away from him, hoping his attention was focused on at last spewing all the poison he harbored deep in his soul. "Dad took you and your mom in when you had nothing. He paid for your college, law school and everything in between. Doesn't that mean anything to you?"

"He died and left me nothing."

"That's not true. He left you over ten thousand dollars."

His upper lip curled. "A paltry amount. That pittance ran out four months after he died."

Beth eased another two steps back from his hulking form and eyed the knife block four feet away on the kitchen counter. If she could only divert his attention for a couple seconds, she could make a run for it and grab a knife as she raced out of the room.

"Is Cynthia in on this, too?"

"Are you kidding? She's moving on to the next sugar daddy, as you know." A sly grin flickered across his face. "Actually, she got started on that even before your dad died."

"So I learned today. Cynthia's a lot of things, but at least she isn't a murderer. Like you."

"You're defending her?" Genuine puzzlement creased his forehead.

Beth grasped at the straw that had presented itself. "Yes. No matter what else Cynthia's guilty of, she loves you, Aiden. She's always been the one to rush to your defense in every situation. Even managed to convince my own father to let me be the sacrificial goat when the cops showed up and found pot and alcohol at the party. Remember? The night you cut out and left me to shoulder all the blame."

He smirked. "Couldn't have planned it any better. I called up all my friends and acquaintances and told them to get over here. The more grass, booze and other drugs they could bring, the better. Then, I called the cops myself to tip them off and gave them the address."

"You planned that all along?"

"Of course."

Another step back. She was so close to the knives. But she dared not make a sudden grab while his attention was all on her. "Like I was saying, Cynthia loves you. If you kill me, Sammy will catch you and make sure you're put in prison for the rest of your life. What would that do to your mother to have to come visit you at a penitentiary?"

"I prefer to think of it as eliminating an obstacle, not a murder. Don't worry about her. She won't live long enough to worry about it. I can't have Mom needling me for her cut of your inheritance."

"Wh-what are you saying?"

"Mom's next."

Her gasp filled the kitchen. If Aiden was capable of killing his own mother, he was truly mad. "Think, Aiden. Please. Think this through. You're not as smart as you believe. How's it going to look that I signed a will the day before my death? You'd be the person with the best motive to kill me. Sammy would target you in a heartbeat."

"The will's dated a year earlier, dumb ass."

"And it just happens to come to light now?"

"What better time than after someone dies? That's how wills work. Sign it and I'll safely tuck it away in a file cabinet."

There was no reasoning with a madman.

Aiden turned his back to her and toward the papers on the counter. Now was her chance—maybe her only chance. Beth leaped forward and lunged for the knife. Her right hand closed over the wooden base and she pulled one from the block. A subtle rush of air must have alerted Aiden and he wheeled around.

Beth brandished the large carving knife in front of her as she carefully backed toward the foyer. Aiden advanced, a coaxing smile on his lips.

"We both know you aren't going to use that," he said soothingly.

"Do you really want to try me?"

He frowned and shook his head. "I didn't put enough drugs in that tea."

"Mortal danger is a powerful counteractant to any sedative." Adrenal hormones were probably flooding her body. Beth kept the knife raised as she contemplated her next move. Even if she managed to reach the front door, Aiden would be on her before she could unlock it and run into the yard. Her best bet now would be to pivot, run upstairs, and then try to lock herself in one of the bedrooms. And after that? If only she could grab her cell phone to call the police—it sat, tantalizingly close, charging on the counter. But she'd have to figure out the next step once there was a locked door between her and Aiden.

The shrill ring of the landline phone buzzed through the tension between them.

Beth didn't wait to see if Aiden turned in the phone's direction. Damned if she'd just stand there and let him overtake her. Good chance he'd grab her arm before she could get a lethal cut in.

She ran. As fast and furious as she could pump her legs. She felt his breathing behind her as she climbed the stairs but couldn't risk a look around to gauge how close he was. She made it up the short flight of stairs and began running down the hardwood hallway. Aiden's footsteps pounded close behind. Oh, God, she was never going to make it. The first bedroom was on the right and she headed to it. Only three more steps…two…

Over two hundred pounds of solid flesh knocked into her back, and she hit the floor headfirst. The knife slipped out of her grasp and clattered across the floor. Beth extended an arm, desperately stretching to reach it, but Aiden easily scooped it up first. He rolled her over onto her back and pinned her down with a knee to her stomach. The metal tip of the knife pressed into her throat.

"Let's start over. Shall we? We're going to go downstairs, you're going to sign those papers, and then we're taking a little night ride. Got it?"

Beth blinked up at the brother she'd never truly known. He didn't even appear to be all that angry, merely annoyed that she was causing so much trouble with his plans. But the absence of rage only chillingly brought home how truly crazy he must be.

"Please, Aiden," she whispered, hoping to reach some small sane part of him that might be buried in his soul.

He drew back the knife and pulled Beth to her feet. "No more nonsense now," he chided. "Can't leave a mess behind."

That was the only reason Aiden hadn't killed her yet. He didn't want to leave behind any evidence of foul play, plus he wanted her authentic signature. Once he had that, he'd drive her to a remote area in the hills and…kill her and dispose of her body.

An inexplicable calm settled over Beth as she let him lead her back into the kitchen. It almost felt as though this whole ordeal was happening to someone else and she was observing from afar. Her survival instinct had kicked in, providing a chance to try and think through her predicament and seek possible opportunities for escape.

Let him believe she'd been frightened into meek compliance. He'd be all the more startled when she seized the perfect moment to try and escape again. Wasn't that what Sammy had taught her that day in the woods? In the kitchen, Aiden sat her roughly down in a chair by the table. Without a word, he shoved the papers in front of her and handed her a pen.

She began writing her name. Should she try to signal something here? If Aiden was successful, if he killed her, shouldn't she leave behind a breadcrumb trail that would lead Sammy to her killer? *Sammy.* The surreal calm crumbled. He would be devastated. He'd find some crazy reason to blame himself for not protecting her. And if he never caught the killer? He'd probably never forgive himself. She didn't want that. Not for anyone and especially not for him.

Slowly, she wrote her first name with, hopefully, enough of an exaggerated script that might raise eyebrows at close inspection—but not so exaggerated that Aiden would notice. Would it be enough? Beth began to write her middle name, deliberating leaving out a letter to further make it look suspicious. She stole a quick peek at Aiden, who was watching her and not the writing. A mad desire arose to scribble the word *help* somewhere on the page, but she didn't dare take the chance.

"Hurry up," he demanded.

She finished her name and set down the pen. He gave it a quick glance and nodded. "Very good. I'll put these up in a good place later."

Beth swallowed hard. *Keep him talking.* "When you visited me at the W Hotel—you were going to kill me that day, weren't you? I wasn't drunk. You'd spiked my drink then, too."

Aiden scowled. "I had you right where I wanted. Didn't have you sign the will, but I would have forged your signature after. Another ten seconds and you would have plunged headfirst down the hotel stairwell. Damn Sammy for showing up when he did. What a pain in the ass."

Beth shivered, realizing how close she'd come. What did he have in mind for tonight's killing? What would his new method for murder be? Her glance strayed to the knife he'd laid on the table. *Don't dwell on that now.* "Speaking of Sammy, you underestimate him if you think he won't figure out what you've done."

"Sammy Armstrong? The same genius who believes Dorsey Lambert is behind all your accidents?"

Her eyes widened. "You mean—"

"I'm the one who cut the brake line on your car. I'm also the one who threw that pipe bomb in the cabin. Did you really think I wouldn't hunt you down there? I used that old cabin so much for partying as a teenager that it's the first place I thought of for you to run and hide. " He slammed his hand down on the table. The loud *tha-wump* echoed through the kitchen. "I can't believe it didn't kill you both."

The confession confused her. "But Dorsey's cousins were there. They ran from us."

"Oh, the Lamberts have been stalking you all right. At first, I was annoyed. Then I realized I could use that fact to my advantage. Why would anyone suspect me of killing you when Dorsey had motive and opportunity? And *that*, my dear Beth, is what Sammy is going to believe. That Dorsey or one of his kinfolks is responsible for your disappearance.

"Disappearance?" A small hope bloomed inside her chest. Maybe Aiden planned on letting her live, perhaps allowing her to assume a new identity in another country.

"Disappearance or death." He shrugged. "Depends on whether or not they find your body."

With that chilling remark, Aiden stood and grabbed his coat off the back of a kitchen chair. "And now we go for a ride."

"Where are we going?"

"You'll find out soon enough."

No way in hell she'd cooperate without a fight, like a lamb led to the slaughter. Beth jumped to her feet, grabbed a vase on the table and swung it at Aiden. The fragile glass exploded on his right temple. Blood and glass shards splattered through the air. Aiden shook his head, momentarily stunned.

Again she ran. This time she made it to the backdoor and had even managed to release the dead bolt on the lock before a sudden, searing pain exploded on her scalp. Her body was jerked back into Aiden's chest and he twisted her hair locked in his grip.

"Nice try."

She tried to remember the move Sammy had taught her when grabbed from behind, but she couldn't manage anything with the violent pull at her scalp.

He dragged her across the den and then threw her onto the sofa. Beth kicked at him, even landing a few blows to his chest and gut before he wrestled her onto her stomach. His large hands tightly gripped hers, then she felt the rough hemp of rope cut into her wrists. In short order he bound her hands, and then her ankles.

Beth rolled over onto her back and stared up where he lurked above, breathing hard and gushing blood from the head wound. Aiden swiped at the crimson streaks and winced; evidently a few glass shards had embedded into his skin.

At least I made a mess, she thought. Hopefully, enough of one that it would make her disappearance look suspicious. Because right now, it appeared that Aiden had won. She was defenseless and entirely at his mercy.

Aiden tapped a finger against his lips, studying her.

"What?" she asked breathlessly. Maybe he was rethinking his plan. Was he going to kill her right here, right now? *No, no. I'm not ready to die.* Tears poured down her cheeks, hot and salty.

"I'm debating whether or not to duct-tape your

mouth shut." He shrugged and dropped his hands to his sides. "Guess there's no need to. No one will hear your screams where we're going."

"Where are you taking me?"

He wagged a finger at her, as though scolding a mischievous child. "You'll see soon enough."

"Please, Aiden…"

But he'd already turned his back, snatching an afghan from the recliner. He threw it over her, smothering her face. Beth rocked her head to and fro, frantic to fight against the sudden darkness and feeling of claustrophobia. Her warm breath was trapped underneath the knitted blanket. Was the end coming now? A death blow to her head? A gunshot wound to the heart? Strong arms gripped underneath her knees and shoulders and he carried her out the front door.

Maybe a neighbor will see him, she thought, grasping at the slight thread of hope. Unlikely given the time of night, but she prayed for it nonetheless. The door of his vehicle opened, and he flung her into the back seat as carelessly as though she were a sack of potatoes. A door slammed shut behind her. Moments later, the front door of the vehicle opened, and Aiden settled behind the wheel. Christmas music blared from the radio and he dialed down the volume, whistling along with the tune. The sedan pulled out of the circular drive.

Beth struggled and slowly managed to sit upright. The car screeched to an abrupt halt. Aiden threw back his head and laughed. "I'm an idiot," he said in apparent amusement. He threw open the driver's-side door and walked past her. The trunk clicked open from behind.

No, no, no.

Aiden flung open her door. In his hands he held a roll of duct tape and a knife. Her gut seized, and she began screaming. "Don't put me back there. Help! Somebody help me!"

Aiden peeled off a strip of tape and then sliced it with the knife. "Knew I should have done this to start with," he grumbled, leaning toward her with the improvised gag.

She rocked her head violently back and forth, but Aiden still managed to slap the tape across her mouth. *I can't breathe.* Her lungs burned. Would she die from asphyxiation before they made it to wherever he was taking her? She inhaled as much oxygen as she could through her nose, but it didn't feel like nearly enough.

"The front gate guard isn't there now, but they might have a camera recording my coming and goings," Aiden mused aloud, as calmly as though deliberating a move in a chess game.

Then he picked her up and carried her once again. She wiggled, trying to leverage her bound body to either butt him in the head or twist from his grasp, but Aiden was too strong, too determined, for her struggles to even slow down his inevitable next move.

Aiden stuffed her in the trunk and slammed the lid shut. Cold darkness enveloped her, and even though no one could possibly hear, Beth whimpered, her screams smothered and trapped under the tape. The closed confines felt like being entombed in a metal casket. *Stop. Get ahold of yourself. There must be something you can do.* She quit screaming but her loud, labored breathing roared between her ears—and still she couldn't seem to suck in enough air. Giving in to hysteria and hyperventilating would not help her live to see the morning.

Beth controlled her breathing to a slow, diaphragmatic pace. Her eyes adjusted to the darkness and in the taillights' pinprick glow she discovered a large metal toolbox in the right corner. She kicked it with her bound feet and it toppled over, its contents spilling out—rough lengths of cord, several knives, black gloves and rolls of duct tape.

Aiden had come prepared.

Beth held her breath, wondering if Aiden had heard the toolbox fall. But he drove on, still humming along with the loud radio music, as though he hadn't a care in the world. And why not? He thought he was smart enough to get away with murder.

But despite all his cool, deadly arrangements, Aiden hadn't factored in her desperate will to fight for her life, or her ability to devise a plan of her own. As far as he was concerned, she didn't have the brains or the brawn to fend off an attack.

She'd just have to prove him wrong.

With the toolbox knocked on its side, Beth discovered another tiny source of light that shone in the trunk's dark interior—a small handle with a dim glow. She stared at it, wondering what it opened.

Understanding thundered in her brain. A release handle! For at least the past decade, all vehicles made in the United States were required to provide an interior trunk release mechanism. She wanted to cry with relief.

Beth rolled over to it and tried to maneuver her body into a position where her bound hands could pull the handle. Her first priority was escape. She'd work on her bindings next. But no matter how she twisted, her hands couldn't quite grasp it. At last she gave up, panting through her nose, exhausted with the effort. Beads of sweat dribbled down her forehead, stinging her eyes, yet she couldn't swipe them away.

The sedan came to an unexpected halt and Beth stilled, dread churning in her stomach. Seconds later the vehicle rolled onward, and she realized Aiden had stopped at the stop sign at the bottom of Falling Rock. What kind of psychopathic killer obeyed traffic signs in the dead of night when no one was around?

She tried to keep her bearings and figure out where they were going. If—no, *when*—she got out of this damn trunk, she needed to know where she was. How awful it would be to have a chance of escape only to run around in circles and get caught by Aiden again.

If Aiden stayed straight on this road, they'd soon be in town. If so, it would be her best opportunity to kick the trunk lid and hope that the noise would attract attention. But who would hear her? No one would be on the streets at this hour. There had to be another way. She'd read newspaper stories of people escaping from trunks. What had they done?

An image flashed through her mind, a television reel of a kidnapped child who'd kicked the taillights out of his abductor's vehicle and then stuck his hand through the resulting hole, alerting other motorists that he was trapped inside. She'd do the same, but she'd have to wisely choose her timing. Aiden would surely hear the noise of the taillights shattering. The most opportune moment to make her move would be at the first traffic light in town. With luck, there would be a few late-night travelers for the holidays and someone would see her desperate signal for help.

But instead of going through town, Aiden took a sudden left. Her small ray of hope immediately extinguished. They were on County Road 18, heading away from Lavender Mountain's town area. What ungodly, remote place did Aiden have in mind for her murder?

Okay, scratch the whole kick-out-the-taillights plan. No way would there be a stray vehicle on this lonely mountain road. If she was going to get out of this alive, it was all on her.

Beth searched in the semidarkness until the palm of her right hand came into contact with sharp, cold metal. Now was the time to try to cut her hands free of their bindings. More likely she'd slice her wrists open in the awkward, blind attempt and then proceed to bleed out. But anything was preferable to whatever Aiden had in mind for her.

Cautiously, Beth gripped the knife's handle and began to saw at the rope binding. The top of the blade pricked into her wrist, but she gritted her teeth and re-adjusted her aim. It was painstaking work and she repeatedly stabbed at her own flesh in the process, but what choice did she have?

To help keep her mind off the pain and the imminent danger of her predicament, she continued to try and map their location. Did he have their burned-down cabin in mind? They were headed in that general direction, but going there didn't make sense. There was no reason to choose it as a murder scene. Perhaps Aiden would arbitrarily stop on this lonesome road whenever he decided the time was right.

The rope bindings began to ease under the wet slickness of her wrists. The sedan suddenly swerved, and she lost her balance. Searing pain sliced through her skin as she fell against the knife blade. Beth moaned and caught her breath, trying again to slip out of the restraints. Her time was short. Aiden had turned onto Witches' Hollow Road and that only led to one place.

She knew exactly where they were going. This was a dead-end lane that ended at an old abandoned gravel pit. Estimated at over sixty feet deep, this time of year the pit would be filled with icy water from melted snow.

Her brother's intention couldn't be any clearer. The only question now was whether he intended to kill her before throwing her into the icy pit.

Branches raked against the vehicle in an eerie grinding that set her teeth on edge. The road was narrowing, and the sedan jostled as it ran over potholes.

The binding at last gave loose and Beth freed her hands. Quickly, she ripped the duct tape from her mouth, barely registering the tear of flesh on her face. She gulped in a lungful of fresh air, grateful for the small mercy.

The sedan hit a deep pothole. Her entire body lifted and then dropped. At least this time her arms were free, and she could stabilize herself from rolling all over the trunk. The vehicle slowed as the terrain worsened. Aiden couldn't continue much farther down this path without a four-wheel-drive truck. She was almost out of time. Beth hurriedly cut off the rope binding her ankles. It was now or never.

She located the trunk release lever and popped it. A sweet click, and the top of the trunk flung open, blasting her with the night's frigid air. Beth grabbed one of the knives and lunged forward. The sedan came to an abrupt halt.

"What the hell?" Aiden thundered, opening up the driver's-side door.

Beth scrambled out of the truck and began to run. Her ankles and feet were numb from being bound, but she stumbled forward as fast as she could.

"Stop running," Aiden shouted.

Hell, no. Why should she make her murder more convenient for him?

A shot rang out, exploding into the night. She kept running, waiting for the shock of the bullet as it rammed into her, but nothing happened. She dared not glance behind to see what was happening. Aiden must have fired that warning shot straight up in the air. Beth cut away from the road, slipping into the cluster of trees and dense foliage. Aiden was hot on her tail as she rushed forward, branches and vines cutting into her face, hair and body. This must be what it was like to be a deer or rabbit fleeing from a hunter—only she was the one out of her element here in the bleak, alien woods. Her left foot caught under a root and she fell. Her ankle twisted and burned beneath her. The knife fell from her hands. Beth hunkered down, gathering her body into a tight ball under a knot of woody bramble that cut through her clothes and into her flesh. Her fingers searched for the knife, but all she felt was snow melting into her bare hands.

Dead leaves and twigs crunched all around where she lay on the wet ground. Closer and closer he came. Beth closed her eyes, awaiting the inevitable. All she had left was to try and land a good kick or punch once he discovered her hiding place.

And he would find her.

She knew the moment Aiden spotted her. All sound ceased. A whoosh of air and then a bruising grip ground into her right forearm. Aiden placed a knee against her back. She tasted snow and leaves.

"There you are. Did you really think you could get away from me? Damn, killing you is more trouble than I thought it would be."

"Aiden. Please. You don't want to do this."

"Got no choice now. We've come this far."

The distinctive sound of duct tape unraveling rent the air. Seconds later, her shredded and bleeding wrists were taped. Tears gathered in her eyes. She'd worked so hard to be free and now she was right back where she started.

"I won't tell anyone what happened tonight."

He snorted, not even bothering to point out how ridiculous she must sound. With a grunt, he yanked her to her feet.

"At least you wouldn't get the death penalty if you stop now," she persisted, hoping to reach him by some wild chance. Deep down, she believed some shred of humanity still existed beneath his charming, lighthearted manner. "Quit and maybe you'd end up with only a few years in prison for kidnapping."

Past his shoulder, a cut of light strobed through the trees. It lasted only seconds, then vanished. The dark seemed darker and more absolute from its absence. Had she lost it? Had desperation and fear conjured an illusion? Aiden whipped his head around and surveyed the woods, then shrugged. "Must have been lightning."

Lightning was an unusual phenomenon in winter, though. She didn't have time to dwell on it as Aiden began dragging her back toward the road.

"Don't give me any more trouble," he warned. "Accept your fate and you won't have to suffer. It will all be over quick. But if you do fight me, I'll knock you out cold. Your choice."

Some choice. Stay conscious and face Aiden while he killed her in order to have one last shot at begging for her life and praying for a miracle, or take being knocked out and spared the final horror. Beth decided to fight until the end.

"Someone saw us, Aiden. Those were headlights flashing through the woods. They'll report it. A car with a popped trunk on a dark road? They're probably calling it in right now. Let me go and you can get away."

Aiden ignored her. He crammed her into the front seat and then settled beside her. "I want you where I can see you. How the hell did you manage to get free?"

She didn't answer and rapidly scanned the center console and dashboard for either a cell phone or a makeshift weapon. Only a couple of empty beer cans lay scattered on the floorboard.

"I don't want a blood trail everywhere," Aiden continued. "I'm hoping they never find your body. That way, there's less risk anything will ever be traced back to me."

He cranked the car and the sedan lurched forward. They proceeded slowly, but with the deteriorated condition of the road the sedan scraped ground a couple of times. Beth's gaze switched from Aiden's profile to the wild landscape. In minutes, the car headlights shone on a faded metal sign that read Lavender Mountain Pit & Quarry. Just beyond the sign was a ramshackle wooden building that had once served as the company's modest headquarters. She'd visited the place many times over the years as a teenager. Local legend maintained that the structure was haunted, and it had become a Halloween attraction for older teens looking for spooky thrills. Beth never imagined the creepy place would be the sight of her own violent death.

The car shuddered to a stop and she cast him a quick glance. *Wait until he pulls you from the car, then make your move.* That would be her best shot at making contact.

Unexpectedly, Aiden reached across her and pushed the passenger door open. "Get out," he ordered. She froze, unsure if now was her moment to strike.

"I said get out." Aiden gave her a violent push and

she tumbled out. Aiden immediately followed suit. "Turn around," he commanded.

Slowly, she obeyed. He stood before her, illuminated in the car's elliptical beams. He had a gun raised and aimed directly at her. Beth's heart beat painfully in her chest. With his head, Aiden motioned her forward. Behind him, the black abyss of the pit awaited.

But they weren't alone. Someone was watching. She heard a twig break, as if snapped by a foot. She felt them staring, watching in the darkness like a wild beast. Beth crept forward at a snail's pace. Past Aiden's shoulder, a figure emerged out of the woods. Moonlight glowed on his ginger hair. Recognition slammed into her.

What the hell was Dorsey Lambert doing out here? Were he and Aiden working together?

Aiden studied her startled face and then whipped his head around. But Lambert had already disappeared into the shadows.

He chuckled. "You really think that old trick's going to work on me?"

Chapter Seventeen

The phone rang, jostling Sammy from an uneasy sleep. The alarm clock by his bed blinked neon-green numbers—2:46 a.m. Nothing good ever happened at this time of day. Could it be Beth? He picked up his cell phone from the nightstand and frowned at the unfamiliar number. Not Beth then. His racing heart quieted several beats. But an Atlanta area code was on display. Perhaps there was some news about Dorsey Lambert. Quickly, he swiped the screen and spoke. "Officer Armstrong."

"Sammy?" A woman's hesitant voice sounded. "I'm so sorry to bother you at this horrible hour but I'm afraid."

"Who is this?"

"Cynthia Wynngate, Beth's stepmother."

Sammy stood, pulling on his uniform pants he'd flung at the foot of the bed only a couple of hours ago. "What's wrong? Is Beth hurt?"

"I—I'm not sure."

"Explain yourself."

"We, um, had a bit of a falling-out earlier today. I don't know if she told you?"

"She did," he growled impatiently. "Go on."

"So I asked Aiden to go over and try and help smooth things over between us like he always does."

His heart slammed in his ribs before he remembered Beth was spending the night at Lilah's. Sammy pulled on socks and slipped into his uniform shoes. "Your point?"

"I—I think Aiden might be planning to hurt Beth."

Sammy stilled, hands frozen over the shoelaces he'd been tying. All his niggling doubts and suspicions about his old friend rushed up and merged into a knot of dread. "What makes you say that?" he asked past the lump in his throat.

"It wasn't so much what he said, it's how he said it. His practice hasn't been going so well and when I called him this afternoon, I asked how his firm was doing. He admitted it was in dire straits but that he had a plan to fix everything." Cynthia paused. "He sounded strange… I—I can't explain it exactly. I pressed him what that meant, and Aiden claimed he'd be coming into a large sum of money in the next few weeks. I asked if a big lawsuit settlement was due and he laughed, saying he had a major score to settle with someone."

Sammy cradled the cell phone between his shoulder and right ear as he slipped into his uniform shirt. He wished Cynthia would hurry with her story, but suspected that the more he interrupted and pressed her, the longer it would take.

"Anyway, I asked when he'd leave to see Beth today and he said he had a few supplies to pick up first before leaving the city. Then—and this is what makes me nervous—Aiden said tonight was the night his plan would be set in motion and that people like Beth, born with silver spoons in their mouths, didn't deserve to have such easy lives when people like him had to struggle."

Sammy scowled. What a strange woman Cynthia was to report her son to an officer of the law on the basis of so little. "And from that conversation you suspect your own son…of what, exactly?"

Her voice chilled a notch. "I'm just saying maybe someone should check on Beth. I awoke from a disturbing dream over an hour ago and I've tried to call both of them but get no answer. I even tried the landline at Falling Rock."

Why hadn't Beth answered her phone? Probably only because she saw Cynthia's name on the screen and didn't want to talk to her, he suspected.

"I'll check it out," he told Cynthia, abruptly ending their call. Immediately, he punched Beth's number on speed dial. It rang four times and went to voice mail. "Call me," he said roughly, not expecting to really hear from her. Beth was either asleep or had her phone ringer turned off. To be safe, Sammy called Harlan to make sure all was well.

"Sampson here," Harlan grumbled into the phone. "Sammy?"

"I'm calling to make sure Beth's safe and sound. I got a call from her stepmother warning she might be in danger from her stepbrother."

Harlan muttered an expletive. "She's not here. She left hours ago, insisting that she wanted to stay in her own home. Sorry, I should have called you. Do we need to—"

Alarm coursed through him. "I'm going over now to check it out. I'll call you later."

Sammy buckled his belt and headed to the den where he grabbed the Jeep keys off the fireplace mantel. Recrimination rose and battered his conscience. He should have asked Beth if he could spend the night with her. He couldn't rest now until he'd either seen Beth or heard her voice.

Chills skittered down the back of his neck as he raced out the door and into his Jeep. Sammy zipped down his neighborhood street and then sped through town. At the entrance of the Falling Rock subdivision, the unattended gate opened automatically, and he shook his head as he drove through. Months ago, their homeowners' association had cut back on manning it with a security guard on duty at nights, citing the difficulty of finding and funding personnel. In his opinion, the gatehouse was now merely a pretentious show of wealth and security that held no real teeth.

Most of the homes were tastefully lit with a Christmas tree placed in an open window and outside strings of white or pale lights draped across porch and roof lines. A few homes had mangers or decorated yard trees that glowed from a single white spotlight. Driving through the elegant neighborhood felt like slipping into a fairyland. Could anything really bad happen here?

Oh, hell yes. Sammy recalled the human trafficking ring they'd uncovered a year ago. A wealthy Atlanta couple had used one of these mansions as a holding pen for kidnapped young women. While there, the victims were physically and emotionally broken down and eventually sold as sex slaves. His partner, Charlotte, had been the one to crack that case.

He turned the corner to Beth's street and gave a brief, involuntary smile at the corner house, which sported over a dozen inflatable holiday cartoon characters, including a twenty-foot-tall Grinch. The home was lit with a mismatch of bright colors on every available surface. Some might unkindly call it "tacky," but he secretly loved it.

Sammy's amusement was short-lived as he pulled into Beth's driveway. His knot of anxiety wouldn't unravel until he saw she was unharmed. Leaving his truck running, he ran to the front porch and stopped, his heart sinking.

The front door wasn't completely shut; it gaped open an ominous inch. Sammy withdrew the revolver on his belt clip and stepped to the side of the door before pushing it open all the way with his foot.

There was no sound or movement from beyond. Slowly, he eased into Beth's home, gun drawn. He stole past the unlit dining room, down a hallway and into the den where a lamp burned near the sofa. At first glance, all appeared in order. Sammy peered closer at the sofa where Beth might have recently sat. Semidry droplets of a dark liquid spotted the floor and couch cushions. Had Beth had an accident of some sort? Or had something worse befallen her? His own blood ran cold at the thought.

Sammy raced upstairs to check out the bedrooms. All were empty and there were no signs of a struggle. Beth's bed was unmade, as though she'd been in it for a time before being awakened. Where had she gone in the middle of the night? He hurried back downstairs and opened the garage door. Her rental car was parked inside. Sammy strode over to it and placed his hand on the hood. It was cold and unused. He opened the door and took a look. Nothing unusual there.

Sammy returned inside, his concern mounting. He called Beth's phone number again and heard it ring nearby. He found it plugged into a charger on the kitchen counter, next to her purse. His shoes squeaked, grinding against some small object. His eyes followed the trail to several large fragments of broken glass. Behind the kitchen island were larger pieces of broken glass, perhaps a vase.

He called her name, then Aiden's. Nothing. Just the sound of his own voice in the empty home.

Beth had not left her home willingly. Not without her purse and phone. He called Charlotte on speed dial. She answered almost at once, although her voice was drowsy with sleep. Sammy found himself suddenly unable to speak past the massive pressure weighing on his chest.

"Sammy? What's up?" Charlotte's voice sharpened. "What's wrong?"

"It's Beth," he said roughly. "She's missing. Foul play suspected."

A muttered curse and then "Where are you? I'm coming over."

He gave her the address. "Call Harlan, too," he added. "We need a manhunt with all available officers."

"Should I put out an APB on Dorsey Lambert?"

"Yes. And also on Aiden Wynngate."

"The man in the videotape. Beth's stepbrother, right?" Charlotte asked.

"Right. I'll explain everything later."

He hung up the phone and swiped a hand through his hair. Who had taken Beth—Lambert or her stepbrother? Were they working in tandem? It would make sense. Aiden's firm represented persons charged with a crime. As the tape had shown, Aiden had plenty of opportunity to make connections with the criminal underworld.

Think. Where would Aiden or Lambert have taken Beth? Trouble was, there were dozens of remote roads in these mountains. All suitable for murder and burying the victim in a shallow grave that might or might not be discovered by hunters one day. His heart pinched, imagining Beth at this moment, scared out of her mind, believing she was about to die.

Or she might already be dead.

Sammy drew a long breath and shook his head. He couldn't go there, couldn't entertain the thought of Beth not being in this world. They'd find her. There had to be a clue here somewhere. He scanned the kitchen and his eyes rested on a stack of papers on the table. That was as good a place as any to start his search. He glanced at the typewritten words and blinked.

Last will and testament of Elizabeth Jane Wynngate.

Frost flowed through his veins and his heart froze. Abruptly, he rifled through the papers and found what he was looking for. Aiden Wynngate was listed as the primary beneficiary, with his mother, Cynthia, also inheriting a significant percentage. If Aiden had an accomplice, it was Cynthia, not Dorsey Lambert. But why would Cynthia have called him if she was in on it? Maybe she wanted to make sure the finger pointed at her son and not at her?

Unless this was an elaborate red herring planted by Lambert. Sammy immediately struck that idea as not being credible. Everything pointed to Aiden. His strange behavior, association with criminals and one terrific financial need. Greed was always a slam-bang murder motive.

Where would Aiden take her? He knew all these backroads. Even with a full-blown manhunt it would take hours to check every narrow dirt road that crisscrossed the mountains. His cell phone rang, interrupting his racing thoughts. He glanced down at the screen before answering. It was Charlotte.

"We've got a tip," she said without preamble. "An anonymous caller at the station claimed a woman had been abducted and taken to the old Lavender Mountain quarry."

The old abandoned pit. Of course. He should have thought of that straightaway. "On my way," he said tersely, tucking his phone in his back pocket, then fishing the Jeep keys from his pocket as he ran to the door.

He could be there in ten minutes, twice as fast as any officer in town. But would that be quick enough? It had to be.

Sammy sped out of Falling Rock and raced on the snowy rocks with reckless abandon. *I'm coming, Beth. Hold on, sweetheart.*

He hadn't been to the quarry in years and he almost missed the turnoff. Sammy slammed on his brakes and took the turn like a NASCAR driver on the final lap of a race. The Jeep swerved to the far left, almost plunging into a ditch before he jerked the steering wheel to the right and returned to the road's center. Headlights illuminated recent tire tracks in the snow.

Almost there, Beth.

The truck bounced and rattled on the rough road. All at once, he came upon an unmoving sedan and had to slam his brakes to keep from plowing into its rear fender. Sammy swerved to avoid the collision and the car beams spotlighted two persons standing near the edge of the deep pit—Aiden, eyes wide with shock and bleeding from a cut at his temple, and Beth, looking equally as shocked, her brown hair whipping in the wind.

Sammy retrieved his gun and flung open his truck door, using it as a shield. From the side of the door, he pointed his gun at Aiden. "Hands up, Wynngate."

Aiden pulled a gun from his jacket and fired a round.

Pain exploded in Sammy's left shin and his leg gave out beneath him.

"Run, Beth!" he screamed, rolling under the Jeep bed for protection. But he wasn't fast enough. Another bullet slammed into the front of his left shoulder, dangerously close to his heart. He lay on the ground, exposed and vulnerable. The next shot would take him out for good. Had Beth run? Was she safe? A black film seemed to form over his vision, and the world grew fuzzy and unfocused.

A shrill scream pierced through the ringing in his ears. *Beth.* He opened his mouth to urge her again to run, but the words would not come. He struggled to his feet. If it was the last thing he did, he had to shoot his old friend. Had to protect Beth at any cost. Her life was all that mattered. Tamping down the pain, he picked up his gun in his right hand and focused.

Aiden had walked closer to him and only stood a few feet from where he lay, gun raised for the lethal shot. Beth lunged at Aiden's back and he fell. A shot exploded, and Sammy felt a bullet whizzing by his ear, narrowly missing his face. Beth was still in danger. Why wouldn't she run while she had the chance? Aiden's gun lay on the snow-covered ground between them. Sammy began crawling toward it. Aiden also crept forward to retrieve his weapon. Beth lay sprawled on the ground, stunned from the impact of hurling her body at Aiden.

He was going to die. They both were.

From his right, a figure sprang from the dilapidated quarry headquarters. Was he hallucinating? Just as Aiden's fingers grasped the weapon's handle, the man kicked the gun away. Beth scrambled to pick it up.

"Sammy! How bad are you hurt?" she cried.

Dorsey Lambert's eyes locked with his. What the hell was the man doing here? Were the two in league after all? No, that made no sense. Lambert had saved his life.

In the confusion, Aiden jumped to his feet and began running. Dorsey took off his jacket and pressed it against Sammy's wound. The pain was excruciating but necessary. He could feel the warm blood soaking his shirt and jacket.

"Backup on the way?" Dorsey asked. "I called the cops earlier."

"Yes."

Beth dropped to her knees beside him. "Sammy!"

"He's going to be okay," Dorsey said. "That bastard was trying to frame me for murder. I knew I had to keep an eye on him."

Sammy hoped Lambert was right in his pronouncement that this shot wasn't fatal. Even now, sirens wailed in the distance. But his head swam, and strength oozed from his body with every drop of blood lost. And still Beth wasn't out of danger. "Aiden might return," he warned them. "We..." His words began to slur. "Not safe yet. Still in danger."

Chapter Eighteen

Still in danger.

Beth cast a quick glance over her shoulder in time to see Aiden hightailing it to the woods. She knew what she had to do. She'd already witnessed her stepbrother's persistence. He'd come back to finish them off if he had the chance.

"I'll stay with him until the ambulance arrives," Dorsey said with a nod at Sammy. "You go on. Know how to use that gun?"

"Yes." But she hesitated, staring down at Dorsey's hands pressed over Sammy's wound. Blood had soaked through Sammy's jacket and covered Lambert's fingers. Sammy's eyes were closed shut and his face was pale as the snow. Fear clinched her gut. She didn't want to lose him. Not when her heart had begun to love.

"Go!" Lambert shouted, thrusting a flashlight into her free hand. "There's nothing you can do here."

Beth rose to her feet and ran, gripping the gun's handle in her right hand. She knew how to use it but hoped she didn't have to. All she needed was to keep Aiden in sight and make him quit running. The cops could arrest him then and take care of the rest.

She shone the flashlight on Aiden's footprints in the snow. He couldn't escape. Not after all the hell he'd put her and Sammy through. She'd brought this trouble into Sammy's life. Aiden was *her* stepbrother and he'd been after *her* money. Only fair that she be the one to bring him down in the end.

She entered the woods, and the thick tree canopies blocked most of the full moon's light. If Dorsey hadn't had the good sense to bring a flashlight, she wouldn't have had a chance at tracking Aiden. Surprisingly, a narrow trail ran through the terrain. Probably forged by deer hunters, she surmised. Aiden had somehow found the trail. Had he scouted this area ahead of her abduction? Had he devised contingencies in the event he was forced to flee? What if he'd deliberately drawn her into the cover of the woods?

Beth flicked off the flashlight. What she'd imagined an advantage might prove her undoing, since the elliptical beam spotlighted her every move. Her heartbeat went into overdrive and she felt the roaring of blood in her temples. Despite the cold, a sweat broke out all over her body. She strained her ears, listening for the slightest whisper of Aiden's breathing, of an unexplained twig snapping.

But there was only the persistent, haunting howl of the wind rattling through the treetops. An owl hooted, and she bit back a scream. Seemed she'd gone from hunter to hunted. *I'm the one armed with a gun. Aiden's the one who should be frightened, not me.* Yet her mind didn't buy the argument. He was close, she could feel it. She had to know where he was. Waiting in the darkness for him to pounce was the worst torture. Beth snapped on the flashlight and circled around.

No Aiden in sight.

Her legs went weak with relief and she leaned against the rough bark of a pine tree. Chasing Aiden was a fool's errand. She'd go back to Sammy and wait for the cops to mount a search. They were the experts. She straightened and turned for retreat.

Straight ahead, the flashlight illuminated a large obstacle that hadn't been there seconds before. *Aiden.* The light trembled in her hands and she almost dropped it. He'd been so quiet in his approach. So lethal.

He grinned. "Hello, Beth."

How could he be so calm—so confident? He'd greeted her as though he'd just stepped into her home for a chat, as though they weren't standing in the woods after he'd attempted to kill both her and Sammy. The grip on the gun at her side tightened. Did he have a weapon, as well? One he'd hidden here earlier?

He stepped forward and she took a step back, raising the gun. "Stay where you are."

A smile ghosted across his lips. "You wouldn't hurt me."

"Don't be so sure."

He didn't take another step, but he didn't retreat, either. "Why, Aiden?" she said gruffly, past the lump in her throat. "Have you hated me all these years?"

"Not always. At first, you were merely an inconvenience. But once your father died, you were in my way."

His words were more chilling than the December night. *In the way. An inconvenience.* How could she never have seen past his easygoing facade? She wanted to believe there was some good left in him. A modicum of decency.

Aiden stretched out a hand. "Give me back my gun."

She shook her head, trying to wake up from the surrealistic nightmare of the last hour. "Why should I? So you can shoot me?"

"I won't hurt you. I just want to escape. I can't go to prison. It would kill me."

The sirens sounded louder, and he uneasily glanced behind his shoulder. But would they get here in time? She had to keep Aiden focused on her, not the approaching cops.

"Did Cynthia murder my dad?" she asked, hoping the question disarmed him and returned his focus to her.

He faced her again and chuckled. "Good ole Mom. She's inventive, you've got to give her that. Put her LPN training to good use."

"What did she do to Dad?" Beth fought back her tears, her horror. "How did she kill him?"

"*Kill*'s a strong word. Come on. Your dad was old and had a weak heart. He'd have died soon anyway. Mom only helped him along a little."

"How did she do it?" she insisted, her voice tight and hard. "I never heard even a whisper of suspicion on the cause of death."

"After his heart attack, Mom finished him off with an air embolism. Killed by thin air." Again he chuckled. "All it takes is a well-administered syringe of oxygen." He held up a hand and pointed his thumb and index finger like a pistol. "Poke that tiny needle in an inconspicuous place and voilà—an easy solution." He jabbed his index finger above his kneecap and made a tiny, swishing sound. *Whoosh.* "Like I said, she picked up a thing or two at her old job."

The callous description of her father's murder almost shattered the little bit of her composure that remained. Her knees jellied, and the gun wobbled in her hand. Beth struggled to understand why this had happened to her family. "But why? He loved you. Both of you. He took you in and shared everything he had."

Aiden shrugged. "Stop making him out to be a damn saint. He was a dirty judge, remember? You always were in your own little world, painting and drawing. But to answer your question, he got suspicious of Mom having a boyfriend. She denied it, of course, but Mom was afraid that since he was onto her, he'd hire a private detective and find the truth."

Aiden took a step forward, but this time Beth didn't step away. Anger steadied her hand and gave her strength. The sirens kicked up a notch, their ghastly wail drawing closer. The longer honk of a fire engine blasted, as well as the high-low pitch of an ambulance alarm. *Please let them get here in time for Sammy.* He'd have been so much better off if he'd never gotten involved with her. But on the heels of that disturbing realization, Beth realized she could never regret a moment of their time together. The memory of every second—every kiss and every touch—seemed incredibly precious.

"One last question."

He quirked a brow and stilled.

"Does Cynthia know about…about your plans tonight? Are you two working together?"

Aiden flashed a grin, his teeth gleaming as white as the snow in the darkness. "Are you kidding me? Her methods are more subtle. More untraceable. Mom doesn't have the stomach for the nitty-gritty work."

If she couldn't appeal to Aiden's humanity, perhaps she could reason with his avarice. "You know she gets a large hunk of my money when I die, right? You don't get it all."

"Do you think I'm stupid?" His mouth tightened, and his chin lifted an inch. "I'm an attorney, for Christ's sake. I can read a damn legal document. I know exactly how much she'd receive. But she won't live to enjoy it."

Matricide. Cynthia was a lot of things, but she adored her son. Aiden was her golden child that she protected and defended. Maybe that was the problem. She'd raised him to believe that he deserved anything he wanted and to claim it at any cost.

Aiden was upon her, his breath smelling of bourbon. "Give me the gun. Now. You'll never see me again."

"I don't believe you."

"It's true. I've got a car and a driver waiting for me down the road." He pulled a small leather binder from the inside pocket of his jacket. "Got a passport and a plane ticket, too."

"Where do you think you can run?"

"Like I'd tell you?" He shook his head. "All I'll say is it's warm and their cops turn a blind eye to extradition requests. But I need my gun. I can't outrun the cops without a weapon. There's going to be a standoff."

Alarm chimed through Beth. He'd need more than a weapon. He'd need a human shield. He'd need…*her.*

The woods were suddenly alive with blue and red cop lights strobing through the icy trees and dense underbrush, sirens shrieking in the frigid air—the moment of reckoning was upon them. Aiden's arm began to rise, and she made a move of her own. Her left arm hoisted the heavy steel flashlight in an arc, catching the right side of his face in a crushing thump of bone.

Aiden screamed and staggered backward, holding his head in his hands.

Beth dodged around him, navigating clumsily through the copse of trees. *Head back to the main road.* She didn't need the flashlight now; the glare from first responder vehicles cast a spotlight on the clearing ahead. Aiden clomped behind her, as fast and furious as a bull and gaining on her with every second. Her wet slippers were useless for gaining traction.

She reached the clearing. Several police cars snaked across the narrow road and a couple of them left the road and bumped across the field. Their headlights stung her eyes and she blinked, trying to orient herself in the temporary blindness.

Oomph. A solid mass of weight slammed into her back. An arm encircled her throat, pushing her neck back in a choking hold. She could hardly breathe.

Aiden had gotten just what he wanted. He'd take her down with him if needed. What else did he have to lose?

"Give me the gun," he growled in her ear.

The gun. Thank heavens she hadn't dropped it. He might be faster and stronger, but she wasn't defenseless. Cold metal practically burned into her numbed hand and fingers. Could she do it? Really shoot somebody? Hell, yes. He'd left her no choice. As best she could in the awkward hold, Beth aimed the gun backward and pulled the trigger.

The explosion rang in her ears. The hold loosened, and Aiden screamed in agony. She gulped in a lungful of fresh air. Cops seemed to shout at her from every direction, but she was too wired to make out the words, only the frantic urgency of their voices. *Run.* Aiden wasn't through with her yet. Just as her legs obeyed her brain's command, Aiden lunged at her, knocking her to the ground.

The gun fell out of her hand and she grabbed it. Aiden loomed above her, his dark eyes aglow with desperation and madness and anger mixed with fear. He raised an arm, his hand gripped in a fist. She tried to wiggle out of his grasp but his knee lodged firmly in her gut and his left arm anchored her upper torso. The snow was wet and freezing, seeping through her bathrobe and pajamas. In two seconds Aiden would deliver a knockout punch, take her weapon and make his wild dash to freedom while dragging her along as a hostage. He'd kill her at the first opportunity when she was no longer useful to him.

Beth lifted the gun, not sure if she'd even get off a shot before Aiden's fist shattered her face. With numbed, stiff fingers, she pulled the trigger and fired. The reverberation of the gun tingled in her palm and the blast deafened all sound. All sensation seemed frozen in the frigid night. A chiaroscuro of black, white and grays punctuated with slashes of red.

There was Aiden's widened eyes and slackened jaw;

…the crimson patch blooming on his chest;

…the black nighttide lit by red sirens;

…the white snow falling swiftly and silently—a silent witness to murder.

Oh, God. She'd killed him.

Aiden's body toppled backward several inches and then fell forward. She watched his descent in horror. There wasn't time to move away. Dead weight crushed her chest. Beth screamed until her throat burned raw. Pandemonium erupted as cops and rescue workers arrived, their voices calling out sharp commands and urgent warnings. A volley of camera flashes strobed the area from officers recording the crime scene.

It was all a jumbled mess echoing round and round in her brain. Strong arms rolled Aiden's heavy, slack body away. "Is he…?"

She couldn't form the word, but the man nodded. He had a kind, grandfatherly face that was worn and wrinkled. He awkwardly patted her arm. "Sammy?" she asked.

"They've already taken him to the hospital. Are you hurt?"

Beth eased up to a seated position and blinked at the swarm of people standing above. Two men placed Aiden's lifeless body on a stretcher. She averted her eyes, not wanting to witness the shell of a man she'd believed had cared about her all these years.

"I'm okay but I want to go to the hospital. I need to be with Sammy."

She struggled to her feet, surprised to find her limbs weak and her vision blurry. Two people rushed forward and supported her from either side.

"Need a stretcher?" one of them asked.

She stiffened her spine and cinched the wet, dirty bathrobe closer against her waist. All she needed was Sammy. She had to be with him, to touch him and see his eyes open again.

Not ten yards away, an ambulance awaited, its back door open and the interior lit. She glimpsed two stretchers and lifesaving equipment on shelves. But there was also another vehicle—the side of it emblazoned with the County Coroner seal. Several workers loaded a stretcher with Aiden's body wrapped in a tarp.

The cops waved an EMT crew over and she was encircled. Safe and protected. But a tight knot of anxiety cramped her stomach.

Please, God, let Sammy live.

Chapter Nineteen

Beth laid her head beside Sammy's chest on the hospital bed where he rested. Despite the uncomfortable chair, she was afraid that if she fell asleep it would be days before she awakened. The weariness went bone-deep. She'd showered in Sammy's private room and Lilah had brought her dry clothes to change into. Her friend, mother hen that she was, had also insisted that she eat a bowl of soup. Now, warmed and sated, her body wanted sleep. She fought the drowsiness, wanting to be the first thing Sammy saw when he awakened.

The doctors had assured her that the surgery to remove the bullet and staunch the internal bleeding had been a success. A couple of nights in the hospital for observation and Sammy could go home.

Home. Beth realized that she thought of Lavender Mountain as her home now. Boston seemed far, far away. Her heart was here in Appalachia—with Sammy. The hospital door opened and Lilah poked her head in, eyebrows raised in question. Beth shook her head no, shuffled to her feet and entered the hallway where Harlan and Lilah stood guard.

"He's still sleeping, which is a good thing. Sammy needs lots of rest." She cut Harlan a stern glance. "He's in no shape to be giving statements or making reports tonight. Probably not tomorrow, either."

Harlan nodded. "Of course. Besides, I spoke with him just before he went under the knife and I know everything I need to for the time being. I also spoke with Charlotte before she was admitted here."

"What happened to her?" Beth hadn't even known Sammy's partner had been on the scene. Dread weighed on her chest. Had something awful happened to the pregnant cop?

"She's fine," Lilah assured her with a quick squeeze of the hand. "Just delivered a nine-and-a-half-pound baby boy. James is beside himself. It's their first baby."

Lilah and Harlan exchanged a tender, knowing smile as Beth sighed with relief. At least something good had come out of this night. "Y'all should go on home," she urged them. "Sammy's out of danger and I'm fine."

Lilah leaned into Harlan's side, patting her round stomach. "I'm not going to argue with you. I'm beat. Come by whenever you're ready. The spare room's yours."

Harlan extended a hand toward her. "You'll always be welcome in our home."

She shook his hand and his unexpected kindness had her blinking back tears. No wonder Lilah was so in love with this man. He often appeared taciturn and aloof on the outside, but underneath, Harlan was a solid, stand-up kind of guy. Lilah had chosen well.

Beth tiptoed back into the room and resumed her seat by Sammy's bed. Some color had returned to his face and the chalk-white paleness was gone. His breathing was smooth, deep and regular.

She huddled under a blanket. After all the hours outside in the winter cold, it seemed her body just couldn't get warm enough. Her lids were heavy, and she gave in to the pleasant lethargy.

Something tugged on her hand and she startled awake. Beth gazed at the unfamiliar, sterile room in confusion for a moment until her eyes focused on Sammy. He smiled at her, his brown eyes warm and gentle. "They told me you were okay," he said. "But nothing beats having you right here in front of me where I can see for myself."

"Ditto," she said past the lump in her throat. "You gave us all a scare."

"Nothing compared to what I saw when I found you with Aiden."

She nodded slowly. "You know he—he's dead now."

"Harlan filled me in on everything. Don't you dare waste a moment of grief for his sorry ass. You did what you had to do."

"I know, but…"

Sammy held out his arms, and she leaned forward, laying her head on his chest and allowing him to comfort her. For the first time since she'd arrived at the hospital, tears slid down her face. But they were good tears this time, healing tears. Sammy's fingers caressed her scalp and then his fingers stroked her hair. Beth sighed and felt peace settle over her at last.

Long, long minutes later, she pulled away. "Forget about me. You're the one who's been shot. How bad does it hurt?"

"I told you I'm fine," he said gruffly.

"If something had happened to you…" Beth squeezed his hand.

He narrowed his eyes. "Sure everything's all right with you? You must be exhausted. And devastated."

"Aiden's not the worst of it. It's what he said about Cynthia that I can't get out of my head."

"Cynthia?"

"Oh, that's right. Harlan didn't get a chance to fill you in on everything. Aiden claimed that she killed my father by injecting him with oxygen. Apparently, an air embolism did him in."

"Damn it. None of us even suspected there was foul play, Beth. Given his age and history of heart trouble—"

"Of course you couldn't have known." Beth stood and began pacing. "I don't know what to believe anymore. If what Aiden said is true, I want Cynthia to pay for what she did to Dad."

Sammy frowned. "Don't expect a confession from her. And I seriously doubt that there's any evidence after all this time."

What about justice for her father? Had her stepmother gotten away with murder? Beth hugged her arms into her chest. "Do you think Cynthia killed him?" she asked Sammy.

"We may never know for sure, but I'm inclined to think the answer is *yes*."

"Me, too." She recalled the grim amusement on Aiden's face as he described how his mother had caused the fatal heart attack. "Harlan told me she called you and rang the alarm about Aiden. Why do you think she warned you I might be in danger?"

"Could have been one of two things. Either she wanted Aiden caught in the act and arrested, leaving her with your inheritance—"

"Or she truly cares about her son and wanted him to get caught before he killed me and possibly ended up on death row," she said slowly. "I'm guessing it's the first option."

"And she might have tipped us off to cover her bases in case an investigation implicated Aiden. That way, she could claim she acted in your best interests over her son's, even throw doubt on any stories he would tell about her possible involvement in your father's demise."

"I bet she hates me now," Beth muttered. "Not that I particularly care about her opinion. Unless she decides to come after me for shooting Aiden."

"You'll never have to see her again, whether or not she's ever convicted of murder. I won't let her hurt you," Sammy promised, his face grim and his eyes flashing in fury. "Soon as I'm able, I intend to have a little chat with her. I guarantee you by the time I'm finished, she'll never want to step within miles of anywhere you might be. If she knows what's good for her, and I suspect a person like her always has their best interests at heart, Cynthia Wynngate will never again step foot in the State of Georgia."

Beth believed him. "There's only one thing left that troubles me."

"What's that?"

"Dorsey Lambert."

"No need to worry on his account. The man saved both our lives tonight."

"That's what I mean. I feel like I owe him."

"You don't owe him a thing. But if it makes you feel better, we can write a letter to the parole board recommending he be released from parole."

"I want to do more than that. After all, my Dad did take his money and placed an undue hardship on his family." She stopped pacing and nodded her head, decision made. "I'm going to provide him a reward. Enough money so that he can start over in a new life."

"That's incredibly generous. Probably more than

he deserves. He and his family did stalk you, remember? They also broke into your home and tried to extort money from you."

She cocked her head to the side and regarded him with a smile. "But they weren't killers. And Dorsey saved your life. For that, he deserves a fresh start."

Beth resumed pacing, her heart growing lighter as she thought of the future. There were so many things she wanted to do, so many wrongs to right. As the daughter of a judge, no matter how much her father had erred later in life, her sense of justice ran deep. And she had her dad to thank for it. For many, many years he'd been honest and fair. Whatever had corrupted him later, she'd grown up with his strong role model of integrity.

It was how she'd choose to honor and remember her father.

Her right foot knocked against something on the floor and she glanced down to find what she'd stumbled upon. A black duffel bag was positioned at the end of the hospital bed.

"Harlan brought it over," he explained. "I asked him to bring that and—"

"What's this?" She lifted the square canvas that had been leaning against the bag. She held it up to the fluorescent overhead light and chuckled with surprise. The edges were charred, and soot blackened a good portion of the bottom, but she recognized it as one of the paintings she'd been working on at the cabin.

"I can't believe you kept this."

"Are you kidding me? I risked life and limb to get them."

She laughed. "Crazy man. It wasn't worth it."

"Sure it was. It's beautiful. And you painted it."

She couldn't tear her eyes from the ruined painting.

She could redo it, or even try and repair the damaged parts. But Beth decided she wanted them to remain. They were a reminder of the day Sammy had run out of the burning cabin with a handful of her artwork.

The day she'd fallen in love.

"Come here," Sammy demanded gruffly, patting the hospital bed.

Beth propped the painting on the metal nightstand and climbed into bed beside him. She ran a hand through his hair, and he planted a kiss on her forehead. "So you think I'm a crazy man?" he teased, his chest rumbling with laughter. "I'll admit, I'm crazy in love with you."

It was hard to believe her heart could go from the depths of despair from only a few hours earlier, to feeling as though it would burst with joy. His admission left her speechless. She knew how deeply his parents' divorce had affected his willingness to make commitments.

"I'm not asking you to stay here," he said quickly. "I know you have a life in Boston. But we could see each other long-distance. Plenty of couples—"

She kissed him, long and hard. At last she pulled away. "I don't want a long-distance relationship. I want to stay right here in Lavender Mountain."

"But won't you miss the excitement of Boston?" His brows drew together in consternation. "What about all your artsy friends and visiting museums? We have nothing of the kind to offer here."

Did he want her to stay or not? Was he still afraid of love and commitment? "I see unparalleled beauty in the Appalachian Mountains that no museum painting can ever replicate," she said quietly.

Sammy appeared unconvinced. "What about all your friends? Your art classes?"

"I can teach anywhere, including Lavender Mountain. And as far as friends and family, all I ever want, or need, is one person who loves, supports and believes in me." She jabbed a finger playfully in his chest. "And that person is you. I love you so much."

"I love you more. But are you sure? Really sure?" Hope flickered in his dark brown eyes, but she also read a worrisome, nagging doubt.

"One hundred percent positive," she assured him. Then she pressed her mouth against his, expressing all her love in the kiss. She was where she was supposed to be, now and forever. Sammy held her in his arms, and long after he'd finally fallen asleep, Beth lay beside him in utter peace and joy as she watched the snow fall on Lavender Mountain.

* * * * *

COLTON'S AMNESIA TARGET

KIMBERLY VAN METER

Chapter One

"You're gonna love this," Reese Carpenter promised with a subtle quirk of his lips that pretty much guaranteed his partner, Jordana Colton, would not agree. "John Doe at the hospital, all banged up, unconscious, no ID. And—wait for it—nothing but your name on a piece of paper clutched in his hot little hand."

Jordana, Braxville police detective, looked up from her report and narrowed her gaze. "Come again?"

Reese wagged the phone receiver at her. "Yeah, line four. All yours, practically gift-wrapped."

Jordana rolled her eyes and switched the line. "Detective Colton here."

"Detective, we've got an unconscious male Caucasian with no identification that we might need your help identifying down here at the hospital. Think you can come down and take a peek?"

"Sure thing," Jordana said, perplexed. "I'll be there in a few minutes."

Jordana clicked off and returned to Reese with an annoyed sigh. "Guess I'm heading down to Braxville General to unravel a mystery." Like she had time to spend on a John Doe when there was a case potentially involving her family on the desk. Sidenote: she hated mysteries of any sort.

"Oh, your favorite," he quipped, to which Jordana shot him a look that said, *I'm going to spit in your yogurt if you leave it unattended*, then grabbed her keys to leave. "Hey, call me if you hear back from forensics, yeah?"

"Sure. Let me know if your mystery guy is an old boyfriend looking to rekindle a lost love."

"Screw you. I don't have old boyfriends," Jordana returned, adding with a smart-ass grin, "None here, anyway."

Reese chuckled and Jordana exited the building. The sticky heat of Kansas in September clung to her face and body as she climbed into her car, the steering wheel burning hot to the touch. God, she'd be so happy when the weather turned to cooler temps. She'd had enough of this fall heat-wave crap.

Hot weather made people cranky and mean-tempered. Just last week she'd nearly been clocked by a mean drunk standing in his skivvies outside his place, waving a whiskey bottle, ranting at the world, sweat dribbling down his sun-weathered face.

In a small department, even detectives had to do fieldwork and that meant answering disturbance calls if none of the street cops were available.

As luck would have it, Jordana plucked the short straw on that one.

Heat and booze, a combination guaranteed to bring out the worst in people.

Braxville General loomed ahead and she pulled into the emergency loading zone reserved for cops bringing in perps with medical issues.

She waved at Rosie, the front desk volunteer, a living fossil if there ever was one, but hers was a face Jordana would associate with Braxville General until the day she died.

"Hi there, honey," Rosie called out. "Say hello to your mama for me."

Jordana offered a short smile and a thumbs-up, saying, "Copy that, Miss Rosie," before going through the double doors to the emergency room where her John Doe was being held.

Jordana knew this place like the back of her hand. Before she retired from the Navy and became a cop, as a kid she'd been a regular at this place.

In spite of her mother's ardent attempts to change her, Jordana had been a straight-up tomboy, more content to spend time running with the boys than hanging out with the girls.

As a precocious twelve-year-old Jordana had come to the conclusion that girls were boring. As opinions went, nothing had changed much since she was twelve. Shocker: Jordana didn't have many girlfriends. But that suited her just fine. She didn't have anything in common with most of the women in Braxville and small talk was excruciating.

So, *best to avoid it* was her motto.

Dr. Cervantes saw her enter and waved her over to a bay. "Sorry to break up your day like this but all he had was this in his hand." He handed Jordana a slip of paper. Sure enough, her name and cell were scrawled in masculine handwriting, plain as day.

Jordana took a closer look at the guy who remained knocked out, an IV drip feeding fluids into his body, but otherwise he seemed in relatively stable condition. "Head injury?" she surmised.

"Yes, concussion with some minor brain swelling. He should regain consciousness soon but I thought you might want to come down and take a look. I was hoping you might recognize him."

But Jordana was looking at a stranger.

Older, best guess in his mid-thirties, some salt-and-pepper seasoning in his sideburns but an otherwise strong head of dark hair. It didn't take a rocket scientist to deduce that this man wasn't from Braxville.

Also, she didn't have a clue who the hell he was or why he'd been looking for her.

"Sorry, drawing a blank on this end," Jordana said to Dr. Cervantes, but offered to run his prints. "Something tells me this guy ain't living off the grid. His prints ought to be in the system." Jordana pulled her fingerprinting device from her pocket. One of the fancier gadgets the department had purchased with some help from a Homeland Security grant. It was all digital and it went straight to the database.

Jordana gently pressed his fingers against the pad, recording his prints. No messy ink, no cleanup. Sometimes Jordana loved technology. Other times she missed the days when everyone wasn't so heavily connected.

While the device ran a search, Jordana asked for details about the John Doe. "So, what happened to him?"

"Someone found him out on Range Road, like he'd been dumped. Looks like someone thought they'd done the job with that crack in the head but he's a lucky bastard because it didn't fracture the skull, just knocked him around plenty."

"He ought to run out and buy some scratchers with that kind of luck," Jordana said. "That blow could've killed him."

Dr. Cervantes agreed. "Like I said, lucky. I wish I had that kind of luck. If it weren't for bad luck, I wouldn't have any."

Jordana chuckled at the doc's wry humor even if he was full of bologna. Dr. Cervantes seemed to live a charmed life. His wife, Valeria, was a Peruvian beauty and his kids all looked like they were plucked from a magazine photoshoot. On the surface, he had it all.

Jordana knew better than to trust appearances. Still, she hoped that all was as it seemed when it came to Dr. Cervantes because she genuinely liked him.

"Your wife is too pretty for you," Jordana quipped with a snort. "Take your blessings where you find them."

Dr. Cervantes chuckled with a nod. "Such wisdom from someone so young," he said, a twinkle in his eye.

She barked a laugh. "Young? I feel every second of my thirty-one years. Some days I'm pretty sure I might be sixty."

"Someday someone is going to turn you from a cynic to a romantic," Dr. Cervantes prophesied. Jordana laughed because it was highly unlikely but the doc was certain of it, saying, "If I were a betting man…you're too attractive to spend your life chasing criminals."

Jordana wagged her finger at him. "Ahhh, watch out, Doc, your sexism is showing. I happen to like chasing criminals."

Dr. Cervantes sighed as if he'd never understand but said, "I stand by my words. I'm never wrong about these things."

A soft ding alerted Jordana that the search was finished. "Saved by the bell," she teased, lifting the device to read the results. *Oh, damn.* She, sort of, did know him. Well, not in person but she'd spoken to him on the phone two weeks ago. "His name is Clint Broderick, thirty-six, from Chicago."

Clint Broderick was the last living relative of the

dead body fished out of the wall of a warehouse scheduled for demo by Colton Construction. The body was identified as Fenton Crane, a private investigator with a shady past, with only one living relative: Clint.

"So you do know him?"

She couldn't get into specifics, not with the Crane investigation still ongoing. "Yeah, part of a possible murder investigation. Mr. Broderick was supposed to meet with me two weeks ago but then I didn't hear from him."

"Seems he must've tangled with the wrong people," Dr. Cervantes said.

"So it would seem."

Instead of solving the mystery, the mystery had deepened.

If Clint Broderick had been on his way to see Jordana, what happened along the way? The fact that the only living relative of the dead guy walled up in an old warehouse ended up bashed in the head and left for dead didn't seem like a coincidence.

Did someone want to protect a secret? Did Broderick know something someone wanted to keep quiet?

She had questions only Broderick could answer—but the man was still out cold.

To the doc, she said, "Can you move him to a private, secure room?"

"That can be arranged. Should we post security, too?"

"Might be a good idea. At least until he wakes up."

Dr. Cervantes nodded. "Consider it done. We need the emergency room bays, anyway."

Jordana took one last lingering look at Broderick, noting with reluctance that even unconscious the guy had an impressive bulk about him. Those nice rounded shoulders and well-defined, broad chest gave away his dedication to the gym.

The man had discipline.

Everything about him told a story without his mouth saying a word.

The only thing it wasn't saying was how he'd ended up in a Braxville hospital instead of in her office like he was supposed to.

More questions.

Another damn mystery.

Oh, goody.

CLINT BRODERICK AWOKE to dimly light darkness in a place he didn't recognize, hearing sounds he couldn't place.

Panic threatened to bloom, tightening his chest as he sat up with a jerk, nearly upsetting the IV cart attached to his wrist by the thin tubing.

What the hell?

Then the pain hit. His head felt as if a badger were trying to gnaw its way free from his skull using nothing but blunt chompers and a will to succeed. He cupped his head gingerly and found a large bandage covering a knot that throbbed like an angry protestor at a political rally. His mind swam as he blinked back the vertigo that threatened to make him puke.

He was in a hospital? How'd he get here?

The night nurse came in to check his vitals and realized with a start that he was awake.

"Oh, goodness, you gave me a fright. How are you feeling? You have quite the nasty bump on your noggin."

He didn't know how to answer, admitting gruffly, "Hurts. Can I get some water?"

"Of course." She filled a cup from the pitcher at the end of the bedside table, handing it to him. "Careful now, you've been out for quite a while."

"How long?"

"Almost twenty-four hours. Are you dizzy? Faint?"

"All of the above."

"Understandable. Head injuries hurt like the dickens and they do some kooky things to the brain. Lucky for you, you only had minor swelling but only God knows what kind of damage that can do. Do you know your name?"

"Of course I know my name," he grumbled, but when he tried to produce it from his memory, there was a scary blank spot. "It's..." He struggled to remember. "My name is, um..."

But the nurse seemed to expect his memory gap. "No worries. Short-term amnesia is also common for a head injury like yours. I can help you out. Your name, according to your fingerprints, is Clint Broderick. Does that ring any bells?"

Clint Broderick. Sounded right but he couldn't be sure. Still, he took her word for it. *Fingerprints don't lie.* "Yeah, sounds about right."

"Well, you try to get some rest. The doctor will see you in the morning."

Rest? He'd just been unconscious for nearly a day. Lying in a hospital bed for another couple of hours until the doctor made his rounds wasn't appealing but what else could he do? He didn't even know his damn name; he couldn't exactly check into a hotel room.

"Where am I exactly?" he asked, wincing against the throb in his brain.

"That would be Braxville General, in Braxville, Kansas. Just outside of Wichita and pretty as a picture if I ever saw one. We have a lot of community pride around here."

He couldn't muster a polite smile; instead, he took a swallow of water to wet his dry throat, then said, "I'm guessing I didn't have my wallet or anything when I was found?"

"Nothing but the clothes on your back, sugar. Sorry about that. Someone must've been right mad at you to do you like that."

Yeah, guess so. Too bad he couldn't remember who the hell he was or who might be so pissed at him that they'd knock him into next week and leave him for dead. Talk about waking up in a nightmare.

He nodded to the nurse. "Thanks. Can I get something for this headache?"

"Sure thing, sugar. Doc has cleared you for light pain meds if you should need them. Be right back."

The nurse left him and he eased back on the pillow, staring up at the ceiling. He had no idea who he was or how he'd gotten here.

But someone had tried to kill him. What if they tried to come back and finish the job?

Yeah, sleep? Not gonna happen.

He lifted his arms to stare at his hands. Smooth, strong and capable but not callused. Something told him manual labor wasn't in his wheelhouse. So, a desk guy of some sort? Did he push paper all day? Had he discovered some shady dealings and someone thought to clip loose ends?

The throb in his head intensified when he tried to push too hard on the memory button.

Ah, hell. He wasn't going to find the answers tonight.

Hopefully, tomorrow brought more clarity—or at

the very least an end to this vicious stabbing pain in his brain.

One could hope.

Because that was all he had right about now.

Chapter Two

The next morning Jordana received word from Dr. Cervantes that Mr. Broderick was awake and she hustled back to Braxville General. True to his word, the doctor had sequestered her victim in a private section of the hospital with a security guard at the door. She flashed her badge and entered the room.

The man who'd been knocked out cold the last time she saw him glanced up at her entrance and she was hit with a pair of stormy blue eyes that complemented his brown hair and revealed an intensity she could feel with a glance.

That presence she'd sensed about him bloomed when he was fully aware. This man could probably command a boardroom or lead an army without breaking a sweat. Her military training recognized authority when she saw it, even if he couldn't remember who he was yet.

"Mr. Broderick, I'm Detective Jordana Colton." She extended her hand and he accepted with a perfunctory shake. "How are you feeling?"

"Confused."

Damn. She'd been hoping perhaps his memory had returned by morning, but she kept her disappointment from her voice, explaining, "The doctor says you have some short-term memory loss caused by your head injury. It should pass with a little more rest."

"Yeah, I guess so. Gotta say, not sure how to think about this situation. I may not know my name but I remember that my mother's name was Daisy. How can I remember that?"

"Long-term memory is stored in a different section of the brain," she answered. "You should be able to remember the parts of your life that are stored in long-term memory, such as your childhood, but anything in the short term will be affected."

Her explanation seemed to make sense as he nodded. "Yeah, I remember the house I grew up in, the street even, but not being able to remember my name? It's messing with me."

"I can only imagine," she murmured in support, but got right to the point. "Mr. Broderick, I was able to identify you through your prints, but actually, you and I had a conversation two weeks ago with plans to meet up."

He furrowed his brow, regarding her in question. "I'm sorry…were we…supposed to meet for a date?"

The awkwardness of his question only made Jordana blush. "No, it wasn't a personal call," she assured him. "I'm afraid I was calling with unfortunate news."

"Yeah? Like what?"

It was some kind of karmic kick in the ass that she was having to deliver this crappy news twice to the same person. "A body was found in the walls of a warehouse scheduled for demolition and I'm sad to be the bearer of bad news but the victim turned out to be a man named Fenton Crane, a relative of yours."

He digested that information for a minute, but in the end he shook his head, saying, "Sorry, doesn't ring a bell. Was he a close relative?"

"Well, an estranged uncle but you came up as his only living relative."

"So, was I coming to talk to you about this dead uncle when someone waylaid me?"

"It would seem that way."

"Do you know who might've done this?"

She shook her head. "No. The investigation is still early. We don't have much information to go on. I was hoping that you could give us some additional insight when I contacted you. You were planning to meet up with me but then I never heard back."

"I guess I must've had some kind of information worth sharing if I was willing to drive here." He paused a second to ask, "Wait a minute…where's my car? The nurse said I was found on the road?"

"Yeah, dumped along Range Road. Sorry, no car, though. Do you remember what you were driving?"

He thought for a minute, then shook his head. "No, sorry. Another big blank." Frustration laced his tone. "How long is this amnesia supposed to last?"

"I don't know. I think it varies. You'll have to ask Dr. Cervantes about the specifics." She wished she could be more helpful but they were both hitting cement walls. Finding Fenton Crane's body in the walls of a warehouse her family's company was scheduled to demo had planted a frenzy of suspicion on her family's doorstep and she'd hoped that maybe Clint Broderick could shed some light into why Fenton Crane was in Braxville in the first place. "It's possible you might regain your memory within a few days," she said, trying to be helpful.

An awkward silence followed. She should leave. There wasn't much more that could be said until he regained his memory but she wanted to hang around.

Her gaze strayed to his ring finger. No wedding band. At least no one was waiting and worrying about him at home. *Some men didn't wear their rings.* She shifted against the inner dialog in her head. "You don't remember anything? Nothing at all?"

"I remember that I hated strawberries as a kid. Does that help?"

"Not really."

"Yeah, then I don't have much more to share. Sorry."

He had arresting blue eyes, like two vibrant blue paint chips with flecks of variegated color blended in a creative swirl. Or a turbulent ocean reacting to a summer storm, churning the seabed with its violent motion.

Someone had to be waiting for him at home. There was no way a man like him was unattached.

Get a grip, unnecessary personal information. Stop wasting energy on something immaterial to your case.

The realization that she was hanging around for a less than professional reason made her stiffen and refocus. "All right, then. Well, I suppose until you regain your memory…there's not much we can do to help each other."

"I wish I was of more use to you."

The genuine timbre of his voice tugged at her in a disconcerting way. He had no one here and he had no one to help him. Where was he supposed to go? Presumably, he'd come to Braxville to help *her* and then someone had tried to kill him.

Not your problem.

But he could be an important key to the puzzle. In the interest of the case, shouldn't she keep him as close as possible?

Don't say it, just turn around, keep walking. Don't be stupid and reckless.

But the words fell from her mouth, anyway.

"Look, I don't want you to get the wrong idea or anything, but seeing as you don't know anyone here in Braxville and you don't even know who you are, if you need a place to crash, I have a spare bedroom you can use for the time being. Until we figure something else out."

Had she just invited a stranger to come bunk up with her?

Had she lost her mind?

She could practically hear the incredulous protests of her five siblings when they found out. It was brash. Dangerous, even. And yet she didn't regret offering. It was about the case, nothing else. Besides, it was just for a few days and maybe it could provide a break in the case.

This went against protocol, another voice argued—a voice that sounded a lot like her partner's. No one in their right mind would, or should, volunteer to house a stranger, but her gut was pushing her to do exactly that. She'd learned to trust her instincts even when all signs pointed the other direction. *So, here's putting those instincts to the test...*

"Yeah, so...if you're not allergic to cat dander...my door is open."

THE CUTE COP had just offered him room and board.

His first impulse was to answer with an enthusiastic yes but was that wise? He didn't even know who he was or who *she* was for that matter.

What if she was a dirty cop who knew who'd done this to him? What if she was keeping him close to protect his attacker?

What if she planned to finish the job and cover up his murder with her cop connections?

Likely? Probably not but he'd never been attacked and left for dead before, either.

Or at least he didn't think this had ever happened to him before.

Damn, paranoia was an ugly thing. But given the fact that he'd nearly died and he didn't even remember how it'd happened, a little paranoia seemed understandable.

The long pause caused her to fluster, saying, "Forget it, I was just—"

He quickly jumped in. "No, I appreciate the offer. I was just thinking, I have no idea if I'm allergic to cat dander. I guess there's only one way to find out, right?"

A short smile and a sudden flush in her cheeks only made her more appealing but he didn't need to be thinking like that about Jordana Colton. *Detective* Colton, that is. Gotta keep the facts of the situation front and center. "Oh, right," she acknowledged. "Well, yeah, you'll know right away whether or not you're allergic because either you'll start sneezing like your head is going to pop off or you'll be fine. I also have Benadryl on hand in case things go from bad to worse."

"Yeah, I'd hate to survive a blow to the head only to die choking on cat fuzz."

Her smile widened, almost reluctantly, and he realized he might not know who he was but he did know what he liked—and he liked Jordana Colton.

"So, the doc should spring me today… It's embarrassing to ask but could you pick me up later this afternoon?"

She answered with a professional nod. "Of course."

"Cool. Yeah, that'd be great. I appreciate your offer. Very kind of you."

She nodded, clasping her hands in front of her as if conducting a very proper business transaction with heads of state. "Um, so, of course, there is nothing romantic offered or expected or solicited. Just to keep things as clear as possible to avoid any awkward moments."

"Got it. I don't think you're my type," he said with a slight tease to his voice. When her brow arched ever so slightly, he added, "Or at least I don't think you are."

"Good." She scribbled her name and number on a piece of paper, pausing before handing it to him, a small wry chuckle escaping, murmuring something about the irony, which was not lost on him, then said, "Call me when you're ready to leave."

He nodded. "Thank you for doing this. I appreciate your kindness to a stranger. I promise I don't think I'm a bad guy or anything."

Her quick smile revealed a nice set of white, straight teeth as she quipped, "If you are, I'll just shoot you and that will be the end of that."

A private thrill chased his thoughts as he watched her leave. She had a trim, athletic figure, strong and agile. She could probably disable a bad guy in seconds. That was a little bit hot.

He probably shouldn't have taken her offer.

The smart thing to do would've been to find where he lived and then get his ass home. But the unexpected benefit of not knowing who he was relieved him of the burden of expectation or obligation.

Hell, he could be the president of the United States and it wouldn't matter because the slate was blissfully empty. Kinda like when he was a kid. No one looking to him to keep their bills paid. No one expecting him to solve their problems. No one badgering him for signatures or payroll.

He was just like a kid again, floating through life, looking forward to the next day or adventure. He liked that idea. He liked it a lot.

Also, maybe it wasn't right or appropriate but Jordana Colton…he wanted to know her better.

Hopefully, with any luck, he wasn't allergic to cats.

Chapter Three

"Any luck with your John Doe?" Reese asked when Jordana returned to the station.

"No, his memory is still shot," she answered, going to her desk. "But the doctor thinks it should only be a few days before he recovers fully. Just gotta be patient, I suppose. Head injuries are tricky."

Reese grunted in agreement. "Back in high school, I took a nasty blow to the head during a football game. My brain was fuzzy for weeks, but I never lost my memory. Kinda wished I had. Would've made my dating history a lot easier to stomach."

She smiled, privately happy that Reese was returning to some semblance of himself. Not that he'd ever be that happy-go-lucky guy again after losing his last partner, but maybe he'd find his smile again.

He was a damn good cop, though, and Jordana liked working with him.

"So, what's the guy going to do in the meantime? Stay at the hospital?"

She swiveled in her chair to face Reese, knowing he was going to hate what she was about to say. "Actually, in the interest of the case, I offered up my spare bedroom for a few days until he got his memory back."

Reese's expression turned into a scowl. "You did what?"

"Calm down, it's just for a few days and he seems harmless. Besides, the guy doesn't have anywhere to go and he doesn't even remember his name."

"You know this is stupid," he growled. "This guy could be a murderer for all you know."

"He's not a murderer," she disagreed, but she could see how her decision might seem brash. "Look, I get it. Under normal circumstances, I wouldn't dream of doing something like this but my gut says the guy isn't dangerous and what he knows about Fenton Crane might be the key to cracking how the hell he ended up dead in that warehouse."

"Your connection to this case is blurring your judgment," he said. "I understand that you're willing to do whatever it takes to clear your family but that's exactly why you shouldn't be running this investigation."

She was well aware of the conflict of interest, but the saving grace was that they were in a small department and there weren't many backups. She'd assured the captain that she could handle the investigation without losing her objectivity, but granted, this decision seemed to fly in the face of that assurance.

"Okay, yeah, on the surface it looks stupid but whatever happened to just being nice to a stranger who got the short end of the stick in a situation? I mean, he's here because of me. He was coming to Braxville to talk to me about this case and then something happened to him."

"You're not responsible for his bad luck," Reese argued, still not on board. "I'm not trying to be an ass but I'm not going to see your side on this. It's reckless and foolhardy—two things I never thought I'd have to worry about from you."

Ouch. "I appreciate your concern but I got this. Don't

worry. Besides, if he gets out of line or I get a bad vibe, I'll just kick his ass into the ground."

"So there's no way I can talk you out of this?"

"Not really."

He shook his head. "I guess there's nothing more to say, right? You're going to do what you want to do no matter what I say."

"Pretty much."

Reese exhaled a long breath but knew it was pointless to keep arguing. "If you're hell-bent on ignoring any common sense, at least let me look into his background so you're not walking blind into this situation."

"Fine. If that helps you relax, run a detailed background on him and text me anything alarming."

"More alarming than the fact someone tried to kill him and left him for dead for unknown reasons?"

"Yeah, more than that."

Jordana chuckled and returned to the report on her desk. Yeah, she knew it wasn't protocol to let a stranger into her home who may or may not have information related to the dead body.

What they knew about Fenton Crane was frustratingly little. They knew he'd been hired by Rita Harrison to search for her missing daughter, Olivia.

Olivia Harrison turned out to be Body Number Two walled up in the warehouse.

In a town with a relatively low crime rate, finding not one but two dead bodies in an old warehouse was downright jarring.

They were keeping the details, such as they were, as quiet as possible. They didn't need the crackpots to crawl out of the woodwork with their own theories, but then they also needed leads, and sometimes the most unlikely source turned out to be the key that busted a case wide open.

People were easy to rile up and hard to control, something she learned in the Navy, which was why she kept those "in the know" within a very small circle.

"Forensics come back on Oliva Harrison yet?" she asked.

"Yeah, best guess midtwenties, cause of death likely a blow to the head. Skull fracture shows blunt force trauma. Been dead a long time, though."

"Man, that's rough. So, the vic turned out to be the mother of someone here in town, Gwen Harrison, an elementary school teacher?"

She nodded, chewing on her pen. And then her brother Brooks got involved and, in true Colton fashion, couldn't stay in his damn lane. Like the situation wasn't complicated enough with their dad owning the warehouse where the bodies were found, Brooks had to go and get involved with the dead woman's daughter.

What twisted webs we weave, right?

"I can't imagine how horrible it must've been for her family when she went missing without a trace, only to be found by accident twenty years later," she murmured.

"Yeah, horrible tragedy," Reese agreed. "Do you ever think of how many dead bodies might be hidden right beneath people's noses, walled up in the buildings we enter every day?"

She made a face. "That's macabre."

"But true. Hell, we have no idea how many people have met their Maker early thanks to some evil asshole with a twisted childhood. It's a sobering thought. Probably why I'll never have kids. This world is a dumpster fire."

"And you're a bowl of sunshine," Jordana quipped with a wry expression before reaching for the phone.

A text message awaited. Well, it looked like her new roomie was ready to be sprung from the hospital. She pocketed her cell and rose. "I gotta go. Broderick is ready to leave."

"Text me when you get home or I'll show up with guns blazing ready to execute justice with extreme prejudice."

She laughed. "You watch too much television. I'll be fine."

Jordana left and headed for the hospital. She didn't like mysteries but there was something about Clint Broderick that made solving his more appealing.

Was that a red flag?

Probably.

Was she going to stop?

Not likely.

CLINT GESTURED RUEFULLY to his thrift store hand-me-downs the volunteers had rustled up for him so he didn't have to walk out with his backside showing, and Jordana laughed. "I don't know for sure but something tells me I have better fashion sense than this because damn, this is embarrassing," he said.

"It lacks a certain…"

"Style?" he finished for her, staring down at the trousers that looked like they'd been plucked from some old guy's 1970s wardrobe after his clothes had been donated to charity following his death. "I'm pretty sure this hasn't been in fashion since disco was cool."

"You might be right. It might've even come from Rosie's husband's closet, but look on the bright side, at least it's better than the Braxville General blue robe special."

"You got me there," he agreed, dusting his trousers

with a gingerly motion that smacked of a little awkwardness and Jordana didn't blame him. This was a little strange. "So, you sure you want to do this?"

"Of course," she answered. "My gut tells me it's the right thing to do."

"Well, I'm thankful to your gut. I've never been in a position like this. I mean, not that I can remember. The emergency techs had to cut my clothes free but they gave me a bag filled with the remnants. I think I started off well-dressed."

"If that's the case, that means you're probably not homeless. My partner is running down your identity to see if we can find anyone who can help put together the pieces."

"Probably also to check and make sure I'm not a lunatic," he supposed, and Jordana grinned without apology. He chuckled. "I don't blame you. I'd question how good of a detective you were if you didn't."

"Glad to know I've passed the test."

"Well, that one, anyway," he said with a wink. Was he flirting? Like he was in any position to flirt with the cute detective. That blow to the head had scrambled his neurons. Something told him that he wasn't usually this easygoing but it felt good.

Maybe he was acting out of character. Maybe before he got jumped he was a stiff, rigid asshole with a chip on his shoulder.

God, he hoped not.

"All right, paperwork is finished. You're sprung, Mr. Broderick," Jordana said, gesturing for the open door.

But before they went any further, Clint had to set down some ground rules. "You have to stop calling me Mr. Broderick. Even though I don't know who I am, I know it feels weird to be called something so formal.

Please, call me Clint. Let's pretend we're old acquaintances or something. It might make things less weird. How about we try that?"

She graced him with a curious smile, cocking her head as if trying on his idea in her mind for size. "Okay, that might work for now. Unless I find out you're, like, a serial killer or something."

"Such escalation. What if I'm just your garden variety thief? Or a white-collar embezzler? It doesn't always have to be so violent."

Jordana laughed. "Okay, but if I find out you're anything but the unfortunate victim of a crime, I'm putting you in handcuffs before you can even slather cream cheese on a bagel."

"Mmm, bagels. I think I like those."

All jokes aside, it was impossible to forget that someone had tried to kill him, possibly someone in this town, and he had no clue who to watch for. Not to be paranoid but being bashed in the head and wiped of your memories made for some jittery peripheral glances.

Danger could lurk anywhere—with anyone.

All he had was Jordana Colton on his side for the time being, and having a cop watch his back seemed like something he ought to hold on to.

Now, he just had to pass the first test.

Lord in heaven, please don't let me be allergic to cats.

Chapter Four

Jordana unlocked her front door and welcomed Clint inside. "Well, here it is, in all its glory," she said with a self-deprecating shrug. "I'm not much for knickknacks and frou-frou stuff. I like it clean and simple. Less to worry about."

Her sister Bridgette had once described her personal style as utilitarian and, by her tone, it hadn't seemed a compliment, but Jordana didn't care, which was probably why the military had appealed to her. Everything had a place and a purpose. If only life were that way, it would make solving crimes so much easier, but no, humans were messy and often did things for no particular reason aside from emotion, and emotion was impossible to rein in with logic and reason.

She dropped her keys in the small bowl perched on the table in the entryway. "Okay, so the house is small enough so no worries getting lost. Bathroom is over there, adjacent to the spare bedroom, and my bedroom, which is, of course, off-limits, is opposite the spare." She returned to Clint, who was still surveying his new surroundings. "Any questions?"

"Seems pretty straightforward. I've yet to see this potentially allergenic cat you mentioned," he said.

"Ah, that's Penelope—I didn't name her so don't

judge—and she's probably hiding. She's not a huge fan of strangers or anyone aside from me. You might not see her at all."

"Penelope…okay, good to know." He gestured to the spare bedroom, asking, "May I?"

"Yes, certainly," she answered with her own gesture, following him as he walked into the tidy spare. To her trained eye, she saw her military training in action. Crisp, tight hospital bed corners, zero clutter in sight, floors clean and countertops dusted. Keeping things in order gave her a level of comfort. "It's not the Ritz but it'll keep you warm and dry until we find out more about you."

"It's great. You didn't have to do this and I'm grateful for the kindness." He glanced around, adding, "I don't know for sure but something about your style feels complementary to my own. I don't understand the appeal of knickknacks, either. Dust collectors, if you ask me."

"Exactly. If only I could convince my mom the same. She's always trying to fob off her collections of nonsense on to me in the guise of 'family heirlooms.'" Jordana made air quotes with a quick shake of her head. "Nope, it's just junk, Mom."

He chuckled. Jordana's breath caught in her chest at the sound. Time to exit gracefully. "Okay, well, I'll let you get settled and get out of your hair. Feel free to help yourself to the kitchen, though I don't really keep a well-stocked pantry because it usually goes bad before I have the chance to eat it." She clarified, "I eat a lot at the station, late nights."

"Anything is better than hospital food," Clint said with a wry grin. "I might not remember much but I definitely remember not appreciating the cuisine at Braxville General. Much to be desired unless you're a big fan of reconstituted split pea soup with the grainy consistency of a puddle after a hard rain."

She laughed. "Can't say that I'm a fan. I'm more of a burgers and fries kind of girl."

"Me, too."

"Burgers and fries girl?" she teased.

"Exactly."

Jordana smiled until she realized with a start this sounded way too much like flirty banter. "Okay, then. You have my cell. Holler if you need anything. I'm going to head back to the station to catch up on some paperwork."

"Yeah, sure, no problem," Clint said, but a frown creased his brow, prompting her to pause. "What I'm about to say sounds like the opposite of manly but it just occurred to me...what if whoever tried to knock out my lights comes back to finish the job? I'd like to think that I'm a badass with ninja skills when I get my memory back but the reality is... I'm probably not? I guess, what I'm trying to say, really badly, I might add, is that maybe I shouldn't be left alone right now."

That had to be really hard to admit, she realized. Clint also had a point and she was embarrassed that she hadn't thought of it first. For crying out loud, who was the detective in the room? Her cheeks flushed but she nodded in agreement. "Valid point. I'll have my partner bring my paperwork here. I can work from home."

"I hate to be a scaredy-cat about it but—" he rubbed the back of his head ruefully "—seems kind of foolish to tempt fate with unnecessary risk."

"Right. Very true." Okay, now that she was thoroughly embarrassed for seeming like a rookie— "Like

I said, kitchen is all yours"—she disappeared behind her bedroom door.

Maybe Reese was right. Was it reckless to bring Clint into her home like this? She didn't know anything about him and she seemed to forget basic common sense when he was around. Losing her good sense could be a liability for them both.

Clint was a handsome guy—and everyone in Braxville knew she was single as a Pringle. Tongues would wag, which meant if Clint's attacker was still in town, it wouldn't be difficult to narrow down his location.

She'd have to stay extravigilant for many reasons. Some of which had nothing to do with the case and more do with the fact that her heart rate seemed suspiciously rapid when he smiled.

A handsome man with a healthy sense of humor—that's how panties ended up on the floor.

She rubbed her forehead. It'd been a while since she actively dated (translation: had sex) and apparently Clint flipped whatever switch she had inside her brain that regulated that area. No wonder Reese had side-eyed her when she told him her plan. Good grief, she sounded reckless *and* thirsty.

Hot, single guy with no memory? Suuurre, I can take him in—into my bed!

That last part was delivered in her head with a smarmy leer. Great, now she was bullying herself in preparation for the jokes that would invariably happen somewhere down the road.

The best offense is a good defense.

She'd go the extra mile to make sure no one had reason to question her integrity or her motivation. It was all about the case. Not his broad shoulders, muscular build and charming smile.

Definitely not that.

But the fact that he checked *all* her internal boxes? Well, that made for a perfect foundation for potentially awkward feelings to brew.

And that was just Jordana being honest with herself.

CLINT CLOSED THE door and took a better look around his new digs. Clean, orderly and functional. What's not to love? *Better than a hotel room, right?* And considering that he didn't have access to his money (hopefully, he had some), Jordana's offer came free of charge.

He sat on the bed, testing the springs. Firm yet supportive. Definitely better than a hospital bed. In addition to the knot on his skull, his spine felt permanently kinked from being folded into a bed too small to accommodate his frame.

Speaking of skull, he gingerly touched the angry bulge still deforming his head and grimaced. Definitely not a great look but he was alive so that kept his vanity in check.

So, his name was Clint Broderick. Seemed like a decent, strong name. He opened the hospital bag with the remnants of his clothes. The linen felt fine, maybe high-end. Definitely not a thrift store find like the rags he was wearing right now. First order of business, find something else to wear. He couldn't continue to sport this 1970s ensemble for much longer or else people were going to start asking if he was planning his Halloween outfit early.

But seeing as he had no cash, it made purchasing difficult.

He didn't want to borrow money from the only person he knew in this tiny town but he didn't see a more viable option.

Clint groaned. Was the universe going out of its way to emasculate him? The only thing that would further demolish his sense of masculinity was if Jordana discovered he'd been brained in the head by someone's pint-size, rolling-pin-wielding grannie.

He much preferred the theory that he'd been attacked by a hardened criminal or an international assassin.

All kidding aside (sort of), he was trying not to dwell too hard on the fact that someone had tried to kill him. Who had he pissed off so bad that they wanted to snip his thread?

Was he an asshole? Did he do dastardly things to innocent victims? What kind of person was he? The kind of person who used the word *dastardly*? He didn't have any answers. A sense of panic hovered at the edges of his thoughts. Hell, he didn't have a clue as to who he was or what kind of person he was.

For all he knew, he could be a real jerk who never donated to good causes, or sneered at the misfortune of others.

God, he hoped not.

What if he was the kind of guy Jordana would never actually invite into her home if she knew his true character?

Talk about a spiral into serious mental health danger.

Good or bad, a person's identity was everything.

Breathe. Chill out. You're not Hitler.

He'd know if he were a bad person, even if his memories were gone. If he were a terrible human being, he'd be drawn to do more terrible things, right? That's logical. *Right.* Clint paused a moment, waiting to see if terrible desires jumped into his head. When nothing unseemly took center stage in his mental theater, he nodded with satisfaction at his own deduction.

Conclusion: normal guy with memory loss. No hidden Hannibal Lecter lurking in his psyche.

Okay, so time to make a plan. He couldn't sit in Jordana's house like a caged canary, waiting for the next shoe to drop. Jordana's partner was running a background check on him. Details would reveal themselves and he'd hopefully find someone who actually knew him and could help put the pieces together.

And, much like a normal guy, he had eyeballs in his head. Eyeballs that really enjoyed the view of his new roommate.

But that was a hot stove best left alone. He didn't need his memories to figure out that messing around with the cute detective was a bad idea.

She didn't seem attached to anyone, but then, maybe she preferred to keep her house separate. He knew nothing about her aside from the fact that she appeared dedicated to her job, focused on keeping boundaries between them, and that she had the most beguiling smile when she chose to share it.

For all he knew, she could be a crooked cop keeping him close to protect those who had bashed his head in. Sure, it was a theory but he really couldn't give it much weight. Jordana had a straight and narrow sensibility about her. She probably never lied on her taxes or took an extra dinner mint at a restaurant.

She'd also probably never mess around with someone under her care—and he was relieved. Mostly because his conviction toward her wasn't quite as strong. He was way too intrigued by the intensity of her stare and the subtle curve of her lips to say that he wouldn't ever cross that line.

With Jordana keeping the lines tightly drawn, he didn't have to worry about anything unprofessional happening. All he had to worry about was finding who tried to kill him before they tried to come back and finish the job.

Chapter Five

"I got intel on your houseguest," Reese announced, sliding over in his office chair to Jordana's desk, dropping a folder with a grin. "Background check came in this morning. Seems your guy—"

"Not my guy," she corrected him with a warning scowl. "But go on…what about Clint?"

"Seems Clint Broderick is some big fish from Chicago. The guy is loaded. Owns a big tech company. I'm talking easily worth millions."

"That explains the fine threads," she murmured, digesting the information. She returned to Reese, dreading the answer to her next question. "So, is Mr. Moneybucks married or something? Someone waiting and worrying back in Chicago?"

"Nope. Only family was the dead guy walled up in the warehouse. Tough break, that. It's the old trope—the lonely rich boy with only dollar bills to keep him warm at night."

Jordana tossed a balled-up paper at Reese's grinning face. "You're finding way too much enjoyment in this."

"A sense of humor is important to keeping one's sanity," he drawled with a subtle smile. "So where is your rich houseguest? I thought you said he didn't want to be left alone?"

She chuckled at how her answer would be received. "Actually, I lent him some money so he could buy some clothes. He couldn't keep wearing what the hospital discharged him in."

"At least you know he's good for it," Reese quipped, to which Jordana agreed. "It could be worse—he could've been a con artist and just bilked you out of a couple bucks."

"My gut told me he was an acceptable risk and, as it turned out, I was right," Jordana said with a pointed look toward Reese because she wasn't above rubbing in her victory. "What else did you find out?"

"Well, he might not have any family but he does have a business partner, Alex Locke. Contact information is in the file."

Business partner. Immediate suspicion fell to those closest to the victim; that was just standard operating procedure. "Anything come up on Locke?"

"I didn't go deep but from the surface he looks pretty boring. The business seems to be doing well enough. There isn't a giant red flag waving around that points to motive, but like I said, that's just surface values. I can keep looking."

"Yeah, go ahead and poke around a bit. Make sure Locke is clean. I don't want to send Clint from the frying pan to the fire."

"Any particular reason you're so hot to protect this guy?" Reese asked.

"I'm doing my job," she answered, shifting against the implication that she was doing anything above and beyond what she'd do for anyone. But even as the words dropped from her mouth she knew it was a hard pill to swallow. "Okay, fine, I feel bad for the guy," she admitted. "He came here to help my investigation into a homicide that turned out to be his only family and then he gets whacked in the head and loses his memory."

"It's not your fault," Reese reminded her. "You can't carry that burden on your shoulders forever. What are you going to do, marry the guy to prove how sorry you are that he got jumped while trying to aid an investigation?"

She glowered. "Don't be stupid. Of course not."

"I'm just saying, it's a little much what you're doing for this guy. Feels more than professional. There, I said it and you can be pissed but I'm not sorry for being honest."

Maybe she was being a little more accommodating for Clint but she also knew she wasn't going to kick him out or do anything that might jeopardize his safety. "Well, we all have our opinions," she said, scooping up the file folder. "Thanks for the legwork. I have to go."

"Let me guess, Clint needs a ride after his little shopping trip? Maybe share a sandwich for two over at Harvey's?"

Her cheeks heated. She was meeting Clint for lunch but she hated the way Reese made it sound. But whatever, Reese could suck an egg. Jordana lifted the folder, saying over her shoulder, "Thanks for the support, buddy. You're a peach," as she marched out of the station.

Harvey's deli, located within the newly built Ruby Row shopping center, was a convenient place to meet after Clint did his shopping but it bothered Jordana that Reese had framed this meeting like a date of some sort, which it absolutely was not.

If anything, this was a working lunch and there was nothing social about it. She grabbed a table to wait for Clint, her knee bouncing with nervous energy. Maybe she should've suggested that Clint meet her at the station instead of a restaurant. She could've scarfed down a microwave burrito like she's done countless times in the past and Reese wouldn't have had cause to give her the side-eye.

But what did it matter? Clint was already living in her house for the time being; it wasn't as if meeting for lunch was going to soften the reality of her new living arrangement.

A deep throb had begun to pulsate behind her left eye. If everyone would just lay off her decision, that would be great. And by everyone, she meant Reese.

She looked up to see Clint enter the restaurant. Immediately, her breath caught. He made jeans and a T-shirt look like high fashion. She blinked against the very real warm sensation sending tendrils of awareness through her body. *Oh, good grief, so he can rock a casual look, big deal. Nothing has changed.* She schooled her expression before he slid into the seat opposite her with an unsure grin. "Did I do okay?" He surprised her with the question.

She affirmed with an efficient nod. "Jeans and a T-shirt are appropriate for the early fall in Kansas, yes."

"Good, good," he murmured. "Honestly, I don't know if I'm a jeans and a T-shirt kind of guy because I was drawn to the slacks and polos but, you know, when in Rome, right? I think I'll stick out less if I dress like the natives."

"Braxville is not the untamed wilderness," she grumbled, taking mild offense. "If you wanted to wear slacks and a polo, you would've been just fine. No one would've given you a weird look."

"Good to know," he said, seeming to sense that he'd offended her. "I'm sorry if I implied anything—"

"No, you're fine," she said, wanting to move on. She was being prickly and picking a fight for the wrong reasons. *Get back on target.* Jordana produced the file folder. "I have some good news. My partner, Reese, was able to dig up some information that might help jog your memory."

Clint perked up. "Yeah? What'd he find?"

"Well, it seems you're…let's just say you're not worried about how you're going to pay the light bill." She waited for Clint to open the file before adding, "You're pretty much loaded. You own a tech company in Chicago with a business partner, Alex Locke. Ring a bell?"

A part of her hoped she'd see the light of recognition dawn in his eyes but the other part, the inexplicable part, hoped he remained blank.

Girl, you are walking a dangerous path. Get off while you still can.

Excellent counsel. Except she knew she wasn't going to.

And that was worse.

CLINT WAITED FOR that spark of memory to burn away the fog of his amnesia, but as he stared at the facts on the printed page, he felt nothing. Frustrated, he pushed the folder away with a heavy sigh. "Sorry, I don't remember any of this. Damn it. When is this going to end?"

"Dr. Cervantes said it could happen anytime. It isn't likely going to be permanent," she assured him. "I would wait on contacting your business partner until my partner can do a little background check."

His face screwed into a confused frown. "Why?"

"Because those closest to the victim are usually the first to fall under suspicion," she said.

"That's messed up. Seems like a penalty for being close to the victim."

"Sometimes but it's really just a way to clear away the obvious. Detective work is often a process of elimination until you get down to the most plausible suspects. As much as I hate to remind you, someone wanted you dead. Your business partner needs to be cleared before we can successfully check him off the list of possible suspects."

That made a certain amount of sense, but he didn't like the idea of someone whom he shared a business to fall under suspicion because it called into question his judgment. "Doesn't feel very good knowing someone tried to kill me," he said, settling back with a sigh. "I was kind of leaning on the theory that it was a robbery gone wrong. I mean, they did take my wallet."

"But no charges have been made on your credit cards, which tells me they likely just dumped your wallet."

"Guess that doesn't jive with a thief's mentality to steal something only to throw it away before using it."

She nodded. "Yeah, pretty much, but hey, think of the bright side—you don't have to fill out a bunch of bank paperwork to prove fraudulent charges. You just need to cancel your cards as lost and order new ones."

"Yeah, that's the bright side," he replied, his good mood squashed. He thumbed through the paperwork. "Is there any way you can clear my partner quickly? I need to get access to my funds and I don't even know where I bank. I'm guessing my business partner would know that information."

"I understand that it's hard to accept help, but if you're just patient, we can get this figured out. In the meantime, I'll keep track of expenses if it helps ease your discomfort and you can pay me back."

"With interest," he added, needing something to lessen the uncomfortable feeling that he was freeloading, even though he knew he wasn't. He might not remember jack about his life but he recognized the prick of pride.

"Interest isn't necessary," Jordana said, ready to move on, but Clint wasn't.

"No, I need to do something a little extra to feel better about landing in your lap. I know this can't be a cakewalk for you. I've completely disrupted your life and I need to do something to make up for it." He held Jordana's stare, feeling her push back, but he wasn't going to budge. He tried a different angle, saying with persuasion, "Look, you said yourself, I can afford to be generous. Let me throw a little extra your way. It's the least I can do for everything you've done for me thus far."

"I'm just doing my job," she protested. "It wouldn't be right to accept money from you above what you owe."

"C'mon, be honest, you've been a little extra accommodating," he said, gesturing to his new clothes. "And I sincerely appreciate the effort even if it's not something you do for everyone."

"I don't like the way that sounds," Jordana said with a subtle frown. "I don't need anyone saying that I'm giving you special treatment. It's hard enough to prove that I'm walking a professional line without you throwing money in my purse. It doesn't look right."

"Not to point out the obvious but you already said I'm liquid and I think there might be a huge disparity between my income and yours. I don't feel right putting the burden of my room and board on your shoulders without properly compensating you."

"Why are we arguing about this? Fine, if it puts an end to this conversation, I can donate whatever you give me to charity." She relented with an exasperated exhale. "Can we move on?"

Clint could tell Jordana was at her tipping point. If he pushed any harder, she'd shut down and he didn't want that. Besides, he'd earned the victory, no sense in belaboring the point.

"Yes." He nodded, satisfied and ready to eat. "I'm starved. What's good here?"

Chapter Six

Jordana wasn't accustomed to having another human being rattling around in her house. She struggled with the need to play the hostess at all times—something her mother had never failed to point out was not her strength—but Clint was surprisingly chill about their unorthodox situation.

She'd brought home case files, but as she sank into the sofa, her head still throbbing from the stress of the day, she couldn't bring herself to look at the files just yet.

Clint was in the kitchen making an awful racket. *What is he doing? Remodeling?* She rose to investigate and found Clint wearing a cooking apron her sister Bridgette had bought her as a gag gift (because Jordana hated to cook) and making a huge mess in her usually orderly kitchen.

"What's happening?" she asked, trying to hide her dismay. "Looks like the apocalypse blew through here."

"Yeah, turns out I'm a bit of a messy chef," he agreed with good humor. "But I think I'm doing an okay job on the actual cooking front. I think I know what I'm doing. I mean, I'm kind of going off instinct but it smells pretty good, wouldn't you say?"

It did. "I don't feel the need to vomit if that's what

you're asking," she said, sliding into the barstool at the island. "So what are you whipping up, Gordon Ramsay?"

"Pasta carbonara with bacon and peas tossed with garlic and olive oil." He paused to ask with alarm, "Are you a vegetarian?"

"Nope. All meat for this girl," she answered, countering with, "How do you know *you're* not vegetarian?"

"Well, the bacon smells pretty damn good so I'd say if I were vegetarian I'd be repulsed, right?"

"Sounds plausible. What if you're not eating meat for ethical reasons and not for reasons of taste and texture?"

"I'll just have to take the risk," he said. "If it turns out that I am a vegetarian, I'll find a way to repent, but until then, I'm going to eat my weight in this pasta because it smells like carb heaven."

She laughed. "Judging by your physique, I don't think you carb-load very often."

He grinned in acknowledgment. "Then today is my cheat day, I guess, but you know the best part about losing your memory?" He paused for dramatic effect before answering. "You don't remember anything to feel guilty about."

That was an interesting way to look at his situation, she mused. Rising, she pulled a bottle of red wine and uncorked it to pour a glass. She gestured and he nodded. "Guess we'll find out if you like wine, too," she said, raising her glass in toast before taking a much-needed sip. *Ahhh, good stuff.* She watched as he took an exploratory drink. When he nodded in agreement, she smiled.

Was she really sitting in her kitchen drinking wine with Clint Broderick while he made dinner? This smacked of inappropriate. Nothing about this situation was protocol. She didn't know the rules. Everything felt suspect and out of joint. She ought to excuse herself and get back to work but she didn't get the chance.

"I hope you're hungry," Clint said as he dished up her plate and slid it over to her. He took a minute to dish his and then took a seat at the island with her. Clint rose his glass for a toast. "Here's to discovering who the hell I am and why someone wanted to kill me."

She clinked her glass with his, murmuring, "Here, here," and took another fortifying sip. Jordana knew she ought to thank him for dinner and then excuse herself to her bedroom for the night but she didn't want to.

For one, she liked spending time with Clint. For two, it seemed rude to grab her plate and scurry off like a raccoon stealing someone's dinner.

People had to eat. Simple biology. She stabbed the pasta with her fork with a little too much force, startling Clint.

"Whoa there, careful. There's enough for seconds if you're that hungry," he teased.

She blushed, mortified. "Sorry. It's not… Forget it. Smells delicious. Thank you." When in doubt, fall back on good manners. At least her mother would be proud. "Oh, that's really good," she admitted, surprised. "I was a little worried it might be inedible."

Clint chuckled. "Thankfully, it seems I do know my way around a kitchen, which is a relief. I'd hate to think I was completely useless in a real-life sort of way."

"What do you mean useless?" she asked, confused.

"Just the stereotype of a bachelor being all thumbs in the kitchen. Especially a bachelor with means. I like knowing that I can navigate a hot stove without panicking and calling for takeout. Feels good. I don't know, maybe it's stupid but losing my memory has made me insecure about a lot of things. This—" he pointed at his plate "—makes me feel a little less so."

She smiled. "You have nothing to feel insecure about—you are a very good cook." To prove her point, she took another bite and moaned with genuine appreciation. "Don't tell my mom but this right here might have replaced her mashed potatoes and meat loaf as my new favorite dish."

"I've replaced a mother's meat loaf? That feels like high praise. I'll take it. Sorry, Mama Colton."

Jordana broke into a giggle midbite. "Lord help me, but my mom would probably love you."

"What's not to love?" he said with a grin. "I seem pretty damn awesome to me."

Jordana rolled her eyes at his cheesy confidence but the guy had a point. A beat of silence followed as Jordana pushed around her pasta, thinking. Was this his actual personality or was this a consequence of his memory loss? She looked up to find Clint watching her.

"Where'd you go?" he asked as if he could see right through to her personal thoughts.

"How do you know I went anywhere?" she tried teasing. "Maybe your amazing pasta has rendered me speechless."

He shook his head. "You're a terrible liar. Do you know that everything you think and feel flows right across your face? I don't advise you take up poker. You'll lose your shirt."

"And are you a good liar?" she countered.

Clint shrugged. "I haven't a clue. Maybe. Maybe not. I guess I won't know until I regain my memory. Is that what you were wondering?"

"No," she admitted. "I wondered if this is who you really are or if this is just a consequence of the memory loss. People who sustain head injuries…personality changes aren't uncommon."

"I've heard that, as well." He took a moment before adding, "But I can't imagine that I'm so different than I am now. I think some things are just part of who you are."

"Yeah, but you don't even know what that means for you."

"It's hard to describe but I can tell when something feels off. It's like trying to put on a shoe that doesn't quite fit—everything feels wrong."

"But how could you possibly know?" she insisted. "You literally have no clue who you are or who you *were*. You don't know why you were coming to see me or what information had been so important that you'd make the trip."

"All I can do is give you an example," he said, moving to face her. "When you first offered up your place, my first instinct was to say no. Even though I had no idea where I was going to stay or how I was going to manage, I didn't want to put you in a bad position. That's an inherent value that I think is part of your long-term imprinting, which wasn't affected by the head injury."

Jordana was surprised by how relieved that logic made her feel. "I suppose that makes sense," she said, breaking into another smile. "I'm sorry you haven't regained your memory yet. I know it must be aggravating."

"It's no picnic but…having you around makes it easier to bear."

His admission created havoc in her belly that had nothing to do with the fact that she was mildly sensitive to gluten.

On that note, Jordana knew she ought to gracefully excuse herself but she remained rooted to her stool, loath to leave, wanting to stay.

Yeah, this was definitely a problem, but at the moment…she didn't really care.

CLINT KNEW HE shouldn't have dropped that truth bomb but there was something about Jordana that made him want to be honest and raw with her. He found her blunt pragmatism invigorating, and her badass sensibilities turned him on.

Yeah, as in completely aroused when she was around, but he was trying to keep himself in check. She'd been pretty clear: nothing romantic was offered or appreciated.

He wasn't going to ruin her trust in him but that didn't mean he wasn't fantasizing about her lips on his behind closed doors.

Keep things on solid ground.

"So, tell me what you can about the Crane case—that's the one you were investigating, right? The one with my relative?"

She seemed relieved to switch gears. Detective Colton was back in the room. "Well, it's an active investigation so I can't share too many details. I can tell you what I initially told you when we spoke on the phone."

"It's all new to me so go for it," he said, winking. "Every time is like the first time right now."

Jordana chuckled but quickly sobered, saying, "It feels disrespectful to joke about the circumstances. I mean, Fenton Crane was your relative."

"Yeah, but even if I did remember him, from what you told me, we weren't very close. I mean, it sounds like I never really knew the guy. Don't get me wrong, it's terrible that he ended up in a wall—that sounds like a bad way to die for anyone—but I don't feel any grief or loss."

Jordana accepted his explanation. "Yes, it seems Mr. Crane was an uncle but that in itself is really sad." She leaned against her elbow to regard him with curiosity. "What's it like to be such a lone wolf? I can't imagine not having brothers and sisters or extended family all around me. Actually, it might be nice at first but after a while… I would imagine that it would get lonely."

His childhood had been lonely. His parents, decent folk, if not a little absent, had figured out early on that having a clutch of kids wasn't in their wheelhouse. It was probably a blessing that he'd grown up an only child. He didn't like playing the lonely kid card, though. "It was fine. Being an only child gave me certain advantages. I never had to share my toys," he said with a playful smile.

"How many siblings do you have?"

"Ready yourself."

His brow arched. "Go on."

"I am one of six Colton kids," she admitted. "And there's a set of triplets in that number."

"Triplets? Holy crap. What a handful for your parents that must've been."

"Yeah, I think it made my mom neurotic. My dad was a workaholic so he wasn't around much for the child-rearing part. I can't remember my dad ever changing a diaper. Not his generation, I guess. My mom shouldered the load. It made me want to never have kids, that's for sure."

"Seriously?"

"Yeah, maybe. Well, maybe that's too harsh. I'm just

not cut out for that life. I prefer chasing criminals to toddlers."

He laughed. "Is it sexist that I assumed all women at some point want to get married and have kids?"

"It is and you know it," she said, calling him out. "I can tell by the way that dimple pops out on your right cheek that you're full of shit and you know that, too."

He laughed. "Okay, guilty. I guess sometimes I'm a sexist asshole," he confessed, shrugging his shoulders with mock apology.

"Well, you had to have some kind of flaw," she said, rising as she gathered their plates. "Because a man who can cook like this and looks like you…is some woman's dream."

Some woman? But not yours? Ah, Jordana, you kill me.

But he liked it.

Chapter Seven

Jordana returned to the house at lunch with good news. She found Clint reading the local newspaper with an expression of amusement. "There's a section in the local paper called 'Cop's Corner' that lists select calls to Dispatch. Listen to this one—'11:25 p.m. Report of petty theft on Georgia Lane. Reporting party saw neighbor take lawn ornament.' This is hilarious! Is this for real? Or is this someone's column full of made-up stuff?"

She sighed. "It's real. Some people are very invested in what goes around. A lot of nosy neighbors calling in their grievances, honestly."

"Oh! Here's another one—'2:30 p.m. Report of suspicious circumstances on Mockingbird Lane. Reporting party wants to report an unknown person parking in front of his house. Wants officer to tow unknown vehicle.'" Clint looked to Jordana with eyes brimming with laughter. "This is what constitutes crime around here?"

"Aside from the two bodies that were found walled up in an old building owned by my family? Yeah, it's pretty quiet around here."

Clint sobered. "Ah, right. Something tells me that discovery wasn't printed in Cop's Corner."

"No, we asked the editor if she would respectfully keep that entry in the dispatch log, out of the media."

"Only in a small town would that work," he said. "If you tried that in Chicago, you'd get laughed out of town."

"Privileges and perks," Jordana said, adding, "And I know exactly what that Mockingbird Lane call was about. You'll find this funny. So there's this old man who thinks he owns the street in front of his house. He calls every time someone parks there. We've tried explaining that the street is owned by the city and anyone can park there but he's stubbornly refused to listen. So we get a call each time. It's a pain in the ass. He needs a friggin' hobby. We actually draw straws to determine whose turn it is to talk to old man Bryce."

"That's his name? Bryce?"

"Yep. Bryce Riggens. You don't need a neighborhood watch with old man Bryce peeking through his blinds at all times." She chuckled. "Not sure how many people will show up to his funeral when he finally goes. He's pissed off quite a few people."

"Sounds like an unhappy man," Clint said. "Ah, well, too late to change that leopard's spots. So, what was your good news?"

Jordana smiled, happy to share something positive. "Seems you did have someone waiting and worrying at home—your assistant. Reese tracked down some names and numbers and came across your personal secretary, Jeana—does that ring a bell? Jeana Erickson?"

His brow furrowed as he searched his memory. "It sounds vaguely familiar, but when I push harder for details, the information slips away," he said, his tone laced with frustration. "So, did she realize I was missing? Why didn't she file a missing-persons report?"

"She wanted to but, according to her, she was afraid you might not approve, especially if it turned out to be nothing. Apparently, you don't like untoward attention."

Clint digested that information before saying, "Well, that makes sense. I own a big company. I probably have investors, and investors need to feel safe and secure in order to keep the flow of money going. I think she did the right thing not filing. Besides, I'm clearly not missing, just my memory is."

"That's circular logic but okay," she said derisively. "Anyway, I have her contact information for you." Jordana handed Clint the paper in her hand. "Feel free to contact her. You can share what happened to you, but if you could keep details to a minimum, that would be helpful."

"Right," he agreed, staring at the name and number on the sheet. "It's weird to stare at something you should know but have no recollection of its importance. I feel bad for my assistant."

"A suggestion if you wouldn't mind," she said, waiting for his nod to continue. "I wouldn't mention the amnesia. I don't know anything about your business but knowing the boss has lost his memory might affect your company. I'd just keep that intel on a need-to-know basis until you recover."

"Solid advice," he said. "Makes sense. Thanks."

Jordana nodded and headed for the kitchen to find a deli sandwich on sourdough waiting for her. "What is this?" she asked.

"Unless that's a trick question, it's clearly a sandwich," he answered, joining her. "I've got nothing but time on my hands when you're at the station and I like to tinker in the kitchen. It's the only thing that makes me feel a little normal."

"But you shouldn't feel you have to make me dinner or lunch every time I turn around," she said, biting her lip. "Although that looks pretty good and I'm starved.

I was going to pop a burrito in the microwave but now that doesn't seem very appealing."

"Please, eat." He gestured to the barstool. "It's the least I can do to help out, okay?"

She understood the need to feel useful but she was wary of the tickle in her stomach when he did things like this. It was hard to keep lines drawn when they kept inching closer and closer past the point of no return.

And what exactly did that look like?

Well, if it looked like the dream she had last night, then it looked like two naked people twisted around each other like there was no tomorrow.

Her breath hitched in her throat at the memory. *That does it, no more chocolate before bed.* She slid onto the barstool and pulled the cellophane free. "How do you manage to make a roast beef sandwich look like art? Are you sure you're a tech guy?"

He chuckled. "Well, maybe I made my money in tech but secretly yearned to be the next culinary sensation."

Jordana smiled with amusement before taking a bite. She nodded with appreciation, "Okay, yeah, this is pretty good, damn it," she said around her bite. "If you keep this up, I might not want you to ever get your memory back."

Clint laughed at her joke but a part of her—the part she kept under lock and key—realized she was a little serious.

She liked having Clint around.

More than she wanted to admit.

HE LIKED FEEDING JORDANA. There was something primal and caveman-ish about his enjoyment of "providing sustenance" to the woman he found attractive, but he kept his feelings in check with a simple reminder:

she'd stated her boundaries and they excluded anything romantic.

So, he'd have to satisfy his growing feelings by stuffing her face as often as possible.

And he wasn't lying when he said it made him feel useful. He might not remember his life but he knew that he didn't like being idle.

"Any movement on the case?" he asked, biting into his own sandwich.

"No, not really. It's a challenge when the victim doesn't remember anything," she answered with a teasing smile that tested his ability to keep his lips to himself. "We've got some feelers out, to see if anyone saw anything on Range Road where you were found, but these things take time. People have a tendency to keep to themselves, especially when dealing with something like this."

"What happened to the small-town stereotype of neighbors helping neighbors?" he asked.

"If you were local, that stereotype would apply, but there's nothing more cliquish than a small town," she said.

"That's discouraging," he admitted. "What are the odds you'll be able to catch who did this?"

She winced a little. "Not very good."

He accepted her answer, appreciating her honesty. Now it was his turn to be forthright. "Can I be frank with you?" At her nod, he continued. "I'm not really expecting anyone to come forward with information, which means at some point I'm going to have to admit that my case might go unsolved and I have to get back to my life in Chicago."

"That's a healthy expectation but I'm not ready to give up just yet. Someone might still come forward."

He wanted her to want him to stay for reasons that had nothing to do with the case. *Ugh. Pathetic, much?* Was he a stage-four clinger in his normal life? Was that why he didn't have a wife or a girlfriend? The paranoia was hard to shut down when you knew next to nothing about yourself.

"I appreciate the effort," he said, switching focus. "Maybe if you told me more about Fenton Crane, it might help jog my memory."

"What we do know about Fenton isn't all that flattering. Are you sure you want to know that kind of detail about your family member?"

He assured her with a smile he could take it. "I didn't know the guy, remember? Just because we shared DNA didn't mean he was coming over for Thanksgiving dinner. Go ahead, hit me."

"Okay, from what we know, Fenton was a bit of a sleaze. Definitely no moral boundaries. He was motivated entirely by money. He'd take any job for the right amount of cash."

"Just playing devil's advocate here, aren't we all motivated by money?"

"Fenton was a private investigator who set the bar pretty low if the money was good enough," Jordana said.

"Yeah, but the PI business…not exactly a cash cow. Sometimes you gotta do what you gotta do to survive."

She cast a wary look his way. "You sound pretty defensive for a guy who claims he didn't know the victim."

He held his hands up, laughing. "I swear, I didn't know him. I'm just saying, passing judgment on the poor guy for trying to make a living seems a little harsh."

"Some of us have higher moral and ethical standards, I guess," she said a bit stiffly.

Was this their first disagreement? Was he weird for enjoying that flash of spirit in her eyes? The thing about Jordana that he was starting to realize was that she kept a lot under lock and key. He sensed a passionate woman hiding behind that buckled-down exterior.

It wasn't his place to try and jimmy that lock but couldn't fault a man for trying, right?

"Sorry, sorry, didn't mean to offend you," he promised. "Just trying to offer perspective."

Jordana's expression lost some of the tension but he could tell the energy between them had changed. "I appreciate your help," she said, rising to clear her spot. "And lunch was great but I have to get back to the station."

He didn't want to leave things ruffled between them. Clint reached out to gently grasp her hand. "I shouldn't have stepped on your toes. It's your investigation and I don't know what I'm doing so take my opinion with a grain of salt."

Her smile seemed strained around the edges as she slowly eased her hand free. "It's fine. You did nothing wrong. Maybe talking to your assistant will jog some memory loose. I'll see you tonight."

And then she was out the door.

Maybe he shouldn't have pressed those buttons. He didn't want to ruin the trust they were building but something inside him urged him to push a little.

Was he a jerk in his pre-memory-loss life? According to Jordana, he'd built a large, successful company. Success came at a cost. Sometimes you had to be aggressive. Maybe that's why someone had tried to kill him. Maybe he'd pushed the wrong person too far.

Not a far-fetched theory. People have turned violent

for lesser reasons. But he was grabbing blindly at anything in the dark and it didn't feel good.

He grabbed the paper. Time to see if a voice from his past triggered some recovery.

Chapter Eight

Jordana liked to think of herself as calm and rational, definitely not prone to theatrics or melodrama. As the second oldest in a family of six, there simply wasn't room for a personality that sucked all the oxygen out of the room.

But there was something about Clint that made her feel irrational. It definitely made her want to act in a way that was out of character.

When he grasped her hand, she nearly froze. Her heartbeat practically shattered her rib cage. His hand, smooth and warm yet big and commanding, felt perfect against her skin. It was all she could do to calmly and reasonably withdraw without looking like a crazy person.

Her knee-jerk reaction was to yank her hand free as if scalded. But not because his touch repulsed her. No, quite the opposite.

You need to encourage him to return to Chicago, her inside voice reasoned.

That was the last thing she wanted. She liked having him around.

Aside from his awesome kitchen skills, she liked coming home knowing he was there. The smile that found her lips the minute she pulled into the driveway was hard to smother.

You're losing objectivity, that damned voice chided her, *time for him to go.*

All good advice, and yet, she kept finding new justifications to keep him there.

But not every justification was personal, she wanted to protest. She currently had two unsolved crimes on her desk: the warehouse murders and Clint's attack. What if they were related? It was foolhardy to send him packing because she was harboring some misplaced attraction that would surely fade with a little distance.

All she needed to do was to stay the course, keep her head on straight, avoid doing anything that would blur the lines and everything would work out.

She didn't dare confess her concerns to Reese. He'd tell her to pull the plug, *pronto*, on their living situation because he hadn't been a fan from the start.

Jordana hated being wrong and Reese loved being right.

That's what we call an impasse.

She'd have to buckle down and figure things out on her own.

When in doubt, focus on work.

Jordana strode into the station, heading for her desk, when the brand-new captain pulled her into his office. After her previous boss left the position, longtime lawman Michael Placer was put in charge.

Captain Placer, a man with a stern Wilford Brimley look about him, left his officers to their jobs and rarely micromanaged, but she could tell by his expression he'd heard that Clint was living in her spare bedroom.

Damn that small-town gossip.

"What can I do for you, Captain?" she asked, standing at attention, her naval training demanding nothing less when speaking to a commander.

"At ease, Detective," he said, going straight to the point. "Is that amnesia guy, Clint Broderick, living in your house?"

No sense in lying. "Yes, sir. I thought it prudent to keep him close given the circumstances of his assault."

"Your house is not a certified safe house," Placer reminded her. "If you've located his people, turn him loose. The department can't afford the liability of you harboring him under your roof."

"The department didn't assume any liability. I took him in under my own recognizance."

"Did you run that by me?" he returned pointedly.

"No, sir."

"Right, because you knew the answer would be no."

"He didn't know anyone or have access to any resources. It seemed…cruel to toss him onto the street."

Placer waved away her explanation. "Be that as it may, it wasn't your job to house him. You don't know anything about the man. It was foolish and reckless on your part, and frankly, I find that surprising coming from you. You're not usually this foolhardy. Do I need to worry about you, Detective?"

"Of course not," she answered with a clip to her tone. "As it turns out, Broderick is a respected businessman in Chicago. We only just discovered his contact information, which I gave to him today. I respectfully ask for a little leniency in this regard. It should only take a few more days before he can safely return to Chicago."

That seemed to soften the captain's hard line. "A few days?" he repeated.

"Yes, sir," she answered, assuring him, "I understand

your concerns. I promise he's been a perfect gentleman and a polite houseguest."

"That's not the issue. I'm concerned that you made the offer in the first place."

"Sometimes you have to listen to your gut," she said, refusing to allow herself to be second-guessed. "Besides, his case is still unsolved. Someone tried to kill him. I'm still the detective on his case. I thought it best to keep Broderick close for his own safety."

"We're not the FBI, Colton. We're a small-town police force with enough resources to keep the peace, but we're not equipped to take on cases that require that level of protection for the witnesses. Look, I admire your heart. It's one of your best qualities, but I can't have you set a precedent of bringing home victims to lodge at Chez Colton. It's just not sustainable or smart. Understand?"

"Of course," she answered, but she felt the captain was making a bigger deal out of her decision than it warranted. It wasn't as if she were opening her doors to every person in Braxville with a sad story.

"So we're clear? Broderick goes home ASAP?"

"Unless I have a break in the case, yes," she replied.

"Detective," Placer warned, irritated by her stubbornness. "I'm not playing around here."

"Understood."

He sighed as if knowing she was going to do what she felt best, no matter what he said. "I can tell by that look in your eye that you're gonna do what you damn well please. Look, the only reason I'm not putting Broderick on a plane right now is that your gut is usually right, but I don't like this, not one bit."

"I feel a certain level of responsibility for what happened to Broderick. He came to Braxville to tell me something about the Crane case. He got whacked and left for dead because of me. Letting him crash in my spare bedroom, for the time being, was the least I could do. As it turned out, it was an acceptable risk."

"Lucky for you he didn't turn out to be a serial killer."

"That would've worked out badly for him if he were."

Placer's gruff expression broke around a grudging smile. "Can't argue with you there." He leaned back in his chair, his girth causing the chair to groan. "Okay, you've got your few days to put the pieces together, but after that, I'm pulling rank and putting Broderick on a plane back to his people."

"That's fair," she conceded. "Was there anything else?"

"No, one shitshow a day is my limit. Keep me in the loop if anything pops up on either case. I've got too many eyes on our department and it's giving me indigestion."

She smiled. "Or it could be the pastrami on rye that your wife has told me you shouldn't be eating."

"And I'll tell you what I tell her, 'Don't waste your breath. Some things ain't worth living without.'" With that, he shooed Jordana out of his office.

When she sat down at her desk, she narrowed her gaze at Reese and mouthed the words, *Big mouth.*

Reese just grinned without so much as a mouthed *Sorry* back because she knew he wasn't, and he wasn't going to pretend otherwise. Okay, she kinda liked that about Reese but not when it backfired on her.

She only had a few days to produce some kind of results.

Nothing like an impossible goal to galvanize one's motivation, right?

CLINT STARED AT the paper with the phone number. He'd spent the last fifteen minutes vacillating on whether or not to place the call.

Sure, it seemed an easy decision—make the call, possibly trigger a memory, maybe even go home.

But what was waiting for him back in Chicago? Who was he? Did people like him? Was he a jerk boss who everyone secretly hated and talked about behind his back? The loss of his memory wasn't a cakewalk but it certainly freed him up to be whomever he chose without the burden of the past.

He was being a baby and delaying the inevitable. He couldn't play house with Jordana forever. At some point he had to face the music back in Chicago.

No matter the tune playing. With a heavy sigh, he picked up the phone and dialed. Within the first ring, a female voice answered.

"This is Jeana Erickson, may I ask who's calling?"

Well, that was the name Jordana had given him. He supposed he was on the right track. He cleared his throat and threw his cards out there. "Hi, Jeana, this is…uh, Clint Broderick. I heard you might be looking for me."

The sharp intake of breath on the other end wasn't surprising. "Mr. Broderick! Where have you been? When you didn't answer your phone for several days I became worried. Are you okay?"

He waited a beat for recognition to hit him like a thunderbolt, and while there was something about the timbre of her voice that sounded familiar, he couldn't picture her face or recall any memories.

Clint smothered his disappointment by assuring the woman he was fine. "I'm sorry, Jeana, I didn't mean to worry you. I had some business here in Kansas and then lost my wallet and cell. I've had a bear of a time trying to sort the details in this town but I can't leave just yet. I still have some unfinished business to take care of."

"Oh, heavens! Do you need me to call and cancel your bank cards?"

"Yes, that would be great. Thank you. Also, I can't get access to my accounts right now. Can you wire me some cash?"

"Right away. Just tell me where to send it."

Clint gave Jeana the information for the Western Union in town with the amount. When she didn't seem to blink an eye, it seemed to support Jordana's intel that he wasn't hurting.

"Is there anything else you need?" Jeana asked. "How long will you be staying in Braxville? Should I cancel your upcoming meetings?"

He must've told his assistant where he was going, but had he told her why? "Yeah, go ahead and cancel. I'm going to be here for a few more days."

"Yes, sir. Oh, Mr. Locke has been asking for you. Should I let him know that you're still in Braxville?"

His business partner. Jordana hadn't cleared Locke of being a suspect. He hated to be so paranoid but losing his memory had made him second-guess everything. "No, I'll give him a call later, tell him myself," he told her. "Hey, quick question, what did I tell you about why I was going to Braxville?"

The confusion at his question was evident in her voice as she answered, "I don't recall you saying why. What I remember you saying was that you had private business to deal with and that you'd be gone a day or so. Did I miss something?"

Clint let the poor woman off the hook. She sounded like she ate antacids for breakfast. "No, no, you're fine. I was just wondering. You're good."

Her relief was evident. "Thank you, sir. I'll get that wire transfer to you immediately and take care of your bank cards. Is this a good number for further contact?"

"No, I'll get in touch after I buy a new replacement phone."

"All right," Jeana said. "I'm so happy you're safe. Everyone will be so relieved."

"Thank you, Jeana. You're a big help."

"Oh! Gosh, yes, of course, I'm on top of things on this end." Then the flustered woman clicked off. Clint replaced the phone on the receiver, silently amused that Jordana still had a landline and wondered if Jeana's reaction was proof that he was seen as a real jerk back at the office.

She'd been practically tripping on herself to please him. If that were the case, maybe the list of people who wanted him dead was deeper than he thought.

And that wasn't a nice feeling at all.

Did he have more in common with his dead relative, Fenton Crane, than he cared to admit?

He had to find out.

Chapter Nine

Jordana planned to spend her day off working on background files for both cases but Clint had other plans.

"We need to get out of this town for the day," he announced, causing her to look up from her notes with a quizzical expression. "Now that I've rented a car for the time being and I have some cash in my pocket, I say you let me treat you to a distraction."

"You really shouldn't draw so much attention to yourself," she warned, worried that whoever had been after him still hadn't left town. She had a hard time believing someone local had perpetrated the crime but she remained open to the possibility.

"What? I needed a car to get around."

"Yes, but did you need to rent something so… flashy?"

"A convertible Mustang was the only vehicle they had in an upgraded coupe," he apologized. "I'm not trying to be flashy. It was either the Mustang or some kind of boxcar that looked like it wouldn't withstand a stiff wind. At least the Mustang is made from steel."

She supposed she could understand that explanation. The rental agency in town was notoriously small without much of a selection. "You're lucky you didn't end up with a Buick LeSabre. That's Bonnie's favorite car in her fleet, which no one wants to ever rent but she won't replace it."

"Do they even make LeSabres anymore?"

"I don't think so." She shook her head.

He clapped his hands, rubbing them together, excited to get back on topic. "Back to my original suggestion. Let's distract ourselves from the noise and do something fun."

She frowned. "A distraction is the last thing I need. I need to focus," she said, pointing at the piles of paperwork all around her. "I need to double down if I'm going to find answers."

He immediately countered with, "Actually, you'll be *more* productive if you give your mind a break to recharge. Right now you're spinning in mud and not getting anywhere."

"How would you know this?" she asked dryly. "You can't even remember if you like pineapple on your pizza much less what makes someone more productive."

He paused for a minute to give her statement some thought, then decided definitively, "I do not like pineapple on pizza. Just thinking about it gives me hives. Seems unnatural. And, Miss Negative Nelly, I actually just read about a study conducted by the University of Illinois that concluded taking breaks helps the brain to reboot and aids in the formation in critical problem-solving."

She regarded him with a curious frown. "Are you pulling my leg?"

"Not even a little bit. So, it's science. Time to take a break."

The warning from the captain rang in her head, but if Clint was right and taking a break actually helped her with the case, it seemed warranted.

A break would be great, though. Her eyesight was swimming from all the paperwork she'd been wading through with little to show for it.

"Let's say I was open to the idea in theory—what did you have in mind?"

"I did a little digging around and there's an indoor climbing place in Wichita that looks right up your alley."

"Like, rock climbing?" she asked.

He nodded with a grin.

"What if I'm afraid of heights?"

"Are you?"

"No, but what if I was?"

"Then I guess I'd say, time to conquer your fears," he answered, his grin widening.

Jordana bit her lip to keep from smiling. She knew all about the place he was suggesting. She actually went there when she could spare the time away. Since the warehouse bodies were found, it'd been a while since she could sneak away.

Was she impressed that Clint had accurately guessed what she'd find relaxing and enjoyable on her day off?

Okay, yes, a wee bit.

Was she going to take him up on his offer?

Not sure.

"I probably shouldn't," she hedged, still mulling the idea in her head. "I'm not sure it's a good idea to be out socially together."

Clint balked. "Am I not good enough for you, Detective?" he asked with mock offense. She couldn't stop the laugh that followed. Jordana shook her head and rolled her eyes. His gaze met hers, a twinkle matching the dimple in his cheek. "Look, it's just an offer to climb a fake rock and sweat our asses off, not a marriage proposal. It'll be good for both of us to blow off some steam. I may not remember much but I do recognize the signs of cabin fever and I definitely have it."

Jordana should say no but she wanted to go. A day away from Braxville at her favorite place to hang out and, as Clint put it, "sweat their asses off" seemed like the perfect plan to her.

"Fine," she relented, but not before reminding Clint of the ground rules. "This isn't a date by any stretch of the imagination. We'll pay our own way. I can pitch in for gas. Understood?"

"Buzzkill," he teased, but nodded. "Understood. Like I want you slobbering all over me, anyway. You probably kiss like a Saint Bernard."

She laughed harder at his obvious overkill in that department. Popping from her seat, Jordana grabbed her purse and jacket, saying, "I guess you'll never know."

Clint smiled. "Guess not," he agreed, but there was something about his tone, or maybe it was his expression, that told a different story.

She suppressed a shiver and forced a bright, completely unaffected smile, saying, "I can't wait to critique your driving skills. Not to make you nervous or anything but I'm a harsh critic. Between military and police training, I'm a stickler for the rules of the road."

But Clint just laughed, taking her challenge with a level of confidence she found alluring. "Bring it. I'm impervious to intimidation."

That shiver she was trying ardently to keep under wraps morphed into a full-body warmth that raced from her toes to the top of her head. She recognized trouble when she felt it but it was like trying to fight a food craving when she was starving. Even though she knew she ought to stop, Jordana couldn't fight the urge to reach for the very thing she knew was bad.

Bad for so many reasons.

The man had amnesia, for crying out loud. He couldn't possibly know what was good for him. It didn't matter that his energy matched hers—he wasn't in a position to act on those feelings.

But even if he wasn't working on two instead of four cylinders, the fact didn't change that she was investigating his case. There simply wasn't any wiggle room for *feelings*.

"Ready?" she asked.

"Woman, I was born ready… I think," Clint answered with a wink.

A CHANGE OF scenery was just what the doctor ordered—a fact hammered home the minute they got out of Braxville. In spite of her promises to the contrary, Jordana was quiet and seemingly relaxed as a passenger. He liked to think it was because she trusted him but it was likely because he hadn't been the only one needing an escape.

"What's it like to grow up in Braxville?" he asked, making conversation during the drive. "Is it stereotypical to think that small-town life is all bake sales and community picnics?"

She chuckled, admitting, "Sometimes. I did go to my share of community barbecues and picnics. Also participated in quite a few bake sales." Jordana smiled in memory. "I've definitely eaten my weight in chocolate chip oatmeal cookies in my day."

"Are you an oatmeal raisin fan?" he asked.

Jordana made a face. "God, no. Throwing a raisin in a cookie is a quick way to ruin a perfectly good cookie."

He laughed. "Okay, so tell me more about being a Braxville native."

"Well, growing up in a large family in a small town is very insulating. It's like you can't breathe without someone asking you about your business. It's bad enough when you have your siblings poking their nose into everything you do, but it's made ten times worse when the neighbor down the street does, too."

"Sounds like hell."

"For a kid who wanted some space, it was, which was why I left and joined the Navy."

"That must've been a culture shock," he said.

Jordana nodded. "At first, yeah, it was overwhelming, but I liked the idea of a new adventure, seeing places I'd never been and meeting people outside of my bubble."

"So you enjoyed your time serving?"

"Mostly, yeah."

"So why'd you leave?"

"Because at the end of the day, I realized I wasn't cut out for a lifetime in the military. I wouldn't say I have a problem with authority but I definitely don't like someone telling me what I can and can't do every single moment of the day."

"Makes sense. Do you miss anything about the service?"

"The structure," she answered wistfully. "I liked that there was order, which was something I never had growing up. No matter how hard my mom tried, a houseful of six kids is going to be chaos at a certain level. I craved structure when I left home. I definitely got that and more from the Navy."

"Why'd you come back to Braxville?" he asked.

"Turns out I missed home," she replied with a small laugh. "And I wanted to go into law enforcement. When an opportunity to join the Braxville Police Department popped up, I took it."

"Are you happy with that decision?"

"Of course," she answered, but there was the faintest hesitation he sensed. Everyone had regrets, even people who said they were blissfully happy. "Sometimes I wish there was more action, but now I've got two cases without easy answers and I'm wondering if I should be careful what I wish for."

"There's a possibility my case is a simple robbery gone wrong," he reminded her. "If it weren't for the knot on my head and the amnesia, you probably wouldn't be spending so much time on trying to find who did it."

"You were assaulted. In a town as tight-knit as Braxville, an assault doesn't go unnoticed. People feel safe here for a reason. I can't just shrug off your case on the assumption that it was probably a failed robbery."

He admired her dedication. There was a lot to admire when it came to Jordana. Damn, he wished he could remember more about his own life. It felt like half a person with his memory gone. "I thought this amnesia thing was something they made up in the movies. I didn't know it happened to real people," he said. "Being on the receiving end, I can tell you, zero stars. I do not recommend."

She laughed. "I can only imagine. I'm sorry your memory hasn't kicked in yet."

"Yeah, me, too. It's disconcerting not being able to tell if I like raisins or not."

"Take from me, raisins are gross. Shriveled up little husks of former grapes…they're not only gross but macabre, too."

At that, he laughed. "Maybe I'll take your word for it."

They arrived at the place and exited the car. Jordana gave him a quick smile before saying, "You passed your driving test. You might not remember much about yourself but you remember how to drive. I consider that a good sign."

He gestured to the massive building. "I guess we'll see how good I am at climbing. If I fall on my face, promise not to laugh?"

"I promise no such thing."

"Harsh."

She winked as she pulled the door open. "Don't fall."

Excellent advice.

Don't fall. He watched as Jordana walked with easy familiarity to the counter, throwing down some cash to enter. She wore tight leggings and tennis shoes and a formfitting top that showed off her trim figure. He didn't know what he liked as far as women went but he liked what he saw in Jordana. Why was she single? Were all the men in Braxville dumb and blind? A lesser man might be intimidated by Jordana.

He found her breathtaking.

She turned to him, waving him over. "C'mon, pay up! I'm about to show you how it's done."

Clint grinned. "I love a woman with balls bigger than mine," he quipped, throwing down his own cash. "But don't worry, honey, I'll go easy on you."

"Challenge accepted, big man," she taunted with a darling smile that made him want to throw her over his shoulder and claim her as his. Damn, it was a good thing he was about to get his sweat on because he had way too much testosterone pickling his brain.

As he watched her attack the hardest climbing wall in

the place, lithe muscles working, determination etched on her expression, that reminder came floating back.

Don't fall for her.

What if it was too late?

Chapter Ten

Jordana was covered in sweat, muscles loose and worked out, her hair a damp mess—and she couldn't stop smiling.

For one, she smoked Clint on the climbing wall, and two, a shirtless Clint was an image she'd savor for months to come.

"Not bad," she told him, throwing him a bone as she wiped herself down with a small towel. "I think you can respectfully hold your head up in mixed company."

"You're too kind. You shimmied up that rock wall like you were a monkey in a past life. I was just trying to keep up so I didn't lose my man card."

She laughed, tossing him a clean towel. "Your man card is safe," Jordana assured him, her gaze lingering a little too long on the firm muscle cording his stomach. A whole lot of man was hiding beneath those buttoned-down shirts. Jordana forced herself to look away as he finished. Once he'd thrown the used towel in the bin, they checked out, the mild fall air caressing their faces, practically inviting them to take a picnic at a park.

What would people say if they saw them? That niggling voice of doubt was less strident away from Braxville but it was still there.

"You're an amazing woman, you know that?" Clint

said, that grin sending tendrils of need and want curling through her body. He was so damn nice to look at. She couldn't remember the last time she felt drawn to another person like she was drawn toward Clint and she didn't know how to handle herself.

"You're no slouch yourself," she murmured, glancing up at him through her lashes. She never flirted but she was doing it now. *Kiss me, damn it, before I come to my senses and shut you down!* The energy around them crackled with tension. She could almost hear their heartbeats beating as one.

"Am I off base or…" He looked to Jordana, his gaze fastening on hers with the same energy. When Jordana gave him the green light with a small, breathless nod, he looked like he'd won the lottery. He reached, pulling her into the cove of his arms, saying, "Thank God. I've wanted to kiss you for longer than I should admit but, you know, *boundaries*."

"Shut up and kiss me," Jordana said, lifting her mouth to meet his. His lips, soft and firm, brushed across hers, setting her soul on fire. She willfully ignored that anyone could see them, taking the chance that the odds were slim that someone from Braxville might recognize her. His tongue swept her mouth and she rose on her tiptoes to deepen the kiss. The sharp musky smell of man rose beneath the notes of his aftershave, tickling her senses.

He tasted and smelled like a snack she could happily enjoy for the rest of her life.

They broke the kiss but she continued to cling to him, his arms around her feeling like the home she never realized she was missing. "We've really done it now," she warned with a breathless laugh. "I can hear rules breaking all over the place."

"I only care if you do," he said.

She met his gaze and realized with wonder, "I don't really care."

"Good because I know exactly what I want to do with you," he said, slipping her hand in his as they walked briskly to the car. She laughed and eagerly followed where he led.

Climbing into the car, fastening her seat belt, she asked, "And what did you have in mind?"

"The closest hotel."

Her opportunity to cool the heat between them flashed before her eyes but she didn't want to stop. In one breath, she tossed all the good reasons why this was a terrible idea right out the window.

You barely know him.

You're breaking all the rules—yours and the department's.

You shouldn't open a door you can't close.

The gossip hounds will eat you alive!

Oh, yeah, all excellent reasons to pump the brakes but Jordana couldn't imagine a better idea than to end up skin against skin with this man. The heat between them could warm a small country and she couldn't wait to throw more kindling on the fire.

She ignored the shrill little voice at the back of her head and instead played his willing navigator. "There's a small motel off Greenberg Avenue. It's quiet and off the main road. It's also clean and cheap."

"And you know this because…?"

Jordana laughed. "Because a few officers from the department stayed there for an interagency conference. It was easier than driving home each day."

"Works for me," he said, pulling onto the main road, the tension between them humming.

A few minutes later—after a hurried detour to the closest pharmacy for condoms—they were checked into the motel, and before they even reached their door, they were all over each other. Hands, mouths, breath mingling and fingers fumbling for the door. They finally burst through the door. Clint kicked it shut with his foot, tossing the keys to the dresser, and they tumbled to the bed.

Hunger and desire blotted out rational thought as she stripped out of her clothes, watching with rapt anticipation as Clint shed his, as well. She rose on her knees, admiring God's handiwork on the male canvas before her. A light dusting of hair furred his chest, traveling down his belly to pool in a dark but neatly trimmed nest where his erection sprung, hard and ready.

"You might not remember who you are but I like who you are right now," she said, gently cupping the warm, soft flesh of his sac while she nuzzled the spicy length of his manhood. She wanted the taste of him, her mouth hungering for the feel of his length. He groaned as her mouth closed over the soft head, her tongue playing with the slit at the top, tasting the faint saltiness of his excitement. "Mmm, I love the way you taste," she said, thrilling at the feel of his fingers threading through her hair, his breath short.

After a few moments of teasing, taking his length down her throat, he groaned and gently pulled away, his gaze dark and consuming as he stared down at her. "Not so fast, you little devil. Your turn," he said, giving her a gentle push and sending her tumbling backward into a soft cloud of bedding. He opened her legs and stared with hungry appreciation before saying, "Damn, woman, I think I died and went to heaven."

She didn't have time to roll her eyes with a blush because Clint was serious about taking his turn, only he was determined to make her climax. Jordana twisted her hands in the bedding as Clint's tongue worked masterful strokes against her swollen nub, sucking, nipping and pushing her ever closer to that cliff, only to pull back and start over.

Oh, God, had she ever been so thoroughly mastered by a man's mouth? No, never, but Clint was quickly proving he was a man above all others.

Fresh sweat broke out across her skin. A low moan escaped her parted lips. Her hips lifted as he held her against his mouth. She couldn't escape what was building. Her nipples pearled, tight and hard, as she crashed into a climax so hard her toes curled and a cry fell from her mouth as she gasped his name over and over. Everything inside her clenched and released in a rhythmic dance that stole her breath and left her shaking.

Holy hell, what'd just happened? The answer came swift and with stunning clarity as she struggled to catch her breath.

I think I just fell in love.

HEARING JORDANA KEEN her climax was music to his ears. Going on instinct, he followed her cues as he drove her closer to that edge so that when she finally tumbled over, she would lose her ever-loving mind in the fall.

And it was sweet.

She tasted like honey, and he already wanted more. He didn't care about anything but this moment. Clint couldn't say for sure but this felt different than anything he'd ever known. He wanted to consume Jordana, to become one with the delicious woman beneath him until neither knew where one stopped and the other began.

It was the craziest feeling but he also knew he could trust it as genuine.

But now, he needed to be inside her. He climbed her body, pausing to slip a tight, budded nipple in his mouth, sucking and teasing as he'd done to her clit, and then continued on to seal his mouth to hers. She groaned against him, her tongue darting to taste herself on his lips.

The heat between them seared the air. After sheathing himself, he positioned himself at her entrance and slowly pushed deep, groaning as she swallowed him whole. *Oh, God, it felt so good.* He wanted to make her climax again but his eyes were crossing from the pleasure. She clenched herself around him, sending stars whizzing across his vision. "If you keep doing that, I won't last long," he bit out a rueful warning, sweat dotting his hairline. "You feel so damn good, woman."

Jordana giggled, low and throaty, pulling him deeper inside her. "You can make it up to me," she said, nibbling at his neck as his muscles strained.

He kissed her long and deep as he slowly thrust against her, building that heat again. Before long, she was clinging to him, whimpering as he kept hitting a good spot.

And damn, was it good for him, too.

Just a few more minutes, he pleaded with himself, clenching his jaw, as the pleasure ramped up, building to that inevitable moment. *Puppies, kittens, basketball, runny oatmeal*—he tried pulling anything and everything into his mental theater to stall his orgasm but it simply felt too good between her thighs; that wet heat was more than he could ignore and he came hard.

"Jordana," he gasped, thrusting against her like a wild man, losing all semblance of control. He fin-

ished with a gasp and collapsed against her, his member throbbing inside her with residual waves of pleasure. He groaned and rolled off, his heart beating with the speed of a runaway train. "I think I'm about to have a heart attack," he said with an exhausted grin. "But man, but what a way to go."

She laughed, shaking her head. "You know we've really screwed things up by doing this, right?"

"Don't care."

Jordana rolled to her side, propping herself up on her elbow. "Is that so?"

He wasn't lying. "Nope. It was worth it. You're worth it."

She sobered, her eyes like twin seas after a storm. "You say that now but…"

Clint met her gaze. "And I'll keep saying it. Nothing will change my opinion on that score." He sealed his mouth to hers before she could launch a counterargument. Something about her felt right, more true than anything he'd ever known. Given that his life had been turned upside down and he could trust very little, he was going to be greedy about holding on to what felt real. Breaking the kiss, he murmured, "Any questions?" and Jordana shook her head in answer. "Good."

He knew all the arguments against what they'd done—as well as the ethics—but none of that mattered to him. He may have come to Braxville for different reasons but Jordana was his reason to stay.

At least for now.

It seemed his business partner, Locke, had things well in hand back in Chicago, so who was to say that he couldn't take a minivacation with Jordana? He was the boss. He could do as he pleased. And nothing would please him more than spending days in bed with this incredible woman.

"Do you think we could get a restaurant to deliver here?" he asked in all seriousness. "I'm starved."

"This isn't the Ritz," she reminded him with amusement. "But I think there's a vending machine down the hall. You might be able to find some chips and a soda."

"That's not good enough for the fuel we're going to need," he said, bounding from the bed, aware of how she watched him with unabashed hunger. "We can order a pizza, then."

"And just what exactly do you plan to do that you need to carb-load?" she asked with a provocative slow roll to her belly, glancing at him with playful seduction.

That beautiful, heart-shaped ass with its soft, rounded cheeks begged for his hands, lips and tongue, and he had to swallow first before he could rejoin her with a promise. "Oh, woman, the things I'm going to do to you might be illegal in some states."

He was suddenly thankful he'd grabbed the big pack of condoms because damn if he wasn't ready to go again right now.

"Ah, hell, food can wait."

And suddenly he wasn't thinking about his stomach anymore.

Chapter Eleven

"You know we can't stay holed up in this motel forever," Jordana said around a hot bite of take-out pizza. "At some point we have to go back to Braxville, or at least I do. My boss might start to question if I've been kidnapped if I don't clock in within a few days."

Clint responded with a regretful sigh. "I know but let's enjoy our illicit moment a little while longer."

Jordana and Clint had spent the night and following day hiding from the world, having sex, showering, ordering takeout and starting all over again, but Jordana knew reality wasn't too far behind.

"I don't want this to end," he said.

"I don't, either, but I can't have people questioning my integrity if they find out we're sleeping together. I just want you to know, I've never done anything like this before," she said, worried Clint might think this was a normal thing for her. "I'm straight as an arrow, most days. I don't even claim an extra shirt on my uniform allowance like most people."

He chuckled, "Calm down, Dudley Do-Right," he said, putting her at ease "I know you're not that kind of person. We have insane chemistry and that's hard to fight."

"Insane is right," she agreed with a worried frown.

"But what does that mean? I mean, what's happening right now?"

"Do we have to define it?"

"Yeah, I think we do." She wasn't the kind of woman who did things spontaneously or rashly, and the fact that she'd fallen into bed with the victim in an assault case she was investigating left her feeling off-center. "I'm not saying I want you to put a ring on my finger but… I don't know, this is outside of my comfort zone."

"I like you," Clint said. "I want to keep seeing you. To me, it's that simple."

"There's nothing simple about that at all," she disagreed. "If my captain finds out about this, I could get kicked off both cases. I shouldn't have done this. I don't know what I was thinking."

"Do you want to keep seeing me?" he asked.

"Of course I do, but—" Clint cut short her tailspin by pulling her to him and kissing her quiet. Jordana stilled, surprised at how easily his touch calmed her overactive brain.

"It's going to be fine," he promised, and when he said it, she believed him. "The thing about not growing up in a small town? You don't worry too much about the opinions of strangers."

Jordana wished she had that freedom. "If only it were that easy." She exhaled a short breath, refocusing. "We have to keep this on the down-low. You might have the freedom of not caring about what people are saying but I have to care. My reputation is on the line. You understand that, right?"

Clint sobered. "Of course I do. I will keep my hands to myself when we're not in private," he said, but added as he pulled her into his lap, "but when we're not in the public eye, that's a different story."

She melted beneath his touch. "I'm good with that compromise."

"Excellent," he said, brushing his lips against hers, "because I plan to spend as much time as possible in your naked company. Have I mentioned you have the most amazing body?"

She blushed. "You have. Several times."

"Well, it bears repeating. Over and over and over again."

Jordana laughed. "You're too much of a charmer to be completely single. Are you sure you don't have someone waiting for you back in Chicago?"

"Not that I'm aware. I think Jeana would've mentioned something, like, 'Oh, Tina has been calling nonstop,' or 'Do you want me to let Rhonda know you'll call her soon?' but she never said anything similar, which leads me to believe I'm footloose and fancy-free."

Jordana was skeptical. "That's not a convincing argument. She might just be respecting your privacy."

"I could just ask Jeana if I'm seeing anyone. As my assistant, she'd probably know."

"That would be a really weird question to ask, don't you think?"

Clint shrugged. "If it eases your concern, I'll do it."

"No, I'm fine. I don't want you to do anything that will tip off your people that you've lost your memory. Something like that could affect confidence."

He tightened his embrace, pleased. "I love that you care. You're really sweet."

"I'm not actually," Jordana confessed with a chagrined expression. "*Sweet* is definitely not a word used to describe me."

"I disagree," he said, his voice dropping to a husky murmur.

She blushed again, saying, "That's not what I meant."

Clint chuckled, the sound a low rumble against her body. "When you blush, it shows off the tiny smattering of freckles dancing across the bridge of your nose."

Jordana rubbed her nose with a gasp. "I do not have freckles."

"You do and I love them." He grinned. "You also snore a little."

Now she was truly mortified but she didn't have time to dwell on it because Clint was determined to make good on his promise of keeping her occupied when they were alone.

Her head fell back on a groan as he nuzzled her neck and nipped at the tender skin. Goose bumps rioted along her forearms and her nipples stood at attention, ready for his mouth.

To which he obliged.

Oh, good God, did he oblige.

AS MUCH AS Clint wanted to hole up in that tiny motel room, they had to check out and return to the real world—a world that left him still wondering who had knocked his lights out.

After another round of naked fun, a shower and a quick bite to eat on the road, they headed back to Braxville. Each mile closer to town brought a change in Jordana. Away from the stress and expectation, Jordana was a different person. She laughed more easily and the tension coiling her in knots disappeared.

He hated that he felt half a person with the loss of

his memory. Clint liked to pretend that he was taking the situation in stride but, deep down, a niggling sense that he really needed to return to Chicago was becoming more insistent.

The doc had suggested memory exercises, which he wasn't sure was helping. The truth of the matter was, the best way to trigger his memory was to return to the place where he'd made memories. Braxville was an empty slate.

But he didn't want to leave Jordana. She created a light inside him that felt new and intoxicating, brightening all the dark spots that he hadn't known were there.

"I'm going to leave a five-star review on Yelp for our little motel," Clint said, winking at Jordana.

She laughed. "Make sure you use an assumed name. I don't need people connecting the dots."

"You are thorough," he said with an appreciative whistle. "Have you considered a career in the FBI?"

"I did," she replied with a cheeky grin. "I decided to stay local but I like to keep my options open."

"I love a dangerous woman," he quipped.

"That's what they all say until she's better with a gun than he is."

He didn't know about other men but that excited him. "Maybe you've been hanging around the wrong men."

"Maybe so," she agreed.

They got back to Braxville by evening and Jordana was already in work mode, as if feeling guilty for taking a few days off. He sensed he ought to keep his thoughts to himself at the moment because Jordana had a wall up around her in spite of everything they'd shared.

Something about that drive felt familiar to him. Maybe in his previous life he'd been a workaholic, too.

While Jordana buried herself in work files, Clint found a quiet place to call his assistant.

"Hello, Mr. Broderick," came her pert reply even though it was considered after-hours. Maybe he always expected his assistant to work the same hours as he did, no matter how late. That pinched at his conscience a little, but in this instance, he needed to ask a few questions.

"Sorry for the late call," he said.

"No trouble at all," Jeana assured him, which told Clint he probably needed to make some changes in his life for the benefit of his most trusted employee. He'd have to work on that later. For now, he had more pressing issues. "Jeana, I need to trust you with something that no one else knows. Can I trust you?"

He was taking a risk in confiding in Jeana but he had to start trusting someone who knew him from before the assault. If he couldn't trust his assistant, he was in sorry shape.

"Of course, Mr. Broderick," Jeana replied without hesitation. "Is there a problem?"

"Yeah, a pretty big one actually," he admitted, glancing up at the ceiling with a sigh. "Seems I lost my memory."

"Come again?"

"Yeah, you heard me right. I was assaulted when I arrived in Braxville and the damage to my head was enough to knock my memories sidewise. Mostly short-term memory. I can remember stuff about my childhood, but I can't remember much about my adult life, especially within the last year."

"Oh, Mr. Broderick," Jeana gasped with genuine horror. "What can I do? Shall I call your doctor? What do you need? How can I help?"

"That's the thing, I don't really know what I need except that I need someone I can trust to help me through this without alarming anyone within the company. The doc here says it's temporary so I just have to find something to jog my memory back into place."

"Perhaps you should come back to Chicago," Jeana suggested, which wasn't far from what his own counsel had advised, but he didn't want to leave.

"I appreciate the advice and you're probably right but I have things I need to do here for the time being. I need to ask, what's my relationship like with my business partner?"

"Mr. Locke? Well, you seem like close friends. He's been your right-hand man since you started the business. Why do you ask?"

"Just trying to get the lay of the land." He didn't want to admit that Jordana had planted a seed of suspicion in his head because he couldn't remember much of his relationship with Locke to defend him. Now, to the next awkward question. "Uh, okay, so I'm just going to come out and ask, am I currently dating anyone?"

God, that was hard to get out of his mouth. *Please say no.* It was going to get real ugly real fast if it turned out he had someone waiting for him when all he wanted to do was be with Jordana.

But Jeana gave him wonderful news. "No, sir. You were dating a woman named Iris Yearly but you broke it off about three months ago. Since then, you've preferred to bury yourself in work rather than date."

Relief coated his voice as he said, "Thank God." He hastened to clarify, adding, "I just mean, I'm glad no one's sitting at home worried about me."

"Of course, sir."

Another question popped in his head. "Are you always this formal with me? All the 'yes, sir, no, sir' makes me feel like I'm from the IRS or something."

Jeana answered carefully. "Well, you do prefer a certain level of decorum between us but I don't mind, sir. I appreciate your professionalism."

"How long have we been working together?" he asked.

"Going on six years."

"Six years and you still call me 'sir'? Good grief, Jeana, was I an asshole?"

He didn't expect her to be truthful but the answer was evident to his eyes even if his memory was faulty. "Look, can I apologize for the person I was before I got knocked in the head? I sound like a real jerk. No wonder someone was trying to kill me."

"Oh, no, sir. You're very kind and a good boss. I can't imagine who would want to hurt you. I enjoy working for you and most of everyone who knows you seem good with your authority."

He ought to drop it but he was bothered. Maybe the person who tried to kill him was a disgruntled employee? What if he'd been ruthless and cold to the wrong person? Had he brought this on himself?

The only way to find out was to return to Chicago. But he wasn't ready. Not yet.

"I'll be in touch," he told Jeana. "Remember, keep this between me and you. Don't tell Locke, even."

"Of course, sir."

And stop calling me sir.

But really, that was the least of his problems. Going forward, he needed to figure out who he wanted to be and if that was the same person he'd been when someone tried to put out his lights. Hell, who was he kidding? Right now, all he wanted to do was fall asleep with Jordana in his arms and think about all this crap tomorrow.

Good plan.

Chapter Twelve

Jordana walked into her parents' house and found her mother, Lilly, in the kitchen, scrubbing a pot with an agitation she recognized from her childhood.

Lilly Colton had always exorcised her stress through the power of elbow grease—a coping mechanism Jordana had inherited, as well—but seeing as their home had always been spotless in spite of six kids, that said a lot about the level of stress her mother had endured.

And now she was back to scrubbing.

"What's wrong?" Jordana asked, going straight to the point.

Lilly looked up with a warm but strained smile. "Nothing, darling, so good to see you," she answered, presenting her cheek for a kiss, which Jordana dutifully provided. "I just needed to get these pots cleaned before starting dinner. You know I can't cook in a dirty kitchen," she reminded Jordana.

"Mom, by no stretch of the imagination would anyone dare to call your kitchen dirty. I'm pretty sure your kitchen is cleaner than most hospitals."

"Hospitals are dirty places," Lilly said with a scowl. "That's hardly a welcome compliment."

"Sorry." Jordana shook her head, knowing she wasn't going to win. "So, what's new? Aside from Bridgette being here again. Are you two getting under each other's skin yet?"

"I love having Bridgette home," Lilly insisted. "It's been so long since we've had any decent visit with that job of hers."

"Well, being a public health official has its demands on her time," Jordana said, defending her sister, but added, "Don't you think it's interesting that a cancer cluster popped up in Braxville?"

"Oh, whatever." Lilly waved away Jordana's comment. "Can't hardly blow your nose somewhere without someone saying something is going to give you cancer. Can't drink the water, can't eat the vegetables, can't breathe the air…it's exhausting if you think about it. For my own mental health, I've resolved to *stop* thinking about it. If the good Lord sees fit to send me home, that's what happens."

"Mom, I hardly think people getting cancer is God's will. That's pretty macabre, don't you think?"

"Jordana, let's not argue," Lilly said, resuming her scrubbing. "Did you come over to snipe at me or did you come to actually visit?"

A wave of guilt made Jordana soften her tone. She reached for a freshly baked cookie from the display plate. "Of course not, Mom. I wanted to pop in and say hi, see how you're doing. By the looks of the force you're putting on that poor pot, I'd say something is bothering you."

"Nothing is bothering me," Lilly insisted with a slight clip. "Just trying to get this house in order in time for your uncle Shep, is all."

She paused with the cookie midway to her mouth. "Uncle Shep? What do you mean? He's coming home?" Jordana's uncle Shep was an infrequent visitor to the

Colton homestead because he was too busy with his naval career, a path she'd followed, in part because of her admiration for her uncle. "Why didn't you tell me he was coming?" she asked, excited.

"I wasn't sure until yesterday. Your father offered the carriage house, though I don't know why Shep can't find his own place. He has plenty of money seeing as he had no children of his own."

True, Uncle Shep had never married but Jordana had understood because Uncle Shep had been married to the military—happily, one might argue—given he'd risen through the ranks with a stellar reputation.

And Jordana idolized her uncle Shep. "I can't wait to see him," she said with a bright smile. "So I'm guessing he finally retired, then?"

"Yes," Lilly answered, wiping away a small bead of sweat with the back of her hand. Her restless gaze swept the kitchen as if searching for something else to direct her attention but everything gleamed as if on display, a fact which dismayed Lilly. "Yes, retired. And he'll probably be underfoot the whole time, pestering me."

"Pestering you? Mom, Uncle Shep is hilarious and sweet. I doubt he'll pester you for anything," Jordana disputed, shaking her head at her mother. "Did you and Uncle Shep get into it or something?"

At Lilly's sudden sharp look and subtle flushing as she murmured, "No, don't be silly," Jordana recalled a hazy memory that popped in her head for no reason she could figure.

It was the summer her dad was working long days and nights—barely home at all—and Uncle Shep was helping out around the house, filling in the gaps for Fitz. She remembered her mom laughing a lot with Shep, something she rarely did with Dad. Dad was a hard man to please and that critical eye fell on his wife often, particularly after the triplets arrived.

To be fair, triplets would've put a strain on any family. And then her baby sister, Yvette, came along—it was a lot of kids.

But there was love, too. There had to be for Lilly to stick around; that was always the argument Jordana made when people whispered under their breath about Fitz Colton being a raging maniac.

Fitz was as different as one could be from his half brother, Shep. Maybe that's why Jordana had gravitated toward her uncle. Uncle Shep had been encouraging and entertaining whereas her dad…well, he was so focused on work that he'd had little time for the six kids all clamoring for a bit of his attention.

Again, six kids was a lot.

She didn't fault her dad for being overwhelmed.

"You don't want Shep moving into the carriage house?" Jordana surmised, curious as to her mom's reaction.

"I'm too old for a roommate, Jordana," Lilly said stiffly.

"Mom, the carriage house isn't even attached to the main house. You're hardly roommates. You and Dad had talked about renting out the carriage house for extra cash."

"Yes, and ultimately we decided against it," reminded Lilly, straightening the dish towel for the third time. "Honestly, I just don't understand why your dad couldn't have encouraged Shep to find a nice apartment in town."

"Maybe because we're family and there's no reason? The carriage house isn't doing anything but collecting dust. It'll be fine, Mom."

But Lilly looked more agitated than ever. "Yes, of course. You're right. I'm just feeling out of sorts today." And then she did what she always did, pasted a blinding smile on her lips as if nothing had happened because Lilly Colton had the steel spine of a soldier who made living through chaos look like a walk in the park.

WHILE JORDANA WAS OUT, Clint made use of the empty house to study his own business, Broadlocke Enterprises. He figured it was time to make that call to his partner, Alex, but he wanted to have some kind of idea what they might have to talk about.

Dialing the number Jeana gave him for Alex, he made the call.

Alex picked up on the fourth ring, as if he were on the other end trying to figure out who was calling.

"Alex Locke," he answered.

"Hey, Alex, it's me, Clint. Thought I'd reach out to you and see how things are going without me barking orders all the time."

The surprise in Locke's voice was evident as he answered, "Clint, where the hell have you been? No one's seen or heard from you in days. I was starting to get worried. Not even Jeana knew where you were."

"Needed a few days off to decompress," he lied. "The stress was getting to me. It was either take a few days or start drinking my breakfast. I figured I've earned a few days of R and R but I'm sorry for worrying everyone."

"You take a few personal days? Who is this pod person? Clint Broderick doesn't take vacation days unless ordered to because he's banked up too many," Locke refuted with a chuckle. "Seriously, are you okay?"

"I'm fine. Went rock climbing two days ago," he said, amending, "Well, indoor rock climbing but it counts. It was hard as hell and my fingers are still jacked up. Not sure I'll take it up as a hobby."

"Rock climbing? Little early for a midlife crisis, don't you think?" Locke teased. "You should stick to golf, even though a five-year-old could beat your swing."

So he golfed? Golf sounded boring. Hit a ball and chase it. Over and over. It was aggravated walking. But he played it up to Locke. "Yeah, maybe you're right. So, everything good while I've been gone?"

"See, there's the guy I know and love—can't keep business off the brain," Locke said. "Yeah, of course. I've always told you that the world wouldn't stop spinning just because you weren't there to micromanage it."

Micromanage? "I'm a changed man," he told Locke. "I've had…an *epiphany*."

"Yeah?"

"Yeah. I know I was a workaholic and a bit of a control freak," he said, taking an educated guess at his own habits, "but you know, life is short and you can't take it with you. I'm going to start spending more time making memories that matter."

"Are you joining a cult? Oh, God, you joined a cult, didn't you? Please tell me you didn't pledge your assets—*our* assets—in your initiation?"

"What the hell is wrong with you? I said I wanted to create memories and you think I've joined a cult?"

"Hey, if you were on this end, listening to Clint Broderick wax philosophically about stuff he generally didn't care about until now, you'd start to freak out, too."

Clint was beginning to realize maybe it wasn't farfetched to theorize that whoever had tried to kill him probably worked for him.

Jesus, talk about a rude awakening.

"So, when are you wrapping up your little impromptu 'Finding Clint' tour and returning to Chicago?"

"Not sure. I still have some things to do here in Braxville."

"I don't understand how you managed to find your zen in a small nothing town in Kansas. As far as anyone is concerned, the only thing you can find in Braxville is tumbleweeds."

He chuckled. Locke had a good sense of humor. "Actually, Braxville is kinda nice. The small-town atmosphere is a nice change from Chicago."

"I'll bet you can't get a decent deep-dish there," challenged Locke, and to that Clint couldn't argue.

"The pizza situation here is marginal at best but I did have an incredible burger the other night and that made my taste buds happy."

"You, the foodie? I don't believe it. You're impossibly picky. You made the chef at Harold's want to quit."

Clint didn't remember the chef or Harold's but he played it off. "Well, if you're going to call yourself a chef, you better be prepared to accept criticism."

"The man fed heads of state but apparently your palate was more sophisticated," Locke returned dryly. "Anyway, kudos to the burger man for managing to please Clint Broderick."

Ouch, there it was again, proof that maybe he'd been an insufferable ass before getting the stuffing knocked out of him.

He shifted, discomfited. Maybe getting assaulted would turn out to be a blessing in disguise?

Never in a million years would he ever have imagined thinking or saying anything like that statement.

But here we are.

"Okay, I gotta run. This is my new number. Lost

my old phone. Call me if there are any issues you can't handle."

"Enjoy your tumbleweeds and five-star burgers."

"Will do."

And Clint clicked off. So, Locke sounded like a decent guy—the opposite of himself apparently. Maybe that was their dynamic. Locke was the good cop, Clint was the bad.

Their dynamic must've been successful. If he wasn't that same guy anymore, would their dynamic still work?

He supposed he'd just have to play it by ear.

Chapter Thirteen

Jordana was at her desk while Clint did some business around town when Reese popped in, dropping a blue file on top of the papers she was reading. "What's this?" she asked, opening the folder.

"Information on Broadlocke Enterprises." He gestured for her to start reading. "The business owned by your roomie and his partner, Alex Locke."

"Yeah? Is there something amiss?"

"Well, just that someone has been siphoning cash off the top for years."

"Who?"

"That is a bit trickier. I don't know. Whoever is doing it is pretty sneaky about it. Almost didn't catch it. I happened to call in a favor with a forensic accountant who works for a law firm in Wichita and they pointed out the discrepancy in the books."

"So whoever attacked Clint could've been the one cooking the books."

"Or Clint could be the one and someone found out."

She frowned. "That makes zero sense. Why would someone try to kill Clint if he was the one stealing from his own company?"

"Maybe it was his business partner who tried to off him, pissed off because he was stealing."

"Stop saying that Clint had something to do with the books," she said, irritated.

"What if he did? We don't know this guy from Adam. Need I remind you, he's a stranger with one helluva weird situation. Who gets amnesia? Is it even real? I heard somewhere that true amnesia is so rare it's practically almost fiction."

She dead-stared Reese. He was getting on her nerves. "You're acting like a jealous boyfriend. Dr. Cervantes diagnosed him with amnesia because he treated his head injury. I didn't make up his diagnosis and Clint certainly didn't. Is that what this is about? What is your deal?"

Reese immediately went on the defensive. "I'm just saying, you're putting a lot of faith in a guy you don't know. Seems unprofessional at best and dangerous at worst. I'm trying to look out for you."

She couldn't exactly admit that her feelings were personal. Sleeping with Clint may have been a bad idea, especially now with this new information. But her instincts said Clint wasn't the one behind the embezzling and Reese was grasping at straws trying to find a way to paint Clint in a bad light. "Look, it makes more sense that someone connected to the business is behind the embezzling. A disgruntled employee? Maybe even his partner. What do you know about Locke?"

"Common garden variety upwardly mobile white male," Reese answered with a shrug. "On paper, pretty boring. Competent but nothing particularly extraordinary jumps out at me."

"And you think he doesn't have motive?" Jordana asked, exasperated. "You and I both know that anyone closest to the victim falls under suspicion first."

"Yeah, well, I can't exactly check his alibi when you've told me to keep the details of Broderick's attack under wraps." He affected a mock questioning tone, saying, "Sir, can you tell me where you were the night your business partner may or may not have been attacked on Range Road in Braxville, Kansas? Why do I ask? No reason."

She knew the right thing to do would be to question Locke but Clint didn't want his partner to know the details of his injury. Ordinarily, business concerns would take a back seat to her investigation but she justified honoring his request by saying that they were waiting to see if Clint's memory returned before questioning Locke.

It was flimsy at best and she was embarrassed.

Worse still, Reese knew she was handling Clint's case with kid gloves. "All right, let's question Locke," she said with a sigh. "We need to get some movement on this case."

"Finally!" Reese dropped into his seat, ready to rock and roll. "Now we're cooking with gas."

But she stopped Reese just as he scooped up the phone. "Can you wait until tomorrow? I want to give Clint a heads-up that it's going to happen."

Reese frowned. "Why?"

"As a courtesy."

"He could be a suspect," he returned, exasperated.

"C'mon now. Get real."

"No, in the embezzling," Reese answered, equally irritated.

"Yeah, well, we're not investigating that part. We're investigating his assault. Stay on task, okay?"

"Stay on task?" he repeated, incredulous. "I'm not the one stalling and making all kinds of excuses not to follow the usual protocol."

"I'm asking for one day," Jordana said, gritting her teeth. "Not a month."

"If I didn't know better, I'd say you were letting your personal feelings get in the way of your judgment," he muttered, clearly not on board with her suggestion. "I don't understand why you're going soft on this Clint guy. You let him move into your place and now you're giving him undue courtesy. Is he blackmailing you or something?"

"Do you really think I'd let someone blackmail me?" she asked. "No. I just feel bad for the guy. He's a victim, try to remember that. Think of it this way—what if he'd been a woman assaulted on Range Road and I offered her the same deal while she recovered? Would you be all up in my business, accusing me?"

"A woman is different," Reese answered with a shrug, not caring that he sounded sexist as hell.

"So because it's a man, I can't control myself?" she asked, getting hot under the collar. "Seriously, you can shove your sexist BS up your ass, and while you're at it, stop worrying about my personal life and what I choose to do with it."

"If the situation were reversed and I was the one offering up my place to a female victim, would you be good with it?" he countered.

Jordana hated that he made a fair point and she didn't have an equally strong counterpoint. She grabbed her stuff. "I'm taking a half day," she muttered, needing some fresh air and to get away from Reese.

Jordana exited the building, still fuming. Reese had never been such a jerk before. She gave him some latitude because he'd lost a partner and that made him a little overprotective but she was fully capable of taking care of herself. She didn't appreciate being coddled or managed and Reese had put it upon himself to do both.

Everything about this case had flipped her on her head and she was done feeling out of control.

She saw Clint coming toward her, two shopping bags in hand, ready to meet her at the car parked alongside the main road.

In slow motion, she noticed Miss Ruthie Garrett—a little old lady that should've had her license revoked years ago—career toward Jordana's car in her beat-up Buick like a drunken sailor on leave, neatly clipping the driver's side door before tootling off as if nothing had happened.

Jordana opened her mouth to shout at Ruthie but seconds later a loud explosion threw her to the ground as her car burst into flames.

CLINT'S EARS WERE RINGING. It took a moment to realize he was lying on the ground, smoke all around, shouts and sirens finally piercing the fog in his brain. *That can't be good*, he thought muzzily as he climbed to his feet. The scene was something of a gangster movie, except this wasn't 1930s Chicago but a small town in the middle of nowhere Kansas.

And Jordana's car had blown up.

Dropping the bags, he half ran, half stumbled to where Jordana was lying on the ground, unconscious from the blast. She'd been closer to the explosion and the blast wave had knocked her back a few feet.

"I need an ambulance," he shouted, gently cradling Jordana's head where a giant gash seeped gobs of blood onto his hands. "Goddamn it, I need a doctor! Somebody call 911!"

Jordana's partner, Reese Carpenter, skidded to a stop

and helped Clint carry Jordana to the sidewalk and out of the street. "What happened?" Reese asked, waving over the paramedics. "Did you see anything?"

"No, man, she was walking to the car and then this other car, a freaking boat, came out of nowhere and sideswiped Jordana's car and seconds later it was in flames."

"Goddamn Ruthie Garrett," Reese cursed under his breath. "The woman needs to get off the road but her damn family has a lot of money and somehow she gets to keep her license."

"If this isn't enough proof that she's a menace, I don't know what is. I thought cars only blew up in the movies. Was it the gas line or something?"

"I'm not a mechanic," Reese snapped, moving so the paramedics could load Jordana onto the stretcher just as her eyelids start to flutter open. Reese pushed Clint out of the way, saying, "Jordana, can you hear me? You're going to the hospital. You've got a head injury and they need to check it out."

Clint knew Reese wasn't deliberately trying to be obnoxious, but he felt a little territorial at the most inappropriate moment. He forced himself to take a step back and let Reese handle things.

But then just as the paramedic was about to shut the doors, he popped his head out to ask, "You Clint? She's asking for you. Hop up, you can ride with her."

And he didn't have to be asked twice. He ignored the look of suspicion clearly stamped on Reese's face and climbed aboard, going straight to Jordana. He didn't care what it looked like; he needed to be with her.

The double doors closed and Clint gently grasped her hand. She squinted against the pain. "Hurts," she admitted as the paramedic prepared an IV line. "What happened?"

"I don't really know. Some old lady in a giant Buick hit the car and then it blew up. You're lucky you weren't closer when it blew, otherwise..." He didn't even want to finish his sentence. Clint looked to the paramedic, needing reassurance. "She going to be okay?"

"Head wounds bleed like the dickens but her vitals are good. She'll need a CT scan to be sure there's no bleeding on the brain."

"I doubt it's that bad," she said, her voice a weak croak. "I don't need—"

"Will you let the doctors do their thing? You were just nearly blown to smithereens and I need someone to tell me you're going to be okay."

Maybe it was the shake in his voice or the fear in his gaze but Jordana quieted and gave a small nod of understanding. "Maybe it's not a terrible idea to get checked."

He knew she was doing it for his benefit but he didn't care. Whatever it took to get her to the doctor and treated was fine by him.

"I'll buy you a new car," he promised, kissing her hand. "One that's supersafe and not prone to blowing up."

Was that even a thing? How would he know?

"State of the art, the safest on the market," he said, kissing her hand again. "I swear to God, the safest I can find, and if I don't find one that is deemed safe enough, I'll hire engineers to build me something."

She had the wherewithal to chuckle because he was being ridiculous but it was good to see her smile through the pain. "It was probably just a fluke. I was planning to buy a new car, anyway."

Logic told him yes, it was likely a fluke but a tiny, scared voice whispered the possibility that someone had meant that fiery end for him, and Jordana was simply collateral damage.

He wasn't sure he could live with the possibility that something he was tangled up in had endangered Jordana.

First things first: fix his girl.

Then, like it or not, it was time to go home.

He couldn't afford to walk around in the dark anymore.

Chapter Fourteen

"That's one hard head you have there," Dr. Cervantes said with a smile. "But one completely normal brain scan. You conked your noggin and you're bound to have a nasty headache but otherwise you're good to go home."

Jordana smiled with relief. She hated hospitals. Clint exhaled, looking as if he'd been holding his breath the entire time. She was tired and her head was throbbing but she wanted to go home.

She didn't want to think about anything aside from a soft pillow and falling asleep in Clint's arms. Tomorrow would come soon enough and all the trouble that came with it. For one, she had to talk to Reese. She'd jumped on him when he'd called her out for doing things that were out of character. He was a good detective and a great partner. He didn't deserve her guilty conscience.

She'd have to come clean and let the chips fall where they may.

Clint hadn't left her side. Tears crowded her sinuses for no good reason. The head injury was making her loopy. Dr. Cervantes signed her discharge paperwork and she was dressed and ready to leave when Reese appeared.

Clint shared a look with Jordana and she gave him a subtle hint to give them a minute.

Once Clint left the room, Jordana was surprised when Reese folded her into a grateful hug. "Jordana, I thought you were going to die in the street. Puts things in perspective real fast."

She felt awful for Reese. Seeing her like that must've triggered some really bad memories of his last partner. She pulled away to regard him with a solemn apology. "I'm sorry I was so awful to you. You were right. Your instincts were right. I am sleeping with Clint and I've lost some objectivity. I didn't mean for it to happen but it did and I don't regret it. I only regret not being honest with you."

Reese took a minute to absorb what she'd said and then nodded, accepting her apology and her confession. "You're a good detective, too. If you think he's a good guy, I'm sure you're not wrong. I just want you to be safe."

"I know you do. I'm sorry I put you through needless worry. I appreciate that you've got my back. I'm sorry I didn't trust you with the truth from the start."

"It's okay. You're forgiven. So what's your next move?" he asked.

"Honestly, my bed. My head feels like it's about to pop off. Now I know how Clint felt when we pulled him off Range Road. Head injuries are no joke."

Reese affected a mock-serious tone as he asked, "Do you know who I am? Do you know who you are? Do you have amnesia?"

"I remember that you're a smart-ass so I must be okay," she said, smiling, glad that things were good between them again. She needed her partner. Fighting and keeping secrets from him hadn't felt right.

Clint reappeared, peering around the corner to see

if the coast was clear. She motioned for him to enter. "It's okay. Reese knows," she told Clint.

"Thank God. I'm not very good at keeping my feelings a secret apparently," Clint admitted, assuring Reese, "I'm not a bad guy, I promise."

"You better not be or I'll take you down without losing a minute of sleep," Reese said with a smile that was both good-natured and a little dangerous. Clint might not know it, but Jordana did—Reese meant every word. He took his partners very seriously. "All right, I'll leave you two kids to it. You don't need a ride?"

"I left and came back with my car. We're good."

Reese gave them a thumbs-up and then left.

"I think he likes you," Jordana said.

"Yeah, well, what's not to like, right? I'm practically a basket of kittens."

She laughed and then winced. "Oh, please, don't make me laugh. My head is killing me."

Clint left and returned with a wheelchair, which he directed her into in spite of her protests. "I can walk perfectly fine. There's nothing wrong with my legs."

"Oh, I know that," he said with an appreciative glance that made her blush. "But you're getting the royal treatment. I mean, check out these wheels. Top of the line chrome and medical-grade leather. This is—" he fiddled with the brakes until they disengaged, pushing her out the door "—the only way to travel."

Jordana waved at Dr. Cervantes as they headed out, trying not to laugh as Clint made a terrible nurse, but even as she climbed into the car and waited for Clint to return after he took the wheelchair back into the hospital, she couldn't shake the sinking feeling that Ruthie Garrett's vehicular mishap hadn't caused the explosion.

Because cars didn't just explode.

Someone had either tried to kill her or Clint.

The question was…who?

Clint tucked Jordana into bed, fussing over her like he would an injured bird until she glared at him with exasperation. "Okay, okay," Clint conceded, and climbed into bed beside her. "I'm so glad you're safe." Wrapping his arms around her, she settled into the cove of his chest. The warmth of her body against his soothed his ragged nerves. The subtle scent of her shampoo tickled his nose. When he thought of how badly things could've ended, fear curdled his guts. "I'm so glad you're okay," he murmured, brushing a kiss across her crown.

"You were knocked out, too," she reminded him. "Maybe you should've had your head rechecked. You're the one with the preexisting head injury."

"I'm fine," he promised her. "My concern is for you."

"You heard Dr. Cervantes. My head is too hard to sustain any damage."

"Yeah, well, that blast was intense."

Jordana fell silent and he tightened his arms around her, her head lying on his chest. In such a short time this woman had become so important to him. How that'd happened, he'd never know, but he couldn't question the way he felt because it was as real to him as the blood flowing through his veins. But with that realization, he also felt the crushing weight of guilt. If he was the cause of Jordana getting hurt, he'd never get over it.

"So, cars don't usually blow up like that, right?" he asked, half joking even though it wasn't funny in the least. When she affirmed what he already knew with a small shake of her head, he exhaled a long breath and said, "I didn't think so."

"Does that mean you're not buying me a new car?" she teased.

He chuckled. "I probably have a fleet of them somewhere in Chicago. I'll have one shipped to you."

"I'm kidding and don't you dare. I have insurance."

"I've never thought to check—does your insurance policy cover explosions?"

"I guess I'll find out tomorrow," she murmured with a sleepy yawn. "Let's go to sleep. Tomorrow will be here soon enough with all its problems."

That was the truth.

Tomorrow he had to tell Jordana the news that he was going to return to Chicago but he hoped he could persuade her to come with him. It was crazy—they hadn't known each other very long—but the idea of leaving her behind was unsettling and he knew he couldn't stay.

He needed answers. It was selfish of him to hide out in Braxville knowing that he wouldn't find the answers he needed here. Chicago held the key to regaining his memory and he couldn't afford to ignore that fact any longer.

Life gets real when cars start blowing up. But even more real was the way he felt about Jordana. He knew it was fast but there was something about her that felt right. His gut said, *Hold on to this one*, and he knew he had to do just that. He had no idea how he was going to convince her to leave Braxville, though.

She was stubborn and attached to this place. Her roots went deep. Asking her to uproot herself to follow him to Chicago felt selfish on his part, and yet he couldn't bring himself to leave without her.

Damn, maybe the old Clint was slowly rising to the surface. A certain level of ruthlessness urged him to say or do whatever possible to get her on that plane with him.

He wouldn't manipulate the situation, he told himself. If she didn't want to come on her own, he wouldn't force her hand. Not even if it killed him to leave her behind.

Jordana was fast asleep in his arms, making those soft noises that he found adorable but fairly mortified her when he brought it up.

Good night for now. Tomorrow is a big day.

Clint let his eyes drift shut, joining Jordana within seconds.

Chapter Fifteen

"Go to Chicago with you?" Jordana repeated, staring dumbfounded at Clint from across the island bar in her kitchen as the morning sun cast golden light around her and the coffeepot gurgled to life. She may have bonked her head but surely Clint wasn't asking her to run off with him? What about her job? What about her life here? Stunned, she replied with a shake of her head, "I can't. I have responsibilities and a life. I can't just drop everything to go play house with you in Chicago."

"That's not what I'm asking you to do," Clint said. "I'm asking you to come with me to Chicago to help me sort out who's trying to kill me. I can't find answers until my memory returns and my memories won't return until I leave Braxville. Somewhere, deep down, you know I'm right."

Of course she knew he was right. Didn't mean she liked the idea of him leaving or that she could traipse off into the sunset without a care in the world. Frustration laced her tone as she shut him down. "Clint, as much as I would love to be with you, I have a job here and people who rely on me. I can't leave with you."

Clint bracketed his hips, his lips pursed. He wasn't a man to take no for an answer. He tried a different tactic. "Okay, I get it, your job is important to you—as it should be—but what if your captain signed off on your absence as part of the investigation?"

"He won't."

"But what if he did?"

She sighed with exasperation. "Trust me, he won't. It makes zero sense for me to follow you to Chicago on Braxville's dime. We don't have that kind of budget."

"What if I contributed to the Braxville personnel budget?" he said.

"That's not even funny. It's also illegal. Private citizens aren't allowed to make contributions or donations to city budgets," she said, casting him a short look. "You can't buy me, Clint."

He realized he'd made a misstep and quickly tried to correct. "Of course, you're right. That was crappy of me to even suggest such a thing. Can you tell I'm desperate to have you with me? It's not a good look or feeling but I'm being honest. I don't want to leave without you but I have to leave."

Jordana rose from her seat to wrap her arms around him, truly sad that he was going. "I'm sorry, Clint. If it counts for anything, I hate the idea of you leaving."

"It does count," he admitted, but the determined set of his jaw told her he wasn't giving up. He gazed into her eyes. "Someone tried to kill me, Jordana. I don't trust anyone but you to find out who's behind this murder plot."

"How do you even know I'm a good investigator? Clint, you don't even know me. I have an investigation on my desk right now that's growing colder by the minute and I'm no closer than I was when I got the call that two bodies were found walled up in my family's warehouse. Maybe I wouldn't even be that much help."

She wasn't usually insecure about her skills but now

wasn't the time for bravado, not with Clint's life on the line.

"You're the one I want. I have a sense about people—I don't know how I know it but I do. From the first moment we met, I had a good feeling about you. You're strong, confident and capable. I want you by my side."

Jordana felt it was necessary to point out an alternate theory. "Look, I know the circumstances are unusual but there's still a possibility that it was an unfortunate coincidence. My car might've been a ticking time bomb and all it took was one swipe from Ruthie Garrett to set it off. It might have nothing to do with you. If forensics doesn't come back with anything that suggests someone tampered with the vehicle, we have to accept the possibility that coincidence was in play."

He released her with an exhale filled with irritation. "C'mon, Jordana, don't patronize me. You and I both know that someone rigged that car to blow with me and you in it. The only reason I wasn't in that car when it blew up was because I made an impromptu decision to pick up a few things at Ruby Row Center. That car was going to be our funeral."

He was right, she had patronized him when he was strong enough to handle the truth and they were running in circles. Maybe her reluctance to follow him to Chicago had less to do with the reasons she gave and more to do with her reluctance to admit that she had deep feelings for a man she barely knew.

"I need you, Jordana," Clint said, reaching for her hands. "I don't trust anyone else. You're the only person I have in my life that I trust one hundred percent. Given the fact that someone is trying to kill me, that gives you the number one spot in my life."

"What would I do in Chicago?" she asked, wavering. "I don't have any privileges with Chicago PD and they certainly wouldn't appreciate me poking around without clearance."

"I know. What I'm asking is for you to be my second pair of eyes. Tell me what your gut instinct tells you about the people around me. I'm too close to the situation. I'm not asking you to walk away from your career—hell, that's the last thing I would ever ask of you. I'm just asking for a little help and a little time to figure this out together."

He made a damn persuasive argument. She had some personal time banked up seeing as she never used her vacation or sick days. Human resources would be overjoyed to see her use up some of that banked time. But it felt foreign to skip off with a man she'd only met two weeks ago to go undercover without permission or clearance to catch a criminal. If she was considering this wild idea, Clint had to know everything.

"Someone is embezzling from your company," she blurted out.

Clint drew back in surprise. "Come again?"

"I was going to tell you but then the explosion happened. Reese found some banking discrepancies in your books. He had some fancy forensic accountant take a look and they found that someone has been siphoning money off the top for years. It's easy to miss but it's there."

"Why was Reese poking around in my books?" Clint asked, frowning. "Seems a little bit of an invasion of privacy."

"He was looking for motive. An investigator always looks to the financials. Money is a great motivator to kill someone."

Clint regarded her with wary curiosity. "And what

do you think about that? Do you think someone within my company tried to kill me over money?"

"I can't deny it's a compelling lead."

Clint accepted her answer with a nod. "About how much money are we talking?"

"Hard to say exactly but a rough estimate is in the millions. I mean, your company has been doing well for years. It's no wonder no one caught the siphon."

But Clint looked ready to punch something. She could only imagine how it must feel to realize someone was dipping into his bank account. It might even bother him more than the murder plot, judging by the storm building behind his eyes. His gaze swung to her, determined more than ever. "I understand if you don't want to come but I could use your help."

Jordana felt herself slipping. Was she going to do this? And if she did go, was she going for the right reasons?

From the moment Clint Broderick had come into her life, nothing had been the same.

SOMEONE WAS STEALING from him. He narrowed his gaze, cursing his inability to remember jack shit about his own life. His memory loss was a coup for whoever was putting their hands on his cash box.

The knowledge that someone was embezzling from him felt like a double insult. The attempt on his life had to be connected to the theft. He was a loose end. Had he discovered who was dipping in the books and everything that'd happened to this point was simply someone trying to cover their tracks?

Hell, he'd become a TV crime drama plot. That didn't sit well with him.

The urgency to return to Chicago was like a dull roar in his brain.

He took some solace in that Jordana had agreed to leave with him. Her agreement left him with no small amount of gratitude. There'd been nothing he'd said that wasn't true. He trusted no one like he trusted her.

He'd sift through the meaning of that understanding later. For now, he was just overjoyed that he wasn't facing what was coming alone. And he was under no misconception that he was walking into a storm with blinders on.

How had he let this happen? What kind of man had he been before his head injury that someone would do this to him? Was Alex a part of this? From what he'd gathered, he and Alex went way back. They'd built the company from scratch. Why would Alex steal from their company? He couldn't imagine how any scenario with Alex at the forefront of a murder plot made sense, but he was holding on to what he knew with a tight grip.

A part of him was starting to understand that he used to be ruthless because for a split second it had been second nature to try and bend Jordana to his will. That wasn't right. If he was that man before coming to Braxville, he sure as hell wasn't leaving as that man.

But with someone gunning for him, he was going to have to bring some of that edge to the fight if he wanted to survive.

Jordana returned from the station with a tension he recognized. He knew he was the cause of that turmoil.

"Everything okay?" he asked.

"No." She didn't sugarcoat it. "I asked for the time off. My captain agreed to it, but in the meantime, Reese is going to take over the Fenton case."

It made sense but he knew that must've stung. He

went to her and grasped her hand, making a point to meet her gaze. "I know what you're sacrificing to come with me and I want you to know I appreciate it more than I can put into words. When this is all done, I swear I'll make it up to you."

"I made the choice," she said. "I believe it's the right decision but it still stings, I'm not going to lie."

"I won't say I understand but all I can say is thank you and mean it."

Some of the tension left her shoulders and he pulled her into his arms, holding her tight. "You are an amazing woman, Jordana Colton. I think getting bashed in the head was a blessing in disguise because it brought me to you."

"I wouldn't go that far," she said with a rueful chuckle against his chest. "Let's just get this done so we can move forward. Hopefully, the minute we set down in Chicago, your memory comes back like a ton of bricks so we can make short work of who's behind the attempt on your life. I'm only willing to put *my* life on hold temporarily."

He understood and accepted her terms.

"You and me both," he murmured, hoping for the same shock of memory rushing back. If not, he didn't know how he'd hold on to the life someone was trying to take from him.

Chapter Sixteen

After winning an argument with Dr. Cervantes to clear her for flying, Clint arranged a first-class flight to Chicago, which in itself was a culture shock for a girl who lived a more modest life.

Sure, her parents had money on paper but everything was always tied up in their assets and her father's business. Plus with six kids, there'd been times Lilly had had to get creative to make ends meet. So traveling in the lap of luxury wasn't something Jordana was accustomed to and she wasn't sure if she liked it, either.

Champagne during the flight, soft, comfortable chairs with ample legroom and a little curtain divider to separate the Haves from the Have-Nots…it was all too ritzy for her tastes.

But Clint seemed to settle into the comfort as if he were born to it, which made her a little anxious.

Reese had warned her that she didn't really know Clint. He owned and ran a multimillion-dollar company; he wasn't a lost stray without a family to care for him.

And even if he seemed lost and alone at first, that'd been temporary.

Now, they were headed back to his world and Jordana hadn't a clue what that world looked like, except she was willing to bet her eye teeth it looked nothing like her own.

They touched down at O'Hare International and immediately a sleek black town car awaited them. Clint's assistant, Jeana, had made all the arrangements and Clint fell right into step with every accommodation as if using muscle memory. Already he seemed different, more confident and assured of himself, but also colder.

His gaze took on a sharp look and that smile she'd come to love was replaced with a tight, contained set of his jaw that spoke of control and authority.

She suppressed a shiver. Seeing him like this was a different kind of sexy but the change made her wary.

Would she like the person he truly was when he regained his memory? What if this entire relationship they'd built in record time was an illusion that wouldn't stand up to the glare of reality? Had she put her life on pause for something that was doomed to fail?

There were too many questions in her head to enjoy the flight. By the time they landed, she was rigid with tension, a fact Clint noticed.

"I'm nervous, too," he admitted, slipping his hand into hers. "We'll face this together."

That helped a little bit. Some of her tension melted away. She risked a short smile as she nodded with a murmured, "Together."

The town car, drenched in understated wealth and privilege, looked like something a movie star would find appropriate. Jordana felt underdressed in her comfortable jeans and sweatshirt but she tried to keep her insecurity at bay. She didn't like the idea of people staring at her, which would no doubt happen as curiosity provoked interest.

Clint might not remember his life here but everybody else in his world did.

Not only had the king returned but he'd brought a plus one.

The town car pulled up to a stately building and a sharply dressed doorman promptly helped them exit the car.

"Pleasure to see you home again, Mr. Broderick," he said.

"Thank you, good to be home," Clint said, handing the man a crisp bill for his troubles. Clint waited for Jordana and then, holding her hand, they walked into the building, which his assistant, with whom he'd shared his secret, provided all the relevant information to gain entrance to his penthouse.

The *freaking* penthouse.

Yes, of course Clint lived at the very top of a very posh building. Where else did she expect him to live? A hovel? A small shack in a depressed neighborhood? Of course not. But again, the shock of reality was a sharp one. Everywhere she looked, she saw evidence of extreme wealth, a world she'd never get used to being around.

"Not bad," Clint joked as he opened his front door to reveal a spacious, tastefully decorated but definitely masculine decor. Tones of gray, black and white with steel accents dominated the space with cold, hard marble countertops that gleamed in the overhead light. "Too bad I don't have any family to impress because this is worth showing off, am I right?"

She forced a smile. "It's pretty top-shelf. Where's the bathroom?"

"I haven't a clue but let's find out together." He gestured and they traveled down a long hallway. Art created by artists she couldn't identify hung on the walls but Clint barely noticed. They found the master bedroom and Jordana sucked in a wild breath at the vision of male dominance and sexual prowess that practically dripped from the room.

"Jesus, Clint, who the hell were you? Christian Grey?" she muttered with a grimace. Definitely not to her tastes. She turned to Clint. "If you have a secret room of pain hiding behind a closet door, I'm catching the first plane out of here."

"It's a little much, isn't it?" Clint agreed, glancing around. "Very 'executive privilege.'"

"Yeah, not to be rude but it's not very homey."

"I agree. I like your place better," he said, shocking her. He smiled for the first time in a way that reminded her of the man she'd fallen head over heels for and reached for her. "I don't know the guy who signed off on this pleasure palace but I do know that you being in it automatically makes it ten times better."

She grinned as he sealed his mouth to hers. His tongue darted to taste her and she opened willingly, needing something to ground her in this new environment. His touch, his scent, the way his mouth fit perfectly against hers, was exactly the touchstone she needed to breathe more easily. "I needed that," Jordana said, smiling. "Thank you."

They ended the kiss, somewhat reluctantly, because both had to use the restroom after the long flight, but after a quick shared rinse in a massive shower that looked bigger than her entire bathroom back at home, Clint was ready to put that sumptuous bed to good use.

"Let's break it in," he said, dropping his towel to reveal his ready erection. The lustful grin curving his lips was predatory and sexy as hell. He gestured to her own towel covering her. "Your turn."

She cast him a sly glance and then, turning, let the towel slide slowly to the floor. "Come and get it," Jordana said with a demure glance over her shoulder.

Clint growled. "Oh, baby, consider yourself *gotten*."

He was on her in seconds.

Damn, the man was fast—and oh so good with his hands and mouth.

CLINT STARED UP at the darkened ceiling of his bedroom, Jordana sleeping softly beside him. Moonlight caressed her half-revealed naked body as she lay twisted up in the silk sheets.

They'd christened this bedroom with extreme prejudice. Bits of memory came to him unbidden at unexpected moments. He'd known about the stash of condoms in his bedside drawer. Remembered putting the fresh box in the drawer. He remembered that the hot water spigot was sensitive and would pour lava if he twisted it too hard.

He remembered the doorman's name—Fred—and that Fred had a wife and two grandchildren. He also remembered that he always gifted Fred a thousand dollars for a Christmas tip.

So, he could be generous when it suited him, it appeared. Or maybe he was generous with those he deemed worth the extra effort.

Tomorrow he was going to the office. Jeana had it arranged so that she could brief him on the business end. She'd already pushed his business meetings for another two weeks to give his memory time to bounce back with familiar immersion. He made a mental note to compensate Jeana generously for her discretion and her invaluable help.

Clint also had a meeting with Alex at some point but he wanted more time before meeting with his partner. There would be no way he could hide his memory loss from Alex and he wasn't comfortable revealing that handicap just yet.

Maybe it was his ingrained sense of competition or maybe he wasn't sure how secure he felt about Alex's loyalty but he felt it was the right decision to hold back details.

Or maybe he was just being paranoid and Alex would never do a thing to hurt him.

It could go either way. The downside to amnesia was he couldn't tell who was trustworthy and who was likely to stab him in the back when he wasn't paying attention.

The upside to amnesia? Well, it might sound crazy but when he was in Braxville he felt more relaxed than he ever thought a person could with the whole of their life wiped away.

But now that he was back in the Windy City, he understood. He could feel the responsibility settling on his shoulders, the familiar weight of expectation weighing on him. Getting away from all that? Felt pretty good. Even if he had to get bashed in the head to achieve it.

He was Clint Broderick—CEO and cofounder of Broadlocke Enterprises. By all accounts, he was a very wealthy and powerful man with questionable design tastes. He couldn't imagine signing off on this look now. After staying with Jordana in her cozy little house, the penthouse felt cold and detached.

Did he really *live* here? As in, did he come home from a long day at the office and find sanctuary here? Nothing about this place felt relaxing. Sure, it was a great place to host cocktail parties to schmooze with powerful people and it certainly made for a perfect place to hook up with women he didn't plan to keep around but it wasn't a place he'd happily bring someone he wanted to build a life with.

Again, his gaze strayed to Jordana and a warm smile immediately followed. She made love like a voodoo priestess summoning an unearthly force but there was something sweet and tender about her that she tried to hide.

She didn't trust easily or quickly and yet, for some reason, she'd taken a chance on him.

He didn't want to do anything to lose that trust. He'd also do anything in his power to make her stay with him more comfortable. If she wanted, she could rip out everything in his place and start fresh with her own vision of comfort and security.

Hell, he clearly had the money, and what good was money if you couldn't spend it on the things that mattered most?

Jordana mattered to him.

All this—his stare perused his bedroom—meant nothing if Jordana wasn't happy.

Sighing, he pulled her sleeping body against his. She snuggled against him, those lovely, perfect breasts baring to his gaze. Immediately, he hardened but he'd already exhausted his pretty, long-legged detective and she needed some rest.

He chuckled as she moaned softly, the sensual sound sending the blood pounding to his already hardened member, but he deliberately closed his eyes and forced himself to relax.

There'd be plenty of time tomorrow morning to remind her how happy he was to have her here.

And he couldn't imagine a better way to start the day than inside Jordana.

After that, he could conquer the world—with or without his memory.

Chapter Seventeen

Within minutes of waking, Clint's head was between her thighs, lapping at her sensitive nub and sending sweet pleasure cascading through her body. She moaned, threading her fingers through his hair, barely able to breathe as he pushed her toward that cliff before she'd even had a chance to chase the wispy remnants of her dreams away.

In such a short time, Clint had learned her body's language and he spoke it fluently. He teased, sucked and nipped at her most sensitive spots until she had no choice but to succumb to the thigh-shaking pleasure that only Clint could provide.

She came quickly with a tight gasp, her body spasming with release, a moan rattling in her throat. *Holy Mother of God...*she was nearly delirious.

Clint rose from beneath the bedding, his mouth slick, a grin curving his lips. "Good morning, gorgeous," he said before kissing her fully awake.

He had this way about him that drew her like no other. If she were smart, she'd pack up and leave. She wasn't stupid or naive. These kinds of love affairs burned bright and hot and left scars when it was all said and done.

But she wasn't going anywhere, not yet.

"That's better than pancakes," Jordana said with a satiated grin as she wrapped her arms around his neck. "You're going to spoil me. That's how I want to wake up every morning from now on."

"How can I say no?" he asked.

"You can't."

"Good, because I can't imagine anything better than tasting you for breakfast every day."

She blushed, teasing, "I bet you say that to all the girls."

"I don't think I do," he said with genuine honesty, "but even if I did, I only mean it with you because I don't remember anyone else."

Jordana laughed. "That's terrible."

"But truthful."

He kissed her again and her hand moved to remove his boxers but he stopped her. "That was just for you," he said. "Besides, if we start that engine we'll never get out of here. I have to get in the shower. Care to join me?"

She glanced at the alarm clock and realized she'd better get up and moving, too. "Sure," she said, stretching like a cat. His gaze heated and she caught his full erection barely contained behind his boxers. With a quick movement, she pulled him down until he tumbled to the bed. Jordana rolled on top of him, grinning with a counter: "But you need to get dirty first..."

"Oh, I'm already plenty dirty—" Clint lightly tapped his head "—but I like a woman who goes after what she wants," he said, his hands bracketing her hips as she rubbed against his hard length.

Everything about Clint felt so good, so addictive. She'd never been one to place such a high priority on sex but that might change with him. In a blink, his boxers were off and a condom was on.

"So much for not starting the engine," he said with a groan as she slowly sank down on his length.

"Stop talking," Jordana demanded, her eyes fluttering shut on a moan as she seated herself fully on top. He drove up, his hips flexing as he anchored her with his big hands. "Oh, God, yes, just like that!"

"Bossy woman," he bit out with a sexy grunt. "I like it."

Yes, she realized with a groan, sex like this was addictive.

And like most addicts, she was willing to do things she never thought possible just to be with him. It was heady, dangerous and thrilling.

He rolled her over, skewering her, hitting the best spot deep inside until she panted with desperate need. He made her wild, insatiable. She clutched at his shoulders as he drove into her, his thrusts becoming more and more intense. She tensed as the pleasure built to an indescribable level until she crashed into her climax, shuddering and crying, almost babbling as wave after wave washed over her.

Clint followed seconds later with a growl that she felt deep in his chest before collapsing; the weight of his body while he remained firmly lodged inside her was the best feeling in the world.

"I can't get enough of you," he admitted with a rasp. "My God, woman, what have you done to me?"

Jordana felt the same but she held the words back. Instead, she smothered the potential of more talk with a searing kiss. He tasted of her, he smelled of sweat and sex. Together, the spicy blend aroused her to new levels.

Was this insanity? Had she tumbled into a crazy new world where chaos replaced order?

Maybe.

It was too late to turn back now.

Slowly recovering, Clint rolled from the bed with a command, "You, me, shower," and he padded naked across the bedroom, giving her a lovely view of his perfect ass as he went. The water started and he hollered, "Are you coming?"

She grinned and bounced from the bed. "Hold your horses, now who's being bossy," she said, pausing to glance at herself in the bedroom mirror.

For a full half second, Jordana didn't recognize herself. She looked the picture of a well-screwed woman. Her hair, tousled and wild, almost to the point of rat's nest territory, fell around her shoulders, and her cheeks were pink and rosy.

Who was this person? She envied her.

The woman in the mirror wasn't afraid to run off and live a life of luxury with the man she adored. The woman in the mirror wasn't plagued with fears and anxiety that her family might somehow be responsible for the death of two people. The woman in the mirror wasn't trying to walk the line between keeping up professional pretenses while secretly screwing the man whose case she was investigating.

The woman in the mirror didn't have any worries or cares.

But she wasn't the woman in the mirror, was she?

She was Jordana Colton—a woman with a complicated family life and a stalled personal life—and at some point, she'd have to leave the woman in the mirror behind.

CLINT ARRIVED AT his office, Jordana in tow, apprehensive that someone would figure out something wasn't right with him, but as it turned out, everyone was too busy with their own workload to focus much on him.

Jordana murmured as they took in the room, "You definitely had a preferred style."

"It would seem so," he agreed with a slightly pursed frown. He must've used the same decorator for his office as he had for the penthouse because it had a similar executive tone, lots of grays and steel accents. Everything screamed masculine power, in an overt way. Almost as if trying too hard. There was no time to fret about his interior decorating choices but he made a mental note to make some changes when the dust had settled. "Now we'll see where the rubber hits the road," he said, preparing to learn what kind of boss he was.

Maybe they'd been relieved by his absence. He didn't have long to think about that possibility for Jeana appeared, the woman who was his right-hand man, so to speak, and she looked as efficient as she sounded on the phone.

Medium height, brown hair pulled into a no-nonsense bun, glasses perched on her nose, wearing a sensible skirt and light jacket, a scarf tied artfully around her slender neck. Her blue eyes were kind but sharp. "Mr. Broderick, so happy to see you back after your business trip. Shall we discuss your itinerary?"

Of course, that was code for going to his office so that Jeana could debrief him further on his life. He was so glad Jordana was there with him, as well. He'd need the extra set of ears and eyes to keep everything straight. He felt as if he were cramming for a test on every subject he'd ever taken in school but he had no idea which subject the questions would be about.

Jeana led them to an expansive executive office with

a glorious view of downtown Chicago, closing the doors quietly behind them.

More grays, some navy blue and variations of gray met his eye as he perused his office. It was cold and impersonal but also imposing, which was probably the tone he'd wanted to convey in his previous life but now felt like an ill-fitting suit. *One bump on the head and everything changes*, he mused with sardonic wit.

"You must be Jordana Colton," Jeana said, extending a hand. "I hear we have you to thank for keeping such close watch on our intrepid leader."

"Quite by accident, I assure you," Jordana answered, shaking Jeana's hand. "But I'm happy to help. We're going to find who made the attempt on Mr. Broderick's life."

Jordana was playing it cool, keeping the professional lines drawn, but Clint didn't want to keep his affection for Jordana secret. To Jeana, he said, "She's my girl. Anything you can tell me, you can tell her, too. I trust her implicitly."

Jordana flashed him an aggrieved look but didn't say anything to the contrary.

Jeana, to her credit, didn't blink an eye. "Very good." She gestured for Jordana to have a seat while Clint settled in the high-back leather chair behind the modern executive stainless-steel desk. The desktop gleamed without a single fingerprint or smudge, the room smelling faintly of polish. A memory flashed: selecting this desk. He remembered thinking it looked impressive and intimidating, appropriate for someone of his position. Jeana handed him a folder. "I compiled some pertinent information you might need. Basic background of the company, current projects, challenges and obstacles, as well as some personal information, as I know it."

Jordana shot Clint a look as if wondering exactly how close he and Jeana had been. He wanted to reassure Jordana that there was nothing between him and his assistant; he wasn't that much of a cliché. He actually knew this to be true. Slivers of interactions with Jeana started coming back as if pushing water through a rusty bucket full of holes.

He snapped his fingers, excited. "I bought you a Hermès scarf last year for your birthday!"

Jeana broke into a pleased smile. "Indeed you did. Such an extravagant gift but much appreciated."

He was nearly giddy. "I'm remembering things. Not all at once but they're starting to fall into place, one by one." Clint jumped from his chair to peruse the library lining the wall. He picked up a leather-bound book, a first edition of *The Adventures of Tom Sawyer*, published in 1876. "I bought this at auction. I narrowly beat out my competition by ten thousand dollars." He grinned at Jordana, adding, "I paid a hundred grand for this book."

Jordana's gaze widened. "Are you kidding me? You paid how much for an old book?"

"What can I say, I'm a huge Mark Twain fan. Reminds me of my childhood. Remember, I was an only child. Kinda lonely. Books made it bearable. This book was the start of my love for reading."

Still, Jordana murmured, "Seems a lot for a book. Just saying."

He chuckled, returning to his chair, feeling much better, more hopeful than before. Clint rubbed his hands together. "All right, let's get started. Jeana, tell me what I need to know."

They spent the next hour going over the tidy file Jeana provided, and by the end, he'd gained more memory just by going over the information. There were still gaps but they were getting smaller by the minute. He'd known familiarity would help jog his memory. All he'd needed was to immerse himself in his previous life and it would all come tumbling back.

"Jeana, I need to take my girl out and celebrate. Would you make us a reservation at Boka? I want to show her a good time."

"Clint—"

But Clint's mood couldn't be dampened. "Wait until you experience the culinary mastery of Chef Pierre, you'll think you died and went to heaven."

Jeana nodded and left them alone. Judging by the frown on Jordana's face, she wasn't on board to be wowed by Chef Pierre.

"Do you really think it's wise to be out and about when your memory is still compromised?"

"That's the thing, it's coming back. I remember things. I remember more and more with each interaction. I think it would be beneficial to go to places I'm used to going, and I remember Boka being one of my favorite restaurants."

It was solid logic, but honestly, his reasons had more to do with treating Jordana than triggering more memories. He wanted to show her a good time. He also didn't want to give her a reason to regret coming with him. He was willing to take out all the stops to impress Jordana. Maybe if he did a good enough job, she might want to relocate to Chicago…permanently.

Chapter Eighteen

Jordana stared at the black floor-length, formfitting dress Clint purchased for her to wear to dinner. Was she going to prom? Who went to dinner dressed so fancy? And it was itchy. She preferred burgers and beers where jeans and a T-shirt were appropriate but she permitted herself a wistful sigh at the sheer beauty of the designer gown. *Okay, twist my arm, it's gorgeous*, but was it her? She wobbled a little in the heels, wincing at the subtle pinch on her toes. Whoever created high heels was a sadist.

She gave a final critical perusal and came to the inevitable conclusion that, even though it wasn't her style or comfort zone, Clint had excellent taste. It was hard not to feel like *Pretty Woman* wrapped in such finery. She didn't want to even know how much this dressed had cost him but she imagined it was worth a small fortune. She could almost hear her frugal-minded mother's voice chiding, "No dress needs to cost that much when there are children going without food in the world."

But when in Rome, right? What was done, was done. Maybe she could donate the dress to charity tomorrow to ease her guilt. Tonight, she was going to wear it with a smile because her date was the hottest man on the planet.

Especially now.

Clint appeared, dressed in a sharp tailored suit, black with a midnight blue tie, dress shoes polished to a shine. He was almost beautiful, too pretty—definitely the most handsome man she'd ever seen—and he took her breath away.

But she wasn't the only one affected.

Clint walked up behind her, his breath on the nape of her neck as he murmured in awe, "You, in that dress, should be a crime. Incredible."

She turned with a shy smile. "It's very pretty, isn't it? You have very good taste."

"To be honest, I think you could wear a potato sack and still turn me on but I'm happy to let the rest of the world be envious of what I have." He offered his arm, "Shall we?"

Jordana drew a deep breath to steady her nerves, and accepted his chivalrous invitation. "You're very charming when you want to be," she told him.

"With you, I always want to be. You make me want to be better."

"What makes you think you're not a good man to begin with?" she asked, faintly amused. "Amnesia doesn't change who you are, just blots out your memory."

"Yes, but memory is an essential part of who we are. We are shaped by our experiences. Without them, how are we supposed to know how to react to a situation?"

Jordana stilled. He made a good point. Clint noticed her sudden disquiet and pressed a lingering kiss on her bare shoulder. "Don't worry, I don't think I was a bad person but I'm beginning to realize I was a workaholic. Now, all I can think about is spending time with you."

She glanced at him, faintly troubled. How did this

end happily for either of them? Clint seemed so well-suited to this environment, whereas she felt distinctly out of place. There was no way she could ever picture calling Chicago home, just as asking Clint to adjust to the slower pace of a small town seemed ludicrous.

Clint sensed her disquiet. "Everything okay?" he asked.

Answering to stave off the inevitable, she said, "Just a little nervous about walking in heels." She wasn't going to ruin the night with an argument she knew they couldn't solve. Tonight was about enjoying each other's company. Maybe it was foolish to ignore the elephant in the room but she couldn't help herself.

"If you trip, I'll catch you," Clint promised, and her traitorous heart fluttered a little faster. How could she not fall for a man who knew exactly how to charm the socks from her feet? With Clint, it seemed she was destined to ignore every red flag flashing before her eyes because her usual rules didn't apply.

"You are a ridiculously sweet talker," she teased. "But I'll hold you to it. It would be my luck to be dressed this fancy only to land on my behind."

"And such a fine behind it is." Clint dragged a knuckle lightly down her arm, admitting, "All I know is that you matter to me in a way that shouldn't make sense but feels right." She shivered, angling to receive the most tender brush of his lips against hers. Clint smiled, murmuring, "We should go if we're going to make our reservation."

Right, dinner. She scooped up her clutch, ready to go, but not before reminding him that as fun as it was to get dressed up, it might not be wise. "You look amazing and I'm proud to be on your arm but I want to go on record to say that I don't know if going to dinner is a good idea. We don't know if it's safe yet."

He chuckled. "Turn off that detective brain of yours and just enjoy a lovely evening with your favorite person," he said, winking.

Turn off her detective brain? Not possible but she'd let that go for now. She dazzled him with a bright smile, determined to enjoy the moment. "Wow me, Mr. Broderick. I'm ready to be amazed."

"That's my girl," he said, causing her to warm all over. They walked arm in arm as if they were a couple used to such outings together, but in the back of her head, Jordana was still struggling with how different his life was compared to hers back in Braxville. How could he ever find Braxville interesting when he was accustomed to this level of opulence?

She supposed the reality was that their time together would end sooner than she would be ready but that was life. Nothing lasted forever.

But as much as Clint wanted her to shut down the investigator in her, that wasn't something she could do. It was just a part of who she was, even when she was wearing an evening gown.

CLINT COULDN'T IMAGINE a more beautiful woman sitting across from him. Jordana had swept her dark hair up into a messy bun with curling tendrils that drifted to frame her face, exposing that long, graceful neck he wanted to spend the evening kissing.

The fact that he had to convince her to leave her gun back at the apartment only made him want her more. She was the perfect contradiction—exquisite lady on his arm, deadly if needed.

The urge to be greedy, to keep her all to himself, was a struggle to keep at bay.

Pride puffed his chest when he caught envious glances as they walked into Boka. *That's right, she's all mine. Keep staring because you can't have her.*

But he immediately tempered that thought process because he knew Jordana wouldn't appreciate being thought of as a possession to be coveted.

She slid into her seat with grace but her gaze remained sharp and on point, as if scanning the crowd, ever watchful for threats.

"No one is going to gun me down before the entree," he assured her with a playful smile. "You can take the night off, sweetheart."

"Force of habit," she murmured with an embarrassed smile. "Of course, you're probably right. This is a very nice place. Do you remember coming here often?"

"I do," he answered, happy to be able to recall that information. "I know it sounds silly but I'm almost giddy that I can remember such a small detail."

Jordana smiled more broadly. "Don't apologize. There's nothing silly about being excited to recover your memory. I think you've handled your situation with more grace than I ever could've. Frankly, the fact that you haven't run screaming into the streets is a miracle."

"Don't let my cool facade fool you. There were some private panic attacks in the bathroom. I just didn't want you to see me break down. I wanted to preserve my manly image."

She rolled her eyes. "That's ridiculous. If your penchant for slippers didn't ruin your man card, nothing will."

He pretended to be affronted. "There's nothing wrong with slippers. Cold toes are irritating. Especially when a certain someone wants to warm said toes against someone's back when they go to bed," he replied, arching his brow pointedly at her. She giggled, knowing she was guilty. "I know what you're getting for Christmas, Miss Frosty Toes."

"Slippers make your toes sweat. My toes have to be free."

To be honest, he'd endure her cold toes any day but he didn't want to admit too fast that he was crazy about her. Jordana wasn't like any woman he'd ever met. She wasn't impressed with his wealth or stature, which he found refreshing.

Now that his memory was returning, he recalled why his last relationship ended. Iris, a stunning woman with culture and class, had been more in love with his bank account than him as a person. She delighted in extravagant gifts and the glitzy social scene when he'd been more interested in staying home, curled up on the sofa watching a movie or, as in the case with Jordana, spending the day sweating on a climbing wall.

At the end of the day, they'd simply been incompatible.

He privately chuckled at the very idea of Iris breaking a sweat doing anything beyond her yoga class. Her body had been practically perfect—sculpted and pristine without a single blemish—and yet Jordana's body, crisscrossed with nicks and battle scars, strong with hard-earned muscle, made him shake with arousal.

"You have a look on your face that doesn't seem appropriate for a fancy restaurant," Jordana warned, her gaze lighting with conspiratorial understanding. *Oh, yeah, baby, you know what I'm thinking.* But she was right. Damn if his thoughts weren't running like a ticker-tape parade across his forehead. "You're going to set the table on fire if you don't stop."

"Not my fault you look like a smoke show in that dress," he countered, reaching for his wineglass, needing something to put out the fire smoldering between them. "Remind me who's idea it was to leave the apartment when we could've ordered takeout and spent the rest of the time naked?"

She lifted her glass in salute, her expression saying, *That's on you, sucker*, and he wished she were beneath him, naked. It took a minute to calm the hunger clawing his groin but he managed to reach a respectable mind-set by the time their food arrived. His taste buds rejoiced as the memory of Chef Pierre's signature culinary style exploded in his brain. Taste, touch, smell, all-powerful catalysts for memory, as Dr. Cervantes had told him.

Jordana groaned as she sampled the couscous. "That might be the best thing I've ever had in my mouth." At Clint's raised brow, she blushed. "You're incorrigible."

"Only with you," he said.

"Oh, my goodness, laying it on a little thick, aren't you, Broderick?" She laughed, her eyes twinkling with wit. "One might think you're trying to butter me up for a little after-dinner action."

"Am I that transparent?" he said, pretending to be shocked until his grin gave him away. "Okay, caught. I want you naked in my bed for all time. There, I said it. And I don't apologize for it, either."

"I hate to be a wet blanket but my captain might have a problem with that," she returned with a wink.

He waved away the unwelcome dose of reality. "No wet blankets allowed." He didn't like to think about Jordana leaving. Maybe he could convince her that Chicago wasn't so bad, after all. But that was a problem for another night.

Clint was riding a high until they went to leave. Climbing into the town car idling at the curb, a plume of exhaust curling into the chilly night air, something caught Jordana's eye, causing her to do a double take.

"What's wrong?" he asked.

"You ever get that feeling that you're being watched? Well, I just got that feeling."

He relaxed. "Of course you're being watched—you're the most beautiful woman within everyone's direct line of sight. Let them stare, you're all mine," he said, kissing her cheek as he helped her into the car.

But Jordana was still troubled. She twisted to peer out the back of the town car window. "My instincts have kept me alive. Something feels off."

"Honey, I love how diligent you are but I think we're okay," he assured her.

Jordana settled in the seat, dragging her gaze away from the rear. "Maybe it was too soon to be out and about," she said, worrying her bottom lip.

Clint chuckled. "My little detective. I told you, tonight we were taking the night off from intrigue and drama. We are celebrating." He pulled her into his lap to kiss her. She gentled in his arms as his tongue swept her mouth. "There's my girl," he murmured with approval. "Do you have any idea how hard it was to keep my hands to myself throughout dinner? I think I deserve a medal."

She laughed, the sound like happiness in his soul. "We didn't even stay for dessert. I had my eye on that tiramisu. I feel cheated."

"I'll have it delivered," he promised, going to nuzzle her neck. "Whatever you want, it's yours."

Jordana dropped her head back with a throaty giggle, giving him better access to the sensitive spot where her neck met her shoulder. She moaned as his lips traveled the soft skin, his nostrils flaring at the intoxicating tease of her unique scent beneath the artfully applied dab of perfume at her pulse points. He groaned, his hand sliding up her thigh, baring the toned skin beneath the thin sheath that whispered across her flesh.

But as his fingers climbed farther beneath her dress, inching their way toward the apex of her thighs, Clint was thrown forward as something impacted them from behind. He held on to Jordana to keep her from falling but she was already twisting free from his grasp to peer behind them.

"Goddamn Chicago drivers!" the driver shouted as he righted the wheel. "I'm sorry, Mr. Broderick. Everyone all right back there?"

"What happened?" he demanded, wiping the sweat from his brow.

"I knew something felt off," Jordana said. "Did you notice if the car was trailing us before it hit?"

"No, ma'am."

"It was probably just a bad driver," Clint said, trying to calm the storm behind Jordana's eyes. "Driving in Chicago is like driving downtown New York—you take your chances."

"You don't think this is connected to the attempt on your life?" Jordana queried, not convinced.

Admittedly, the first thought that jumped to his mind was filled with paranoia, but now that his heart rate was settling down, he didn't think the hit was deliberate. "It was just bad luck that it was our vehicle that was hit. I doubt it was connected."

"I disagree," Jordana said flatly, unwilling to budge.

"We need to report it and I need to bring in my brother Ty for additional security."

"Whoa, whoa, let's hold up for a minute. The last thing that will help is overreacting to a situation that's likely unrelated. I don't need your brother showing up trailing my every move."

"Ty owns a security company. This is literally what he does for a living. I'd feel a lot better if he were here watching your back."

Did he really want a shadow? No.

Did he think Jordana was overreacting? A little bit.

Was he willing to do whatever he could to put her mind at ease? Yes.

He sighed, relenting. "Fine. If it'll make you feel better. Get your brother on the line. I just hope it's not a waste of his time."

"Your safety is not a waste of time," Jordana said sharply. "And you're wrong…someone is still trying to kill you. My gut is never wrong."

He wasn't going to argue.

What if she was right?

And just like that, the evening was ruined.

Chapter Nineteen

Money was a great motivator. Jordana asked Ty and his team to come to Chicago to watch over Clint, and after she offered him double his usual rate, he made it happen.

But to be honest, Ty might've come whether she'd offered him money or not because big brothers were like that—even when their little sisters were all grown up.

Or maybe he was just as curious as the rest of the family to find out why Jordana had packed up and split with a guy she barely knew.

Everyone had questions—questions she hadn't answered before leaving town. The thing was, she didn't want to get into a deep conversation about her motivation when she wasn't sure how she'd gotten to this place. Sure, the investigation was an easy excuse, but it didn't take a trained investigator to see that it was flimsy as hell. Jordana didn't relish the idea of admitting to her family that she was crazy about Clint, and yes, it'd happened fast but she couldn't deny how she felt.

Her mom would lecture her about being impulsive, her dad would yell about her lack of professionalism, her sister Bridgette would frown and ask if she'd thought things through, the triplets would grab some popcorn to watch the show, and her baby sister, Yvette? Well, she'd probably watch the ensuing chaos with detached interest without offering much more than a shrug because Yvette was ridiculously contained with her feelings.

So yeah, Jordana hadn't been superexcited about sharing what was happening in her personal life when she didn't know if it was going to last.

Why shake up the fishbowl if this thing with Clint was short-lived?

But now Ty was coming and he'd have questions. If she wanted him to stick around, she'd have to be honest.

She picked up her brother at the airport. His team was taking a later flight. Clint had offered the guest bedroom but Ty preferred a hotel, which suited Jordana fine because it felt awkward to be cuddling with Clint with her brother watching. *Ugh.* Big brothers remained protective no matter how many birthdays she'd had.

"It's been a while since I've been to the Windy City," Ty said, folding Jordana in a hug before they climbed into the town car. She'd missed the big lug. Of her brothers, Ty was her favorite. He had a way about him that was hard to ignore. Between those incredibly dark blue eyes that didn't miss a single detail and that slightly unruly shock of dark hair, it was hard to find anyone who wasn't intrigued or drawn to Ty. His only flaw? The man had a serious streak a mile long that could be a real buzzkill at times. Still, she loved the butthead.

"Thanks for coming," Jordana said, gesturing to the awaiting town car. Clint had insisted they use the car service for traveling around the city, even though Jordana would've preferred to use Uber.

Ty paused at the luxury with a knowing grin. "Moving on up, sissy?"

"Shut up," she growled, climbing into the car.

Today, she was the one cutting short the laughs,

which was a change. When he saw she wasn't in the mood for jokes, he sobered quickly. "Okay, what's the situation? You can handle yourself on most days. It must be serious if you're calling me in."

She drew a deep breath, then as quickly as possible, she gave Ty the backstory of their current situation, ending with, "And that's why I think last night's *accident* was no accident—along with everything else that has happened."

Ty took a minute to digest what she'd shared. "I agree," he said to her relief. "I don't think it feels like coincidence, either."

"I'm so glad you agree with me," she said. "Clint refuses to believe that he could be in real danger in spite of everything that's happened. I think he thinks if he doesn't give it the appropriate weight, it'll stop being true."

"Denial is a powerful thing. Maybe he knows you're right but he doesn't want to further alarm you."

"Too late and that tactic does not work on me. If anything, it makes my anxiety worse."

He chuckled. "Well, I guess he doesn't know you well enough yet." Ty paused before saying, "And about that…kinda moving a little fast, don't you think?"

Ah, the big brother talk. She knew it would come sooner or later. It didn't matter that she'd served in the Navy, been on her own for quite some time and worked as a police detective, Ty would always see her as that kid in pigtails. *Boy, that got annoying.* "Yes, it's very fast," she acknowledged, meeting his gaze without flinching. "But I know how I feel and I know myself well enough not to second-guess. The way I feel about Clint is unlike anything I've ever known. I'll do anything to keep him safe. Will you help me?"

It was the simplest way to get Ty to understand that she wasn't messing around nor was she taking her own actions lightly. She knew how it looked from the outside and she knew how she'd react if someone she loved were doing the same. She didn't fault her family for being apprehensive, but in the same breath, she hoped for their understanding.

Ty smiled, reaching for her hand to give it a short squeeze. "I'll do what I can to help your man. I hope he's worthy of your love."

Jordana smiled, so happy Ty was there with her. "Thank you. Your support means everything."

Ty gave a short nod, acknowledging the moment, and then switched to business mode. "Okay, so I'm going to need a list of associates, his itinerary and any pertinent information you picked up during your investigation if we're going to do this right."

"Perfect. I can get that to you tonight after you get settled at the hotel. When is your team coming in?"

He checked his watch. "Flight is scheduled for eight o'clock."

"That gives us some time to squeeze in some visiting. Deep-dish pizza, maybe?"

"Oh, girl, you're speaking my language and I'm starved. I miss the days when flights offered actual food instead of peanuts and a ginger ale."

"Who drinks ginger ale?"

"I do."

She made a face. "Reminds me of Granny when we were sick. Always forcing ginger ale down our throats."

"It's supposed to settle your stomach," he said, chuckling.

"Well, it had the opposite effect for me. Gross stuff."

"You and your picky palate."

It felt good to banter with Ty. They'd always been close even if they had bickered hard enough to bring the roof down. Now, as adults, they were just as close but their lives kept them apart for long periods of time. Ty was always off doing cool stuff with this security business and Jordana was focused on her law enforcement career.

Ty broached a subject Jordana wasn't keen to touch but she supposed it was the hot stove that threatened them all.

"What's the deal with those bodies being found in one of Dad's warehouses?"

"It's been a nightmare, honestly."

"I'm kinda shocked that you're the investigator. Isn't that a conflict of interest?"

"A big one but the department is small and there just isn't anyone else qualified to run the investigation. I have a partner, Reese Carpenter, who's working the case with me. Captain said Reese will keep me honest," she answered with a wry chuckle. "Reese is a good man. He won't let me lose perspective."

"What does Dad say about all this?"

"Not much. I think he's just hoping it goes away. Dex has been up my ass about the investigation, though."

"Of course he has," Ty quipped, not surprised. "He's always been about the image of the company. This situation is probably a PR nightmare."

"It doesn't bolster confidence, that's for sure."

"Has Dad lost any contracts because of this situation?"

"Dad hasn't shared that information with me. You know how he is. Dad is a subscriber to old-school misogyny. He thinks women should stay in the kitchen and out of men's work. Oh, and Uncle Shep is moving into the carriage house. Mom is all in a tizzy about it. I caught her scrubbing the stainless steel out of her pots and pans the other day."

"Uncle Shep? Has he retired from the Navy?"

"Yep, and I guess he's ready to spend his retirement fishing and doing whatever it is retired people do."

"Good for him. He's earned a little R and R." He recalled a memory. "Remember that summer Uncle Shep was home before Yvette was born? Mom was pulling her hair out with the triplets and dad was absent, as usual. If it weren't for Uncle Shep I think Mom would've had a nervous breakdown."

"Yeah, it was the best summer actually. Uncle Shep made things bearable. Mom is too high-strung for her own good. I swear someday her head is going to pop off if someone leaves the bathroom without straightening the bathroom towels."

Ty laughed. "You're always so harsh on Mom. Cut her some slack. I can't imagine running a house with six kids practically on her own while holding down a nursing job. It's a wonder she didn't become a closet alcoholic."

"And relinquish some control? That would be a nightmare for Lilly Colton," Jordana returned with a snort. "And you've always been a mama's boy so your opinion is invalid. You don't have Mom always nitpicking at you like she does me."

"I think you nitpick each other," he said.

That was a circular argument that Jordana didn't have the energy or desire to continue. Ty would always side with their mother, end of story. By this point in their lives, she'd accepted that fact.

"You know Bridgette is home, right?" she said.

"Yeah, she mentioned something about coming

home for a while to follow some kind of lead about a cancer cluster?"

"Yeah, in Braxville. It's pretty serious. She's staying at the house and Mom and Dad are always driving her nuts. I told her I'd help her look for a different place to stay while she's in town."

"All this talk of cancer makes me want to get a full checkup."

He wasn't joking. Jordana had no doubt Ty had already scheduled that checkup appointment but she didn't blame him. It was unsettling to hear that Braxville might be an epicenter of a cancer explosion. Maybe it wouldn't hurt to follow his lead.

"Hey, did you ever hear the rumor about Colton Construction being responsible for a few workers getting sick?"

Jordana did a double take. "No? What do you mean?"

"It's probably just people talking but I remember hearing something about Dad's company being the root cause of people getting sick."

"That's ridiculous. People will say anything when they're bitter and mean. Dad's made plenty of enemies in his time. He's not exactly the most personable guy in the world but he did an amazing job with the Ruby Row Center. You'd think people would stop spreading rumors when the man has actually done something great for Braxville. Besides, do you really think Dex would be out there pushing for more jobs if he thought Colton Construction was a liability?"

"That's true. Dex the Dealmaker loves money."

"Well, when running a business, at least one person should know how to network," Jordana said with a sigh, "because Dad would probably push away more people than gain them if it weren't for Dex."

Ty agreed. "Hopefully, it's all resolved soon. The stress can't be good for Dad's heart."

A chill settled in her bones. She didn't like to think of her dad being vulnerable to anything, much less the aging of his body, but the stress weighing on his shoulders was more evident each day. "He'll be fine," Jordana declared, refusing to think otherwise.

They arrived at the penthouse just as Clint arrived, as well.

Time to get this show started. Hopefully, Clint made a good impression on Ty, otherwise…things were going to get awkward.

CLINT KNEW MEETING the older brother was a big deal to Jordana so he wanted to be on his best behavior, but as it turned out Ty was a cool guy and he liked him immediately.

"Flight good?"

"As good as can be expected with only peanuts to chew on for the long flight," Ty grumbled. "According to my dad's business partner, Dex, they used to offer full-course meals on long flights. When did that stop? Jordana said something about deep-dish pizza. You know a good place?"

"Do I know a good place?" Clint repeated with a big grin. "I know of *the* place to get the best deep dish and I insist that you let me take you."

He caught the subtle roll of Jordana's eyes because she knew he was trying to make a good impression, but he also sensed that she appreciated his effort so he wasn't about to stop.

"Luigi's, owned and operated by the same family since the 1930s, emigrated from Italy and brought all their culinary secrets with them. One bite from a Luigi's pizza and you'll wonder how you survived without it."

"Sounds like a moral imperative that I find out for myself if the claim is true," Ty said dryly. "But you honestly had me at family owned and operated. Any business that can survive working with family must be doing something right."

Jordana excused herself to freshen up before dinner and that gave Clint an opportunity to talk frankly with Ty.

"I really appreciate you coming out here to put Jordana's fears at ease. She's been wound up pretty tight about this whole situation."

"I agree with her," Ty said, surprising Clint. "Look, my sister has some killer instincts, and if she says something isn't right, I'd listen."

"It's not that I'm not listening, but the odds of all this being connected seem astronomical."

"Not really if you think about it. First and foremost, we're going to dig into your associates. Money is a big motivator for foul play. We will need to clear all the people closest to you before we can widen the circle."

"Jordana said the same. She's mentioned concerns about my business partner, Alex Locke, but I really can't see him doing something like this. We've known each other for years and created the company from scratch together. Aside from business partners, we're friends. He'd never do something like that to me."

Ty looked sorry to be the bearer of bad news. "In my experience, it's always the person you least expect who's screwing you over. Jordana said you also have an assistant?"

"Yeah, Jeana, but she's been my rock through this.

When you meet her, you'll understand, there's no way it could be her."

Ty nodded but kept his judgment to himself. Jordana reappeared from the bedroom and Ty clapped his hands together, ready to eat. "I can practically taste that melting cheese already. Let's do this. I can't think on an empty stomach."

"Bring your credit card—my brother can eat twice his weight in food. Mom used to always say that Ty was going to eat her out of house and home."

Ty puffed up, almost proud as he patted his stomach. "What can I say? I was a growing boy."

Clint chuckled as the two bantered back and forth as they went downstairs to get into the car, but his thoughts were stubbornly stuck on the realization that maybe he ought to stop downplaying everything that'd been happening.

Maybe he couldn't keep denying the fact that someone was actually trying to kill him.

The thought was a sobering one that not even the best deep-dish pizza in Chicago could budge.

Chapter Twenty

Having Ty in Chicago with Jordana lessened some of the homesickness that popped up unexpectedly, but as they dug deeper into Clint's business and associates, the strain of having someone over his shoulder all the time was starting to show.

"Ty is using the information found by the forensic accountant to dig deeper into who is embezzling from your company," Jordana said as they settled onto the sofa with their Thai takeout. "Whoever is behind this scheme is pretty sophisticated—"

"Can we not talk about the investigation tonight?" he asked with a touch of irritation. "We can talk about other things, right?"

She drew back, stung. "Of course but I thought you'd want to know what Ty has been doing. You are paying him to do a job—a pretty important job, in my opinion, which seems far more important than how much I don't care for the weather here in Chicago."

"What's not to like? The weather is temperate, practically California weather. Cool enough in the evenings for a light jacket but warm enough in the day for a short-sleeved shirt, or a dress," he said, trying to lighten the mood, but Jordana wasn't having it.

"I don't wear dresses," she said flatly. "And no, I

don't care for the weather here and I miss Braxville. Why did I put my life on hold to help you when you're not willing to give just as much as I am to see your case solved?"

"It's not that black and white," he argued, realizing Jordana wasn't in the mood to play nice right now. "My memory is returning in fits and starts but I'm still struggling in the deep end of the pool having just learned to swim. I'm doing everything I can to keep the company moving smoothly while I recover."

"I get that but your life is more important than board meetings and new account acquisitions."

"Easy for you to say," he said. "You don't have the weight of everyone's livelihood sitting on your shoulders. If Broadlocke goes down because of all this, people will lose their jobs. I help put food on people's tables. I can't ignore my responsibility."

"But you're asking me to ignore mine?" she countered sharply. "I brought Ty here for a reason. I asked him to put you as a priority above his other cases because I care about you. Don't make me regret my decision to come here."

"I didn't force you to come," Clint said, rising to throw away his carton. "Don't turn this into some scenario where I'm the bad guy who dragged you away from Hicksville, Kansas."

Jordana's mouth dropped. This was a side of Clint she'd never seen: cold and detached.

She didn't like it one bit.

Jordana shook her head. "I don't know who you are right now, but I'm not interested in finding out. Good night," she said, leaving the sofa to toss her carton and retreat to the bedroom.

Once she was safely behind closed doors, she let the

tears flow. She didn't believe in fairy-tale endings but it was shocking how much it hurt to hear Clint speak to her this way. She wanted to pack her suitcase and bail but she was wise enough to know that was hurt feelings talking. No one was perfect and people lost their tempers but she hadn't been ready to see that side of Clint yet. Was anyone ever ready to see the darker side of the person they were crazy about? No, but it happened just the same.

She didn't want to call Ty but she needed to vent. Picking up her cell, she rang up Bridgette.

"Hey, how's Chicago?" Bridgette asked as soon as she answered. "Please tell me you're eating your weight in amazing food. Chicago is such a foodie town."

"Yeah, there's a lot of good places to grub," she agreed, but Bridgette could tell by her tone that something was wrong.

"What's up? Everything okay?"

"No, everything is a mess actually," Jordana admitted, tears clogging her voice. "Clint and I just got into an argument. I know he's under a lot of strain, but I didn't sign up to be his emotional floor mat."

"What'd he say?"

Jordana gave Bridgette the abridged version of their earlier conversation, finishing with a sniffled and woeful, "And he hurt my feelings."

"Oh, honey, I'm sorry. Sometimes men are stupid."

And just like that Bridgette managed to make her laugh. "Yes, they are." She wiped at her eyes, chuckling at the irony that her younger sister seemed to have more wisdom than she did. "I just don't understand how he can be so stubborn about this whole situation. It's like he doesn't want to find out who is out there trying to kill him. Am I crazy for insisting that he make that his top priority?"

"Of course not, but you don't know what's going through his head. Maybe he's overwhelmed with everything and he has poor coping mechanisms. Everyone has their way of coping. Mom cleans like a maniac. Maybe Clint hides in denial."

"Yeah, I know, but his kind of coping mechanism is going to get him killed. Ty agrees that someone is out to get him, but Clint is treating the situation like it's nothing. Honestly, I couldn't care less about his business right now. I want Clint to be safe. Broadlocke Enterprises can suck an egg for all I care."

Bridgette laughed at Jordana's vehement reply. "He built that company from dirt, right?"

"Yeah, so?"

"You of all people should understand why he's being so stubborn. Look at Dad. Is he not the most stubborn person in the world? And wouldn't he do anything for Colton Construction?"

Bridgette had a solid point. "Are you saying I'm attracted to the same kind of man as our dad?" she asked, groaning. "How did that happen?"

"Genetics, social imprinting, take your pick. The fact is, you're going to have to work around him if you want to keep him safe for his own good, of course."

Jordana smiled. "Kinda like how Mom slips Dad his vegetables in things he won't taste?"

"Exactly. She knows if she serves up a plate of zucchini he's going to give a hard pass but if she puts it in his favorite bread? He's going to gobble it up and ask for another slice. You need to start working with what you've got instead of pushing against what you don't."

"Jesus, Bridge, when did you get so damn wise? Aren't I supposed to be the big sister?"

"While you were off being a hero serving our country, I was out making dumb mistakes. Wisdom doesn't come free."

"Ain't that the truth," Jordana commiserated. "Okay, so you're saying I need to do what I do and ignore Clint when he's being an ass."

"Pretty much."

Jordana sighed, knowing it was solid advice, but there was a sadness to the realization that the bubble had popped. "Does this mean we're officially out of the honeymoon phase? Damn, that was short. I thought we should get at least three months before we showed each other our bad sides."

"It sucks when the love goggles fall off," Bridgette agreed. "But you went to Chicago to do a job. So the job had side benefits. Doesn't change the original reason you left Braxville, so stick to the plan. If the benefits end, that's the way it goes."

She accepted Bridgette's counsel and thanked her for listening, but as she hung up, she crawled into the bed, still a bit sad. Had she thought Clint was The One? *Truthfully, yeah.* Was it most likely going to end as quickly as it began? *All signs point to yes.*

And that's why she fell asleep feeling as if the truth were her enemy.

CLINT COULDN'T BRING himself to apologize for snapping even though he felt like a jerk.

The truth was he was starting to chafe at the constant presence in his life, the shadow of uncertainty that hovered above his head like an unwelcome thought.

Ty was doing a good job of staying out of sight, doing

his work behind the scenes, but one of his team was planted within the head office for visuals and Ty had wired his office to catch any conversation that might be useful.

He wanted nothing more than to crawl into bed beside Jordana and pull her into his arms but he'd left things ugly and raw between them. Jordana wasn't the kind of woman to forgive and forget so easily.

Nor was she swayed by overt gestures.

It wasn't like he could buy a huge bouquet of roses and expect her to melt. That was one of the things he admired about her. She was strong, tough and smart. He knew she was right. The investigation needed his full attention but so did his business. There was only so much of him to go around. But Jordana meant so much to him. He needed to swallow his pride and apologize. As he rose to head to the bedroom, his cell lit up.

It was Alex.

"Hey, man, sorry to bug you so late but I'm a little concerned about something I need to talk to you about."

He paused with a frown. "Yeah? What's up?"

"What's with the security detail snooping around the office? I just had a run-in with a guy named Ty Colton, says he's on the payroll for security. I don't remember talking about anything like that. Is there something I should know?"

Clint swore beneath his breath. He'd hoped this case would be resolved before he had to talk to Alex but it seemed time wasn't his friend.

"Sorry about that. Yeah, I hired Colton's security team to watch my back after the situation in Braxville."

"You said it was a mugging. That could've happened to anyone, man. Don't tell me you've gotten paranoid all of a sudden," Alex said, half joking. "Do you need a night-light, too, buddy?"

"You get mugged and tell me how secure you feel at night, and yes, I would like a night-light," he quipped.

"Oh, hell, what am I talking about? You have a detective keeping you safe at night," Alex teased with a chuckle before continuing in a more serious tone. "Look, I'm all for you feeling safe but I think this is a little overboard. We have security. Nothing is going to happen to you at the office."

"Yeah, I know, but they thought it was a good idea, more of a precaution."

For reasons he hadn't fully examined, he hadn't shared the full details of his attack in Braxville with Alex. Mostly it was because he didn't want to seem weak or vulnerable in front of his business partner but there was something else that he didn't quite know that kept him from spilling the beans.

"Is there anything else I need to know about this security detail?" Alex asked.

"No, I'll probably send them home in a week or so. It's mostly to make Jordana feel more secure. You know how it is. Women worry." He cringed, knowing if Jordana had overheard him right now, he'd likely be dodging a plate whizzing past his face. "I'm sorry if they were disruptive in some way."

"No, no, I understand. Of course you have to placate her. I get it. Next time, a heads-up would be appreciated. I don't like being blindsided."

"Right, that's reasonable," Clint said. "Thanks for understanding."

"Yeah, no problem. I'm here for you, man. I mean it. You can tell me anything. We started this company together and we're friends."

Clint chuckled. “Yeah, I know.”

“All right, glad we got that settled. See you at the office tomorrow. It’s your turn to bring the bagels.”

“Got it.”

Alex clicked off and Clint tossed his phone to the table with a long exhale. When would this all end? He wanted to get back to normal so he could put all this behind him. Maybe then, he could focus on Jordana like he wanted. Until then, he had to tread water and hope Ty or Jordana found answers soon.

Chapter Twenty-One

Clint was knee-deep in paperwork when Ty showed up at his office the following day. After his conversation with Alex last night, Clint was on edge about having Ty walking the halls. He gestured for Ty to close the door behind him so they could speak in private.

Ty dropped into the chair opposite Clint with a frown. "I heard your partner, Locke, isn't so keen on having my team poke around."

"Yeah, to be fair, if the shoe were on the other foot, I wouldn't much like it, either."

Ty shifted in the chair, all business. "Look, we need to talk about some of your inner circle. We've cleared most of the people on the payroll except a handful who work closest with you."

"And?"

"And we've found nothing to support that they might be involved with the embezzlement or the attack on your life."

"That's good news," he said.

"All it does it narrow the playing field. The people closest to you are the ones who stand to benefit if you aren't around. At some point we need to talk to Locke."

"I know but let's try and leave him out until we absolutely can't anymore."

"Okay, there are others we can talk to before Locke. Starting with your assistant, Jeana. It's time to question her."

He wanted to protest that Jeana would never do anything to hurt him—she practically adored him—but he knew it would be a waste of breath.

"Okay, I understand," Clint said on a sigh. "I'll let her know you'll be calling."

"Thanks." Ty paused before saying, "We did find some more information on the money. The transactions were tied to a terminal located within this building but narrowing down which computer was used takes time."

Clint's heart sank. It hurt to know that someone he worked with was stealing from him. He tried to create a good work environment and Broadlocke was considered top tier in the employment bracket for competitive wages.

And yet, someone was still stealing from him. Anger followed. "I want this person found. Who else is on your list aside from Jeana?"

Ty pulled a folded sheet of paper and carefully unfolded it before handing it to Clint. "That's the short list we compiled. Everyone on that list needs to be cleared."

Clint perused the list. Some names were familiar but others were hazy, as if he should know them, but his memory was still glitching. Of course Alex and Jeana were at the top.

"Another theory we're working on is, do you have any disgruntled employees that come to mind who might feel justified in helping themselves to the piggy bank?"

A name jumped to his memory, Derrick Rochester, an analyst who used to be in charge of the old computer system before they upgraded. Rochester hadn't been happy about the change, loudly protesting. In the end, Clint thought a different place might be a better fit and he was let go.

"Sounds like a good foundation for motive," Ty said, jotting the name down along with contact information. "Anyone else?"

"We like to pride ourselves in being a good place to work," Clint answered, searching his memory. "We don't have a lot of people who don't stay. We hire good people and good people stay."

"Fair enough. We'll look into Rochester and see if he's keeping his nose clean."

Clint nodded, unsettled by the conversation. He'd always been a straightforward guy. He tried to be fair and consistent, but there would always be someone who thought you were the worst no matter what you did.

Was that the case? Was there someone out there hating him so much that they wanted him dead?

"What about past lovers?" Ty asked. "Sometimes matters of the heart get messy."

"There's only one woman I dated in the recent past, Iris Yearly, and she's already moved on to someone else. I doubt she cares about what I'm doing enough to cultivate this kind of scheme."

"We should check it out, just in case. When it comes to emotion, things are never as black and white as we want them to be."

He knew that to be true. This situation with Jordana had him twisted in knots. Clint nodded and jotted down Iris's contact information. God, he hoped it wasn't Iris. He exhaled a long breath. He wanted this nightmare to end. "Do you need anything else?"

"No, I think this will keep us busy for a few days."

"Good." Clint wanted to focus on work; that was

something he understood. He had a major meeting with a new client and if they landed their account it could mean a lot to their company. He didn't want to let anyone down and he still felt insecure about his memory. There were patches, blank spots, in his memory that cropped up at unexpected moments and he sweated the possibility of losing something vital at a crucial moment.

It was why he'd been staying late at the office. It could also be that he wasn't entirely proud of his mumbled apology for being a difficult ass. Sure, Jordana had accepted his weak defense but he hadn't let himself off the hook because he knew she'd deserved some groveling on his part. The thing was, he wanted to be able to show Jordana that they were both safe from any real threats, but he couldn't do that unless he could prove it.

While Jordana worked with Ty, he poured over past accounts, refreshing his memory, reading mountains of memos, texts and emails so that his recall was up to date.

But all that "homework" took a toll on his time with Jordana, which he hated, but he couldn't see a way around it. He'd much rather spend his time curled around her luscious body, listening to her laugh, making her sweat, but he couldn't risk losing everything because of his memory loss. It was a full-time job keeping that information under wraps, particularly from Alex. If it weren't for Jeana, he never would've been able to pull it off.

Speaking of Jeana, he hoped and prayed Ty was able to clear her. It would stab him in the heart if Jeana were found to be the one behind all this drama.

Also, if it was Jeana, he was in a whole lot of trouble because she knew everything.

She also knew when would be the best time to strike again.

He was living on the edge of a sword but he didn't know who was doing the swinging.

JORDANA WAS RESTLESS back at the penthouse. She felt like a caged bird in a pretty prison but she couldn't leave unless she knew Clint was safe. She wasn't the type to go shopping or sightseeing. She preferred having a job. So when Ty showed up at the penthouse and invited her to come along to question a former employee, Derrick Rochester, she couldn't dress fast enough.

Meeting Ty downstairs in the lobby, she grinned when he ushered her into an awaiting rented car. "You have no idea how you are saving my sanity right now," she said.

"I figured you were going stir-crazy when Clint said you were staying behind at his place."

"You got that right," she replied. "I'm beginning to question if it was a good idea to come to Chicago. I'm not being all that useful and I can't just sit at home like a good little puppy waiting for its master to come home."

"Which is basically what everyone was thinking when you decided to leave with Clint. He seems like a great guy, don't get me wrong, but everyone who knows you…well, this kind of gig just isn't your thing."

She knew he was talking about the completely different world Clint inhabited in comparison to her own. "I know," Jordana said, shaking her head. "I care about him a lot, maybe I even love him, but I don't know how this works out in the long run. I've been thinking, maybe I should go back to Braxville."

"Is that what you want?"

"I don't know what I want. I just know that I'm not doing any good here. He doesn't want to work on the case with me and he's so distracted with the business that he doesn't have time for me on a personal level so why the hell am I staying?"

"What do you mean he doesn't want to talk about the case?"

"He says he's overwhelmed and just needs a break when he comes home, which I can understand, but sometimes I feel he doesn't give sufficient weight to the fact that there's someone out there trying to kill him."

"If it makes you feel any better, I don't think he's trying to ignore that fact. I think he's trying to keep a lot of balls up in the air and a few keep dropping. I feel bad for the guy, honestly."

"Yeah?"

"I do. He's trying to balance a new relationship in spite of a bunch of different and equally time-consuming situations. I think anyone would be overwhelmed."

Jordana digested her brother's comment, nodding. "Yeah, that makes sense, but even so, it does draw attention to the red flags that are waving all over the place."

"Such as?"

"Such as, I don't belong in his world. I don't fit. I'm not ever going to be some society girl or a 'lady who lunches' and I don't see myself joining the Chicago PD. I like the pace of Braxville and maybe that's not ambitious enough for some people but I liked my job back home. Hell, I miss home. I miss my bed. I miss my judgy cat."

"Ugh, that cat. He *is* judgy," Ty agreed.

"But I don't want to leave unless I know Ty is in good hands."

"Do you want to leave Clint behind?"

"Not really," she admitted with misery. "But I don't think I can stay, either."

"Why not?"

"Because if I stay, I'll become more resentful and eventually it'll just tear us apart. I'd rather leave before we hate each other."

He chuckled. "Maybe it won't come to that."

"No, it will. I can't stay," she realized, her sinuses clogging with the sadness of that conclusion. "Maybe it's true that if you truly love someone you have to let them go. Staying would be a disaster for us both."

"I want you to be happy, sis. If you think leaving is the best for both of you, I know I won't be able to change your mind. All I can do is promise that I'll keep your man safe while you're gone."

Jordana wiped at her eyes. "Thank you."

"When are you going to tell him?"

"Probably tonight, after I make my flight plans. I don't want to give him the chance to change my mind."

"For what it's worth, I think he's a good man. I like the way you light up around him. I've never seen you so happy…or so sad. I think it's real between you."

She smiled, appreciating her big brother's support. "I think it's real, too."

But staying would be a mistake. As much as she loved Clint, she wasn't doing him any good here and she was needed in Braxville.

Sometimes being an adult meant making hard choices.

Leaving Clint behind before she knew who was behind his attack was a thorn in her side but she knew she was leaving Clint in good hands.

Ty would do whatever was necessary to catch the person responsible.

She wasn't looking forward to that conversation when she told Clint she was leaving.

Until then, she was happy to distract herself with a little old-fashioned investigative legwork.

Chapter Twenty-Two

"I don't want you to leave," Clint said, facing off with Jordana, even as she stood with her bags packed and her Uber waiting downstairs. "C'mon, Jordana, talk to me. What's this about?"

"It's about me being in the wrong place for the wrong reasons," she said, wiping at her eyes.

Clint was at a loss. One minute things were great and the next Jordana was bailing? "Is this about our argument the other night?"

"Yes, but no."

"I should've apologized better. I knew you deserved a better apology but I got caught up in work—that's no excuse, I'm sorry. I was rude and insensitive," he said, trying to make things right.

But Jordana shook her head. "It's not that. I'm not so petty as to decide this over one fight. The fight was just what opened my eyes to what is happening here. I'm dying not being able to be useful. I'm not the kind of person who can spend hours shopping and being frivolous with my time. I like to have a job. I'll never have that here and it doesn't matter how much I love you—"

His heart leaped at her admission. "You love me?"

She pressed her lips together as if pained, admitting, "Yes, I do. Maybe it's crazy to fall for someone as quickly as I did but, Clint, I do love you, whether it was too fast or not. However, sometimes love just isn't enough. You and I are old enough to know that it takes more than just feelings to make things work. The logistics between us are a nightmare."

"I'll fix it," he promised. "Give me a chance to fix things."

"It's not something you can fix or you should fix. You belong here. I belong in Braxville. C'mon, we both knew that this was a fairy tale that wouldn't have a happy ending. I should've listened to everyone who told me that it was a mistake to come here. I'm just coming to my senses and righting the ship."

"So, I'm a mistake? Your feelings for me are a mistake?" he asked, stung.

Jordana looked exasperated and sad at the same time. "Of course not, but maybe a little? I'm sorry, I know I'm not making much sense. All I know is that I can't stay but I'm leaving you in good hands. Ty will figure out who's threatening you, and your life can get back to normal. I'm not a part of that normal life. If you stop to think about it, you know I'm right."

"Bullshit, Jordana, you're running away from your feelings because you're not ready to admit that I'm the game-changer in your life. You don't like surprises or things you can't control. I'm sorry I threw your life into a tailspin but I'm not sorry for the way I feel—and you shouldn't be, either."

She didn't argue his point. "My Uber is waiting. I have to go if I'm going to catch my flight."

"Screw your Uber. You're not leaving."

"I am leaving," Jordana said, grabbing her suitcase and carry-on. "Don't make this harder than it already is."

"Please, don't go."

Tears welled in her eyes but she didn't waver. "You'll realize this is best when you've had some distance."

"I love you, Jordana."

"You'll get over it," Jordana said, her voice strangled. "Goodbye, Clint."

And he watched her leave. His heart cracked in two but his feet remained rooted to the carpet. He should run after her, beg her to stay, but he couldn't do it.

Wouldn't do it.

If she wanted to go, he couldn't tie her to a chair and make her stay.

Was it his pride? Maybe.

But maybe it was because he didn't know how to convince her that he wanted her more than anything else if she didn't already know it. Or deep down, he knew she was right at a certain level, in that place where he didn't want to acknowledge or see.

Chicago wasn't her town, wasn't her vibe. He'd seen her slowly withdraw, and when she'd tried to reach out to him, he'd been too focused on work to make the effort.

Hell, maybe love wasn't in the cards for him. If it wasn't going to happen with Jordana, he didn't want it with anyone else.

Clint cursed under his breath and wiped at the tears on his cheeks. *Screw it, if she wants to leave, that's her choice.*

He had plenty to keep him busy.

Even though it hurt, Clint shoved Jordana from his mind. He had bigger problems than his fractured love life.

Time to focus on what mattered.

JORDANA CRIED THE entire Uber ride to O'Hare. Barely managed to wipe her tears away long enough to board her flight and then quietly sobbed through most of the two-hour flight back to Kansas.

By the time she reached her house, it was late and she was emotionally exhausted.

Falling into her bed, she took comfort in the familiarity but then caught a lingering whiff of Clint in her bedding and she started crying all over again.

At some point, she fell asleep, but by morning, she felt run over by a truck. Still, routine offered some semblance of calm as she showered, dressed and headed to the station.

Reese looked up, surprised to see her.

"What are you doing here?" he asked. "You're supposed to be in Chicago."

"I'm back and ready to jump into my caseload," she answered with false cheerfulness. "Turns out the Windy City wasn't for me. I'm excited to get back to work. Any leads on the Fenton case?"

She didn't want to talk about Clint or Chicago, a vibe that Reese caught right away and followed her lead for the time being. She was sure he'd have plenty of questions later but she appreciated the fact that he knew her well enough to leave it alone.

"Maybe. So forensics came back on both the bodies. They tested positive for chromated copper arsenic, an unusual chemical to be found on bodies that are twenty-plus years dead."

"Arsenic of the deadly sort is found usually in soft tissue but there wasn't any soft tissue left," she said.

"Exactly. So that begs the question, why was it found on the bones?"

"Unless it was an environmental property within the surroundings where the victims were found," she supposed.

"That's what I was thinking. I did a little digging and it turns out that chromated copper arsenic is a pesticide/preservative used to prevent rotting in lumber that's going to be used outside. CCA is usually found in pressure-treated wood."

Jordana mused over the information, apprehension replacing her previous determination to focus on nothing but work. She had a bad feeling about this new development.

"Tell me more about CCA. Is this a normal building material?"

"Maybe back when the warehouse was built but not since the EPA put the kibosh on CCA-treated wood in 2003." He looked to Jordana. "Do you know when that building was built? If it was built in the 1970s up until 2003, then it makes sense that it might have CCA-treated wood."

"I don't know when that building was built," she murmured, worrying her bottom lip. "I could ask my dad. He should know."

"Do you want me to ask him? Just to give you some separation from your family with the case."

Her dad would not appreciate Reese poking around his business and it was not likely to end with her dad's cooperation without a warrant. She sighed. "No, I'll ask him. My dad can be difficult at times."

She returned to the bodies. "Okay, let's assume that the bodies were close to CCA-treated wood and that's why the chemical compound showed up in the lab. It doesn't give us much information on who killed them."

"No, but most killers don't leave calling cards," Reese quipped.

Jordana allowed a short smile but she didn't feel like joking around. Her heart was heavy and now her mind was cluttered. There was something about that CCA showing up that bothered her but she couldn't quite put her finger on why. "So CCA-treated wood was a commonly used building material until 2003?"

"From what I can tell."

"So why'd the EPA ban the use of it after 2003?"

"It's sick. Chromated copper arsenic, as it turns out, is dangerous to humans. Like, as in real bad. Of course, it took some people dropping like flies for the EPA to figure out that maybe humans shouldn't be around that poison before they dropped the ban hammer. Hey, as we all know, government agencies run slow as molasses in winter."

She agreed, still thinking. Did her dad know about the chromated copper arsenic in that warehouse? She couldn't imagine that he had. Her dad liked to do things by the book. If he found out that the materials being used were harmful, he'd take care of it. Her dad was a lot of things but he wasn't a monster.

"So, everything okay?" Reese asked, tentatively broaching the subject she wanted to avoid. "I didn't expect to see you back so soon."

"It just didn't work out. Turns out I was more of a distraction than a help so my brother Ty is there running down leads and I came back here where I'm useful."

"Oh, so everything's cool with you and Broderick?"

"Um, I'd rather not talk about it, honestly. I just want to focus on work," she answered, struggling to keep the tears at bay. Reese nodded, letting it go, and she was grateful. "Hey, so, does it matter when that warehouse was built? It's not like chromated copper arsenic killed Fenton and the other victim, right?"

"Yeah, I guess not. I was just curious. Seemed an interesting find on the forensics."

Jordana breathed a secret sigh of relief. She didn't want to talk to her dad about the warehouse even though it was inevitable at some point. He owned the building where two bodies were found. She'd been the one to stop construction, which hadn't been the greatest conversation she'd ever had with her dad.

And as long as the investigation was ongoing, she couldn't let construction resume, which was putting a strain on her dad's budget, but she didn't have a choice. It was her job.

Now was a complicated time in her family's life with Uncle Shep coming home and Bridgette back in town.

Honestly, sometimes she understood why her mother was always scrubbing the kitchen.

A clean kitchen was something she could control.

Maybe she ought to give her kitchen a good scrubbing.

Lord knows, she could use the outlet.

Chapter Twenty-Three

Clint stared morosely into his Scotch, asking Ty, "Why'd she leave?" but he knew Ty didn't have any answer that was different from the one Jordana had given any more than his fourth Scotch had the answer. "I don't understand. We had something good and she just up and left me behind like I was nothing to her."

Now he was repeating himself. He'd turned into the weepy kind of drunk he hated but his heart wouldn't accept the truth as it stared him in the face. He wanted a different answer, something that made him feel better but there wasn't anything that would make him feel any different and he knew it.

"I think you've had enough, buddy," Ty said, signaling to the bartender for the tab, but Clint wasn't ready to leave. He wanted to get hammered and forget that the woman he was crazy about had left him. But Ty wasn't taking no for an answer. "You'll thank me in the morning," he promised, helping Clint off the stool. "Besides, no one needs to see you like this."

Ty made a fair point. He was the boss. People depended on him. He signed the checks. Being sloppy drunk wasn't a good look. If only his heart didn't feel like it was being torn in two by dueling rottweilers.

"Fine, we'll go but only if you promise to call Jordana for me and put in a good word. Maybe she's not mad anymore," he said, his mind swimming. "I mean, how long does your sister stay mad?"

"She didn't leave because she was mad," Ty said, maneuvering him out the pub door and into the awaiting Uber. He slid in beside Clint and shut the door. "She left because she wasn't getting any traction here and you didn't exactly help her feel like she was needed."

"What are you talking about? I need her. I need her like nothing I've ever needed before in my life. Do you even know how hard it is for me to admit that?"

Ty chuckled. "Yeah, I can guess, but Jordana needs a job. She's always been that way. Maybe this was for the best."

"Stop saying that," he growled. "Does it look like it was for the best? Do *I* look like I'm at my best? You don't even have to answer—I can tell by your face that I'm a mess. I know it, you don't have to lie."

"Okay, I won't lie," Ty said. "You are a mess but my sister's not one to stick around to prop up broken men. Figure it out, man."

"I didn't say I was broken," Clint muttered, drawing away only to smack his head on the glass by accident. He cursed loudly as he rubbed his forehead. "This car is too small. Why are we riding in a shoebox?" To the driver, he said, "No offense, my man, I'm sure it's great," and returning to Ty to whisper in a not so whispery voice, "Seriously though, what the hell? I have a car service with adult-size cars at my disposal. Why are we riding in a toy car?"

Ty laughed. "You are messed up. Shut up and enjoy the ride. You're lucky I like you enough to get you safely home. I promised Jordana I'd look out for you but I'm not sure that extended to drunken binges after-hours."

"I miss her," Clint admitted in a sad voice. "I miss the smell of her hair, the taste—"

"Whoa, hold up, that's my sister, remember? I'm going to try and pretend that I don't know how close you two were, okay?"

"Right, right," he said, apologizing. "I've never had a sister. Or a brother. My parents weren't the prolific type. I'm not even sure how they made me. Separate beds my entire childhood," he shared in a slurred whisper. "Never the two shall meet. Seriously, how'd they make a kid if they didn't share a bed? It's a mystery, right?"

Ty grinned because he was being an idiot but Clint didn't care. He was sloppy drunk, no sense in denying it. But that's what happened when you had to numb the pain of losing someone. "Tell me something about Jordana that I don't know," he said, almost desperate to hear anything about her.

"Like what?"

"I don't know…what was her favorite cereal as a kid?"

Ty did a double take. "Cereal? Hell, I don't know. She wasn't much of a cereal eater that I can recall. She was always bitching about how everyone left an empty box in the pantry. Now that I think about it, she liked Cream of Wheat. Not cereal per se, but a breakfast meal. But she liked it lumpy. Out of all us kids, she was the only one who liked her Cream of Wheat with big ol' lumps in it. No one liked it when Jordana made it for everyone, which I think she did on purpose so she could eat the whole pot herself."

"That's my crafty girl," Clint said, happy and proud for no particular reason, only that it was a story about Jordana. "She's a go-getter."

"She is," Ty agreed. "One time for a science fair project she proved that ants' stomachs were transparent by collecting a handful of ants and then feeding them colored sugar water. Bugs never bothered Jordana—she was a bit of a tomboy. Afterward, she released the ants back into the ant hill where she'd collected them but the colony rejected the ants because of their colored abdomens and tore them apart. It was brutal. She was more fascinated by the ants' reaction than the results of her science fair project."

"No wonder she went into detective work," Clint said, impressed and a little scared of twelve-year-old Jordana. "Ants' stomachs are transparent?"

"Yeah, well, at least the ants she collected. Not sure about the specific species and whatnot. Too many years between now and then. I remember our mom being freaked out about the ants being in the house. She found it macabre and disgusting at the same time."

"I think it's cool," Clint said.

Ty nodded. "Me, too."

They arrived at the penthouse and Ty dutifully made sure that Clint made it inside before telling him to hit the bed and he'd call in the morning.

Ty left Clint for his hotel room in spite of Clint's offer of the spare bedroom to crash in.

"You probably snore and I'm a light sleeper," Ty joked. "I'll talk to you tomorrow. Sleep it off, buddy."

But it was Clint who slept in the guest bedroom. There was no way the ghosts in his bed would allow any sleep.

Some battles you just couldn't win.

AS MUCH AS Jordana tried to get out of a family dinner, Bridgette's pitiful begging forced her hand.

"Please don't leave me alone with our parents. All

they want to talk about is why I haven't started dating yet, and no matter how many times I tell them I'm simply not ready, they don't seem to hear me. I'm going to need backup."

"There's no time limit on grief," Jordana said, being supportive. "I think it's a testament to how much you loved Henry that you're reluctant to step back into the dating pool."

"It's like people expect me to just move on and that's not happening. I planned to spend a life with him. Now that he's gone, I don't know how to pick up the pieces again without feeling guilty for snatching some happiness."

"Never feel guilty for happiness," Jordana admonished. "Henry loved you so much. He'd never want you to wallow in sadness for the rest of your life."

"No, he would've told me to move on," Bridgette agreed with a watery laugh. "Henry was laughter personified. The man never met a person he couldn't make a friend. It's not fair that he's gone and terrible people are walking around fresh as a daisy."

"Life isn't fair," Jordana agreed sadly. "Yes, I'll be there tonight and be your backup if our parents start in on you."

"Thank you, sis," Bridgette said with a sigh of relief. "I owe you one."

Jordana chuckled. "You still owe me for that time I didn't tell Mom and Dad you snuck out your freshman year to be with your boyfriend at the time who was a senior. Your ass would've been toast."

"Oh, my goodness, I forgot about that." Bridgette laughed. "What was I thinking? That could've ended badly."

"Yeah, and I didn't sleep all night until you slipped

in at five in the morning. I wanted to ring your neck. I had finals the next day and I was exhausted from worrying about you."

Amusement colored Bridgette's voice as she retorted, "It's not my fault you never took any chances or risks in high school. You were so straitlaced. No one was surprised when you decided to go into the military right out of high school. Why didn't you go career military?"

"I liked the structure and the strong sense of duty, but in the end, I just couldn't see myself toe the line under someone else's command until I retired. As much as I wished I had Uncle Shep's resolve, I knew it wasn't going to be for me in the long run. I don't regret a single moment in service, though."

"Makes sense. For all your determination to follow rules, you have a rebel streak buried inside you. I see it now and then and I fully support seeing it more often." She paused a minute before asking, "Have you talked to Clint since coming home?"

"No, and I don't plan to," she answered, losing her smile. Clint was the hot stove that she couldn't quite touch yet. "Ty gives me updates so I know what's happening with the investigation, but other than that, I steer clear."

"Do you miss him?"

"Yes." That single word wasn't big enough to convey what she felt in her heart but it was all she had. "More than I thought possible."

"Then swallow your pride and *call* him," Bridgette said.

"No, it's better this way. A clean cut. We can both move on," she said, holding the line. "Trust me, chasing after something that's doomed from the start is a really bad idea."

"I think the reason you're running away is because you're scared of the big feelings you have. You're always the one in control, but when you fall in love, the things you thought you could control go out the window."

"I've been in love before," she corrected her sister, but it hadn't felt like this. From the start Clint made her feel something different. Her feelings had been wild and untamed, definitely something she wasn't used to, but she wasn't running. "Trust me, he's much better off finding a woman who's content to be arm candy. You know that's just not me."

"He fell in love with you," Bridgette insisted, refusing to let it go. That was the thing about family—particularly sisters—when they had a bone, they never let it go. "If you're hurting, he must be, too. Think about that."

She didn't want to think about Clint at all. She just wanted him to be safe. "Can we change the subject?" Jordana asked. "I'm not in the right frame of mind to have this conversation. Besides, I'm going to need your backup with Dad. I know he's going to ask me again when I can let him resume construction and I don't have the answer he wants."

"Yeah, that's a tough one."

"Gee, thanks, you think?"

"I'm sorry. You're right. We both need to have each other's backs. It's going to be a rough one. Do you want me or you to pick up the wine?"

"I'll do it."

"Cool. See you at six."

"I'll be there with bells on—with alcohol in both hands."

"You're the best big sister," Bridgette said.

"I'm your only big sister."

"That's what makes you the best."

They ended the conversation on a shared chuckle but Bridgette's advice to call Clint stuck in her head. Closure was important for them both. Calling him would only reopen wounds that were trying to heal.

But she missed the sound of his voice.

The way that cute dimple popped out when he grinned.

And the way it felt to fall asleep in his arms, safe and secure that all was right in the world for at least that moment.

No, she wouldn't call.

Even if she thought about it every day.

Chapter Twenty-Four

Jordana's first response to her mom's invitation of dinner was to make an excuse to avoid a sit-down with her parents given the uncertain situation facing the investigation, but she chickened out and caved. Mostly for Bridgette, so she wasn't left sitting through an awkward dinner alone. But Jordana could've timed her watch to her dad's launch into the "nonsense" holding up his timeline and she wished she'd followed her first impulse, sister or not.

"Do you realize how much money I'm losing each day you hold up demolition on the warehouse? I've got investors that are chewing on my ass wanting answers and I don't have any to give them."

Jordana shared a glance with Bridgette before answering carefully, "You know I can't talk about an open investigation, Dad. We're moving as fast as we can, that's all I can say."

"I don't understand why you've got to keep the demo shut down. You've got the bodies. Why do you need the site any longer?" her dad persisted, ignoring the pointed look from his wife. "It's total bureaucratic red tape and it's costing me millions. I could lose this bid if it keeps up. You want that to happen? You enjoying the food on this table? Well, if I lose this bid, you can bet things are going to change around here."

"Dad, it's not Jordana's fault two bodies were found in your warehouse," Bridgette piped in. "Just let her do her job."

Their dad swiveled his gaze to Bridgette, pointing his fork at her, "And you, missy, you're no better in all this. What's with all the questions about chemicals with my business. If I didn't know better, I'd say my whole family was trying to bankrupt me."

"Fitz!" Lilly gasped, appalled. "Stop it. We're not talking business at the dinner table."

"Well, Lilly, my business is under attack," he shot back, not willing to back down. "Dex told me the other day that Bridgette's office is poking around in our supply chain, asking questions about history that has nothing to do with today. I never thought I'd see the day when my own family had a knife to my throat."

"Daddy, that's not what's happening," Bridgette insisted. "It's standard procedure. You know I'm here because of the cancer cluster. Every business is under scrutiny, not just yours. I promise you it's not personal. Besides, why are you worried? I'm sure you've done nothing that's going to turn up bad."

"That's not the point. Of course I'm not worried about that—I'm worried about losing this contract, which my business sorely needs. Construction jobs are down, the economy is depressed and I had to fight tooth and nail to win the bid. The last thing I need is a cloud of suspicion hanging over my head scaring off future investors. You're only as good as your last job and I don't want the Ruby Row Center to be the last job Colton Construction gets to call finished."

"It won't be," Bridgette assured their dad, but Jordana shifted against the feeling that their dad wasn't being entirely honest.

"Dad…when was the warehouse built?" she asked, remembering her earlier conversation with Reese.

He looked up from his plate, annoyed. "What?"

"I'm just wondering…when was the warehouse built?"

Her dad waved away the question. "What does that matter?"

"I was just curious." She couldn't share that CCA was found on the remains without getting into the details of the investigation. "I thought you might know."

"I don't know, mid-1970s," he answered gruffly. "Somewhere around there."

She breathed a secret sigh of relief. If the EPA hadn't banned the use of CCA-treated wood until 2003, her father was in the clear as far as the chemical showing up on the bodies.

"I don't want another word about business," Lilly declared, putting her foot down in a firm tone. "I want to enjoy a nice dinner without all the shouting and bad energy. Am I clear?"

But without work to focus on, Lilly was quick to jump to Bridgette. "Darling, we're so happy to have you home again. I know it's been hard without Henry. How are you doing?"

"I'm fine, Mom," Bridgette answered with a bright smile, but her eyes told a different story. "Just keeping focused on my career. This assignment was a huge coup for my promotion. It was coincidental that it landed in Braxville but I'm happy to be home for a bit. Nice change of pace."

"And we're so happy to have you home. Oh, I ran into that nice boy you used to date, Vincent Hogan, the other day. He works at the Feed 'N Seed now. Runs it for his dad. Very nice young man. You should see if he's free for lunch sometime. I always thought you made a nice couple."

Jordana was ready to jump in to deflect their mom's direction but it was Fitz who shut her down first. "Lilly, give it a rest. Stop trying to play matchmaker all the time," he growled with irritation. "The girl can find her own dates. She doesn't need you throwing eligible bachelors at her."

Lilly's mouth pressed together as she shot daggers at her husband. The tension between them was uncomfortable. Jordana felt for Bridgette being stuck in this house with the two of them. "I'm just making conversation, Fitz," she replied stiffly.

"It's okay, Mom," Bridgette assured Lilly, trying to salvage their ruined dinner. "Vince was always very nice but we had nothing in common. We were better as friends."

"Being friends first is important," Lilly said, slipping one last comment in before moving on. "Anyway, it might be nice to catch up. As friends, of course."

"Maybe. If I have time," Bridgette said with a smile for Lilly's sake.

Mollified, Lilly rose, saying, "I made pie from apples picked at Applegate Orchards. Frannie says this batch is probably the best they've had in years. Well, you know they had that worm infestation that one year. Terrible stuff. But they're all good now." She smiled, hands on hips. "So, who wants a slice?"

Fitz wiped his mouth with his napkin and rose without answering. When he left the room, Jordana tried not to see the pain in her mom's eyes. Why was her dad wound so tightly?

"I'll have some, Mom," she said, prompting Bridgette to join in.

"I can't turn down pie."

Lilly nodded, her smile strained but appreciative. "Two slices coming up." She disappeared into the kitchen.

It wasn't until her mom was clear of the dining room that Jordana looked to Bridgette in question. "What bit Dad in the butt?"

"I think this demo situation is hitting him harder than we realized. I've never seen him strung so tight, which is saying a lot."

Jordana nodded. "I'm working as fast as I can," she promised, but in light of her dad's meltdown, she couldn't help but feel the pressure.

And no amount of apple pie was going to fix that.

CLINT WAS DOING everything he could to distract himself from Jordana's absence but seeing as he wasn't sleeping in his bed—and the guest bed wasn't quite as comfortable—he had a crick in his neck that didn't help his surly mood.

He eyed the phone as if it were a traitor for not ringing with Jordana on the other end. How could she just walk away as if what they'd been to each other was nothing?

Was it so easy for her to slip back into her routine as if he'd been nothing more than a momentary distraction, a blip on her emotional radar that warranted little response?

Jeana walked in, the picture of efficiency with a permanent pleasant smile etched on her face. Suspicion narrowed his gaze. Could Jeana be the one poised to stab the knife in his back? Clint was still doing background checks so he didn't have an answer. For now, he was supposed to act like it was business as usual.

"Good news, Nortec is ready to negotiate their newest tech contract and Broadlocke was their first choice. Should I set up a meeting?"

He grunted in answer. "Make sure you cc Alex. I want him there, too. Alex knows Nortec's CEO, Byron Zucker, and it could help to have a friendly face across the table."

"Certainly. I'll make sure Mr. Locke is present. I picked up your dry cleaning and hired your new cleaning service as requested."

He couldn't remember asking for a new service. "When did I ask for that?"

"Oh, right before you left, sir. Seems the prior cleaning crew wasn't up to your standards. This new service comes highly recommended."

How hard was it to clean up after a bachelor who was rarely home? And what the hell kind of bad job had the previous service done in his eyes? His memory had returned for the most part but some lingering patchy spots made him feel like an old man losing his marbles. He nodded at Jeana with a short smile. "Thank you, Jeana."

She nodded, jotting some notes in her folder before snapping it shut and peering at him with concern. "May I speak freely, sir?"

Clint leaned back, curious. "Of course. Is something bothering you?"

"Not at all. I'm more concerned about you, sir. You've been…preoccupied since Miss Colton returned to Kansas. I wondered, if I might be so bold to suggest, that you try and smooth things over with her."

A wry smile curved his lips. "I appreciate your concern but that ship has sailed. I'm sorry I've been preoccupied. I'm working on it. I'll try harder."

"Oh, sir, I don't mean to imply that you've been less efficient. However, you do seem sad."

"Jeana…was I good boss? I mean, I'm starting to remember things that make me think that maybe I was a jerk. If I was, I apologize. You're an asset to my team and I don't know what I'd do without you."

Her pale cheeks flooded with color as she ducked her head, flustered and pleased at the same time. "Thank you, sir. That's the nicest thing you've ever said to me."

"You see, right there, that comment… Was I horrible? Please be honest. I need to know what public opinion of me is like around here."

He could tell she was choosing her words carefully as she shared, "Well, sir, you were certainly a boss who knew how he wanted things done and you were fairly rigid in how you would expect people to do them. I'm sure some've chafed under that kind of leadership, but to be fair, you're very good at what you do and with that skill takes a certain level of confidence, which can be off-putting for some."

"But not for you?"

"Oh, goodness, no, I appreciate a firm hand. I like guidelines and structure. You have always provided both."

There was something about the way she looked at him, both adoringly and shy, that made him wonder if Jeana had a secret crush on him. From what he knew of Jeana, she would never act on it even if she went to bed with a life-size pillow with his face plastered on it.

Unrequited love could be dangerous.

He regarded Jeana with quiet speculation. "Jeana,

may I ask you a personal question that may sound out of line?"

Jeana's expression faltered but she nodded. "If you think it will help, of course."

"My memory is still spotty in some places… Did we ever…what I mean to ask is…well, I don't remember if we ever…had…"

Jeana's eyes widened as she caught where he was fishing. She blushed harder and shook her head vehemently. "No, sir, never! You've always been the picture of a gentleman. Never improper with any of your employees. I can say with authority that your moral character is beyond reproach."

He breathed a short sigh of relief. God, it was shocking how worried he was about her answer. "Good, good," he said, tapping the top of his desk lightly. "Very happy to hear that. Thank you, Jeana. I appreciate your candor."

"Will that be all, sir?" she asked, lifting her chin, returning to the efficient assistant within a blink, as if she clung to that persona as a life raft when the seas turned choppy.

"Yes, thank you."

Jeana smiled and nodded, turning on her heel, click-clicking out of his office with short efficient steps filled with purpose.

Jeana was an odd duck but was she a killer?

Either she was the world's best actress or Jeana was exactly as she seemed—a stellar assistant with a possibly mild but ultimately harmless crush on her boss.

Being wrong could prove to be a fatal mistake.

Chapter Twenty-Five

"A blind date? Are you insane?" Jordana asked, staring at Reese as if he'd grown a second head. After that disastrous dinner with her parents, the fire to solve the warehouse murders was burning bright, but Reese was too interested in setting her up with a buddy to be serious for a minute.

"You need to get out there, shake things up a bit," Reese said, undeterred.

Good grief. Jordana made a concentrated effort to return the conversation to solid ground. "Oh, I talked to my dad about the warehouse, and it was built in the 1970s. He couldn't remember the exact date but it doesn't matter because the EPA didn't ban CCA until 2003 so the point is moot."

"C'mon, Jordana. The best way to get over a guy is to get onto a new guy," Reese said, stubbornly refusing to drop it. "His name is Blaine and I think you'd dig him."

"First of all, gross. Second of all, I would never agree to a blind date with a guy named Blaine. Where'd you meet him? The country club?" She'd had her fill of wealthy men.

"Does Braxville have a country club?" Reese asked, momentarily distracted.

"Yes, of course we have a country club. Even people

in Braxville like to golf," she answered, exasperated, gesturing back to the case on her desk. "Can we please talk about the case? We need to focus. I think we should go over what we know, a recap of the facts to refresh our memories. Sound good?"

He groaned. "No, it does not sound good. You might've taken a break but while you were gone I did nothing but eat, sleep and dream about these bodies and that damn warehouse. Maybe I need a break this time."

"Well, playing matchmaker isn't going to help you relax. You should stick to something you're good at." She paused to question, "What exactly are you good at?"

"Ha. Ha. Very funny." Sighing, he swiveled back to his desk and pulled his research file. "Fine. Here's what we know so far—two bodies, one male, one female. The male, approximate age mid-to early fifties, and the female, mid-to late twenties. Both suffered blunt force trauma to the head, which suggests foul play. The male, Fenton Crane, was a private investigator related to your John Doe, later identified as Clint Broderick, and the female, Olivia Harrison from Kansas City, was reported missing by her mother, Rita Harrison, but never found. Dental records were used to positively identify both."

Jordana rubbed her forehead. It was impossible to untangle her family's connection to all the players in this case. Gwen Harrison, Olivia's daughter, showed up in Braxville looking for answers and instead fell in love with Jordana's younger brother, Brooks.

Not the most convenient love match but she supposed you couldn't help who you fell in love with. Tiptoeing around all the conflicts of interest in this case was turning into a tap-dancing competition.

"And Fenton was hired by Rita to look for her daughter, Olivia, which unbeknownst to her had been walled up in an abandoned warehouse owned by my father."

"Yep."

"And it would seem that Fenton met the same fate as Olivia, possibly by the same perp, seeing as both died from blunt force trauma."

"The evidence would suggest as much."

"The question that keeps bouncing around in my head is why someone would kill a young mother?"

"Statistically, probably the father of her child, but seeing as Olivia was tight-lipped about who she was seeing, I don't know how we'd figure that out. Rita is too old now to remember much detail from back then."

That was true. They'd questioned Rita Harrison about the disappearance of her daughter, Olivia, but twenty-plus years was a long time to hold on to small details that could make or break a case.

The sad fact—and one she wasn't ready to embrace—was cold cases with murdered women were hard to solve without DNA left behind at the scene. Forensics hadn't pulled anything from the body aside from the chemical CCA and those bones weren't doing much talking.

"We've taken DNA samples from Gwen and put it into the database, but unless the DNA of the father pops up somewhere, we're poking around in the dark," Reese said.

"It bothers me that whoever killed these people has been walking around scot-free. It's not right," Jordana said. "I hate injustice. There's too much of it in the world. Sometimes it's overwhelming. Are we making a difference at all?"

Reese's gaze met hers with conviction. "Of course we are. Little things add up to big things. Sure, maybe we're not the FBI or some bigger municipality but we make a difference here, in Braxville. People look to us to keep them safe and that's what we do every day to the best of our ability."

"But that's just it, Reese… I'd say Fenton Crane and Olivia Harrison might disagree that Braxville is a safe place. Right now people are looking for answers, not so much because they care about the case but because they need to feel safe again. If we can't solve who killed those people, we're going to lose the faith of people we are about."

"We're going to do our best," Reese maintained, refusing to let Jordana's pessimism leach into his belief. "Jordana, you're one of the most stubborn, most dedicated, officers I know. It's the reason you're lead detective on this case. The captain believes in you but so does everyone in this station."

"I appreciate the vote of support but let's be honest—the reason I'm in front of this case is because we're short-staffed. You and I both know, the conflicts of interest are so complicated and entangled that there's no way I should be lead detective."

"Don't look a gift horse in the mouth," Reese warned with a half smile. "I'll be honest, I didn't think you should be involved at first but you're incapable of being shifty. Your need to seek justice is part of your spine. I do not doubt that you'd haul in your own father if it turned out he was involved."

A shiver slithered down her spine at Reese's supportive statement. She murmured her thanks but in her mind's eye she saw her dad's obvious agitation from dinner and that chill turned to a cold freeze.

What if her dad knew more than he was letting on?

And if her dad was guilty, could she put handcuffs on her father and take him to jail?

She swallowed the sudden lump in her throat.

Please don't make me cross that bridge.

ALEX STRODE INTO Clint's office, a storm crossing his features that didn't bode well. "Do you want to tell me why a security agency is snooping around my personal affairs? Is there something I should know?"

Ty was making discreet inquiries but it was just a matter of time before Alex found out. That time was now.

"I hired Ty Colton for personal security. He's just doing his due diligence. It's a formality. I'm sure you're fine. Once he can scratch you off the list, it'll be like it never happened."

"I don't appreciate being watched," Alex growled. "You should've given me a heads-up that my privacy was going to be compromised."

He could understand Alex's ire but he couldn't tell Ty to back off. "If you can do me this favor, I'll owe you one."

"This is more than just buying someone a beer for a favor. He was asking questions that implied I might be a criminal or something. I'm a cofounder of this company. I'm not going to stand by and let some jerk-off disrespect me like that. I'm insulted that you would even suggest such a thing."

"C'mon, Alex. No one is asking you to stand naked in front of a stranger so he can give you a cavity search. I think you're overreacting a little bit."

Alex's nostrils flared. "Easy for you to say. It's not happening to you."

Clint knew Alex wasn't going to let this go unless

he gave him some backstory but he was taking a risk sharing the full details of his time in Braxville before Ty could clear Alex. He supposed in the interest of keeping the peace, he had to try.

"Sit down for a minute," he said, gesturing toward the open seat. When Alex dropped into the chair, his expression still hard, Clint said, "I wasn't entirely honest about my time in Braxville."

"What do you mean?"

"I mean, something happened to me while I was there that I tried to keep under wraps for the company's sake."

"What happened?" Alex asked, frowning with confusion. "I thought you went to Kansas to talk about your estranged uncle, the one they found walled up in a warehouse."

"Yeah, I did, but before I could talk to the detective, I was waylaid. Someone bashed me in the head and left me for dead. It was pure dumb luck that someone saw me crumpled on the side of the road."

"You were attacked?" Alex repeated, dumbfounded. "What the hell, man? Why didn't you tell me this earlier? I could've put a security detail together."

"I wanted to handle it privately. I didn't want anyone to lose confidence in my abilities to run the company. You know how scared investors can get when something upsets the status quo. I didn't want you to worry about me when you had to work on landing Nortec."

Alex waved away Clint's answer. "You're my best friend, not just my business partner. If someone was harassing you, you should've told me. I hate that you thought you had to shoulder that alone. Are you okay?"

"Yeah, all good. I was bruised and battered for a short while but I recovered and now I just want to make sure whoever attacked me isn't looking to finish the job the next time."

"Wait, you think this was more than just a random attack?"

"Honestly, I don't know, but in this case, I'd say it's better to be safe than sorry, right?"

"Sure, sure," Alex agreed, nodding. "Hey, I'm sorry I came in so hot. I didn't realize what you were going through."

"I know, it's okay. I wanted to tell you but I also wanted everything to go back to normal. Business as usual. It's bad enough that I have to deal with the aftermath. I don't want to deal with my business landing on shaky ground because of it."

"*Our* business," Alex corrected him with a wink.

"You know what I mean," Clint said. "Of course it's our business."

Alex accepted Clint's correction and said, "Okay, well, I think it's safe to say I'm not a threat. We've been in business together for too long. If I was going to kill you, it would've happened before now."

They chuckled together. Clint adding, "Yeah, a lot of water under that bridge."

"Damn straight. Remember when we were first starting and you didn't want to take that contract with Greger Corp? It would've been our first big contract and we needed the money, bad."

"Yeah, because when you get in bed with dogs, you end up with fleas," he said. "Besides, we ended up getting a better contract with a better class of people right after."

"Lucky break. Aaron Greger might not have been the kind of guy you wanted to share a dinner table with but that account would've put us on the map far earlier than we had on our own."

But Clint had dug his heels in and threatened to walk if Alex continued to chase after that contract and eventually Alex caved, which probably saved their friendship.

"See? If we could come out the other side after that major blowup, we can handle anything," Alex said.

Clint smiled, nodding. "Yeah, everything else feels like smooth sailing."

"We work well together," Alex said. "I mean, I wish you'd let us take some more risks, but you know, that's an old argument that we'll probably never resolve."

"You're already a wealthy man." Clint chuckled, shaking his head. "What's a little more in the bank going to do for us?"

"More is always better."

"Not always."

"And that's where we agree to disagree," Alex said, rising. "About that security detail…would you mind sending them in a different direction? I don't usually let someone that far up my ass unless they're paying for dinner first."

"I'll talk to Ty," Clint agreed, waving him off. "Get out of here and do some work, you heathen."

Alex laughed. "Takes one to know one, brother." He left Clint's office.

But once Alex was gone, Clint wondered if he'd just made a big mistake sharing that intel with his oldest friend. He didn't know who he could trust.

Damn, he missed Jordana. She was the one person he knew had his back.

If only his pride would allow him to beg for her return.

Chapter Twenty-Six

Jordana did anything she could to remain busy, even if it meant doing busywork at home that only a lunatic would jump feetfirst into—such as organizing her spice rack by alphabetical order. Her justification was that she didn't want to search for what she was looking for when cooking. She wanted to be able to go straight to the spice in question. Quick and efficient.

But then that job turned into a consolidation of spices, making sure that she didn't have duplicates, checking expiration dates and making a list of replacement spices as well as adding new ones. Her small project had turned into a major ordeal but she was happy to keep her mind occupied with anything other than fighting her urge to pick up the phone and call Clint just to hear his voice again.

As if summoned by her subconscious, her cell rang and she nearly ran to it, hoping against hope that it was Clint calling her.

When she saw it was Ty, her hope turned to dread.

"Hey, Ty, are you calling me with good or bad news?" she asked.

"Depends on your outlook. It could be considered good news but then it could also be very bad news."

"You know I hate ambiguous answers," she said with a groan. "Spit it out."

"I found the embezzler, if not who attacked Clint."

Her heart stopped. "Yeah? Who is it?" Someone he knew? Someone in his business circles? A past lover? The suspense was killing her. "C'mon, don't drag it out."

"Alex Locke is the one siphoning from the business accounts and he's been doing it for a long time. I'm talking millions. The guy has been living large on Broadlocke's purse."

Jordana let out a breath of disappointment. Clint was going to be crushed. "Have you told Clint yet?"

"No, not yet. I was going to do that this afternoon but I wanted to tell you first."

"Don't tell him yet. I'll deliver the bad news. He should hear it from a friendly face."

"Do you think that's a good idea? You left for a reason. I'm not sure you ought to rip open that wound all over again. Not just for you but for him, too."

"What do you mean?"

"The guy's been a mess since you left. He's only just now starting to pull it together. I'm not sure it's a good idea for you to come out here when he's finally doing better."

"I wouldn't be coming to reignite anything romantic. I just know that this news is going to devastate him. He should hear it from someone he knows has his best interests at heart."

Ty sighed, knowing that Jordana wasn't going to listen. "Fine. That works out. I have to cut things short here, anyway. I've got another case that's blowing up and needs my attention. My flight leaves tonight. How soon can you get here?"

She checked her watch and then her gaze met the spice mess on her counters. Forget the spice project. It could wait. "I'll take the next flight out."

Ty offered to put her flight on his expense account and Jordana let him. She wasn't going to let pride get in the way of getting to Chicago. Following a quick message to Reese explaining the situation, she quickly packed, smothering the little voice in the back of her head that cautioned against doing this. Ty was probably right but she couldn't bring herself to stay back. Clint needed her. She wasn't going to let him face this terrible news alone. Reese would be able to handle anything on the warehouse murders until she returned but Clint was in grave danger and needed her.

But what if, when she arrived, she was the last person Clint wanted to see? It wasn't as if she expected him to welcome her with open arms but she hoped he wasn't hostile. People with broken hearts were unpredictable in their reactions. It would crush her if Clint said awful things and pushed her way.

Judging by what Ty said, Clint had been suffering. She hated that she was the cause of that pain, but ultimately, it'd been best for them both. At least, that's what she told herself when she white-knuckled her urge to pick up the phone and apologize for running away.

The heart could justify just about anything. Such as making a trip to Chicago to deliver bad news.

Ah, for crying out loud, who was she trying to convince? She missed him. She missed Clint in a way that defied logic, the pain of his absence like a physical thing.

Trying to ignore the pain of his absence was like trying to ignore a knife in her side.

So, it was probably really shortsighted of her to jump

onto a plane to see the man she was trying to put in her rearview mirror. These circumstances weren't ordinary, though, she reminded herself. It wasn't as if she were traipsing off to see an ex-boyfriend for funsies or just to see if the spark was still there because she saw him on Facebook and he looked pretty good.

That was what her friend Layla did. Left her life in Braxville to go see an old boyfriend who had relocated to Washington state. For her, it worked out. Layla and her guy were living happily in that soggy state as if the years apart meant nothing.

But that was a fairy-tale ending that wasn't going to work out for Jordana and she wasn't expecting it to.

What was she expecting? First things first, she needed to make sure Clint was safe. Then they'd navigate the choppy waters of getting justice.

Of course Alex should go to jail but white-collar crime was usually given a slap on the wrist. Pay restitution, do some community service.

But if Alex was behind the attacks on Clint's life? That was a whole different story. Alex was in deep trouble if that was the case. Honestly, Jordana wasn't sure which scenario she hoped for more. A friend can forgive a lapse in judgment fueled by greed. It's a lot harder to forgive attempted murder.

JEANA ENTERED HIS office to announce, "Miss Colton is here to see you," and if he hadn't looked up in shock to find Jordana walk in, he would've sworn he'd misheard her. But there she was. Looking as beautiful as ever with her kissed-by-the-Kansas-sun skin, her eyes bright and those long legs that he remembered quite clearly kissing the length to find the promised land, and striding into his office with purpose. An Amazon warrior queen—that's what she looked like. That is, if an Amazon warrior queen was licensed to carry a gun instead of throwing a spear.

He blinked, half-afraid he was imagining Jordana, but when Jeana quietly closed the door behind her, leaving them alone, he knew he wasn't dreaming. Jordana was here.

And he couldn't play it cool. He was overjoyed. "You came back?" he asked. "Is everything okay?"

"I came to deliver you the news personally about who's been embezzling from your company," she said, her expression chagrined. "I wanted you to hear it from a friendly face."

"That doesn't bode well," he said, losing some of his joy. He held his breath, afraid of her answer. "Why didn't Ty tell me?"

"He was going to but I told him I'd do it. Seemed appropriate that since we started this journey together, I should be here with you when it ends."

"Don't say it like that—sounds like I'm dying or something."

She chuckled. "Sorry about that."

"At any rate, I'm glad you're here," he said, coming toward her. The tremulous smile on her lips told him she missed him, too. He wanted to fold her into his arms but there was also something about her body language that told him she wasn't there to pick up where they left off. He folded his arms across his chest, ready for the bad news. "All right, hit me, who's been stealing from me?"

"Ty found evidence that… Alex Locke has been stealing from the company for years. I'm so sorry."

He wasn't prepared for that punch to the chest. He'd half expected it to be a disgruntled employee looking to get even or a current lower-level employee with a grudge.

But Alex? Why? That couldn't be true. "Alex has no reason to steal from me. Ty is wrong."

"He's not wrong. Ty is very good at what he does. Ty sent me the documents." Jordana pulled her phone from her purse and queued up the files for him to see.

He accepted the phone in disbelief. Scanning the documents, he saw what he couldn't bring himself to believe. *Alex?* "I don't understand," he said. "Alex does not need to steal from the company. His net worth—"

"Is all on paper. Alex Locke is cash poor and he's teetering on the edge of bankruptcy. I'm sure he thought he didn't have a choice."

"He could've asked me for a loan if he was struggling." Clint, still reeling, was having a hard time wrapping his head around this information. "He's my oldest friend. I would've helped him out."

"Pride is a powerful thing," Jordana said sadly. Drawing a deep breath, she continued. "But now that we know, we need to alert Chicago authorities. They need to take over from this point."

"Turn him in? No, I don't want to do that. The bad press will kill this company. No, I'll handle it privately."

"I know you have to think about your company but you need to let the authorities in because there's a chance that Alex was the one who tried to kill you."

"No, I don't believe that at all. Sure, money problems I can understand. Bad judgment, whatever. But Alex would never try to kill me. That's absurd."

"I know how it feels to want something not to be true but the evidence is right here. Alex is the thief but he could also be the one who is trying to kill you. You can't take that chance. Once he figures out that you know, he might get desperate. Desperate people do stupid things. Don't let your friendship blind you."

"I need a minute to process," Clint said, leaning against his desk. He couldn't deny he was seeing the paper trail leading straight to Alex's doorstep but he couldn't accept that Alex had tried to kill him. "What does Alex have to gain if I'm dead?"

"Sole ownership of Broadlocke?" Jordana guessed as if it were a no-brainer. "He has money problems. Think of how it would benefit him to have you gone. Maybe he's tired of running plans by you or having to share the responsibility of decisions. I don't know, people do terrible things for less reasons."

Clint had a hard time accepting that Alex would do this to him but a niggling sense that Alex often chafed against Clint's decisions gave Jordana's theory a little more weight. Sure, he and Alex didn't always agree on which accounts to take, but in the end, they always managed to make it work.

Betrayal tasted bitter in his mouth. Jordana's expression softened, and she reached out to him, placing a hand gently on his, offering a simple, "I'm sorry," but he couldn't produce an appropriate response because his throat was choked up. Finally, he managed, "Meet me at the penthouse. I need to talk to Alex," but Jordana wasn't having it.

"No, that's a bad idea," Jordana protested, but his mind was made up. He and Alex had started this business from the ground up. He deserved answers and he wanted the man to look him in the eye when he gave them. But he should've known Jordana wasn't going to hang back. "If you're hell-bent on making a stupid decision, I'm not letting you go in without backup."

He already knew he loved her but in that moment, eyes shining with grim acceptance, willing to face an uncertainty with him, he loved her that much harder.

When this was all said and done…he was going to make things right with Jordana.

Chapter Twenty-Seven

Jordana knew there was a high probability of things turning bad once Clint confronted Alex. She'd seen too many instances where people got hurt. And against her better judgment, she didn't alert the authorities as she wanted to. Clint wanted to handle this himself. Jordana wouldn't dream of letting him walk into the lion's den alone, even if it meant things could go seriously sidewise.

Alex, similar to Clint, lived in a posh building on the top floor, but the immediate difference between Clint's place and Alex's was stark. For one, it looked as if Alex had been burglarized and just forgot to call police and report it. What little furniture remained in the room lay toppled as if someone had thrown them in a rage. One chair rested on its back with a broken leg. A wall mirror was shattered as if it'd been punched. Beyond that, the place was relatively bare but there was evidence on the walls that art or decor had once hung there. There was an air of sadness and ruin that was hard to miss.

"What the hell, man?"

By the look on Clint's face, it'd been a while since he'd been to his friend's place and the last time he was there it hadn't looked like this.

"Hey, uh, what are you doing here?" Alex asked,

his gaze darting from Jordana to Clint, trying not to squirm. "I wasn't expecting guests tonight."

"Or ever, if your place is any judge. What's going on?"

Alex ran a hand through his hair, irritated. "It's been a rough night. How about we talk about this in the morning. I've been getting ready to remodel, is all."

But Clint was already piecing together the puzzle. "You've been selling your stuff. Why?"

"No!" Alex barked a short, nervous laugh. "Why the hell would I sell? No, I mean, I got rid of a few things because I'm going in a different direction. You know me, I bore easily. Probably why I can't keep a girlfriend for longer than six months."

The attempt at a joke fell flat. Jordana shifted against the tension in the room. Clint held Alex's stare as he said, "I know you've been embezzling from the company. Upward of millions." He took another glance around. "Judging by the sparse furnishings, I'm guessing you've had money problems for a while. What is it? Drugs? Gambling? What's your vice, man? Something made you take that leap. What was it?"

"I don't know what you're talking about," Alex said, becoming defensive. "Is this what that crap private investigator told you? He's messing with you. Probably trying to get some more billable hours by sending you on a wild-goose chase. It's all crap, man. I would never steal from the company. That would be like stealing from myself."

"Or stealing from me," Clint replied, unfazed by Alex's denial. The paper trail was hard to ignore. "You've got five seconds to come clean before I call the Chicago PD and report you. Help me understand what the hell you were thinking."

Alex sent a sharp look Jordana's way. "This is probably her doing. She's got her brother sending you bad intel for some reason. Maybe you ought to look a little more deeply into her background before you start pointing fingers."

"Leave Jordana out of this. Right now, she's the only thing standing between you and my fists because I'm seeing red. Start talking."

Jordana's muscles tensed. If things were going to go down, this was the moment. Razor wire separated them from all hell breaking loose and calm, rational thought. A tic spasmed Alex's right eye. The air practically bristled with taut energy. Clint held Alex's stare. "Don't make me report you," he warned.

Finally, Alex crumpled under the pressure, releasing a pent-up breath as he walked away from Clint to drop onto the sofa, the picture of a broken man who couldn't run any longer.

"It started innocently enough," Alex started. "A game here and there to win over clients, networking to bring in new business. A few wins, a few losses, no big deal. It was all business."

"You're addicted to gambling," Jordana finished for him.

Alex didn't want to admit it but he grudgingly nodded. "Not sure how it happened, but before I knew it, I was up to my eyeballs in debt to some shady people. The only way I could pay them off was to dip a little in the company books but I fully planned to pay it all back."

"Except you didn't," Jordana said.

"No, I didn't," he said bitterly. "And then I had to borrow more. I had to keep up the flow or else I'd sink. It was like trying to swim in quicksand. I could never get a foothold and I was barely keeping my head above water."

"Why didn't you come to me for help?" Clint asked. "You have a problem. I would've helped you before it got to this point."

"Hey, I don't need Clint Broderick coming in to save the day, all right?" Some of that earlier bristling returned. "I can save myself. And I did. I was doing good for a while. My luck was turning around, I could feel it."

"Spoken like a true addict," Jordana said. "It's always the next game, or the one after that, that's going to make everything right again."

Alex didn't appreciate her input but he knew enough to keep his tongue in his head. Clint rubbed his forehead. "So how deep are you?"

"Uh, a million."

Clint swore under his breath. "Jesus, Alex, what have you done?"

"Look, I know it was stupid. I couldn't seem to stop myself. I'm underwater, man. There's no stopping what's happening at this point."

Jordana's ears pricked at something in Alex's statement. Taking a chance on her gut, she said, "So, when did you hire the hit man to take Clint out?"

Clint looked sharply to Jordana but then slewed his gaze at Alex, awaiting an answer. Jordana knew Clint wanted Alex to deny that part, to prove that he wasn't a murderer, just a thief. But when Alex's eyes watered and he choked on his admission, Jordana knew with a sinking heart her gut hadn't been wrong.

"Man, I'm so sorry. I wasn't thinking! I was desperate, out of my head, scared. I was messed up. I wanted to take it back but it was too late."

"What was too late?" Jordana asked.

"The hit was paid. I couldn't take it back without it coming back on me. I didn't know how these things worked, and when I called to cancel I got a message that there were no refunds, and if I tried to do anything to cancel the hit, I'd be next."

"Who is this person?" Jordana asked, immediately grabbing her phone to call Chicago PD. "We have to call the police."

"No! They'll kill me for ratting them out. Besides, I don't have a name, just a number, and it's a burner phone. It's not like you can just flip through Yelp and find a contract killer. There are channels you got to go through and they don't mess around."

"You hired someone to kill me?" The pain in Clint's voice tore at Jordana. "How could you? We were friends. You were my *best* friend. Stealing money I can understand but to want me dead?"

Alex buried his head in his hands in shame. "I'd do anything to take it back, man. I regretted it the minute I set the plan in motion. When I heard that you'd been attacked in Braxville but you thought it was a robbery gone wrong, I was relieved. I thought maybe the hit man might've thought he got the job done and moved on. But I got a message saying, *Attempt two*, and then your car got hit. That's how I knew that it wasn't over yet. I've been trying to think of a way out of this but I'm spun out of ideas. I'm so sorry, man."

"I need everything you have on this contract," Jordana said to Alex, disgusted by the man's weakness. "I can run a trace on the phone and see who it leads to."

"It's a burner phone. You're not going to find anyone," Alex insisted. "Look, you should do yourself a favor and take a vacation while I sort this out. I'll figure out how to fix this, but in the meantime, get out of town."

"Sorry if I don't take advice from you right now," Clint said coldly. "If you'd come to me before you started this, maybe we could've fixed it together. It's too late now."

"What are you going to do?"

"The only choice you've left me," Clint answered, his phone going to his ear. "I'd like to make a report of embezzlement and attempted murder."

Alex broke down and sobbed. There was nothing more to be said.

CLINT'S LIPS WERE numb as he watched Chicago's finest take his best friend into custody. He still couldn't wrap his head around the fact that Alex had screwed him over for money.

"I didn't see this coming," he admitted to Jordana, his voice hoarse from trapped tears he couldn't cry. Alex didn't deserve his tears. "He was willing to see me dead over money. How could he betray me like this?"

Clint knew Jordana didn't have the answers but her pained expression told him that she wished she did.

One of the officers broke away to ensure Clint was going to come to the station to make a statement.

"First thing in the morning," Jordana jumped in, sliding her hand through his, explaining to the officer, "It's been an overwhelming night."

"Of course." The uniform nodded and handed Clint a contact card. "Ask for Detective Milton."

Clint nodded and the officers took Alex away. Clint locked up Alex's apartment and they walked out of the building. Jordana started to hail a taxi but he stopped her. "Can we just walk for a minute? I need to clear my head."

She nodded and wrapped her arm around his. "Walking is good."

They fell into an easy step together with no particular destination in mind. Clint couldn't go home with everything swirling around in his head. He needed an outlet or he would lose his mind.

As it was, his heart was howling.

"We met freshman year in college," he shared, needing to talk. "He was the fast-talking, smart-ass kid with the jokes. People just flocked to him. I was the exact opposite. Somehow we fit together."

"Opposites attract, even in friendships," Jordana said.

"I should've seen this coming. Even in college, Alex had always been looking for shortcuts. He almost got busted for stealing tests. Skated past that collision by the skin of his teeth. At the time we laughed about it. Now, it seems cheating the system for his gain was ingrained in his DNA."

"Some people change, some people don't. You couldn't have known that Alex had a character flaw that big."

"Couldn't I, though? I missed that red flag even though it was waving in front of my face. My blindness nearly got me killed. I trusted the wrong person with everything I had. What if Alex had bankrupted Broadlocke? What, then? It's just stupid luck that we haven't gone under now that I know Alex has been sucking off the books like a damn vampire."

"You'll be able to fix this. What's most important now is finding who this hit man is before he tries to finish the contract." She shivered, glancing around. "I'm not sure it's a great idea to be wandering around in the open. You never know if you've got a target on your back. You should come back to Braxville with me. It's not safe here."

"It's not safe anywhere," he reminded her.

"Yes, but the odds of the hit man getting to you are significantly lower if you're where I can protect you."

"I'm not going to run and hide."

"Don't look at it that way," she said, frustrated by his refusal. "This is about more than your male pride."

"I don't want to argue with you." But he wasn't going to let anyone run him out of town.

"You're impossible," Jordana growled, but her eyes were soft with concern. "At the very least, we should get you inside. Let's get you home."

He supposed Jordana was right but he didn't relish the idea of spending the night alone. He stopped, turning to meet her gaze. "Stay with me tonight."

Jordana winced in a subtle movement as she shook her head. "I'm not sure that's a good idea. I have my hotel room."

"Forget the hotel. Stay with me."

"I've already paid," she said, fishing for reasons.

"I don't care. I'll give you the cash. I just don't want to be alone right now."

"I don't want your money. I want you to be safe."

"I need you, Jordana," Clint said with a catch in his voice. God, he'd never needed anyone more than he needed her right now. "I don't know what to think anymore. I need someone I know I can trust with me tonight. You're the only person I trust in this entire world."

Jordana softened and relented. "Just tonight," she warned when his relieved smile widened too far. "We already know how this doesn't work out. I don't want a repeat of before. I'm not staying in Chicago."

He'd take those terms. "Just tonight," he agreed, closing his eyes before pressing a kiss to her forehead, repeating in a cracked murmur, "Just tonight."

It was a devil's bargain. One night of comfort would only soothe temporarily but the heartbreak of watching her leave again would only twist the knife deeper into his heart.

It is what it is. He'd take what he could get.

Chapter Twenty-Eight

It was a wordless exchange, an offer without sound. Jordana knew accepting his offer would mean one thing—she wasn't sleeping anywhere but beside him. And she was shaking with the desire that heated her blood. It was one thing to pretend she was over Clint when she had work to distract her. It was completely another to be in his arms, his body pressed against hers, as her heart awakened with a painful jolt.

"Clint," she said with a soft cry as he hoisted her onto his hips, carrying her to the bedroom. Memories washed over her from her time there, both good and bad. He laid her down gently as he quickly stripped, his eyes centered on her as if he were afraid she might disappear if he blinked. She let her gaze wander the exquisite planes and valleys of the man she adored with all her heart but would never get to keep, and reached out to him, almost desperately. "I've missed you," she whispered a confession as he helped her out of her clothes.

"Baby, you have no idea how much I've missed you," he returned in a feverish tone. He lavished attention on her bare breasts, taking care to gently drag his teeth against the sensitive nipples, causing them to pearl into hardened tips that he sucked into his greedy, hot mouth.

Jordana gasped as his tongue rasped along the tender skin, suckling at her breast as his hand slid down her belly to find the softness of her mound. She curled around him, cradling his head, before he released her breasts to travel where his hand rested. He inhaled her scent, driving himself wild. His groan of appreciation sent goose bumps of awareness rioting through her nerve endings, awakening a hungry beast inside her.

He parted her legs, pressing sweet kisses down her inner thighs until he settled on the swollen bud between her folds. Her sharp gasp as her hands curled into the bedding was the encouragement he enjoyed. "That's it, baby," he murmured against his damp skin, "come for me, sweetheart."

She cried his name as pleasure washed over her in a crashing cataclysm that left her toes curled and her womb clenching as everything spasmed in beautiful unison. Jordana fell back, damp and spent, breathing hard as the final waves of pleasure continued to ebb around her. Clint climbed her body to plant a deep, soul-searching kiss on her awaiting lips.

This was heaven and hell. Heaven to know that perfection existed within another's arms; hell to realize it would never work between them.

Tears sprang to her eyes and Clint seemed to understand, wrapping his arms around her, rolling to his back so he could gaze up at her. "You're so beautiful," he murmured. "I love you, Jordana."

"I love you, too," she said, choking on her tears. His hardened length burned beneath her, hard and insistent. Jordana was desperate to feel him inside her, to merge with him in the most primal way possible. Positioning him at her entrance, she slowly descended on his hot staff, taking each inch with deliberate intention, sinking into the pleasure of being filled by the man who owned her heart.

He groaned as her wet heat enveloped him on all sides, gripping his length as he bracketed her hips, guiding her as she rode him, finding her pleasure as he took his.

"Jordana." He gasped her name like a prayer, his fingers curling into her flesh, creating delicious disharmonious sensations to compete with her nerve endings. She found the rhythm that suited her best, moaning as she neared her climax. Sweat broke out across her hairline, her breasts swelling, nipples hard. She shuddered as heat washed over her, pleasure rippling up and down her body as she crashed into an orgasm that exploded from a deep place inside.

Stars alive, I'll never meet anyone like you. Falling to his side, limp and out of breath, Clint threw one leg over his shoulder, bending her in half as he impaled her again on his length. His name escaped on a cry as Clint thrust against her with a fervor that spoke of a man running from grief, heartache and betrayal. All she could do was be his vessel, his conduit to some sort of relief.

But even as he neared his climax, Jordana felt the beginnings of a new orgasm rumbling through her nerve endings, tingling and ringing as loudly as a bell atop the church tower. There was no escaping the pleasure as it gripped her around the throat, sending sweet surrender cascading through her body, wave after wave until they were both drenched in sweat and breathing hard as they recovered.

Moonlit skies filled the bedroom window, bathing their naked, glistening bodies in a pale glow.

She met his gaze, her fingers finding his, curling together. In this moment, perfection was a tangible thing, a tangle of arms, legs and souls. She'd never been one to spout poetry or over-the-top proclamations, but she suddenly understood the impulse. Clint was unlike anyone she'd ever met. He was not replaceable. How cruel was fate to introduce them, only to tear them apart?

Just as she couldn't ask him to leave everything he knew where he was established, he shouldn't ask her to do the same. They lived in different worlds and neither were compatible.

Fresh tears welled in her eyes. Clint pulled her into his embrace with a murmured, "Shhh," as if to say he understood but now wasn't the time to talk about it. Jordana nodded and settled against his chest, her naked body fitting so well against his.

If tonight was all they had, why ruin it with the reality of tomorrow?

Her eyes drifted shut on a sigh.

CLINT KNEW THE minute Jordana fell asleep. Her breathing slowed as her body relaxed, followed by light snoring that he found incredibly endearing, though she would likely disagree.

A smile found him even though he knew she was fully planning to leave him again. It was no use to try and convince her to stay. It'd been wrong of him to drag her to Chicago in the first place. She was a beautiful wildflower that only grew in the country. Chicago, with its cement forests and cacophony of human life, had been slowly killing her. But he wanted to ask her to stay. He wanted to sleep beside her every night, listen to the minutia of her day and argue about stupid stuff, like whose turn it was to wash the dishes.

The reality that Alex had betrayed him in the worst possible way left him with the realization that Jordana was the sole person he trusted completely, and she was going to get on a plane and leave him behind. Fate and circumstance were nasty bedfellows. And he had to find a way to stop beating himself up for missing the red flags that'd been waving in front of his nose.

Loved ones are always our blind spots. He loved Alex like a brother. The fact that that street had been one-way hurt more than he wanted to admit.

He tightened his arms around Jordana, needing her warmth to permeate the winter chill on his heart. Only Jordana made him feel like happiness was possible, that trust was rebuildable. Not with Alex, of course, but with others. He had details to work out with the lawyers, business entanglements to sort out, protections to put in place as they went forward without Alex.

Attempted murder coupled with the embezzlement came with a hefty sentence. Alex would likely go away for a very long time. Tears stung his eyes. Betrayal was a bitter taste on the tongue. Tomorrow he'd have to give a statement to the police. He'd have to tell in great detail everything that'd happened since his assault in Braxville. Word would likely get out quickly that Alex Locke of Broadlocke Enterprises had been busted. Company morale would be shattered. Investor confidence would be tested.

He had to have a plan to save his business before Alex's actions completely tanked a dream that took years of grueling work in the trenches to create.

Fresh anger flooded Clint. What the hell was Alex thinking? Was he thinking at all? Like Jordana said, addicts didn't think about the people they were hurting, only the fix. He knew more heartache was coming when he had to face Alex in court, to stare in the eyes of the man he'd thought had his back only to find out that same man was his enemy.

A sigh rattled out of his chest and Jordana stirred with a faint whimper. He pressed a soft kiss on her exposed neck and she settled. Was there a way to convince this strong, independent woman that their lives could intertwine without sacrificing either of their interests? She'd want a plan; he didn't have one. Saying "But I love you" wasn't going to cut it. Ignoring the selfish part of himself that wanted to do whatever was necessary to keep her with him was a struggle.

But he'd never ask her to stay when she wanted to leave. He'd respect her wishes but nothing could stop him from wanting her. Until then, he'd just have to savor the moment until it was gone.

Chapter Twenty-Nine

Morning came and, with it, the sad acceptance that she had to go back to Braxville.

She woke before Clint, giving her the chance to watch him sleep. He had a classically handsome face with a hint of ruggedness. His chest rose and fell with each heavy breath. Muscles that had no business residing behind a button-down shirt and jacket made her hunger for something other than food.

His eyes slowly fluttered open, a smile following as he reached for her. "I'll never tire of waking to this face," he said with a sexy sleep-roughened voice.

Jordana didn't want to talk. She wanted to spend this last morning with Clint, loving him without words.

She slid her hand down his stomach to find his erection, already hard and ready even if he was barely awake. Smiling, she burrowed under the blankets to take him into her mouth.

He groaned, his hips thrusting gently against her mouth. Jordana worked him until he was ready to burst. Clint threw the covers aside and fell back against the bedding with a harsh moan, his muscles tensing as he neared his climax.

A raw sense of power rippled through Jordana as she held this powerful man between heaven and hell.

She teased him, pushing him to the brink, only to slow down before starting again.

"Oh, God," he moaned.

Finally, she pushed him to the edge. Clint stiffened, going rigid as he came. It was primal and raw.

She rose, her hair a mess but a smile wreathing her lips. Clint looked more in love with her than ever. That expression was the sweetest memory she'd take with her. Jordana kissed him, then rose to drink some water. She took her fill and handed Clint the bottle. He guzzled the bottle, finishing it. He fell back on the bed, inviting her to return to his side, but Jordana had to get to the airport.

"If I climb back into that bed, I won't leave." At Clint's raised brow, she clarified, "And I have a plane to catch."

His expression dimmed and she hated to be the one to ruin the moment. "You know, if you're ever in Kansas…you can always look me up."

It was an attempt at brevity but they weren't friends with benefits, happy to leave each other behind until the next time. Their lives were so complicated there was no easy answer for either of them.

"Is there anything I could say that would make you want to stay with me?" he asked plainly.

"It isn't a question of wanting to be with you," she answered. "It's just that we tried it already and your world isn't compatible with mine."

"Maybe we didn't try hard enough."

"Maybe we ignored what we should've seen from the start."

"Which is?"

She gazed at him with love and sadness. "That I'm a police detective for a small town who loves her job and you're a wealthy business owner who has to wine and dine clients for future contracts. You need someone on your arm who will help you achieve that. I'm not that person."

"You make it sound like I'm the kind of guy who uses a woman for an advertisement. I've never been the type to chase after a trophy wife. If I'd wanted that kind of partner, I would've stayed with Iris."

"Maybe that's the person you need."

"Don't patronize me, Jordana," he said, his temper flaring. He rose from the bed and pulled on his loungers. "I understand your world. Maybe you're right that I wouldn't fit in a small town and you don't fit in a city but you never asked me if I could try and make it work, either."

Jordana frowned. "Why would I ask you a question that I already know the answer?" she asked in confusion, hating that the morning was turning sour. She tried to smooth things with an apology. "I shouldn't have said that about Iris. I didn't mean to patronize you. Sometimes my mouth gets away from me." She peeped a sidewise glance at Clint. "Sort of like this morning..."

The sexy reminder softened the hard edges of his expression. "You might be the devil," he growled, walking toward her. He pulled her into his arms for a tender kiss that belied his rough touch. "But I like whatever you are."

Jordana threw her head back to give him better access to her neck. He nibbled and kissed until he returned to her lips, announcing with an impish grin, "We should shower," then shocked her when he scooped her up, carrying her to the bathroom.

She knew what was going to happen the minute they were both naked. And she wasn't complaining. She still had plenty of time to catch her flight. Or she could reschedule. Either way, Clint was doing his best to make her forget all about Braxville.

For now.

CLINT KNEW THAT no matter how many epic orgasms he gave Jordana, she was determined to be on that plane back to Braxille, but he gave it the good ol' college try. In the end, all he managed to convince her to do was share a late breakfast with him at his favorite restaurant after she confessed her secret love of eggs Benedict.

His favorite breakfast place was world-renowned for their eggs Benedict, and if that's what his woman wanted, that's what she was going to get.

Once seated, he said, "So tell me about the case with my uncle. Have you found out anything new?"

Pleased to talk about anything other than boarding that plane, Jordana nodded with a smile. "Actually, yes, but I'm not sure if it was a lead or anything. The bodies were found with an odd chemical on the bones, CCA, which stands for chromated copper arsenic. It was a common enough chemical treatment in the '70s but the EPA banned its use in 2003."

"When was the building built?"

"Well, as it turns out, my dad said the building was built in the mid-1970s so that tracks, but between you and me, I can't shake the feeling that CCA is some kind of clue. I just don't know what, though."

"Why'd the EPA ban the chemical?"

"I guess it's a carcinogen but they didn't know that until later when people who were exposed to it started getting cancer."

Clint nodded. "A lot of building materials were later found to be dangerous around humans. Did you know the EPA has only banned nine chemicals in spite of the thousands on the American market?"

"That seems an underwhelming use of an agency created to protect people from chemical harm," Jordana said.

"Well, chemical makers aren't in a big rush to admit that their product could be dangerous. Proving that a chemical is harmful to humans is a long and lengthy process. Polychlorinated biphenyls, or PCBs as we call them, were banned in 1978 but you can still find some banned chemicals coming in from China where the regulations are different."

Jordana frowned. "How would you know if something was treated with an illegal chemical?"

"Aside from testing it, you have to rely on the honesty of the seller where you're getting your materials."

"Why would anyone buy tainted materials?"

"Money," he answered with a shrug. "Cheaper materials lower the bottom line. I remember Alex and I getting into a disagreement about some tech parts we were sourcing and he wanted to buy from a Chinese distributor, but even though they were cheaper materials, I didn't get a good vibe from the distributor as far as their chemical compound usage. Ultimately, we passed and went with a different distributor."

"You didn't trust Alex to make the right choice," she surmised.

"No, I guess I didn't. As it turned out, Alex had a bit of a moral and ethic ambiguity that didn't mesh with mine."

She reached out to squeeze his hand, assuring Clint, "He's going to get what's coming to him."

Clint nodded, appreciative of her gesture. "So that's the only lead so far?"

"Yeah, it's a little disheartening. My dad is up my tailpipe, pressuring me to release the crime scene so he can demo the building, but I can't do that until I can solve those murders."

"Cold cases are notoriously hard to solve," he said. "I can understand your dad's frustration. As a business owner, I'd go nuts if I couldn't do my job because of someone else being in my way."

"And if that someone is his daughter, he feels it's perfectly acceptable to harass her at a family dinner," she said. "Totally ruining my mom's apple pie reveal."

"I'm sorry, babe."

"I feel bad for my mom. My dad is a tyrant some days. I don't know how she put up with him all these years. Oh, and my uncle Shep is moving into the carriage house, which has further put my mom on edge—not that she needed help in that department—and my dad seems oblivious to anything that doesn't directly affect him and Colton Construction."

"Does your dad care that none of his kids went into the family business?"

"Oh, yes. It's a point of contention but he mostly saves that beef for my brothers. Thankfully, they know how to let it roll off their backs."

"I can't see Ty being bothered by something like that." Clint chuckled.

"No, Ty is his own man. On one hand, I'd think my dad would be proud that his sons and daughters are so independent but he only wants us to be headstrong with other people, not him. With him, he wants us to jump when he snaps his fingers."

"As stressful as that all sounds, having your family around is a blessing. I wish I had siblings to argue with or a father to butt heads with over nothing. It's weird what you end up valuing. Alex was the closest I had to a brother. Now, he's gone, too."

"I'm so sorry, Clint," she murmured. "I wish things had turned out differently."

"Me, too. You know, I was half expecting the culprit to be a disgruntled employee or maybe even my assistant."

"Jeana? She's practically perfect," Jordana said, chuckling. "And she has a mad crush on you."

"You know… I think I figured that out, too. She's a good woman but, well, boundaries."

She blushed. "Is it terrible that I hate the idea of you dating anyone but me?"

"Yes," he said, shocking her. He grinned, showing that he was joking. "Hey, you're breaking my heart by leaving. The least you could do is suffer the heartburn of knowing that I might be out there dating."

"You're the worst," she chided around a laugh just as their food arrived. "You, sir, have been saved by the server."

He chuckled and watched with pleasure as she moaned after her first bite. Mission accomplished. At least he knew that the eggs Benedict hype was real. They made some small talk while they finished their breakfast and then, after paying the bill, they walked arm in arm out onto the sidewalk.

The weather was nearly perfect today. Birds skimmed across blue skies like skipping stones on water. The temperature was moderate, almost vacation weather. But on the day he was saying goodbye to the love of his life, it ought to be raining like the apocalypse was about to crash down around their ears. He glanced up at the sky with a subtle scowl but he couldn't blame Mother Nature for his bad luck.

Parking for this particular restaurant was always a bear, but instead of using the car service, he wanted to drive Jordana himself. Something about the act of driving made him feel more in control of the situation, even though it was an illusion.

It didn't matter if he drove or the car service drove, Jordana was still going to head to the airport.

But as it turned out, the parking garage wasn't exactly the kind of place he would've chosen. Even to his own eyes, the place wasn't well-lit and there were too many dark areas for his comfort. Still, it was broad daylight—what could happen?

They were nearly to the car when, out of nowhere, someone wearing a ski mask popped from the shadows, the glint of a knife catching his eye before he went down to the ground with a hard thud. Jordana screamed and he realized his attacker had come prepared. Another man held Jordana while the man on him tried to gut him like a fish.

They scrabbled against the filthy cement. Clint struggled to keep the knife blade from his throat. Sweat broke out across his body as adrenaline powered the fight-or-flight defense mechanism. He could hear Jordana struggling with her attacker but he was too busy himself to help.

Please don't let me die like this.

"You know why I picked a knife?" the man said between grunts as Clint tried to overpower him. "Because it's more personal. You've been a real pain in my ass. I'm going to enjoy spilling your insides and then I'm going to have fun with your hot girlfriend as a bonus."

But just as the man went to shove the knife deep into Clint's chest, he went flying to land in a crumpled heap, knocked out cold.

Jordana stood, bruised and bloodied, looking like an avenging angel with a helluva roundhouse kick, the other assailant suffering the same fate as the first.

"Jesus, you're a badass," Clint breathed, wiping at his bloody nose, surveying the scene. "This must be the hit man or there's someone else out there who hates me enough to want me dead."

Jordana wiped the trickle of blood from her mouth with a wry smile and pulled her cell to call 911. While they waited for police to arrive, Jordana found some rope in Clint's car and quickly bound the men like trussed-up pigs ready for the fire.

Clint couldn't stop staring at Jordana.

"Are you okay?" Jordana asked, starting to check him for knife wounds, but he stopped her with a gingerly placed kiss around bruised lips.

"I will be," he answered. "Right now, I just want to kiss you until you tell me to stop. You saved my life. Again. If I wasn't so damn happy to be alive, I'd be embarrassed as hell that you had to save me instead of the other way around."

Jordana barked a short laugh as if he were ridiculous, saying, "Baby, kicking ass and saving lives is equal opportunity." She blotted at her bleeding lip with the edge of her shirt. "But I think I'm going to need stitches."

"Is it weird that I think that's the hottest thing I've ever heard you say?"

She laughed, howling as her lips protested. "Yes. Very."

He grinned, pulling her into his arms just as the cops screeched into view, lights and sirens blaring as if they were the ones saving the day.

They shared a wry look, both thinking the same thing, before pointing to the prone men tied and ready.

Chapter Thirty

Clint managed to convince Jordana to stay a few more days while her lip healed but soon enough she was mended and it was time to return to Braxville.

The last few days, aside from healing from a brawl, passed with little drama or stress. They ordered take-out, made love, laughed, watched movies, talked about the mysteries of the universe and forgot about the rest of the world outside of their four walls.

It was magical. But it was also unsustainable.

The outside world awaited even if they had no interest in participating. Jordana knew that Clint thought everything had changed but it hadn't.

Finally dressed after four days of minimal clothing, Jordana met Clint's gaze and prepared for the heartbreak of goodbye.

"What are you doing?" he asked, perplexed. "Do you want to go out to eat this time? I thought we could order Greek tonight."

"Clint, as much as I would love to stay in this apartment, in your bed, for a lifetime, eventually real life would intrude. We both have lives we have to get back to. Now that I know you're truly safe, I can leave with a clear conscience."

"Whoa, hold up, not so fast. Let's talk about this."

"No, nothing has changed. I have a job to return to, an investigation that I'm up to my eyeballs in with my family, and I can't just bail. They need me to figure out what happened."

"I thought, maybe, things were different now," he admitted. "Felt different."

She cupped his face, meeting his sad gaze with equal misery. "I love you, Clint. I always will. You are probably the love of my life and I have to let you go. Our lives are so different. Eventually, one of us would become resentful of the other, no matter what decision was made. If I stayed, or you came to me, it would end the same."

"You don't know that," he said, stubbornly refusing to listen. "You're making a judgment on the future, and as far as I know, neither of us has a crystal ball."

"No, but I have experience. I know who I am and I know I already ignored my misgivings to follow you here only to have it end in the same way."

"I was distracted and I didn't give you the attention you needed. I'll be better this time."

"Stop." She held a finger to his lips with a stern expression. "I'm not a fickle houseplant that needs constant tending or else I will wilt. But I'm also not the kind of person who can be idle. I need a purpose, a job, a reason to greet the dawn with enthusiasm. I can't get that here."

"You could get a job at the Chicago PD."

"I don't want a job with the Chicago PD. I have a great job in Braxville."

"It feels like you're running away."

"I'm not."

"Then what is this?"

"It's being responsible enough to ignore the pain in my heart and doing what's best for both of us."

"That's very saintly of you," he said with a harsh look that cut her to the core.

"Don't be ugly," she pleaded, hating that his pain was coming out with a harsh tongue. "Don't make this harder than it already is."

His expression lost some of its anger. "Baby, I don't know how to watch you leave. You're a part of me. You might as well lop off an arm or a leg. It'll feel about the same."

She reached for him, resting her forehead against his. "I know. I feel the same. We both know in our hearts this is the right decision. I don't want to ever see resentment in your eyes when you look at me, and I don't want to feel it when I look at you."

"So a preemptive strike is the best option?" he asked in disbelief. "Preparing to fail?"

"No, just honest about life and how it usually turns out when people ignore the reasons why they shouldn't uproot their lives for someone else."

Jordana stepped away, tears stinging her eyes. "Please don't make this harder than it already is."

"If you're asking me to make it easy to leave me, I won't."

"C'mon, Clint…this isn't fair."

"Damn straight it's not fair. Not fair to either of us. I'm asking you to give us a shot. You're saying what we have isn't worth it for you to take the risk."

"I'm not saying that," she disagreed on a cry. "How can you say that?"

"Because that's what I hear you saying. There are no guarantees for anyone. Sacrifices, compromises, they're all part of a functioning relationship. You gotta try, put in the work, do everything you can to meet your partner in the middle. That's how things work out in the end."

"Really? How would you know that, Clint? Your parents are dead. My parents are stuck in a dysfunctional marriage, eaten up by resentments, and only sheer stubbornness keeps them tied together, not love. I've known for a long time, and I swore I'd never have that kind of relationship."

"And we won't," he said, bewildered. "We love each other."

"You think my parents didn't start wildly in love? Oh, trust me, they were at one point. You don't have six kids without being into one another at some level. But it changed. Life changes people. Circumstances out of our control changes people. Why would I start a life with someone that I'm almost guaranteed to end up resenting at some point because one or both of us were required to give up something important to the other to make it work? I just won't do it. I can't."

"I won't resent you."

"I'm not willing to take that chance."

He groaned with frustration. "We're going in circles."

"Exactly." She bent to pick up her luggage. "I was hoping you'd drive me to the airport but maybe it's best that we just part ways here. I can call an Uber."

"That's cold," he chided. "Seriously, Jordana. Don't be ridiculous. Of course I'll drive you."

"Thank you," she said, wishing she didn't have a golf-ball-size lump in her throat. "I appreciate it."

Clint just shook his head, muttering, "Give me a few minutes to get dressed," and then disappeared into the bedroom.

She supposed that was as good an ending as she could hope for.

Still hurt like a bitch.

TRUE TO HIS WORD, he saw Jordana off to the airport, but he didn't kiss her goodbye. He didn't think he could do that without embarrassing himself in front of strangers. He left her there with a curt goodbye, walking away before he could see the tears shining in her eyes. She was leaving as a preemptive strike against a possible future breakup. It was crazy and messed up but he couldn't change her mind.

He wasn't ready to admit that he'd lost her. Wasn't ready to lose.

Losing his memory had been an incredible experience. He'd been able to rediscover who he was and who he didn't want to be.

He wanted to be a better person. But he couldn't—and wouldn't—beg a woman to be with him if she was determined to leave. If Jordana couldn't see that he was the only man for her and vice versa, there was nothing he could do to change her mind.

For God's sake, he'd never had to think twice about finding a date for an event or an evening of no-strings-attached sex. But then Jordana came along and changed everything.

Damn her for cracking open his heart and showing him what love was really about. He'd never been in love with Iris. Breaking up with her had been a blessing to them both. To be fair, he didn't think Iris had loved him, either, but a love match in certain circles wasn't as important as connections, similar backgrounds and matching goals.

Why couldn't he have loved Iris? It would've made his life easier by half.

Of course, there was no way Iris would've been able to roundhouse kick his assailant into next week, either. They both would've died gruesome deaths if Iris had been the one walking beside him when they were attacked.

He shuddered.

So what happens now?

He goes on with his life as if he hadn't fallen in love with his soul mate?

Yeah, sure.

In the short term, he had a company to keep afloat in the aftermath of Alex's actions and investors to keep assured that it would continue to be business as usual at Broadlocke. He had lawyers to meet with, financials to break down and, at some point, to testify against his former best friend and business partner.

On the surface, it would seem falling in love with a woman from tiny town in Kansas would be bad timing. But wasn't that life in general? Was there ever a good time to fall in love? Love was complicated and messy. It burned with the same fire that lights your soul from within. By its very nature, it can't be tamed.

For all her bravery in the field, Jordana was afraid of getting her heart broken. It was better to be the one breaking hearts rather than the one getting broken.

He had no way of proving to her that he would've held her heart in the most gentle of hands. She would've needed to take that leap of faith. Faith was something Jordana didn't have—and he couldn't give it to her.

Hell, maybe she was right.

Even so, why did he feel the urge to buy a ticket and follow her stubborn ass right straight back to Braxville?

He'd put a ring on her finger, give her babies, build a farmhouse, whatever…if only she'd say yes.

In the end, he forced himself to keep walking. Just as Jordana had done.

It was truly over.

And he'd have to find a way to get over it.

Chapter Thirty-One

Back in Braxville, Jordana spent days trying to piece together her life without Clint in it. Her house was spotless. *Thanks, Mom, for passing on the neurosis.* However, no matter how hard she scrubbed, reorganized and decluttered, nothing seemed to brighten her day or let her forget that the ache in her heart wasn't going anywhere.

Bridgette showed up on her doorstep on her day off, dressed in sneakers and her hair pulled in a ponytail. "Get dressed. We're going for a hike," she announced with a cheery smile.

"A hike?" Jordana repeated, confused. "What do you mean?"

"Not a complicated statement. You need to get out of this house before you start tearing down walls and trying to rebuild something when you don't have the time for that kind of DIY project."

Bridgette had a point. Just this morning she'd been eyeing her dated tile countertops, wondering how difficult it would be to demo and replace by herself.

A person could find how to do anything on YouTube, right?

"You know me too well," Jordana said with a sigh. It

wasn't worth the effort to lie when Bridgette saw right through her. "Okay, give me a minute to get dressed."

"Excellent."

Jordana found her hiking shoes and exercise gear, dressed and climbed into Bridgette's rental car.

"I thought you were going to drive Dad's old truck while you were here?" Jordana commented, snapping her seat belt into place.

"And listen to Dad bitch about how I'm not driving properly in his beloved Ford? Hell, no. I'd rather pay half my salary in rental fees than listen to that noise. Besides, that Ford is a gas-guzzler. This baby will drive forever on a full tank of gas."

She chuckled as they hit the road, saying, "Fair point. Sometimes I think Dad only offers things that he can use as leverage later."

"That's our dad for you."

"Have you ever wondered if we're bound to have 'dad' issues when looking for partners? You know, they say that the most difficult parent is the one you'll end up marrying in the form of someone else. I'd stab myself in the eye if I married someone like Dad."

"Henry wasn't anything like Dad," Bridgette reminded her. "Henry was kind and gentle, compassionate and sweet. Can you honestly imagine someone using those words to describe Dad?"

"No. Not even in my wildest imagination."

"So, I don't know if that theory tracks for everyone."

"Or maybe you're just more well-adjusted than I am?"

Bridgette laughed. "Maybe. You are a hot mess."

"Hot mess? How so?"

"Look, don't get your feathers ruffled but I think what you're doing with Clint is stupid. You love him and he loves you but you broke it off because...you might resent each other later? Nobody knows what the future holds. You could be wrong and losing the love of your life on a possibility."

"I know it's hard for you to understand. You and Henry had a fairy-tale marriage until he died. You've seen our parents. I won't end up like that."

"Please don't compare anything to our parents' marriage. They've been unhappy for years but neither will do anything about it," Bridgette said. "And don't paint me and Henry as some paragon of married life. We had our moments just like anyone else."

"Yeah, but you were so in love."

"No more so than you and Clint," Bridgette pointed out. "I think you're cutting your nose off to spite your face."

"Trust me, I'm not. Clint isn't a househusband. He's used to commanding a big tech company worth millions. He's not going to be happy in the long run moving to a tiny town in Kansas without a true purpose."

"But you don't know that. You ran away before you even gave him a chance to figure things out on his own."

"Damn right I did. I don't have to be hit on the head to know that it will hurt. I wasn't going to stick around so I could get my heart broken when he finally came to his senses. No thank you."

"I never knew you to be such a pessimist," Bridgette said, shaking her head. "Where's your sense of optimism, that starry-eyed belief in the power of love?"

"Please, I'm not a teenager. I'm not looking for a prince to sweep me off my feet." Although the times Clint had done exactly that had stolen her breath. He had a body that haunted her dreams. Shaking off the direction of her thoughts, she added, "Besides, with some distance and time to reflect, we'll both come to the same conclusion that not all love stories end with the white picket fence, two dogs and a few kids running around."

"Since when do you like dogs?" Bridgette quipped.

Jordana laughed. "You jerk, I like dogs. As long as they're not too yappy, too big, too small, needy or shed too much."

"Please stick to cats."

They pulled off the road and parked. This spot was a favorite among locals. The trail was easy enough and the view was glorious. Jordana took a big, cleansing breath of the fresh air and smiled. "This was a good idea," she admitted. "I needed a change of scenery."

"I know."

Jordana rolled her eyes. "I love how humble you are."

Bridgette grinned, gesturing with wide arms. "Why be humble when you've got all this?"

Jordana wasn't sure if Bridgette was talking about the vista or herself but she didn't have time to question because Bridgette had already set off at a brisk pace.

"Hold up, speed racer," she grumbled, jogging to catch up.

They walked in silence, enjoying the view, making small talk in between breathing heavy through the hilly terrain, and when they popped out at the top of the low-rise ridge, they had an excellent view of the grasslands below.

"Some people don't know the beauty of Kansas," Bridgette murmured, appreciating the landscape. "I miss this."

"Yeah? I thought maybe you might not enjoy coming home again."

"No, I've missed Braxville and you guys, but I don't miss enduring the constant tension between our parents.

I swear they never get along. I wish they'd just divorce and get it over with."

"You know Mom will never divorce Dad. She's still stuck in a more traditional time where divorce was shameful."

"She needs to get over it. Dad is unbearable these days."

Guilt stabbed at Jordana. "It's because he's so stressed about the investigation. I think he's really in trouble."

"What kind of trouble?" Bridgette asked.

"Financial. I know he doesn't like to talk about those things with us but I think he's been struggling for years and this is the final blow. I think he blames me for how the investigation is going."

"It's not your fault."

"I know but I can't help but feel that I'm letting him down. I don't know what else to do."

Bridgette reached for her hand. "Something will pop up. You're a good detective. Trust your process."

Jordana wished she had Bridgette's confidence. She drew a deep breath, scanning the vista. The light breeze kissed her cheek. She closed her eyes, trying to soak in the calm, letting it permeate her soul to allow some semblance of peace, but Clint was always there in the background, reminding her of what she'd given up.

Tears sparked her eyes as she admitted to Bridgette, "I loved him. I mean, really loved him."

"I know you did," Bridgette said with true sorrow in her gaze. She went into her sister's arms for a tight hug. There weren't enough beautiful vistas in the world to make her forget that simple fact. She supposed she'd just have to let time do its thing.

And try not to break down and sob with each new day that he wasn't there with her.

CLINT LEFT HIS attorney's office numb to the emotions battering his soul. He had to stay focused. One foot in front of the other. Trudging forward like a solider on a mission.

Soldier.

Navy.

Arrgh. Why did everything he thought of lead him back to Jordana?

He entered the building and went straight to his office to find Jeana waiting for him with a full schedule on the books, which suited him just fine because it kept his mind occupied.

Jeana, business as usual, didn't pry about the details regarding Alex but Clint felt it was only fair to let her know all the gory details, even up to the attack in the parking garage.

"Oh, heavens," Jeana exclaimed, her hand flying to her throat in alarm. "Thank goodness Miss Colton was there to handle those miscreants."

He smiled. Jeana was born in the wrong decade, but he appreciated her soft-spoken efficiency and Victorian sensibilities. He found her comforting in a world that had been tipped upside down.

"Yes, very fortunate," he murmured in agreement. "The upside is that the man who attacked me, both in Braxville and here, is in custody and I don't have to keep looking over my shoulder anymore. Police have assured me he's not going to be released on bail so I feel good about moving forward with a clean slate."

"Excellent, sir." She paused before asking, "And will you be joining Miss Colton in Braxville?"

He looked up and held Jeana's gaze, realizing she was asking if she was going to have to start polishing her résumé.

"My business is here," he answered, hopefully putting to bed any fears she might have. "But I've come to realize that it's important to place value on the people around you. I've decided to give you a raise."

"A raise?" Jeana's eyes widened. "Oh, sir, that's not necessary. You're already quite generous."

"Not generous enough. For everything you've done, you deserve so much more."

She blushed. "I'm flattered. I enjoy working here at Broadlocke and with you."

"Good. I don't want to lose you to someone else waving more money at you."

"I would never—"

"Better safe than sorry," he cut in, refusing to take no for an answer. This was the right decision, especially when he found out that Jeana was living on such a modest salary considering her level of importance to his company. "I want to do this for you, Jeana. As a thank-you for being there for me."

She blushed a little harder but jerked a short nod. "My pleasure."

"I've already talked to payroll, so you should see your raise on your next check. I'm doubling your annual salary and then we'll work from there."

Jeana gasped, her knees wobbling a bit and causing her to reach out to steady herself. "Double?"

"Yes, and that might not be enough, either. The truth is, with Alex gone, I'm going to lean on you heavily in the coming months. It's going to be rough waters and I need you to help me keep the ship afloat. It's only fair to compensate you for your time."

"I don't know what to say."

"No need to say anything. It's what should've been done a long time ago. I'm sorry it took me so long to figure out who was worth keeping around."

Her eyes took on a shiny glaze but she held it together. Stiffening her back and squaring her shoulders, she said, "It's an honor to work with you, Mr. Broderick. You've always been fair and honest. In this day and age, those qualities are hard to find in someone of your stature."

He smiled, accepting the compliment. "Thank you, Jeana. Coming from you, it's high praise that I'll work to keep deserving."

Jeana, not one to gush or simper, settled back into work mode, saying, "You have a ten o'clock waiting. Shall I show them in?"

He nodded. "Conference room, please."

"Excellent." She turned on her heel and started to leave, only to pause to say, almost haltingly, "Even if you were to leave for Braxville, we could make it work. Broadlocke is a well-oiled machine. It will weather any adjustments."

And then, having said her piece, she went to collect his next appointment.

She was saying that if he wanted, he could make changes and it would still be all right. Was it true? What if he leaped to move to Braxville and Jordana still sent him packing? She'd already made it clear that she didn't want him uprooting his life for her. He understood her concerns. He didn't want to admit it but in the back of his mind he had the same worries.

He couldn't say without a shadow of a doubt that he wouldn't resent the move at some point.

Braxville was a huge difference from Chicago. He liked his conveniences.

But he loved Jordana.

He chewed on the dilemma for a moment longer before shelving it completely and heading to his meeting.

Chapter Thirty-Two

"Jordana, just the person I wanted to see."

Jordana mentally cringed at the sound of her father's business partner, Dex. When they were growing up he was Uncle Dex because he was around so much, but now that they were adults, he was just Dex.

She'd hoped to talk with her mom about Uncle Shep but she was waylaid before she could slip out of reach.

"C'mere, girl," Dex said with a good-hearted chuckle as he wrapped her in a hug that she allowed but wished she could disappear. She knew why he wanted to talk to her and there was nothing she could say. "You're a sight for sore eyes. Why are you still single? You're much too pretty to be all alone."

Only Dex could make her cringe like this. She forced a smile, answering, "Just haven't found the right one, I guess."

"You gotta get out there, put on a pretty dress, a little makeup. You'll catch a keeper eventually but you better hurry or else you'll end up on the shelf."

She couldn't resist. "That's sage advice—if it were the 1800s. Times have changed, Dex. Try to keep up."

Jordana caught her father's expression, and if she weren't mistaken, she saw a sliver of amusement shining in his eyes. Maybe he got tired of Dex, too.

Sobering, Dex said, "Actually, I was just talking to your dad and he said we're still holed up with the demo on the warehouse. What's going on? I don't understand what the holdup is?"

"It's an active investigation. We can't release the site until we're through with the investigation."

"Honey, these people have been dead for quite a long time from what I understand. They can't get any deader."

"It's not that—the site is an active crime scene. We still have forensics searching for anything that might be tested for DNA."

"DNA? Like what?" Dex screwed his expression into a perturbed frown. "Like eyelashes or something?"

"Something like that. We're still processing," she said, hoping Dex dropped it.

But her luck wasn't that good. "Now, now, honey, that's just not going to work. Surely your daddy has told you that we're losing business on this holdup? That's no lie. We're in some hot water and we gotta get moving or we're all going to lose our shirts. You don't want that, do you?"

She ground her teeth, hating that Dex was smothering her with guilt she didn't need. "Yes, my dad has told me that the investigation is hurting the bottom line. There's nothing I can do to speed things up unless you want to tell me who killed those people?"

"Well, honey, you know I don't have that kind of information." Dex huffed, adjusting his belt. "But surely I would tell you in a heartbeat if I thought it would move things along any faster."

She smiled. "I don't doubt it. But we're moving as fast as we can. Forensics isn't like they show on television. It's a slow process."

"Let's get real here. I could make a call to the mayor and see if there's anything he can do help but I was trying to give you the chance to do your thing. I just don't see how much longer we can wait around."

"She said she's doing all she can," Fitz interjected with a sharp rebuke. "Stop hounding the girl."

Jordana could forgive her dad calling her a girl because she was too shocked that he'd taken her side instead of Dex's on this issue. Particularly when he'd taken a chunk out of her ass just the other day about the same subject. She supposed her dad didn't care for someone else disparaging his daughter.

"It's time to put this to bed," Dex growled, undeterred. "We're getting a black eye all over town over this situation. You have no idea how I'm trying to keep our heads above water all the while little missy here is dumping buckets back in the pool."

"She's not doing that, she's doing her job." Fitz folded his hands across his chest. "We'll talk about this later."

The tension between the two men grew to an uncomfortable level until her mom breezed in with a bright smile, announcing she'd just made a fresh pot of coffee to have with her famous coffee cake. "Dex, I know you can't resist my coffee cake," she said, giving him a look that dared him to refuse.

But of course Dex caved with Lilly. She had this way about her that managed to disarm most difficult men. Maybe that was her secret or superpower.

"You know me too well," Dex admitted, breaking into a smile. "I'll have me a slice, darlin'."

"Fitz?"

Fitz grunted with a nod, dropping into his chair to wait for Lilly to serve them.

This was her chance to bail. She'd have to talk to her

mom another time. Checking her watch, she made her excuses, kissed her mother's cheek and practically ran out of the house before Dex could start all over again.

Forensics would be finished soon, she told herself when the fear and guilt became too heavy to bear. She had to be patient. Rushing would help no one.

Especially not the two dead people who were still waiting for justice.

CLINT WASN'T SURE what he hoped to gain by visiting Alex in jail while he awaited his arraignment but he supposed he needed some kind of closure.

Cook County Jail wasn't a place he'd ever thought to visit, and after being thoroughly searched for any contraband, he was certain he never wanted to return.

The razor-wire cyclone fence enclosing the drab facility was a reminder that no one was getting in or out without clearance. It was a far cry from what Alex was accustomed to. The reality that Alex was going away for a very long time hit him in the gut. He shouldn't but he felt bad for the guy.

Hell, it was hard to forget that he'd been his closest friend. As much as he wanted to, he couldn't.

Alex shuffled into the visitor booth. His ill-fitting khaki scrubs hung from his frame as if he'd lost twenty pounds in the weeks since he'd been arrested. Dark circles ringed his eyes and his head was shorn. Alex picked up the receiver and Clint did the same. The jail smelled of sweat, urine and sadness.

"You look like hell," Clint said, leading with the easiest observation. "What happened to your hair?"

Alex ran his hand over his nearly bald head. "Lice outbreak. It's easier to shave the inmates than treat the lice. One and done, problem solved." He paused a beat, then asked, "What are you doing here?"

"I don't know," Clint admitted, feeling like an idiot. "I just wanted some closure, I guess."

"I've already told you everything. My lawyer said I'm not supposed to say anything else."

"I'm not looking for a confession."

"Then what are you looking for?"

"I don't know," he answered. "Still trying to wrap my head around what happened. What you did."

"Yeah, welcome to my hell. If I had an answer for myself, I'd give it to you. I don't know. Addiction is a terrible thing. It takes your normal thought process and turns it upside down."

Clint nodded. It was an honest answer. "You okay in here?"

"Hey, it's my reality and I earned it. I'm not shying away from what I did. Whatever happens is my karma."

"Stop being so damn apologetic," Clint growled, knowing he sounded irrational. "It's hard to hate you when you're all pathetic behind this glass."

"I hate myself enough for the both of us. I got you covered, buddy."

In spite of everything, Clint chuckled. "Good." His smile faded. "Everything else okay?"

"I've been put in solitary for my safety. I'm considered a white-collar criminal, and since I paid someone to do my dirty work, I'm real low on the totem pole. My lawyer is working on getting me transferred to a different facility. One that's not quite so rough."

"I hope it works out for you," he said, meaning it. The threat was over. He couldn't hold on to the hatred eating him up inside. Alex messed up and he was paying for it. Even though Alex had done something terrible, Clint couldn't hate him.

"You okay?" Alex asked, surprising him. "Are you safe?"

"Do you mean is your hit man still out there gunning for my ass?"

"Not in so many words, but yeah."

"You can sleep easy. Your hit man tried to attack me in a parking garage with a buddy. Jordana took them both down. Chicago's finest came and arrested them."

Alex seemed relieved. "I'm sorry. I wish I could take it all back."

"You and me both. You still owe me for that stupid bet you lost. I'm never going to see that money now."

Alex chuckled. "I guess I'll just have to catch you in twenty years when they let me out."

"Do me a favor, keep it. I'm not sure I'll be inviting you over for dinner," Clint quipped with dark humor. When in doubt, make a joke to lessen the tension. Old habits died hard. "It's not the same without you. I landed the O'Hare account but I could tell I wasn't the showman you were."

"You never gave yourself enough credit. You'll do fine without me."

Clint shrugged. "I guess I have to. Not a lot of choice in that decision."

"I'm sorry."

Clint waved away his apology. He had to keep his composure even though his best friend had betrayed him and his girlfriend had left him to go back to Kansas.

As if honing in on Clint's private thoughts, Alex asked, "What's the situation with Jordana? Nothing hotter than a badass woman, right?"

He agreed but admitted, "She's gone, went back to Braxville."

"You doing the long-distance thing?"

"Nope." Was he discussing his love life with a prisoner behind safety glass? Man, his life had taken a weird turn. "She said she couldn't stay and I couldn't leave—one of us would end up resenting the other. She's probably right. Hell, I don't know anymore. Nothing makes a lot of sense in my life right now."

"What do you want?"

"I want her," Clint answered.

"So stop whining about it and go get your lady."

"My lady doesn't want to be gotten. I'm not going to chase after someone determined to push me away." He exhaled a long breath, adding, "And I'm not sure taking advice from you is the best thing. You never held on to a relationship longer than six months."

"Exactly. I know why I couldn't keep a girl and it has nothing to do with your issue."

"Which is what?"

"You're used to women throwing themselves at you. This one you have to work for and you're bailing. C'mon, man, I've seen you fight harder for a parking space than the fight you're putting up for the love of your life."

He had let her walk away. Even though everything in him shouted to follow and convince her that she was wrong.

"How am I supposed to be in two places at once? Braxville isn't a short commute to Chicago."

"A two-hour flight," Alex told him "You can make it work. Split your time between Braxville and Chicago. Let's face it, Broadlocke can be managed via telecommute if need be. All you need is a solid person at the

Chicago office to manage the day-to-day and then you can conference call most of the client meetings."

Clint stared at Alex. How had this man just solved his problem? This is what Alex had always been good at: creative problem-solving. Tears welled in his eyes but he sniffed them back, pretending that he had something in his eye, but Alex seemed to understand.

"I'm sorry," Alex said quietly. "I can't say it enough. I wasn't thinking straight."

Clint nodded, needing to go. "Take care of yourself," he said, rising. "Do you need anything?"

"A file, some dynamite and a new identity if you've got 'em," Alex quipped, forcing a chuckle from Clint. *Same ol' Alex.* Smart-ass to the end. Alex offered up a brief, pained smile before adding, "Money on the books would be nice. I might be able to save my ass if I can trade something."

"Sure thing, buddy."

Replacing the receiver, he took one last look at his best friend before walking away.

No one told him closure would hurt like a bitch.

Chapter Thirty-Three

Jordana walked into Bridgette's makeshift office to pick her up for lunch. It was nice having her sister home again. They used to be so close but then distance and busy lives had gotten in the way of their relationship.

Of her two sisters, she got along the best with Bridgette. Yvette, the baby, had a personality that tended to rub Jordana the wrong way at times, but Lilly always seemed to favor her, which also stuck a thorn in Jordana's side.

So even though Yvette lived in town, they rarely spent time together unless it was a family dinner at their parents' house.

Bridgette looked up and waved her over with a smile. "Sorry, I just have to finish up these notes before I lose my train of thought. My superior is asking for an update and I want to get everything down."

"Have you had any breakthroughs?" Jordana asked.

"Well, right now we're taking soil and water samples, preliminary stuff. Then we'll start talking to neighbors who are situated near the clusters. We need to document how many people were potentially affected, which means a lot of interviews."

"Except with the people who have already died,"

Jordana said, frowning. "Have you ever heard of the chemical CCA?"

"Chromated copper arsenic? Of course, it's one of nine chemical compounds banned by the EPA for commercial use." She glanced up in question. "Why?"

Jordana vacillated between sharing privileged information or not with Bridgette. Given the fact that Bridgette was an investigator for the state, she relented. "Well, CCA was found on the bodies."

"Interesting. When was the building built?"

"In the mid-1970s so it was grandfathered in, I suppose."

"I wonder how many other buildings have CCA-treated building materials?" Bridgette mused, mostly to herself. "I think I'll look into that."

Alarm spiked Jordana's voice as she asked, "Why?"

"Well, we have a documented case of esophageal cancer that might be connected to exposure to CCA. I'll need to follow up."

Jordana voiced her secret fear. "What if Dad is somehow involved in all this?"

"How could he be?" Bridgette asked, confused. "Dad would never knowingly do anything that would hurt anyone."

"I know but something about this case gives me a bad feeling."

"You're just under a lot of pressure. It's twisting your perspective. Dad is probably fine. Now Dex, on the other hand—he's always seemed shady to me."

She wasn't going to argue that point because she wondered the same. "Dad would never let Dex do anything that would come back on his family," Jordana said, clinging to that hope. "But what if Dad is somehow affected by all this? Dad said he felt his own family was attacking him right now."

"Dad is being dramatic. It's all procedure. He got hot under the collar because I told him I needed to take samples near Ruby Row."

"Why?"

"I don't know. He doesn't trust all this "cockamamie science BS' as he calls it. He does things old-school and doesn't like being told how stuff needs to be done now. Honestly, I've said for years that Dad should retire. Maybe this will be the thing that forces his hand."

Jordana made a face. "Can you imagine Dad without a job to occupy him? He would be unbearable to be around."

"Speaking of, please tell me you know of a rental I can look into? I can't live with them much longer or I'll go Lizzie Borden on their asses."

Jordana laughed. "We don't want that to happen. I'll keep an eye out. Do you think our parents will divorce someday?"

"Not a chance. Mom would never leave Dad. No matter how grumpy he gets. You do realize, our dad is going to be that stereotypical grouchy old man who's always railing about 'those damn kids' as he waves his cane at them."

Jordana, affecting a crotchety old man voice, croaked, "Get off my lawn!" and they both laughed because they knew it was like looking into the foreseeable future. "Can you imagine Dad being young and happy? I mean, people don't spring up out of the dirt angry old men."

"Mom was beautiful in her day. He had to do something to charm her. I'm sure she had her pick of eligible bachelors back in the day."

"Oh, God, you just made me think of the reality that our parents used to have sex."

"Used to? You think they don't anymore?"

Jordana quipped, "Don't you think Dad would be less grumpy if they were?"

Bridgette gagged. "Please, you're ruining my appetite."

But Jordana was enjoying this and teased Bridgette, "Hey, you're living with them. Have you heard them going at it late at night?"

"Oh, my God, Jordana, I would pour hot oil into my ears if that ever happened. And thankfully, no, I haven't heard any late-night nookie." She shuddered. "That would be enough to put me off from ever having sex again."

Jordana laughed, enjoying messing with Bridgette, but she was starving and her lunch hour would be over if they didn't hurry up and get to the restaurant. "C'mon, you prude. Lock up and let's go. My stomach is starting to eat itself."

Bridgette made quick work of closing down her office and they popped into their favorite deli for a quick bite.

Afterward, Jordana dropped Bridgette off and headed back to the station. She worked hard to keep thoughts of Clint at the back of her mind but there were times when it seemed nearly impossible to stop the intrusion of memories.

Today reminded her of the day they went to Wichita and rock climbed. That'd been the best day. She and Clint had been compatible is so many ways, except the most important—where they called home.

Privately, in her weakest moments, usually late at night when she couldn't sleep, she entertained the fantasy that everything had worked out between them and she got the privilege of falling asleep in his arms every night.

The fantasy gave her momentary pleasure until reality popped the bubble. She couldn't imagine Clint enjoying Braxville full-time. He hadn't minded visiting but to live here? He'd go insane.

That painful circle of reason was usually the point where she reminded herself that she'd made the right decision and tried to forget.

It never worked.

No matter how hard she tried, shaking free of Clint's ghost was damn near impossible.

She supposed this was her life now. Forever pining for the one who got away. The one she pushed away.

Yay, me.

BIG DECISIONS SHOULDN'T be made on the fly, but after seeing Alex, Clint realized what he wanted to do. There was still the fear that Jordana would reject him, but he had to take the chance. Otherwise, he'd spend his life wondering what might've been if he'd just grabbed his balls and went for it.

Hell, when he and Alex started Broadlocke, they hadn't much between them aside from a determination to succeed shared by a common goal. If he could create a multimillion-dollar company, survive three different attempts on his life and put away his best friend, he could do anything.

His dark sense of humor was turning out to be a good coping mechanism for what he'd had to endure. But he couldn't deny—didn't want to deny—that he missed Jordana in a way that wasn't going to fade if he gave it more time. He knew the signs of real love even if he'd never experienced it before now.

They had a kind of love that burned down to the soul, leaving a mark for the rest of a person's days. If he didn't do his best to convince Jordana that they were meant to be together, he'd live in regret for what could've been. After everything he'd been through, he wasn't going to live half a life.

He'd convince Jordana's stubborn ass that she was meant to be with him and vice versa. The only trouble was he didn't know how he'd make that happen, only that it needed to. Creative problem-solving had been Alex's field of expertise.

Alex would say one problem at a time. He had to find someone he could leave in charge while he was in Braxville, someone he trusted. The obvious choice hadn't been so obvious, but once the lightbulb went off, it was nearly blinding. He just had to put his plan in motion and pray he wasn't doing it all for nothing.

Chapter Thirty-Four

Another painfully tense family dinner. She needed to come up with a reasonable excuse to bow out the next time her mom sent an invitation. The only problem with bowing out was the guilt of leaving poor Bridgette to face their parents alone. For some reason the boys always got out of family dinners, but the girls were expected to show up.

Well, except Yvette. The baby always got special treatment. Mom never badgered Yvette for not showing up. It seemed that judgment was reserved mostly for Jordana these days.

The emotional toll of spending time with her parents when the investigation was all but stalled was excruciating. She never thought she'd long for the days when all she had to deal with was her parents' ordinary gripes about her never settling down—as if they were living in the Victorian era and she was in danger of becoming an old maid.

Jordana fell back onto the sofa with a groan, wanting to veg out on some mindless television before bed.

An idle thought crowded her mind as she flipped through channels.

What kind of impression would Clint have made on her parents? Her mom would've immediately been impressed by his wealth. Her father would've been his usual standoffish self, and if Dex were around, he'd probably sniff out any potential investing possibilities.

Dex was always hustling.

She supposed she shouldn't give Dex too hard of a time. If it weren't for Dex always looking for the next bid, Colton Construction would've gone under a long time ago.

"Uncle" Dex was an integral part of Colton Construction, no matter how he irritated her most days.

She grabbed her cell and began flipping through her photos, looking for the ones with Clint. Logically, she knew she should've deleted them. The best way to get over someone was to remove reminders.

She couldn't do it.

Her memories with Clint were the secret fuel in her engine. Only in the privacy of her thoughts could she openly admit how much she missed him. She couldn't count how many times she'd stared at her phone, so close to calling yet ultimately didn't because there was nothing more to say.

Hearing his voice would be a knife to her heart.

She missed his laugh; the low rumble deep in his chest when he chuckled was the sexiest sound she'd ever known. Not to mention how he made her bones melt when they were alone.

Jordana grabbed a throw pillow and hugged it to her chest. Had she made a mistake? Had she pushed away the one she would've happily grown old with? How was she to know that she hadn't taken a gamble on the wrong flip of the coin? The military taught her to never second-guess her instincts, but she wasn't so sure that she'd been listening to her instincts but rather fear.

Fear of ultimately losing a part of herself if and when

Clint realized he couldn't make a life work as her partner. Fear of putting in the work to only discover they were truly incompatible. Fear of looking like a fool when she didn't fit in with his circle of wealthy friends.

Jordana exhaled on a groan, her mind spinning in circles. "No sense in looking backward when you know you're not going that way," she murmured to herself as she tossed the pillow, restless.

She glanced at her phone. It works both ways. She hadn't called him but he hadn't called her, either. Was he even missing her? Had he washed his hands of everything they'd been to each other? Yes, it was unfair for her to criticize his methods of closure, but she didn't care. If there was one lesson that'd been hammered home from the time she was young, it was that life wasn't fair.

Just once, she would've liked the pendulum to swing her way.

Enough with the pity party, she admonished, rising. Her gaze roamed her tiny house. There had to be something that needed cleaning or reorganizing. Maybe she would start that tile project, after all. She'd always wanted granite countertops.

No time like the present. Especially when her brain wouldn't let her rest, her heart ached like a bitch and guilt dogged her every step for not being able to close this case.

Adulting was hard.

Right now, she wanted to crawl under her blanket fort and block out everything and everyone.

Seeing as that wasn't an option…*tile project, it is!*

CLINT WALKED WITH purpose into the office, his plan set in his mind, his feet ready to put the plan into action.

He asked Jeana to join him in his office and to shut the door behind her.

Perplexed, Jeana followed his instruction, awaiting his disposition. "Have I done something wrong, sir?" she asked, concerned.

"I'd say so," he answered, steeling his fingers. "I did a little digging into your personnel file and discovered you have a degree in business management with a minor in robotic tech. Tell me…why are you my assistant and not on my development team?"

She blushed when she realized he was paying her a compliment. "I applied for a management position when I first came on board with Broadlocke but Mr. Locke thought I should spend some time as your assistant to learn how Broadlocke operates. I was lucky to land a position with Broadlocke and I was grateful for the opportunity to prove myself."

"That was five years ago. How long were you supposed to 'learn' the ropes?" Clint asked, confused. "Alex never mentioned your qualifications. If I'd known I would've rectified that oversight way before now."

"At first, I was a little disappointed that I wasn't headed straight into management as I'd hoped but there was some wisdom in Mr. Locke's direction. I did learn the ins and outs of Broadlocke in ways that gave me a particular insight."

Clint could see the value, but he didn't like that Alex had been a little sexist by throwing a highly capable female employee in the assistant role. Well, that was about to end. "Here's the thing, I can't do anything about the past but I'm looking toward the future and I need someone here who can help keep Broadlocke running smoothly when I'm not around. Someone I trust."

"Sir?" Jeana blinked, cocking her head to the side

in question. "Are you hiring someone new? Should I contact the headhunting agency?"

"Nope. I did my headhunting, but as I turns out, I didn't have to hunt all that far."

"Oh. Okay?"

"You, Jeana, I want you to operate the Chicago office and not as my assistant."

Jeana's lip trembled as she swallowed. "Are you serious?"

"As a heart attack," he answered solemnly. "Look, you're already the engine that makes sure that this office is a tight ship but what I didn't realize was that you weren't being used to your best potential. If you're willing to take a lead role in the management side, it will come with a substantial raise, some perks, as you know, and a lot more work. Are you up for that?"

She didn't even hesitate. "Yes. Oh, yes!"

He nodded, pleased. "Good. Then you need to start headhunting for your replacement because you're going to need a 'you' by your side as you move into more responsibilities."

Jeana, beaming, took a moment to contain her happiness, then asked, "May I assume you will be opening a Braxville location?"

"You assume correct. A two-hour flight is nothing if I'm needed here. It's time I start creating a solution to my problem instead of just staring at it."

"Seems like a sensible course of action, sir."

"And another thing, no more 'sir,'" he admonished. "As soon as you sign your paperwork for HR, you're on my level. From now on, it's Clint. With Alex gone, I'll be needing a new partner. Understand?"

She smiled, nodding. "I do."

"Excellent. Glad that's settled. Now, if you wouldn't

mind me asking you a tiny favor…could you book me a flight to Braxville on the next available plane? I've got a woman to woo and I've got my work cut out for me."

Jeana's smile grew. "I would be delighted to book you a flight. Consider it done."

Jeana spun on her heel and left his office with a little more spring in her step and it did Clint's heart good to make a positive difference in someone's life. Especially someone who deserved good things.

With the decision made, he no longer felt any reservations. He'd never give much thought to where he would raise a family if he were to have one, but he knew now that Chicago wasn't where he wanted his roots to grow. He wanted for his kids what Jordana had had growing up—stability and a firm understanding of where they came from.

He wanted to complain about small-town life, such as a neighbor with a noisy rooster, or a pig that'd escaped the farmer's pen to root around in his vegetable garden. Hell, he wanted to learn how to grow vegetables and plant fruit trees.

He wanted to attend Friday night football games for the local high school and get to know the townspeople on a real level. The kind of life that entails knowing people by name and being able to chat with them in the supermarket aisles. And he wanted it all with that stubborn, hot-as-hell detective who haunted his dreams and made him realize what he'd been missing all those years. He wanted the white picket fence, the DIY projects, the PTA meetings and corny office Christmas parties.

As long as Jordana was by his side, he'd do it all.

Now, time to problem-solve the biggest obstacle to that promised land: Jordana.

Well, he had a two-hour plane ride to figure something out. Good thing he'd always been light on his feet. And he didn't plan to leave Braxville until he'd convinced Jordana she was The One.

Even if it took a lifetime.

Chapter Thirty-Five

"You look like someone just ran over your dog," Reese commented, prompting a sour look from Jordana. "Case in point. What's eating you, Gilbert Grape?"

She hadn't slept well. She might've dipped her toe into insanity last night, admitting, "I demoed my kitchen around ten o'clock last night."

"What?"

"And accidentally broke a water pipe," she answered, wincing at the nightmare her kitchen had become. "I managed to get the water main shut off but now I need a plumber to come and take a look to repair it."

"Your dad's in construction—can't he do it for you?"

"I don't dare ask my dad for anything right now," she said, shuddering at the thought. "I'd rather pay the money for someone else to take care of the problem."

"You don't think your dad would put aside petty grievances to help you out?"

"You haven't met my dad, have you? And no, I'm already on thin ice because of the investigation."

Reese seemed to understand. "You're doing everything you can. We're going to get a lead soon. Something will pop up. They always do."

"From your mouth to God's ear," she quipped, hoping it was true. She needed a win at some point or else her relationship with her dad might be forever ruined. Difficult personality aside, she still loved the man.

For her sake, Reese moved on. "Okay, my next question is fairly obvious…why in God's name are you starting a demo project in the middle of the week at ten at night? Are you doing crack? Cooking meth? Should I be worried? You know they drug test here."

"I'm not doing crack or meth, you idiot," Jordana said, rolling her eyes, but the motion gave her a headache. She rubbed at her temples. "I think drugs would be easier to explain. I kinda went a little nuts last night. I wasn't planning to start the demo for the countertops but I wasn't able to sleep, and one thing lead to another and before I knew it I was swinging a mallet like a crazy person."

"Which is how you burst a pipe," Reese guessed, to which she confirmed with a nod. "Okay, so maybe some therapy instead of wrecking your home before you know what you're doing?"

"Thanks for stating the obvious. I already told you that I kinda went crazy, but to be fair, I've been under a lot of pressure. Eventually, the top is going to pop."

"Most people do normal things to let off steam, like garden or watch true-crime documentaries on serial killers."

She leveled a sardonic look at Reese. "That's only you. Nobody else does that."

He countered, "I'm fairly certain they don't go full-on wrecking crew late at night completely sober. At least tell me there was alcohol involved with your poor judgment."

She sighed. "Sober. Not even a glass of wine."

Reese chuckled, shaking his head. "Do you have a countertop replacement picked out?"

"Nope."

"Do you have a project budget?"

"Nope."

"So you basically got a wild hair up your butt and started swinging?"

"Yep."

He exhaled a long breath, pinching the bridge of his nose as he implored, "Jesus, Jordana. Just call the guy already."

Jordana stared, wishing she wasn't so transparent. Also wishing she hadn't lost her cool and raged at her poor kitchen without an actual plan as to how to finish the project. Now she had a nonfunctioning kitchen, water damage and no idea how she was going to put it all back together again. If that wasn't a metaphor for her life, she didn't know what was. She glanced away, finally saying, "I can't call him."

Reese sighed. "And why is that?"

"Because you don't get closure by repeatedly opening a wound. He needs time to heal, too. I wouldn't disrespect his privacy by badgering him for no discernible purpose."

"You make a lot of excuses for a woman who is normally pretty straightforward about things."

"I do not."

"You do. Look, I'm your partner. Trust is an essential component of our relationship. I wouldn't lie to you. So you can trust me when I say, you're better *with* him than without. And you're driving everyone crazy with your dour Eeyore routine. It's a bit of a drag."

Jordana glared Reese's way, not because he wasn't right but because she hated that she was *that* person. "Getting over Clint is turning out to be harder than I thought it would be," she admitted. "I just need more time."

"Maybe you can't get over him because you're not supposed to get over him. I don't think anyone would accuse me of being overly romantic but, you know, you and Clint seem pretty well-matched."

She snorted. "Not hardly."

"Forget all the surface stuff—I'm talking about the way you act with one another. He brings out the best in you, which is how it's supposed to work. At least, if rumors are to be believed, of course. Anyway, all I know is that you're making a big mistake by holding a line you drew in the sand over something colossally stupid."

"Did you just call me stupid?"

"Pretty much." Reese shrugged, giving zero "effs" as they would say. "I call it like I see it."

"You should mind your own business," Jordana told him.

"Sorry, can't. You're my partner so I'm forced to deal with you and whatever nonsense you manifest, both good and bad."

"Is there such a thing as good nonsense?" she asked, mildly amused.

"Sure, like your near-baffling belief that *The Wizard of Oz* is one of the best films ever made. That's bull that, although inherently wrong, is harmless, which is *good*. Get it?"

"Your logic is dizzying and you're wrong—*The Wizard of Oz* is a classic in film history. Anyone with a brain would agree."

"My point being, I'm willing to deal with all of it because I'm your partner and I'm tired of seeing you sad all the time. Even when you're pretending to be happy, I know you're not."

Jordana's eyes welled unexpectedly. *Don't do this*

here. Her throat closed up and she couldn't manage a comeback. "I—"

"*The Wizard of Oz is* a classic," a voice with authority said behind her, choking her words in midsentence. She jumped from her chair to see Clint standing there, a half grin on his face, that adorable dimple popping out. "If we're throwing around facts, that is."

"What are you doing here?" she found her voice to rasp, but she was so happy to see him that all she could do was stare. "I mean… Chicago…why?"

He started to walk toward her, and her gaze never left his. The station seemed to disappear around them. Her soul stared with hunger at the man she wanted above all others. Reasons for why it wouldn't work, logical arguments against being together, all the things she had clung to in his absence, dissolved like mist in sunshine. He was here. Standing in front of her. Like the answer to an unspoken prayer.

And she couldn't say a thing.

Clint seemed to understand and reached for her hands to hold in his grasp, his stare never leaving hers. She was mesmerized by those eyes, drinking in his presence like a woman dying of thirst.

"Well, this is awkward," Reese broke in. "But I'm going to stay because I need to know how this turns out. Carry on."

That break was the catalyst to cause her to blink and come to her senses. After shooting Reese a look, she asked Clint again, "What are you doing here?"

"Coming to convince the love of my life to stop pushing me away so we can start our lives together."

Her heart stuttered. "What do you mean?"

"I mean, I'm looking to put down roots with you. Right here in Braxville."

"You can't do that," she protested, flushing with distress. "I told you that was a bad idea."

"Well, I gave it some thought and I realized you were partly right."

"She was?" Reese asked, surprised.

Jordana whirled on Reese. "I swear to God, if you don't shut up I'll shoot you."

Reese held up his hands in mock surrender. "Fine. So touchy."

Returning to Clint, she tried to understand what he was saying. Impatience colored her voice as she said, "Please clarify."

"You said if either of us moved permanently for the other, it would cause resentment. I couldn't deny that could be true. Then I realized I'm not giving up Chicago. I can live wherever I want and telecommute or hop a plane if need be, and be at the Chicago office in two hours. That's hardly giving up Chicago."

Jordana's heart sped up at the implication of his solution. Was it possible that she and Clint could make this work? She didn't want to get her hopes up but… the possibility filled her with elation. "But what about your Chicago office? Who will run it with Alex gone?"

"Turns out Jeana is the most qualified. I leave Chicago in highly capable hands. Probably even better than before. I'm excited to see what she can do. Powerful women are sexy as hell."

She trembled as the full import of what he was saying hit her. "So you're saying…"

He pulled her to him, and she immediately softened. When Clint wrapped his arms around her, she felt home. "What I'm saying, Miss Colton," Clint said in a low rumble, "is that I want to make a life with you here. In Braxville. What do you say to that?"

She felt the tension in the room as everyone seemed to wait for her answer. There wasn't time to be embarrassed at being the center of attention. Her future happiness depended on her answer.

To say yes would be to throw caution to the wind and embrace the now, regardless of the potential outcome.

To say no would be to condemn herself to knowing she'd pushed away the man of her dreams out of fear of the unknown.

She wasn't a coward. She needed to stop allowing fear to dictate her actions.

Jordana slowly looped her arms around Clint's neck, smiling as her heart fluttered with joy, saying, "I say… how good are you at kitchen demo?"

"I'm pretty good at writing a check," he answered with a grin. "But if it's something you want to do together… I'll figure it out."

That was exactly the right answer. As she lifted her mouth to his, the station erupted into applause. The loudest being Reese, the cheeky bastard. Partners were a pain in the ass but Reese was a good one.

"Take her home," Reese called out. "She needs a good…well, I think you can figure it out."

Clint hoisted her up on his hips and carried her out of the station amid the laughter as he called out over his shoulder, "I know exactly what she needs!"

And boy, did he.

Sigh.

* * * * *